the BOULDER WOLVES
the complete trilogy

OLIVIA WILDENSTEIN

A PACK OF BLOOD AND LIES

BOOK 1

PROLOGUE

The astringent tang of ammonia and glass cleaner stung my nose, but I powered through the smell, rubbing the glass table until it reflected the modern high-rise across the street. Six years ago, I could barely be in the same room as a spritz of Windex, but distance had dimmed my acute sense of smell.

Stretching my stiff neck from side to side, I moved away from the table to pack the cleaning supplies and roll them out of the conference room.

"Evelyn, I'm done!" When I spotted a dyed-black mane, I released my cart and draped my forearms over the top of the cubicle's laminated wood siding. "Want help out here?"

"No. I'm done, too, *querida*." The bright silk scarf knotted around Evelyn's hair tonight made my throat constrict.

Mom had owned few things of value—her wedding band embedded with diamond chips that I wore on a leather cord around my neck, and the designer scarf Evelyn never parted with since Mom had gifted it to her. I was by no means jealous that Evelyn had gotten it. If anyone deserved such a beautiful present, it was the woman who'd taken care of us since our arrival in Los Angeles six years ago.

Our neighborhood was, to put it nicely, rough, which meant I was to open the door to no one. When Evelyn knocked two days after we had moved in, I stared at her through the peephole and told her to go away. She did, but then she returned.

The next time she came, she slipped me a folded piece of stationery on which she'd scribbled her name and unit number. When Mom got home from a job interview and saw the paper I'd left out on our dining table, she shot up the stairs like a bullet, racing past the poorly rendered violet boob graffiti that graced the concrete stairwell, and then pounded on Evelyn's door to demand what interest she had in an eleven-year-old girl.

Turned out, Evelyn just wanted to help. Mom had flown back down, a blur of red cheeks and crazed eyes, yelling that we didn't need anyone's charity...that we were *fine!*

We weren't fine.

Thankfully, Evelyn remained persistent and returned again, placating my mother with dishes suited for a crowd and clothing that had been gathering dust in the back of her closet. Naïvely, I'd determined Evelyn was a hoarder with terrible math skills.

Evelyn unplugged the vacuum, then limped back to it and toed the knob that wound up the cord. It coiled into the belly of the apparatus as quick as a prairie rattlesnake. Before she could bend over, I grabbed the handle and heaved it onto her cart. Together, we walked our carts back to the janitorial closet, Evelyn gritting her teeth the entire way. Although she never complained, her right shoulder had been bothering her for some time now. Coupled with her constant limp caused by the stray bullet that had hit her calf two decades ago, Evelyn had slowed down considerably.

"I made your favorite tacos, but do not feel obliged to eat with me, *querida*. If you have a date—"

"Nope. No date." I hadn't gone on one since Mom passed away.

At first, I stayed away from boys because depression was eating me whole, but then paying rent and bills overtook my life, and I picked up as many hours of cleaning jobs as I could find. Some days, the commuting wore me down more than the actual workload and chemical odors. I found no solace in rolling on buses through gray city blocks, leaning away from passengers who smelled like the lunch they'd put away hours before or the perspiration they'd accrued during the day.

Tonight, at least, Evelyn sat next to me, large-knuckled fingers clasped in her lap, chin dipped into her neck, lids closed in rest. A couple seconds before we reached our bus stop, I gently rubbed her forearm and murmured, "We're home."

She startled awake. Hooking her arm through mine for support, we got off the bus. The deep-blue streets were not especially busy at this hour. The regulars were out, though—the army vet with the thick aura of liquor fumes, talking to his runt of a dog that perpetually bared his fangs at me; the two sex workers sporting torn fishnets and caked-on drugstore makeup, who reeked of sweaty vinyl; and the hooded men sought out in equal measure by the police and their twitchy customers.

Except for the dog, they were all pleasant enough.

One of the hooded dealers whistled at me. "When you gonna give me some sugar, Ness?"

Months ago, I'd stupidly worn my name pinned to my chick-yellow cleaning uniform.

Smile tugging at the corner of my lips, I flipped him off, which had his two associates snickering. Every night I passed by them, they'd either whistle or make kissy noises, and every night I'd show them what I thought of their subtle advances.

One night, one of them hadn't been on the corner, and I worried the cops had nailed him, but Suzie the prostitute assured me the boy's pops had gotten out of jail and come to collect his son to start a new life.

Sometimes I wished someone would whisk me away to start a new life, too.

As we stepped into the dirty cement cube we called home, I pushed away thoughts of desertion and told Evelyn, "I'll be up in a minute."

The elevator was out of order...*again*, so she started her slow ascent to her second-floor unit, the menthol salve she rubbed into her sore joints wafting over the tang of fresh urine. Her shoulder wasn't the only thing that worried me. Her bad leg, too, seemed to be causing her pain.

Once I heard her keys jangle over the shouting match of my next-door neighbors and the cartoons blaring from Mrs. Fletcher's place, I walked toward my apartment and pulled out my keys, but then I froze in the middle of the hallway.

I sniffed the air—cigarette smoke, potpourri, and evergreen. The tangled scents jolted my pulse.

My front door was closed, but yellow light slanted onto the steel-gray floor. I turned the knob, then gave a hard shove.

Two people were crowded around my flea-market dining table.

The man jumped to his feet so fast his chair skidded backward on the linoleum. He caught the wooden top rail before it hit the ground. "Ness."

"How did you get in?" I sounded calm, which was surprising, because I was *not* calm. Every nerve in my body twitched.

My uncle tipped his head toward the window over the denim couch. Shards of glass glittered on the threadbare seat cushions.

I backed up. Smacked into a wall.

Not a wall.

Hands came around my biceps and pinned me in place. "Hi, Cuz."

I twisted my neck and gaped up into a familiar set of hazel eyes, then stared back at Uncle Jeb and Aunt Lucy.

"We've come to take you home," Lucy said, finally heaving herself out of the chair.

When I'd hoped for a new life, this wasn't what I'd had in mind.

I shrugged my cousin Everest's hands off and tried to lope around him, but his body filled the exit path. "Like hell I'm going back there!"

"Why didn't you call us when Maggie died?" My aunt wiped the corners of her eyes with a tissue. She hadn't cared about Mom when she'd been alive, but now Lucy was suddenly heartbroken? *The nerve of her.*

"Why *would* I tell you?"

"Because we're your family," Jeb said.

"You lost that title the day you forced us out of Boulder."

My uncle scratched a spot behind his ear. "Ness, there were reasons we urged your mother to leave."

"Oh, I remember them: *Ness is fragile. She shouldn't run with boys. It's dangerous.* Am I misquoting you, Uncle?"

Jeb flushed.

"But now you suddenly want me to come back? Why would I go with you?" My voice rang so loudly in the corridor that my neighbor stopped beating up his wife long enough to stick his head through the door. Probably to check for cops. He didn't ask if I was okay. He wasn't concerned with my well-being; he was scum.

Just like my uncle and aunt.

"You have to come with us. You're a minor," Lucy said.

"I'll be eighteen in September."

Lucy balled the tissue in her dimpled hand. "Until then, we're your legal guardians, so we call the shots."

Disbelief raked over me. "How did you even find out about Mom?"

"News travels," Everest said.

I had no more ties in Boulder, which had me wondering if Mom's death certificate was on the internet for all to see.

"Your school principal called," Jeb said. "You neither attended your graduation, nor picked up your diploma. He was trying to reach your mom, but her phone was disconnected. Since I was listed as next of kin, he phoned me."

Anger and shock warped my sight. Anger that Mom had listed my uncle on my school file, and shock that it was my own error that had led these people to me.

"How long have you been living like"—Lucy wrinkled her nose—"*this*?"

Where I lived wasn't a palace. I was aware of that, but having her state it with such distaste raised my hackles. Her gaze roved over our faded couch, over the chipped white veneer of the countertop, over the yellow water stain that had bloated and cracked a piece of the ceiling.

"Move your arm, young man." The familiar voice had me wheeling around. Evelyn held out a can of pepper spray to Everest's face.

"Whoa, chill out, lady." My cousin lowered the palm he'd planted on the wall to corral me.

Keeping the can directed on Everest, she said, "Get behind me, Ness."

When I didn't, she stretched out her arm and tried to force me back. Worried about my uncle's reaction, I pressed her arm down and whispered, "It's okay," even though it wasn't.

A frown worked itself onto my aunt's smooth, milky skin. "Who's she?"

Evelyn glared at her. "Who are *you*?"

"People I used to know," I muttered.

"We're her family," Jeb said.

Evelyn cocked a penciled eyebrow up.

"They're the reason Mom and I had to leave Boulder."

"And you are, Ma'am?" my uncle asked.

"Evelyn."

Lucy crossed her thick freckled arms, and a column of metal bangles clinked against each another. "And you know Ness *how*?"

"She's been playing the role you guys failed so miserably at," I said through gritted teeth. "If anyone should be my legal guardian, it should be her, not you."

Evelyn glanced over her shoulder at me, then back at my uncle. "I will gladly be her legal guardian. Entrust her to me."

My heart bounded at the possibility.

"I'm not entrusting Ness to a person I don't know from Eve or Adam." Jeb shook his head.

"Why not?" I asked. "*I* know her."

Jeb slapped the kitchen countertop. "That's not how it works. Now you start packing right away, young lady, or—or—"

I could tell from the strain around my uncle's eyes that I was chipping away at his patience, but he had to understand I wasn't the submissive pup he could kick around anymore.

I raised my chin. "Or what?"

"Or Everest will carry you out to the car," Jeb said in a quiet roar.

"He wouldn't dare."

Everest shot me a brazen smile.

Crap. He *would* dare.

"Evelyn's been here for me when you guys haven't! I am not leaving her." She wrapped her calloused fingers around my wrist. "Shh, *querida*."

"Then I guess we'll be taking her along," Everest said.

I blinked at my cousin. "No one's taking anyone—"

Jeb tipped his head toward Everest. My cousin slapped the can of pepper spray out of Evelyn's fingers, then shackled the fists I swung at him, pinning them against my back.

"Take your hands off me!" I tried to tear my wrists out of his grasp, but the action was as futile as a hanging man trying to loosen a noose.

"Sorry, Cuz. No can do."

"We are not the enemy, Ness," my uncle said, stepping on the can of pepper spray Evelyn was reaching for.

"Well, you're sure acting like it!" I bit out.

I tried to headbutt my cousin, but he must've predicted my move because he added space between our bodies, all the while keeping my wrists in a vice. "I don't want to hurt you, Ness."

"I will go with her." Evelyn's declaration made everyone freeze.

"What? No." Lucy's head jerked back, and it made her double chin wobble. She'd gained weight since I'd last seen her; not that she was ever a size eight, but she used to be firmer.

"You surely can't just up and leave, Ma'am," Jeb said.

"I surely can and surely will. Now release her before I call the police and have them observe how unfit you are to be her guardians."

"We're not afraid of cops," Everest said, a lilt to his voice.

I was so furious I wanted to spit on him. On him and on his pride.

My uncle raised an open palm. "Release her, Everest."

Everest let me go. I rubbed my wrists and glared at him, funneling everything I thought about him and his little stunt into that one look. I didn't spit though.

"Can you cook, Ma'am?" Jeb asked. At first, I assumed the drive had made him hungry—my uncle and cousin were always hungry—but then Jeb added, "We need a new cook at the inn."

Lucy startled. "Jeb, we can't just—"

"She's an incredible cook," I said.

"But—" Lucy started again.

"Dad's right. We need a new cook, and Ness won't come without Evelyn. It's a win-win."

Lucy gasped. "We can't just pick someone off the street."

"We're not *on* the street, Mom," Everest said.

My cousin's support was startling and reminded me of another time when he'd stood up for me, but my gratitude whizzed out like air from a popped balloon when I recalled how he'd just manhandled me.

"We can't promise it will work out," Jeb said.

"But she'll stay with me until I'm eighteen even if it doesn't." Evelyn was my life. At fifty-eight, living alone with decreasing mobility, there was no way in hell I'd let Jeb kick her to the curb. "You'll give her a room in the inn."

"You're a very demanding girl," my uncle said.

"You're uprooting me from my life." *Again.* "I have a right to be demanding."

Jeb glanced at his wife, but Lucy was too busy scowling to meet his gaze. "We'll supply her with a room, but it'll impact her salary. *If* it works out."

Lucy finally flicked a creamy hand, contaminating the air with the essence of nicotine that had yellowed the white crescents of her nails. "All this is well and good, but shouldn't we sample the woman's cooking first?"

"The woman has a name. Evelyn. And she made fish tacos," I said.

"I could eat," Everest chirped.

Of course he could. My cousin's appetite was a monstrous thing when we were growing up.

"I'll go fetch the tacos with her," I offered.

"No. I'll go," Everest said.

"Like I'd trust you to do that," I said.

"Everest goes with you." Was Jeb afraid I'd make a run for it?

The thought had crossed my mind, but another one had quickly taken its place: Evelyn wouldn't be able to run. Besides, where would we go? I had never made good enough friends I could phone for help. I'd tried back in middle school, but kids found me odd and kept away. I remembered wondering if they could somehow sense what I was, smell what I was the same way I could smell their acne serums and tinted lip balms. I'd never dared ask Mom. I was afraid she'd burst into my school and punch the kids for shunning me, which wouldn't have improved my social status.

Evelyn, Everest, and I went upstairs, and then we came back with the taco dish. While Evelyn warmed it in my microwave, I packed. Gathering everything I owned took me fifteen minutes and two blue Ikea bags.

"That's it?" Jeb picked up one of the bags and tried to wrestle the second one from my hands, but I held on tight.

"That's it."

As Jeb and I walked to the black van with the golden Boulder Inn logo, we discussed my last rental payment and the cost of a new window, and then he asked if I had a car, and I shook my head. I didn't even have a license.

"A boyfriend or friends to say goodbye to?"

I thought about my drug-dealing admirers and the sympathetic prostitutes for all of a second. "No."

"Really? No one?"

His concern surprised me. I supposed acting as though I hadn't had a life here wouldn't serve him.

"I have Evelyn," I ended up saying so he would stop pitying me.

Lucy and Everest were sampling the tacos when we returned. Evelyn offered my uncle a plate and watched as the tangy goodness vanished down his throat.

"If all your food tastes this good, you won't have to worry about job security," he finally said.

Evelyn smiled at me, and her expression dissolved some of the tension that had gelled inside my veins since I'd busted open my front door and set eyes on the past.

A past I dreaded revisiting.

1

ONE MONTH LATER

The inn was packed.

Brawny men of all ages had arrived sometime before lunch, alone or accompanied by their wives, girlfriends, or sons.

I recognized many of the men, but they didn't recognize me. In my gray housekeeping uniform, I blended with the rest of the staff. Every time someone looked my way, I disappeared into the kitchen where Evelyn was cooking up a feast, or entered one of the unoccupied bedrooms I'd helped prep for the occasion.

Energy crackled in the carpeted hallways, in the living room with its high-beamed ceilings and two-story glass panes, and in the tartan-covered adjoining dens. Every Adirondack on the sprawling porch held a reclined body. Voices chirped. Laughter rang. It was as though the Boulder Pack hadn't come together in years. But I knew for a fact they met once a week. Well, the men did. The women and children were not invited to regular pack gatherings.

"If you go at it much longer, the metal will start peeling."

I froze, and the feather duster I'd been using on the sconce next to the elevator tumbled onto the burgundy runner.

That voice...

Deeper, but nonetheless familiar.

Slowly, I turned to face Liam Kolane, one of the men who'd opposed my plea to join the pack the day my father was shot. I wasn't short for a girl—five-seven like Mom—but I still had to crane my neck.

I hid my loathing for him underneath a smile. "Sometimes the filth is not visible to the naked eye, but it doesn't mean it's not there."

A small crease appeared between the dark brows shadowing his reddish-brown eyes.

I picked up my feather duster and continued down the hallway, swiping the long gray feathers over the other sconces.

He didn't move. "Have we met?"

I looked over my shoulder at him, fake smile still in place. "Not in this lifetime."

That made his entire forehead groove. I tossed him a wink as I turned the corner.

The second I was out of sight, I dropped the smile and hurried to the bedroom my aunt and uncle had loaned me. I shut my door and sidled against it. My heart was thumping so hard it threatened to derail. Liam hadn't recognized me. I was safe.

At least, that was what I believed for the next few minutes.

Two knocks on my door made me spring away from it.

"Open up."

I sniffed the air. Evergreen. *Not Liam.* I turned the knob to let my cousin in.

It had taken his girlfriend almost dying for me to forgive my cousin for being such an ass back in LA. I hadn't forgiven his parents, though. They'd yanked me out of my life one too many times to forgive.

"I just overheard Liam mention to his buddies that he ran into a hot blonde housekeeper." Everest dropped into the flannel-covered armchair in the corner of my bedroom. "Was it you?"

I crossed my arms. "I'm offended you need to ask."

"Only reason I'm asking is 'cause I thought you were planning on holing up in your bedroom until the pack left."

"Can't a girl change her mind?"

"You *can* change your mind, but if I were you, I'd stay the fuck away."

"Noted."

"I'm serious, Ness. Especially from Liam Kolane. He's cut from the same cloth as his dad."

A chill whorled beneath my ribs. "He rapes women too?"

"There are rumors..." Everest dragged his long fingers through his red hair.

I hated that I'd just reminded him of his girlfriend's fate—raped by Liam's father, Heath...the horror.

I sat on the edge of the duvet I'd fluffed upon waking, folding one leg underneath me. "Go against Liam."

"What?"

"For Alpha. Go against him."

Everest exhaled a rough breath. "I have no desire to lead the pack."

"You'd rather have Liam lead you?"

"No."

Ever since Everest's girlfriend had attempted suicide the week I arrived in Boulder, I'd softened toward my cousin. His pain, although different, reminded me acutely of my own. Maybe that was why I'd found it in my heart to overlook Los Angeles. Gone was his cockiness, replaced by this oppressive despondence that had turned him into a bit of a recluse.

"I can't stop thinking about what Heath did to Becca," he whispered, hazel eyes slickening with emotion. Not many things got to me, but a man crying...yeah, that got to me.

I leaned across the narrow space and touched his clasped hands. "Heath is gone, Everest. He got what he deserved."

Even though Heath had died a week ago, the realization hadn't settled in Everest yet. Perhaps because Liam had decided to bury his father in an intimate ceremony to which only a handful of pack members had been convened. Although brutal, seeing my mother's body lowered into the earth had brought me closure.

"He may be gone, but so is Becca," he muttered.

"She's not gone-gone."

He cocked an eyebrow. "Her odds of waking are fucking ridiculous."

"Ridiculous is better than no odds at all."

He snorted. "Can't believe *you're* the optimist."

He was right. I was a half-empty sort of girl.

He sighed then stood. "I should go. The meeting starts soon."

"Think about what I said. About tossing your name in the hat."

"There won't be a hat. No one's going to go up against Liam."

"You don't know that."

He shot me a *how-many-shades-of-clueless-are-you* look.

And here I thought the pack had balls. Many pairs of them. Was there truly no one to challenge a Kolane?

2

The second Everest left, I swapped my gray housekeeping uniform for skinny jeans and a white tank top. Mom's wedding band drummed against my chest as I headed for the inn's common area. Conversations and laughter frothed through the closed doors and filled the hallway. Steeling my nerves, I pumped the sculpted copper handle and drew the door open.

Squares of sunlight dappled the airy room. People were huddled in large groups, either sprawled over the leather sofas, or standing by the buffet of sweets and drinks set up next to the massive stone fireplace. No fire snapped in the blackened hearth, and yet the room smelled of warm smoke, as though the scent of winter fires had penetrated the pale-yellow stucco walls and Native-patterned area rugs.

As I dragged my gaze over the crowd, I caught Lucy's attention. She shot me a look that could've withered one of her prized rose transplants. She wasn't the only one glaring. I garnered many a glare. For example, Liam and the two guys standing on either side of him gave me the stink-eye.

I was the new kid all over again. Good thing it didn't frighten me.

Lucy elbowed her way through the sunlit room toward me, then latched onto my bicep and tugged me aside. "What are you doing here?"

I shrugged her off. "I've decided you were right. That I should get out and meet people."

Lucy dipped her chin into her fleshy neck. "Ness…"

"Yes?"

Her warning died in her throat. My aunt wouldn't dare make a scene, and considering how quiet it had gotten, she chose silence over a messy confrontation.

One of the guys broke away from Liam's little group and approached me, black eyebrows slanting over piercing green eyes. He stopped mere inches from me and tipped his head down. I crossed my arms, expecting him to tell me to beat it.

"Dimples? Is that you?"

If I were the type of girl to blush, I would've turned crimson at the nickname. Not because it wasn't true...I had deep dimples—craters really—but because it was spoken loudly.

"I go by Ness now. And you are?"

He grinned. "Shit. Ness. You're all grown up."

"Six years does that to you." I raised an eyebrow as I studied his face, took in the light-brown skin with the dusting of freckles, the prominent but straight nose, the dark stubble, the cropped black hair, the hazel eyes. "August?" I asked hesitantly. "August Watt?"

He smiled wider.

And then I smiled, because August had been my absolute favorite person in Colorado after my parents. When I'd asked the pack to allow me into their ranks, he and his father had fought in my favor, joining their voices to Everest's. They'd been drowned out by the chorus of *absolutely-nots.*

A girl in an all-male pack? What a revolting idea.

I couldn't help that I'd been born a girl. And it wasn't like I could pledge myself to a neighboring pack, because werewolves couldn't switch packs. The only thing werewolves could do was either be a part of their own pack, or move away—far away—so the distance prevented their bodies from changing. Those who stayed—lone wolves —were loose cannons hunted down by all.

August shook his head. "I didn't think you'd ever come back."

"I wasn't planning on it, but shit happens."

He got that look that drove me insane. Pity. I probably shouldn't have mentioned the *shit-happens* part.

"You okay?"

"I've had better days, but I've also had worse ones."

His frown deepened.

I ran my hand through my long hair because, heck, now *I* was uncomfortable.

Slowly, slowly, his chiseled face smoothed out. "Are you here to stay?"

"Haven't decided yet." My skin pebbled from the vent blasting cold air over my head. I hugged my arms to my chest. "Want to take the conversation outside?" I was chilly, but I also wanted to get away from my aunt's prickly glower.

"Sure."

As we walked through the open sliding-glass doors onto the overhanging porch that was almost as spacious as the living room, I said, "You don't *need* to talk to me by the way."

He draped an arm around my shoulders and tucked me into his side. My entire body tightened at the contact.

"Shut up. I just got my favorite girl back. Let me enjoy her."

I snorted softly. "Favorite girl?"

He amended, "Woman."

I peered up into his face. His freckles seemed to have darkened. "I imagined you'd have plenty of *new* favorite girls. I mean, look at you. You're like a real man now."

"A real man?" He chuckled. "If everyone wasn't staring at us right now, I'd put you in a headlock and rough up that pretty hair of yours."

"Don't you dare."

"Fine." He looked down at me, still grinning. "Seriously, it's so good to see you."

"Likewise." When we reached the guardrail fashioned from a tangle of sanded branches, I ducked out from underneath his heavy arm. "How've you been?"

"Pretty good. I enlisted a year after you left. It paid for college."

"Navy or army?"

"Marines."

I ran my fingers over the knots in the tawny wood that Dad and August's father had put in after Jeb bought the inn. Dad had been a talented carpenter. He'd taught his trade to August's father who purchased Dad's company after he died.

I placed my forearms on the thick balustrade and squinted at the dense copse of pines running up the sharp ridges of the Flatirons. The view from the inn definitely beat the one from the unit I used to call home. Not that I would *ever* admit this to anyone.

"Heard you were working with your dad now," I said.

"Yeah." August stroked the wood, his fingers moving carefully over the knots, and then he turned and leaned against it.

"How's business?"

"Booming. Want a job?"

"A job?"

"I remember you loved whittling wood."

"That was"—Dad's face flashed inside my mind—"a long time ago. Besides, I have a job. I work here."

I wanted my uncle to pay Evelyn her full wage, so I'd offered to help with the housekeeping. My suggestion had made my prim aunt balk, but rather rapidly, when she observed how effective I was, she changed her mind. If Evelyn caught wind of this trade, she'd unleash a torrent of Spanish on me. Every time she became emotional, her mother tongue spurted out like steam from a geyser.

At the beginning, I'd helped with the actual cleaning, but after a week, my sense of smell had gotten so acute I had to stay away from cleaning products. I stuck to laundry and ironing and occasionally helped out with vacuuming and assisting Evelyn in the kitchen.

August's thick black eyebrows almost joined together. "Something just occurred to me."

"What?"

"Did you run into Liam earlier?"

"Why?"

As his gaze settled on a spot behind me, a vein throbbed in his temple.

"I do believe we've met in this lifetime, Ness Clark."

Speak of the devil. I turned around slowly.

Liam glowered at me. I swear...little lightning bolts were zipping out of his eyes. "Where's your feather duster?"

I cocked my head to the side. "Did you want to borrow it?"

The lightning bolts turned into electrical discharges.

A loud clap resounded, disrupting the thick tension, and then Lucy exclaimed, "All pack members are asked to make their way to the conference room."

Reluctantly, August pressed away from the balustrade. "Catch you at dinner?"

I nodded. He'd *catch me* sooner than that.

Liam's jaw moved as though he were about to say something. In the end, he backed away without speaking.

I watched the men leave, allowing them a head start. Whether they liked it or not, I descended from this pack, so their decisions would affect my life. I hadn't had a say in returning to Boulder, but I wanted a say in what would happen now that I was back and out of hiding.

3

I forded through the clusters of women sipping drinks from copper goblets, the heady mix of perfumes and spirited juices making my nose twitch.

"Ness?" Someone tapped my shoulder.

I pivoted.

"It's me. Amanda."

I studied the brunette with the bluntly cut curly hair, the long-lashed tawny eyes, and the heart-shaped face.

"Amanda Frederick," she went on.

At last, I placed her. Miss Popular back in elementary and middle school. Not a mean girl. Just someone interested in everything I wasn't.

Her lips bent into a satisfied smile once she noted the recognition. "Are you back for the summer or longer?"

"Not sure yet."

Two other girls pushed in beside her. They tossed their names at me. *Taryn* and *Sienna*. Sienna reminded me of a piece of pale silk with her wispy blonde hair, latte-colored eyes, and flawless complexion. Taryn, on the other hand, was all harsh angles and stark contrasts. Her face was as narrow as an axe blade, her hair tar-black, and her eyes an icy blue.

"Who did you come with?" I asked.

The pack didn't have daughters—hadn't had any for over a century until me—so these girls had to be plus-ones.

Taryn raised her pointed chin. "Lucas Mason."

I remembered Lucas: shaggy black hair, serious acne, and surly attitude. He used to be Liam's best friend. Maybe still was.

Amanda said, "I'm with Matthew Rogers."

The name conjured up a blond giant.

"Sienna..." Amanda tilted her head toward the delicate blonde. "She's with August." It sounded like a warning.

"You and August seem close." Sienna's voice gusted softly toward me. I'd never met anyone whose voice matched their appearance until today.

"August is the brother I never had," I explained.

"You have Everest," Taryn snapped.

What was that supposed to mean? That I shouldn't hang out with August? "If you'll excuse me, I have somewhere to be."

I started back toward the doors of the living room when Lucy stopped me. I was about to utter an exasperated *what*, when she asked, "Where are you going?"

"To my bedroom."

She scrutinized my face. "Evelyn could use some help in the kitchen."

Without a fight, I walked in the direction of the kitchen until Lucy moved to the buffet. Then I doubled-back and set course for the basement. When I burst into the conference room, forty faces spun my way. Expressions ran the gamut: I got annoyance, anger, shock, curiosity.

But mostly annoyance.

"Ness?" my uncle said in a strangled voice. "Is everything all right?"

The salty, tangy scent of male was overpowering.

"Great." I looked for a free chair but found none. "Sorry I'm late, but Matt's girl is a talker."

A large blond boy with a neck as thick as his face crossed his beefy arms in front of his fridge-sized chest. I suspected he could crush a tree trunk with those arms.

"What are you doing here?" Jeb asked me.

"It's a pack meeting, isn't it?"

"It is."

"You have to be a member of the pack to sit in on it," someone said.

"Good thing I am, then."

An elder with bushy white hair and bushier white eyebrows linked his hands together before him in a business-like manner. "Ness Clark, you're not part of the pack."

"But that was under Heath Kolane. Now that he's gone, you've surely amended your misogynistic ways."

Everest made a little sound in the back of his throat. He wasn't the only one. Matt turned a shade darker, as though soaked with wood stain. August and his father gaped at me. Where Nelson tapped his fingers nervously against the laminated wood, August fought off a smile.

"You would have had to pledge yourself before puberty to become part of the pack," one of the elders said.

The mix of nerves and anger loosened my tongue. "What makes you think I hit puberty?"

Half the room checked me out. In their defense, I'd invited the attention.

"Okay, fine. I hit puberty. But it's a dumb rule. Besides, I was physically absent from Boulder, so I should get a free pass."

"Rules are rules." The declaration delivered by a bald elder was like a whip. Scorching.

Bastards.

Silence descended upon the room, punctuated only by the sound of denim rustling against leather.

Jeb turned pained eyes on me. He was going to ask me to leave. I could sense it in my bones. "Ness—"

Everest blurted out, "Alphas can bring new pledges into the pack at any age, as long as they have pack blood and can change at will."

All eyes were on him now. Everest's cheeks, neck, and ears glowed crimson.

I mouthed a *thank you.*

"You've been away a long time. Can you access your wolf form at will?" Liam asked.

"Yes," I lied.

I hadn't changed in six years, but now that I was back in Boulder, in proximity to the pack, I supposed it was a question of days until my nails turned to claws, my hands turned to paws, and the fine hair on my limbs thickened to fur.

"When was the last time you became a wolf?" he continued.

"Three days ago." From the corner of my eye, I could see Everest's lips pinch. Hopefully no one else caught his expression.

"The issue remains that there is no Alpha yet," the white-haired elder said. "Once one is chosen you will be able to plead your case. Until then"—if he said *shoo* or flicked his fingers, I would punch him—"you are not privy to pack discussions."

"Who are the contenders?"

Exasperated sighs grated up corded necks.

"Liam Kolane." The elder gestured to Liam as though I didn't know who Liam Kolane was.

"And?"

"That's it."

I scanned each and every face around the table. Didn't all wolves long to be leaders? Especially when the opportunity to become an Alpha so seldom arose? This would probably be our generation's one and only chance. After forty, a werewolf was no longer eligible because his body couldn't morph at will.

I looked at Everest. Challenged him to give Liam a run for his money. Heath would've hated that.

The elder with the gleaming bare scalp cleared his throat. "Kindly leave."

Jerk. "What are the requirements?" I asked. "Besides the age, what are the requirements?"

"The requirements for what, Ness?" Nelson asked, his ebony skin crinkling.

"For becoming Alpha."

"You must be under forty and have pack blood in your veins," Everest said.

"So I qualify?"

The planes of my uncle's face tautened. "Ness—"

"It's just a question, Uncle."

"It's a very specific question," Bushy-Eyebrows said.

August had paled, or perhaps it was the contrast to his father's much darker complexion that made my friend seem paler.

"You qualify," Everest declared.

The realization that I ticked all the boxes drummed against me like soft rain. But like rain, it also splashed a good deal of sobriety into me. What exactly was I thinking?

To put my name into the proverbial hat to annoy Liam Kolane was a dangerous game. One I wasn't sure I wanted to play, and not because I was afraid of losing—I had *nothing* to lose—but because, what happened if I won? I'd have to stay in Boulder and lead a pack I abhorred until I died or was demoted.

That wasn't the life I wanted.

At least, I'd never wanted it before.

4

As I applied a thin coat of mascara to my lashes, someone pounded on my door. Pounding was never good. It meant I was in trouble. After the stunt I'd pulled, I wasn't surprised. Actually, that wasn't true. I'd assumed the deafening knocks would've come earlier. Then again, I'd been helping Evelyn out in the kitchen, so maybe my haters hadn't known where to find me.

Lips squeezed into a smile to hide my hammering heart, I drew the door open. My rigid lips slackened. I'd expected Jeb or Everest.

I leaned against my bedroom door, draping on an air of boredom. "To what do I owe the pleasure of your visit, Liam?"

He shoved past me.

I pressed away from the door but didn't close it. "Come right on in…"

He whirled on me. "What the hell was that?"

I cocked an eyebrow.

"Are you seriously entertaining the idea of challenging me?"

"Oh. *That*." I strolled back into my bathroom and lined the insides of my lower lids with kohl.

Oblivion irritated people. I had every intention of irritating Liam and trampling his inflated ego.

He filled the open doorway, eyes flashing to mine in the mirror.

"I'm thinking about it," I said sweetly.

"If it's just to get into the pack, I'll consider your candidacy once I'm Alpha."

"How generous of you." I tossed my eyeliner into my makeup bag and spun, leaning back against the cold porcelain sink top and crossing my arms.

He lowered his brows. "Do not go against me."

"Or what? You'll hurt me?" I walked up to him and jabbed my finger into his chest. "I lost both my parents *and* was forced to come back to this hellhole where people look down on me because I wasn't born with the right blend of chromosomes. What exactly do you think you can do that will hurt me, huh?"

He stared down at my finger. Stepped back so it fell off his rock-hard chest. "I wouldn't *hurt* you, but you'll lose."

"You don't think very highly of me, do you?"

His eyes darkened.

"What if *you* lose?" I asked.

"I won't."

I hadn't decided what to do yet, but that...*that* decided me. "I see cockiness runs in the Kolane family."

He scowled as he backed out of my bedroom. "You know what? Go for it. Challenge me." He rolled his fingers into fists and cracked his knuckles. "It'll be my pleasure to teach you a little humility."

I felt the color rise in my cheeks. When he left, I slammed my door shut and stared at the wood paneling until my breathing no longer came in rough pants.

I DEBATED a long while whether to head down to dinner. Going would show Liam I didn't care that he'd come inside my bedroom to threaten me. But going also meant having to bust out small talk, and I was in too foul a mood to carry on any conversations.

I yanked off my jeans and black swing top, then pulled on leggings, sneakers, and an exercise bra. Sticking my hair into a ponytail, I tore through the empty hallway, down the deserted stairs, and straight for the cavernous gym.

I shut the door then flooded the room with light and music. I dragged the dummy from where it lurked in the shadowy corner like a stalker and thrust my hands into a pair of boxing gloves. Jeb and Lucy stocked this place with more exercise gear than the shoddy gym I'd spent hours in before Mom got sick.

I squinted at the dummy, replacing its blank face with Liam's. I kicked and jabbed at it. It shifted on its springs as I pummeled my fists and feet into it, but it didn't bleed and it didn't bruise.

Liam thought I didn't stand a chance. He was wrong.

Wrong.

Just because I was a female didn't mean I was weak.

Asshole.

I pounded my fists at dizzying speed into the dummy. Sweat slicked down my spine, soaked the back of my exercise bra, dripped down the sides of my face. I swiped my forearm over my brow, then wound my arm back and let my fist fly. A hand hooked around my bicep and wheeled me around. I reacted with a direct punch to the gut. A breath whooshed out of August's mouth as my glove connected to his abdomen. He released me and rubbed the spot.

"I'm so sorry," I yelled over the thumping music.

Tearing my gloves off, I crossed the room toward the water fountain to saturate a towel with ice-cold water, then brought it back to him, but he shook his head at my offering.

A crooked smile replaced his grimace. "Where'd you learn to punch like that?"

"Self-taught." I used the towel on my face and neck, chilling my flushed skin. "Is dinner already over?"

"No. We're at the main course."

"Then why are you here?"

"Because the seat I saved you was empty."

I lowered my gaze to the black rubber flooring. "I wasn't hungry."

"You're not hungry or you're mad?"

"Maybe both."

"What did Liam tell you?"

I whipped my gaze back to his. "How do you know he came to see me?"

"I heard him ask your aunt for your room number."

So that's how Liam knew where to find me... The fact that Lucy had doled out this information peeved me. Did she think his visit would be pleasant, or was she happy to encourage his intimidation technique? Probably the latter.

"Yeah. He dropped by."

"Look, I didn't come down here to discuss him."

"I hope you didn't come down here to drag me to dinner, because I'm not going."

"As much as I admire your spunk, I think you shouldn't go up against Liam. You don't want to be Alpha, Ness. Even *I* wouldn't want to lead the pack."

I tried to steady my breathing, but my larynx felt snarled. "Why not?"

"Why not what?"

"Why don't you want to lead the pack?"

"Because dealing with overblown egos and temperaments takes a toll on you. Even though Heath was...*well,* not the finest specimen...he gave a lot to the pack."

"He might've given a lot to the pack, but he took a lot from people who weren't part of the pack."

August's full mouth thinned.

"Everest's girlfriend tried to take her own life from shame," I continued.

"He's gone now." August's voice was low. "He paid for what he did."

"*He* might be gone, but Liam Kolane isn't."

August touched my bare shoulder. "Liam isn't Heath." When I didn't shrug his hand off, he closed his fingers over my rotator cuff and squeezed gently. "Let him have this."

A new aroma ribboned over August's sawdust and Old Spice scent—flowery, watery. In the open doorway, I spied a pale face set with glittery eyes.

"Your girlfriend's here," I muttered.

He didn't release me. "If you want a place in the pack, I'll make sure you get it, but don't do this."

The beat-heavy Drake song faded. Just before a new song came on, Sienna spoke August's name. He didn't acknowledge her.

"You will lose," he said.

Like claws, his words scraped against my self-esteem. I straightened my spine and squared my shoulders. "Did Liam put you up to this?"

"No."

I backed away from him.

A shadow muddied the green in his eyes. "Ness—"

"I'm a big girl, August. I'll make up my own mind." I walked toward the hamper and chucked the towel inside. "Thanks for your concern, though."

"You're going to go through with it, aren't you?"

"I like proving people wrong."

"This isn't a game."

"I'm aware of that." I drew the door wide.

Sienna scrambled out of my way and flattened her back against the mirrored wall. At least I inspired fear in someone. Not the right someone, though.

"Sorry to have kept your date away," I muttered.

Not that it was my fault. I hadn't asked August to come and tell me how foolish I was.

From anyone else, I wouldn't have cared. But August...August's opinion mattered.

I hated that it mattered.

I hated that it made me question my decision.

Halfway back to my bedroom, I crossed paths with Everest. "If you're here to talk me out of it, don't waste your breath."

He kept up with my hurried strides. "Are you kidding? I'm totally on board with you going up against Liam."

That took me by surprise. I stopped. "You are?"

"Hell yeah. But if you're sure, you need to tell the elders before midnight."

"Why? Do they turn into pumpkins after that?"

Everest smirked, and it shook off the cloying anxiety that had marred his face since Becca swan dove off her roof. "The blood oath happens at midnight."

I remembered my father telling me about blood oaths, but it was in the context of electing the Alpha. Pack members needed to slash their skin, then touch their seeping wounds to the Alpha's. Once the contact happened, the magic took place and turned an ordinary wolf into a true beast. I wasn't sure how it worked in terms of competing for the title.

"Get cleaned up and meet me on the deck," Everest said.

In front of the dining room entrance, I spied Liam exchanging words with Matt, the blond giant, and another boy who was as tall as Matt but built narrower, with shaggy black hair and an ugly scar across one of his eyebrows.

When they caught me staring, I turned my attention back to Everest. "I'll be there in a sec." And then I jogged away to get ready.

I'd give the jerk a run for his money.

Did I want to win? Sure. Who wanted to lose? Did I want to lead a bunch of jerks? No. But if I did win, I could probably nominate someone else to run the pack. I wondered what my father would've thought of my decision. Would he question my sanity, or would he be proud?

My mother had raised me to go after what I wanted. And what I wanted was to stop another Kolane from being in a position of power. I held on to that as I readied to fight for my beliefs.

5

Dessert and drinks were being served on the spacious deck when I arrived. Flickering candles in giant hurricane holders cast eerie glows and moving shadows over the faces angled my way. Conversations halted. The only sound was the instrumental jazz whirring from hidden ceiling speakers.

Jeb shifted toward me, a tumbler of whiskey clutched between his fingers.

"Sorry I missed dinner," I said.

"You want to eat something?"

"I'll eat later."

He lowered his glass to his narrow hip, and the ice clinked. "Ness—"

"Please, Uncle. Don't tell me what to do."

"A month ago, you didn't want to come back here. You wanted nothing to do with the pack, and now you're vying for—for Alpha." He joggled his hand, and whiskey splashed out.

"Let me guess... I shouldn't compete, because I'm a girl, and according to you, girls are mangy little things."

Color crawled up his throat.

"I might've been weak when you kicked me out of Boulder, but I'm not anymore."

"Stop saying I kicked you out, will you?" he hissed.

"Well, it's true."

Through gritted teeth, he added, "It was to protect you."

I dropped my voice. "Because of what Heath did to Mom?"

White appeared around Jeb's iris rings.

Although people were near, they were too busy gossiping to listen to us. Or maybe they'd heard.

Like. I. Cared.

More whiskey dribbled along his wrist. "You—You—"

"Know about it? Yeah. Mom told me. I also know you didn't do shit about retaliating. Besides getting us to leave, that is. Better Mom not tempt your revered Alpha again, huh?"

At first, I'd believed the cancer had made Mom delirious, but then Everest had confirmed it during one of our late-night chats after Becca's attempted suicide. The confession came out almost at the same time as Mom's last breath. Once she'd untethered herself from the lurid secret, her soul slipped out of her body and left me to deal with the aftermath of the terrible truth.

I'd been angry with her. But then Evelyn reminded me anger was one of the stages of grief, so I allowed myself to feel angry. With Mom and with Heath. Where I'd forgiven my mother for not telling me, I hadn't forgiven Heath.

"So this—you entering the contest—it's a personal vendetta?" Jeb asked.

"Not only."

His Adam's apple bobbed. "Liam is not like his father."

Gosh, how many people were going to tell me that? I gave a sharp nod and went to find Everest. Crossing the deck was like walking past a firing squad. Even though the slanted gazes pricked, I raised my chin and pretended to be unaffected by the petty glares.

"I'd forgotten how friendly Coloradans were," I muttered once I reached my cousin by the stainless-steel drinks dispenser.

He poured coffee into a mug, then handed it to me. "Did Dad try to talk you out of it?"

"I didn't give him time to." I took a sip of the charred-tasting beverage. "He knows I know. About Mom."

The clink of metal against glass interrupted our quiet conversation.

The bushy-eyebrowed elder stood from his Adirondack. "Usually pack matters are discussed among the pack, but since the choice of Alpha affects all our lives, not only our fellow members but also our partners, we decided to discuss the subject with all of you. As you're all aware, Liam Kolane offered to replace his father as Alpha, but he's been challenged." The elder's gaze slid to me, but then it skittered toward the beefy blond beside Liam. "Matthew Rogers"—next, the elder tipped his head toward the lanky boy with the mean white scar and mop of black hair—"and Lucas Mason have decided to go up against Heath's boy."

My shoulders pinched together. I bumped my arm into Everest's. "Did you know?"

My cousin shook his head.

The elder's gaze returned to me. "I believe they aren't the only contenders, though."

Silence entrenched the patio.

While Matt and Lucas leered at me, Liam's face was blank, calm. Too calm. Too blank. If anything, his expression bothered me more than theirs. And then it hit me that he must've orchestrated this, asked them to enter their names in the contest to dissuade me from entering mine.

Smart.

If I hadn't spied them talking, I would most probably have been swayed to drop the charade, but I could bet anything Lucas and Matt were going to suddenly back out and leave Liam in charge.

The elder's gaze was cemented on me. "Anyone else interested in the role of Alpha, speak now or forever hold your peace."

August was standing on the opposite end of the deck next to his father. Both had their arms crossed tightly, but only August scowled. His father kept wetting his lips, nervous, concerned. For the briefest of moments, I shut my eyes. When I opened them, determination chased away the hesitation.

I stared at Liam, and in a clear voice I said, "Sign me up."

Intakes of breaths traveled through the women, followed by breathy exclamations. No one looked more surprised than my aunt, though. Her face, which she already kept out of the sun, had become as white as the sheets I'd spent all morning ironing.

Jeb downed the dregs of his whiskey in one long gulp.

Contempt was stamped in many a gaze. And then there was the look August shot me. Disappointment. If I'd learned one thing about life, it was that pleasing everyone was impossible.

I lowered my gaze to the black liquid rippling inside my mug, rippling because my hands were shaking. I tightened my grip.

"You are one ballsy chick," Everest murmured.

"Anyone else?" the elder asked.

I raised my chin and scanned the faces surrounding me. So many of them were still looking my way. So many still whispering. Amanda and her two besties were smirking. Would they have smirked if they'd been werewolves or would they have supported a sister's endeavor?

"I will convene with the elders to discuss the rules of this competition. After breakfast, we will deliberate with the four contenders in the conference room. But before we leave, we need to collect a drop of your blood to guarantee your candidacy."

Bushy-Eyebrows crooked a finger. I handed my mug to Everest and joined the other three who'd already approached the white-haired elder.

"Wrists." His nail had lengthened into a claw.

Liam, Matt, and Lucas extended their arms.

"Ness?"

I jutted my hand out.

"With blood, you will bind yourselves to me so I may know your whereabouts and keep track of your vitals during the contest. Once an Alpha rises, your connection to me will be severed."

He slashed his wrist, and then slashed all of ours in turn. I gritted my teeth at the shock of pain. Bushy-Eyebrows pressed his blood to ours.

"Well, that's sanitary," I mumbled.

"Wolves don't carry disease, Ness," the elder reassured me.

The wolf in me knew that; the human still saw blood as a vehicle for disease.

Almost instantly, the edges of the boys' skin knitted together.

Lucas snorted at my still-gaping nick. "Not healing very fast, are you? Want a bandage for your boo-boo?"

Shooting him a glare, I returned to the table set with desserts and grabbed a paper napkin, pulse pounding against the torn skin. *Heal*, I instructed my wrist; it didn't. That wouldn't help my street cred. I pressed the napkin to my wrist and watched the white turn crimson.

"We will meet in the morning to discuss the contest." Trailed by four other elders, Bushy-Eyebrows walked off the terrace.

Amanda tore away from her friends and strutted over to me, her heeled booties clucking against the hardwood floor. "Hun, hun, hun. Going against our boys is one dumb idea."

"*Your* boys?" I asked.

"Yeah, *our* boys. We grew up with them; we stuck around; we were there to comfort them when they needed some TLC."

My fingers cinched around my wrist tighter.

"We are as much part of this pack as you are. Actually, that's not true. You're not part of the pack."

"Enough, Amanda," Liam said.

So engrossed was I by her pettiness that I hadn't seen him advance.

She twirled, and her curls fanned out around her, littering the air with the aroma of apricot. It blended with the smell of the coffee cooling in my discarded mug, the scent of the blood drying on my wrist, and Everest's evergreen cologne. My stomach swished from the sensorial assault.

"I was just voicing everyone's thoughts," Amanda chirped.

Liam's lips were pressed so tight that when he said, "Leave her alone," I thought it was Everest speaking.

Liam was defending me? Surely I'd heard him wrong. Or he had an ulterior motive. After being a bastard, the only reason he'd act kind would be to confuse me. "I can fight my own battles, Liam."

"I'm sure you can, but we don't talk down to each other. Other packs might, but not us." He sounded so freaking noble. I understood why no one challenged him. He spoke like he was already an Alpha. But if he'd learned that from Heath, then I could only imagine the rest of what Liam had been taught.

Amanda pursed her glossy lips just as a large hand landed on her shoulder. She tipped her neck up and smiled up at Matt, who stood a full head and a half taller.

He extended one large paw. "Don't know if you remember me—"

"I do." I stared at his hand a long while before shaking it.

He didn't crush my fingers like I imagined he would.

As though the contact with Matt's hand had thawed the invisible ice encasing me, others approached. Introduced themselves, *reintroduced* themselves. Six years changed teenage faces, yet I recognized most...remembered most.

A smile crooked Lucas's lips. "We should bond."

My spit went down the wrong hole, and I coughed. "Excuse me?"

"We should do a bonding exercise." He tucked Taryn into his side, his hand almost on her breast. Classy.

His words combined with his sly smile had caused my mind to form indecent images full of leather fetters and iron chains. Why in the world was I thinking about bondage?

"Paintball," a young boy with shoulder-length copper hair said.

"Exactly what I was thinking, little J. We should totally go paintballing tomorrow." Lucas was still simpering at me. "Ever paintballed, doll?"

"Don't call me doll."

Lucas's white scar writhed at my reproof.

"And *no*, I never paintballed."

Amanda stroked Matt's thick fingers, while Taryn whispered in Lucas's ear. I looked for Sienna, found her speaking quietly with August. Unlike the other two couples, they weren't touchy-feely. If anything, their rigid body language told me they were arguing.

There were other girls on the terrace, but they were chatting away, either oblivious or uninterested in participating in the conversation going on around me. I wondered if Liam's girlfriend was among them. I assumed he had a girlfriend, considering the number of girls who'd come to the pack event.

I returned my gaze to Lucas. "Is *everyone* going?"

Lucas's smile snuck back over his lips. "Just the pack and *you*. Feeling intimidated by so much testosterone, Clark?"

What I felt was hot. Probably from the wall of massive bodies encasing me. Or from the blood loss. I lifted the reddened napkin and noted the cut was shallower, the skin less puckered. The wound was closing. That was a good sign.

I retied the tissue, then pressed my palm against the nape of my neck, but my clammy hand did little to cool me down. "Not much intimidates me, Lucas. But thanks for your concern."

That seemed to make Liam smile, or at least I thought amusement had contorted his lips, but I must've imagined it.

Man, it was hot. I needed air. And space. I backed up, bumping into a chest. Brackish sweat and floral perfumes assailed my senses.

I concentrated on breathing through my mouth. "You all have yourselves a good night."

My stomach swished harder, and my head... My head felt as though my brain were being kicked around with cleats.

"Excuse me." When no one moved, I elbowed my way through the throng of bodies.

My sneaker caught on a big foot, and I stumbled, knocking into Liam. His drink sloshed from the glass and spilled over his black t-shirt.

"S-sorry."

He wrapped a hand around my arm to steady me.

Had someone slipped something into my coffee? I bristled and yanked my arm out of Liam's grasp, then traipsed across the deck like a drunk. I made it into the living room without vomiting, and then I bolted to my room on legs that felt detached from my body.

What was going on with me?

6

Cold sweat slicked down my tingling spine. I jammed my key against the lock, but the metal slid uselessly against the wood. I tried again. Again I failed.

"Ness! Wait up." Everest was barreling down the hallway.

There were two of him.

Three.

I didn't want to be sick in the hallway. He grabbed the key from my fingers, opened my door, then helped me in. I scrambled to the bathroom and knelt in front of the toilet just as a jet of vomit spewed out of my mouth.

"Did you eat something bad?" Everest asked.

I hadn't eaten anything since lunch. I shook my head, but that angered the throbbing.

Another wave of sick spurted out of me.

My vision blurred and readjusted. Unfortunately, my sense of smell didn't blur. The acrid stench of vomit was so acute it made my nostrils flare.

Everest took a seat on the edge of the bathtub. "Was it true what you said earlier? That you changed three days ago?"

"Are you really grilling me right now?" I hoisted myself from the floor, flushed the toilet, and turned on the tap.

"No, I'm not grilling you. I'm asking because I have a theory. Did you or didn't you change yet?"

I splashed cold water over my face then squinted at my reflection. My eyes looked wrong. I blinked. My irises glowed like the neon sign over the ice-cream parlor August would take me to on hot afternoons when our dads needed to work.

I spun toward Everest. "It's—It's happening!"

He sighed. "I take it you didn't change three days ago..."

I lifted my hands in front of my face and slowly turned them. My nails had lengthened and were curving.

I stared in horror at Everest. I couldn't become a wolf here. Not in my bathroom. I would destroy it. In beast form, my muscles would grow and my movements would become choppy and rough. When I'd changed for the first time at eleven, I'd destroyed my bedroom and clawed through the living room couch. It took me weeks to master my wolf form.

Would it take me weeks again?

As though someone were carving out my vertebrae, blinding pain vaulted up my spine. I arched backward and gritted my teeth. Pointy canines dug into my lower lip and split the soft tissue. Blood dribbled down my chin. As my shoulder blades popped out of their joints, I bit back a scream and fell forward, landing hard on my palms and knees.

The seam on my wrist burst open and blood gushed out. A crimson river trickled in the grout between the stones.

"It's going to be okay, Ness. I'm right here. It's going to be okay..." Everest's voice sounded like it was coming from another room. He crouched beside me, his palm cool against my scorching neck.

The blood from my lip slopped onto the slate flooring and mixed with the blood from my wrist. I sagged and blinked. Had it been this painful six years ago, or was the pain augmented because of the years I'd deprived my body of its transformation?

Tears dripped off my cheeks and tangled with the blood. "I can't. It hurts..." My voice was more howl than words.

My mind turned hazy with ache, and my elbows gave in. I yelped and flailed forward, smacking my cheek against the cold stone floor. The blow felt as though it had shattered the cartilage in my face, but perhaps it was the wolf within that was shattering my face, just as it was altering my bone structure, dislocating my joints, and hardening my sinews. I closed my eyes and willed it to stop.

Begged for it to stop.

And it did.

THERE WAS an incessant jangling inside my skull. *Ugh.* I pressed a pillow over my face and squashed my lids tight, my lips tighter. Searing pain radiated over my mouth. I pitched the pillow off my head and sat up so fast my bedroom swam before my eyes. I touched my throbbing lower lip. My fingers came away red, wet with blood.

It hadn't been a dream.

The night poured back through me. I shivered, even though I was still fully clothed. Everest—I assumed it had been him—had put me to bed, but he hadn't stripped my clothes off. The seams of my jeans dug into my skin, and the wire frame of my bra felt engraved into my ribs.

I peeled myself from the warm bed and padded to my bathroom. I flicked on the lights, smelling blood before spotting it. Balled pink tissues littered my wastebasket. I moved to the sink and peered at my hellish reflection. My bottom lip was split and swollen, my right cheek was bruised, and my wrist, although no longer torn, sported a purple hematoma.

I turned the shower on and stripped. Red lines streaked my skin, but the imprint of clothing would vanish quickly, unlike my tattered flesh. That would take a couple more hours to heal—if I was lucky. The worst part was that, even if I managed to camouflage the bruise on my cheek, there was nothing I could do about my lip. Everyone would see it. If they learned I'd bit my own self, they'd realize I had no control over my wolf form, which could disqualify me from the Alpha contest.

I returned to my bedroom, grabbed my cell phone that was snoozing, turned off the alarm, and typed a message to Everest. **I passed out because I was sick, and my lip split from the fall. Come see me in the kitchen when you wake up.** I sent that off, then added: **Thank you for staying with me. And for putting me to bed.**

And then I got ready for the long day ahead, feeling like my body had been rubbed against the metal ridges of the washboard nailed to the wall of the laundry room, a memento of early life in Colorado.

7

The second I entered the kitchen, Evelyn gasped. "*Dios mio!*"
She clapped a hand over her mouth and set down her whisk. The runny milk and eggs dripped onto the scratched but gleaming stainless-steel island.

"Who did that to you?" Even though we were alone in the kitchen and probably the only ones awake in the entire inn, her voice was quiet.

I didn't move my gaze off the trickling whisk. "I fell."

She narrowed her eyes at me, irises darkened by skepticism. "Against whose fist did you fall?"

"No one. I promise. I was sick, and you know how I get when I'm sick...I pass out." Which was true. I always passed out when I threw up.

She walked around the island and caught my chin between her fingers, turning my face left and right, inspecting my cheek. I bit down on my lip before remembering the tiny stab wound. I released my lip instantly, then removed my face from her hands.

Her thin, penciled-in eyebrows drew together when her gaze moved over the rest of my body and spotted bruises on my elbows and wrist. "The truth, *querida*."

The truth... Could I tell her the truth, or would she run back to L.A. screaming? Or worse, would she stop loving me for who I was? Why hadn't these things occurred to me before I made her leave everything behind for me? Did I think I could hide my dual nature from her forever?

"It is why you left Boulder in the first place?" she asked. "Someone was hurting you?"

"No one was hurting me." Had Mom told her about Heath? "But it's the reason we left Boulder."

Her eyes glittered furiously as she took in my skin that carried the same camo pattern as the tank underneath my gray uniform. I should probably have gone with long sleeves.

I sighed. "Can you promise not to hate me once I tell you the whole truth?"

She pressed a hand against her chest, over her heart. "Hate you? It is too late for me to hate you."

I sank onto the stepladder Evelyn used as a chair when her knees ached and hung my head in my hands. "You're going to think I'm crazy."

"I would never think such a thing."

"Yes, you will. And you'll leave." I'd told Liam nothing could hurt me anymore, but that wasn't true. Evelyn shunning me, leaving me, that would cause me tremendous pain.

"I will never leave you."

"You swear?" I tipped my head back to stare into her gentle eyes.

"On the Lord above, I swear it. Now tell me."

"I'm a"—I gulped—"a...*werewolf*." My voice was quieter than the fan whirring over the stove.

Evelyn's rouged mouth gaped. Closed. Gaped again. She reminded me of the trouts Dad and I used to catch fly fishing in the mountain streams. "*Un lobo?*"

She'd taught me enough Spanish for me to understand *lobo*: wolf. Even to me, who'd grown up with the knowledge that such fantastical creatures existed, it sounded outrageous.

With shaky fingers, I tucked a strand of hair behind my ear. "Yes."

She didn't back away from me, didn't run screaming, but confusion rippled over her features.

"How hard did you bump your head?"

"I'll show you." Concentrating hard, I lifted my unsteady hands and willed my nails to turn into claws. Nothing happened. I tried again. Still nothing. I tucked both my hands underneath my thighs. "I used to be able to change at will, but being away—"

"Oh, sweetheart..."

"Evelyn, please. I'm telling you the truth."

She shot me a look filled with such pain and sympathy that I grabbed the phone from my tunic pocket and dialed Everest.

After a couple rings, his sleepy voice came on. "Hello?"

"Come to the kitchen now," I said.

"Ness, it's not even six."

"Please."

He grumbled. "Fine."

Silence slipped between Evelyn and me. I could tell a thousand words formed on the tip of her tongue, but she didn't utter any of them. She just stared, her face stamped with as much worry as the day we'd finally let her into our ground-floor unit.

Five long minutes later, Everest arrived. "What?"

"Show Evelyn," I asked him.

"Show her what?"

"What we are."

His eyes widened. "Ness…"

"I can't keep this a secret from her any longer."

He turned his face toward Evelyn. Alarm deepened the little lines around her eyes and mouth.

"Please," I whispered.

"Okay." He raised his hands. In seconds, his nails lengthened and curled, and then his fingers retracted into his palms.

Evelyn became as pale as her pancake batter. She crossed herself, and then…and then she fainted.

Everest caught her before her head could knock against the tiles. I scrambled off the stepladder and helped him situate her there. I rushed to the sink, wadded up some paper towels, and wet them.

"Why did you *have* to tell her?" Everest muttered, his voice still a bit groggy.

"Because she would've found out. It's not like our existence is that much of a secret in this part of the world."

"Just because people suspect we exist, doesn't mean they all believe it."

I crouched beside her and moved the damp compress across her forehead. "I needed her to believe it."

Her eyelids fluttered, and then her mascara-laden eyelashes lifted. She blinked as she came to. And then her black eyes settled on me. An emotion—I couldn't tell if it was fear or astonishment—flitted through them.

"Please, say something, Evelyn." I dabbed the wet towel along her neck.

"Breakfast," she murmured. "I need to make breakfast." She pressed my hand away, latched onto the island for support, and wobbled onto her feet. Everest hadn't released her, but she brushed his hands off as though they were spiders.

She picked out a serrated knife and turned toward me. I backed up and fell, my buttocks hitting cold tiles. Was she going to kill me?

"Can you cut the bread, Ness? Make thick slices."

Working on evening out my thudding pulse, I scrambled back up to my feet and reached out to seize the knife. The serrated blade whispered through the air and gleamed in the bright lighting.

Evelyn returned to her batter and picked up the whisk as though my reveal hadn't happened, as though Everest's hands hadn't morphed into paws.

"If I'm no longer needed, I'm going to go crash a couple more hours." Everest pivoted toward me. "Unless you want me to stay?"

"No. Go. Thank you." Before he left, I told him, "Read your messages."

"I read them."

I plastered on a weak smile as he passed through the swinging door, and then I walked to the cutting board topped with three loaves of challah.

"Evelyn, are you—" I was about to say angry when she stopped me with a raised palm.

Tears pricked my swollen lids. She didn't want to talk to me. She was horrified, and how could I blame her?

We worked in silence next to each other. While she tossed thick slabs of bacon in a cast-iron skillet, I soaked the slices of bread I'd cut in egg and milk, prepping them for the griddle Evelyn had already buttered. Not once did we look at each other. I was afraid of what I would see there, and probably, so was she.

While she cooked, I sunk my hands in rubber gloves and soaped up the toppling tower of bowls and cooking paraphernalia. Then I aligned the stainless-steel containers and helped Evelyn arrange the golden triangles of French toast, the fluffy pancakes, the crispy hash browns, the fried sausage, the glistening bacon, and the scrambled eggs.

As I carried the lidded metal containers into the deserted dining room, dawn fanned out over the mountains and raked through the majestic pines, tinting the rock lavender and the bristly leaves blue. Dawn had always been my favorite time of day. Perhaps because it was the quietest, or perhaps because it felt like a piece of blank paper upon which anything could be drawn.

But not today. Today its blankness felt barren and smudged by Evelyn's silence.

After I slotted all the dishes into their cradles and lit the small candles that would keep them warm until the pack descended upon the dining room, I brewed coffee and tea in the pantry and filled several thermoses with the dark, steaming liquids, going through the motions robotically.

The swinging door flapped.

"Do you know where I could get—" Liam's gaze collided into mine.

I raised a thermos. "Coffee?"

Slowly, he nodded and extended the ceramic mug clutched between his long fingers.

I filled it for him. "How do you take it?"

"What happened to your face?"

I licked the scab on my lip. "I fell. Do you want milk? Sugar?"

His dark eyebrows pressed together. "Just milk."

I poured some into his mug. "More?"

He was still looking at my mouth.

"Do you want more milk?"

He shook his head, then tugged a hand through his brown hair, mussing it up. I didn't remember his mother in great detail—she died when I was five and he was nine—but I remembered she was a beautiful, gentle woman. Instead of looking for Heath in Liam, I looked for her, but the square, chiseled jaw, the brown eyes, the dark eyebrows, those were all Heath.

"Ready for today?" Liam asked as I set the milk down on the large wooden platter.

"For the meeting with the elders or the paintballing?" I lined up the jugs and thermoses, then filled glass pitchers with ice and tap water and placed those on the platter.

"Both."

I shot him a cocky smile, which sent a jolt of pain through my face. No more smiling for me today. "I was born ready." I latched on to the horn handles of the tray and heaved it up.

"Want help with that?"

Even though my joints smarted a little, I said, "I don't need anyone's help." I gave him a wide berth so our arms wouldn't graze, then pressed my shoulder into the swinging door.

The only thing I needed was for Evelyn to keep loving me in spite of the beast I was.

8

I changed out of my work uniform before meeting with the five elders. I slid on skinny jeans and a pair of much-loved, scuffed-up Timberlands that seemed appropriate footwear for paintballing.

Lucas, Matt, and Liam were already in the conference room when I arrived, lounging on the springy office chairs.

"Close the door, Ness," Bushy-Eyebrows instructed.

Even though the idea of being locked in a room with eight men was unpleasant, I shut the door before making my way to the free seat next to Matt. I felt his gaze rake over my face. Lucas looked too.

The bald elder leaned forward and clasped his hands. "Did someone...hurt you?"

"No." I didn't offer details. "So what's on the agenda?"

Chairs squeaked as bodies shifted.

Bushy-Eyebrows took a swig of water from the glass in front of him. "Okay. Let's get down to business. There will be three tests. The first, endurance. You will have to run twenty miles in wolf form over a terrain set with obstacles and traps. The last person to arrive at the marked destination will lose. And anyone who switches into his or her human form will be automatically disqualified."

My pulse jackhammered inside my veins. To compete, I would need to change. Fully change. Not the pathetic attempt I'd gone through last night.

Praying the assembled werewolves' heightened senses wouldn't pick up on my nervousness, I asked, "When will this take place?"

"The sooner the better. Would next weekend work for everyone?"

That gave me one week to master my wolf form. Not ideal but better than a couple hours. I toyed with Mom's ring, slotting it around one finger, then slipping it over another.

Everyone nodded.

"We will test your cunning next. The details of that trial will only be given to the three winners of the first contest," Bushy-Eyebrows said.

I could do cunning. I released Mom's ring and tucked it back into my tank top where the warmed metal rested against my heart.

"And then we'll end with a test of strength. A fight between the last two contenders."

"A fight?" I croaked.

"Did you think this was some sort of beauty pageant, Ness?" Eric asked.

I squashed my aching lips tight to seal off the sharp comeback that threatened to pop out. A fight wasn't fair, but I supposed the elders knew that. Even though I was strong, how much damage could a hundred-and-twenty-pound girl inflict on a two-hundred-plus-pound monster like Matt? I could hurt him, sure, but beat him... unlikely. But maybe Matt wouldn't be the one in the ring.

Maybe *I* wouldn't be the one in the ring.

Bushy-Eyebrows leaned forward in his seat. "Does anyone have questions?"

The other three shook their heads. I neither shook my head nor nodded. I stayed perfectly still.

"Now let's talk rules. Eric?" Bushy-Eyebrows nodded to the bald elder.

Eric started, "Non-pack members—"

I bristled. "So these rules only apply to me?"

"Just the first one. If you lose, Ness," Eric said in a voice that sounded like he'd eaten gravel for breakfast, "you cannot ask the future Alpha to bring you into the pack."

I narrowed my eyes. "Which means I'll have to leave Boulder?"

"Yes."

Even though I'd planned to leave, I wanted it to be my choice. Not theirs. "But if any of the others lose, they get to stay in the pack?"

"Correct."

Well, that's fair.

"You will all be civil to each other. We don't want any fighting outside of these trials," Eric said.

Bushy-Eyebrows continued, "Internal discord will only weaken the pack. Already not having an Alpha for such a prolonged period of time has hurt us and bolstered the self-worth of neighboring packs. Let's not give them more ammunition."

Last night, they'd all been civil to me. This morning, Liam had been borderline kind. Would this go on? The pack had shunned me when I'd needed help after Dad was shot. I had a long memory, and that memory had wedged deep trust issues inside me.

"Okay, Ness?" Eric asked.

I didn't appreciate being singled out. *Again.* I shoved my shoulders back hard against the leather seat. "I can be nice."

"Can you?" Lucas asked.

I shot him a taunting smile. "If I want to be, yes."

"Well, we do hope you'll want to be," Bushy-Eyebrows said. "Any uncivil behavior reported to us will incur serious consequences. Elimination being the gentler consequence."

His name suddenly slotted into my mind. *Frank.* Frank McNamara. He used to be the Alpha when my father was my age. Dad had always spoken highly of him. I wondered if Frank would've allowed me into the pack had he been Alpha instead of Heath. But I quit wondering fast because what was the point in musing over something that couldn't happen?

"I believe you kids have something fun planned, so we'll adjourn this meeting."

Yeah, fun. Not.

"Next Saturday, come to the pack headquarters at noon. Don't be late." The elders rose.

As Frank passed behind my chair, he placed a palm on my shoulder. "Jeb told me about your mother this morning."

Great. Lucy was giving out my room number to strangers, and Jeb was informing people of my loss. So much for respecting my privacy. Sadly, my aunt and uncle were meeting my expectations...my very low expectations.

"Maggie was a good woman," Frank added.

My throat felt like someone had gone at it with a fist.

Frank squeezed my shoulder once then went on his way.

"What'd she die of?" Matt asked as I got up.

I pushed a lock of hair behind my ear. Even though I didn't want to discuss my mother with anyone, I also didn't want them to get their information from other places. "Ovarian cancer."

"Is that why you're so bitter?" Lucas asked.

Matt and Liam both shot him a look.

Lucas raised his palms in the air. "I was just wondering if she was biting off our heads because she couldn't stand the look of them, or if her behavior was out of the ordinary. Am I not allowed to ask?"

"*Damn.* And here I thought I'd been coming across as charming." I smiled. "I should probably work on my social skills." My phone vibrated in my back pocket. I fished it out, but when I saw the number on the screen, I rejected the call and shoved it back inside my pocket. "So, paintball?" I asked, my heart loping around my chest.

If only I could've quieted it with a press of a button, too.

A SMALL BUS was waiting outside the inn, already crammed with animated pack members. Sucking in a breath, I climbed on, Everest close behind. I slid into the first row so I didn't have to ford through the entire bus. Everest dropped down next to me.

I caught sight of August across the aisle. He seemed intent on deciphering the slogan in bold block letters on the driver's cap.

Everest bent toward me and dropped his voice to a low whisper, "He broke up with Sienna last night."

That explained the surly curve of August's mouth.

"How long were they dating?" I murmured back.

"A couple months. Wouldn't know why he ended things, would you?"

"Me?" I frowned. "Why would I know anything?"

Everest gave me a *come-on* look.

"I didn't even know her…"

He narrowed his eyes so much they looked about to collide against the bridge of his nose.

"What?"

"*Dimples?*" he whispered.

"You think it's because of *me?*"

Everest shrugged. "Maybe they were having trouble before he called you his favorite girl."

I jabbed my elbow into his ribs because he'd said that way too loudly. So loudly that August glanced my way. I highly doubted he'd broken up with his girlfriend over me. Everest was giving me way more importance than I had.

The bus door closed after Liam, Lucas, and Matt walked on. Matt slid in next to August, while Liam and Lucas sat behind me. I sank a little lower in my seat. I heard Matt ask August how he was holding up.

August grunted. "Fine."

"How was the meeting?" Everest asked.

As the bus pulled out of the inn's driveway and rolled west, I told him about the first trial and the rule—the one that only applied to me. And then I told him about the last trial. And his eyes went as wide as his mouth.

"You can't win a physical fight," he whispered.

"Thanks for the vote of confidence." He was probably right, though.

Lucas leaned forward, his greasy black hair flopping in my peripheral vision. I half expected him to mention the trials. He didn't. "I was remembering the last time I saw you in your wolf form. You were this scrawny ball of white fur."

The bus went over a pothole, and my breasts jiggled. I folded my arms to block them in place. "You sure you didn't mistake me for a kitten?"

He smirked. "I know the difference between a cat and a wolf. Both have claws, but only one bites."

My phone vibrated in my lap. I could tell Everest had recognized the number from the stiffening of his body. I flipped the phone over.

"Who you avoiding? An ex?" Lucas inquired.

"Exactly."

"Got many exes back in… Where was it you lived again?"

Matt filled in for him, "Los Angeles."

"Got many exes back in L.A.?" Lucas asked.

"Maybe."

"You know, Ness, the elders didn't state this rule, probably 'cause there hasn't been any girls in the pack for over a century, but there's no dating among the pack. We don't shit where we eat, if you get the gist."

I cocked an eyebrow. "In what screwed up world do you think I'd be interested in dating *any* of you?"

He tipped his long chin toward Everest. "You and your cousin look awfully chummy."

Shock rushed through me that he would think I would screw my own cousin.

Everest spun and smashed his fist into Lucas's simpering grin, which had Lucas shooting to his feet.

Liam grabbed a fistful of his friend's t-shirt and yanked him back into his seat. "Enough!" His eyes gleamed dangerously. He probably didn't want his little friend to be kicked out of the running for Alpha for being *uncivil*.

"You punch like a girl, Everest," Lucas muttered under his breath.

"Stop being a dick, Lucas." August's retort rumbled like thunder.

The bus had gone extremely quiet, so quiet I could hear Everest's leaden breaths. I wound my fingers around his wrist, but he ripped his hand away, then sulked the rest of the trip to the paintball arena.

Lucas didn't try talking to us again, but he did talk. To Liam. Told him about the explosive orgasm he'd given Taryn that morning, which had me wrinkling my nose. And then he asked Liam if they were still on for tonight, 'cause Tamara was *extremely* eager to see Liam.

I wasn't the type of person who eavesdropped, but this conversation was in no way a secret. I bet Lucas was thrilled I was hearing it. I bet he thought it made them look appealing. All these girls throwing themselves at shifters because they were muscled and powerful and could turn into fierce creatures.

Few humans were privy to our existence. Most people still believed we were fictional beings, which packs perpetuated because not everyone was hot and bothered over a person who could morph into a beast. There were those who despised what we were.

Like the hunter who'd killed my father with a silver bullet.

People often hated what they didn't understand.

No one understood why a girl was born to the pack, and that inspired hatred.

9

The paintballing arena resembled a post-apocalyptic junkyard. A rusted old bus with blown-out windows sat at the center of muddy earth strewn with various corroded car parts and scraps of metal tall enough to shield a body —and sharp enough to slice through one, too. A plastic tunnel linked the north part to the south part of the arena. A row of brick walls arranged like a labyrinth ran the length of the western fence. A log cottage sat along the arena's northern fence. The rooms were dusty, the furniture disemboweled and overturned, the cabinets crooked and broken, their doors flapping like broken bird wings.

On the east side, there was a narrow tower with a winding staircase, and a plat-form with a plank leading down into a wooden boat that seemed to have washed up from a playground. The round windows were grimy and the corridors tight and dark.

A couple minutes ago, we'd been given long-sleeved overalls, walkie talkies, helmets with visors, heavy guns loaded with paint pellets, and a mission. Besides defeating the enemy team, we had to locate five clues hidden amidst the junkyard.

Everest's grumpy mood lifted. Even August seemed somewhat less encumbered. These boys loved playing wargames.

Everest was on my team, but not August. He was on the red team with Lucas. Liam and Matt were greens like me. The teams had been predetermined before we showed up. Not that I would've chosen to be on the red team. I was plenty happy to have Lucas on the enemy team.

I had my back to the brick wall. On the walkie talkie tuned into a special band-width only accessible to our team, I heard Liam's voice crackle, asking for Matt's position. Matt mentioned the tower. I looked up and spotted him, and then I spotted the barrel of his gun aimed straight at me. Something hard blasted against my stomach.

The bastard shot me!

I was his freaking teammate. He grinned, and then his voice grizzled on the walkie talkie, "Oops. I shot one of ours. Sorry, Clark."

I glared at him, which just increased his wolfish grin.

I walked off the field, gun and hands raised to indicate I was on a timeout. Two pellets flew at me. One from a red. The other from a green. Did these assholes not know the rules? I'd never played before, but I'd listened to the briefing.

I sat in the green camp, waiting for my coach to give me the go-ahead to return to the field—not that I wanted to return. I listened to the voices crackling over the walkie talkies. Heard one of my teammates announce that they'd located item number two and were bringing it back to the camp. Then heard another one announce he was on a timeout. A couple seconds after he walked in, I went back out and raced toward the wooden boat, where I found Everest.

"Fucking Matt shot me."

"I heard." He pulled open a trapdoor just as footsteps sounded above our heads. Dust flaked off the low ceiling. "The rusted pipe's somewhere in the boat apparently. Search the back."

I walked toward the hull, bumping into a hard body steeped in shadows. The green light on his helmet told me he was on my team, even though I couldn't see his face.

A pellet burst against my back. I jerked, then gritted my teeth as I turned. Through the fog forming on my visor, I met Lucas's pleased leer. "You're out, Clark."

Lucas didn't shoot my teammate. He kept the gun leveled on me. "Better run along before I shoot you again."

"Play nice, Lucas," I heard the person behind me say. *Liam.*

He circled around me and then retreated, the weathered boards groaning beneath his footfalls. I hadn't expected him to stay, but I had expected him to be shot. He wasn't.

I marched past Lucas, shoving him with my shoulder, and he chuckled.

"Asshole," I muttered.

I walked back to the camp, not bothering to lift my gun. I was hit six more times, once on the jaw. The pellet broke the skin.

After a minute of stewing inside the camp, nursing my newest wound, I decided that if they weren't going to play fair, I would play dirty too.

The second I was back in the game, I went to find Lucas, disregarding direct orders from our team captain—lo and behold, that was Liam—to assemble on the north side to strategize. I noticed Lucas's black hair first, peeking out from underneath his helmet, and shot him square between the shoulder blades. He turned, arms raised. I shot him again. And again. I took great pleasure in seeing the colorful paint splatter his overalls.

When I was blasted on the waist by one of his teammates, I didn't even care. I stalked back to the camp and refilled my ammo.

"Don't know north from south, Clark?" Liam asked, barging into the camp seconds after me, a large splash of paint on his chest.

"Are we playing as a team now? Because if memory serves me, Matt and two other people from the greens shot at me. You probably didn't notice, though, too wrapped up in barking orders."

"Matt thought you were—"

"Oh, don't give me that! I have a freaking green light flashing on my forehead." I wiped the fog from my visor. "Who got you?"

"August."

I smiled.

We didn't speak after that. Liam was way too busy studying the video feed of the arena. Our coach radioed in that I was clear to reenter the field.

"We're still missing the compass and the pair of yellow pliers," Liam said without turning away from the monitor. "I think the compass is in the tunnel. Want to come with me to find it?"

"Are you planning on shooting me in the back?"

"I don't shoot people in the back."

Sure you don't.

He held my gaze. "I'm not sure what you heard about me, but from the way you've been treating me, I'm guessing it's all bad."

I didn't answer him.

"I'll cover you," he said. "Come to the tunnel with me."

"Whatever. Fine. But know that if you shoot me, I'll make your life hell."

He had the audacity to smile. "More than it already is?"

I erupted from our bunker and headed toward the plastic tunnel. While Liam radioed in our position and asked if anyone had eyes on the exit, I peered inside. An, "all-clear," crackled over the walkie talkie.

"Search the middle of the tunnel," Liam said.

"Sending the girl in first. How gentlemanly."

Liam's eyes flashed behind the fog in his goggles. He pushed past me and flopped onto his stomach and started creeping down the tunnel. "Cover *me* then."

So I shielded him. I thought I caught the glow of red. Sure enough, someone from the enemy team shifted inside the dilapidated cottage. I raised my gun and fired through the window. My pellet hit its mark. The guy turned in my direction. I couldn't see who it was, but did it matter? He retreated into his camp's bunker with his gun and hands raised. On the other side of the tunnel, I noticed another red light. I clambered over the dirt piled atop the plastic tunnel and shot at the person before they could duck and locate Liam.

I hit the person's helmet.

He raised his hands and gun just as a pellet smacked the base of my spine. "Got you again, Clark."

I grabbed my walkie talkie. "I'm out. Lucas is at the south entrance of the tunnel, Liam."

Just as I spoke that, Lucas raised his gun to me again, but before the jerk could get another shot in, a pellet hit him on the thigh.

I wheeled, half expecting one of my teammates to have shot him, but found one of his own instead.

"Stop picking on her, Mason," August growled.

Lucas glowered at him before prowling off.

"Thank you, but you didn't have to do that," I said.

"This is a preview of the trials, Ness. They'll stab you in the back the first chance they get. Drop out. You hear me? Drop. Out."

"I drop out, and I have to pack my bags this afternoon."

"I'll talk to the elders."

"I'd rather you didn't."

He huffed. "I won't stand around to watch you get hurt."

I laid a hand on his forearm. "It's a game, August. They're not going to kill me."

"They might not kill you, but they'll—" His body jerked as a pellet smacked his back.

Liam had crawled out the other side of the tunnel and opened fire.

"What will we do to her, August?" His voice was as harsh as his close shot.

"You won't hesitate to hurt her," August bit out.

"Didn't you hear? Nothing can hurt her." Liam was tossing my words back at me with such a derisive tone, that for a second, I tightened my gloved grip on the gun, tempted to shoot at him.

But I took the high road; I spun and walked away.

If this *was* a preview, then at least I knew what to expect.

10

My body resembled a sheet of blotting paper. Like ink smudges, bruises marbled almost every limb on my body. The worst one was on my inner thigh.

My team ended up winning. Not that I'd felt in a celebratory mood. After the game, I'd vanished into my bedroom to take a hot bath, then donned leggings and a super soft off-the-shoulder tee. I skipped wearing a bra because the wires dug into my bruised ribs. On the upside, my cheek and jaw were looking a lot better. My werewolf blood was kicking in and working its magic.

I simply prayed my body wouldn't decide to change tonight. I didn't think I could take any more pain.

A text from Lucy had me heading to the laundry room in the late afternoon. Now that the weekend was over, all the beds had to be changed.

I loaded up the industrial-sized washers with sheets and pillowcases and duvet covers, trying not to gape at certain stains. I washed my hands twice then started on the ironing of the loads that had already been washed and dried. I fed sheet after sheet through the rotary iron, watching the furrows smooth out of the fabric, feeling them smooth out of me, too.

I cracked my neck, working out the kinks brought on by lugging heavy gear and constantly watching my back. As I reached for a bulky duvet cover, I felt a disturbance in the air, caught a whiff of sawdust and Old Spice. I turned to find August standing in the doorway, knuckles raised.

He froze. Without knocking, he slid his hand into the pocket of his sweatpants. "Your aunt told me I might be able to find you here."

Of course she did. "Did you come to tell me how stupid I am again?"

Surprise carved his face. "I never said you were stupid."

I grabbed the duvet cover, folded it in half, and thrusted it into the iron. I heard him approach...smelled him approach.

"Ness"—his voice was on my neck—"I don't think you're stupid."

I didn't turn. "So why are you here?"

"I'm here to tell you that I've decided to return to active duty."

I let go of the duvet and whirled. "You're going back out there?"

"Just for a few months."

"Why?"

His eyes raked over my face. "I miss it."

"Is that why you broke up with Sienna?"

"News travels fast."

"Is it?"

"It's part of the reason. The other part is that she's a sweet girl who deserves a good guy."

"And you're *not* a good guy?"

"I'm not good"—he watched the rotary iron spin—"for her." He wet his thick bottom lip.

I'd never noticed August's lips before. He had really nice lips.

"Will you give me your phone number?"

"You want my number?" I breathed.

"Yeah. You know"—he smiled—"so I can call you."

"You're not leaving because of me, are you?" I realized how conceited that sounded only after it popped out of my mouth. I raked my hair back. "You know, because you don't want to see my ass handed to me." A spot of heat spread over my jaw and throat and spilled into my chest.

Shut up, Ness.

Shut. Up.

A groove appeared between August's eyebrows. "No," he said after a long pause. "I just need to get away from Boulder for a while. I've been here for three years. I don't like staying in the same place for long stretches. I have my entire life to grow roots, but until I have to, I'd rather run wild."

"And going to fight in... Where are you going?"

"It's classified."

"And going to fight is your idea of running wild? Why can't you run wild in the Rockies or in the Appalachians?"

A smile grew on his face. "Worried about me?"

"Um, *yeah*." I felt the tips of my ears heat up. "You're going God knows where to fight God knows who. Of course I'm worried."

Amusement twinkled in his eyes. "Quit stalling, and give me your number."

He had his cell phone poised in his hands. It was unlocked, so I lifted it from his fingers, created a new contact, and typed in my number.

"Don't run too wild, all right?"

His Adam's apple bobbed in his throat. "You too."

I felt all torn up over his departure. Ten years my senior, August Watt had been like a big brother to me way back when. He'd taught me to play backgammon while our parents had never-ending meals. He'd taught me to climb my first tree. He'd walked with me to the ice-cream parlor, and when the weather was crap, he'd collect me from school in his pickup.

Before good sense could knock into me, I hooked my arms around his neck and pressed my cheek against his chest, against the heart that beat there, strong and steady.

"Thank you for being nice to me. Since I came back, but also during all those years before I left."

For a second he didn't move, but then his arms wound around me and pulled me in tight. "Don't ever thank someone for being nice. Especially not me."

We stayed locked together until one of the dryers beeped so incessantly I broke the embrace to power the machine off.

"Keep in touch, okay?" His voice was a little thick.

I raised a paltry smile—the best I could muster. "I'd need your number for that."

He pressed on his phone's screen, and my cell phone started ringing.

"Pick up," he said.

I frowned. "Okay." I swiped my phone off the top of a pile of clean sheets, then slid my finger across the screen. When I saw him raise the phone to his ear, I raised mine too.

"Hey," he said, and then he winked and turned around, disappearing the way he came. "What are you up to?"

Silly. This was so silly. But it got me smiling. "Laundry."

"That's always code for something else."

"Is it?" I laughed. "What's it code for?"

"Everyone knows what it's code for."

I touched my navel, which suddenly felt tight and hot. "Enlighten me, why don't you?"

THAT NIGHT, just as I was falling asleep, a knock resounded softly through my bedroom. Since the pack had left, I imagined it would be Everest, but as I walked toward the door, I smelled menthol and bacon grease.

Evelyn.

Had she come to tell me she was leaving? My heart thumped as I drew open the door. Hugging her arms, she stood in the darkened corridor, her face free of her usual heap of makeup. The red rims of her eyes told me she'd been crying.

My fault.

My *selfish* fault.

She pressed her arms tighter in front of the plush black bathrobe Mom had given her for Christmas a few years back. To avoid parting with it, Evelyn had mended almost every seam. Would she impart on our relationship the same treatment she'd given her robe?

As her eyes raked over the bruises marring my skin, she pursed her lips.

I wanted to explain, but when I opened my mouth, a tiny sob lurched out instead. Evelyn's arms came loose, and then they laced around me. She pulled me against her chest, combing my hair back as I soaked the fluffy fabric with my tears.

"You won't leave me?"

"No, *querida*. I will never leave. Just as I could never hate you, even if you transformed into a dragon."

A wheezy chuckle glided out between my blubbering. "Those don't exist."

"*Gracias a Dios*." If she hadn't been holding me, I was certain she would've crossed herself.

The corridor lights flickered and buzzed.

"I am ready to hear...*more*. Will you tell me?"

I nodded and tugged her inside. Once the door was closed, once she'd settled on the bed next to me and dragged her lotion-softened fingers through my hair, I told her about how I'd tried to become part of the pack after my father was shot in his wolf form by a hunter. I told her about Heath and what he did to Mom when she'd begged him to train me.

What I didn't tell Evelyn was that I'd entered the contest to become Alpha. I neither wanted to worry her nor have her tell me how dumb it was.

11

When my phone rang on Wednesday morning, I answered without even checking the number. For the past three days, all my calls had originated from August. We talked every day, and when we didn't talk, we texted.

I'd never communicated with anyone as easily. He made me laugh. He also made me feel things...things that were apparently against pack rules. Things that made me wish he'd come back to Boulder sooner than planned.

"Candy, you're alive!" a chirpy voice said.

I rolled into a sitting position so fast I had to clutch the nightstand to avoid keeling over. "Hi, Sandra."

"I've got a job for you, girl."

"A j-job?"

"A client saw your profile—"

"I thought you took it down!"

"I did, but he screenshot your pic and begged me to get in contact with you."

Creep. "I'm not interested."

"Hun, you got gypped out of your last payment because of the unfortunate demise of the customer. This is me trying to make it up to you."

"It's okay, Sandra." It's not like I would've taken said customer's money.

"What about all those bills you still need to pay?"

I let go of the nightstand. I did need money for the overdrafts on the joint bank account I'd shared with Mom, but I didn't want to earn it doing...*that.*

"Why d'you think Everest insisted I pair you up with Heath Kolane?" she continued.

Sandra believed my cousin, whom she'd met through Becca—one of her *girls*—had pimped me out so I could earn fast cash. I hadn't played escort for Heath's money, but explaining my true intentions would've earned me a restraining order instead of a job.

"Real shame he died. He was one of my best customers. Real shame. Anyway, the customer I'm calling 'bout is offering three grand."

I coughed. "Three grand?"

"You interested now, hun?"

Escort was a job like any other, right? Besides...*three grand*. I couldn't exactly turn that down. I still had debts, plus I wanted to reimburse Evelyn for the money she'd loaned me to pay for Mom's funeral. Even though she insisted she would never take a dime for it, the funeral had been pricey, because we'd wanted to give my mother an ending worthy of the woman she'd been.

"Can you tell me more about the gig?"

"Dinner at Pelligrini's."

"No sex, right?"

"*Absolutely* no sex! I don't run a brothel."

I could do dinner. Dinner was safe. "Why would someone pay three grand for dinner?"

"Can't give you any details until you agree to it. So, what'll it be?"

If Evelyn found out... I couldn't even finish that thought without shuddering. I wasn't a prostitute—this was just about being arm candy to men who didn't want to spend time getting to know a person—but most people wouldn't see the distinction.

I hadn't, until Everest explained it to me. He'd met Becca through the agency. Too shy to ask a girl out on a date, he'd paid someone else to do it for him.

"Okay. But, Sandra... Don't keep me on the roster after this, okay?"

"You got it, Candy."

She finally proceeded to give me the details of my date, which I jotted down on the small pad of paper next to the bed, and told me to wear something fancy.

I had two nice dresses: one was the black sequin number I'd worn for my "date" with Heath Kolane; the other was a cherry-red silk slip with spaghetti straps that used to be Mom's.

Even though donning something of hers sent a chill straight through my breast-bone, I went with the red.

I didn't want to be reminded of Heath tonight.

I WAS READY EARLY. I'd applied foundation to my fading bruises. Most had already vanished anyway. And I'd swiped mascara over my lashes and lipstick as red as my dress to my healed lips.

Instead of lingering inside the inn and incurring more of Lucy's inquisition: "Where was I going dressed up like a...like a..." She hadn't finished the sentence, but I'd heard the end loud and clear. I told her I had a blind date and not to wait up. Not that she would have waited up. She told me not to get knocked up. I thanked her for her unsolicited advice.

I waited in the inn's driveway, eyes closed, face raised toward the dying sun. The weather was unusually warm for early July, which suited the L.A. girl in me. Winter in Boulder—if I stayed that long—would be especially brutal now that I was used to mild temperatures.

"Someone's looking mighty fancy."

I snapped my lids open and found Lucas hopping out of the passenger side of a dark Mercedes SUV decked out with oversized off-roading tires. And then Liam was there, too, in a short-sleeved, black V-neck, his hair artfully tousled, as though he'd finger-combed it back with styling wax but missed a couple locks.

How I wished he was covered in warts; it would've made disliking him way easier.

"Where you going, Clark?" Lucas drawled, coming to a stop in front of me.

I was glad I'd worn heels, glad for the extra inches. "I'm going to dinner with a friend."

"You have friends?" he asked.

Jerk.

Liam jabbed his companion. "You look nice, Ness."

I frowned, unsure what to do with the compliment. I tightened the black leather jacket I'd added to my dress. "Thanks?" Why, oh why, did it have to come out as a question? "What are you guys doing here?"

"We just came to have a couple beers at our favorite inn," Lucas said. "Did you think we were coming to hang out with you?"

I balked. "Why would you ever think I'd want to hang out, Lucas?"

He disregarded my comment. "Ready for trial number one?"

"Absolutely." I wasn't ready. I still hadn't changed into my wolf form—I hadn't even tried. I'd been too busy licking my wounds from paintballing to worry about much else. I'd worry about it tomorrow, and if by Saturday I couldn't change, I'd fake an illness. They wouldn't force me to compete sick.

Or would they?

Lucas rubbed his hands. "So...excited to go back to L.A.?"

"Why is everyone so convinced I'm going to lose? And don't you dare say it's because I'm a girl."

His stupid grin widened.

"Leave her alone." Liam shoved Lucas toward the revolving doors just as a black limo pulled into the driveway.

My ride had arrived. I traipsed down toward it. An impressively large driver came out and drew the back door open for me.

I thanked him and got in.

"Mr. Michaels is waiting for us at the restaurant." His voice was as big as he was.

I'm pretty sure Liam and Lucas, who were rooted by the entrance of the inn, had heard the driver speak. They seemed star-struck by the limo, which I guessed wasn't a common car to see in Boulder.

Sandra had sent me a little background information about Mr. Michaels. He was a hotel promoter who owned five-star resorts in Denver, Beaver Creek, and Las Vegas. An extremely wealthy sixty-year-old who'd grown up in Boulder but dropped out of high school at seventeen and moved to Vegas, where he worked his way up to management, then gambled his way to a large bank account, before receiving a consequential amount of money from a deceased grandmother.

I was sort of excited about meeting him, not because of his wealth or status, but because I assumed that anyone who could ascend so far up in the world was worth meeting...worth learning from.

The restaurant was thirty minutes away, in a barn that had been refurbished with cowhide banquettes and lacquered black tables. Modern glass chandeliers swathed the dim interior in a tawny glow that made everyone look handsomer.

The romper-clad hostess led me to a table all the way in the back, toward a man sipping an ochre drink with a snowball-sized ice cube.

Aidan Michaels stood when I arrived, looking me over through wire-rimmed glasses. "Your picture doesn't do you justice, Candy."

"Thank you, Mr. Michaels."

"Sorry I couldn't pick you up myself, but I had an important call with my lawyer."

"That's fine."

He walked around and held out my chair. "Would you like some wine? Or maybe a glass of champagne?"

"Champagne would be nice."

He asked the hostess for a glass of their best champagne, and then he tucked my chair under the table before returning to his seat. "You don't look like a Candy. What's your real name?"

"You're not paying me enough to get my real name."

His gaze tightened, but then his teeth flashed, and he laughed.

"Can I ask *you* something?"

He leaned back in his chair and raised his tumbler to his lips. "Go ahead."

"Why does a successful man like yourself go through an agency to find a dinner date?"

"Aha. The million-dollar question. I was married once, and she broke my heart. So I decided never again, and I've stuck to that thanks to treating dating like I treat my businesses." He shifted forward and placed his drink down. "A tidy social transaction."

His honesty had my shoulder blades un-pinching.

"My turn. Why is a pretty young thing like yourself doing this?"

I unfolded my napkin and laid it on my lap. "I need the money."

He nodded his understanding. "How much is it that you need?"

I bristled. "That's private."

"I apologize. It was brash of me. I was simply considering how many more dates I could get with you." He ran a hand through his silvery hair, then readjusted his glasses and leaned in. "So tell me about yourself, Candy."

Candy wasn't Ness. I didn't want her to be anything like Ness. "I lived in New York until a month ago."

"What a fabulous city! Did you enjoy it?"

"Yeah. I had a great place on the Piers."

He frowned a little. "The Piers? You mean, *Chelsea* Piers?"

Without breaking eye contact, I said, "Yes."

"And what brought you back here?"

I'd been about to say college, but I was supposed to be twenty-one. "Family."

"*Ah*...family."

"Do you have family?"

"My wife's gone, my father's dead, and my mother has Alzheimer's. So no. No family. I have a dog though." He handed me his phone, where he'd prepped a slideshow of images showcasing his pet.

I liked animals—after all, I was one—but Aidan's love for his dog was something else.

"Do you like hunting?" he asked.

I sucked in a breath. "Hunting?" I took a bread roll from the basket and chomped on the chewy crust. Hunting reminded me of my father. I swallowed the lump of masticated dough. "Not especially."

"You're not a Greenpeace advocate, are you?"

"No. I'm just...I don't like guns." *Act normal, Ness,* I chastised myself. "What do you hunt?"

"Bears, cougars, deer...wolves. Have you noticed how many of them we have in our forests?"

I forced myself to look him straight in the eyes. "I never noticed," I said, just as the waiter came back to take our order.

My appetite had vanished, so I ordered a salad, which led Aidan to ask if I was watching my weight, because if I was, it was silly. I answered that I wasn't, and he went on to tell me about all the diets he had to go on when he was married because his wife was a terrific cook.

"Only damn thing she was good at." A smirk ghosted over his reedy lips. "I take it back. She was good at keeping secrets."

I stiffened. The man had serious baggage. What he needed was a shrink, not a date. But I supposed, for three thousand dollars, I could provide him with a dinner's-worth of therapy.

12

After the main course, I excused myself to go to the bathroom, even though what I really wanted was to bolt. Before each bite of food, Aidan would wipe his fork down on his napkin. And then, every couple seconds, he'd rub his earlobe.

I felt his heavy gaze on me as I crossed the crowded restaurant. I eyed the exit with longing, but I'd sat through most of the meal. Only dessert remained—I wouldn't order any and hopefully he wouldn't either—and then I'd get paid.

I asked a waiter where I could find the bathroom, and the man pointed me toward the bar. As I walked past it, a pulse erupted in my temples. There, aligned on the cowhide barstools, sat Liam, Lucas, Matt, and Cole, Matt's older brother, another massive blond with a buzz cut.

I crossed my arms. "Did they run out of beers at the inn?"

Lucas spun on his barstool. "How's your date? Looks mighty cozy." He twirled the neck of his beer bottle between his long fingers.

"Is it a coincidence you're all here?" I asked.

Cole cocked one of his honeyed eyebrows up. "Aidan Michaels is as sleazy as they come, Ness."

"And what? You came to warn me?"

Matt leaned back against the bar. "Yeah. We take care of our own."

"Your own? I'm not even part of the pack."

"You could be, if you drop out before Saturday," Liam said.

"Like I'd ever trust your word."

"Ouch." Lucas slapped a hand over his heart.

"Look, thanks for the warning, but I'm fine."

Liam and Cole hopped off their barstools and walked over to me.

"You *will* be fine." The smell of cold cigarettes clung to Cole's sunburned skin. "If you come back with us."

"I can't."

Liam frowned. "Is he forcing you to be here?"

"No one's forcing me to do anything, but I can't leave."

I tried to step around him to go to the bathroom, but Liam clamped his hand around my bicep. "*Why* can't you leave?"

"Sorry. Did I say can't? I meant I don't want to."

"You can't hang out with a guy like Aidan Michaels."

I shrugged Liam off. "No one tells me what I can or can't do."

He glowered down at me.

"The dude is sixty and only dates whores and call-girls," Cole said.

"Maybe that's why she's here," Lucas drawled.

Liam's eyes widened.

"I'm not a whore," I snapped.

Lucas raised a cocky grin. "Which leaves call-girl."

"He's paying you to be here?" Liam's voice was dark, as though the shadows crowding his face had creeped down his throat.

"Just leave me alone. All of you. And stop fucking pretending like you have my best interest at heart. None of you do."

I started toward the bathroom, but Liam grabbed my arm. *Again.* "Do you need money?"

"That's none of your concern."

"You're a Boulder wolf, so it is our concern," Matt said.

"I'm not a Boulder wolf," I bit back.

"Is there a problem, miss?" the bartender finally asked.

"I'm fine," I gritted out. Then, to Liam and the other three, I said, "You...*all of you*... you all better be gone when I come back out."

"Or what? You'll throw a tantrum?" Lucas sneered.

"Maybe I will."

Finally I went to the bathroom. When I was done, they weren't gone, but at least they were sitting back down. I returned to the table where the waiter had set out a giant chocolate sundae and a thick slice of apple tart topped with cinnamon cream.

"I didn't know which you'd like, so I ordered both."

I glowered at the desserts.

"We can order something else if you—"

"No. No. It's fine. Thank you." I dunked my spoon into the sundae and took a bite to settle my swishing stomach.

"Are those boys friends of yours?"

My breathing hitched a couple notches.

"I noticed you chatting with them." He rubbed his ear.

"They're not friends. Just acquaintances."

"I own a lot of land and concessions. Money and power attracts detractors." Even though he smiled, it looked strained...and I felt a twinge of pity for the man who had no friends and no family, just a dog, a couple rifles, and a real estate empire. His smile vanished, and his eyes deepened to navy as he tilted his neck. "If it isn't Liam Kolane in the flesh."

My gaze climbed up the length of Liam's rigid body and then landed on his incendiary glare.

"My deepest condolences," Aidan continued.

"I'm taking Ness home."

I cringed at the use of my real name.

"I'll be the one taking her home." Aidan reached under the table and crinkled the red silk hem of my dress.

I jerked my knee so hard his hand fell away. *Just yuck.*

"Have you considered that she might not want to go home?" he continued.

I hoped Aidan had said that simply to annoy Liam, because there was no way in hell I was going anywhere else.

"Ness, now." Liam's voice brooked no argument.

"Liam, you're being rude. I'll grab a cab." Dinner was minutes away from being wrapped up. I couldn't leave now. Because he was still standing there, glaring, I said, "Liam's been very emotional since his father...passed away."

"It's understandable. Especially considering the way he died. Have the police caught the murderer yet?"

"Murderer?" I blurted out. "I thought Heath committed suicide."

Liam's face turned to stone.

I blinked at him, then blinked down at the pool of cream surrounding the half-eaten slice of pie. Heath *hadn't* committed suicide? Someone had killed him? A chill curled deep inside my belly.

"Oh, no." Aidan's eyes sparked. "Apparently someone killed him."

Liam muttered something under his breath and then yanked me up by the bicep.

"Liam!" I tried to bat his hand away, but he held on tight.

Aidan didn't cause a scene by interceding, but he glowered. I dug in my heels as Liam tugged on me. Even though Aidan was a strange man, the least I could do was be polite. Plus I needed my bag and jacket.

I grabbed both. "Thank you for dinner, Mr. Michaels."

Aidan studied the place where Liam's fingers connected with my skin. "I see you treat your women the way your father did."

Aidan's comparison made Liam free my arm. Staring at the skin he'd gripped— the skin I was now rubbing—he muttered, "Let's go. *Please.*" It sounded painful for him to add that last word.

Without hesitation, I headed toward the exit.

The second we were outside, he said, "I can't believe you went out on a date with that...that rat."

I stopped rubbing my arm and fished my phone out of my bag.

"What are you doing?"

"Calling a cab."

He gestured to his mammoth-wheeled car. "I got a car."

"I make it a point not to get into cars with strangers."

"And yet you got in that limo earlier."

"That was different."

"Get in, Ness."

I started scrolling through my cell for the number, but Liam plucked the phone out of my hands. "Hey!"

"Just get in already."

"No."

"Look, if you don't get in, I'll toss you in."

"You wouldn't dare."

A bold smile appeared on Liam's dusky face. "Do you want to test that theory?"

I huffed a breath, trod to his car, and climbed in. "You're a real pain, you know that?"

He pitched the phone on my lap before I shut the door. As I strapped myself in, he climbed into the driver's side.

"Where did the others go?"

"I don't keep tabs on my buddies."

"Just on me, then?"

He didn't answer, but his eyes flashed to mine before settling back on the road.

"Lucky me," I grumbled.

Music drifted from his stereo, punctuating the silence with a heady beat.

In the darkness, my phone flashed with the agency's number. I sighed, anticipating the reason for the call. I turned toward the window and answered in a low voice, "Hello."

"Candy, is everything all right? I just got a text from Aidan to complain that you'd rushed out on him."

"Family emergency," I grumbled.

"Oh. Okay. Anyway, hun, he asked for a discount, and since he's a real good customer, I had to grant it. I hope you understand."

"How much less?"

"Half."

I squeezed my fingers around the phone.

"He was happy with you otherwise. Asked if you'd be interested—"

"No."

"If you change your mind—"

"I won't."

"Okay then. I'll wire your wage to your account. Bye, Candy."

A deep sigh rattled out of me. I'd sat through an entire dinner, all the way through dessert, but the dude had the gall to haggle. And it wasn't like he didn't have the money to pay me. I was incredibly tempted to tell Liam to turn around so I could give Aidan a piece of my mind.

"How long have you been doing this?"

"Doing what?"

Liam's eyes gleamed in the darkness. "Dating for money."

"Just this once," I lied.

"Do you have debts?"

"Doesn't everyone?"

"How much do you owe?"

I plopped my elbow down on the armrest and cradled my head. "A lot."

"A lot is not a number. Fifty grand? A hundred?"

I blinked at him in horror. "No!" If I owed a hundred grand, I would...I would...God, I didn't even know what I would do. "Six grand."

"For college?"

"No."

"Credit card bills?"

I huffed. "Past rents. Mom's funeral. Not everyone has an unlimited supply of money like you."

He braked so suddenly my seatbelt dug into my chest. "Ness, can you give me a break? I just lost my father too, all right? I've got my own shit to deal with. But I don't go around being nasty to everyone and debasing myself for a couple of bucks."

Shame surged through me.

He put his hazard lights on and heaved a ragged breath. He clenched his fingers around the steering wheel. "I'm sorry. That came out harsher than intended."

He touched my leather sleeve, and I shifted my arm away.

"Don't touch me." I stared at the crimson flashes punctuating the darkness. "Can you please drive me home?"

"Do you want me to loan you the money?"

I whipped my head around. "And be in *your* debt? No thank you."

"You'd rather keep doing...?" He gestured to the back of his car, but I knew he meant being an escort.

"No. I'm going to look for a real job."

"Don't you already have one?"

I frowned.

"You're working at the inn, aren't you?"

"They're not paying me."

"Why not?"

"Because. I'm not doing it for me."

"Who are you doing it for?"

"For someone else."

He wet his bottom lip that was thinner than his upper one, and it glinted in the darkness. "Do your aunt and uncle know about your debts?"

"They're aware of some of them."

"And they won't help?"

"I would never accept their help." Jeb offered to loan me the money for the rental payments, but I'd refused. I'd let him foot the bill for the window he'd broken, though. "By the way, they don't know about what I did tonight, so don't you dare tell them."

"I won't say anything about your *date*." He spoke the word as though it tasted bad. After a long moment, he asked, "Would you have slept with him if he'd paid you extra?"

I wrinkled my nose. "I would never sleep with someone for money."

Even though I could barely make out his face in the dim light of his dashboard, I could tell he was weighing my words.

"Why?" I asked. "Would you?"

"Sleep with someone for their money?" He let out a soft snort. "Thankfully, I don't need to resort to that."

"I meant, have you ever paid for sex?"

"No."

"Your dad—"

"I know what my dad did. But just because *he* did it doesn't mean I do it." He made a sound halfway between a growl and a sigh. "I'm *nothing* like him."

"That's what everyone says. That you're not like him."

"But you don't believe it?"

"I like to make up my own mind."

He finally angled the car back on the road. "Seems like you already did."

My pulse sprang like a livewire inside my veins and knocked against the side of my neck. I almost apologized, but he was a Kolane. He might not be *all* bad, but he was still the flesh and blood of the man who'd laughed at an eleven-year-old girl in need of guidance and who'd raped a bereft widow after she'd begged him for help.

13

After an uncomfortably quiet ride home, I left Liam without saying goodbye, my throat and chest too congested with anger and grief.

I headed straight to my bedroom, to the small terrace with the single Adirondack. I dropped into it and watched the heavy starlight bathing the serrated crowns of the pines.

Maybe I wasn't being fair to Liam. After all, his father had been murdered. Not that Heath's death was my fault. I'd simply gone to his place posing as an escort so that he'd let me in. If I'd gone as Ness Clark, he would've turned me away at the door. After playing nice for an agonizing stretch of time, Candy told him she knew what he'd done to Ness Clark's mother, to Becca Howard, and to a handful of other women, and warned him she was going to press charges. Heath laughed at her.

At *me*.

And so I'd slapped him. Hard. Which turned his dark eyes frosty. But at least he hadn't shifted, thanks to the crushed pills I'd slipped into his Manhattan. I drugged him, afraid he'd kill me once I revealed my true identity.

In skin, he was frightening, but in fur, he was a monster.

When I told him who I was, he growled, "Get...out," and I got out.

And someone must've gotten in right after me.

Murdered.

The eight-letter word iced me. I wrapped my arms tighter around myself and stood to go inside when a howl echoed deep in the night.

A shadowy shape moved at the edge of the forest—a large black wolf with glowing eyes. The wolf looked at me across the grassy expanse and howled again, and his howl scattered goose bumps over my forearms, over my entire body. Another deep keening made my muscles spasm and my nails turn into claws.

"*Shit. Shit. Shit,*" I whispered, backing into my room.

I yanked off my jacket, threw off my dress as my torso twitched, and tore my necklace off. Heat engulfed my skin, and then fur—white, silky fur blanketed my burning arms and sprouted over my legs. My thighs hardened and shortened. My teeth sharpened. I felt them with the tip of my tongue that had grown thicker, longer.

I tried to pull off my underwear, but my hands were paws.

Paws with sharp claws.

A bolt of pain hit my spine. I arched and threw my head back as my lips stretched and stretched, like my nose, like my ears. I growled, and it vibrated against my narrow, rubbery muzzle. My bones shifted underneath my skin, my shoulder blades turning in.

I dropped to my knees hard. The black pads that had replaced my palms absorbed the brunt of my weight. A tail surged from my backbone, shredding my underwear, whipping against my desk and bed. My knee joints cracked, snapping inward, until they became lupine hocks.

Adrenaline shot down my spine and into my limbs, electrifying every inch of skin, sharpening each one of my senses. I heard conversations from all the way inside the living room. I caught the hoot of an owl, the caw of a raven, the rustle of pine needles. I smelled Lysol and detergent and the green scent of the swaying forest beyond my first-floor balcony. I felt the heartbeat of tiny things—bugs and rabbits and owls.

I ran toward my open balcony doors, crouched low, and then sprang over the balustrade. I soared through the frizzling night air, body thrumming from the release of the wolf that had lain dormant beneath my human skin.

I hit the soft grass on all fours, and then I was galloping through the clearing that led to the forest, kicking up clumps of earth and grass. Behind me, on the large terrace, loud gasps and small cries rang out, followed by captivated chatter. I swiveled my head, and sure enough, a handful of bodies were pressed tight against the wooden railing, pointer fingers raised toward my receding form.

Wolf-watching was an attraction mentioned in the inn's brochure. Visitors were rarely disappointed.

I lifted my nose to the wind and sniffed to pick up on the other wolf's trail, but became distracted by the chitter of a squirrel spiraling up the trunk of a tall cedar. The furball stopped to watch me, its lithe flesh pulsing deliciously beneath the dusting of tawny fur. I'd hunted a squirrel once, had torn through its warm body and crushed its bones in my jaw. I was a sentient beast, but a beast nonetheless.

I observed the squirrel a while longer, until a new fragrance tickled my senses—sultry and spicy and fresh, like hot musk and crushed mint. I ran toward the scent, my paws kicking up pinecones, my claws digging into moss and clattering against downed logs, splashing into engorged, moon-lacquered streams. I dove into one, rolled on the bank, and then wrung myself out.

Free.

That's what I was...wild and untethered.

I sprinted. Away from the inn. Away from the girl I'd left behind. The girl weighed down by guilt and debt. I ran until my heart threatened to derail, and still I ran. Only when I passed under a rocky ridge did I slow. The seductive fragrance of mint and musk churned in the air above me. I craned my neck and met the gaze of an impressive black wolf pawing the stone ledge dozens of feet up from where I stood.

Beneath a cover of matted leaves, a mouse shuffled. I didn't chase it—mice were more cartilage than meat. The wolf made a soft keening noise that traveled toward me slowly. There were no words in that sound...or perhaps my lupine brain hadn't yet reawakened to our tongue.

Was it Liam?

If it was, had he tracked me, or was it a coincidence that he was there?

I thought of Heath again before remembering that wolves could read minds, so I sprinted away, the forest smudging into one long strip of wild darkness. Only hours later did the inaccuracy of my memory hit me—wolves weren't mind readers. They could, however, speak into minds, but only the Alpha possessed that ability, and I had no Alpha.

My secrets were safe.

14

On Friday night, my stomach swarmed with butterflies. In less than a day, the first trial would begin...and end. Even though I'd managed to transform, did I stand a chance against wolves that hadn't been on a shifting sabbatical? I stared around my bedroom, wondering if I should pull the blue Ikea bags back out of my closet. My mother would be ashamed of my defeatist attitude. She was a staunch believer in mind over matter.

For all the good that did her.

I crushed her wedding band in my fist as I left my bedroom. On my way to meet Everest, I stopped by the kitchen. Ever since the night Evelyn had curled into bed next to me, and I'd confessed everything to her, we hadn't spoken about the pack. We'd discussed safe subjects like food and college—she wanted me to apply, but I hadn't done my SATs. Tonight again, she was on my case about colleges.

"I have some savings—" she began.

"No." I shook my head, and my hair brushed my bare shoulders. "I'm not taking your money anymore. Not unless you let me reimburse you."

"Ness..."

"Have you been to see the doctor?" I gestured to her knees. Lucy had given me the name of her physician, which I'd passed along to Evelyn.

"My arthritis is better." She ladled gazpacho into wooden bowls, then topped them with golden croutons, tiny squares of raw vegetables, and a drizzle of olive oil.

"Really?"

"Really." After finishing off the soups and ringing the buzzer to get one of the servers' attention, she busied herself with making my favorite dish: chicken quesadil-las. "You're getting too skinny."

I *had* lost weight, but I'd gained back some of the muscle I'd lost working two, sometimes three, jobs back in LA. I gobbled up every last golden triangle filled with melted cheese set before me.

Evelyn checked the order sheet the server had dropped off, opened the fridge, and removed thick slices of creamy salmon which she laid on the already smoking griddle.

"Who is singing again tonight?" she asked.

"The Lemons."

"Are they good?"

"They—" The door swung open, cutting off my answer.

Everest had arrived, but not alone.

"Frank wanted to meet our new cook," Everest said.

Evelyn dropped the metal spatula she'd been using to flip the salmon. The utensil clattered loudly against the tiled floor, festooning her white apron with oil. Ever since we'd arrived, Evelyn had barely strayed out of the kitchen, let alone the inn. She'd never been a particularly outgoing person, but moving to this unfamiliar town had made her downright skittish. And here was my insensitive cousin bringing someone —not just someone, Frank McNamara—into her safe haven.

Frank bent over to pick up the fallen spatula. "Evelyn, right?"

She gaped at him as he tendered it to her, but her fingers had balled into fists. He placed it on the island.

"I forced Everest to introduce me to the new cook. The Clarks are lucky to have found you."

Since Evelyn's feet had become part of the floor, I grabbed a handful of paper towels and wiped the tiles.

She finally moved, touching my shoulder. "It is okay, Ness."

As I straightened up, I raised my eyes to hers. Two pink spots had appeared on her high cheekbones, dimmed by her foundation, but still bright.

"We better get going," Everest said, "or we'll miss the opening act."

I waited for Frank to leave.

Frank's light-eyed gaze darted my way, then back to Evelyn. Finally, he moved toward the swinging door. "I hope you'll be staying, Evelyn."

Evelyn still hadn't said a word, but she nodded.

Frank offered her a demure smile, then left, the door flapping behind him.

"Are you okay?" I murmured.

Evelyn's lips were slow to unbuckle, but when they did, they arched upward. "I am fine." She slid a knuckle across my cheek.

"Ness?" Everest said.

His voice made the smile wilt off her lips. Where disgust no longer stained the way she looked at me, there was something guarded in the way she observed my cousin. It was as though she couldn't see him without seeing the beast inside. Would she look at me the same way if she bore witness to my other shape?

Note to self: never shift in front of Evelyn.

"Is all of Boulder going to this thing?" I asked Everest as we walked out of the inn and hopped into his convertible Jeep.

He'd taken off the black fabric roof, and the breeze twisted my hair. I wound it up and clutched the ends so that I didn't arrive at the music festival looking like I belonged in the band. Mullets and pompadours had been untrendy for years, but it didn't deter The Lemons from sporting them.

"You sure you want to go to this thing?"

"Yeah. I like The Lemons."

He side-eyed me, one lid a little lower than the other. "You really know who they are?"

"I wasn't living in a cave back in LA."

"Not a cave but—"

I hummed one of their songs as proof that I knew the band and to stop him from making an upsetting comment. Mom had worked hard for everything we had. At some point, I asked, "How's Becca?"

"The same."

A long line of vehicles had formed up ahead. Blinkers striated the dark woods. The drive to the field converted into a parking lot was a crawl, but we finally made it. Like ants, the cars trolled over the grass and dirt.

I climbed out of the Jeep and tugged at the hem of my short, white eyelet dress. A glance around reassured me that most girls were showing way more skin than I was.

"Well, well, if it isn't contestant number four." Lucas's oily voice had my spine straightening. "I bet Liam that you'd be catching up on your beauty sleep before the trial."

Giggling ensued. The girlfriends had come.

My pupils felt like they were warping. I snapped my eyes shut a millisecond, then opened them. "Did you think I was planning on distracting the three of you with my looks to win?"

Taryn, who clung to Lucas's waist as though her balance depended on it, narrowed her blue eyes at me. Of course Liam was there too. And next to him stood a ravishing redhead. Was that the girl they'd spoken about on the bus the other day? What was her name again? The outer corners of her green eyes slanted upward, which lent her this fierce feline look. God, I already disliked her, for no other reason than because she was stunning and surely knew it.

"Is that *her*?" she whispered to Liam, perky nose crinkling.

Liam didn't say anything. Didn't even look down at her. He was looking at me. No. Not at me. Through me. As though I wasn't even standing here.

"Hey, Tammy," Everest said, walking over to me.

Tammy latched on to Liam's hand. "Hey, Everest."

My ribs cinched at the sight of their twined fingers.

"Aidan couldn't make it?" Lucas asked.

Everest cocked an eyebrow. *Right.* I'd failed to mention my *date* with Aidan Michaels. Instead of answering, I spun around and threaded myself through the throngs of festival-goers. If I didn't lose the pack, tonight would be far from fun.

Everest caught up to me and tugged on my elbow. "What the hell was that about?"

"I had a date with Aidan Michaels."

"You what?" His eyes grew as wide as the flashlights the security guards were shining into bags.

I unzipped my cross-body bag. Once the guard let me through, I handed my ticket to the woman scanning them.

"How do you even know him?" Everest asked.

"How do you think I know him?"

"Sandra?"

"Bingo."

"I thought—"

"He offered 3K. Couldn't exactly turn that down."

"3K?"

"Yeah."

"He only paid half because Liam—who *happened* to be at the restaurant—made me leave. He says Aidan is a major creeper. Is it true?"

Everest's face creased, in concentration or in surprise or maybe in something else entirely.

"What?" I asked, combing the air to push away the thick smoke billowing from a food truck.

Slowly, as though he were trying out the words for size, he said, "Aidan Michaels hated Heath."

Bass jolted from nearby amplifiers, making my heart skip a beat. If Aidan hated Heath and I hated Heath, then maybe Aidan wasn't such a bad man.

"But is he a creeper?"

"I'd stay away from him." Everest rubbed his hands on his jeans. "Want a beer?"

"Sure."

He marched ahead of me toward a bar truck. Hollers and whistles pierced the purple air as the server filled two large plastic cups with the foamy liquid. I pulled a long swallow, then licked my lips. Exactly what I needed.

We traipsed through the thickening crowd. The opening notes of one of the band's most popular songs rang out, and people went crazy. Bodies writhed, people shrieked, hands came up and pumped the air. I drank more of my beer so that it wouldn't slosh all over me as we neared the stage. The drummer pounded on the percussions, and the orange-mulleted singer jumped in the air, belting out the lyrics.

I shifted my hips and raised one of my hands. The alcohol flowed through my veins, swirled through my body, and muted the thoughts and worries running on a loop inside my head. I drank deeper from my cup. By the third song, the entire content of my cup swished inside me, heightening the delicious beat and smoky voice of the band.

I felt a tiny bit happy. Even Everest smiled. He didn't dance, but his head was bobbing to the tune. I bumped my elbow into his side.

"Thanks for taking me! This is awesome!" I yelled so he would hear me over the group of chanting girls.

He grinned, then grabbed my empty cup. "I'll go get us refills. Don't move, or I'll never find you."

"Not going anywhere." I swung my head from side to side, the music thrumming against my bones. The night air was warm and pungent with a thousand smells—hot dogs, ketchup, grass, beer, sweat, jasmine, apricot...

I looked for the origin of that scent, fearing I'd find Amanda. Sure enough, she was standing a couple feet away, enclosed in Matt's beefy arms. Next to them stood the rest of the pack. A couple of the guys looked my way, eyes glowing in the darkness. Tamara was grinding up against Liam's rigid build. His hands didn't touch her body, but that didn't deter her. Maybe he wasn't into public displays of affection.

I'd promised Everest I wouldn't move, so I stayed put and tried to pretend they weren't all right there. As I directed my attention back toward the stage, my gaze landed on some guy in a white wifebeater and low-slung jeans. Instead of facing the stage, he was looking at me, and so were his two friends. I frowned when I saw them raise their chins and sniff the air. They whispered to each other, then casually approached me.

My spine clicked into alignment, all of my nerves on high alert. Before they'd even reached me, I knew they were wolves.

"Ness Clark?" Wifebeater asked.

I squared my shoulders. "And you are?"

"We heard the pack bitch was back, but damn, we hadn't heard how hot she was."

For the first time since I'd returned to Boulder, I disliked someone more than Liam and Lucas. "You might call your females bitches, but I prefer she-wolf."

Wifebeater smirked and took another step in my direction.

"Come any closer," I hissed, "and I'll make sure you can never breed."

"The bitch has attitude."

Anger dripped inside my veins like fuel. My limbs hummed. "Just leave me alone."

He raised his palms in the air. "One question, and then we go."

"I'm not answering any questions."

His head was so close to mine I could smell his ripe breath. "Is your ass very sore from being the only bitch in your pack?"

My gaze narrowed to a sharp point. I punched his Adam's apple and kneed his groin. Hard. And then arms were hauling me back, and a wall of bodies darkened the space between me and the asshole. I tried to shrug away from the arms, but they banded tighter.

"What did he say to you?" Liam's voice was low.

Like I would ever tell him. He'd probably wonder why I'd turned violent at such a petty taunt. Or worse, he'd use it as ammunition against me.

"Nothing," I grumbled.

"Justin Summix is an asshole, Ness. So I repeat, what did he say to you?"

Justin Summix. I committed the name to memory. "It doesn't matter."

Liam finally released me, and I turned to scan the sea of faces for Everest. When I couldn't locate him, I stared back at Liam, caught him nodding. I pivoted, just as Matt tore through the line of bodies.

"What was that about?" I asked.

"Nothing."

"My ass, it was nothing."

His pupils throbbed in the gleam of the strobe lights. "You don't talk; I don't talk."

"Ugh." I growled, raking my hands through my hair.

Yelps rose around me as the pack moved through the field of festivalgoers, chasing Justin and the other two. And then three security guards broke away from their postings around the stage to jog after the boys.

"They're going to get arrested!" I bellowed.

Liam gazed intently at his crew, lips thin, jaw set.

"Liam, call them off."

"I'm not Alpha. I don't give them orders."

And yet, that's exactly what he'd just done.

The singer from The Lemons stumbled on one of the lyrics as he witnessed the crush of bodies at the edge of the field, but then he flung his attention back to his twisting crowd and smoothed out the lyrics.

"Have you seen Everest?" I asked.

"Not since he left you alone out here."

"Liam," Tamara whined. "You're missing—"

Amanda elbowed past the redhead. "What the hell just happened?"

I wasn't sure if she was asking me or Liam.

His gaze raked over my face. "The Pines insulted Ness."

"What'd they say?" Amanda asked.

Goose bumps popped up on my flesh, and I rubbed my arms. Amanda tipped her head to the side as though trying to see inside my brain. She was a girl; she probably guessed what boys could say that would set a girl off.

I started sidestepping around Liam, but he caught my wrist. Tamara's eyes zeroed in on her date's fingers.

"Where are you going?" he asked.

"I'm going to look for Everest so he can take me home."

Matt and the others stalked back toward us, all of them a full head taller than everyone else. Their faces flashed with bloodlust and satisfied smiles. For a fraction of a second, I thought they might've killed Justin and the other two shifters, but then I chased that thought away. They were werewolves, not monsters.

"They won't be bothering you anymore, Ness," Matt said as Amanda skipped into his arms. He reeled her in tight and kissed her so hard I had to look away, but not before seeing the blood coating his knuckles.

Lucas's white t-shirt had a sprinkling of blood too. *Shit.*

I bit down on my lip, gnawed on it. "You guys didn't need to do...whatever the hell you did to them."

"I told you: we protect our own." Liam's voice was soft even though his grip wasn't.

"I don't need your protection."

He dipped his mouth toward my ear and said, his voice husky, "Well, you'll get it, whether you want it or not. That's the way the Boulder Pack operates."

My heart pounded unevenly. "I need to find Everest."

I didn't want Liam to be nice. Nice people were harder to hate.

I shook his hand off. "I want to go home."

"I was leaving. I'll drive you."

"No. Please. You have a date."

"I need to be on top of my game tomorrow."

Tamara, whom I'd all but forgotten, huffed. "Fine, let me say bye to the girls."

I would have rather snaked a clogged toilet than be stuck in a car with Liam and his girlfriend. Where the hell was Everest?

"Stay here, Tammy. Have fun," Liam said.

She batted her eyelashes at him. "I want to have fun with *you*."

That was a picture I didn't need in my head. I texted Everest, praying he would see my message and rescue me.

"Not tonight." Liam pried her hands off. "I'll see you tomorrow. Lucas will get you home."

"I don't want Lucas to take me home," she whined.

I checked my phone. *Seriously, Everest...* How long does it take someone to buy a beer? I texted him: **Are you OK?** Because now I was worried.

"I'm ready when you are?" Liam said.

I looked up from my phone and pushed a lock of hair behind my ear. Tamara was whispering angrily at Taryn. Even though I couldn't hear what was being said, from the way both girls glared my way, I guessed it had to do with me.

I sighed. "I should really find Everest first though."

"We'll look for him on our way out."

I chewed on the inside of my cheek, combing each food truck we passed for Everest. Just as I spotted him sitting at a picnic bench next to a girl, I got a text back: **I'm fine. Just ran into a friend. You OK?**

Liam must've followed my line of sight, because he said, "You want me to tell him I'm bringing you home?"

He started toward Everest, but I touched Liam's arm to stop him. "No. Don't interrupt him. He's had a tough month."

I typed back: **I'm fine.** I would send him a message once I was at the inn.

I walked alongside Liam, drained from the strange night. I was glad I was going home early. If I didn't sleep and relax, I'd be a complete mess for the run.

"Are you black?"

He cocked an eyebrow. "I think you have me confused with August."

"Funny. I meant as a wolf."

A lopsided smile formed on his lips. "Yeah."

Even though the air around Liam shimmied with the crisp, warm scent of mint and musk, I wanted confirmation. "Were you out in the woods on Wednesday?"

He nodded.

We passed boisterous groups of teens—slightly younger than I was—and it reminded me of high school, of the cliques I'd never been a part of. I wondered if Liam had been popular back in school. I bet he was. I bet all the guys in the pack were.

"Do you go to college?" I asked, turning away from the gaggle of tweens pointing at Liam, faces flushed from the sight of him.

"I graduated a month ago."

"And now?"

"Now?"

"What are your work plans?" I asked.

"I'm planning on picking up where my father left off."

"Real estate?"

He nodded. "What about you?"

I drew in a long breath of sweet, sticky air. "I don't know. I just want to get through this summer, and then I'll see where I'm at in September."

"Not so certain about winning anymore?"

I wasn't certain of anything anymore, but I didn't tell Liam this. Instead, I stared quietly ahead of me, at the long lines of parked cars bathed in starlight.

"How are your bruises?"

I blinked at him. "My bruises?"

"From paintballing." He glanced at my legs, which made me strangely self-conscious.

I frowned at his concern. "I'm healing quickly again."

"Again? Was that not the case when you were away?"

"I wasn't getting banged up much when I was away."

As he beeped his car open, something flickered through his eyes—remorse, or maybe it was just the reflection of his bumper lights. I could feel him hesitate to follow me toward the passenger side. In the end, he must've remembered I wasn't a date he had to impress, because he got behind the wheel while I opened my own door and climbed in.

As he pulled out of the lot, I asked, "How long have you and Tamara been dating?"

"We're not dating."

"Are you sure she knows that?"

"She knows it."

I didn't ask what they were doing if they weren't dating. I was a virgin, not an idiot. They might not have been dating, but they were most definitely hooking up. My phone thankfully pinged with a message, tearing me out of my strange deliberations. When I saw August's name in the message box, I smiled.

He'd sent me a selfie with some of his Army buddies. They were holding makeshift mics to their mouths—bananas. The picture was captioned: **You're missing one hell of a concert. How's yours?**

"What about you and August?"

I glanced away from my phone. "Me and August?"

"Are you together?"

"Me and August?" I sounded like a broken record. "No. We're just friends."

Liam's features were smooth as stone. "Are you sure he knows that?"

"Of course he knows that."

A sound scraped the walls of his throat, like a grunt, but not a grunt.

"What?"

"He just seemed awfully happy to see you, that's all."

"August used to babysit me, Liam. He's ten years older than I am. Trust me, he doesn't see me as anything other than a little sister." I picked at a loose thread on the hem of my dress. "Were you hoping *everyone* in Boulder would dislike me as much as you do?"

His dark gaze leaped off the road and ground into mine.

"Don't put words in my mouth." He didn't talk to me after that, just drove way above the speed limit.

The pines hedging the roads blended together in an endless juniper-colored smear. Someone was in a hurry to get rid of his passenger. Not that I wanted to spend a single minute more than necessary cooped up in a car with Liam Kolane. Why was I in his car again? *Right*...because Everest had looked like he was enjoying himself.

My cousin owed me big time.

When Liam came to a screeching halt in front of the inn, I pumped my door handle. Before jumping out, I said, "Thanks for the ride."

Liam didn't respond. He didn't even look at me as I climbed out, and the second I'd shut the door, he was off, tires squealing against the asphalt road, taillights burning blood-red in the black night.

15

I didn't sleep. Not a wink. I tossed and turned and tossed some more. The night spun on a loop inside my mind. Every damn part of the night too, from my encounter with stupid Justin Summix, to my drive home with infuriating Liam Kolane. Tamara popped inside my head a couple times too, and even though I tried to picture her with acne and buckteeth, somehow she always morphed into a gorgeous siren.

Ugh!

I finally got out of bed at the crack of dawn. Although I didn't want to overexert myself before the treacherous marathon the elders had set up, I hit the gym to stretch, and then I went to the kitchen and asked Evelyn for a high-protein breakfast. I mentioned I was planning on going for a run this afternoon. I didn't clarify in what form I'd be running or the reason I was running, and God bless Evelyn, she didn't ask.

She boiled three eggs, grilled fat slices of whole wheat toast, and fried two sausages. I took my breakfast back to my bedroom and ate on the small balcony, watching the sun rise and fill the world with color.

Trailing in the smell of fresh cigarettes, Lucy dropped by my room around nine, and it wasn't to wish me good luck. She came to ask me to tidy the guest bedrooms.

"But I have to be at the headquarters at noon."

My aunt had styled her red hair, and it fell in almost child-like ringlets over her milky shoulders. "Better hurry then."

She swiped her fingers across my desk as though inspecting it for dust. She wouldn't find any.

"What did you do with the potpourri jar?"

"What?"

"The mason jar I fill with potpourri. The one I put in every bedroom. What did you do with it?"

"Oh. It's on the balcony. The smell is a little...*strong* for me." Which was true, but the reason I'd set it on my balcony was because the desiccated, flowery scent reminded me of Lucy. Sharing a roof was grating enough without the constant olfactory assault.

"The petals will rot," she muttered as she traipsed to my balcony door and rammed it open. Heels clicking on the plywood floor, she scurried to recover her precious, eye-watering mix.

How could Jeb stand the smell? And Everest? Didn't it bother them?

She walked back into the room and then headed toward my bedroom door, clutching the jar to her bosom.

"Lucy, can I work tomorrow instead of today? Please? I'll put in a double shift."

"You might not be physically competent to work tomorrow. Besides, Saturdays are always busier than Sundays. You should know that by now." She leveled her hazel eyes on me, daring me to complain again.

She wasn't being fair, but perhaps this was the reason she was making me work. As I donned my gray uniform, I called Everest to ask him if he was still taking me to the meeting, but he didn't answer.

I texted him.

No answer.

An hour into my morning chores, I texted him again.

The headquarters was a good fifteen miles away from the inn, up mountain roads where driving faster than twenty miles per hour was downright treacherous. It would take me close to an hour to get there, and it was 10:30, which meant I would need to leave in thirty minutes to make it on time.

At 10:45, I finished cleaning the bedrooms and loped to my own room to change back into shorts and a t-shirt. I called Everest again, my patience dwindling. When five minutes later he still hadn't answered, I jogged toward his suite and then banged on the door.

No answer.

Fuck. I ran to the front desk, ready to grovel with Jeb to take me, but Lucy informed me he'd left with Everest on an errand.

"An errand?" It came out shrilly.

"Keep your voice down."

"Everest promised to bring me to—"

"He must've forgotten. Why don't you borrow one of the vans?"

A breath snagged inside my throat. "I don't have a license."

"You don't say." From the lilt in her voice, I gleaned she knew this.

The clock on the wall behind her ticked so loudly I felt it inside my chest. "Could you drive me?"

"I might not seem busy, but I have a business to run. I can't just get up and leave to take you to a silly contest."

Heat pricked my eyelids. "This isn't a silly contest."

"Isn't it?" She leaned over the check-in counter. "You've set your expectations on an unreasonable goal. Women don't lead packs of men; it's emasculating."

My scudding heart came to an abrupt halt. I blinked at my aunt, stunned to silence.

"Did you expect me to pat you on the back?" She shook her head. "You should've contented yourself with being their equal. Or married one of them."

I backed away because my fingers had closed into tight fists, and my nails were elongating. Before I started howling at my aunt or slashing at her tubby throat with my sharp claws, I pushed through the inn's revolving doors.

I dragged in lungfuls of air to calm my flaring anger and contemplated running, but racing fifteen miles before running a marathon was nonsensical. Besides, there was no way I could cover fifteen miles in one hour, even in wolf form. I whipped out my phone so fast I almost dropped it, and then scrolled to the saved number of a taxi company. I was put on hold before a woman informed me that my ride would arrive at the inn in ten minutes. It was already 11:05. I would never make it.

Never.

I wrote Everest a dozen hurtful text messages but deleted them all. Mom once told me communicating whilst angry was a terrible idea. Considering the things I'd written—things that could irreparably damage my relationship with Everest—she was right.

Finally, a yellow cab drove up the winding path. I tapped my foot. Before he'd even stopped, I lunged into the backseat and gave him directions. We were halfway through the drive when I realized I hadn't taken a bag, which meant I hadn't taken a wallet. I decided not to mention it until we arrived.

As the yellow cab climbed the mountain roads at a cautious fifteen miles per hour, I stared at the red digits escalating on the meter. "Could you drive any faster? I'm a little late."

The needle rose to eighteen miles per hour. How I wanted to jump in front and jam my foot on the gas pedal. I'd told Liam I wasn't sure what I wanted to do, but at this moment, I knew—I wanted to get a driver's license.

I researched this, since watching the minutes and dollars tick by was wreaking havoc on my fraying nerves. At 11:58, the Boulder headquarters rose before us like an oasis in a desert. The squat gray stone structure surrounded by the rusted fence and sunburned grass hadn't changed an iota.

"Word around town is that this place is crawling with wolves." The cabby was gazing at the large wooden sign carved up with the words: *Private Property*.

"I heard, but I also heard they aren't aggressive."

He grunted—obviously not sharing my belief—then turned in his seat. "That'll be forty-eight dollars."

"About that...I forgot my wallet. Can I pay you tomorrow?"

"What? No."

"But I don't have cash."

"Maybe your friends can pay me."

"My friends?"

He jerked his bearded chin toward Matt, who'd stepped into my line of sight. He glowered at the cab. Liam and Lucas came to flank him. Relief flooded through me when I noticed they were all still in skin.

"I'd rather not ask them, but I promise—"

"I got a family to feed, insurance to pay, not to mention taxes and schooling fees. If I accepted promises as payment, my family would starve and get evicted."

Geez. "Do you take PayPal?"

"No, I don't take PayPal, but even if I had an account, I wouldn't accept electronic cash."

"Fine." Cheeks heating up, I kicked the door open, then trekked toward my welcoming committee.

"You're late," Lucas chirped, chewing on a toothpick.

"Why isn't the cabbie leaving? Did you invite him to watch?" Matt asked.

Without taking my eyes off the overgrown grass that smelled like piss, I mumbled, "I forgot my wallet. Can anyone lend me a fifty?"

"Already spent all that hard-earned cash of yours, huh?" Lucas drawled.

I jerked my narrowed gaze toward him. "I forgot my wallet. If someone has PayPal, I'll wire them the cash right away."

"Here." Liam extended a green bill. "Get the guy out of here."

I took it from him, mumbling, "Thanks."

I ran back to the cabdriver and tossed the bill through his window, then waited for him to leave. Once his tires spun, spitting dirt and pebbles against my ankles, I made my way back to the others.

"You look like hell," Lucas said.

God, if only I could bash his tiny skull in. Sensing he'd riled me up, his smile grew grotesquely wide.

"What's your PayPal account, Liam?" I asked.

"I don't have one."

Why did no one freaking have a PayPal account? "I'll pay you back later."

"Sure." He shrugged without looking at me. He was entirely focused on Frank, who was traipsing back up the hill that led into the thick woods. "Should we get started?"

Frank nodded, slipping his phone into the holster hooked on his belt. "Get into your wolf forms."

Matt ripped off his t-shirt then pulled down his pants. Soon, Lucas and Liam, too, stood there only in their boxer-briefs.

Lucas leered at me. "Planning on ogling us or joining us?"

I went pale. Unless I wanted to tear my clothes apart, I would need to take them off also. My pride was dying a slow, agonizing death.

"Why don't you go change behind the building?" Liam offered as my fingers rolled up the hem of my tank top. "No one's inside."

"Alphas change with their packs," Matt said.

Liam glowered at him. "Ness isn't an Alpha."

I thought about turning around and going through the change with my back to them, but that had my stomach in knots.

As I hurried toward the back of the house, Liam's voice rose. "Watch out for the grate. It's pure silver."

A silver grate? I turned the corner, stepping lightly, carefully. I caught the metallic tang of silver before I even saw what Liam had mentioned. There, flush against the squat building was a grate twice the size of a sewer cap. I peered through the sturdy metal netting, at the excavation that was as deep as a well.

"Ness? Are you ready?" Frank's voice made me jerk away from the hole.

I put some distance between me and the silver grate, then chucked off my sneakers and clothes and concentrated hard.

Nothing happened.

I tried harder.

Still nothing.

After everything I'd gone through to get here. And now this! *Traitorous body.*

"Please," I begged.

But apparently beseeching my wolf was pointless. Minutes ticked by, and I remained pale flesh and taut human limbs.

16

I wasn't the type who gave up, but it had been ten minutes, and I was still in skin. Why the others hadn't rounded the building to find me yet was beyond me. I reached for my underwear just as a howl pierced the buzzing air.

And then another wolf howled.

And another.

The base of my spine tingled, and then my bones began to shift underneath my skin. Tears of relief coursed down my cheeks as my ears migrated to the top of my head and my mouth elongated into a muzzle filled with teeth that could scissor through bark and bone. The dusting of hair on my body thickened to summer fur. I fell onto my forepaws as my hind legs shortened and readjusted, as the wolf in me replaced the human.

In my four-legged form, I jogged around the house.

A large gray wolf with sharp blue eyes—Lucas, I imagined—howled, and this time I understood him. *Did you have to take a shit or what?*

I snarled at him.

Matt was more bear than wolf, butter-colored with vivid-green eyes. Next to him, I looked like a scrawny pup. Liam was much larger up close than he'd seemed in the woods. His glowing yellow-amber eyes raked over my unimpressive body before settling back on Frank. The elder crouched beside us, a strip of crimson fabric gripped in his hands.

"You're going to head south." He pointed toward the thick forest coating the side of the mountain. "We've spread pieces of this throughout the woods. Follow the trail until you find Eric. The rest of this shirt is tied to him. He's your finishing line." He passed the piece of fabric around so we could soak in the smell—sweet cigar smoke and cedar. "Now, the quickest way is straight down the hill, but it's also the most hazardous. If you get stuck in a trap, we will free you at the end of the race. Remember: do not turn back to skin. I will feel it if you do." He tapped his wrist as he straightened and rolled the cloth up into his palm.

I was glad for the blood oath then, glad someone could track my whereabouts and vitals. I rotated my withers then crouched low, the tall grass tickling my thumping chest.

"Ready. Set." Frank's voice rang out like a starting pistol. "Go!"

We sprang into action.

Lucas's hind paws sprayed dirt into my eyes. I blinked wildly, slowed, then switched course. Frank had mentioned the shortest path was the most treacherous. Was it true or a trick?

Lucas dashed through the tree line, vanishing into the forest that spilled down the flank of the mountain. He was apparently not worried about the traps, or maybe he'd change course at a later point. Soon Matt and Liam were lost to the trees, too. Although I could hear the soft thuds of their paws and sense the hectic beats of their faraway hearts, I could no longer see them. Which was better. I needed to funnel my awareness onto the ground.

I ran almost leisurely, stepping lightly through the underbrush. Spooked raccoons scampered out in front of me, and birds flapped out of trees, wings dark against the dazzling sky.

At some point, I forgot this was a race and flew heedlessly down woodchip-covered trails. The distant rumble of a car reminded me to melt back into the forest. I cut across a billow of spiky ferns and came out crowned with a cloud of frisky black flies. I flicked my ears and swiped my tail, then growled until they buzzed off.

Dense brushwood raked over my chest and leaf litter snagged in my silky white fur as I jogged toward a stretch of glittering water. My muscles became greedy for speed, so I ran faster. When my paws hit the chilly stream, I halted and lapped my fill. And then I pounced inside to cool my flushed limbs. I bounded down the riverbank, hopping over rotting trees and smooth rocks.

I thought I saw a blur of black fur to my left, but when I looked, there was nothing but a giant boulder. If I hadn't drunk water, I could've blamed my delusion on thirst, but my mind was clear. I was making up company to comfort myself into thinking I wasn't lagging behind. *Was* I lagging behind?

I raised my face and sniffed the air, caught the musky scent of another wolf. I looked for him but didn't see him. I sped up, slaloming through the trees, sliding over patches of dry dirt. I sniffed the air again. This time, it was the blend of tobacco and cedar that netted my senses. Sure enough, tied to a low branch, flapped a piece of red fabric. At least I was heading in the right direction.

I ducked past the branch but stumbled when my paws tangled on something. I backed up. Transparent fishing line glinted in the sunlight. Was this one of their traps or a vestige of a fishing expedition at the nearby creek? I bucked to unravel the plastic filament, but the knot tightened around my pastern.

I growled at the increasing jumble of thread, slid my fangs between it and my skin, and tugged. The fishing line sliced through my skin before finally ripping on my serrated teeth.

I moaned with relief then backed up to change routes. Another thread, this time taut, pressed against my hocks. I bounded forward, but not before hearing something click.

The ground rumbled as though a herd of Mustangs were stampeding down the hill. I twisted my neck.

No wild horses galloped.

The noise was coming from rocks.

Huge rocks.

They smashed against each other as they rolled. Sharp debris rained down on me, whipping my back. I sprang into action just as a large rock skimmed my hind paw. I faltered but recovered my footing fast. Desperation converted to pure adrenaline. As the stones thundered closer, I sprinted, the world blurring green, brown, gray. Thorns and rough bark frayed the pads of my paws, but I kept running.

I tried to change course, but a small boulder arced through the blue air and pounded into my spine, shredding my breath. I went down, down…down, rolling over and over. As the world spun out of focus, as up became down and down became up, I thought of the elders and the cruelty of their little game. Were they watching? Were they enjoying my grievous fall?

My mom's face swam through my mind, eyes as blue as cornflowers, hair fluttering around her face like stalks of wheat caught in a breeze. I drifted in the beauty of the memory, finding comfort in her bright smile, in the low timber of her voice as she spoke my name. As my name transformed and distorted into something else entirely.

A roar.

An inhuman roar that had me snapping my lids. A black shape floated between sky and earth. Another boulder? I blinked, but shards of rock sprayed my face, spoiling my already poor sight. Another roar, more wolf than stone, shook me fully awake.

I dug my claws into the earth, but I wasn't on soft earth. I was on solid rock. And not just a rock. *A Flatiron.* Oh God…

From my vantage point, there was no telling how steep the fall. Calling on the last dregs of energy, I channeled all of my weight into my paws, mincing my claws on the searing rock. My muscles screamed as my speed decreased, as my claws were sanded down and my pads ribboned. I was still coming at the edge of the cliff too fast.

Gritting my teeth, I locked my muscles and dug what remained of my filed claws into the rock.

An inch from the edge, I came to a stop. I kept my head down until the rubble stopped walloping my battered body.

Shivering, shuddering, heart pounding against the sun-soaked Flatiron, I waited for silence to replace the pitter-patter of rock. Once it finally draped over the land, I lifted my head and squinted upward at the gritty trail of blood and chalky scratch marks.

I'd survived the fall, but would I survive the rest of this brutal contest?

17

I licked my wounds a long time. It wasn't as though I could possibly win anymore. Unless another contestant had run into a trap more perilous than mine. I doubted it. The others were surer-footed and more attuned to the land than I was, thanks to the years of experience I lacked.

After a lengthy interlude of self-deprecation, I pressed my battered body up onto my shredded paws. I groaned, feeling as though I weighed a ton more than I had at the start of this godforsaken race. I took a step and whimpered. Another step. Another whimper.

Well, this'll be fun.

And slow.

I hope you're all enjoying this, you asswipes, I howled into the inert air.

Running was out of the question. Tripping repeatedly, I hobbled down the grassy sides of the Flatiron then headed back toward the evergreens. At least, at this pathetic speed, I couldn't possibly run into another trap.

The sun baked my hide as I traipsed clumsily toward the trees. After what felt like a day, I reached the dappled forest. Shadows cooled the bitter heat, and damp moss alleviated the pain that was each step. Moss and shadows could unfortunately do nothing for my sore spine. I wondered, more than once, if the stone that had landed on my back had dislodged a vertebra.

Could I still move with a dislocated vertebra?

I was no doctor, but I guessed my spine must be intact.

My breaths were no longer coming in short spurts. They were lengthening like the shadows as the sun dipped a little lower in the sky. I sniffed the air to make sure I was still heading in the right direction. I caught the sweet smell of tobacco and the crisp scent of cedar, but it was muddled by that of blood.

Fresh blood.

I stopped and sniffed my paws. It wasn't my blood I smelled.

I sniffed again.

Then I followed the tinny trail through the trees, through a shrub of wild roses that layered their sultry perfume over that of the blood. I pushed past them, their thorns snagging in my flesh, and almost tripped on a mound of blond fur.

Matt whipped his head toward me, leveling his green eyes on my face and letting out a low growl. I backed up, but then my gaze snagged on the metal snare jammed around his forepaw.

The jagged trap had bitten into his flesh, revealing bits of white bone and pink sinew. He snapped his teeth at me. I gnashed my own teeth and barked, *I didn't come to gloat. I mean, look at me.*

He looked me over. Grasping I wasn't a threat, he lowered his muzzle to the metal, trying to pry it open with his fangs, but all it did was steep the fur of his face in blood.

I stood motionless for a moment.

I could still win.

The realization fluttered through me as delicately as butterfly wings.

I could leave him behind.

Even if he managed to break free, he wouldn't be able to beat me with a mangled leg. I turned southward and stared at the green hollow covered in deciduous trees. The race would end somewhere in those woods. I could reach them in minutes—fifteen, twenty at most—and once I found Eric, I could inform him of Matt's whereabouts.

Low whines lanced through the air.

I closed my eyes.

Matt was crying.

This bear of a man was crying.

There goes winning.

I twisted back to find the brute gnawing on his forearm. Was he planning on chewing off his paw to get out of the trap? It wouldn't regenerate. We were wolves, not lizards.

I moved back toward him. *Stop.*

A pitiful snarl rose from his reddened muzzle. *Go away.*

I shook my head then dipped it toward the snare. I'd get no pleasure in winning if I left him behind. The smell of Matt's blood, of his agony, overwhelmed my senses. I almost retched.

Matt snapped at me with blood-soaked teeth. Growling, I rammed my head into his chest to get him to back off. *Stop your yapping, Hulk. I'm trying to help you.*

He froze. I placed my paws on either side of the snare and drove my weight down hard on the levers. Besides sending explosive bolts of pain into my bones, it created a thin opening, but failed to release Matt's paw. I tried again, wincing. Matt must've shifted his paw, because when the metal jaw clamped back shut, he let out a low, mournful keening, and fresh blood gushed down his fur.

Don't move, I grumbled.

He snarled at me. I shot him a look that must've translated well because he shut his muzzle. I heaved on my paws again, and again the trap opened, but not wide enough for him to shimmy out. Why the hell did he have to have giant paws anyway?

Ugh.

I tried again.

Nothing.

Again.

My attempts were paltry and clumsy. If I had hands instead of paws—

I sucked in a breath just as Matt's eyes took on a glassy sheen like the marbles I used to roll on the hardwood floors of my childhood home.

Whoomph.

Matt went down so hard I jumped.

Fuck. Fuck. Fuck.

Matt!

His flattened ears didn't flick.

I howled, hoping someone would come, but they hadn't come for me, so they most probably wouldn't come for him. Still, I waited. Wasn't Frank worried? When no voice answered mine, I loosed a rough breath, shut my eyes, and willed my body to change.

I would be disqualified, but at least I'd be able to live with myself, wherever it was I would be living.

18

I'd been half-right about what my body would look like. Where I wasn't entirely mottled with bruises, my palms and soles were in bloody tatters. For the first time since Matt had become unconscious, I was glad for it. After all, I was standing over him in my birthday suit.

Even though I felt and looked like roadkill, I was still prudish roadkill. I kneeled next to his massive, inert form, and worked my blood-soaked fingers nimbly around the levers, prodding them. In one swift jerk, I jammed my palms against them and the trap's jaws opened like a night-blooming flower.

Sweat trickled down my neck, down my smarting spine, as I delicately lifted Matt's ravaged paw and set it on the grass next to his head. I tossed the trap aside, and it clinked shut.

"Piece of crap mousetrap," I grumbled.

Matt stirred, and I jumped behind the wild rose bush. They weren't dense enough to shield me, but beggars couldn't be choosers. The thorns felt like piranha teeth against my skin. I plucked them out, letting out a slew of choice words. Compared to the pain radiating inside my bones, being a human pincushion was peanuts, but still. A twig breaking had me snapping my gaze up, straight into a set of no longer glassy eyes.

I blinked dumbly at Matt. His paw dragged, yet he was already up! *How?*

Remembering I was naked, I spun around, willing fur to cloak my curves. I squinted so hard that anyone passing by would think me constipated. Thankfully, besides Matt, no one was even around.

When I felt a wet muzzle on the knobs of my hunched spine, I almost jumped out of my skin. "Go away!"

Matt made a noise my human ears couldn't decipher. And then he released a soft wail that made my skin pebble.

Not pebble.

Change.

His howl made me change back.

Once cloaked in fur, I turned and nodded to the paw. *Can you walk?*

Not well.

Want to stay here while I go get help?

And let you win?

My shoulders locked up. Hulk's competitive streak had apparently not suffered from the snare. *You're going to win anyway. I broke the rules, remember.*

To help me.

Still, I changed.

I swear he rolled his eyes at me. *Come on, Little Wolf.*

I snorted, which earned me an amused sideways glance. We began to limp down the hill. Where Matt no longer whimpered, I did, and I felt absolutely no shame. *I feel like I crawled through a garbage compacter.*

Your back is one solid bruise.

There goes wearing most of my wardrobe in public.

Wolves didn't laugh, and yet Matt made a sound that sounded almost like a chuckle. And then he asked how I'd gotten the bruise, and I told him about the rockslide.

Even though we moved at a slow pace, we moved nonetheless. Soon we'd reached the trees. I caught the scent of cigar and cedar. It was strong.

Almost there, Matt said, limping beside me.

A slash of red broke through the greenery. It flapped around Eric's wrist.

I can't believe we made it, I whispered.

Figures shifted through the trees like ghosts. I recognized Liam and Lucas and Cole and countless others.

Matt faltered beside me, then landed with a hard thump.

I stopped walking. *Come on, Hulk, get up.*

He whined.

I shoved my muzzle against his furry shoulder. *Get up.*

Slowly, like a mountain rising from two tectonic plates, Matt got up. And even slower, he limped beside me.

Don't tell anyone you saw me naked or I'll stick a snare in your bed.

He let out a small grunt.

Metal blinded me as I focused on the scrap of red fabric. There were cars. Lots of them.

Good, because I was done with walking.

Probably for the rest of my life.

I thought of my driver's license then. At least now that I was out of the stupid running, I'd have plenty of time to get it.

Matt slowed. I waited.

Just go, Little Wolf.

I shook my head. *Stop growling and move your furry ass. I'm out; I changed.*

But they don't know that.

I took the blood oath same as you. Frank knows.

Matt gave me a lingering look, then finally set forth toward Eric. We reached him at the same time. I was finishing this race for myself. I'd cheated, but at least I hadn't quit.

A shiver of pride pulsated through me as I collapsed at the man's feet. Sunlight and loud voices danced around me like dandelion florets. I made a feeble attempt at getting back up, but I...just...couldn't.

A paltry thought inserted itself inside my mind. If I changed while unconscious, everyone would see my naked ass. I almost laughed.

Almost, because I was still a wolf, and wolves didn't laugh.

But then, my muscles slid and slotted back. Unable to fight off the change, I let it sweep through me.

What a pitiful sight I must've been. Thankfully, darkness enveloped me before I could hear anyone laugh.

19

I woke up to Evelyn glowering at me. If I'd thought her eyes were black before, they were a whole new shade of black now—sewer-hole-at-night-black.

"Thank *God!*" She lobbed the book she was reading on the table next to the armchair and stalked over to me on slippered feet. "Ness Clark, I am so mad at you! If you were my daughter, I would ground you until your thirtieth birthday! Rock-climbing alone! *Sola!*" Even through her layers of foundation, her cheeks were the same dark pink as the sky behind her. "When that *chico* carried you into the inn—"

"What boy?"

She blinked a great many times, seemingly startled I'd interrupted her rant for something as silly as the identity of the person who'd handled my naked body.

"Liam Kolane."

"Liam?" My neck felt hot; my jaw too. Fucking crap. I groaned from embarrassment.

"*Sí*, and you were unconscious and covered in blood. *Mi corazón* stopped beating. My heart stopped!" Her Spanish always bled through her English when she was agitated. "I thought...I thought your spine was *rota!*" Her brash voice was trembling. Her hands, too. All of her was quivering.

Even though I was still dying a little from the fact that Liam had carried me back, I reached out and enclosed her cold fingers in mine. The contact wasn't enough for her, and she sandwiched her other hand over mine.

Tears cascaded down her cheeks, dragging tiny clumps of mascara off her wet lashes. And then a sob racked her body. I sat up, and the momentum had her stumble and plop down on the bed next to me. The momentum also had me gritting my teeth. I don't know how long I'd been out, but apparently not long enough. My flesh felt like someone had clobbered it with a meat mallet before rubbing it against a cheese grater.

"I'm sorry, Evelyn. Sorry I put you through this." I let go of her hands so I could hug her. My arms felt like they were attached to fifty-pound dumbbells, but I fought through the pain to pull her in close.

She crushed me against her, and I yelped from all the bruises her grip awakened. She didn't loosen her arms—probably hadn't heard me yelping over her sobbing. "Never again. Never again. You promise? Two days of being by your side. Of watching you—"

I pressed her away. "It's been two days?"

"*Sí*, two days!"

"I've been sleeping for two days?"

"Yes!"

Whoa.

"Your bruises, they've been going away...quickly...but—"

Abruptly, I stood. My legs felt wooden, but at least they held me up as I shuffled toward my closet. I pulled open the door to get a full view of myself in the built-in mirror. I lifted the hem of my tank and pivoted. The backs of my thighs and spine were tinged a yellowish-green. Could've been worse. Could've been black. The worst part of me was actually my hair, which was crusty and tangled and matted in God only knew what. My nails were in pretty dire shape, too—ragged like pinecones.

Evelyn appeared in the mirror behind me, her face ghostly-pale compared to my tanned one. At least *rock-climbing* and slumbering for forty-eight hours had given me a healthy complexion. Mom was always on my case about finding silver linings. She used to say that was how she'd made it through life. *Here's to you, Mom.*

I turned away from the mirror and closed the door.

"I soaped your body, but I did not dare wash your hair. You had a big gash here." Evelyn pressed lightly on a spot on the back of my head that felt incredibly tender. I half expected her fingers to come away wet with blood. They didn't.

"Even though it is still hard for me—what you are"—she gave a small shrug—"I think that if you were not...I think you would not have lived." She wiped her red-rimmed eyes.

I gathered both her hands in mine. "I'm not going anywhere."

No more death expeditions on my agenda in the near or far future. But there would be an expedition. I was going to have to leave town now. Jeb would have to release me back into the world—minor and all. I didn't broach the subject with Evelyn. She'd had her fair share of stress for the day.

Instead, I said, "I love you."

Her crying started again, and even though it felt like I was being quartered, I hugged her.

After she left, which took much prodding on my part—Evelyn needed rest—I took a blisteringly hot bath. As I steeped, I thought. Which made me anxious because most of my thoughts revolved around how many people had seen me naked after the run.

I slid beneath the bathwater, wishing soap could cleanse my brain of its petty anxiety. After all, I'd almost died. *Died!* And here I was worried about nudity. My priorities were massively skewed.

After washing my hair, a task that felt tougher than racing down a hill chased by boulders, I stepped out of the bath, towel-dried my body, and patted lotion over every inch of skin, as though moisturizing my sore muscles could somehow soften them. It didn't, but at least I smelled good—like toasted coconut.

I was about to pull on PJs when there was a knock on my door. In my bathrobe, I pattered toward the door. I imagined it was Everest. Evelyn must've told him I was conscious again.

Note to self: stop assuming things.

It was not my cousin.

20

"Amanda?" I yelped.

"You're alive." She tucked a long curl behind her ear and shot me a cheery smile.

Why was she smiling at me? Was she playing a trick on me? I checked the hallway for a raised phone but found only a couple leaving their bedroom hand in hand.

"Why are you here?" I finally asked.

"One, to check if you were doing better. When I stopped by yesterday, your grandma said you were still recovering. And two, to thank you."

"Thank me?"

"For helping Matt."

I frowned.

She raised an eyebrow. "Do you have a concussion or something?"

"No."

"Well, then, you must remember you saved my baby's hand."

"Oh." I nibbled on my bottom lip. "Is it still...functional?"

"Uh-huh. They've stapled his skin. The nerves and tendons are regenerating."

My stomach flipped at the mention of stapling flesh.

"Anyway, we're all going out to play some pool and grab a couple beers."

I released my lip. "And you're inviting me?"

"No. I came to give you a play-by-play of my evening to make you jealous." She rolled her brown eyes. "Of course I'm inviting you! Scratch that. I'm here to *take* you."

"I don't really feel like going out."

"You're alive. And clean. You're going out, so get dressed."

I furrowed my forehead. My hair was still wet, and I hadn't had time to file my nails down—that last part felt superficially important.

"We'll wait for you in the car."

"Amanda—"

She tsked. "Would you rather we all come to you?" She snuck a look behind me at my bedroom. "Might get a tad crowded in here."

I blanched. "You're joking."

"I never joke." Even though one side of her mouth was pulled up in a smile, her eyes were deathly serious.

I sighed. "Fine."

"You got ten minutes."

"What happens in ten minutes?"

"I send Matt to lug you out of your bedroom."

The girl was not only crazy bossy but also mercurial. A week ago, she wanted me to stay away from *her* boys, and now she was forcing me to spend time with them. Since I was a little worried she'd throw a party in my bedroom, I finally accepted. "Fine. I'll get ready."

After I shut the door, I tried pulling on a pair of jeans, but the simple act of tugging them on felt like rubbing my legs with sandpaper, so I settled on leggings and a t-shirt. Wearing a bra was out of the question, but my nipples weren't *too* visible—I hoped. Okay, they were a little noticeable, but one really had to look.

Hopefully no one would. They'd all surely gotten enough eyefuls on Saturday.

Oh God...

And Liam had carried me back...

Oh great freaking God.

Trying to stifle my embarrassment, I swiped mascara over my eyelashes and red gloss over my lips, ran a brush through my damp hair, then filed my finger and toenails to the quick. I grabbed my bag, my phone—which Evelyn must've plugged in for me—and my room key. As I made my way down the corridor, I checked my messages. Found five from August.

Ness?

Call me back?

I heard what happened.

Ness? Send me some fucking news.

NESS CALL ME.

I smiled at my screen. He was roasting on some desert base or ambushing enemies, and yet he was thinking of me. August was as sweet as they came.

I feel like a freight train just rolled over me, but I'm alive. Thanks for checking on me.

I hesitated to send a heart emoji. August was my friend. Did girls send heart emojis to boy-friends? I'd never even sent one to Everest, and he was family.

"You gave us all a fright."

I looked up from my phone and locked eyes with my uncle who was manning the bell desk. He rubbed the back of his neck. Was he expecting me to apologize?

"Lucy was out of her mind with worry—"

"Lucy was worried?" My voice sounded slightly unhinged. "She tried to stop me,

Jeb. She told me girls shouldn't play at boy's games. Wonder where she got that from."

Jeb blushed. Like a full-on blush. "We were trying to protect you, Ness. We didn't want you to get hurt, and you did. You weren't supposed to find a way of getting there."

"So that's why Everest vanished from the face of the Earth?"

He nodded.

"I may be your ward, Uncle, but this is my life."

"So we should just stand back and watch you kill yourself? You think this is what your mother would've wanted?"

"I'm not going to die."

"You kids… You think you're so invincible, but you aren't. Look at that sweet girl Everest was dating."

"She tried to commit suicide. I'm taking part in a competition. Besides—"

"A competition no one wants you to compete in! *No one*. And I'm not talking about Lucy and me. I'm talking about the whole"—his voice dropped to a hiss—"pack."

His comment hurt. "I'm out of the running anyway," I mumbled. "And for your information, the whole *pack* just invited me to go out with them tonight."

He drew his shoulders back until they formed a perfect T. "I thought you wanted nothing to do with them. I thought you weren't looking to fit in."

Outside, a car honked, and then Amanda waved from the passenger window of a silver Dodge sedan.

"I thought so too, but I'm trying to make the most of my time here. But don't worry. I'll be out of your hair soon."

What I'd wished for the most had finally come true, except leaving wasn't what I wanted most anymore.

Matt honked again.

"I'll see you later," I said.

Jeb pinched his lips together. Either he was all out of unsolicited advice or he'd understood giving me any was useless.

I pushed through the revolving doors, the deep-blue night air slapping my warm cheeks, then pulled open the back door of the Dodge. Someone was already sitting in the backseat.

Sienna. Her fingers worked the hem of her baby-doll top, rolling it over and over.

"Hi," I said.

Keeping her gaze cemented to her hand, she murmured, "Hey."

I wasn't certain why, but I felt guilty all of a sudden. As though entering the Alpha contest had prompted August to leave—which wasn't true. He'd left because he'd needed to get away. It had nothing to do with me.

Matt spun around and gave me a wolfish grin. "Little Wolf's in the house!"

I smirked at the nickname. "Should you be driving?"

"I'm a righty." He wiggled the fingers of his good hand. "Thank goodness for Amanda."

Amanda flicked his big arm and tittered.

I didn't catch the correlation between his fingers and his girlfriend, until Sienna said, "TMI, guys."

Oh. "Eww." I wrinkled my nose.

A soft smile settled on Sienna's face.

Matt belted out a laugh that was as large as his ribcage, then spun the dial of his stereo until a rap song shook the car. And then he revved up his engine and took off, headlights zipping over the darkened landscape as fast as laser beams.

"You might want to put your seatbelt on," Sienna yelped, strapping herself in. I think she added, "Not that you can die from a car crash," but the music was so loud and her voice so soft I wasn't sure.

Couldn't I, though?

Werewolves were stronger than normal humans, but they weren't immortal. If Heath could drown in a pool, couldn't I die from a car crash? Couldn't August perish from a detonating grenade? I filed the question away for later.

I would ask Everest.

After yelling at him for ditching me, I would ask him.

21

The pack along with two bartenders and a couple grizzly-faced beer drinkers made up the small crowd at Tracy's.

As I walked inside, I started regretting coming along. Wherever my enthusiasm to hang out with the pack had stemmed from, the second I crossed the threshold, it shrunk like the Colorado River during hot, dry months.

I straightened my spine and raised my chin. I was here now. Might as well make the most of it. Besides, I was leaving, so it wasn't like they'd have to endure me much longer.

Several gazes raked over me as I trailed behind Amanda and Matt. Even though I was mad at Everest, I desperately sought him out, but encountered Taryn's narrowed blue gaze instead. She elbowed Lucas, who leaned on his cue stick as he turned toward me. On the other side of the felt table, Liam was lining up his pool tip to the cue ball. He was so concentrated on making the shot that a deep wrinkle plowed the spot between his eyebrows. Next to him stood Cole, and next to him, Tamara.

Whereas Tamara looked at me as though I were a leper come to contaminate her, Cole sent me a smile.

"You got Ness to emerge from her lair." Cole pumped his fist against his brother's uninjured one.

"Can't take credit for that. It was all Amanda's doing." Matt draped his arm around his girlfriend. "Everyone knows you can't say no to my girl." He craned his neck to look at me. "I tried when she pursued me. She was relentless."

"Poor baby." She pouted up at him. "You're such a victim."

He laughed and kissed her temple, then tightened his grip. "A real content victim," he purred into her ear.

"They're annoyingly cute those two," Sienna said, her tone slipper-soft. There was no jealousy in her voice, though, just genuine affection.

"When did you move to Boulder?" I asked her.

"In my junior year of high school."

"Where from?"

"Tucson."

"You like it here?"

She shrugged a freckled shoulder.

"First round's on me." Matt made a beeline for the bar that was decorated with sticky ring marks.

The hygiene freak within me cringed. How hard was it to wipe down a bar?

"Name your poison, Little Wolf."

That nickname. I shook my head. "Sam Adams."

"Coming right up."

I was tempted to follow him to the bar, feeling strange just standing here next to the pool table, especially after Sienna and Amanda had flocked over to Taryn and Tamara. I watched Liam finally hit his shot—miss it, to be exact. The tip of his stick skidded right off the cue ball, which spun on itself without making contact with any other ball.

"Performance anxiety, Kolane?" Lucas's gaze sparked with delight, while Liam scowled.

He straightened, studying the cue ball as though it were a live thing that had dissed him.

Cole chuckled, then lined up his stick. He hit the eight ball and sunk it in.

When he leaned over for another shot, I asked, "Isn't that a foul?" I wasn't a huge pool player but was pretty certain the black ball was supposed to go in last.

"We're playing cut-throat," Liam said, chalking up the tip of his stick.

"How do you play that?"

Without taking his eyes off the game, he explained the rules: each player had a section of pool balls and they had to sink their opponents' balls in. Matt arrived then and handed me a sweaty bottle of beer.

"Thanks." I took a sip and felt it drip into my empty stomach. I needed food. And I probably needed it before I drank the beer. "I should eat something," I told no one in particular, but then I offered to get the others food. I prayed no one would ask for anything, or my bank account would take a serious hit.

After everyone said they were good for now, I walked over to the bar, sat on a stool, and then grabbed a laminated menu that was as sticky as the bar. I ordered nachos with cheese and bacon, then spun on the stool and watched the pool game. Again, I wondered what got into me to come tonight. I heaved a sigh, then wheeled back toward the bar and took my phone out of my bag.

August had answered me. **Glad you're okay. Heard you're Matt's favorite girl now too.**

I smiled. **No. Still just yours. He has Amanda.** Only after I pressed send did I realize how flirty that sounded. I dragged a hand through my hair that was now completely dry.

August sent me a smiley face.

Not for the first time, I wished he were here instead of across an ocean. That thought filled me with abrupt guilt. Guilt that made me glance at Sienna. She was laughing at a story Cole was telling her. I studied her a moment, analyzing her body language. Her eyes glittered a little as she looked up at the mammoth blond with the buzz cut. Maybe her eyes always glittered. Or maybe she was over August.

I ducked my face back down and wrote: **You'd be proud of me. I'm at Tracy's with the pack. I'm trying to be social.**

A couple seconds later: **I hope they're on their best behavior.**

No one's called me any names yet.

And if any of them do, you tell me, OK?

I'll be fine. Concentrate on staying alive out there. Which had me thinking… **Are we as killable as humans?**

Don't get your question.

I took a swig of beer, then set it back down and typed: **Can we die of something other than drowning or silver poisoning?**

Dot-dot-dots appeared. Then: **Silver, fire, or asphyxiation. Why? Are you planning on killing Lucas?**

I grinned. **LOL. Even though I wish you'd taken him with you, no. No homicidal plans on my end. I was just wondering.**

Strange thing to be wondering about.

The bartender came back with my dish and the bill. As I dug out my wallet, I remembered I owed Liam fifty dollars. I paid for my meal, then took out the owed amount and slid it inside my bag's front pocket.

When I looked back down at my phone, August had written: **Want me to call you?**

I frowned.

One more line of dialogue appeared: **For a refresher course. Wolf 101.**

I did need one. I was about to type yes when Matt sidled up next to me at the bar. He ordered more beer and filched a soggy tortilla chip from my bowl. "Who you sextin'?"

The chip I'd been chewing on went down the wrong hole. I coughed, then grabbed my Sam Adams and took a long gulp.

"I wasn't *sexting*," I wheezed out.

A goofy grin slashed his jaw. "Sure you weren't."

"Seriously, I wasn't."

He snatched another chip. "Who were you *texting*, then?"

"Everest."

"Liar."

My spine tightened.

"You couldn't have been texting Everest 'cause he's right there, sucking face with some chick."

I spun on my stool. Everest was here? Sure enough, he was sitting on a brown leather couch in a dusky corner of the room, making out with the girl from the music festival.

"So? Who were you really talkin' to, Little Wolf?"

"No one, *Hulk*."

His smile grew larger. "As long as it ain't that creep you went out with the other day, I'm cool with it."

I snorted. "It wasn't, but thanks for your consent." Even though I would sooner swallow a live goldfish than admit this to Matt, I was sort of touched by his concern.

"You looked out for me, so now I look out for you... Only fair. Unless someone's already doing that?" He looked at Everest again then, and I did too.

Like the hunger crimping my stomach, Everest's fickleness pinched my heart. It had barely been a month since Becca's suicide attempt, and he was already kissing someone new. Sure, I'd thought it was healthy for him to be flirting, but making out with someone...that was too much too fast.

"August just wrote back," Matt said.

I whipped my face toward Matt and swiped my cell off the bar. I didn't check the text message, just stuffed the phone inside my bag. My heart had leaped a good couple inches into my throat. "We're just friends."

As he paid for his beers, he said, "I'm not judging. I like the guy."

I wanted to add don't tell Sienna, but that would've sounded incriminating. I scooped up some plasticky cheese and crunchy bacon bits with a chip and stuffed them inside my mouth.

"Lucas wiped me out." Liam was suddenly here, right next to me. He swiped a beer from Matt's stash and drank half of it. "Your turn, Mattie." As though just noticing me, he asked, "Unless you want to play, Ness?"

My heart performed a strange little twist as I looked up at Liam, as I imagined him carrying my limp, naked—*ugh*—body in his arms. They'd probably had to draw straws, and he'd gotten the shortest one.

"I can barely move my arms."

He settled on the stool next to mine, gaze roaming over my arms. "You got a serious thrashing out there. All those rocks."

Had he been there?

Before Matt left to play, he tossed out, "If Liam annoys you, call out my name. Or Hulk. I'll respond to both."

I smiled.

"Did Ness Clark just crack a real-ass smile?" Matt winked at me, which had me shaking my head. He scooped up the three beers and then returned to the others.

"I heard I had you to thank for getting back to the inn." I twirled a chip in the air, twisting the string of cheese glued to it until it snapped off.

Liam didn't say anything.

Without taking my eyes off the chip, I said, "Tell me I wasn't naked." Some people could sweep things under rugs; I was the type who'd rather vacuum them.

"You weren't."

I exhaled a long breath.

"They covered you up the second you changed."

Another breath rushed out of me. "I wonder how the other packs—the ones with females in them—I wonder how they...operate."

"You mean does everyone get naked together?"

Heat curled up my throat.

"I would imagine nudity isn't such a big deal for them."

I finally dared look away from my chip. Liam raised his beer to his lips and tipped it, his Adam's apple bobbing sharply under his dark stubble.

"At least I don't have to worry about that anymore."

He laid a long, muscled forearm on the bar. "What do you mean?"

"Now that I'm out of the pack." *Out of Boulder...*

"You're not out."

"They said that if I failed, I couldn't get into the pack."

"But you didn't fail."

"I did. I changed during the trial."

"Ness, you're still in the running. Matt's the one who's out."

I knocked my beer over, and it spilled onto Liam's jeans.

"Shoot." I grabbed a handful of napkins and dabbed his thigh.

He wrapped his hand around my wrist and stilled my fingers. I froze as something pulsed against my knuckles.

I snatched my arm back. "Sorry," I mumbled, ogling the row of backlit liquor bottles and wondering how many of those I should ingest to forget that my hand had just connected to a very private part of Liam Kolane's anatomy. I wiped my shaky fingers on a napkin. "I broke the rules..." My disloyal voice was wobbling. I prayed Liam would think it was the emotion of not being disqualified that was affecting my larynx and not—

"To save his hand," Liam said huskily.

I feigned great interest in the baseball game on the TV hanging from an articulated arm over the liquor shelf. "He wouldn't have gnawed it off."

"He might've. In wolf form, we can act like animals."

I side-eyed him.

Pale arms slid around his chest. "Baby, you abandoned me." Tamara tried to kiss him, but he twisted his face, and her lips landed on the hard line of his jaw.

I ogled my half-eaten basket of tortilla chips. When minutes later she was still trying to coax him off the barstool, I stood.

"Before I forget." I slid out the fifty-dollar bill and extended it to him.

Tamara stared at the bill, nose crinkled. "Are you paying him for his company?"

I frowned. "What?"

She shot me a sweet smile that was anything but sweet. "Isn't that how you make your living? Cash for company?"

She could've thrown a glass full of ice at my face, and it would've chilled me less than her comment.

Liam pried her arms off him.

"Excuse me?" I said, playing dumb in case I was reading too much into what she'd insinuated.

"The boys said you were a wh—"

"Tamara!" Liam's complexion went a little ruddy.

She pushed out her lower lip in a pout. "What?"

In what world did I think I had friends here? I backed up, and then I turned, emotion burning on my lids. My ears buzzed as I stepped onto the street. I felt drunk and sick to my stomach, but I was neither. What I was, was ashamed. And angry. It wasn't like I could explain what I'd been doing on an escort service website in the first place.

I started walking, not caring where I ended up. I just needed to get away.

"Ness!" someone called out.

Even though my legs ached, I quickened my pace, but someone stepped out in front of me, blocked my path.

22

I tried to sidestep Liam.

He shuffled, blocking me again. "Ness, I'm sorry."

"About what? Telling your girlfriend I was a whore? It's true, isn't it? So there's nothing to be sorry about." I walked off, but Liam stalked next to me.

"We never said you were a whore."

They'd probably used the word escort—big whooping difference. I started to cross the street to get away from him when a car honked at me.

Liam yanked on my arm, reeling me back onto the sidewalk. My shoulder screamed in pain from the sharp tug.

I gritted my teeth as I flung his hand off and rubbed my sore joint.

"Shit." Liam palmed the back of his neck. "Did I hurt you?"

"Don't give yourself so much credit."

"Oh, will you stop acting like you're fucking made of steel. A rock almost spliced your spine Saturday. You're allowed to be in pain."

So he had seen me... He *had* been there. "Thanks for your permission."

He grumbled some unintelligible words. "I don't get you. Really, I don't." He shoved a lock of hair off his forehead.

"What don't you get, Liam? Did you think I'd enjoy everyone finding out that I went on a date with a guy for money?" I hugged my arms against me, trying to squelch the tremors shooting through my limbs. I was cold and I was mad. Not a good combination.

"You said you didn't sleep with your customers, so there's really nothing to be ashamed about. Unless you do...sleep with them."

My stomach bottomed out. "*Them?*"

He held my gaze. Did he know about his father? He couldn't, could he?

Keeping my eyes fixed on his, I said, "I only went out with Aidan." Technically, it was true. I hadn't *gone out* with Liam's father; I'd stayed in. "But I'm not doing it anymore, so if you can stop telling people—"

"I'm sorry."

"Whatever." I tried to step around him again, but he whipped his arm out to stop me.

"Come back inside. Let me buy you a drink to make up for being a prick."

"In what world do you think I'd want to go back in there?"

"Then let me buy you a drink someplace else."

I tightened my arms. "God, Liam, I don't need a pity drink."

"It wouldn't be a pity drink. It'd be an apology drink."

I shook my head. "Thanks, but no thanks. I just want to walk around."

He lowered his hand, and I passed by him. But then he was striding next to me.

"The bar's the other way."

"Maybe I want to walk around, too."

"There are plenty of other sidewalks."

"I like this sidewalk."

"Liam—" I huffed.

"What? You don't have to talk to me."

"That's not going to be weird at all."

I thought I detected a smile, but it could've been a twitching nerve.

"Why?" I asked.

"Why what?"

"Why are you walking with me? And if you say it's to protect me from a handsy passerby—"

"My earliest memory is of your birth."

"My birth?"

He glanced down at me. "Your dad came over to our house to announce that he'd had a kid, and that kid was a girl. I remember how appalled my father was."

His strange confession unsettled me. "You were four."

"So?"

"That's young to remember something."

Liam's gaze dropped to my collarbone as though not daring to meet my eyes. "My father advised your dad to take a paternity test."

I gasped. "My mother would never—"

"It gets worse, Ness." Liam palmed his hair uneasily.

Worse than implying my mother had betrayed my father?

"He also told your dad that he should take you out into the woods"—the volume of Liam's voice dropped so suddenly I had to strain to hear the rest of his sentence— "leave you there, and then try again."

"Leave me in the forest? To do what?" I frowned but then I didn't. Then I opened my eyes so wide my lashes hit my brow ridge. "Oh... He told my father to *kill* me?" I all but shouted. "Because I was a girl?"

Liam's gaze finally climbed back to mine. "Your father was outraged. My mother, too."

"And you?" I snapped.

"Why do you think it's my earliest memory, Ness?" His voice was as thick and dark as the fur that cloaked his wolf form.

Heath had made my father doubt my mother and then suggested I should be murdered because of my gender! If Liam's father weren't already dead, I would've found a silver blade and wrenched it inside his black, black heart.

"What's *your* earliest memory?" Liam asked, whisking my mind off my homicidal deliberations.

I racked my brain. When the memory slotted into my mind, I blinked. It couldn't possibly be my earliest recollection. I hunted through my mind for another but found none.

"Your mother's funeral."

He flinched.

I'd been five at the time. I could still remember what I'd worn—a scratchy black wool dress with thick white stockings and black patent mary-janes. The air had smelled of overturned earth and tears, and there hadn't been a dry cheek.

Except Heath's.

He didn't weep, but Liam cried enough for the two of them.

Liam had been a gangly boy with features too large for his face. He'd grown into his body, grown into his features. He didn't even resemble the narrow-faced sixteen-year-old boy I'd last seen on the winter day I begged the pack to accept me.

"I remembered wondering if you had a hole in your heart," I said as we crossed the street toward a little park. "But now I know." Mom's gaunt face flashed into my mind. "I'm sorry."

He glanced down at me. "For what?"

"For reminding you of her."

"Because you think I forget? Not a day goes by where I don't think about her, Ness." His voice contained the same shadows that had collected over his face.

We carried around the same pain, he and I.

"You never forget the people you love, but I guess you know this now," he said softly.

A snare snapped around my heart.

I thought about my mother, about my father—who was *most definitely* my father—as we passed by the playground of my youth. It had changed, gotten a shinier swing set, but the monkey bars I spent hours scaling were still there. Dad would swing alongside me sometimes, while Mom looked on, shaking her head and laughing, telling him he looked ridiculous—a gorilla in a hamster cage.

I didn't realize I'd stopped walking, didn't realize I'd started crying, until I felt the swipe of a thumb over my cheek.

I drew in a sharp breath when Liam did it again.

Oh, no, no, no.

His face took on such an intent look that I jerked backward. His fingers slid off my cheek and fell slowly, curling into a fist at his side.

My heart whizzed around my chest like a stray bullet. I prayed he couldn't hear my pulse, prayed he couldn't see how it made the thin cotton of my shirt quiver.

He shifted his gaze to a plump tree dripping with lilac blooms. "I'm sorry about laying all this on you. I just thought you'd appreciate knowing."

"I do appreciate it, but it doesn't make me sorry your father is dead."

Liam didn't respond for a such a long time that I hesitated to apologize, but I just couldn't. I couldn't apologize for saying words I meant. His father was evil.

"Do you want to go home?" he finally asked.

Did he mean to the inn or to Los Angeles?

Probably to the inn... "Yeah, but I'll call a cab."

He shifted his gaze to me. His eyes were so dark, as though his pupils had stretched from lid to lid and corner to corner. "I'll drop you off. It's on my way."

Was it really? "Okay."

In silence, we made our way to his car that was parked across the street from the pool bar. I could see the pack through the glass façade, wielding cue sticks, laughing, and drinking. I prayed they couldn't see me. I didn't want new rumors to spread.

Liam pulled my door open, and instead of making a fuss, I got in. The tension inside the car was so thick it was stifling. I cracked my window open, but the brisk air did little to deflate the ripe atmosphere.

I rested my cheek against the headrest and watched the darkness unspool outside the car, the same way it was unspooling inside my mind: Liam wasn't attracted to me; he pitied me. He thought I was pathetic and sad and way too proud for my own good. Besides, *I* wasn't attracted to him. Sure, he was handsome, but plenty of guys were handsome. Just because my body reacted to his didn't mean I should encourage the feelings swarming through me.

"The elders want to meet on Wednesday." His voice jolted me out of my deliberations.

I turned to look at him, his profile lacquered by the glow of his dashboard.

"To discuss the next trial."

"I shouldn't be part of the next trial."

His jaw flexed as he slid to a stop in front of the inn. "But you are."

"But I shouldn't be."

"Look, if you don't want to take part in the contest anymore, go to the meeting and have it out with *them*."

I flinched from the harshness of his voice. "Fine. At what time will it be and where?"

"It'll be at my father's house at 6:00 p.m."

A shudder shot down my spine. "Why at your father's house?"

He cocked an eyebrow. "Do you have a problem with going there?"

I clicked my seatbelt and pumped my door handle. "No."

"Aren't you going to ask me for the address?"

"I remember where it is."

"Of course you do."

My pulse became a chaotic mess of heartbeats.

I didn't ask what that was supposed to mean, because I dreaded his answer. Had the agency told him I'd been the girl they'd sent to see Heath, or had Liam figured this out on his own? Or did his father have security cameras? I hadn't seen any, but that didn't mean the sleazeball hadn't installed some.

What did it matter? It wasn't as though *I'd* killed him with my three little anti-shifting pills. They were innocuous. I knew that firsthand, because I'd had to swallow one every day for the first three months after we left Boulder. Even though distance from the pack eventually blocked the change, Mom had used pills to drain the were-wolf magic from my veins. The pills had belonged to my father, who'd taken them to avoid shifting while his bones mended after he'd broken both his legs.

I hopped out of the car and muttered, "I'll see you after tomorrow." And then I slapped the door closed, feeling the vibrations all the way inside my joints.

23

The following day, Lucy stopped by my bedroom at sunrise to ask how I was doing. I wondered if she honestly cared. I shrugged and told her I was better.

"I heard they've kept you in the running," she said, pulpy arms folded in front of her Double-Ds.

"I heard that too."

I waited for her to tell me to quit the contest. She didn't. And I didn't share my intention to drop out.

Her hazel eyes combed over the bare legs peeking from my sleep shorts. "Can you work?"

"Yes." I stretched my arms. They no longer felt attached to dumbbells, but a faint soreness remained.

So she assigned me guest bedrooms, and I donned my gray uniform and tackled her task, scouring rugs with a vacuum, stretching sheets to their breaking point, dusting the mason jars filled with homemade potpourri. The physical exertion kept my mind off what Liam had insinuated.

But only for a while.

By the afternoon, after eating with Evelyn in the kitchen, I paced my bedroom like a tiger locked in a cage. At some point, I picked up the framed picture on my nightstand—a shot of me with my parents. I studied my father's face and compared it to my own. Besides our matching dimples and perhaps the shape of our mouths, I'd inherited all of my features from my mother.

I growled as I realized what I was doing. How dare the Kolanes insert doubt into my brain.

I was my father's daughter.

I was a werewolf, like him!

I set the frame down so hard the glass rattled. Thankfully, it didn't break.

A knock snapped my attention off the picture. I went to the door and then thrust it open. Crossing my arms in front of my chest, I scowled at Everest, then gave him a piece of my mind. I gave him *all* the pieces of my mind.

He dropped a shopping bag on my bed.

"What's that?" I grumbled.

"A dress. I hope it's the right size."

"What the hell? You bought me a dress?" I threw my hands in the air. "You think I'm going to forgive you because you got me a present?"

"I didn't buy it to cajole you. I bought it because you're going to need it tonight."

"Why am I going to need a dress tonight?" I realized I was yelling when Everest pressed a hard finger against my lips.

"Keep your voice down."

"Don't you dare tell me to keep my voice down. You don't get to tell me what to do! You ditched me." My voice caught on a sob.

Everest sighed and tucked me against him. "I'm sorry. My parents." He shook his head. "And then—then I found out something, and I was working on a solution before I came to you. Now calm the hell down, so I can explain."

I pushed him away.

"Liam hired a PI," he explained.

My throat became a dry husk.

"The man's been sniffing around to find out what happened to Heath. Guess where it led him? Straight to the escort agency." His whispers sounded like shouts. "Sandra didn't give him your name. She contacted me, though, when she couldn't reach you. Anyway, she promised not to give you away in exchange for some hush money."

"You paid her off?"

"Yes. I paid her off."

"How much?"

"Don't concern yourself with how much. I covered it." He palmed his mussy red hair.

"I think Liam already knows. Last night, he implied—"

"He doesn't know. He's trying to guess, but he doesn't know."

I dropped heavily into the armchair, rested my head back, and sighed. "I realize my being there the night Heath died doesn't look good, but I didn't kill him, Everest. I should just come clean."

When Everest didn't say anything, I propped my head back up. His lips were so thin and his cheeks so pale my heart stilled for a couple beats.

"What?"

He sat on the foot of my bed.

"You're scaring me... What?"

"Ness, I heard Lucas and Matt talk about Heath's tox screen. How the coroner found drugs in his system."

My spine went rigid. "So?"

"He drowned because those pills... They fucked up his nervous system."

"Are you—are you—" Tremors crawled over my arms and legs, rattled inside my chest, rippled over my skin. I lifted a trembling hand to my gaping mouth. "No," I whispered.

Everest hung his head then craned his neck and shot me the grimmest, most doleful stare in the history of stares. "Yes."

The room distorted. "You mean to say... You mean to tell me..."

"That you killed him? Yes."

My breathing halted as fear clambered down my throat and squashed my lungs. *I killed Heath.*

For all my talk of murdering him, I would *never* have gone through with it.

I wasn't some blood-thirsty executioner.

Everest leaned forward and caught one of my hands. "I have a plan."

I tried to swallow, but jagged lumps clogged my airway like clumps of hair in a shower drain. "I need to...to run away."

"No."

I killed Liam's father. The pack Alpha. The pack was going to come after me and shred me to ribbons.

"I have a plan. A plan that will keep you safe. I promise. It's foolproof."

Nothing was foolproof.

Silver bars materialized in front of my eyes. The Boulders were going to toss me in that hole of theirs. I removed my hand from Everest's and massaged my temples. If the pack didn't kill me, the authorities would lock me up for involuntary manslaughter. It wouldn't matter that it hadn't been intentional.

Shit.

"Ness. I got a big player to help you," he said.

I didn't think the President of the United States could get me out of this mess.

"Julian Matz," Everest said, as though the name should've meant something to me. It didn't.

"Who the hell is Julian Matz?"

Everest flinched from my shrill tone. "The Pine Pack Alpha."

My skin broke out in goose bumps. His plan was to involve the Alpha of the greatest enemy pack? Ice spilled into my stomach as an even more chilling thought settled. "Did you...tell him?"

"I had to."

He had to. I was straddling the brink between fury and anger, and it was giving me a strong urge to gouge my cousin's eyes out. "You told him! How dare you!"

Everest blinked. "Ness, I did it for you."

Fuck. My life was fucked. Maybe I should attempt to fly off a roof like Becca. Or maybe I should turn into a wolf and travel to a distant mountain range and lose myself in the wilderness.

"Look, you're going to meet with Julian tonight, and he'll explain how he's going to go about clearing you." He gestured toward the shopping bag. "Wear the dress and meet me in the driveway at five. I'll take you to him." He checked his watch. "You have two hours to get ready."

He got up and started walking toward the door.

"Why do I have to wear a dress?"

"It's his nephew's engagement party."

Stab me through the heart. Not only did I have to meet with an enemy Alpha, but I had to attend an engagement ceremony where surely the entire Pine Pack would be assembled.

I'd almost rather have died.

Almost.

24

The dress Everest had gotten me fit like a glove…an actual glove. The stretchy black leather hugged each one of my curves, leaving absolutely nothing to the imagination. Nor did it leave any room to strap a knife to my thigh, which I'd considered.

But then I'd reconsidered it.

Bringing a weapon to a werewolf engagement party was surely in poor taste. What would I do with a knife anyway? If the blade wasn't welded from silver, it would do me little good. Everest's revelation made me bang a clenched fist against my mirror. A fissure streaked the glass. I stared at the crack as though it were an omen. What did breaking mirrors mean? *Right…seven years of bad luck.*

I was doomed.

I took one of the pins I'd sandwiched between my lips and stuck it into the bun that was supposed to look sleek but ended up resembling a ball of yarn a cat would've chased down a staircase.

When my updo was done, I grabbed my bag, cell phone, key, and then slid on my black heels. On my way out of the inn, I crossed paths with Jeb. I prayed he had no inkling of what I'd done.

He crossed his arms as I passed by the bell desk. "Where are you going?"

"I'm having dinner with Everest."

His forehead grooved. "Where's he taking you?"

"He said it was a surprise for having forgotten to take me to the first trial."

Jeb's pupils twitched with guilt.

"'Night, Jeb."

He peeked over my shoulder at the parking lot, probably to check whether I was telling the truth about going to dinner with his son.

I climbed into Everest's car with little grace, the dress constricting my movements. "I didn't know they made straitjackets out of black leather."

Everest cracked a grin, one of his incredibly toothy grins, and for a second, it made me forget that this was possibly one of the crappiest days of my existence. And I'd had my fair share of crappy days.

I hooked on my seatbelt. "So, who was that girl you were swapping spit with at Tracy's?"

"Just a girl."

"Same one from the music festival, right?"

"Right."

"And you met her…randomly?"

The tips of his ears flushed. "She's not an escort."

I hadn't meant to imply he'd met her through Sandra. "What's her name?"

He flicked his gaze to me. "Why do you want to know?"

I was a little taken aback by that. "Because I'm your cousin, and your life interests me. But if you don't want to tell me—"

"It's Megan. She's a freshman at UCB."

Glancing outside, at the narrow sunlit road hedged with pines, I rubbed my thumb over my bag's strap. "What about Becca?"

"What about her?"

"What happens if she wakes up?"

"It's been a month, Ness."

"So you're giving up?"

"I'm not giving up, but neither am I going to wait by her bedside for the rest of my life."

I was no relationship expert, but moving on from someone he'd loved after just a month felt incredibly brusque.

"I didn't mean to make you feel guilty," I ended up saying.

"I don't feel guilty." His answer was dry, brittle almost.

For a long moment, we both watched the ribbon of road we were traveling in silence.

When we crossed over into the Pine Pack territory—a border delineated by sour piss and a pristine, ten-foot metal fence guarded by two wolves in skin, I asked, "How come you went to the Pine Pack for help?"

Everest eased his window open and gave the guard our names. The man waved us through, and we set off down a cedar-shaded alley lined with floating white balloons.

"Because they hated Heath."

I mulled this over. "What's in it for them?"

"Julian will tell you."

"Why don't *you* tell me?"

"Because he'll explain it better."

"Do they want something—"

Everest slapped his steering wheel. "God, Ness, have a little patience, okay?"

I bristled from his snappishness. He was delivering me to a den of wolves—literally. The least he could do was hint at what was expected of me.

"Are you coming in with me?"

"No. It wouldn't look good if I were there."

"But my presence won't set off warning bells?"

"You are not a Boulder wolf. You have every right to be here. And if anyone gives you grief, tell them Julian paid you for your company. He'll corroborate the story."

I wanted to scream that I wasn't an escort but reined in my irritation.

He came to a stop in the looping driveway of the Pines' headquarters—an all glass and wood structure that resembled a luxurious country club. A cut above the simple gray stone building the Boulder Pack convened in. Then again, the Boulder Pack made good use of the inn, which was perhaps the reason they'd never invested heavily in expanding their headquarters.

A white-gloved waiter opened my door.

"Are you picking me up?" I asked.

"Julian will have someone drive you home."

"Can't you pick me up?" I sounded like a whiny child, but I didn't like being in unknown territory.

He sighed. "Fine. Call me when you're ready to go."

"Thank you." I shot him a weak smile. "Thank you for everything, Everest." My throat was closing up again.

He didn't look at me as he answered, "What's family for?"

Clutching my bag against me, I turned and ascended the wide, peony petal-dusted stone steps like a prisoner walking toward their execution.

25

I'd researched Julian on the internet to find out what he looked like and what he enjoyed doing. He wasn't a particularly private person, so I'd unearthed plenty of shots of him surrounded by his "family." I even got to see my favorite Pine Pack member, Justin Summix, in a couple shots. I'd had the urge to print one out of Justin so I could stick pins into his face and crotch. Misogyny brought out the worst in me.

As luck would have it, Justin was the first person I laid eyes on. Perhaps I noticed him first because he was the only person I knew. Others were vaguely familiar, but grief and distance had blurred my memories of them. Justin elbowed the boy he was standing next to and pointed me out. *Subtle.*

A girl, not much older than me, with a mass of long kinky blonde curls and lips colored a bright pink, placed a hand on my forearm.

Her nostrils flared. "Excuse me, sweetie, but I believe you have the wrong pack gathering. I smell Boulder wolves all over you." She pressed on my arm to turn me around. "We don't take their leftovers here," she explained sweetly.

I pasted on a pert smile and brushed her hand off my bare arm. "Good thing I'm not a Boulder leftover then. I'm looking for..." His name withered in my throat when I spotted him at the center of the room. Like a pebble tossed into a pond, everyone rippled around Julian.

As though he sensed me looking at him, Julian turned his clear-blue eyes up toward me. A frown gusted over his face, followed almost immediately by a slow, slow smile.

I walked down the steps, my heels clicking on the stone. Nostrils flared, and more than one set of eyebrows hitched as I approached my *date.*

"Mr. Matz," I said.

"My, you are striking, Miss Clark." He picked up one of my hands and held it to his lips as though he were about to kiss it. His lips never met their mark, but his gesture did. The weres I'd felt closing in around me began to back up. He twirled me around so that I had my back pressed against his bordeaux-colored dinner jacket. A tiny gasp escaped my lips, and he loosened the arm he'd wound around my waist.

"Everyone, Ness Clark is our special guest tonight. I expect you all to be on your absolute best behavior."

My gaze crossed paths with many sets of wide, startled gazes. Everyone seemed to wait for an explanation as to why I was their special guest, but instead of adding anything, Julian released me and then offered me his arm. I supposed not taking it would be in bad form, so I looped my arm through his.

"Let me introduce you to the couple of the hour."

He led me through a set of open doors that gave way onto a sprawling, manicured lawn planted with perpendicular hedges. Their corners were so straight I imagined the gardener using a ruler to chop them.

Julian raised one of his hands, where a pinkie ring glittered with a diamond the size of his nail. "Robbie, Margaux!" he called out to the couple who were having their picture taken by a team of professionals.

The photography equipment looked as expensive as the bride-to-be did with her white lace dress and the river of diamonds wrapped around her swan-like neck.

Julian's nephew turned toward me first. He raised his nose the slightest bit and sniffed the air. His eyebrows slanted just like those of his fellow shifters. Obviously Julian had not announced my visit to anyone other than the guards at the gate.

"This is Ness Clark." Julian's pouty mouth curved, which accentuated his nephew's frown.

"Callum Clark's girl?" Robbie asked.

Julian nodded. "The very one." He released me and leaned in toward his future niece-in-law—or whatever she was to him. "Margaux, darling, you look ravishing tonight."

"As do you, Uncle."

"Always a kind word for your graying uncle."

"You are not graying." She let out a tinkling titter, as though her lips were made of crystal.

I sniffed the air, wondering what she was truly made of—skin or fur. She smelled like Robbie, as though she'd bathed in his scent.

When the camera crew asked if they could get a picture of her with Julian, he obliged.

Robbie crossed his arms as he watched his uncle dip his future wife over his arm. She laughed, her eyes glittering for the camera as wildly as her diamonds. I looked up at Robbie and wondered if he worried about the way Julian touched Margaux. After all, Julian was the Alpha, and Alphas liked to take things that weren't theirs for the taking...at least that had been true in our pack.

"You've grown up lots since the last time I saw you." Robbie glanced down at me. "How long has it been?"

"Six years."

"Six years…" he mused, his gaze back on his future wife who was now giggling because Julian had scooped her up. "I always wondered something."

"What?" I asked him.

"Why didn't your pack punish the hunter who killed your father?"

"Excuse me?"

"The last hunter who injured one of ours was mauled instantly. I thought the Boulders abided by the same rules as we did."

My body, which I'd angled toward Julian and Margaux, pivoted fully toward Robbie. "They do. The hunter was killed right after I left Boulder."

He frowned deeply. "The man's very much alive, Ness."

My heart, which had behaved until now, hurdled against my ribcage.

"You were with your father that night, weren't you?"

"I was, but it was dark, and it was one of my first runs, and my sense of smell was still developing, and—"

"So you don't remember the hunter?"

"I never even saw him. At least, I don't remember seeing him." I remembered hearing the gunshot, the hot spray of blood, the metallic smell of it, but that was all that remained of the devastating night. "But the pack sniffed him out. And they"— my voice caught—"they *killed* him."

The pity crinkling Robbie's expression made my skin crawl. "For a dead man, he looks and sounds awfully real."

Bang. Bang. Bang went my heart. Like the rifle that had stolen my father from me. Robbie was lying, trying to get a rise from me.

"How do you even know who it is?" I asked.

"You don't think we carry out our own investigations? The death of a shifter affects us all."

His words rubbed my nerves raw. "Why should I believe the man is still out there? For all I know, you're trying to rile me up so I go and kill an innocent man. A man whose death would be convenient to the Pines?"

"Passionate little thing, aren't you?"

"Answer my question. Why should I believe you?"

"Truth is, you shouldn't. But if I were you, Ness, I'd go ask your pack for the truth."

"I don't have a pack."

He tilted his head to the side. "So the rumors I heard that you were competing for Alpha are deceitful?"

"I'm not competing anymore. I have no interest in being a Boulder."

He folded his strong arms in front of his broad chest. "So a lone wolf it is?"

"No. I'm leaving Boulder."

"Not shifting will shorten your lifespan. It's unnatural for your body not to go through the change. It would be like a woman not menstruating."

His comparison had me wrinkling my nose.

Margaux burst back next to us as Julian posed for a couple shots by himself. She latched onto her fiancé's arm but then let go to fuss with the white ribbon wrapped around his short blond ponytail.

"We should return to our guests, Robbie."

He kissed her, and then to me he said, "Enjoy the party."

Hand in hand, they went back to the crowd that had spilled out the French doors onto the paved terrace where all the faces and finery blurred into a vibrant, glittery cloud.

A hand wrapped around my elbow. "They'd like to take a picture of us. Would you pose for one with me?"

I turned to Julian. "No."

He studied my expression, then flicked a hand toward the photographer's assistant who had trailed after him. The woman scurried away.

"Mr. Matz, who killed my father?"

Julian gave his head a little shake. "Robbie. Robbie. Robbie. Always sticking his nose in matters that don't concern him."

"Tell me his name. Please." I had a violent need for the truth.

He dipped his chin. "If I am not mistaken, you had dinner with him a few days ago."

"*I* had dinner with my father's killer?" My voice was loud, too loud. It echoed inside my ears.

Julian's lips settled into a grim line. "Aidan Michaels."

Every sound, color, flavor, and scent faded as the name sank into my mind.

I'd sat at a table with my father's assassin. I'd made conversation with him. I'd taken his money.

I raised a hand to my neck and gagged on the bitter taste careening up my throat. I clamped my teeth shut, and sweat broke out over my upper lip. An arm wound around my waist, steadying me. The world eddied, before coming back into sharp focus.

"I'm sorry to be the bearer of such dire news, Miss Clark."

Stupidity left a vile taste in my mouth. Here I'd thought my pack disliked me, but if they hadn't avenged my father, then their dislike ran deeper than I'd assumed. Loathing throbbed beneath my skin. Claws curled from my nailbeds.

"Breathe. Your eyes have shifted," Julian instructed.

I breathed, and the simple act of inhaling and exhaling managed to drive my claws back. What it didn't manage to do was ease my fury.

"Heath had too many business dealings with Aidan Michaels to afford killing him." Julian leaned toward me, his whisky-scented breath brushing my ear. "You did the world a great favor by killing him."

My heart felt like a shard of ice. "Everest said you could help me." For the first time since my cousin had informed me I was a murderer, I didn't care.

An amused, almost satisfied expression creased his eyes. Unlike what humans believed, werewolves aged at the same rate as humans, yet Julian looked ancient, like he'd been alive far longer than his forty-seven years.

"I am well acquainted with the PI Liam hired. One word from me, and he will direct the focus of the investigation off of you."

"What will that word cost me?"

"You don't beat around the bush, do you?"

I squared my shoulders, and the leather dress tightened around me like a second-skin. "What will it cost me?"

"You go on with that little game your elders have organized."

I jerked my head back. "I don't want to be part of my pack."

"You wouldn't just be a part of it. You'd rule it."

"I have no desire to rule a bunch of pricks."

"Why did you enter your name in the first place, then?"

"Because I didn't want another Kolane to have that sort of power."

"And you've changed your mind?"

"No."

A slippery smile eased over Julian's lips. "You go on with those silly trials then, and I will not only make sure that your name is cleared, but also that you win."

"How and why?"

"Don't bother yourself with the how. As for the why…" Julian closed his hand over my elbow and steered me up the lawn. "I want there to be peace between our packs, and I believe you are the instrument of that peace. There is something incredibly special about you, and not simply because you are the first female born to your pack in a century. Although, perhaps your sex does color my conviction." He pulled me to a stop on the first step of the grand stone staircase leading up to the terrace. "Do we have a deal, Miss Clark?"

His flattery and backing were honing my ego into a dangerous weapon. "The Boulders detest you. They believe you are the source of all evil."

"I don't doubt this." His eyes flared like silver bullets. "But would an evil man desire peace?"

I tried to glimpse the wolf lurking beneath the human casing of tanned flesh, pouty mouth, and powder-blue eyes that were Julian Matz. I sensed his wolf was an impressive specimen.

"I could sweeten the pot by having my weres deal with Aidan. Would you like that?"

"I like to clean up my own messes, but thank you for the offer."

"So, will you go on with the trials?"

Did I have a choice? Besides hitchhiking away from Boulder, I had no way out. "Yes."

Julian's teeth flashed. He lifted my hand to his mouth and laid a kiss there to seal our deal. "How proud you would've made your father."

Glass shattered against stone, and then screeching voices exploded above us. I wheeled around and found an almost unrecognizable man glowering down at me and Julian. Blood poured from Liam's temple and gushed from his nose.

"Get away from him, Ness!" Liam's voice struck me like a bolt of lightning, but instead of making me tremble, it electrified me.

With an almost clinical detachment, I cocked my head to the side and watched as he struggled against the three shifters restraining him. I wondered if they were the same weres who'd rearranged his features into a bloody, pulpy mask. Liam bared his teeth, then whacked the back of his head against one of them. His captor gasped and teetered back. Blood dripped from his nostrils, mixing with Liam's on the slabs of limestone.

"Release him." Julian's voice cut through the pregnant air.

Liam was freed so suddenly he stumbled forward, but he regained his footing instantly.

"To what do we owe the pleasure of your visit, Liam?" Julian asked.

Liam's eyes roamed over my face. "I've come to collect my wolf."

His wolf? I was *no one's* wolf.

Julian echoed my musings out loud. "*Your* wolf?" His voice cocked in time with his eyebrow.

Color prickled Liam's jaw. "Ness is a Boulder wolf."

"As far as I understand, your pack hasn't let her pledge herself."

"Ness, come on. I'll take you home." Desperation rolled off him and banged into my toughened shell.

Now he cared? I hugged my arms around my torso. In my mind, I whispered, *Go away. You're making a fool of yourself.*

Julian wound a possessive hand around my bicep. "Ness is my date for the evening."

Liam's gaze rocketed toward the Pine Alpha, then slammed back into me.

He waited.

And waited.

For me to deny this. Or perhaps he waited for me to scrub Julian's hand off.

I did neither.

I could see the exact moment it registered with him that he'd wasted his time playing the savior. His entire face hardened, and he backed away. And then he shook his head, lips curling in disgust.

I kept my face blank of emotion as he stepped back and back until he disappeared.

I'd made an ally tonight, but I'd also made an enemy.

26

I stayed at the engagement party another hour. I'd made it a point not to leave with him, just as I was making it a point not to stay too long. I wasn't looking for a replacement pack.

Not that this was a possibility. I dug my phone out of my bag to ask Everest for a lift, but Julian pre-empted my demand by clicking his fingers. "Sarah!"

The wild-haired werewolf who'd told me Boulder whores weren't allowed on Pine territory got tasked with bringing me home. From the annoyance tightening her brown eyes, I could tell she was as glad about this arrangement as I was.

Midway home, she asked, "Did you blow him?"

I pitched my gaze off the dark road and onto her. All her features were fine, especially in contrast to her mass of tousled curls, but I could tell her delicateness was skin-deep, and that her personality matched her wild hair.

I guessed she meant Julian, but I needled her anyway. "You'll have to be more specific."

She wrinkled her pert nose. "God, really? Eww." She narrowed her gaze on the starlit forest. "I meant Julian."

"No."

"But you did do something to him, or he would never have helped you."

"Do you know where Liam Kolane lives?"

She raised one of her already peaked eyebrows. "Is this a trick question?"

"No. I left Boulder when I was eleven. Liam still lived with his father then."

A dimple appeared in her cheek. She must've been biting it. "I do know where he lives."

"Can you drop me off there?"

"Why?"

"I don't owe you an explanation, Sarah."

"If you're two-timing my Alpha, you do."

"Two-timing your Alpha would mean I was one-timing him. Which I'm not. I just need a word with Liam."

"I'm not waiting on your ass, though. I'm not your chauffeur or anything," she grumbled.

"Because you think I'd want you to wait on me?"

"Are you screwing Liam?"

"Do I look like I'm screwing him?"

"Babe, you look like you're open to screwing a lot of things."

"What is that supposed to mean?"

"Who wears a dominatrix dress to an engagement party?"

My eyes snapped a little too wide. I realized I hadn't fit in with the tulle and silks in my skintight leather but hadn't realized what impression it gave others. Then again, I hadn't been too concerned with fashion when I'd donned it.

"I didn't buy it."

"One of your lovers got it for you?"

I tugged on the hem that was riding up. "My cousin bought it for me."

"Yuck. If my cousin ever bought me shit like that, I'd tell her to wear it herself."

I snorted as an image of Everest wearing my dress snuck into my mind. "It's a him, not a her."

"An even better reason to get him to wear it." She smiled, and it thawed some of the stiffness padding her small red Mini.

"You're a wolf, right?" I wasn't sure why I was asking. She smelled like one. Perhaps it was to get confirmation. Confirmation that I wasn't the only female werewolf in the world.

"Damn right."

"How many of you are in your pack? Females, that is?"

"Twenty-eight for seventy males."

The Pine Pack was more than twice the size of my pack.

My pack.

The thought caught me by surprise. I shook my head, but like a fly, the thought stuck to the web of my mind. Boulder blood ran through my veins, but that was it. The Boulders weren't *my* anything. Even if I became their Alpha, I'd never truly belong.

I stuck my elbow on the armrest and cradled my head as what I'd agreed upon—becoming Alpha of a pack I loathed—dug its talons inside of me. My deal with Julian wasn't fair to the Boulders, but fairness wasn't a value upheld by my pack anyway.

I massaged my temple. What was I supposed to do? If only there was someone I could ask. I thought about speaking to Everest, but he'd all but forced me to meet with Julian, so his counsel would be far from objective. I thought of Evelyn next. Perhaps, in not too many words, I could paint a clear enough picture of what was going on so she could advise me.

"We're here. That'll be a hundred bucks." Sarah turned toward me in the car, her eyes glowing in the semi-obscurity.

I raised my head off my fingers. "You're kidding, right?"

"Depends. Do you have money to burn? I could really use new headphones."

"You'd spend a hundred dollars on headphones?"

"I like good sound." She lowered her hand.

"But a hundred bucks?"

"Ever heard of DJ Wolverine?"

"No."

"Have you *not* been to The Den?"

"What's The Den?"

She rolled her eyes. "Only the coolest club in the whole of Boulder. I deejay there on Thursdays and Saturdays. DJ Wolverine." She pointed to herself. "I can't believe you haven't been."

"If it's Pine territory—"

"It's neutral territory. The Boulders go there with their little bite-sluts."

"Bite-sluts?"

"Girls who want to get bitten." When I frowned, she went on, "Some people still believe that if you get bitten enough times by a shifter, you'll turn into one."

I blinked. I didn't remember seeing any bite marks on the Boulders' girlfriends.

"God, you really are a total newbie at this. Robbie wasn't kidding."

"Robbie wasn't kidding about what?"

"That you need an education."

"He told you that?"

She smiled, her teeth glowing so white in the light of the car they resembled pearls. "I'm his baby sister. Robbie tells me everything."

"You're his sister?"

She slapped a palm over her chest very dramatically. "I'm offended."

"That I didn't know you were his sister? Unlike you, I didn't study your family tree."

"What'd they teach you in werewolf school?"

"I didn't go to...werewolf school." Was there even such a thing?

She smirked. "Did you fall for that?" Her smirk became a smile. "You did, didn't you?"

"You're weird."

"Says the only female in her pack."

"That makes me unique. Not weird."

She went back to smirking.

A light came on in a sleek, wood-paneled cabin at the end of a short dirt drive. I caught movement in the floor-to-ceiling windows that boxed in one end of the house. Liam's place wasn't oversized like his father's but looked pricey nonetheless.

The click of the car doors unlocking made me jump.

Sarah squinted at the shifting, shadowy shape. "You seriously not tapping that?"

"I'm seriously not tapping that," I said, pumping my door handle. "Thanks for the ride."

"Yeah. Whatevs." She flicked her hand. Gold rings set with cut stones glinted on two of her fingers. "Ciao."

I got out and started walking.

"If you ever get bored"—Sarah's voice made me spin around—"or have questions about being a she-wolf, you can find me at The Den. Thursdays and Saturdays."

I gave a short nod. That was...*kind*. Sadly, kindness made me suspicious. This was the reason behind my detour. I wanted confirmation that Aidan Michaels *had* shot my father and an explanation as to why there hadn't been any retaliation. I twisted back toward the rectangle of glass and wood, moonlit dust blooming around my heels as I approached Liam's house.

27

I was about to knock when the door opened. Liam had probably smelled me, like I'd whiffed his distinctive musky scent halfway down the drive.

He stood there, a towel riding low on his waist, his dark hair dripping water from a recent shower. Even though he basked in shadows, I noticed that his nose and a large part of his jaw were bruised. The blood was gone, though.

I looked away from his face, focusing on the sharp-lined furniture arranged at ninety-degree angles on a cowhide rug. Liam shifted, his body filling the doorway, surely to block out the sight of his home from my prying eyes.

He crossed his arms. Sinews moved beneath his smooth, golden skin like mooring lines. "What do you want?"

I inched my gaze back up to his face. "Did Aidan Michaels kill my father?"

His expression emptied of its hostility. Clearly, he had not been expecting *that* question.

"So? Did he?"

Frowning, he said, "I thought you knew."

"I wouldn't be asking if I knew."

Liam's eyes raked the darkness behind me, which had me twirling around. Was Sarah still there? Before I could turn back to face him, he yanked me inside then released me and shut his door.

"What were you doing at Robbie's engagement party, Ness?"

My gaze dipped to his glistening, muscled torso before sliding to something safer, something inanimate—a lamp speared into a block of black marble that bowed over the couch's armrest.

"I repeat, what were you doing at a Pine gathering, Ness?"

I looked back up into his stern face. "How did you even find out I was there?"

"Frank sensed you were in their territory. And then I caught a picture of you on one of their Instagram feeds. The Pines are social media whores." His voice was as sharp and stark as his house.

For some reason, that last part made me snort. "You have Instagram?"

"What. The fuck. Were you. Doing there?"

"The agency sent me." The lie slid out as smooth as the leather that ensconced me.

"The fuck they did. Julian would never use a Boulder wolf as an escort. Besides, I thought you were done with that."

"I'm not a Boulder wolf. Plus it was easy cash. *And* it gave me the opportunity to meet them. They're lovely people. Way more civilized than *your* pack."

"I told you I can pay your debts."

"And I told you I don't want your charity."

His hands moved to the towel at his waist. "It wouldn't be charity if I fucked you, right?"

I blanched. "I-I just... It's just d-dates." My throat went dry. "I don't have sex."

He untucked the towel, his long fingers moving slowly. "I have trouble believing that." The gray cotton slid heavily to the floor and pooled around his feet.

I backed up. "I'm not having sex with you, Liam."

"But you'll spread your legs for Julian?"

That made me snap. "I don't spread my legs for anyone."

"Look at you. Look at what you're wearing." He gestured to my dress, and I burned with rage.

I pressed my palms against the leather at my hips, wishing I could transform it into something else, something that stopped giving the impression I was a whore. "You're a real jerk, you know that?"

"At least"—his voice was barely above a vibration—"I'm an honest one."

Nerves skittered underneath my skin.

He took a step toward me, and I took another step back. My tailbone hit smooth wood.

"First..." His lips shut then parted again.

My heart held perfectly still.

"First Aidan. Now Julian." He moistened his lips. "Do you have a thing for older men?"

"They were jobs." My shoulder blades knocked together as I flattened myself against the wall.

Liam pressed one hand on the panel beside my face. His breaths whispered against my forehead. "Prove it."

I gaped at him. How was he expecting me to prove it? It wasn't like I'd documented my evenings.

An inhuman glow devoured his irises and coated the whites of his eyes. And then his nails lengthened into claws beside my face. They clicked against the wood. He snapped his eyes closed. When he opened them, they no longer shone yellow and his nails had receded.

I became acutely aware of his nakedness, of his proximity. He was careful not to touch me with any part of his body, and yet I felt him...everywhere. Smelled him. Heard the blood pound wildly in his neck.

"Damn it, Ness," he growled. "Prove it!"

His tone broke me out of my daze. "I don't need to prove anything to you, Liam Kolane."

"You embarrassed me today."

"I never asked you to retrieve me."

"What's your game?"

A knot of fear pulsed behind my navel. "Get away from me."

I pressed my hands into his torso, but it was like trying to move a tree. An infernally hot tree. His body wasn't on fire but felt like it was, especially in contrast to my clammy palms.

He spun me around and pushed me against the wall until my cheek was flush with the glossed surface, then locked my wrists behind my back with one of his hands.

"Let me go!" I screeched.

"Not until you tell me the truth. Did you or didn't you fuck Julian Matz?"

"Go to hell." A tear snuck down my cheek. And then another. And another.

"You leave me no choice." His knees clicked as he crouched.

Horror shot through me, and I struggled against him. Was he going to rape me? Oh, God, Everest had been right. Liam *was* like his father.

Silence. And then a long inhale. He'd sniffed me!

White-hot rage undid me, and I spun, ripping my wrists out of his grip. He rose, and I slapped him. Not once but twice, and I would've slapped him again if he hadn't caught my flailing hands.

"You are a pig! No worse than a pig!" I shouted. "How. Dare. You!"

His expression went slack. I ripped my hands from his and punched him in the gut. I would've punched him lower, but I didn't want to violate him like he'd violated me.

A groove formed between his slanted eyebrows. "You didn't sleep with him."

I shook, trembled, quaked. "I hate you. Hate you!" I fumbled to find the door knob. "If you ever...*ever*...come close to me, Liam, I will injure you so badly even your wolf gene will be powerless to fix you."

Liam stood perplexed. I doubted it was my threat that was scaring him. I doubted he took me seriously. If he did, he wouldn't have defiled me.

"Ness..." His voice sounded scratchy.

"Don't talk to me." I wrenched the door open and fled into the night, tripping on my heels. I kicked them off.

Anger and humiliation throbbed against my spine, against my heart, against my skull.

"Ness!" I heard him call out to me.

I didn't stop, didn't turn around. I had no idea where I was, but I ran anyway. Any place was better than here. And as I ran, my muscles thrummed, my bones hummed, and my skin prickled. The claws came out first, and then the fur. My body changed so fast it tore my dress, and I fell hard against asphalt.

Headlights blinked into existence up ahead, and I seized up.

The car rolled closer, the light glinting like honey off the ends of my white fur, the beams burning into my retina. I blinked just as an enormous black shape rammed into me.

For a second, I flew and then I landed so hard on my rump I whimpered. The world spun like the car's tires, and everywhere I looked was drenched in the blackest darkness and the shiniest starlight.

28

Fear shot up my spine at the same time as tiny aches exploded around it. And my lungs... They could barely expand underneath the weight of the body crushing mine. I squirmed and the black wolf rose off me and dragged himself a couple feet away.

I waited with bated breath in the shadows of the ditch, half expecting car doors to click open and footsteps to pound the road. But the car didn't even slow, zipping past where I lay hidden, spraying gravel over my dirt-flecked white fur. Slowly, I stirred, pressing up onto my limbs that were once again shaking, and blinked the darkness away. When my sight cleared and sharpened, I made out the gleam of Liam's eyes.

He let out a low-pitched whine. I backed away, but my bruised rump hit the slope of the ditch.

Liam didn't advance on me. He also didn't back away.

In that instant, I realized I owed him my life, but saving me didn't erase what he'd done. I bared my teeth and growled.

He still didn't move.

I barked, *Get away from me.* He didn't, so I shot out around him and into the forest, my sense of smell going haywire as it picked up a myriad of aromas. Dank moss tangled with Liam's musk, and the cold sweetness of wood smoke blended with the crisp scent of insect bodies.

I stepped over rocks and splashed through a creek. At some point, I caught a whiff of white jasmine and something else. Something chemical—Windex. I was approaching a house.

You're going the wrong way.

I froze. I wanted to ask which way was the right way, but I'd chew off my paw before I would admit I was lost.

The Flatirons are to your left. Liam's low drone carried over to me like the buzzing fireflies flitting around my ears.

I'd been relying on my sense of smell but had forgotten to look. I tipped my head up and located the Flatirons. And then I raced over earth and downed logs, muscles smacking against my hide like elastics. When the inn materialized, I slowed my pace. Bodies moved on the spacious terrace, glasses clinked, and fire snapped in a wide copper pit set between the Adirondacks.

I scurried along the lip of the forest, hoping the centennial trees would keep my wraith-colored form hidden from the guests having dinner. The scent of chargrilled meat and tangy barbecue sauce wafted toward me. My stomach gave a violent growl.

I loped around the side of the inn toward the parking lot but froze before turning the corner.

I couldn't enter the inn in wolf form.

I would need to shift back, but I'd be naked. And my bag? Where was my bag? It must've fallen outside Liam's house. I squeezed my eyes closed, my tail whacking the wall in frustration.

Jeb would have a second key.

Craning my neck, I looked around for Liam—I'd lost his scent at about the same moment the inn had come into view.

He was gone.

Finally.

Taking in a deep breath, I closed my eyes and let my human form bleed over my animal form. In seconds, I was a girl again. A bare-assed girl covered in dirt, with twigs tangled in her snarled hair. Thankfully, it was long enough to hide my breasts, revealing only their underside. I rose from my crouch, and shielding my privates, I crept toward the revolving door.

A mother with her child walked by, and I slammed my backside against the wall, praying they hadn't spotted me. Once I heard their voices peter out, I peeked inside again. The coast was clear. I pressed my muddy palms into the glass and pushed the door, then sprang toward the bell desk and dove behind it. Feet—small with copper-polished toenails—appeared underneath my face.

I craned my neck and locked eyes with Lucy. A sigh of relief whooshed out of me.

Her irises were framed with so much white that I could tell the feeling wasn't mutual. "Ness," she hissed, but then she flinched at the sound of approaching voices and all but shoved me inside the back room that stank of potpourri from the shelves full of drying petals. "Are you insane?"

"I lost my bag. And my clothes." Which was self-evident.

"What do you think we run here? A kennel?"

Ouch. "I didn't do this on purpose, Lucy."

"Of course you didn't."

"Can I please get a bathrobe? Or a towel? And another key?"

"Another key?" Her cheeks were so red they looked like candied apples. "You lost yours?"

"It was in my bag."

"Which you lost."

"Which I misplaced. But I'll find it." I stood back up, slowly, covering myself with my hands again.

My uncle's voice floated from just outside. Lucy jumped to block the office entrance, her collection of metal bangles jangling wildly on her freckled wrist. "Jeb, can you grab an extra bathrobe from the linen closet?"

"A bathrobe. Why do you need a bathrobe?"

She shifted to hide the sight of me. "Ness needs one."

A beat. Then. "Oh."

Once he left, she walked to a wall with lots of tiny hooks and grabbed a key—I supposed it was a spare. The hooks weren't numbered, but her system didn't seem very secure. I sensed it wasn't the right time to offer advice, but it increased my longing to have my own place, a place I could stroll into naked if I wanted to.

I thought of my apartment back in L.A., then of my childhood home here. I wondered if I would remember how to get there. Wondered if anyone lived in it.

A white bathrobe smacked me in the face. I hurriedly donned it, tightening the belt until it dug into my waist.

"You can come in," Lucy said, I supposed to Jeb.

My uncle stepped into the room. After he took in my disheveled hair and mud-splattered face, he said, "I thought you were going to dinner with Everest."

Right. "I did, but he had a date afterward. He asked me if I would be okay to walk home." I dragged my hair off my face. "I got lost. And then I changed...and well...I managed to find my way back."

Lucy was shaking her face in disbelief. "That's incredibly irresponsible."

I wondered if she was talking about me or about Everest. I didn't ask.

She huffed. "Oh, and she lost her key."

"Keys are replaceable," Jeb said.

"Was it a master key?" Lucy asked suddenly.

"No. I don't leave the inn with the master key." After cleaning the rooms, I always put it in the safe.

My uncle sighed, a deep, rattling sigh. I didn't think it had anything to do with the type of key I'd lost though. He sounded tired.

"I'm going to call Everest. I'm not pleased with him. Not pleased at all. We raised him better than this." He lifted his phone to his ear and watched me as he spoke into the receiver. Everest must've corroborated my story, because when Jeb hung up, he was shaking his head. "He says he's sorry." He exchanged a weighted glance with Lucy.

"Can I go?" I peeped.

He waved toward the door, and I slid by them, stepping quickly over the wine-colored runner, hoping the sconces weren't casting too much of a glow on my face. The second I arrived inside my bedroom, I sidled against the door and crumpled to the floor.

For a long moment, I didn't move, didn't flick on the lights, didn't take a shower. I just sat there on the floor with my knees tucked against me, and I breathed. Just breathed.

The adrenaline vanished from my body the same way it had come—quietly and completely.

29

Lucy had me start work early the next morning.

She stopped by my bedroom to ask that I vacuum the common areas and rearrange the furniture on the terrace. Neither of us mentioned the previous night's happenings. It was easier to pretend that I hadn't erupted into the inn like a wild animal.

I grabbed my earphones from my nightstand drawer when I remembered I didn't have a phone, which meant I had no music to listen to during my chores. I sighed. But that was the least of my worries. I also didn't have my wallet. And a key to my room was somewhere in the wilderness, etched with my room number and the Boulder Inn logo, which was basically an invitation to visit.

After I finished my chores, I would need to retrace my steps to Liam's house. Would I even recognize the way? Hopefully my wolf scent still clung to the forest floor, and I would be able to follow it back.

The motor rumbled as I pumped my arms back and forth, dragging the nozzle over the thick rugs and hardwood floors. My shoulders ached, but I pressed on. At some point, my body would adjust to my four-legged activities, and my muscles would strengthen. Besides, the ache paled to the pain that had ravaged my body after the first trial.

Which reminded me that I had to meet with everyone this evening at Heath's old place.

Which reminded me that I would have to sit in the same room as Liam.

The thought made me vacuum faster and harder. I crouched to get the nozzle underneath the couches, then plucked off the throw pillows decorated with Native American motifs and vacuumed the seats, before fluffing the pillows and arranging them like dominoes. I turned to start on another sofa when I bumped into someone.

My first instinct was to apologize, but my first instinct fizzled out the second I saw who it was.

Liam's nose and jaw were almost healed. It was his dark eyes that looked bruised. I guessed he hadn't slept much, and I hoped it was because of me...of what he'd done. My thighs clenched as I remembered him sniffing me, and the urge to slap him frothed upward.

"Ness?"

I pretended I hadn't heard him. Heart thumping fast—too fast—I moved around the room, hauling the roaring nozzle over every inch of floor, even the areas I'd already scoured. If only I could suck him up inside the hose.

I heard his slow inhale again, and a bolt of indignation sparked inside my core. In my peripheral vision, I saw him step toward me. I put more distance between us. Finally, he got the message, because he walked out of the living room. It took several minutes for my breathing to return to normal.

I shut off the vacuum, and as I dragged it back through the double-storied room, I spotted something on one of the couches. Something that hadn't been there before.

My bag and my shoes.

Making sure the doorway was still empty, I strode over and checked the contents of my bag. I even unzipped my wallet. I didn't carry around much cash, but the little I had was there. I took out my phone, half expecting it would have died during the night, but it had a full battery. Liam had probably charged it to peruse its contents. Sure my phone was password-protected, but the code was my birthday—it wouldn't take a rocket scientist to crack it.

I had two new text messages.

One from Everest: **Need me to pick you up?**

One from August: **Heard you were still in the running. What's going on? Call me.**

I didn't answer either. I stuffed the phone back into my bag, returned the vacuum to the closet, and tidied up the terrace. Once I was done, I stopped by the kitchen for food. During lunch, I asked Evelyn if she would accompany me on a little trek: to my old house.

Although hesitant, she'd agreed. We left the inn in the early afternoon and walked up a long stretch of winding road that ended in a cul-de-sac.

"One winter, I skidded on ice and fell all the way down the hill. Mom almost fainted when she saw me. I had cuts all over my cheeks."

"Was it ghastlier than the way you were returned to me on Saturday?"

I flashed her a sheepish grin. "Probably not."

She looped her arm through mine, her bad leg slowing our pace. The skid of rocks underneath her sneakers worried me—she wasn't even lifting the foot attached to the damaged calf.

"Is this too hard on your leg?"

"No. It is good for my leg." The ends of Mom's silk scarf, which Evelyn had wound around her ponytail, fluttered in the warm breeze. "I do not exercise enough, and it is becoming stiff."

I kicked a pebble that landed noiselessly inside a clump of heat-bleached grass. The road, which used to be smooth, was pockmarked. I hoped that whoever owned my childhood home was maintaining the house better than the path that led to it.

When slate shingles rose in the distance, my heart sped up and so did my pace. But then I remembered Evelyn's leg, and I slowed.

No smoke curled out from the chimney. Then again, it was summer.

As we neared the house, I told Evelyn the story of how I forbade my parents from kindling a fire one Christmas, terrified it would char poor Santa. I'd believed he was real until we'd left for Los Angeles. After all, werewolves were real, so why wouldn't Santa be?

Moss flecked the purple-gray stone walls, making my house resemble a witch's hut...if witch's huts had broken windows.

I frowned at the shattered glass.

"Was all of the land your family's?" Evelyn ran her finger over the heavy purple blooms of the wisteria that wrapped around the beams of our porch and spilled their heady scent into the hot air. After Mom planted the vine, it took years for it to bloom, and then one summer, it purpled and pinked.

As bees pirouetted lazily next to the blooms, I peered through another cracked, dusty window. There wasn't a trace of life in the house. It was abandoned.

"This was my bedroom," I told Evelyn.

The previous owners had stripped the mint wallpaper from the walls and painted them a blaring sunflower yellow, but the floor was the same faded-honey color with scratch marks they hadn't been able to sand down. I remembered leaving them there the first time I'd changed.

The only feature that remained in the room was a built-in closet that hung open like a gaping, toothless mouth.

"And in here?" Evelyn asked.

I went over to her. "That was Mom and Dad's room."

Only a bare box spring and an iron headboard remained. Like my room, it was barren and grubby. My heart squeezed as memories trickled into my mind: dawn-tinted bedsheets, the space between their warm bodies, soft lips on my forehead, fingers running lazily through my hair.

They'd coddled me—their only child—with unyielding affection and infinite gentleness.

And Aidan had taken that from me. Desire to understand why he'd shot Dad and then insisted on dining with me made me shake with anger.

A hand wrapped around mine.

"Oh, *querida*."

I leaned into Evelyn, and she tightened her grip, tugging me around the empty house to a wall that was all sliding glass doors.

"The kitchen was Mom's favorite room."

Evelyn turned her gaze up to the strip of sunshine pouring through the mottled gray skylight Dad and Nelson had put in one summer. August had assisted our fathers while I'd served them extra-sour lemonade to show them what I thought about not being allowed to help. I'd felt immense satisfaction when they'd all squinted from the bitter taste.

My parents didn't want me climbing high, afraid I'd fall and break my neck. I hadn't shifted yet, so although everyone watched me closely for a sign that I'd inherited the Boulder gene, I was still deemed a delicate human.

One night, though, after Mom had headed into town for a girls' dinner, Dad had let me climb up on the roof with him. With our backs against the sun-warmed slate, we'd gazed up at the sheet of stars. He'd told me how he'd once wished upon a shooting star that Mom would marry him and bear him a healthy baby.

"Are you sad I'm a girl?" I'd asked him.

He'd fixed me with his eyes that resembled the surface of Coot Lake at sunrise—a deep gray that veered to silver—and stroked my cheek. "No, sweetheart. I am terribly happy you were born a girl."

I touched my cheek as his caress ghosted over it.

Evelyn stepped in front of me, the scent of menthol eddying thickly around her... around me. "Enough. We are leaving."

"I'm okay."

"You are not okay." She swiped her thumbs against my cheeks.

Finally, I relented with a deep, rattling sigh. She was right. I was experiencing a sensorial overload and needed distance. As we walked away, my phone vibrated inside my bag. I checked who was calling—*August*. I didn't pick up.

"Boy trouble?" Evelyn asked.

"No. I just don't feel like talking to anyone right now. Except you."

She snaked an arm around my waist and gave me a long squeeze.

"Are you liking it here?" I asked.

She bit her rouged upper lip before answering, "*Sí*. Jeb is a kind man."

"But Lucy isn't?"

"Your aunt is a little...*bossy*, which is not to say she is malicious. I just prefer your uncle." Once we'd reached the junction with the main road, she said, "The boy who brought you home on Saturday...he is handsome."

Her words flicked my heart. *Nope*. I was not touching the Liam subject with a ten-foot pole, or a fifty-foot one for that matter.

"He was very worried when he dropped you off..."

My cheeks burned with the memory of how he'd violated me. I would never dare tell Evelyn what he'd done. She'd be disgusted, but perhaps not only with him. Perhaps she'd be disgusted with me too. Because she'd ask what prompted him to do such a thing.

It was a can of worms I had no desire to open.

Not now.

Not ever.

30

I arrived for the meeting five minutes early, but I was still the last one there. I breezed past Liam sitting at the sleek wooden bar that separated the kitchen from the living room.

Lucas was his usual jovial, annoying self, leering at me from underneath the baseball cap he'd fit sideways on his head. "Have a good time at Robbie's engagement party?"

Instead of freezing up or ignoring him, I pasted on a fake smile. "It was awesome."

The five elders clenched their jaws, and gazes met and lowered to the chopped centennial tree trunk used as a coffee table. I guessed they'd all been brought up to speed about my visit to the Pine Pack.

Lucas's gaze tightened on the elders, their lack of condemnation obviously irritating him. "I have an ethical problem with Ness competing in this trial."

Eric shifted on the tan suede couch. "Perhaps she had a good reason for attending." The clear glass globe pendent suspended over the living room cast a white sheen on his bald head.

"I did. I wanted to get to know our neighbors," I said. "Isn't that required of Alphas? To be aware of everything and everyone around them? Besides, wouldn't it be nice if the Boulders and the Pines could interact without violence?"

"They're calculating pricks," Lucas hissed.

"Because you're not?" I tossed back into his face.

Lucas scowled.

"*You've* been plotting my downfall since I signed up for this, Lucas. That's the very definition of being calculating *and* a prick."

"Aren't you a little firecracker today?" He laid both his elbows on the bar behind him and leaned back. "Why are we even allowing her to continue? She broke the rules."

"She shifted to help Matt," Frank said, his bushy white eyebrows shadowing his eyes.

Lucas snorted. "He would've been fine."

"Still," Eric said, "empathy is commendable."

Lucas's nostrils flared. His hatred for me was as acrimonious as the sweaty half-moons staining his gray muscle tee.

"Ness, why don't you take a seat so we can discuss the second trial?" Frank tipped his head toward the barstool between Liam and Lucas.

Like hell I would sit there.

"I'm good standing." I leaned against the built-in bookcase that was stacked with hundreds of books. Horrible Heath had apparently been an avid reader. Too bad it hadn't made him a kinder person.

Frank rose from the couch and grabbed a wooden box from the coffee table, then walked over to Liam and Lucas. "An Alpha should be cunning." He waved the box in the air. "You might be wondering why we decided to hold the meeting here. There is a reason for our choice of location. When Heath was sworn in, he was ordained to protect a very valuable pack artifact, which rested within these six little walls." He slowly pivoted the box. "I use the past tense because it was stolen."

"Maybe Heath got rid of what was inside," I suggested.

Frank raised a single bushy eyebrow. "Why would he have broken the lock?"

"Because he misplaced the key?"

Eric grunted. "We've known about the theft for some time but haven't acted upon recovering it until now. First we needed to locate the artifact, and we have. Julian Matz has it."

Goose bumps the size of mosquito bites coated my arms. "So someone from the Pines stole it?"

"We don't know who took it; we just know they have it." Frank turned to Lucas. "So you see, Ness's sociability with the Pines might serve her in this second trial."

Lucas huffed.

"What exactly is it that we're looking for?" Liam asked.

Although Frank looked at Liam, I didn't. If I could, I would never, ever set my gaze on his face...*ever again.*

"A piece of petrified wood."

"Seriously? We're hunting down a piece of wood?" Lucas crossed his beefy forearms.

The barstool creaked as Liam shifted on it. "What's so special about it?"

"Its properties only concern the Alpha, and us." Frank pointed to himself and the four other older wolves.

That raised my curiosity a couple dozen notches. "And if we find it, can we know what it is?"

"If you become Alpha, Ness"—he side-eyed the graying wolves—"you'll be privy to the information."

From the way he'd glanced at the others, I could swear that he'd sooner believe in leprechauns prancing around Boulder with pots of gold than in me, Ness Clark, a girl, becoming his Alpha.

Little did he know I had Julian's support.

Julian's support...

Whoa.

Julian had said he'd help me become Alpha. Like the rocks that had trampled my body during the first trial, understanding knocked hard into me. Frank was right. Julian *must've* stolen it. He *must've* known they'd come searching for it.

A new scenario played out in my head: *Heath finds out Julian stole from him, gets angry, threatens Julian, who comes over or sends over a thug—like Justin—and has Heath quieted forever.*

The possibility that *I* hadn't killed Heath thickened my blood, making it slide sluggishly through my organs.

"Do you think"—I moistened my lips with the tip of my tongue—"Julian had something to do with Heath's death?"

"No." It was Liam who answered. There was no hesitation in his voice.

I set my eyes on the black leather boot he'd crooked on his opposite knee. "How can you be sure?"

He hesitated a second before saying, "Because he knows the consequences of killing *or* backing the killing of another Alpha."

"Which are?" The laces on both his boots were untied. I supposed it was on purpose. One boot would've been a coincidence, but not two.

"He and his entire pack can be razed."

"Razed? You mean killed?"

"Yes."

Well, there went my shred of hope. The vein in my neck palpitated with disappointment. I stuffed my hands into the pockets of my white denim shorts so that no one would spot how terribly my fingers trembled.

"What if they destroyed the piece of wood?" Lucas asked, which I hated to admit, was a relevant question.

Frank rubbed the day-old white growth on his chin. "Let's hope they didn't."

"How long do we have to find it?" Liam asked next.

"Well"—Frank glanced behind him at Eric—"Robbie's wedding is next weekend, and they've invited our pack to attend."

"Hell, no. You can't be serious." Lucas flipped the baseball cap on his head from side to back. "It's a trap."

"We've considered this, Lucas, and although we don't believe it's a trap, we've decided that only me, Eric, and the three of you will be attending. It'll give you the opportunity to locate the artifact without breaking and entering." Frank opened the box and held it out toward me.

I frowned as I peered at the bare interior. Did he want me to confirm it was empty?

"Smell it, Ness."

Oh. I dipped my nose and sniffed, and my eyes watered from the rancid odor. It was the way I imagined rotting bones smelled—dry chalk and tangy decay.

Frank moved to Lucas next, who took a deep whiff. "That's foul."

He held the box out to Liam. I didn't look at him but imagined he wrinkled his nose, too.

James, the thick-waisted elder, rose from the couch and hooked his thumbs underneath the suspenders holding up his khakis. While the elders still turned into wolves on full moons, the rest of the time, they were humans with normal, slower metabolisms.

"The wedding's taking place on Julian's estate," he said. "We believe our artifact's stored on the premises, thus our reasoning for sending you all to the wedding. You boys will need tuxes and you, Ness, will need a gown. You all got some?"

"Yeah. Sure." Lucas snorted. "Got a whole closet full of tuxes."

"Rent one, Lucas," Eric said. "Liam?"

"I have one, but I don't know if it still fits. I'll try it on tonight."

"Ness?"

"No ball gowns in my closet. Is there a place I can rent one?"

"I wouldn't know," Eric said.

"Why don't you ask one of your customers to buy you one?" Lucas shot out.

I snatched my hand out of my pocket and flipped him off, which just made him smile.

"I can ask the wife if she's got one," Eric offered. "She's about your size."

I blanched at his suggestion. If his wife was as old as he was, then I couldn't imagine her owning anything I'd want to wear. But beggars couldn't be choosers.

"Maybe Taryn has one she could lend Ness. They're about the same height." Liam's suggestion made me as rigid as the bookcase.

I'd rather wear a vintage dress than anything owned by Terrible Taryn.

Lucas didn't answer. I bet he was glaring at Liam.

I pinched my lips and muttered, "I'll find something."

A thought crawled into my mind. Perhaps I could ask Julian, as part of the package of helping me out.

"Okay, then." Eric clapped his hands once to signal that the meeting was adjourned.

"I have one last question," Liam started.

I scrutinized my grass-streaked sneakers.

He continued, "There's only one thing to find and three of us."

"Good question, son," Frank said. "The person who finds it gets to choose his or *her* adversary for the last trial."

I snapped my neck up, and my gaze collided with Liam's. His dark eyes glinted with brutal hope...hope to disqualify me. I bet Lucas and Liam would even work together to retrieve it. Little did Liam know that Julian would give it to *me*.

I could finally eliminate Liam.

My heart pounded, and the adrenaline bled into my eyes. I felt them shifting. I blinked the transformation away.

When I cracked my lids, everyone had risen.

I peeled myself away from the bookcase and voiced the concern that had been gnawing at me for the last twenty-four hours. "Why wasn't my father's death avenged?"

Everyone froze. Great waves of shame rolled over the elders' weathered faces, excavating their wrinkles. Or maybe I wanted to believe it was shame. Maybe it was simply discomfort. There was an elephant in the room—*me*—and I was forcing them to acknowledge it.

"We haven't avenged Heath's death either," one of the elders said, and a chill spider-crawled up my spine.

My eyesight dotted as blood pounded against my temples. Would the fact that it had been an accident sway them to spare me?

"I'm not talking about Heath right now." Keeping my voice steady, even though my lungs felt vacuum-packed, I said, "I'm talking about my father. Why is Aidan Michaels still alive?"

No one spoke for a painfully long minute. Eric palmed his bald head, and Frank sighed.

"Why—" I was about to reiterate my question when James interrupted me.

"'Cause he's got a detailed file on us, complete with pictures of us shifting."

"So? Werewolves aren't a secret," I said.

"Just because a handful of people know about us in these parts doesn't mean we want the entire world to find out werewolves are real. Do you realize how many crazies that sort of news would attract?"

I chewed on my bottom lip. "But if Aidan is dead, the file disappears. So it would be a win-win."

"If he dies, the file *gets* released."

"How?"

"He's made copies, Ness. He's given it to key people," Frank explained. "Too many to track down. I'm sorry, but we just can't risk it."

I pursed my lips. "Was he punished at all, or did he get off scot-free?"

Frank scrubbed a hand against the back of his neck. "Heath reprimanded him. Told him that if he ever killed again, he'd stop doing business with Aidan."

Heat scorched my eyes. "You're kidding me. All Heath did was *threaten* to end his business dealings?" My voice echoed shrilly against the exposed wooden beams running across the ceiling. "Did he hate my father? Is that it? Did he hate him because he had a girl instead of a boy?"

"Ness..." Frank started, but I held up my palm.

"I thought Alphas were supposed to put the pack before everything else. I guess I was wrong." My chest pounded with fierce breaths and fiercer heartbeats. I stalked out of the living room, out of the house like a wild creature, my gaze going in and out of focus.

I needed to calm down, and I needed to do it fast or my body would shift and rip up my favorite shorts and t-shirt, *and* force me to enter the inn in my birthday suit —again.

I yanked my phone out of my back pocket and typed Aidan's name in the search engine. A second later, pages of data on him spewed over my screen. Only one thing interested me though. The minute I found it, I memorized the information, then I downloaded a recording app.

I would exact my own justice.

31

When night fell, I borrowed a mountain bike from the inn's private fleet and pedaled the three miles of rough trails that led to Aidan Michaels's estate. Maybe he wouldn't be home, but I was a patient person with a desperate need for answers and nothing better to do on a Wednesday night.

I could wait.

Fortunately for me, his palatial glass and stone house was lit up, cutting tall squares of light on the landscaped bushes and peach flagstones tiling the path to the front door. I pedaled harder, checking for security cameras. I was pretty sure I caught sight of several glowing red dots, but that could've been my overactive imagination.

I leaned my bike against the manicured bushes by the front door, then slid my phone out of my bag and turned on the microphone. After carefully placing it back inside my bag, I walked to the front door and punched the doorbell. Like a gong, the sound reverberated against the lofty panes of glass...against the walls of my chest.

As I waited, I licked my lips which felt chapped. Footsteps sounded inside the house, claws skittered on stone, and then a lock clicked and the door opened.

"Ness!"

Aidan grabbed the collar of his dog and held him back. The dog growled, not at his owner, but at me.

I'd forgotten he had a dog. I swiped my tongue against my lips again, praying he wouldn't let the hound charge me. I'd have to kick it, and I didn't like the idea of striking a dog.

"Is this about the discount?" he asked.

I jerked my gaze back up to Aidan. "The money?" I didn't want *that* on tape. "No. It's about my father."

"Your father?" Behind his wire glasses, Aidan's gaze roved over the darkness surrounding me as though searching the night for my father.

"The man you shot six years ago?" I sounded aggressive.

I needed to cool down or he'd slam the door in my face.

Or worse, he'd release his dog.

It growled again, slobber dripping down its jowls. My wolf bristled within.

"You must be mistaken. I've never shot a man." Aidan's navy eyes met mine with a disconcerting steadiness.

"He wasn't a man when you shot him. But you know that. You know everything about *us*. Isn't that why you asked me to dinner? Did you get lots of interesting material for your blackmail file?"

His lips thinned. "Careful, Ness. One phone call to the police, and I'll show them your escort profile. I don't think they'd take too well to a minor—"

"Because you think they'd take well to an old man paying said minor."

His mouth quirked. "I'm not that old. Besides, I never paid *you*."

The money in my account had been wired from the agency, but cops could trace his payment to the agency, unless it was made in cash. "Look, I didn't come here to blackmail you into apologizing for what you did to me or to my father. I don't even care if you took me out to dinner to gather information on my pack. The reason I came here was to get closure. To understand *why* you shot him."

His gaze flicked again to the darkness, and it dawned on me to check the hand that wasn't holding the dog—check for rifles or knives or whatever weapon a crazy, werewolf-hating recluse could wield. The fingers of his right hand were empty, simply toying with his earlobe.

"I shot a wolf that was on my property. I didn't shoot your father."

He was careful with his words, as though he was aware I was recording him. But he couldn't know. My phone was wedged deep inside my bag.

"Then why didn't you shoot the other wolf he was with?" I asked.

Aidan studied my face. "The little one wasn't *threatening*."

"The big one wasn't threatening you either."

"It was on my property," he repeated, as though that was a sound reason for murder.

"So was the little one."

His eyes bore into mine. "In hindsight, I should've shot the little one."

"But you didn't shoot...*me*."

His Adam's apple bobbed and rippled the lax, stubbly skin of his neck. "Want the truth, Ness Clark?"

I crossed my arms in front of my tank top, which stuck to my back. "That's what I came here for." Sweat beaded between my breasts but quickly absorbed into the fabric of my hot pink bra.

"Packs have Alphas. Alphas are larger than other wolves."

I frowned, but then his words sunk into me like the perspiration into my clothes. "My father wasn't the Alpha."

"It was dark. And there was a small wolf next to a larger one. How was I to know it was a pup?"

"So you meant to kill Heath? My father's death was a...a *mistake*?"

Aidan nodded.

Damn. Speak the freaking words! I tried to rephrase my question so it required a verbal response when his hand skidded off his earlobe. In the next instant, he'd released his hound and grabbed a rifle which he pointed at my chest. I shut my eyes, expecting the hound to pummel into me, but it flew toward the tall pines hedging the property.

I started inching backward when he hissed, "You move, I shoot."

His hound snarled, and then it didn't. Bones snapped. And then silence.

I strained to look behind me, but my vision was hazy with fear.

"They just killed my dog," Aidan whispered, a manic inflection to his tone.

Who'd just killed—

He shoved the barrel of his rifle into my chest, jerking my attention back to him. "They leave me no choice but to kill theirs."

Theirs? Was he referring to me? Adrenaline spiked through me, clearing the haze. I gripped the barrel and shoved it upward. A shot detonated. I jammed the butt of the rifle hard into his shoulder blade. His grip faltered, but he didn't drop the weapon.

Growls resonated behind me, and Aidan's eyes turned wild with bloodlust. He cocked the rifle. I tried to ram it into his shoulder again, but sweat had slickened my palms, and my hands slipped. Aidan ripped the rifle from my fingers and pointed it at the wolves behind me.

The wolves who'd just come to help. Who didn't deserve to get shot.

"Go!" I yelled as I stepped in front of the still-warm muzzle.

My heart spun like a flicked top. I shrieked the word again, but neither wolf moved. I could smell them mere feet away from me, like I could smell the sharp stench of gunpowder.

Aidan's knuckle flexed.

My body reacted. My fingernails lengthened into claws. I punched the rifle away again. The shot flew wide. As he actioned the bolt, I swiped my claws over his sideburns, ripping hair and skin. Blood dribbled down his throat.

"You little cunt," he growled.

I bounced away from him as he stared at his bloodied fingers, momentarily forgetting about the weapon in his hands. Why had I stepped back? I shouldn't have stepped back... I needed to take the rifle from him.

I lunged for him again, and he swung the rifle into my cheek. My neck cracked, but I didn't fall. The hot metal barrel scorched my skin, and the blow had my ears ringing.

"Crazy bitch!" He shouldered his rifle again.

"Better not shoot me in human form," I said. "You wouldn't be able to pass it off as a...*hunting accident.*"

He angled the gun's muzzle on my thigh. My ears rang louder. If he spoke, if the wolves behind me howled, the sounds were lost to me.

Aidan smiled, and his knuckle whitened on the trigger.

The stink of gunfire tore through the air at the same time my body rocketed sideways. My head glanced against the flagstones so hard pale stars exploded in the corner of my vision. I blinked sluggishly. The world came back into focus, but all I could see was darkness.

Dense, soft blackness.

I reached out, and my fingertips met fur.

Even though moving made my skull scream in pain, I shifted to see past the fur.

A black wolf lay on top of me.

He'd knocked me out of the bullet's path, but now he was crushing my lungs. I shifted again, this time extricating my body from underneath the beast.

A volley of snarls and screams echoed next to me. Gritting my teeth, I twisted toward the cacophony. A gray wolf was on top of Aidan, fangs bared at the psycho's ashen, pulpy face. Aidan's lips moved. The bastard was still alive. How I wished he were dead.

He spit at the wolf. It struck the man's face with its giant paw. Aidan's cheek slammed hard against the sticky, wet stones. His purple-veined lids slid shut, lashes fluttering against sallow skin.

I pressed my shaky palm against the ground and heaved myself into a sitting position.

The gray wolf magicked away his fur and claws and fangs. *Lucas.* He whipped his head toward me. The area around his mouth was tinged crimson, and his black hair was as wild as his blue gaze.

"Liam!" he yelled as he jumped off Aidan and soared toward me.

Liam?

Liam had saved me?

"Liam!"

He lay still, as still as Aidan and the hound.

A new wave of terror beat at the back of my throat.

Lucas rolled Liam's large lupine form over and pressed a hand against his flank. When Lucas drew his fingers away, his palm was dyed a deep red. "Call Matt!"

Sick chills pulsated through me.

"Ness! Fucking call him!" Lucas hollered.

Hands shaking, I dug through my bag for my phone. I managed to grasp it, but it slipped out of my slick fingers and tumbled on the stones.

Lucas, who'd pressed his hand back against the wound in Liam's side, growled at me. "Are you waiting for him to die?"

"N-No." I seized my phone again. Entered the wrong code. Twice. The third time I managed to unlock it. I began scrolling through my contacts when I remembered I didn't have Matt's phone number. "I d-don't have it."

Lucas barked the number at me.

Fingertips tap-tapping against the screen, it took me several attempts to get the number entered right.

Matt's voice came on before I could even speak. "Who's this?"

I was trying to gather my voice, but it kept jamming behind my jumpy breaths. "M-M-Matt…"

"Ness?"

I nodded stupidly.

Matt couldn't hear me nod.

Lucas growled and tore the phone from my inept fingers. While he spoke, I touched Liam's neck. I felt a soft flutter nip my fingertips.

I smoothed the fur on his cheek. "He-He's alive."

"Barely," Lucas muttered. "The fucker probably used a silver bullet." He twisted to look at Aidan, who hadn't moved.

His chest still rose and fell, but he was out cold.

"If Liam dies, I'm going to shred Aidan Michaels's body with my claws, then tear his carotid out with my fangs, and then I'll watch him bleed the fuck out."

It was petty, but the pack's double-standards stung.

"Fuck. I can't staunch the fucking blood."

"Here." I pulled my tank top off, then balled it up and handed it to Lucas.

He wadded it against the hole.

"Is there an exit wound?"

Lucas blinked at me, and then, clutching my t-shirt, he lifted his friend's leg and felt blindly for a puckered hole. "I can't goddamn see anything!"

I scooted over and prodded the velvety flesh, seeking depressions. Found none. The bullet was still inside Liam.

And if it was made of silver...

I shuddered then returned to Liam's head and pressed my palm delicately against his nose. It was wet and cold, pulsing weak breaths against my clammy skin.

It should've been my leg that leaked blood.

It should've been me.

Why did you do that?

As I stroked his fur, a car engine roared and rubber squealed.

A silver sedan glinted in the darkness.

Matt was here.

32

Matt must've ground his foot into the brake, because the tires shrieked as the Dodge vaulted to a stop. He opened his door, and then, face as pale as the clouds twisting over the moon, he pumped open his trunk, took out a heavy blanket, and jogged toward us. Without uttering a single word, he spread the heavy fabric on the blood-soaked flagstones, then shoved me aside, crooked one arm underneath Liam's neck, and snared his forepaws.

"Ness, hold it down!" Lucas jerked his head toward my tank top still wedged against the gushing wound.

I scrambled to my feet and gripped the sodden fabric.

Lucas hooked his arms around Liam's rump, and on Matt's signal, they hoisted their friend onto the blanket. Then they crimped its edges with white-knuckled fingers and heaved. I straightened in time with them, keeping a steady pressure on Liam's flank.

I only let go when Matt shouted at me to open the passenger door. He placed his end of the body inside, then loped around the car and crawled onto the backseat. Breathing jaggedly, he tugged the blanket until Liam was entirely sprawled on the backseat, then flung the door shut.

I got in next to Liam. Laid his head on my cold, goose-fleshed thighs. And then I resumed pressing my tank against his injury. Car doors slammed, and then tires screeched and headlights burned a white path down the road.

As we zipped through the darkness, I heard snippets of Lucas's and Matt's conversation—*he was trying to shoot her...out cold, but not dead...silver bullet, I think... Greg is on his way.*

"That's not the way to the hospital," I said when Matt hung a left instead of a right.

He twisted around long enough to glare at me.

"We're not going to the hospital. We're not going to a vet either." There was no humor in his voice. Just anger.

He was angry with me. I wondered if it had solely to do with tonight, or if other factors—like the engagement party I'd attended on the arm of the enemy pack Alpha—contributed to his antagonism.

I stared down at Liam, my fingers moving gently through the long, silky black strands on his neck. His fur began shortening, retreating inside his pores. Next, his snout receded, and his ears migrated back to the sides of his face.

"Guys, he's shifting." The dark shape draped over my legs became a human face with sallow skin and a pale, gaping mouth.

"Fuck," Lucas said.

I guessed it wasn't a good thing. But why, I had no—

My hand stilled on Liam's brow.

My father had shifted back when the silver had leaked into his heart, draining his werewolf magic and then his life.

My vision tilted and blurred, and the fingers gripping my balled, sodden top curled so hard around the fabric that rivulets of blood ran over Liam's burnished thigh.

Liam was dying.

33

It had started to rain during the drive over to Liam's house. Soft drops pelted the windshield and then the navy cover wrapped around Liam.

My bare stomach was covered in goose bumps that had little to do with the weather and everything to do with the direness of Liam's predicament, and the memories of another time when another silver bullet had pierced the flesh of another wolf. I crossed my arms in front of me, to cover myself and to ward off the chill in my bones.

Seconds after we arrived, a middle-aged man wearing rubber Crocs and navy scrubs knocked on the door. "Where's Liam?"

I assumed this was Greg, the doctor Matt had mentioned in the car. The man was neither part of our pack, nor did he smell like a wolf. From the way he dressed, I took it he was a real doctor. He blustered in, squeezing a black nylon duffel in one hand. I trailed him inside Liam's dusky bedroom, keeping my eyes averted from the cadaverous-looking body nestled underneath a brown fleece cover.

Even though my gaze was fixed to the painting of an oversized peacock feather that hung over the stone fireplace, cocooned in a Plexiglas box, my attention was on the hushed conversation whirring around Liam.

"You're going to have to help me, Matt," Greg was saying. "Hold him down."

My teeth ground hard as I heard metal clink—probably surgical tools.

"Ready?" Greg asked.

Matt must've nodded because the next thing I knew, a hoarse cry shredded the room. Liam was definitely not dead. As suddenly as it arose, the cry abated, and the room oozed with silence.

Abysmal silence.

"I see it," Greg said. "Hold him down again."

I squeezed my eyes tight.

This time, the cry was muted, as though Liam's ability to form sounds had gotten bogged down in a web of sticky breaths.

Metal pinged against metal. Footsteps. The gush of water. Was it over? Was Greg washing his hands? Had he retrieved the bullet?

I peeked toward Liam, who was out cold. His face was pale and shiny with sweat, like melted candle wax. A matching sheen of perspiration gleamed on Matt's large, furrowed forehead. He was talking softly, steadily, using gentle words and shared memories to bring his friend back to life.

Lucas stood vigil on Liam's other side, wearing a pair of low-slung jeans surely borrowed from Liam. When his murky gaze met mine, I jolted my eyes toward my bare, bloodied midriff.

I was an intruder... I had no right to be here.

So I left.

The living room was bright. Too bright. I rubbed my eyes, wishing I could rub the horror of the night out. Waiting for news, I perched on the edge of the couch. I tried to pray like Evelyn did when I accompanied her to mass, but then remembered how many prayers I'd sent upward for my mother and how deafening the answering silence had been.

The tangle of male voices in the bedroom had me perking up. The conversation was still hushed, but I caught a lilt to the tone. Greg must've gotten the bullet out... Or maybe it wasn't made of silver.

That would be good.

A moment later, Matt emerged from the bedroom, shoulders hunched but forehead smoother.

"Is he— Did—" Nerves tore the volume from my voice.

"Greg got the bullet out. It was whole."

I raked my clammy palms over my thighs and exhaled a deep sigh.

Matt tossed a piece of fabric at me—a plaid shirt. Since he was still wearing his, I assumed it was one of Liam's. I slipped it on, and the scent of Liam enveloped me.

"Thank you." I didn't dare meet Matt's gaze. Just the heavy, reproachful feel of it was painful. "Was it made of silver?"

"Yes."

I shuddered, then rubbed the right side of my skull that tingled from a lump the size of an egg.

The couch cushion dimpled as Matt took a seat next to me. "You okay?"

"I'm fine. Just shook up."

Matt's lips were pinched. "We told you to stay away from Aidan Michaels, but you didn't listen." He shook his head. "I don't get you, Ness. I thought I did. I thought I had you all figured out. I thought you were some shy, sweet girl trying to act all tough to fit into the pack, but I don't think you're shy. And I don't think you're trying to fit into the pack."

I swallowed, twining my fingers together in my lap. Like Matt, I was no longer sure I knew who I was and what I was doing.

"Why did you go see the Pines, Ness? And please don't tell me it was for money, because we'll all pitch in and give you the amount you need. You'd have to ask, but we'd do it." He touched my knee lightly, and I flinched. "Asking for help isn't a weakness. It's not a flaw either."

My eyes went hot. With shame. But also with gratitude.

How I wished I could unburden myself, but if I told Matt my reasons for visiting the Pines, I'd be inking my death sentence.

"It was a job," I lied, and then I repeated the words I'd heard Mom yell at Evelyn, "I don't want charity. " That was true at least. Like my mother, I had my pride. She'd worn it throughout her life like armor, and it had earned her the respect of many.

Matt loosed a rough sigh. "And what were you doing at Aidan Michaels's house?"

This time, I told him the truth. How I'd hoped to understand why he'd killed my father. How I'd planned on entrapping him with a recorded confession.

Matt snorted.

"What?"

"Aidan Michaels is the biggest benefactor of the Boulder PD. He's got every officer crawling around this town in his pocket. If I can give you some advice—which I hope you'll actually listen to this time—don't...*ever*...go to the police. Some people in the department are aware of our existence, and they share Aidan's view—that we're abominations. If they weren't scared shitless of what we would do to their families if they waged an attack, they'd have tried to eliminate us a long time ago."

Lucas came out of the bedroom, and we both looked up at him expectantly. "The good doctor needs alcohol." He swiped a bottle of tequila from the rollaway bar tucked in the corner of the living room. I must've frowned, because Lucas added, "To disinfect the wound. We're not celebrating...yet." He flicked his gaze to Matt, then vanished back inside the dark bedroom.

"How did they know I was there?" My voice was as quiet as the cold air murmuring through the vent in the ceiling.

"Aidan is enemy number one of the pack. We've breached his security system, so we have eyes on him at all times. My brother, Cole, is a tech prodigy. He's constantly monitoring the dude. When he noticed you there, he called me. Liam and Lucas were with me. Liam...he flipped." Matt scratched a spot behind his ear. "He said you got real upset earlier over Heath's decision not to seek retribution. Anyway, he was sure Aidan was going to kill you, or do...worse things to you."

Guilt ravaged me. But then the conversation I'd had with Aidan played in my mind.

"Aidan shot my father because he thought it was Heath. Could Aidan...could *he* have killed Liam's father?" I sounded so pathetically hopeful.

Matt stared long and hard at me.

"Like I said, Cole monitors him," Matt said slowly. "Aidan was inside his house all night."

"Maybe he got someone else to do it for him?"

"Maybe."

That little word buoyed me more than Julian's support.

Lucas padded back out into the living room. He wasn't smiling, but his mouth was softer. "The wound's closing up. He's healing."

Air whooshed out of Matt's lungs. "Thank God."

"I'd thank Greg, not God." Lucas's voice pinged around the glass walls enclosing the living room. "I need to go debrief the pack."

His relief was making him jumpy and borderline giddy. I half expected him to hug Matt and pound him on the back, but Lucas did neither. He just asked his friend for a ride.

As though remembering I was there, Matt offered to drop me back at the inn. I rose just as Greg came out of the bedroom, wiping his hands on a steel-gray towel that reminded me of the one Liam had tied around his waist the night he—

"He's asking for you, Ness," Greg said.

34

I sucked in air so harshly I coughed. "He wants to see *me*?"

Greg nodded, while Lucas and Matt exchanged a silent, weighted glance.

"You staying, right, Greg?" Lucas asked.

"Sure."

Lucas pinned me with his blue stare. "Just until one of us comes back."

Did Lucas fear I would finish the job the bullet had botched, or was he scared Liam might need a doctor on standby? I hoped it was the latter but believed it was the former. Sadly, Lucas and Matt had every right to be distrustful of me.

"I'll stay out here." Greg sat on the sofa, then picked up a large book from the wrought-iron coffee table. *The History of Wolves.*

I wondered if it mentioned werewolves.

"We should be back in a half hour max," Matt said.

"That's fine," Greg said. "I'm not on call tonight."

So he *was* a real doctor.

He put his feet up on the table and feigned great interest in the reading material on his lap.

"You gonna be okay in there, Clark?" Lucas asked.

I doubted he cared if I would be okay. What he cared about was if Liam would be okay with me in the same room. Still, I said, "Yes," before I advanced toward the bedroom. Even though the door was ajar, I knuckled it. "Can I come in?"

A hoarse, "Yes," answered me.

Without looking back at the others, I entered the bedroom, leaving the door open to show I had no ill intent. Liam was propped up on three pillows. Although still pale, some color had returned to his cheeks and some life to his eyes. In the darkness, they gleamed disquietingly bright, their beam ensnaring me. The hard set of his jaw told me he was angry.

Really angry.

The front door banged shut, and I jumped.

"Close the door." His voice was deep and raspy, as though the bullet had scraped his throat.

My heart banged like Aidan's shotgun.

"Please." His Adam's apple bobbed in his corded neck.

I bit my lower lip, eyeing the doorknob. Finally, I wrapped my fingers around the cool metal and pushed it. The click of the latch bolt against the strike plate echoed harshly in the quiet room.

I'd decided never to lay eyes on him after what he'd done to me, and here I was locking myself inside a bedroom with him. The night was stretching the limits of my sanity. I crossed my arms and raised my gaze to his.

"I know you can't stand to look at me after what I did to you." He watched what his words did to me.

My nostrils pulsed. The coppery scent of blood mixed with the smell of his skin was making my head spin. Or maybe it was the intensity with which he was studying me.

"I wish I could erase my actions, Ness. I wish I could go back in time and let you go without acting like a...a"—even though his voice wavered, his gaze didn't—"a savage. I am so deeply ashamed of what I did to you." His voice was soft like the patter of the raindrops tapping against the window.

"Is that why you took a bullet for me tonight? So I would forgive and forget?"

"No." His lids slid shut for a long second. When they lifted, his eyes were even brighter than before. Wolf eyes. "I'd understand if you never forgave me."

My chest tightened like a fist.

"Please say something," he croaked.

Pressing my arms against my abdomen, I said, "I'm glad you're okay."

"Are you?"

"Yes."

He hitched up an eyebrow, as though not truly believing me. But it was true, and he must've seen this on my face because his eyebrow slowly fell back, aligning with the other.

"Why did you do it?" I asked.

"Because I was hurt and"—he looked at the painting of the feather over his fireplace—"jealous."

My arms loosened. "Jealous? Of Aidan?"

His gaze jolted back to me. "What?" A flush creeped over his jaw.

I swallowed. "I asked why you took a bullet for me."

"Oh." Clearly, his answer hadn't been intended for this question. He looked away again and a deep groove appeared between his eyebrows. "I reacted. That's all." His lips barely shifted, yet his words stirred the air that had gone very still.

I barely heard his answer over the loud echo of his previous answer. *Jealous.* "What did you think I was asking you about?"

The tendons in his neck shifted as he sat a little taller, as his shoulders pressed a little harder into the pillows. "Why I lost my mind when you came to my house." He closed his eyes, then leaned his head back against the wooden headboard. "This conversation is more painful than being shot."

A breath snagged in my chest. "You *like* me?"

His eyes remained closed. He was so still I checked his chest was rising with breaths.

Liam had feelings for me?

"Are you trying to torture me some more?" His voice broke the spell of his confession.

"No. I— *Why*?"

His eyes flew open and set on me. "Why do I like you?"

"No one else does."

"First off, that's not true. Second off, I have no clue. I just do. But apparently the feeling isn't mutual." His tone was rough. "So if you can forget I said anything, that would be great." He turned his face so that he was facing his bathroom door.

"I was scared tonight. Scared that you'd die." My blood simmered in my veins, heated my skin.

I toed the tufted rug that stretched over almost every inch of the wooden floor and examined the long fibers, trying to decide if they were purple or maroon. In the obscurity, it was hard to tell.

"I don't hate you, Liam."

Purple. They were purple. A deep, almost electric purple.

Bare feet flattened the looped filaments and stopped inches from mine. My heart-beats quickened like skittish trout.

The heat from his bare skin permeated the slim divide between us. Warmth meant he was better, unless he was coming down with a fever. Was his wound infected? I didn't dare move. Didn't dare look up. But Liam crooked a finger underneath my chin and tipped my face up.

"I almost died tonight, Ness, and that reminded me that I'm not immortal. That none of us are. We might be stronger than humans, but we don't get to live forever."

My throat tightened.

"Do you know what I thought about when the bullet hit me?" His pupils throbbed, burned a path straight into me.

"What?" I breathed.

"That I'd hate to die with you thinking I was a bastard."

I removed my head from its perch. "Liam—"

"Let me finish." His tone was gentle but tremulous, as though severing the connection between his finger and my chin had shaken his confidence.

I'd been about to say that I didn't think he was a bastard. At least, not anymore. Not since he'd taken a bullet for me.

"And the second thing that entered my mind"—he combed an unruly lock of hair behind my ear, and I shivered—"was that I didn't want to die before getting to kiss you."

I blinked. "You want to kiss me?" If I'd heard him wrong, and he'd said *kill me*, then...well, that would be so many shades of embarrassing.

"Yes, Ness Clark. I'd like to kiss you."

It struck me then that Liam didn't think I murdered his father. I closed my eyes. "Don't, Liam. Don't like me. I'm no good. For you...I'm no good."

My eyelashes dampened. *No, no, no*...I couldn't cry. Not in front of Liam. Oh, God, I was such a mess.

"Why shouldn't I like you?"

"Because...you shouldn't." The tears snaked out.

Perfidious tears.

I felt his thumbs swipe over my cheeks, felt his fingers close around the sides of my face, tilt it back toward his.

"You're going to have to give me a better reason."

I looked at him then, and my heart beat so wildly it almost tripped right out of my chest. A better reason was the truth.

"Tamara." I blurted out the redhead's name, not knowing what else to say.

"Tamara?"

"She likes you, Liam. I couldn't do that to her." My excuse was pathetic, eye-roll-worthy pathetic.

"Let me make something very clear, I don't give a crap about Tamara."

"But—"

"Go out on a date with me."

"Liam—"

"One date. And I promise to wear clothes." One side of Liam's mouth quirked up.

Of course, *that* made me acutely aware that he was naked. "Lucas said there was no dating within the pack."

"Lucas is a dumbass, and it's a bogus rule. I know for a fact that two of the wolves in our pack are together."

For the briefest of moments, I wondered who, but then I focused back on the matter at hand. "We're opponents. Opponents can't date."

A nerve jumped in his jaw. "Says who?"

"It wouldn't be ethical."

"Really?" His face loomed over mine.

I licked my lips that felt as dry as my throat. "Yes. Really."

"Drop out then."

That snapped something in me. I ducked away from him. "Is that what this is about?"

"What?" His forehead grooved.

"You're trying to make me drop out?"

His eyes darkened, and he gave his head a little shake.

"Why don't *you* drop out?"

His jaw clenched. "I've been working my entire life toward this, Ness. You only want this to piss me off."

"That's not true," I blurted out. But it was true.

So. Damn. True.

He crossed his arms in front of his blood-flecked torso. "You didn't go against me because you hated the idea of having a Kolane in charge?"

Instead of answering him, I used the momentum of our quarrel to drive in my previous point. "See? We can't date, Liam."

He snorted but didn't disagree with me. Then again, his bedroom door flew open.

As he took us in, Matt's eyebrows shot up. "Everything all right in here?"

Liam glared at me. For someone whose dying wish had been to kiss me, he seemed over it.

"Yeah," I mumbled, planting my gaze on the large oaf of a man standing in the doorway instead of on the infuriating one standing inches from me.

Matt flicked his attention to Liam, who remained as still as glass.

"Can you take me home?" I asked Matt.

"Of course."

I started walking away when Liam's voice made me halt. "Why do you want to lead this pack, Ness?"

My cheeks burned from being put on the spot. "I don't have to explain my reasons to you."

"I just hope your reasons are noble, because these are good men. Men who deserve someone honest, with the pack's interest at heart."

I stared at Matt's dirty boots.

I swallowed over and over, but my saliva kept getting jammed up. Finally, I managed to wheeze out, "And they'll have someone deserving of them."

For the first time in a long time, I was speaking the truth.

Because it wouldn't be me.

I would make sure to lose the next test. I wasn't sure how yet, but I was sure it would come to me. If I lost, Julian couldn't hold that against me. Could he?

He probably could. He'd probably rescind his offer to speak to the PI. Or if he'd already spoken to him, he'd call him back. But it wouldn't matter because Liam would already have heard it from me.

After the next test, I'd confess.

I'd confess it all and free myself of the debilitating guilt. And if that meant groveling for my life, then I would drop to my knees and grovel. My only hope was that Liam would show me the mercy his father had been incapable of showing my mother.

35

I spent every minute of the next three days with Evelyn. If these were to be my last hours on this earth, there was no one I wanted to spend them with more than Evelyn. Several times, she asked me what was wrong. *Nothing.* That was my answer. *Nothing* plus a cheerful smile.

But she knew me better than that. She also knew there was no point in pushing me. That when I walled myself off, there was no breaching my brick-and-mortar shell.

Next week, my fate would be sealed.

I thought about the wedding with a heavy heart. Remembered I still needed a dress. I tried to call Everest for help, but Lucy told me he'd gotten dire news about Becca and that he'd hit the road to clear his mind.

I didn't want to hold his sorrow against him, but I was sad he'd left me behind. I didn't wallow too long in my loneliness, though. After days of avoiding August's calls and messages, I'd answered him that morning. Like a dying person, I was putting my life in order, and part of that order was thanking August for caring, even though I didn't really understand why he cared about me in the first place. I was no longer the innocent little girl whose hair he'd ruffled and whom he'd taught to whittle wood into animal statues.

As I wiped down wine glasses in the pantry, my heart squeezed so tight a sharp pain spread through my chest. I was wallowing again. God, I didn't want to wallow. I drove my focus outward, on the chirpy conversation of the two servers who worked nights and weekends at the inn. They were discussing going clubbing at The Den.

One of them, the one with a pixie cut and a gazillion silver hoops in her right ear —Emmy—must've noticed I was listening, because she asked, "Want to come with us, Ness?"

I almost dropped the glass I was drying. Emmy and the other server—Skylar—

were at least a decade older than I was and had never spoken to me before. I'd assumed it was because I was so much younger than them *and* related to their boss.

"I'm only seventeen."

"You don't look seventeen," Emmy said. "Besides you're too pretty to be turned away from the door. Plus, DJ Wolverine's spinning. She's awesome."

DJ Wolverine... It took my mind a second to connect the dots. DJ Wolverine was Julian's niece, Sarah. She could help me get in touch with Julian.

"Okay. I'm in."

I'D NEVER GONE CLUBBING, so I didn't know how people dressed. Although sporting the black dress I'd worn when I'd visited Heath made my skin itch, it was the only nice thing I owned. Well, that and the red dress, but there was a small tear in the side seam—probably from when I'd ripped it off my shifting body.

The black sequins sewn over the material caught every flick of light, casting tinsels over the dashboard of Emmy's little car that rumbled with club beats.

"You okay, hun?" Skylar asked. She'd swept her bleached hair into a high bun that sat atop her head like frosting on a cupcake. "You seem real down."

I bit the inside of my cheek. "I'm okay."

Emmy turned down the music. "Is it your momma?"

"My mom?"

Just two mornings ago, in that slim moment between sleep and wakefulness, I'd reached for my phone to call her for advice. Only when I couldn't find her contact did I remember she was gone. I'd lain in my bed a long while, watching the dove-gray light of dawn turn pale gold.

Emmy glanced toward Skylar. "We heard you lost her a couple months before coming out here."

Skylar spun around in her seat, her manga-sized blue eyes roving over my face. "I lost mine last year, and although I ain't gonna say our pains are the same"—she didn't sound like she was from around here—"if you ever need to talk, well, you can talk to me, hun. We can bitch and lament together. I'm real good at bitchin' about life."

"It's one of her many talents."

Emmy grinned, while Skylar chortled.

Intent on shifting the spotlight off the woman I missed so much, I asked, "How long have you two known each other?"

"We met two years ago." Skylar placed her hand over Emmy's and brushed her knuckles. "We started working at the inn at the same time."

Emmy loosed a light sigh. "It was love at first sight."

My lids fluttered. "Oh...you two...you're together?"

"For a year and a half already! Time flies," Emmy said. "What about you, Ness? Are you seeing anybody?"

I stared out my window at the moon that was growing fatter and fuller every day. "No."

"No one's caught your eye?"

"Not really."

"Maybe you'll meet someone tonight," Skylar said. "The Den's full of hotness."

"Maybe."

Soon, we were parking across from a brick building illuminated by a huge blue flickering neon sign. A beefy bouncer stood by the closed metal doors, turning away three gangly boys, before letting in a gaggle of chattering girls who wore too much makeup and too little clothes. I'd never felt overdressed before, but in this moment, as I trailed Emmy and Skylar, I felt extraordinarily self-conscious. It didn't help that people from the long line awaiting to get into the club were staring.

I started walking toward the end of the line when Skylar looped her arm through mine and tugged me to the front. Grumbling erupted behind us, but neither Emmy nor Skylar seemed to care.

"Hey, Bobby!" Skylar chirped.

The bouncer turned toward us. "Skysky." He tipped his head down toward me, hiking up an eyebrow. "Who's your little friend?"

Little friend. Skylar had a couple inches on me, but I was far from little. Unless he meant age-wise. That was probably what he'd meant. My palms slickened. *Don't ask to see my ID. Don't ask to see my ID.*

"Ness's my little sister. She's visiting from LA." The lie rolled off Skylar's tongue so naturally that Bobby pulled the heavy metal door open.

Music whooshed out and battered against the dark street.

"Be good," he said.

"Aren't we always?"

"Em is." He smirked at Skylar. "You, not so much." He winked at us as we passed by him and then closed the door.

Swirling neon lights illuminated the cavernous building, which must've housed an old power plant once upon a time. Exposed metal tubing and air vents criss-crossed the high ceiling like a rat maze, reflecting the swinging strobes. In the middle of the dancefloor stood a wide square bar manned by several bartenders. Partygoers spilled around the bar, moving their bodies to the deafening beat. On a metal mezzanine, people sat at tables, pouring long drinks from liquor and juice bottles. Some were leaning against the railing, gazing down at the crowd below.

"Where's the DJ booth?" I yelled into Emmy's ear, my mouth coming in contact with some of her silver hoops.

My lips instantly blistered, and I jerked away. I licked the tiny sores, then squashed my mouth shut when I caught her staring at it.

Nostrils working, she pointed to the top of the stairs that led to the mezzanine floor. There, in an open booth, pink headphones nestled in a mane of wild curls, stood Sarah aka DJ Wolverine.

Emmy tapped my shoulder. "Is it me, or is your mouth smoking?"

I licked my lips. "Must be you."

She frowned.

"I'm going to go say hi to someone," I said.

"Okay. We'll be right here."

I nodded, then strode across the room, slaloming between the bodies.

Another burly bouncer stood at the bottom of the stairs. He stuck out his hand when I approached.

"The DJ's my friend," I said.

He gave me a grumpy, meaningful look. He wasn't buying it.

"Ask her," I pleaded.

"I can't interrupt her set."

"Please. Her name is Sarah. Her uncle is Julian Matz. Her brother—"

The bouncer grumbled. "Fine. But I'm keeping an eye on you."

I slid by him before he could change his mind. When I reached Sarah, she was fiddling with some dials on her turntables.

"Hey!" I yelled.

Since my voice didn't carry through her headphones, I gesticulated my hands. That caught her attention. She looked up from her laptop. A frown gusted over her face, but then she recognized me, and a sizeable smile curved her lips. She held up a finger, tapped on her laptop—probably cuing up the next song—and then she lowered her headphones.

"Welcome to my den. Did you just get here?"

I leaned over the tall booth. "I need Julian's phone number."

"Why?"

"I need to ask him something."

"Ask me instead."

I supposed I *could* ask her. "I've been invited to your brother's wedding, and I need a dress."

She frowned, her thin eyebrows slanting over her wide brown eyes. "Not sure what you heard, but my uncle doesn't wear dresses."

I balked at her answer. "I was just hoping he could help me get one."

"Why would he help you get one?"

"Because he offered to help me the other day." Before she could jump to any conclusions about her uncle's reasons for aiding me, I added, "He pities me for being the only girl in my pack."

Not my best lie ever, but it seemed to appease Sarah because her forehead uncrumpled. She raised a finger again, then set the headphones back on her ears and cued up the next song. The beats overlapped seamlessly, before the new song glided over the fading one.

She pushed the headphones down again, then sized me up. "You're what, a four?"

I nodded.

"You can borrow one of mine. Come over to my place tomorrow."

"Really?"

"Yes, really." She rolled her eyes. "Now, go dance. I need to concentrate on my set."

I started to turn away when I remembered I had no clue where *her place* was. "I don't know where you live."

"Give me your phone."

I entered my password and passed it over.

She typed in her contact information, then handed the phone back to me. "Don't come before twelve! I'm dead to the world in the morning."

"'Kay. Thanks."

She fluttered her hand in a *don't-mention-it* gesture, then stuck her headphones back on and bobbed her head.

I clambered down the stairs, past the bouncer, who'd lost interest in me after ascertaining I wasn't some crazed fan. I zeroed in on Skylar and Emmy's location at the bar and threaded myself through the mass of bodies.

The newest song Sarah was playing had people jumping and pumping their fists in the air. Twice, my feet got trampled. The first time, the person didn't apologize—they probably hadn't realized. The second time, though, the *trampler* caught my arm and leaned over to apologize. The boy's breath reeked of beer and bad dental hygiene.

"It's okay," I said, shrugging him off.

His gaze skimmed over my face, then dipped to the V-shaped neckline of my dress. *Subtle.* "Can I buy you a drink?"

I was about to turn him down when someone beat me to it.

Liam loomed over the boy. "No. You can't."

The boy turned toward him before backing away faster than a spooked rabbit.

"Maybe I wanted a free drink," I said.

Liam's eyes flashed dangerously. "Then *I'll* buy you a drink."

Not the answer I was expecting. "Forget it. I don't want anything to drink."

"Did you come with Everest?"

I shook my head. "He's out of town."

Liam's jaw tightened. "Of course he is."

What was that supposed to mean?

"Did you come alone?"

"No! I came with two coworkers from the inn."

Someone shoved into me, and I momentarily lost my balance. Liam shot out a hand and caught my elbow, steadying me. Once he'd established I could stand on my own two feet, he let go.

I rubbed the patch of skin he'd touched. "I should go find them."

"Females or males?"

My forehead furrowed at his strange question.

"Your coworkers, are they women or men?"

"Women. Why?"

"Just asking."

Uh-huh. Weirdo. "I should go find them."

Heart pounding to the hectic rhythm of the bass spilling from the surround-sound speakers, I made my way toward Skylar and Emmy. They'd met up with another couple—Francine and Lark. Francine was petite and feminine. Lark was something else. In spite of the buzz cut and the baggy AC/DC t-shirt, Lark didn't strike me as a man. But maybe he was.

They were all very nice and included me in every conversation, which was more than the pack did. At some point, I found myself looking upward at the mezzanine, right into Liam's shadowy gaze. His forearms were propped on the metal guardrail. Matt stood next to him, and behind them sat the rest of their posse and their harem of girls.

When a thin, pale arm snaked around Liam's midsection, crumpling his black V-neck, I looked away. Three days ago, he'd proclaimed he'd wanted to kiss me, that he didn't care about Tamara, and yet here she was, wrapped around him like string around a birthday present.

His fickleness stung way more than it should.

36

I'd been standing for what felt like hours in the bathroom line, and it had barely shortened. What did women do in there?

I started tapping my foot to distract myself from the spasms in my bladder. When that didn't help, I took out my phone. I wasn't socially connected—no Facebook, no Instagram, no Twitter, no Snapchat—so I checked the news, especially what was happening overseas. Even though August had said little could kill a werewolf, I worried about his safety. What if a blood-thirsty rebel set fire to his camp?

I shuddered just thinking about it.

By the fifth article I read, I was two people closer to my destination. I contemplated the men's room entrance that swung like a revolving door. Boys were in and out so fast I suspected they didn't wash their hands. At this moment, I wished women would sacrifice hygiene for speed. Just as I had that thought, the boy's bathroom door flapped again, and lo and behold, Liam Kolane stepped out.

I swung my gaze to the short ponytail of the girl in front of me, feigning great interest in her purple hair tie.

When her head swiveled and her mouth fell a little open, I momentarily shut my eyes. I could smell Liam next to me, feel the heat from his hulking body.

"What do girls do in there?" he asked.

I loosed a sigh, then opened my eyes. Why was he always there? Did he have some internal radar that displayed my location at all times?

Barely moving my lips, I mumbled, "Beats me."

"Come."

That made me look up. "Where?"

He nodded toward the guy's bathroom.

"I can't go in there."

"We have toilets too."

They also had urinals and probably a long line of boys doing their business. "With doors?"

One side of Liam's mouth curled up. "Yes."

He leaned down until his mouth was leveled with my ear. I shivered when his hot breath pulsed against my lobe.

"If you become Alpha, you'll need to get over your prudishness."

I raised my gaze toward him. *But I won't be Alpha, Liam. I won't even be part of a pack come next week. Maybe I won't be part of this world either.* I didn't say any of these things. Instead, because I was going to seriously pee myself if I didn't get to a toilet soon, I accepted his proposal and trailed him to the guy's bathroom. Two boys tried to go inside, but Liam told them to wait. He opened the door. Three guys were standing at the urinals. *Great.* Not awkward at all.

"Get out," he said.

My jaw prickled with embarrassment when I realized he was kicking people out. The three guys turned—just their heads thankfully—and gaped at Liam. When they noticed his serious expression, they zipped up quick, and bypassing the sinks, they filed out.

"You didn't have to kick everyone out," I said, going toward a stall.

He leaned against the door to keep it closed and gave me a smug smile. "You'd rather have had an audience?"

No I wouldn't. I locked myself up in a stall, and squatting over the piss-covered toilet seat, I emptied my throbbing bladder. I tried not to think about Liam standing just outside.

As I flushed, there was banging. Liam must've cracked open the door because music blared against the black tiles.

"The bathroom's out of order," he bellowed, just as I came out of the stall. He leaned against the metal door then planted one boot on it.

I washed my hands with the pink soap that smelled like antiseptic and artificial cherry.

"I saw you talking with Sarah Matz."

Of course he'd had an angle for helping me out and clearing the bathroom. He wanted information. Instead of beating around the bush and asking if it was illegal to chat with a Pine wolf, I said, "And you want to know what I discussed, I suppose?"

He didn't respond, just studied me as I approached him, wiping my hands on my dress. The sequins weren't very absorbent.

"I asked her if I could borrow a dress for her brother's wedding," I said.

His eyebrows shifted over his eyes that looked amber in the bathroom's red florescent lighting. "Why did you ask her for a dress?"

"Who else was I supposed to ask? My aunt is twenty sizes bigger than me, and Evelyn doesn't own any fancy apparel. I looked online, but unlike tuxes, there's no shop that rents dresses in Boulder."

The door pulsed behind him. He opened it and barked, "It's out of order," then leaned against it again.

"I'm done, Liam. You can let them—"

"*I'm* not done."

I balled my fingers into fists. "That's all I talked about."

"Taryn must have a dress."

"I don't want Taryn's dress."

"I'll take you shopping tomorrow."

I jerked back. "No way."

His gaze ground into mine, and my pulse skittered. I tried to breathe to calm myself. After the fourth not-even-remotely-close-to-soothing breath, I mumbled, "Stay locked in here with me any longer, and it'll start rumors."

"I don't give a shit about rumors."

"But Tamara will give a shit."

"Please stop using Tamara as an excuse to push me away."

"I'm not using her as an excuse. She was groping you earlier! I saw her."

His pupils expanded and bled darkness into his irises. "You were watching me?"

Heat pulsed against my jaw. "I was looking around and happened to see her *and* you."

"You're the first girl who's turned me down."

So this was what his strange behavior was about? No longer feeling threatened, I unclenched my fingers. "I'd say get used to it, but I doubt you'll ever need to get used to it."

He didn't smile, didn't even react to my indirect compliment.

"Seriously, can you let me out now? This place reeks." When he didn't, I reached around him for the doorknob.

He swiped my arm and spun me around so fast he had me pinned to the door with his forearms bracketing my head.

I'd been wrong to relax. Liam was unpredictable.

"Ness"—the way he spoke my name, all rough and low, had my stomach swishing—"I'm not like my father."

I'd expected him to say many things but not that. "Then don't hold me against my will."

His breaths shuddered against my forehead. Slowly, almost painfully, he pushed himself off the door...off me.

And he let me go.

37

At four the following afternoon, I entered a modern-looking building not too far away from the The Den. I checked my phone for Sarah's floor number and pressed on the button that had a big six on it.

As the elevator rose, so did my nerves. What if her generosity was a ploy? What if she'd called up a bunch of other Pine shifters and they were going to ambush me?

I massaged my temples as the elevator doors swept open on the sixth floor. Where was all this anxiety coming from?

I hadn't slept much last night, getting to bed way too late and getting woken up by Lucy way too early. It was as though she wanted to make me pay for going out. Or maybe she was making me pay for the missing bike—the one I'd left at Aidan's house the night he shot Liam. I told her someone had stolen it while I'd gone into the DMV to get the sign-up forms. It beat explaining what had really happened to it.

I'd contemplated retrieving it, but I didn't want to risk Aidan putting a bullet in my skull…if he was even home. Considering his injuries, he could be bandaged up like a mummy in a hospital bed.

When I arrived in front of Sarah's door, I pressed on the buzzer. A long minute later, there was grumbling followed by footsteps. Sarah opened the door, a pink silk sleep mask that read *Go Away* wedged up on her forehead. Smudged crescents of makeup framed her squinty eyes.

"Shit. Is it noon already?"

I smiled. "It's 4:00 p.m."

"Shit," she said again.

The outfit she'd worn last night was draped over the back of a lavender velvet couch. Her buffed, white stone floors were strewn with various other articles of clothing. She nodded for me to come in.

"For a girl who wanted a hundred bucks for headphones, you live in a mighty fancy place." I studied the crystal chandelier that dangled over a leather coffee table. Each crystal was shaped like a raindrop and hung at different heights. "Are your parents in?"

"No. Why would they be?"

"Don't you live with them?"

"God, no. The second I turned eighteen I was out the door."

"So this is all yours?"

"Yes, ma'am."

"Do you have a roommate?"

She scrunched up her nose. "I don't do roommates."

"I wish I could live alone too."

"You live at the inn, right?"

"Yeah," I said with a sigh.

"Sucks."

"Tell me about it."

Over her black sleep shorts and black tank, she wore a turquoise silk bathrobe with a heron print.

"Want a glass of water? Or coffee? Or—"

I smiled at her attempt at playing hostess. "Just a dress."

"I need coffee first." She padded away toward the open kitchen. The stainless-steel appliances shone as bright as the gray ceramic tiles around them. The place was seriously sick, straight out of a lifestyle magazine. As she filled a percolator with ground coffee, I put my bag down on one of the many stools propped under the marble kitchen island. She flicked the switch, then gestured me toward a doorway that was twice the size of a normal doorway.

Like the rest of her apartment, her bedroom was monstrously oversized and covered in clothes.

"You can't afford a housekeeper?" I asked before realizing how critical that sounded.

Then again, she was a slob, and she didn't strike me as ignorant of the fact.

"I don't like people touching my stuff."

"Yet you're okay with letting me borrow a dress?"

She cocked an eyebrow as though just grasping how egregious that was. Then again, everything about this girl was a contradiction. She drove a Mini yet lived in a marble palace; she DJed in a club yet obviously didn't need the money.

"Dry clean it before giving it back." She flashed me a smile that pried her sleep-filled eyes wider. She slid a mirrored door open with great flourish. "I'm wearing the yellow one. Take your pick from the others."

I stared at the row of hangers dripping with silks and satins and tulle and sequins. "Are you a gown hoarder, or do you really attend that many fancy parties?"

"That many fancy parties. But I do like clothes. A lot."

My gaze swept over the rest of her closet, over the teetering piles of sweaters and t-shirts, over the lineup of jeans in every wash imaginable, over the column of shoes that ranged the gamut of sneakers to crystallized heels to every style of boots on the market.

"You're drooling."

I snapped my mouth shut. I *was* drooling—metaphorically speaking. I didn't have saliva dribbling down my chin or anything.

"Another reason I would never get a roommate... She'd steal all my clothes."

"Only if she was your size."

"She'd probably get to my size to fit into my clothes." She dropped down on her bed, then stretched her arms over her head.

I fingered the material of a black dress.

"You shouldn't wear black to a wedding."

"Okay."

"Or white. Try the red one. Red usually looks good on us blondes." She stuck her sleep mask back on.

I plucked the red one out and marveled at it.

The coffee machine gurgled, and then it beeped, and Sarah rolled back up.

"Stop eye-fucking it, and try it on." She tossed her silken sleep mask on top of her mussed-up sheets, then got to her feet and walked back out to the kitchen.

While she was pouring coffee, I pulled off my t-shirt and slid the fluid, backless halter number over my head. Once the fabric settled, I unbuttoned my cut-offs and kicked them off. I stepped in front of the mirror. The dress was stunning. Too stunning. What if I ripped it or stained it or—

"Told you it would look awesome." Sarah was leaning against the gigantic doorframe, clutching a mug of coffee between her fingers. A gold-foiled word was stamped on it—*Princess*. How appropriate.

"It's really nice, but maybe...*too* nice?" My voice sounded slightly high-pitched.

"Would you rather wear something ugly? 'Cause if that's the case, I don't have anything for you."

"No. It's just"—I smoothed the fabric of the flowy skirt—"it's expensive, isn't it?"

"Probably. Mom gave it to me." She pushed off the doorjamb. "Look, I'm not going to force you to wear something you're not comfortable with, but know that I most probably won't wear it again. I try not to wear the same thing twice. So if you're worried about ruining it, don't. There are plenty more where that one came from."

"That's really generous."

She shrugged, and her silk robe fell off her shoulder. She hiked the slippery material back up, then returned to the bed, where she sat cross-legged. "I had a question for you."

I stopped admiring the dress.

"Why are you the only girl in your pack?"

"I always assumed I was a fluke of nature." I bit the inside of my cheek. "Do *you* know why I'm the only girl in my pack?" It struck me I used the possessive pronoun, so I switched it out for, "I mean, in the Boulder Pack?"

"Nope. No clue." She sipped her steaming coffee. "Must be weird... Weirdly cool."

"It's definitely weird but not cool at all. I wish there were others."

"You get all these hot guys to yourself. Why would you ever want to share?"

"They're not *all* hot. Besides, none of them like me." *Anymore...*

"Babe, pull off your blinkers. You know the way you were checking out the dress. Well, Liam was staring at you the exact same way all fucking night. Seriously, I almost screwed up my beat-juggling because of you two."

"He stares at me because he doesn't trust me. None of the Boulder wolves do. After he saw me talking with you, he was all up in my face about what we'd discussed."

She rolled her eyes. "The Boulders think everyone's out to get them."

"And they're wrong?"

"Well, yeah. Not *everyone's* out to get them. The dudes are Neanderthals. Hot Neanderthals, but Neanderthals nonetheless. What would my *very evolved* pack need with any of them?" She downed the rest of her coffee, then set her mug down next to a half-empty bottle of water. "They don't have anything we don't already have."

"They're all males."

She frowned. "So?"

"They're all stronger than I am."

"Just because your muscles aren't as big doesn't mean you're weak, Ness." She tapped her index finger against her temple. "This'll sound corny as shit, but the greatest strength comes from here."

I pursed my lips, not because I thought she was wrong, but because I thought she was idealistic. It was easy to be idealistic when you possessed everything—from riches to security to status to family. I had none of those things.

She tipped her head to the side. "Here I thought you were this self-confident, arrogant girl, but you're not, are you?"

"I make a good first impression, don't I?" I raised a smile I wasn't really feeling. "You're also surprisingly different than I assumed. You're actually nice."

"Ha. I think you're the first person to say that." She twisted her long curls in a makeshift bun that held by itself. "Can you please tell my mother that on Saturday? I'd *love* a front-row seat to that reaction..."

My smile turned genuine.

Sarah's stomach growled long and hard. "I need food. Want to grab some lunch?"

I glanced at the glowing red digits on her bedside clock. "It's 4:30."

"Perfect time for lunch." She walked over to another doorway and slid it open. Behind it sprawled a white marble bathroom. "So? You in?"

"Sure."

While she showered, I delicately pulled the dress off and folded it neatly, then put on my denim cut-offs and navy t-shirt that felt incredibly ratty in comparison. I asked her twice more if she was sure about the dress. Both times won me headshakes and *yes*es.

We had food at Tracy's, where I expected to run into some member of the Boulder Pack, but instead we ran into a couple Pines. Thankfully none of them were Justin Summix.

When I mentioned his name, Sarah wrinkled her nose and leaned over, burger suspended in midair, meat juice dripping onto her creamy coleslaw. "He's the worst."

I liked her more after that. And I already liked her quite a bit, so that was saying a lot. How I wished she were a Boulder wolf. But then I wondered why I wished she were part of a pack *I* wasn't even part of. And what did it matter anyway? In the end, she was a wolf like me. Just because we didn't answer to the same Alpha—I answered to none for that matter—didn't mean we couldn't be friends.

38

Although we'd made plans to hang out mid-week, Sarah had to cancel for some wedding stuff. The bored sound of her voice told me she wasn't looking forward to whatever her family had planned for her.

I stayed in most of the week, shifting into my wolf form only once to go for a run. I didn't stray too far up the mountain, but I did pound the earth from sundown to twilight, exerting my pent-up nerves.

All week I'd tried to call Everest for news, but he didn't answer his phone. I was beginning to think he didn't want to talk to me. Maybe he thought that associating with me was shameful considering what I'd done to his Alpha. Whatever his reasons, I added his silence to the long list of things that perturbed me.

I spoke to August a few times—always steering the conversation toward him. We talked battle strategies and hot deserts, grenades and religious indoctrination. Light-hearted subjects.

At the end of our last call, I asked him when he was coming home, and he asked me if I missed him, and it triggered a painfully awkward stretch of silence, which he put an end to by saying he needed to get geared up because his squad was waiting for him in a Humvee.

Truth was, I did miss him, but I tacked that up to being a lonely pariah. It was probably better that he was away. If he'd stayed, he might have hung out with me out of pity, and I would've hated that.

When Saturday rolled around, my stomach roiled with nerves. I'd been too nervous to eat, too nervous to do much of anything besides the chores Lucy had assigned to me. I'd asked Evelyn if she wanted to go for a walk, but she told me her head was hurting.

Before leaving for the wedding, decked in my red gown, I stopped by her bedroom where she was watching Law and Order reruns. She blinked up at me from a flowered armchair that seemed as old as the inn, then her eyes glittered and she repeated, "*Que linda*" so many times, the tips of my ears glowed as bright as my dress.

"How are you feeling?"

"How are *you* feeling?" She narrowed her black eyes at me.

"Fine."

Her puckered brow told me she didn't believe me.

"I'm going to be late if I don't hurry." I bent over and kissed her forehead.

She caught my hand and squeezed it. "You'll tell me all about the wedding tomorrow?"

"Yes." I lingered by her bedroom door, staring at her calm, screen-lit profile.

What would happen to her if Liam didn't forgive me? Would Jeb and Lucy keep her on, or would they chase her away?

When she caught me staring, I razed the anxiety from my face and pasted on a smile. I shut the door before she could ask me what was wrong, then walked briskly away in case she decided to go after me.

Jeb, who'd been sitting in the office filling out a spreadsheet, followed me outside to await Frank. Even though the sun was beginning to arc down, it was a couple million degrees out, yet the heat did little to ward off the chill skittering over my bones.

"You don't have to stay out here with me, Jeb."

My uncle squinted at the setting sun. "Today's part of the Alpha contest, isn't it?"

"Yes."

He pursed his thinning lips. "Why are you still competing? Are you trying to prove something to someone?"

As I stared out at the sinking ball of fire that gilded the crowns of the tall pines, I nibbled on the inside of my cheek. "Not anymore."

"You really want this?"

I didn't answer him. Instead, I asked, "Is Everest mad at me?"

A frown touched Jeb's wrinkled brow. "Why would he be mad at you?"

Everest must not have shared what had happened to Heath if my uncle was asking me this.

When I failed to answer, Jeb said, "Lucy told me he got bad news. Apparently, Becca's parents have decided to take her off life support." He sighed. "So sad... She was so young and seemed like such a nice girl."

"Seemed? You didn't know her?"

"Not well. Everest didn't bring her around much. My son is a very private person." I felt him study me in silence for a long second. "Speaking of knowing people, Ness, how well do you know Evelyn?"

His frown made a tremor zing up my exposed spine. "Very well. Why?"

He hooked his thumbs through his belt loops, shifting from one loafered foot to the other.

"*Why?*" I repeated.

He stopped shifting. "The other day, a guest wanted to meet our new cook, and when I introduced them, the woman called her by another name—*Gloria*. Evelyn said she didn't know any Glorias, but her eye twitched. I'm no behavioral expert, but I think—"

"Evelyn's not a liar. She's never even been to Boulder." I was annoyed my uncle was trying to destroy my faith in the only person I trusted.

He nodded. "I was just putting it out there. In case—"

"You shouldn't put things out there if they're hurtful."

His mouth gaped a little. I could tell he wanted to say more on the subject, but my expression must've dissuaded him. Thankfully, a car rumbled up the driveway. Frank was coming. When I spotted giant wheels, the relief I'd felt evaporated.

It wasn't Frank who was picking me up.

The car slowed to a stop next to me. Lucas was riding shotgun, decked out in a black tux that strained in the shoulders. He had his arm slung out the open window.

"Hey, Mr. Clark."

"Hi, boys." My uncle inclined his head before pulling open the back door and holding out a hand to help me up. "You're all looking mighty dapper tonight."

"Well, you know the Pines and their hoity-toity events."

Jeb offered a small smile that didn't reach his eyes. "You boys keep my niece safe, now. I don't like the look of them young'uns."

"Oh, Ness doesn't need us for that," Lucas drawled. "Especially now that she's besties with Julian's niece."

Jeb blinked at me. "You're friends with Sarah Matz?"

"Is that not allowed?" I wasn't in a good mood. Not at all. But it had little to do with Lucas's comment and everything to do with Jeb's.

"Is Ness ever in a good mood?" Lucas asked my uncle.

I growled as I strapped myself in.

My uncle didn't answer Lucas, too busy scrutinizing my face.

Evelyn wouldn't lie to me.

She wasn't a woman called Gloria.

"Are you sensing you're going to fail miserably? Is that it?" Lucas chirped.

Liam glanced into his rearview mirror, and our eyes met for the briefest of moments. I looked away before he did.

"You're so astute at reading people, Lucas." I didn't want to fight with him tonight.

He simpered at me before rubbing his hands together. "Should we get this party on the road? I'm dying for some canapés or whatever dainty shit the Pines feed on."

The entire way to Julian's estate, Liam didn't speak once, but there was never a dull moment, because Lucas was a freaking word-mill. The boy *loved* the sound of his voice.

When we passed through the gates that were manned by two burly wolves in skin, I nibbled on my lip before remembering I'd slicked on bright-red lipstick to match my dress. I checked my reflection in my phone's camera, fixed my lipstick, then smoothed the glossy curls I'd made with my mom's old flat iron after watching ten tutorials on YouTube and failing nine times out of the ten at recreating them.

Julian's home loomed at the top of a knoll like a pale cloud. During the ride over, Lucas had informed me the Pine Alpha's inspiration had been a French castle.

"The dude thinks he's a fucking king," Lucas had said.

As I took in the smooth stone façade and the grid of diamond-cut window panes that seemed to stretch an entire acre long, I had to agree with Lucas—Julian definitely fancied himself a sovereign.

A valet dressed in black pants and a high-collared red jacket drew open my door and held out a gloved hand. Before I could latch onto it, Liam rounded the car, stepped in front of the parking attendant, and extended his own hand.

I hesitated to touch him, and he sensed it because his gaze grew stormy. He didn't lower his hand, though. He held it out stubbornly. I gathered the folds of red chiffon in one hand and then yielded to Liam's will, grasping his fingers. Angering him would work against me when I pleaded for my life.

As soon as my feet touched the ground, I removed my fingers from his. His shoulders tightened, creasing the fine fabric of his tuxedo. Lucas walked ahead of us through the mammoth front doors, his head swiveling from right to left. Either he was ascertaining threats or he was admiring Julian's black-marbled lair. Gold finishes accented the dark furnishings, and crystal vases overflowing with scarlet roses adorned every table in sight.

"Did Julian ever marry?" I asked.

"Why? Are you interested?" Lucas shot back.

I rolled my eyes but caught Liam observing me. Even though I hadn't planned on answering Lucas's inane question, Liam's weighty stare made me say, "Of course not. He could be my father."

"I didn't think age mattered to you," Lucas said.

I snapped my attention to the shaggy-haired male who drove me insane. "Can you cut me some slack tonight, Lucas? I'm really not in the mood."

A server approached us with a platter of champagne flutes. I grabbed one and downed it in a very un-ladylike manner. I didn't care, though. Tonight was going to be rough, and I needed as much liquid courage as I could get. I set the stemmed glass back down on the man's platter before emerging from the black entrails of the house onto the packed terrace.

A hush fell over the crowd as all heads swiveled toward us. Although many stared my way, most looked at Liam. Between his chiseled jaw, his artfully gelled hair, and his black tux, he looked like he'd just stepped out of a GQ spread. Perhaps that wasn't the reason they looked at him, but I bet it was the reason why some of them *kept* staring.

The unremitting gurgle of water from a large round fountain projected noise against the mosaic-tiled floor, chipping away at the oppressive silence. I inhaled slowly, trying to iron out my nerves, but all that did was fill my lungs with the sickly-sweet smell of the roses spilling over the flat wooden trellis that roofed part of the terrace. Orange dregs of sunlight slid around the velvety petals and sharp thorns, dappling the crowd in shards of light. Candles flickered on tall skinny tables wrapped in white cloth, and glowing spheres of frosted glass hung from the trellis like miniature moons.

Lucas stood close to me; Liam even closer. Both narrowed their eyes at the quiet, observant crowd. Julian appeared then, in an emerald tux. He pressed past his people to reach us, a tumbler in one hand, a woman in the other. First I thought the woman was his date, but the resemblance between them was so uncanny that I guessed she was Sarah's mother.

"Welcome, welcome." His voice trumpeted out of him, cheerful and loud. "My sister Nora and I are so glad you could make it." He let go of his sister's hand to take mine and lifted it to his lips. "Ness, there are no words to describe how you look tonight."

"I can think of a few," Lucas muttered. "Red, for example. Half-naked."

"What a poet you are, Mr. Mason," Julian said, tossing a chilly glance Lucas's way. "The women must just love you."

"They do actually."

Liam shifted to stand in front of me, which forced Julian to let go.

A broad smile curled over Julian's face.

"Well, aren't we a little possessive?" he said under his breath.

Liam didn't answer.

Thankfully, Lucas spoke. "Frank and Eric aren't here yet, are they?"

"You are the first to arrive." Julian's eyes sparked as newcomers made their way onto the twinkling patio. "Mingle and be merry." He took his sister's arm, and together they walked to greet their new guests.

Soft string music started up again. Although the Pines remained alert, tossing sporadic glances our way, conversations resumed.

"Is he expecting us to actually chat with his people?" Lucas muttered to Liam.

"Damn, girl, I was right." A burst of yellow popped into my line of sight. Sarah walked over to us, blonde corkscrews tumbling over the buttercup dress that stuck to her curves like a bandage.

She pressed a kiss to my cheek, which had Lucas and Liam gaping. They'd heard we were friends, but apparently they didn't believe it.

"You Neanderthals clean up nicely, too," she said.

Lucas, who'd grabbed a glass of champagne from a passing tray, choked on his drink. "Neanderthal?"

I grinned.

"Yes. Neanderthal. Especially you, Mason," Sarah said. "From what I hear, you're a particularly devolved male specimen."

Lucas's eyes turned a neon shade of blue. "Figures you and Ness get along. Both shrews."

"Lucas..." Liam said.

Lucas turned on his friend. "What? I'm not the one tossing around hurtful observations."

"Was shrew supposed to be a compliment?" Sarah asked.

Lucas smirked. "Compared to what I was really thinking, yes."

Her eyes glittered with mirth.

"Are you deejaying tonight?" Liam asked, and I wondered how painful it was for him to act convivial.

"After dinner, I'm on."

"Damn. I forgot my earplugs." Lucas downed his champagne.

"Oh, I saw you dancing to my beats on Thursday night."

"Must've mistaken me for someone else. I don't dance."

"Not well, but you do."

Lucas rolled his fingers into a fist and cracked his knuckles. "Why were you even looking at me, blondie?"

"It's part of the job. I keep an eye on my crowd. I need to make sure you're all hearing what you want to hear."

"Then you're reading me all wrong."

Sarah crossed her arms in front of her. "Really? What is it you want to hear?"

He scraped his hand through his black hair. "Anything but that crap you play."

"You're an ass, Mason," she said. "A real ass." They glared at each other for so long I started to pull her aside, but she stood her ground.

"Sarah, darling! Come greet our guests." Nora's voice rang over the courtyard.

Still glaring, my friend whipped around and strode over toward her mother and uncle.

"Is it completely impossible for you to be nice, Lucas?" I asked.

His gaze, which had trailed after Sarah, snapped back toward me. "Are her lips and tits even real?"

"Oh my God, shut up," I said.

"What? Am I not allowed to ask? They don't look real."

"Lucas—" Liam started.

"Don't tell me you weren't wondering the same thing..." Lucas turned to look at Sarah again.

"I wasn't wondering the same thing," Liam said in a low voice.

Lucas shifted his attention back to his friend. "Right." His eyes flashed to me then to a waiter carrying a platter of mini club sandwiches. He grabbed three and chucked them into his mouth. "See you kids later."

I didn't ask where he was going, because I already knew. He was going to start the hunt for the piece of decaying wood.

After Lucas left, I asked Liam, "Shouldn't you go?"

"It would look suspicious if I left too, don't you think?" Liam peered at something beyond me.

I turned and found the focus of his attention—Justin and his two cronies from the music festival.

"Do you have any idea why the thing we're seeking is so important?" I asked softly.

Liam's gaze tracked back to my face, then lower, to my collarbone dusted with glittery powder. "No."

My heart scudded. "Not even a guess?"

He shook his head as he lifted his gaze back to mine. The intensity of his attention pressed my lungs hard against my ribcage. No one had ever looked at me so intently. Then again, no one had ever tried to see into my mind as desperately as Liam Kolane. I lowered my lids, hoping the delicate skin would hide my machinations just a little while longer.

39

Lucas returned a few minutes before the ceremony began—empty-handed and pissed. He shuffled past Frank and Eric and the latter's wife to reach the seat Liam had saved.

Lucas exchanged quiet words with his friend, probably telling him where he'd looked. No doubt remained in my mind that they were performing this test as a tag team.

Liam was about to sidestep past me, when he stopped and leaned in, his breath warming my earlobe. "I'm not being very polite. Why don't you go?"

Musk lifted off his smooth skin and slid into me, momentarily hazing my mind. God, he smelled so good. Why couldn't I just be repulsed by him? I tried to put some space between our bodies, but the backs of my knees hit the seat of the chair.

"I want to see what the bride is wearing." I sounded as hoarse as a heavy smoker.

Liam straightened, eyebrows casting shadows over his amber eyes. "Don't you want to beat me?"

"Just because I'm letting you go first doesn't mean I won't win."

The tendons in his neck shifted as he studied my face. Could he tell it was a lie?

He started to dip his head back toward my ear when the first notes of the wedding march began. All those who'd been sitting rose to their feet in a rustle of chiffon.

"You better go," I whispered.

Liam stepped past me and into the outer aisle, distancing himself quickly from the ceremony.

He returned after the ceremony, wearing a disgruntled expression. I took it he'd failed to locate the artifact.

"Wasn't the ceremony just marvelous?" Julian was standing in the petal-strewn aisle by our row.

"It was lovely," Eric's wife said, tucking a short white curl behind her ear.

Unlike Eric, Frank had come alone to the ceremony. Maybe he wasn't married. I realized I didn't know much about the elders. All I knew was that both men had had sons, but only Eric's was still alive, and both had fourteen-year-old grandsons who were part of the pack.

"Are there any weddings on the Boulder Pack horizon?" Julian asked.

Frank glanced at Lucas, then at Liam. "None of our boys are committing yet, but we'll be sure to keep you updated, Julian."

Our boys. Salt in my wound.

Julian smiled a frigid smile then turned his attention to me. "Ness, may I have the pleasure of your company before dinner begins?"

Prickling from Frank's exclusion, I moved past *his boys* and hooked my arm through Julian's extended one. I knew what it looked like but was too slighted to care. We drifted away from the festivities, toward the glossy green hedges forming a manicured maze.

"Ah...the Boulders and their boys." Julian let out a soft snort. "It's a real shame wolves can't pledge their allegiances to another pack. I'd welcome you with open arms."

"That's kind of you, Mr. Matz."

"Julian, please. Mr. Matz makes me sound like an old college professor with a penchant for tweed." He wrinkled his nose. "How's the contest going?"

"It's going." I lowered my gaze to the red chiffon swirling around my ankles.

"Then why are you putting off competing?"

I faltered and would've faceplanted if he hadn't been holding me up. It didn't help that my skinny heels kept burying themselves in the soft earth. "I'm not putting it off—"

"Ness, spare me the lie. I'm not an idiot. While Lucas and Liam roamed my house, you stayed planted on my lawn like a gloomy poppy."

He led me around a sharp, leafy corner, then around another. I was disoriented. Not only by the thriving labyrinth, but also by his admission. He knew why we were here. How? I opened my mouth but not to speak. Just to gape.

"Did you assume my invitation to attend my nephew's wedding was sent out of geniality?"

I tried to shut my jaw, but it hung open, its hinges shattered by shock.

"I possess something dear to your pack, and McNamara knows it. It was a matter of time before he sent his *boys* to retrieve it."

I finally got my mouth to work. "But how... How did you know it would be part of the contest?"

"I made sure it became a part of it by tendering an invitation onto my estate."

A loud squawk sounded. I raised my eyes to the sky to spot the bird capable of releasing such an ear-splitting sound but saw nothing flying overhead.

"If I'd been Frank, and your pack held something of mine, instead of breaking and entering, I'd jump on the opportunity to stroll through the front door."

"So your pack really did steal it?" I whispered into the dusky air.

"No."

"But then...how—"

"Someone gave it to me in exchange for a favor. I knew it was of great importance because Heath had paid me a visit a couple days before he died to demand I return it to him. At that point, I had no idea what in God's good name he'd been raving about. But of course, his request rendered me extraordinarily curious. And when what he'd been pursuing dropped into my lap some time later...well, you can imagine my absolute delight."

Julian stopped walking, pulling me to a stop too. He frowned and released my arm. I assumed someone was coming but heard no footsteps, smelled no other body. Then again, it was difficult to smell much of anything over the sour scent wafting in the air. He reached around me to pluck a leaf that stuck out from the smooth green wall of vegetation.

The reason we'd stopped.

My skin turned bitterly cold as I realized that if I stepped out of the line he'd drawn for me, he'd probably snap my neck like he'd snapped that poking imperfection.

Julian returned his attention to me. I took a step back, my bare shoulder blade brushing against the bristly hedge. What had gotten into me to follow him deep into a maze he knew like the palm of his hand?

The sky had dimmed to a periwinkle blue that matched Julian's eyes as he drank in my dread like a man savoring a delectable vintage.

He held out his arm. "Shall we?"

I swallowed, forcing my limbs to move, even though the mere thought of touching Julian had goose bumps pebbling my arm.

As we started walking again, he said, "Shortly before we met, I contacted McNamara to let him know I held what Heath had been so desperately seeking and promised to hand it over if he explained its importance."

My throat moved with another swallow. "He mustn't have told you if you still have it."

He tsked. "Ye have little faith in me, Miss Clark."

My eyes widened, soaking up the silvery outline of his gelled hair. "He told you?"

"Yes."

"But you didn't return it."

Another loud squawk. I tipped my head upward again.

"I had every intention of giving it back—until I heard what they used it for. Then I had every intention of destroying it, but I held off, waiting for a new Alpha to rise to power in your pack. It is more challenging to barter with ashes."

"What do they use it for?"

Julian stopped walking again, but this time, it was simply to face me. "Have you really no idea?"

I shook my head.

"They grate the wood into the drink pledges have to ingest the day they join your pack."

I frowned.

"Have you never wondered why only males are born to the Boulder Pack? Did you truly think it was an evolutionary trait like your elders claim?"

The world held still for a moment, and then it tipped. Julian slid his palms underneath my elbows to hold me upright.

"I hope this will renew your desire to compete."

A gust of wind cartwheeled through the maze, blowing against the glossy leaves that waved at me like tiny hands. Anger bloomed in my chest, chasing away the chilling numbness I'd felt all week long.

"Once you become Alpha, you can destroy it and change the course of your pack's future."

Color must've seeped into my cheeks, because Julian raised a wide smile that barely crimped his too-smooth, too-shiny brow.

He leaned in close. "Shall I tell you where I'm keeping it hidden?"

"Why are you helping me?"

"I've already told you. I want a friend in your pack, and I think you'd make a good friend."

"You already have Everest."

"I would not call your cousin a friend. Merely an effective purveyor. But if you'd rather not be my friend, then—"

"Where is the damn stick?"

A slow smile drew his pouty lips upward, revealing the perfectly polished enamel of his teeth. "That's my girl."

"I'm no one's girl."

He scraped a dry finger against my cheek. His hand smelled so strongly of acetone and lotion it momentarily dispelled the repulsive scent blistering the air.

I bristled away from his touch.

"Take every right turn from now on. At the center of this maze, you'll find the cage in which I keep my glorious pets. What you're looking for is inside."

A cage? Was that the source of the squawking and revolting reek?

Julian handed me a little key. "You will be needing this."

I closed my fingers around the gold key and started walking away when Julian called out to me.

"After you were born, your father came to me."

I didn't turn around, but I waited, spine tight.

"He asked if I could enlighten him as to why he'd been given a daughter."

"He must not have drunk the celebratory concoction," I said drily.

"Perhaps. Anyway, at the time, I didn't have an answer for him. I told him he should ask his Alpha. He told me that he had. Would you like to know what Heath told him?"

"He instructed him to kill me and try again. Oh... and he also suggested a paternity test." My tone dripped with acid.

The ensuing silence told me Julian hadn't expected me to answer.

But then his voice rose again. "I know you feel guilt, Ness. I sense it weighing heavily on your shoulders. Cast it away. Heath Kolane was not a good man. Besides, think of your father. Think of what a victory it would've been for him to see you, his strong, beautiful daughter, rise to the highest rank of a pack who cast her away because of her gender."

My heart hardened to steel. My resolve too. I didn't delude myself into thinking Julian was my friend. He was an oily, manipulative man, but he'd just given me two tools—courage and knowledge—to right one of the many wrongs inside my pack, and for that I was grateful.

I started up again and took the first right.

The first of many rights.

40

Even if Julian hadn't shared the directions to his birdcage, I would've found it from the smell. His vibrant-colored and cacophonous parrots reeked. As I approached their cage, eyes prickling from the aggressive stench, I lifted a hand to block my nose.

No wonder he'd hidden the fossilized wood inside. The birds' awful stink would cover up the artifact's. I wasn't sure what the old thing I needed to find would look like and regretted not having asked what color it was or where it rested in the cage. When Julian had mentioned a cage, I'd imagined a smallish thing, not one I could step into without hunching over.

The birds turned their beady black eyes toward me, growing still and quiet at my advance. I uncovered my nose and sniffed the air for what I needed to find. My eyes watered, but I kept sniffing, strolling slowly around the cage. I caught a whiff of cold rot and stopped. Both parrots had swiveled their neckless heads to watch me, their sharp beaks buried deep in their puffy red chests.

I crouched to see if the smell emanated from the wood-chipped floor. My nose burned. The rancid odor was definitely worse below. In the pale light of the moon, I tracked my gaze over the woodchips until I found a disturbance in their evenness. Something glinted among the dull carpeting like polished bone.

Pressing one palm over my nose, I made my way back around the cage to the door and slid the key into the lock. When the latch clanked open, I pushed the door open and slipped inside, shutting it back quickly so Julian's prized pets didn't flock out. Keeping one eye out on the quiet birds, I moved toward the irregular patch of flooring and dug out what I'd seen.

Thick. Yellowed. Shiny. Putrid.

The key to gender selection.

How had anyone been able to swallow a drink sprinkled with this was beyond me. I would've thrown up at the mere smell.

Perhaps that's what had happened to my father. Perhaps he'd thrown up the vile thing.

I wrapped my fingers lightly around the disgusting object and exited the birdcage. The parrots hadn't fluttered a single feather. I turned the key, then buried it in the palm that wasn't holding the Boulder relic.

As I turned, I bumped into a body.

A tall, broad body with glowing yellow eyes.

41

Liam stood in front of me, jaw so hard it could cut glass.

My pulse raged from his presence, from his nearness.

"You found it." The low timbre of his voice rolled toward me. He was angry. Terribly angry.

I pressed the key harder into my palm. "I did." I should probably have dropped the key into the grass and prayed he wouldn't see its shine, but I didn't drop it. I didn't dare move. "You've arrived too late."

"You wouldn't have had any help, would you now?"

"Would it matter? The rule of the game was to find the artifact. They didn't specify our method for finding it."

A rough smile perched on his lips. "You're good, Ness. Sneaky, even."

I tried to step around him, but he blocked my advance. "Get out of my way, Liam."

"You cheated."

I glared up at him defiantly. "I used my connection to find it. How is that cheating?"

"Your connection...or your mouth?"

I uncurled my fingers from the piece of wood. It tumbled onto the grass at the same time as my hand flew into Liam's jaw.

How could I ever have considered letting him win? "I've never ever touched a man that way!"

"Then why is Julian helping you?" he asked, rubbing his jaw.

"Maybe because he thinks I'd make a better Alpha than any of you." I crouched to pick up the fossil. Woodchips had caught in the hem of my dress, but I didn't bother brushing them off. My hands trembled too fiercely to do much more than focus on clutching the key and the wood.

I shook my head as I rose and passed by him, knocking my shoulder into his chest on purpose.

"You're going the wrong way."

"It's away from you, so it must be right." My vision had tunneled from anger and adrenaline. I'd find my way outside of this maze eventually. I was in no rush. I walked briskly, my heels poking into the ground and popping out. I took every left turn I could find. Instead of finding myself on the great lawn, I found myself back in front of the birdcage.

I growled out of frustration.

At least Liam was gone.

I tried again, this time focusing. I remembered I'd emerged from the maze on the side facing the cage door, so I walked back that way, and then I took a left, and another left, and another. On the ground beneath my feet I spotted the spindly branch Julian had ripped. Bolstered by the knowledge I was heading in the correct direction, I concentrated on recalling how I'd gotten to that point. It took me three attempts to figure it out.

When I burst out of the maze, I released a deep breath but then sucked in air anew when I caught sight of my welcoming committee.

Liam, Lucas, and Frank stood there. All of them had their arms crossed.

"What? No applause?" Apparently anger made me snarky.

"You had help," Lucas said.

I shot my gaze to Liam who met it straight on. He didn't even flinch. "Perhaps I did, but as far as I can remember, that wasn't forbidden."

Lucas whipped his head to shift his hair off his forehead. "That's cheating."

"I didn't come up with this test, Lucas. The elders did."

"Frank, come on..." Lucas said, untying his arms and waving his hands around. "You can't let her win."

I fixed my gaze on Frank and dared him to disqualify me.

Slowly, his chest rose with a sigh. Even more slowly his lips parted, and he said, "Let me see it."

"Can't you smell it?" I was pretty certain the odor would never wash away from my skin, even if I dipped my hand in bleach.

"I need to ascertain it's whole."

I raised my chin up a little higher and walked closer. I held out my palm and opened my fingers. When he tried to pluck it out, I snapped my fingers closed around the noxious wood and hid it behind my back. "I'm not giving it back."

Frank cocked a bushy eyebrow. "If you don't give it back, you'll be disqualified."

"I know what it does," I said, shaking with anger.

He dipped his chin into his neck. "I assumed as much."

"How could you use this? How could you perpetuate such savagery?" I murmured disgustedly.

Liam and Lucas turned their attention to Frank.

"Could we discuss this in private, Ness?"

"Why? Are you afraid of how *your boys* will react, Mr. McNamara?"

One of his eyes twitched. "No. Actually, go ahead and tell them. This shouldn't be a secret anymore."

He was bluffing. He had to be bluffing. The Alphas and elders had kept this a secret for a century.

"It's too late anyway," he said. "For their generation at least, it's too late."

"What does it do?" Liam asked.

Frank raised his gaze to me. "Shall I tell them, or should I leave you that honor?" When I didn't move my lips, Frank said, "A trifling amount of the wood is mixed into your pledge drinks. It destroys female sperm."

Both Liam's and Lucas's eyes widened. Both their mouths gaped. They'd really had no idea.

"Genius," Lucas said.

I balked at his answer. But of course he'd find it genius. I looked at Liam, waited to see his reaction, but besides a slackening of his stance, he didn't utter a single word.

"Not the reactions you were expecting, are they?" Frank said.

To think my father had had to answer to him as a boy.

"Do you also find it genius?" I asked Liam, loathing how desperate I was for him to say no.

He blinked but didn't speak.

"I don't think the pack could've dealt with more girls," Lucas said, which made Frank's lips quirk up.

I wanted to whack the smile off his face and almost swung the yellowed fossil into his cheek, but I held myself back.

"At least," Frank said, serious again, "we don't kill off female embryos like they do in the other packs. Because that's what happens in the other packs. Women interrupt pregnancies when they find out their offspring is female."

"Not the Pines."

"*Even* the Pines. Why do you think there aren't as many females to males in their pack? They just cover it up better than the other packs."

"That's a lie."

"No, Ness. It isn't a lie."

I wanted to growl, and I did.

Frank held out his hand. "Last chance to stay in this contest."

Shaking my head, I slapped the rancid stick against his palm. He could have his evil gender selection tool back. If I became Alpha, I'd destroy it. And if I didn't rise to the top, I wouldn't have to worry about the damn thing, because I would no longer be part of the Boulder Pack.

"Did Callum not drink it, Frank?" Liam asked. "Is that why he had Ness?"

I held my breath.

"He drank it," Frank said, "but it made him sick. We believe that's why it didn't work on him."

I released the captive air, hating how much relief Frank's explanation brought me.

"Aw, man..." Lucas grumbled. "I had a bet going that Ness wasn't a Boulder."

"You bet that my mom cheated on my dad?"

"Lucas," Frank chided him. "Not only is that inappropriate but—"

"Oh come on, Mr. McNamara. Wasn't that one of the reasons Heath didn't accept Ness's pledge? Because he wanted to spare her the heartache of uncovering her heritage through a communication glitch?"

"What are you talking about?" I all but snarled.

"If you're not a Boulder," Lucas said, "you won't hear the Alpha."

Silence caked the warm breeze. I tucked a long tendril of hair behind my ear before remembering the hand I used had been the one to clutch the pack artifact. The lingering stench made my eyes water.

"Do you also doubt my lineage, Mr. McNamara?" I asked.

Frank hooked a finger into his black bowtie and tugged as though it were on too tight. "Your mother was a good woman."

A non-answer.

"I suppose we'll find out for sure if you win, Ness," Lucas continued. "If none of us can hear you—"

"Enough! Enough." Frank's face was so red it made his eyebrows appear whiter. "Who will you choose as your opponent for the last test, Ness?"

I hated the uncertainty that had again crawled underneath my skin. I exhaled an annoyed breath, then looked at Lucas and Liam—a rock and a hard place.

I finally made my choice.

"Liam," I said. "I pick Liam."

And then I walked away, finding my way home the same way I'd found my way out of the maze.

Alone.

42

I'd tried to drown my overactive mind in a book, but to no avail. After three pages, the contents of which had pinged against my skull without leaving a trace, I tossed the book aside and turned off the light on my nightstand. I shut my eyes and prayed sleep would devour me.

But it didn't. My nerves were too raw to sleep.

"Oh, Mom," I murmured. "Whose child am I?" A tear slid down my nose and into my pillow.

I rolled onto my back, and then I stared at the immaculate white paint on the ceiling, crumpling my comforter between my fingers. I felt a nonsensical bout of nostalgia for the water stains that had adorned our ceiling back in Los Angeles.

A knock on my window had my pulse spiking. I sat up quickly, and the world spun. Had I imagined it? Another knock, this time more insistent. I got out of bed slowly, swiping my room key off my desk and fitting it between clenched fingers.

Who would knock on my window? Everest maybe—

I drew the drapes open.

Liam stood on my balcony, barely distinguishable from the night in his dark clothes. Only his face stood out, pale as the moon behind him.

Nerves shrilled in my ears, and I shut my curtains.

"Ness, let me in." He banged on the glass again, and I felt his fist inside my chest. "I'll wake up the whole damn inn if you don't let me—"

I shoved the curtains aside and opened the door, and then I backed away from him, fingers wrapped tightly around the key.

He thrust the door closed so hard it sucked in a piece of beige curtain.

He scowled as his gaze caught the glint of metal in my fist. "I'm not here to hurt you."

I didn't loosen my grip on my makeshift weapon. "Why are you here then?"

"I'm here for answers." He inhaled a rough breath. "Why are you Julian's puppet?"

"I'm not his puppet."

"Oh, come on!" Liam smacked an open palm on my desk. I jumped. "You vanish into a fucking maze with him, and then you come back out all victorious and smug."

"Is it so hard to believe he might enjoy my company?"

Liam let out a cruel laugh. "It is, actually." His voice was hostile. "Julian is a manipulative bastard, and don't tell me you don't realize that, because you might be a lot of things, Ness, but you're not dumb. Now, please tell me what the fuck is going on, because I am this close"—he held out his index finger and thumb, which were a hairbreadth's away from touching—"to my breaking point."

I pressed my lips shut, not to keep my confession from sliding out, but to keep Liam from seeing how they trembled. I squared my shoulders for the same reason.

"Did you think Lucas wouldn't kill me? Is that it?" he asked.

My heart punched my ribcage. "What?"

"Don't tell me you weren't aware that the last test is a kill game."

Those two words should never have been part of the same sentence. "A-A kill game?"

A shadow lapsed over Liam's brow. "Winner takes all. Including loser's life."

The key tumbled out of my slack fingers and clinked against the wooden floor.

His eyebrows writhed in surprise. "What? You didn't know?"

"They're going to—" I swallowed, but it did little to displace the lump expanding like a vacuum bag inside my throat. "Make us—" I'd convinced myself I'd meet Liam's punishment with my chin raised high—whatever that punishment may be. But that was because I hadn't really believed he would kill me.

I wasn't ready to die.

I didn't want to die.

"Is this some sick joke?"

"No. It's not. I wouldn't joke about something like that." Liam raked his hand through his hair, ramming back a lock that had fallen over his forehead.

A thought whispered across my mind. He'd planned on selecting Lucas as his contestant. Had it been to spare me? "You would've been ready to kill Lucas?"

"I wouldn't have had to kill Lucas, because the elders would've let one of us concede. They wouldn't have wanted to eliminate a pack member."

His words trickled through me like grains of sand in an hourglass, and like those grains of sand, they were marking the time I had left.

I realized then that this was the perfect way to get rid of me for good. "But because it's me—a non-pack member—they'll take conceding off the table?" I swayed a little but caught myself on the back of my desk chair. My knuckles whitened. "Is that why you're here? To finish this stupid contest?"

His gaze turned a forbidding shade of black. "Do you really think I could kill you?"

Silence rang in my ears. "You want to become Alpha more than you want anything else, Liam, so yes, I think you *could* kill me."

He dropped down on the foot of my bed and let out a gravelly sigh. "It's true. I used to want it more than anything else. For my father, for the elders, there was no doubt I would be the next leader. It was what I was reared for."

I tucked a piece of hair behind my ear. My fingers shook. "And you'll make a great Alpha, Liam," I admitted softly. "I didn't use to think so. I assumed you were like Heath, and sometimes, you do remind me of him, but you also remind me of your mother, and she was a good woman who always cared for others more than she cared for herself. At least, that's what my mother told me. I don't remember her very well."

He snorted. "You don't have to be nice to me. I'm not going to kill you."

I released the chair and went to sit next to him on the bed. "I mean everything I just said." I twined my fingers together in my lap and marveled at how quickly my fingernails had grown back, how strong they'd become, almost as hard as my wolf claws. "I entered this contest to spite you but stayed in it because I'm proud and hated to be considered lower than low because I'm a girl. I wanted to prove to you, to the pack, and to myself that I was worth something, but I wasn't planning on even trying to win the last contest. That's why I picked you and not Lucas. Because... because I wanted *you* to win."

"Ness—"

"Let me finish." I squeezed my fingers together. "I don't want this, Liam. I don't want a pack that doesn't want me. And certainly not at the cost of a life."

I'd killed once.

Never again.

Never again.

"I'll leave Boulder and never come back. They can't make you kill me if I'm gone, right?" I turned my head to look at Liam, who was staring back, eyes wide.

"No."

"It won't work?"

He shifted, and one of his knees knocked into mine, creating a spot of heat on my cool skin. "You shouldn't have to leave your home because of me."

"*My home*?" I let out a soft snort. "I don't have a home here, Liam." I lifted my eyes to the untainted ceiling. "I live in a hotel. With an aunt who, for some reason, really despises me and an uncle who doesn't think very highly of me. My only friend was my cousin, but he up and left me. And my newest friend is a girl I keep being warned not to be friends with because she's the enemy. The only other person who was nice to me is off fighting in the Middle East. I might have a roof over my head, and a woman who cares about me like I was her own granddaughter, but I don't have a home."

One of Liam's hands came up to my face, his fingers cradling my chin, angling it toward him.

"You can't leave," he said, his voice a husky whisper.

"Why not?"

His warm breath rushed over my face. "Because then I'd spend my days tracking you down instead of focusing on the pack. What sort of Alpha would that make me?"

I lowered my lashes. "You think they'd make you track me down?"

"No one would make me do it."

The room was so quiet I heard him swallow.

"Do you...*feel* anything for me...besides contempt?" His lips worked on a smile but tumbled nervously back into a straight line.

"Would it change anything if I did?"

Emotion flared over his face, fast and bright like lightning. "It would change *everything*." He spoke the last word so slowly goose bumps erupted over my bare legs and arms, over the slice of bare stomach peeking between my sleep shorts and tank top. "Do you?"

The goose bumps breached my skin and skittered over my ribs. "What do you think?"

"I don't want to think; I want to know. Do you?" Even though his grip on my chin was gentle, his fingers were not. They dipped into my skin as though trying to leave marks.

"Yes," I whispered.

Before my next heartbeat, he'd splayed both his hands on my hips, lifted me, and propped me onto his lap. I bent my knees around his thighs. And then one of his hands was in my hair, his other on the base of my spine. And his lips...his lips were on mine, hard and soft, punishing and kind.

A series of explosions went off in me.

I was kissing Liam Kolane.

Liam Kolane was kissing me.

When his tongue swept over the seam of my mouth, my entire body rocked with a shiver. My hands, which had been resting lightly on his biceps, reached up to grip his shoulders. I burrowed my fingertips into his t-shirt, afraid that if I loosened my grip, I would tumble off him.

I parted my lips and took his tongue in. He growled into my mouth, his hands pressing harder into my skin. In his bruising grip, he scooped me up and stood. I locked my legs around him, locked my mouth on his. He walked to one side of the bed, knelt on the mattress, then lowered my body beneath his. Slowly I untangled my legs from around his waist and stretched them out underneath him. He braced himself on his forearms and pressed his lips against mine, tangling his tongue with mine.

Kissing Liam Kolane felt like running through a starlit field in my wolf form—the purest form of power and sensation there existed in this vast, dark world.

I ran my fingers over the runnel of his spine, then dipped my hands beneath the fabric of his black t-shirt to touch the warm, tanned skin I'd barely ever dared glimpse. His muscles roiled underneath my exploring hands; tendons pinched, flesh tensed.

He broke the kiss.

"Not fair," he whispered hoarsely.

I arched an eyebrow.

He rolled me over so that I was on top, so that his big hands could slip underneath my tank top.

"I've been dying to touch you, Ness. Every fucking inch of you. My turn."

His hands stroked my spine, the sides of my body, the indents of my waist before traveling upward, his thumbs trailing over my stomach, my ribcage, the underside of my breasts, stilling on my nipples. His touch sent so many tremors through my bent arms that I almost collapsed over him. He drew a line of kisses from the edge of my jaw all the way down to the hollow of my collarbone.

I moaned. Embarrassingly loud. And not just once.

He fit his mouth back over mine and swallowed the rest of my sounds, then slid his thumbs back down.

"You are so fucking perfect," he murmured against my lips.

Those words were my undoing. And not in any romantic way.

I began to cry, hundreds of tears.

If he knew what I'd done to his father, he wouldn't think me very perfect.

He wouldn't want to kiss me.

He wouldn't want to touch me.

"Hey." He slid me onto my side, then brushed his knuckles over my face to dry my wet cheeks. "Hey. What's going on?"

A savage sob raked up my chest, erupting from my mouth. I threw the back of my hand against my trembling lips and bit the thin skin to silence myself.

He combed a lock of hair behind my ear. "Tell me what's going on."

The words shivered on the tip of my tongue but never made it out. I couldn't tell him.

I tried to turn my face away from his, but he forced me to look at him.

"Do you also think my mother cheated on my father?" I croaked. It wasn't what had set me off, but it was troubling me almost equally.

The tension burst from his taut features in time with his breaths. "You have his dimples. And his smile."

Were dimples and smiles proof of genetic affiliation?

He caressed the side of my neck. "Is that all that's bothering you?"

I swallowed before I lied, "Yes."

"Good." He smiled, the slow scrape of his nails agonizingly pleasurable.

I shivered, and not because of how good his touch felt, but because I knew, with unfaltering doubt, that the next time his fingers would come in contact with my neck, it wouldn't be to caress it, but to snap it.

43

L iam left a little after midnight. I'd pretended to have fallen asleep so he wouldn't soil his lips further on mine. The guilt of having let him kiss me was tenfold-worse than the guilt of having drugged Heath.

In the gray hours of the morning, glum thoughts turned my mind the same dull shade as the sky. I got up and walked onto my balcony. A warm wind combed through the tall evergreens, making them shiver, making me shiver. My skin itched to shift, and I let it. I pulled off my tank top and sleep shorts and transformed into my other self, and then I jumped over the balcony and raced away from the inn, not caring if any guest had awakened. They all looked forward to wolf sightings anyway.

The lavender sky was no longer littered with stars, and the air was calm, abuzz with the beating wings of oblivious things. By a stream, I ran into a herd of mule deer. Even though I meant them no harm, their perky ears twitched at my approach. When their large, shiny eyes zeroed in on me, they pranced away in a blur of gray-brown fur.

I watched them leave, like everything else in my life.

Only Evelyn remained.

Evelyn...

I needed to get back to her. I needed to speak to her. But what would I tell her? I hadn't decided what to do. To leave or to stay?

I stared at the horizon.

I *could* run.

Right now, I could run. As a wolf, I'd cover a lot of ground.

But Liam could run too. I had no doubt he'd track my scent with ease. Even if I had hours on him, his legs were so much longer than mine that he'd catch up. And then what?

A fly buzzed by my ear, droning loudly. I flicked my ears.

If I could get away, I'd have to relearn to live only as a human, my body frozen in a single shape. I'd done it once. I could do it again, but did I want to? The need to shift had become visceral, part of me, like the blueness of my irises and the blondeness of my hair.

I watched the horizon as it yellowed and greened, and then I turned and started to run back, savoring each tread of dewy earth, each crunch of crumbling rock, each crush of springy grass. I breathed in heavy lungfuls of the sweet dawn, cherishing them as though each breath were to be my last.

I thought of Liam. Of his mouth and hands. And my muscles swelled with adrenaline. I was thankful for last night. Thankful to have felt desired. I almost wished I hadn't pretended to sleep, that I'd stripped Liam of his clothes and let him peel mine off my body so I would finally know what so many accused me of taking against payment.

But it would've been greedy and unfair.

I was grateful for what we'd shared, even though I was haunted by the hatred he'd feel once he knew who the girl he'd called *perfect* truly was.

Ahead of me stretched the hedge of pines that separated me from the inn like a picket fence. I slowed.

If these were to be my last moments in wolf form, I'd savor each second.

I MADE it back to the inn without being discovered, leaping onto the little balcony Liam had scaled just a few hours ago. I trotted back into my bedroom, my claws clicking on the hardwood floors, and then I changed back.

Swift as it had appeared, my fur retracted, leaving behind flushed skin. Sweat salted my lips. I licked it away as I pushed off the ground and rose to my feet. I headed toward the shower but stopped when I spotted a folded sheet of paper by my bedroom door. Muscles tensing, I approached and snatched the letter up, unfolding it in the same breath.

IF YOU WANT TO SEE EVELYN AGAIN,

GO THROUGH WITH THE LAST TRIAL.

SPEAK ABOUT THIS NOTE AND SHE DIES.

My fingers turned as cold and hard as ice chips and crimped the paper. I read the words; reread them. The letters blurred and fragmented, then knit back together and smoothed.

Who would do this to me?

Someone who was aware of how much I cared for Evelyn. I'd never made it a secret, but still...how many people possessed this knowledge? She so rarely left the inn that it would have to be someone close to me.

Who could possibly want to blackmail me into killing Liam?

Or was their intention to get *me* killed by Liam?

Could it be Julian? He'd guessed Liam cared about me—made several allusions to it last night—and wouldn't want to murder me, which would force *me* to kill Liam and become the Alpha Julian so desperately desired as an ally.

But Julian didn't know about Evelyn. Or did he? I'd told Sarah about her when we'd had lunch. Had Sarah been spying for her uncle? Was her friendship an act?

My stomach turned as cold as my fingers.

But Julian had seen how determined I was last night. He couldn't possibly know I'd chicken out of the last test. Unless he'd heard what it entailed...

Something hardened inside my mind. Whoever sent me this note knew what the last test would be. They knew blood would be spilled. Mine or Liam's. Whose death were they rooting for?

Lucas hated me and had never hidden how much he wanted Liam to become Alpha. It wouldn't have been difficult for him to find out about my relationship with Evelyn. I could go to him and confess my plan, but if he hadn't sent me the note...

I brought the paper closer to my nose—crushed flowers. The scent could've drifted from the dirt embedded underneath my fingernails. I sniffed the paper again. There was another scent. Something almost sour but also a little sweet. I inhaled so many times that my head started to spin, and all the smells melded together. I crumpled the paper and tossed it against the door.

A violent chill curled around my skin but was soon replaced with heat. My body smoldered with anger. One person would die today...and it wouldn't be me or Evelyn or Liam.

It would be whoever fucking wrote this.

44

I tossed on the first things I found in my closet and then flew through my bedroom door.

Evelyn's door was unlocked, her bed unmade. Whoever had taken her had snatched her from sleep, because she always made her bed. I touched the creased pillow—cold. And then I crouched next to the bed. The fabric smelled faintly of menthol but also of something else—cold smoke.

Evelyn didn't smoke.

Which meant her captor did.

My phone vibrated in the back pocket of my shorts. I straightened up, staring at the unknown number flashing on my screen. Could it be the kidnapper?

Slowly, I slid my finger across the screen to answer the call. "Hello."

"Ness? It's Frank."

His voice shrink-wrapped my hope.

"McNamara," he added.

As though I could've forgotten… "What is it, Mr. McNamara?"

"We'd like you to meet us at your father's old factory. The one the Watts took over."

Blood beat against my skin, making every inch of it tingle. Just what I needed. A trip down memory lane. "Why?"

"We need to discuss a…*development* with the pack."

I looked toward the sash windows that gave onto the employee parking lot. When we'd arrived, I'd tried exchanging my room with Evelyn's so she could have a better view, but she insisted that being on the ground floor was better for her. I didn't see how it had benefited her in any way considering she so rarely went out.

The edge of Evelyn's curtain fluttered. I lunged forward and drew it open so briskly a handful of tiny hooks ripped off the metal rod.

Heart twitching, I stepped into the parking lot.

"Ness? Are you still there?" Frank's voice sounded tinny.

"Yeah. I'm here." I shaded my sore eyes from the sun spiking through the fir trees lining the lot and scanned the premises.

"Liam came to speak with us."

My stomach knotted like a climbing rope. Had Liam asked them to cancel the last trial? Had he told them I was ready to concede? What would happen to Evelyn if they voided the contest?

"We need you to come see us. The pack is waiting for you. Your uncle said he could take you."

"Now?"

"Now."

His firm response made my fingers curl hard around the phone. "I'll be there as soon as I can."

The warm air smelled of car exhaust, rancid garbage, and evaporated dew. Dark stains dappled the asphalt. My heart gave a shudder. Forcing my stiff legs to bend, I crouched and sniffed.

Oil.

Not blood.

My phone vibrated with a message from an unknown number. Frank must've forgotten to tell me something.

The message said: **Tick tock.**

Not Frank.

A car honked so shrilly I bounced onto the balls of my feet. A black minivan with the Boulder Inn logo backed into the employee lot. Another honk. The strident sound shrilled in my skull.

"I tried to call your room," Jeb said, leaning out the driver's side window to peer at me. "What are you doing out here?"

"I stopped by to see Evelyn."

I watched his face as I said this. He glanced toward the open window, but didn't ask me how she was doing. Did he know she wasn't there?

"Did Frank get ahold of you? The pack's expecting us at the Watts's warehouse."

"I had him on the phone."

"Are you ready to go?"

No. I wasn't ready, but did I have a choice? I threw open the passenger door and got in.

Tick. Tock. The words echoed through me at the same time as a deafening deliberation. My aunt was a heavy smoker.

"Where's Lucy?"

"She's with Everest."

"Where?" My voice was so brusque my uncle frowned.

"I don't know, Ness."

Could Lucy have taken Evelyn? Forcing me to compete in a death match would be a convenient way of getting rid of me. I stuck my elbow on the door handle and cradled my pounding forehead.

"I wish you'd listened to me." My uncle's voice broke, and a thick sob lurched out of him. "I wish you'd never entered this contest."

I pried my head off my fingertips.

My uncle was crying.

Over *me*.

He was crying over me.

Surprise momentarily displaced my raging edginess.

"I failed your mother," he croaked, wiping his eyes.

I didn't think anyone besides Evelyn would ever mourn my death, but apparently I was wrong. Apparently Uncle Jeb would.

"I'm not dead yet." My words were thin, flat. I couldn't deal with his grief or his remorse. Not now. Maybe not ever. To each their own. "Can we please just go? I want to get this over with…"

That set him off all over again. Hearing a grown man cry used to irk me, but as I sat there, watching the tears drip around his mouth, I was numb.

When he still hadn't started driving, I repeated, "Can we please go?"

He inhaled deeply, stared at my stony expression, and finally…finally started driving.

The world smeared into one long strip of color outside the window. I hadn't taken this road in years. It had changed. There was still the Mom and Pop ice-cream shop with the flickering neon cone and the gas station—empty at this early hour, but new buildings had sprouted on the sunburned grass. All of them carried the word Watt.

August and his father had expanded the business. I was glad it had been so profitable even though seeing their name on those plaques instead of my father's pinched my heart.

The flat-roofed gray warehouse—the original workshop—materialized in the distance. It looked the same as it had the dusty afternoon Mom and I had driven over to hand Nelson the keys and the deed.

Jeb parked in front of the loading bay, which was gaping wide. I climbed out of the van and then closed the door.

A figure stepped out of the shadowy workshop, cutting across the lot.

Liam. Mute sunlight played over his handsome face, danced across his lips.

My heart became very quiet. When he reached out for me, I took a step back. If he touched me, I'd break. Shading my eyes, I stared around the lot, then back at him, at the slant of his eyebrows.

He stared around the lot too. "Are you expecting someone?"

"No," I said fast.

Jeb came around the car. "Morning, Liam."

One glance at my uncle's tear-streaked face, and Liam's eyes widened, as though he understood my moodiness.

"The fight's off," he said. "But only if we both concede."

Uncle Jeb squinted his red-rimmed eyes. "Then who becomes Alpha?"

"Lucas," Liam said.

As though he'd heard his name, Lucas stepped out of the warehouse, his black hair devouring the rays of pale sun.

A chill swept up my spine. If he became Alpha, then Lucas wasn't the one blackmailing me.

Unless he didn't want the title.

No. He wanted it. Even though he wouldn't have willingly taken it from his friend, there was no way he would turn this down.

Maybe it really was Lucy, but wouldn't my uncle be aware of his wife's machinations?

Unless Julian was behind the whole thing.

"You need to tell the elders you're conceding." Liam placed his hand low on my back to guide me into the warehouse. His pressure was light, and yet I felt like his fingers were imprinting into my flesh.

Every set of eyes fixed on me. On Liam. On the place where his palm connected with my body.

The warehouse was so quiet. Or maybe I couldn't hear anything over the deafening sound of my thundering pulse. My phone vibrated in my pocket. I jumped. My gaze sped over every man and boy. I checked their hands for phones. None of them held one.

With rigid fingers, I extricated it from my pocket. The silicone cover caught on the crumpled note, which slipped out and tumbled onto the sprinkling of sawdust like a cluster of down. I watched in horror as my uncle crouched to retrieve it. Time slowed as he rose, the paper tucked in his palm.

The world tipped, and Liam's fingers curled around my waist.

"This fell out." Jeb handed it to me without so much as glancing at it.

My knuckles seemed to have fused with my phalanges, yet somehow, I managed to hold the paper and stuff it back into my pocket.

A groove materialized between Liam's eyebrows. It deepened when I stepped away from him to read my newest text message.

I tried to reason that it could be from anyone.

Maybe it was from August.

The number was unlisted. **I see you.**

Nothing else. Nothing more.

My throat locked up.

Someone touched my shoulder, and I jumped.

"Everything all right?" Jeb asked.

I powered off my phone. If they were watching me, that meant they were here. That meant they no longer had to communicate with me through enigmatic text messages. I wanted to yell at whoever was sick enough to toy with me to man up and step forward, but I didn't yell. I barely breathed.

"Has Liam filled you in on what we're offering?" Frank's white hair frizzed around his leathery face like a halo.

I gave a sharp nod.

Eric frowned at me, light pinging off his bald head. "It's a great sacrifice he's making to save your life."

"Do you forfeit, Ness?" Frank asked.

The cement floor shifted, yet everyone remained upright. The strips of lights on the ceiling droned like wasps. Mouths moved, but voices didn't reach my throbbing eardrums. I wanted to scream *yes, I forfeit*, but the words on my phone seared my corneas.

I. See. You.

Julian wasn't here.

Unless he was seeing me through a surveillance camera.

I swallowed, choking on my saliva. I coughed.

Liam stepped in front of me, face tipped down toward mine. "Ness?"

"No." The world lurched out of me like a bullet. "I don't forfeit."

Liam's gaze cut through me like a knife. "What are you doing?"

"But I want to fight in wolf form because I don't stand a chance in human form." I prayed Evelyn's captor wouldn't figure out the true reason I wanted to fight in wolf form.

"You're a cheat, Ness," Lucas hissed. He stood next to Matt. Matt who'd once looked at me with kindness. There was no more kindness in his green eyes. "If you win this, I will never answer to you."

Matt lowered his gaze and then he turned and stalked away, his big body graying in the shadows of the warehouse.

Frank glanced around him. After the other elders nodded, he said, "We agree to your terms."

"I don't agree to them," Liam blurted out.

"You'd rather fight in skin than fur?" I asked him.

His temper flared. "I'm not fighting you."

"Please."

"Please?" He scraped his hands over his face. "What's wrong with you?"

"Nothing's wrong with me. But something's obviously wrong with you if you don't fight for what you want."

"I *am* fighting for what I want."

That splintered my heart. My lids fluttered closed a moment. *Be strong. Be strong.* When I opened them, my resolve was back. "Should we shift, Mr. McNamara?"

"You may proceed. But remember, conceding will no longer be allowed after this."

I nodded, then kicked off my shoes and yanked off my tank top.

Liam stepped in front of me, blocking the sight of my body with his. He radiated anger. His taut muscles pulsed with it. "Ness, this is crazy."

I unbuttoned my shorts and let them fall to the floor. I didn't bother taking off my bra or underwear. I'd never get them back anyway.

The dead had no use for undergarments. Or any garments for that matter.

Before my teeth turned into fangs, I whispered, "Don't make me wait too long."

And then I dropped on all fours.
Come on, I begged, but all he would hear was a whimper.
As wolves, we understood human speech.
As humans, we didn't understand wolf speech.
I pawed at the sawdust, impatient for him to be able to hear my last confession.
My last apology.

45

Liam shouted something at Frank that I didn't try to understand. I was too busy looking around me to see if someone else would shift.

No one shed clothes. No one transformed. Most were too busy gaping between me and Liam.

Sawdust puffed beneath me as a black t-shirt hit the floor. I craned my neck up as Liam kicked off his jeans, swearing beneath his breath.

In seconds, he became a black beast with gleaming eyes.

Don't react at what I'm about to tell you, I said.

His nostrils flared.

I'm being blackmailed. Someone took Evelyn, and they said they would kill her if I didn't go through with the last trial.

He turned so still I bared my fangs and lashed at him, nipping his neck.

Fight me or they'll know I'm talking. I dug the tips of my fangs into his skin. *Damn it, Liam, figh—*

He released a blood-curdling snarl and then tossed me off him with a hard shrug. I yelped as I landed on my haunches, a pale cloud rising around me like smoke.

He advanced toward me.

They sent me a message saying, I see you. *So they're here. Or they're watching me somehow.*

When he started to turn his head—a dead giveaway I was talking—I launched myself on his back like an arrow. He wrung his massive body, and I tumbled off, falling hard on my spine. He stepped over me, pinning me to the ground.

What now? he growled. *'Cause I sure as hell won't kill you.*

Yes, you will.

A deep, guttural sound rose out of him and made my fur stand on end. *The fuck I am!*

You will once you know...once I tell you what I did.

He became as still as an ebony carving. *What did you do?*

I shut my lids so I wouldn't see his reaction. *I...I killed your father.* Nothing happened for so long that I peeked through my lashes at him. *I am the reason he's dead.*

His pupils turned pin-sized. *What are you talking about?*

The crowd tightened around us, but still no one transformed.

*I started working at the escort agency to land a meeting with Heath. I knew he wouldn't let me into his house and listen to me otherwise. I wanted to see him to speak my piece. I slipped him three pills—*I swallowed, but my throat felt wadded up with cotton*—that made it impossible for him to shift. And then I told him that I knew what he'd done to Becca Howard...to my mother.*

Shock rushed over Liam's features, but soon that shock turned into something else. Something that whittled his expression. *What did he do to your mother?*

He didn't ask about Becca, which meant he already knew.

When she begged him to let me into the pack and train me, he...he raped her. I dragged in a rough breath. *I hated your father, Liam, but I never meant to kill him. It truly was an accident. If I could rewind...if I could just—*

Ness, my father didn't die because of any drug.

I know how he died, Liam. I know he drowned. My eyes were so hot that the cold air made them sting. *But he drowned because of their effect.*

You think he fell into his pool and somehow spasmed to death? His gravelly voice turned almost shrill. *Oh, Ness...* He nudged my cheek with his wet nose.

But Everest said—

What did he say? His tone was as dark as his glistening fur.

I didn't answer him. I couldn't. My throat had squeezed as tight as a fist.

My father did die in his pool, but he was strangled to death with a silver cord.

The air eddied between us, cold and hot, loud and silent.

Strangled? I whispered.

Your pills might've slowed him down, but they didn't kill him. Liam's large black face dipped heavily. In a slow, even voice, he added, *I wondered why my father hadn't shifted.* And then, *Everest knew about the pills, didn't he?*

He suggested them. I only wanted to give your father one, but Everest recommended three. He told me Alphas weren't built like normal wolves.

Suddenly, everything made sense. How quickly Everest had been to blame me. How swiftly he'd pushed me toward the enemy pack to make me look like a traitor. How he'd up and left Boulder. Why he'd blackmailed me to compete in the last trial.

My death would mean his secret was safe.

Liam's death would mean my cousin would be free of retaliation.

What he hadn't counted on was for me to figure it out and share my findings with Heath's son.

My head swam, but my heart, it shot up from the depths it had been wallowing in. *I have to go. I have to go.* I tried to wriggle out from underneath him, but he pinned one of my shoulders with his giant forepaws. *Liam, I have to go! Let me go! Everest took Evelyn. I have to save her.*

I spun my face to see my uncle. He was watching on as intently and curiously as the others. Was he in on his son's scheme? Was he the one who *saw* me?

I writhed, but Liam wouldn't get off me. I snarled at him. *I need to find her.*

I'll go with you.

You come with me and they'll know I talked.

What am I supposed to do? Let you leave to face Everest on your own?

Yes.

No. His yellow eyes sparked like fire.

He'll kill Evelyn if you come with me.

He might kill her and *you if I let you go on your own.*

We're wasting time. I writhed like a snake. *You want to help me?* I growled. *Then shift back and tell them I'm running away since I can't forfeit. That'll give me time to find her, and it will lead Everest astray.*

Ness—

I spun so briskly to the side that he faltered. He tried to trap me again but ended up swiping his paw across my face, his claws catching in my cheek. The wound wasn't deep, but it stung.

Liam folded his ears back. *Shit.*

I could see my reflection in his gaze; I could see the red seeping over the white. Using his surprise, I flipped onto my stomach, my cheek weeping blood on the cement floor, and leaped out from underneath him.

I burst into the sunlight, speeding away from the boy who made my heart beat fiercely, from the warehouse that held cherished moments of my childhood, from the pack I'd wanted to become a part of even though I'd claimed otherwise.

46

Liam didn't come after me, which led me to think he'd changed back to his human form and indulged my plea. I prayed his explanation would get back to Everest, and that he wouldn't hold my supposed desertion against Evelyn.

I flew toward the inn like a lightning bolt, pounding the earth so violently I thought my heart would crack. The urgency and the adrenaline dimmed the horror of what I'd just learned...of what my cousin had done.

When I reached the inn's property line, I slowed to make sure there weren't too many humans but then realized I was wasting precious minutes. To hell with sightings. I was not an impressive creature, not like Liam and the rest of the boys. They couldn't pass for real wolves; I could. I muscled my way through the prickly fir trees and bounded into the parking lot. Evelyn's sash window still gaped wide.

As I trotted toward it, I lowered my nose to the hot asphalt and inhaled. There it was again. The ashen scent of a crushed cigarette laced with Evelyn's minty ointment. Everest didn't smoke... Or did he? Did I even know my cousin?

The odor of arthritis cream ran the length of the parking lot, tempered with that of gasoline fumes. He'd taken Evelyn in a car. How was I supposed to trail a car?

I ran, but not fast, clinging to the edge of the road. I discovered a cigarette butt, coated in dry saliva, then picked up more hints of Evelyn's salve. I prayed it wasn't my addled mind conjuring up smells that weren't there.

The sun baked my hide, but thankfully, the whiteness of my fur repelled some of the heat. I walked and walked, losing the invisible trail more than once, but retrieving it each time. Like a fractured chain, it hung in the stifling air. The only explanation I could come up with was that her captor had left the car window open.

A fork split the road in half. I smelled the air but froze as I took in my surroundings.

No…

NO!

I'd followed an old scent. Despair limning my vision, I stared at the steep hill with the pockmarked road that led to my childhood home. My heart thudded. I backed away but stepped in a spot of mud that sucked at my hind paw. I yanked my leg free, noticing tread marks beneath my paw print.

Fresh tread marks.

A car *had* come by here.

Maybe I hadn't followed an old trail.

I sped up the hill, pulse lurching savagely. Tucked behind the house was a black minivan with the Boulder Inn logo. Part of me had held out hope that I'd been wrong. That it wasn't my own family that had done this to me. The van trampled that hope.

Wolves didn't have goose bumps, yet my fur tingled with thousands.

I swayed but steeled my nerves as I inched closer to the house, ears perked up for sound. Through the grimy window of my old living room, I caught a sight that sucked all the oxygen from the air.

Evelyn was strapped to a chair, her snarled black hair spilling over her hunched shoulders. My eyesight narrowed as I took in her legs hooked to the chair rungs with duct tape, her arms taut and stretched backward, her hands bound with a zip tie. I tried to see her chest, see if it still rose and fell, but she was angled away from me.

The desire to sink my fangs into flesh and spill blood seized me so hard my muscles jerked.

One of Evelyn's fingers twitched.

She wasn't dead!

A voice, scratchy yet feminine, rose from within. "She didn't go through with the trial."

My vision blurred and sharpened.

Lucy!

I circled around my house toward the broken window pane of my bedroom. The second the crackled glass would fall against the hardwood floor, Lucy would know I was here.

My stomach seized as the scent of cigarettes and menthol blasted into my pulsing nostrils.

Now!

Glass bit into my flesh and rained over the floor.

Something thumped lightly in the living room. And then everything turned quiet-quiet. I lunged toward my open door and shoved it wide, claws skittering over wood. My aunt's mouth rounded with a gasp as I leaped onto her, slamming her against the floor. Her skull cracked like an eggshell, or maybe it was one of the bones in her body because her eyes were still wide, still seeing. I bared my teeth and growled.

The sharp tang of urine and fear filled the room.

"Ness!" she shouted, but it sounded like static to my buzzing ears.

I barked, and she blinked wildly.

Suddenly, something collided into my side and tore me off my aunt's heaving, urine-soaked body.

47

I was half expecting to see my cousin, but it wasn't Everest who'd flung me off Lucy; it was Liam. He'd caged her underneath his massive furred body.

What are you doing? I hissed.

Lucy was muttering, "It's not what you think."

He growled at her so roughly she shut up and turned as white as the towels I'd laundered for her day after day.

Liam spun his face toward me. *We need to find Everest, and Jeb doesn't know where he is, but I bet she does.*

I stared at him wide-eyed. My uncle wasn't in on it? How could he not have known? How—

The others are on their way.

I turned toward the wrap-around windows, and sure enough, vehicles were rolling up the drive. Suddenly, the room was filled with human bodies.

Frank rushed toward Evelyn, who was shaking with sobs. The second he freed her, she slung her arms around his neck. He whispered into her ear words I couldn't pick up. And then he kissed her cheek.

And she let him.

But then Liam stepped in front of me and blocked out the rest of the room. He licked my cheek, and the warm wetness stung, and then he tried to lick my shoulder, and I realized he was trying to get the blood off me.

I shoved him aside. I'd tend to my injuries later. First, I needed to ascertain Evelyn wasn't hurt.

Cole and Lucas were hauling Lucy up. I felt them look my way, but I didn't look at them, utterly focused on Evelyn. She released Frank and limped toward me. Slowly, she kneeled, pain excavating each one of her wrinkles, and then she extended her arms, and I walked into her embrace.

I trembled when her fingers combed through my fur.

"*Querida*," she murmured croakily. "She told me you needed me, that you were here." She took my face in her hands, then pressed her forehead to mine. "*Lo siento*. I am so sorry for going with her." Evelyn swept her shaky, dry palms over my muzzle.

A bone-deep shudder raked across my body, and tears skimmed off my eyes, tangled with my bloodied fur. Fear, relief, anger, and tension swept through me in waves.

Evelyn was safe.

She was safe.

I tried to tell her I loved her but remembered I was still a wolf. She wouldn't understand me. And then I realized this was the first time she saw me in my beast form, and I froze.

She threaded her shaky fingers through my fur again, stroking my neck over and over.

She wasn't running off, screaming.

I relaxed into her embrace, but then a hand touched my haunches. I snatched my head out of Evelyn's hands and snarled at the person who'd dared pet me. Frank pulled his arm back to his side, as though fearing I would bite.

I licked Evelyn's hand. She stared at the skin my tongue had touched, then stared at me, and I felt like I'd done something wrong. But then her pallid face split with a startled smile, and she wrapped her arms around my neck and crushed me against her.

Her scent rushed through me, reaching the places her arms couldn't, and like the petals on a limp rose, my wolf form tumbled off my spent body.

Several things happened at once. Evelyn gasped. The air turned colder. A shirt whispered over my naked backside. A loud voice rose over all the others, demanding that everyone get out. Frank's. Large hands lifted Evelyn and helped her back to the couch, and then those same large, papery hands wrapped around my taut and trembling arms.

"Someone, get her clothes!" Frank's frantic voice reverberated off the cracked plaster walls. "I'm so sorry. We didn't know."

I bobbed my head, half nod, half tremble.

Frank rose and someone else crouched in front of my huddled, naked form. *Liam*.

"Here," he said.

I kept my eyes on the dusty, water-stained wooden slats my father would oil every two years. Whoever had bought our house hadn't cared for it at all.

Liam fit a roomy t-shirt over my head, then lifted my hands one after the other and guided them through the sleeves. He tugged the hem low over my thighs. And then he crooked my chin on a finger to make me look at him.

"She's safe, Ness. You saved her." He smoothed my hair back, and then he collected my trembling body against his solid one, and held me.

The room swayed and then it blurred and darkened before finally vanishing completely.

48

I sprang awake so fast my head spun and my vision fragmented. "Evelyn!"

"I am right here, *querida*." She eased me back down, then leaned over me, her fingertips curving over the sides of my face, tracking over each one of my features.

I blinked at her. "You're okay?"

"I am okay."

"Did Lucy...did she hurt you?" I whispered.

"No."

I closed my eyes and saw my aunt's protruding eyes, saw Evelyn hunched in a chair. I forced my lids up. My mouth tasted sour, and my body reeked of wet-dog. I stretched my arms and legs then sat up, slower this time, my cheek pulsing. I lifted my fingers and felt a patch of puckered skin.

Evelyn wrapped her hands around my bicep. Although I didn't require her support, I let her guide me to the bathroom...I let her tend to me. She closed the lid of the toilet and sat me down. As she warmed the water, I peeled my t-shirt and shorts away. I didn't remember putting them on.

When steam curled up from the shower nozzle, I stepped into the bathtub, sat, and raised my face, letting the hot water beat down on me. Evelyn squirted soap into her hands and cleaned my body. And then she rubbed shampoo between her palms and washed my hair. She lathered in conditioner next, her careful fingers working out the knots.

She rinsed and rinsed and then turned off the water. As she picked up a towel, I clamped my fingers around the rim of the bathtub and heaved myself up and out. She patted down my body and then my hair, and I felt like I was a toddler all over again. She forced me to sit back down on the closed lid and went to get me clean clothes:

leggings and a tank top. I pulled both on. She dried my hair some more and then combed it out.

As I stood, the world spun a little, and my stomach rumbled as though it hadn't been fed in days instead of hours.

"You need to eat something." She steered me to the armchair that was creased and warmed from her body. "Sit here and don't move."

"I won't." I leaned my head back and shut my eyes, relishing the tranquility.

Sometime later, she was back with thick slices of chewy bread topped with thin slivers of turkey. I ate slowly, the food dropping into my stomach like clumps of blizzard snow. Evelyn pulled the sheets off my bed and tucked in new ones. For a long time, the rustle of fabric and the floorboards creaking under Evelyn's lopsided footsteps were the only sounds inside the room. I thought about the day. About Lucy and Everest and Jeb. And that made me think of what my uncle had insinuated.

She was fluffing my pillows when I finally spoke. "Evelyn?"

"Yes?"

I peeled a piece of crust off the bread and shredded it into dark dust between my fingers. "Can I ask you something?"

Like an articulated toy, she straightened out. "Anything."

"Is your real name...is it Evelyn?"

Even though her pupils were almost indistinguishable from her irises, I saw them pulse, or maybe I sensed them pulse. For seconds that stretched into full minutes, she stared at me. Then her gaze moved off mine, settling on a spot beyond my shoulder. Her long lashes swooped down and skimmed her pallid cheeks.

I hadn't wanted to believe Jeb; I still didn't want to believe him. But her evasion... "Who's Gloria?"

The silence turned barbed. Slowly, she raised her lashes. Tears burned in her eyes as brightly as the stars blazing in the night sky behind her. The plate slid off my knees. It didn't crack, but crumbs peppered the rug, and the remaining slices of turkey dropped like crumpled tissues.

She sat on the foot of the bed and linked her hands in her lap, her black hair falling around her lowered face.

"You're Gloria, aren't you?" I murmured at the same time as she said, "I am sorry."

Heartache bloomed inside my chest. I hadn't wanted my uncle to be right.

I blinked away the sudden blurriness. "Was it a coincidence we met?"

She shook her head.

I gripped the armrests.

Her lips trembled behind the fence of bottle-black strands draped around her face. "It does not change the way I feel about you, Ness."

I studied the perfect arc of light cast by my nightstand lamp on my white wall. "Just tell me everything."

Evelyn—no, not Evelyn—*Gloria* sat up straighter. "My name *used to be* Gloria. I changed it to Evelyn so my husband wouldn't find me."

I frowned. *Husband?*

"I was born in Mexico, but I moved to the U.S. as a child. To pay for college, I took up housekeeping jobs. That is how I met...*him*. I married him for papers, and he married me because his grandmother refused to give him access to his trust fund as long as he was a bachelor."

My gaze leaped off the wall and back onto her.

"The romantic in me believed that maybe we would fall in love. He was handsome and well-educated, but he had a lot of secrets. Dark secrets. He would spend most of his days locked in his office, and when he left the house, he would lock the door. I became so terrified of him that I confronted him." Her mouth set in a grim line. "He told me that if I ever questioned him again...if I ever went into his office, he would have me deported, so I stopped prying and kept my distance. Well, as much distance as you can put between two people sharing a house.

"One day he forgot to lock his office door. I feared it was a trap and almost did not go inside, but I was desperate to know what sort of man I was living with. What if he was a serial killer? Or a terrorist?

"It *was* a trap. He caught me before I could find anything, and then he blackmailed me. He said that if I wanted to stay in America, I had to do something for him." She turned to look out the window. "He made me seduce a man. That man was Frank McNamara."

Shock pinned me in my seat. "Frank?" The memory of their encounter before the music festival flashed inside my mind. And then the kiss he'd placed on her cheek earlier...

"You're from here?" I croaked.

Without turning away from the window, she nodded. "I was so scared, Ness, that I did as my husband told me. Frank was a married man. Seducing him went against all of my beliefs." She held a knuckle underneath her nose and drew in juddering breaths. "Frank fell for my act. But soon it was no longer an act." She closed her eyes, and a tear slid down her pale cheek. "We fell in love, and I told Frank the truth. And it was terrible."

She bit her lip that had started to tremble.

"After I told Frank the location of all the listening devices I had planted, he made me leave. I went back to the house I hated, to the man I detested. I only had months left to get my papers, but I could not stay so I packed my bags. My husband came home then. He already knew I had removed the surveillance equipment. I told him I was done. He said he would call the police, and I told him I no longer cared. I made the mistake of turning my back on him."

She stretched her bad leg in front of her.

"He shot me. The bullet was meant for my heart, but a wolf attacked him, and he missed. And then Frank was beside me. I do not remember much, but I do remember something...something that did not make sense until a couple days ago. I remember seeing the wolf turn into a man. For years—decades—I thought it was a delusion brought on by loss of blood."

Her voice broke on a sob and then on another. For a long moment, she wept.

"I had deceived Frank, spied on him, and yet he saved me."

Every fiber of my being urged me to go over to her, but my muscles had gelled with shock.

"He took me to a man who fixed my leg as best he could, and then he drove me out of Colorado and into Arizona. He had a great aunt who lived in Tucson. He asked her to take me in, and she agreed. She was such a kind lady."

Evelyn—*Gloria*—rubbed her hands together slowly, the same way she did when her palms were dusted in flour.

"Before he left, he got me new papers. I became Evelyn Monroe. I lived with his great aunt for many years, and during all those years, Frank visited only once. For her funeral." She closed her eyes and inhaled a deep sigh. "Frank allowed me to live there, in his house, many more years. I cleaned stores and offices but never made enough money to pay him back for all he had done for me.

"He came back into my life six years ago. I thought he was bringing me news of my husband. That he had finally died." She looked up at me. "But it was not that. He came for a favor, which I agreed to. I would do anything for this man."

My ribs trembled from the rapid drumming of my heart.

I knew what was coming.

"He asked me to move to Los Angeles to watch over you and your mother. He knew that if he sent anyone else to care for you, your mother would have made you move. He did not want to lose sight of you. He did not tell me why you were important. Not that he needed to explain himself to me. Especially not after telling me…"

Silence as thick as my duvet settled between us.

"What did he tell you?" I whispered.

She raised her eyes to mine. Like moonlit ponds, their black depths shivered. "That it was my husband's fault you had to leave Boulder."

My mind whirred with rapid calculations. None of them made sense, and yet I asked, "You were Heath's wife?" Had he had a second wife?

"No, *querida*. I was married to another monster."

There was a more monstrous man than Heath Kolane?

She pursed her lips in shame. "I was married to the man who shot your father."

I swallowed, and my throat smarted as though I had consumed shards of glass, then I sputtered as though the glass had embedded itself into my lungs.

"*El diablo*."

I couldn't draw a full breath. "Y-You were married t-to Aidan Michaels?"

"Keep away from him, you hear me?"

I gave a sharp nod. The dinner I'd sat through made me want to throw up. "Is that why you don't leave the inn?"

She squeezed her lips. "*Sí*."

"You shouldn't have come back here, Evel— I mean, Gloria."

"Do not call me Gloria. I am not her anymore." She stood, walked toward me, then took a seat again, this time in front of me. She held her hands out, palms up. When I didn't touch them, she said, "I might have found you for the wrong reasons, but please do not doubt how much I love you. You are like a granddaughter to me, Ness."

My throat clenched.

"Please, *querida*, do not hate me for my lies. I cannot lose you. *Te quiero tanto...*"

My heart bounded in time with my hands that landed on Evelyn's. She closed her fingers around mine as though afraid I might change my mind, but I wouldn't. I could never change my mind. It didn't matter how she got into my life. What mattered was what she'd done since she'd been in it, and all she'd done was love me. As deeply and fiercely as my parents had.

I had so many more questions, but one took precedent over the others. "You really didn't know what I was?"

A slow smile curved her lips. "No. I did not know that men or women could change into wolves."

"Frank never told you?"

"No. After the night he saved me, I never dared ask him. I think part of me did not want to know the truth." Her mouth stayed curved a while longer. But slowly, her lips settled back into a soft line. "He came by to check on you a few hours ago." Her thumbs traced the tops of my hands. "He asked me to convince you to join the...*pack*."

I inhaled so sharply the air seared my nostrils. Was this a possibility now?

"I told him I would do no such thing. That it had to be your decision. But..." She tapped her thumbs on the back of my rigid hands.

"But...?"

"But I think you should consider it. I worry for you, *querida*. I worry that without the pack's protection, someone could hurt you."

"My father had the pack's protection, and he's dead."

Her thumbs stilled as horror leached the color from her already insipid skin.

"The pack can't protect me from everything, Evelyn. Look at what my own family did. To you." *To me.* Did she know that Everest had made me take the fall for his crime?

"I suppose you are right." She fell silent for a long moment, her eyes directed on the crescents she was sketching over my skin. "Frank says my ex-husband did not murder Heath, but I think he says this to reassure me. It is probably just my imagination." She exhaled a deep sigh. "What a relief that you know everything. What a relief."

I trembled to tell her the truth about Heath—if only to reassure her that it wasn't the monster she'd married who'd killed him.

I was about to launch into that convoluted story when she said, "Liam is outside. He has been waiting to speak with you all day."

I jerked my gaze toward my balcony.

The corners of her lips tipped up further, and then she laughed. "You think I would let a man linger outside your bedroom?" She shook her head. "He has been waiting for you on the inn's porch all day. Frank came, but so did Liam...so did Liam."

49

I didn't run off right away after Evelyn left. I spent long minutes processing everything she'd told me, coming to terms with the facts that our encounter hadn't been motivated by a random act of kindness; that she'd once been married to the man who'd killed my father; that Frank had cared enough to send someone to watch over me. I'd been convinced everyone in the Boulder Pack detested me.

My heart sped up when I closed my fingers over the doorknob and turned it. The walk down the carpeted corridor seemed interminable, and my lightheadedness made the floor feel as though it were swinging like in a fun house. Several times I had to lean against the wainscoting to steady myself.

The cavernous living room was dimly lit and occupied with a couple of guests sipping wine. I was surprised the inn hadn't been shut down after what had happened. Was Jeb even here?

I scanned the terrace for Liam, found him leaning over the balustrade. I stared at him for a long moment, watched how the white moon delineated his long body. The summer night was warm and frosted with a perfect round moon.

The elders must be running with the pack. It was strange to think there would come a time when I could no longer change at will.

Liam hadn't sensed me yet, or maybe he had but didn't dare acknowledge me, afraid to spook me. I walked over to him slowly, then placed my forearms over the balustrade even slower.

He kept his gaze fixed to the sprawling, jeweled immensity stretching before us. "I'm sorry, Ness."

"What are you sorry for?"

"For not catching Everest before he fled. For what my father did to your mother. For having rejected your plea to enter our pack after your father died. For hurting you." He touched my cheek, the marks he'd clawed there, then his gaze dipped lower, and I knew he was apologizing for another night.

"I incapacitated your father, Liam. And then I went after something you wanted just to annoy you. If anyone needs to apologize, it's me." I surveyed the gentle sway of the tall pines that were almost as green as during daylight in this bright darkness. "To think I befriended Julian because Everest told me the Pine Alpha could protect me from your retaliation once you found out what I'd done." My eyes were so hot that the cold air made them sting.

He shifted so that his entire body faced mine. "Is that why? I thought you were having an affair with him."

"God, no." I shuddered.

He mistook my shivers for a chill and coasted his hands up my bare arms. That just made me shiver harder.

He frowned. "Are you cold?"

"No."

A smile started on his face. He glided one of his palms over my shoulder, toward my neck, settling his thumb in the hollow of my collarbone. His four other fingers rested lightly on the knobs of my spine. My frenzied pulse pounded against the pad of his thumb.

"You know, the night it happened—probably moments after you left—my father called me. He was agitated and drunk. And angry. Really angry. He ordered me to set fire to the inn. He said your family would be the pack's downfall. I told him he was drunk and crazy, and that no one was setting fire to anything. And then he called me a coward. A coward like my mother. And then he said—" His fingers clenched almost painfully around my neck.

I wrapped my hand around his and dragged it away.

His lids slipped shut.

"What did he say?" I murmured.

He squashed his lips hard. So hard I thought they would never open again. But they did. "He said that he'd hoped getting rid of her would make me more of a man."

My hand froze against his. "Getting rid of—"

"Dad would beat Mom. Often. The night she died…" His voice juddered. I squeezed his hand to steady him. "They fought because of something I did." His voice broke on a strangled sob. He pressed his lips tight again, but again, they reopened along with eyes blackened by tears. "I always suspected that he'd beaten my mother to death, but I'd never known it for certain. Not until he confessed to it. I lost my shit then. I told him I would kill him. And then I hung up."

My heart shattered like Liam's stance. He sagged against me, sobs rolling out of him. I wasn't sure if they were for his father or for his mother. I led him to an Adirondack before the weight of his sorrow could knock us both over. He pulled me down with him and hugged me like a frightened child hugged their mother, clutching the fabric of my tank, crying against my collarbone.

Liam's sobs finally subsided, but he didn't raise his face from where it pressed against me. "Lucas and August had been sitting next to me, so when my father was found floating in his pool mere hours later, they were convinced I'd killed him. They went so far as to discuss this with Frank. I went ape-shit crazy on them and carried out my own investigation. I hired a PI and had him look into you. I'd smelled you on my father's couch. I didn't think you'd killed him—at least not alone."

I ran my fingers through his hair, hoping my touch could soothe him a little.

"It took Everest leaving town for it to suddenly click into place. I'd learned about Becca by then and made the connection. And then, when Frank told me Everest had stolen the Boulder relic—"

"Everest stole it?"

He nodded.

"Why?"

"I'm not sure. For leverage?" He sighed, and his warm breath pulsed against my skin. "Tomorrow, I'll start looking for him, but tonight... Tonight, I want to spend the night not thinking about my father. Not thinking about Everest. Not thinking about the heart attack you gave me when you asked me to end your life..."

He released the fabric of my tank top and gazed up at me, his hands finding purchase on the small of my back. His breaths slowed, evening out. The heat of them raised goose bumps *everywhere*.

I was suddenly conscious that it wasn't a child who was holding me, and my fingers faltered. His lips connected with the sharp bone in my shoulder and stayed there—not quite a kiss. I never thought a shoulder could be so sensitive, but every nerve ending in my body converged in that one spot.

He raised a hand to the base of my skull and tugged my face infinitesimally closer.

"Frank wants me to join the pack," I blurted out.

"He's not the only one."

With the tip of his index finger, he traced a line down the center of my face, down the middle of my throat, stopping only once his finger reached the patch of skin underneath which my heart beat a fevered rhythm. He spread his fingers and pressed his palm there.

"You really think Frank would have had us fight to the death?" I asked, my voice a little hoarse.

"Probably not, but there was no way I was going to risk your life to find out."

His eyes glimmered in the violet darkness, reflecting the sheet of stars suspended over our heads.

He leaned toward me and fit his lips to mine. The fragrance of his skin tangled with that of the forest and of the moon and of the warm earth. His hold became crushing as his mouth parted mine, as his tongue twirled around mine.

Liam kissed the same way he did everything else in his life, with a deep, savage, territorial hunger.

In the distance, a wolf howled, and I swear my body responded, my skin bristled. Liam's too. Soft, hot skin transformed beneath my fingers into softer fur.

He broke off the kiss to curse.

"Full moon," he explained.

I frowned.

"It makes our bodies crave turning more than anything else."

I was pretty sure I craved *him* more than anything.

"Fuck it. I'd rather stay in skin tonight."

Another howl tore through the dark fabric of the night, alluring and deep, an invitation. My fingers tapered into curved claws. Liam's eyes glowed an inhuman hue, and the slightest hint of fang appeared over his lip.

"Do you have any plans tomorrow?" I asked him.

He frowned, and his teeth shortened. "No."

"Want to spend the day with me? In human form? We could get to know each other...and not just in the proverbial sense."

Heat stained my jaw.

He pushed a strand of hair off my face. "I didn't think Ness Clark ever blushed." He placed a kiss on the base of my neck.

I shuddered. "Run. I need to run."

"Hmm...is that what you need?"

I swatted his shoulder, and he winked. Tightening his grip around my waist, he stood, then set me down.

Another howl punctured the night.

Liam weaved his fingers through mine, and then together, we raced down the staircase that was carved in the side of the wide deck and crossed the moonlit field.

Someone yelled for us to watch out for the wolves. I glanced back at the inn, my hair whipping my face. Guests stood against the railing, gazes plunged on the forest beyond. Their mouths moved, but we could no longer hear them. I guessed they were discussing the reckless girl and boy running toward certain death.

I understood then why the pack hadn't avenged my father. What would these people do to us if they found out magic ran in our blood? Would they be holding rifles loaded with silver bullets or recording devices?

Neither scenario was pleasing.

And yet letting a man like Aidan Michaels live was the least pleasing of all.

50

In the cover of the forest, Liam stripped. My gaze caught on the perfect shape of his anatomy. It wasn't the first time he'd been naked in front of me, but it was the first time I let my gaze slip lower than the sharp dents at his waist.

"Your turn."

I jerked my gaze up to his face. He was smiling, his incandescent eyes more yellow than brown, burning a path straight for me.

"R-Right." I needed to get naked to change or I would have no more clothes left in my wardrobe. Checking that no other sets of eyes glowed my way, I awkwardly removed my tank top, getting my hair stuck in the process.

Not that he'd been far away, but Liam stepped in closer and reached over my bare shoulders to help me untangle the mess of cotton and blonde strands. His chest brushed against my bare breasts. I could tell it was calculated because after he tossed my tank top on the ground, he moved again...

And again...

"Need help with your leggings?" His voice was as soft and husky as a caress.

"No," I breathed, hooking my fingers into the elastic waistband. "Turn around."

His pupils pulsed. "Really?"

"Really."

"I've seen you naked, Ness."

I was about to ask when but remembered. The first trial. He'd been the one to carry me back to the inn. If he'd seen me, it probably meant the rest of the pack had had an eyeful too. *Damn.*

"I was unconscious, so it doesn't count."

He shot me a crooked smile, and ever so slowly, he turned, smearing a hot trail across my navel that glistened in the moonlight falling around the pine branches.

When seconds passed, and I hadn't looked away from the mark he'd left on me, he asked, "Are you sure you don't need my help?"

I hurried to remove my leggings, kicking them aside. However turned on I was, my first time wouldn't be in the middle of the woods against a tree. I shut my eyes and flipped that small switch that transformed me from human to animal. When I blinked, I was on all fours beside a looming dark beast. He nuzzled my neck, and it sent a delicious shiver down my spine. Although chaste, the gesture felt almost as intimate as a kiss.

Liam tipped his face toward the sky and let out a long howl. A moment later, a deep keening answered us. The pack was on the Flatirons.

We took off toward them, Liam gentling his speed to match my own. Every so often, I would stop watching the dark forest floor and glance over at him. The irony of how much I enjoyed running beside him and being with him didn't escape me. I'd spent my formative years despising both Kolane men, believing they were equal in deserving my contempt.

Son and father were nothing alike.

As Liam ran, he looked at me, his eyes glowing so bright they resembled fragments of stars. *Did anything ever happen between August and you?*

His question made me trip and stumble on a sliver of rock that nicked my hock. Liam stopped so suddenly his claws dug into the earth and raised dark dust. Startled, it took me a second to regain my footing.

He bent his long neck toward the warm trickle seeping from the slice on my hind leg and licked the blood away. Again, my whole body quivered.

No. Nothing ever happened, I finally said. *But it's not the first time you ask. Why don't you believe me? Did August say something?*

He shook his head. *I smelled you on him the night he left.*

Weird. But then I remembered my last meeting with August in the laundry room. *I did hug him.*

The fur on Liam's forehead rippled with a frown. *He smelled like you'd mated.*

I blinked at him. *You mean, like we'd had sex?*

He looked off into the distance, as though embarrassed to be asking this question.

Liam, I've never had sex with August, or with anyone else for that matter.

He swung his head back toward me. Gone was his embarrassment. In its place was pure astonishment.

Oh, God, he really thought I'd whored myself off.

Never? He took a step closer, and his nose bumped into mine.

I only became an escort to meet your father.

And Aidan.

Ugh. My shoulders tightened at the sound of his name. *Dinner with him was an accident. Well, not an accident. I told the escort agency I was no longer interested, but apparently Aidan insisted on meeting me. I said no, but he offered three thousand dollars. I regret every second of that dinner.*

You were so mad when I dragged you out.

Because you think I would've admitted to you how relieved I was? I was still convinced you were the devil's spawn.

His eyes turned somber. *I was...I am.*

I'm sorry. That came out wrong. I—

It's the truth, Ness. My father was a horrible man. He didn't speak for a long while after that. Just drew in breaths, one after another.

I licked his muzzle, and that jolted him out of his dark deliberations. *You're nothing like him.*

Well isn't this sweet?

Liam whirled around, stepping in front of me to block me from the sight of the whiny-voiced wolf. It didn't take me long to figure out who it was. A skein of wolves spilled out on either side of the creature who'd spoken.

Julian, Liam said tightly.

I thought one of you would be dead by now. Personally, I was hoping it would be you, Kolane. No offense.

Plenty taken, Liam gritted out.

Julian walked around Liam to see me. Not that I was cowering behind Liam. I was just too busy gauging the intentions of the Pines to move a muscle.

Ness, darling, I believe we need to have a little chat.

I searched for Sarah in the lupine faces and thought I saw her, but it could've been one of the other females of Julian's pack.

I lost. Sorry, I said, distracted by the flash of teeth from a dark-brown creature. I'd lay my paw in a snare it was Justin Summix.

Sorry? Well, then so am I. Shall I tell Liam what you did, or would you like to?

Go right ahead.

The brown wolf snarled at me—probably from the lack of respect I was showing his Alpha; I snarled right back.

Julian remained quiet for so long that I finally looked up at him. He was much more impressive in fur than he was in skin, and yet he inspired no fear in me.

Turns out I didn't kill Heath, I said.

After a long moment, he said, *It was Everest, wasn't it?*

It's none of your business, Julian, Liam growled.

An Alpha killer is every Alpha's business.

My father wasn't targeted because he was an Alpha. He was killed because he was a cruel man.

That took Julian a long, long second to process. He was still and silent for such a slow stretch of time that I started to think he would never recover from his shock. *Perhaps I have misjudged you, Liam.*

He had.

Like I had.

Who will become the next Boulder Alpha then? Julian asked.

Lucas Mason, I said.

My answer elicited intakes of breaths and ragged chuffs. I deduced that Lucas wasn't much admired by the Pines. I shared in their antipathy, but he was Liam's friend. Maybe he wasn't as bad as I deemed him to be; or maybe he was, and Liam was blinded by their shared history.

A feminine voice rose above the others. *Ness?*

Sarah? I asked.

Sorry. I was chasing after a rabbit. She advanced toward us, her wavy gold fur gleaming with sweat and moonlight. *What did I miss?* Blood was smeared over her smile. She licked her muzzle.

Lucas Mason will be sworn in as the next Boulder Alpha, Julian said.

No effing way, she said in a low, rumbling voice.

She stopped beside me, sniffed the air, then sniffed my fur. She frowned, and then her eyes snapped very wide.

Lots of surprises in the Boulder Pack tonight, huh? A wolfish pout-smile flourished over the Pine Alpha's face. *Word of advice, in fur, it is equally pleasurable.*

My body temperature soared so fast the air around me surely trembled. Sarah made a noise that sounded like a chuckle. I shot her a death-glare. She was still laughing softly when Julian called her away.

Julian, why did Everest give you the Boulder relic? I asked.

He stopped and turned his neck to face me. *He said it was to help you.*

Help me? More like help himself. My cousin didn't care about me. He'd been willing to sacrifice me.

May you have a truly enjoyable night, Julian said, and then he was off.

The sound of paws thundered through the forest as the Pines raced after their Alpha. Liam stared after them in silence for so long that I nipped his neck. He twitched back to life. And then his head curved toward mine.

How will you punish Everest? A gust of wind tickled my fur.

That will be for Lucas to decide.

My stomach writhed with nerves. *He'll kill him…*

Liam watched a bird take flight in the tree above us, disrupting the rustling stillness. *Doesn't he deserve to die?*

I hated my cousin. There was no doubt about that. But did I wish him dead?

He nuzzled a spot next my ear. *Don't worry yourself with that now.*

All thoughts of my cousin puffed out of existence as Liam slid his wet nose down the length of my neck and back, taking the scent of me deep into his lungs.

A delicious shiver ran through me as his hot breaths pulsed against my taut flesh. *You marked me on purpose, didn't you?*

He circled around me, lowering his face to mine. *Are you angry that I want everyone to know you belong to the Boulders?*

How hard my parents had fought for me to belong. How hard I had fought for this myself.

To me? he added raspingly.

No. I pressed my cheek into his jaw, feeling the sprint of heartbeats beneath his black fur.

His pulse matched my own.
That wasn't true.
My pulse wasn't sprinting.
My pulse was dancing.

EPILOGUE
THE FOLLOWING DAY

Even though I was still undecided whether to pledge myself to Lucas Mason, I decided to attend the ceremony held at the Boulder headquarters.

I was going for Liam. Sure, he promised he was fine about having lost out on the chance to rule the pack, but I believed he was saying this to assuage my guilt.

"Did you think it over?" He reached out across the center console of his car to take my hand in his. His palm was calloused from his midnight run, his nails jagged, and yet it was the gentlest hand I had ever held. "Ness?"

I jerked my gaze away from our twined hands. "What?"

"Please pledge yourself."

I bit on my bottom lip. I would be lying if I said last night, running with a group of men who were like me in every way, except anatomically, hadn't been magical. Because it had been. But how much of that magic was due to Liam?

If he'd been the one to become Alpha...

"Does the offer come with an expiration date?" I asked.

"Of course not, but I want you with me, Ness." He slowed to a stop at a traffic light. The last one before the winding path that led to the headquarters. "Wasn't last night incredible?"

"It was."

"Then why are you hesitating?"

Keeping my gaze fixed on the windshield, I said softly, "It was incredible because of you."

He tugged on my hand, dragging me nearer. "Look at me."

I looked. At his swept-back hair, his dark eyes, his full upper lip, his slightly thinner lower one.

"I once told you about my oldest memory, but I never told you about the memory that's marked me the most. The one that's been playing on a loop in my mind for the past six years. You, tiny, skinny, fragile you, coming into the headquarters and asking us to train you, to accept you."

The memory crimped the edges of my heart. "You all said no. Well, all of you except August, Nelson, and Everest." I tried to snatch my hand from Liam's, but he tightened his grip. "I let you go once—*we* let you go—and it was a mistake. I would love to blame it all on my father, but that would be unfair. Truth is, we were cowards. Almost all of us. We were a brotherhood. We thought having a girl in our midst would change us, would change everything. And it does change everything, Ness, but the Boulders are ready for change.

"A new Alpha will rise tonight. A new era will begin. Be part of it. You are as strong, as cunning, as resilient as the rest of us. And a hell of a lot better to look at."

"Stop it."

"Stop what? Telling you the truth?"

"You already won me over, Liam."

A smile tipped his lips. "And you won over the pack."

I rolled my eyes.

"I'm serious. Matt still talks about how you saved his paw. And then Frank told us about your life in L.A., how you cared for your mother until the end, and for Evelyn. And then I caught some of the elders discussing how smart and strong you'd turned out, just like your father, but with your mother's fiery temper."

"Seriously, stop it." I knuckled a tear from the corner of my eye but smiled at the mention of my mother's temper. My mother had always blazed brighter and hotter than most women.

"Ness, you've earned their respect. You've earned everyone's respect."

"Except Lucas's."

Not that Lucas's respect mattered. Lucas didn't matter to me.

"Babe, last night, you let me stay out with them. When I insisted on going back with you, you insisted I stay with them. Lucas's greatest fear is that a girl comes between us."

"That's not seriously his greatest fear...?"

"It sort of is. Lucas lost his parents young."

Lucas had been involved in a car crash a couple years after I was born. A shard of glass had sliced through his eyebrow, leaving behind the nasty scar he still bore. He'd survived because he'd forgotten to wear his seatbelt. His father and mother hadn't been as lucky, and when the car tumbled down into Coot Lake, they hadn't managed to unstrap themselves.

"And then, when his granddad died," Liam continued, "we were all he had left. He doesn't hate you."

I blinked wet eyelashes at Liam. The air shimmered around his face. I blinked again, and the shimmer was gone, but his face remained.

Solid.

Real.

I reached out and touched his jaw. "I'll think about it."

He stopped the car on the side of the road. "You're not still worried about not being a Boulder, are you?"

I bit my lip.

Giving his head a little shake, he leaned over his gearshift and closed the distance between our mouths, forcing my lips to open. The kiss dimmed my gnawing anxiety.

When we pulled apart, the sky was a rosy lavender, and the pines a gilded green.

We drove the rest of the way in silence. I wasn't sure what he was thinking about, too concentrated on all I was thinking about. How I longed to tell my mother about Liam, about the trials, about Frank's invitation to join the pack. I closed my eyes and saw her eyes glitter with a smile. The memory flickered behind my lids like birthday candles. I thought about my father next. About how he'd taught me about constellations and crafted stories of strong, alien, warrior princesses sprinting through clusters of stars. His princesses were always blonde, always had dimples, and always had wide blue eyes, like me. Each night, thanks to his boundless imagination, I would live a new life, on a new planet, face new challenges, new enemies. I wouldn't always be victorious, though. *A loss will teach you more than a win*, Dad would tell me on the nights my alter-ego alien-self returned home to her parents, defeated.

I no longer had parents to run home to when I lost.

But I did have Evelyn.

And now I also had Liam.

He stroked the top of my hand. "We're here."

We rolled through the open rusty fence and parked next to a long row of cars. I smoothed my hair into a knot at the nape of my neck, then tucked my mother's ring into my sky-blue camisole so the gold band rested against my heart.

Liam walked around the front bumper of his car and then collected my hand in his. We strode slowly toward the stone building that glowed with yellow light. Bodies milled inside. Excitement rippled through the glass windows that had been propped open to let the warm July evening in.

When we entered the spacious room, gazes fell on our twined fingers. Liam let go of my hand, snaked his hand around my waist, and tucked me closer.

Matt stepped in front of us, holding out a wicker basket full of razor blades. "Less pain than claws." Liam took one, but I didn't—even though Matt waited a long time for me to change my mind.

"The Alpha will slash the skin over his heart, and the rest of us will slash our wrists then touch them to his chest," Frank was telling the younger ones. I felt him glance my way, and then I felt him glance beyond me, and something shifted in his expression.

A new scent layered itself over the ones rising from the broad bodies around us. One I hadn't smelled in weeks—sawdust and Old Spice. It suddenly nulled all the other smells. My heartbeat fluttered as I glanced over my shoulder, daring to hope August was back.

There he stood, in a dusky corner, body steeped in shadows. When our gazes met, a smile broke over my face. He didn't smile; he froze.

I swiveled back. "You didn't tell me August was coming home."

Liam's jaw set a little tightly. Wasn't he happy to see his friend? His brother?

"Give me a second." I pried Liam's rigid fingers from my waist, then walked toward August who seemed to burrow deeper into the wall behind him. "You came back!"

He palmed his buzzed hair, muscles twisting beneath his dark-copper forearms. "Yeah, but just for the ceremony. I deploy in a few hours." His green irises eddied. "So you and Liam, huh?"

I looked behind me. Saw Liam staring at us, shoulders squared, expression stern. Was he still mad at August for having assumed he'd been involved in Heath's death? Or was Liam jealous?

I took a small step back but felt a hard tug forward that destabilized me. I checked August's hands, assuming he'd held me back, but his hands were shoved deep inside the pockets of his army fatigues.

Frank clapped, and I jumped. "We are all here, so let's begin."

A circle formed around Lucas.

August walked off first, and I felt him distancing himself from me like a mooring line stretching tight. *What the hell?* I returned toward Liam slowly, palm pressed against my navel.

Liam watched August, who'd situated himself across from us, arms crossed firmly, gaze sunk on Lucas.

"Are you okay?" Liam asked me.

I nodded, then added a smile when I noticed my nod hadn't seemed to reassure him.

Lucas slashed one of his wrists. Crimson ribbons of blood leaked down the inside of his forearm.

"Your chest, son," Frank said. "You have to slice here." He tapped two fingers against his heart.

But Lucas disregarded his instruction. He walked over to Liam. "Take off your shirt, Kolane."

A deep groove appeared between Liam's eyebrows. "What are you doing?"

"I'm not taking this from you."

"Lucas, I don't—"

"Shut the fuck up and strip, man." Under his breath, Lucas added, "Never thought I'd say that to you, huh?"

When Liam didn't pull his shirt off, Lucas said, "Hope you weren't too attached to this thing." He yanked on Liam's shirt and sliced through it with the razor blade and then shoved the limp material aside and carved a narrow slit over Liam's heart.

I gasped.

Lucas pressed his wrist to Liam's wound and then kneeled before his friend. "I pledge myself to thee, Liam Kolane, for as long as I shall walk the world in fur. Long may you live and rule."

For a moment no one moved, and then everyone moved at once. Even though men shoved me to get close to Liam, to swap blood with their new leader, he held on tight to my hand, anchoring me at his side.

When it was Augusts's turn, a hush fell over the room. He slashed his wrist, then pressed it to Liam's rising chest. Rivulets of red ran down the carved planes of his stomach, absorbed into the waistband of his jeans, tinting the blue a dark crimson. August didn't speak any words. I supposed words weren't necessary for the magic to bind them together.

He tipped his head toward Liam and then left without so much as a passing glance at me. And again, I felt something tighten behind my belly-button, stretch thinly, coming close to snapping when his pick-up's taillights vanished past the rusted fence.

"May you lead us well, son," Frank said, gripping Liam's shoulder and giving it a short squeeze.

The ceremony took almost an hour for everyone to pledge themselves. When it was Jeb's turn, my uncle walked over, eyes and cheeks more sunken than I'd ever seen them. He shot me a pained look, then, trembling, he sliced his wrist and touched his blood to Liam's.

"Thank you, Jeb," Liam said.

Jeb's lips quavered, and then his shoulders hunched and he retreated to the back of the room. Frank went to him. I watched them talk, watched my uncle cry as he nursed a reddened tissue around his wrist.

And then I stared back at Liam and pried the razor blade from his grip. He looked at me, at my fingers guiding the blade over my wrist. When blood beaded there, wonder shimmered in his umber eyes.

I pressed my wound to his slashed skin. His chest pumped harder as I spoke my own version of the pledge. "In fur and in skin, I belong to you, Liam Kolane."

He didn't smile, but he caught my wrist in his hand and held it there, against his heart. Something palpitated inside my chest, but it wasn't my heart. It felt as though a link were clicking into place, fastening me to my Alpha.

He raised my wrist to his lips and kissed it. When he brought it back down, his curved lips red with my blood, I heard words in my head, *As I to you*.

I blinked back tears. "I heard you," I whispered hoarsely. "I heard you."

His smile grew and grew, as did the noise level around us. The air vibrated with the thrill and significance of the moment we had all just shared.

My uncle's soft wail snapped me out of my enchantment. I retracted my arm that was still stretched toward Liam and went to Jeb.

"Did you know what Lucy and Everest had planned?" I asked him.

"No." The word came out garbled. "I swear I didn't, Ness."

Suddenly he hugged me, and I let him. I even patted his bowed back.

"I'm so sorry. So sorry," he kept repeating.

And I believed he was.

"I'm so ashamed of what was done to you."

Frank placed a hand on Jeb's shoulder and squeezed. "You're getting blood all over her pretty top." The elder's smile deepened his crow's feet.

Jeb jerked away from me.

"Don't worry. Evelyn taught me a foolproof way to wash blood out of clothing," I said.

"Meat tenderizer mixed with water," Frank said.

His answer had me gaping, until I remembered Evelyn's earlier confession.

"Thank you for putting her in my life," I told him.

Jeb frowned so hard his brow scrunched up. "Evelyn?"

"Mr. McNamara sent her to watch over me and Mom."

"What?" Jeb gaped at Frank.

"Ness, please call me Frank. As to Evelyn, she and I share a tumultuous history," Frank explained, which just had Jeb gape wider. At least he was no longer sobbing. "I owed it to Callum to take care of his little girl. He was a good man."

At the mention of his brother, a strangled sound jerked out of Jeb's mouth. He dug his fists into his reddened eyes.

"I'm glad you joined the pack, Ness." Frank touched my cheek, then leaned over and placed a kiss on my forehead. "Welcome to the family."

Little butterflies whirled around my stomach, and I smiled gratefully up at him. "Can I ask you something, Frank? Would you have made us kill each other?"

He smiled a little as he said, "That, you'll never know."

But I did know. His expression told me all I needed to know. Frank wouldn't have made us spill blood. That was something Heath would've done.

I stayed next to my uncle after Frank left. "Where's Lucy?"

Jeb drove the heels of his hands into his reddened eyes. "Eric...Eric locked her up in his basement"—his words were labored—"until she talks. Until she reveals where Everest is hiding."

She'd sooner die than hand over her only son. "What happens if she doesn't talk?"

"They'll make the pack track him down."

I'd meant to her, but I didn't clarify my question. This was hard enough on Jeb.

"Let's hope he went far, far away then," I whispered just loud enough for Jeb to hear.

His puffy eyes widened, as though he couldn't believe I wasn't first in line to rip out his son's jugular.

I wanted answers, and corpses don't talk.

I gave Jeb a tight smile, then started to turn away when he called out my name.

"I have something that belongs to you." He dug through his jeans and produced a key that he tucked into my palm. "It took me a couple years to get the money, but I bought back your house."

That was how Lucy had gotten in...

I pushed that morose insight away as he continued, "It's in your name."

"I can't—"

"You can."

"But it'll take me years to pay you back."

"It's a gift."

"Jeb..."

He closed his fingers around mine, forcing the key into my palm. "I couldn't prevent Aidan from killing my brother. I couldn't prevent Heath from hurting your mother. And more recently I couldn't prevent my wife and son from using you to terrible ends. Let me make amends."

"But none of those things were your fault."

"Please, Ness. Please take it. It's in a dire state, but Nelson said he could help you. Or maybe August—"

"Thank you." Heat blurred the sight of his pale features. "What'll happen to the inn?"

He sniffed. "It'll keep running. I'll hire a new manager." He stared down at his brown loafers. "Maybe after the summer, maybe I'll close it down for a little while. I don't know yet."

I supposed working would keep him from dwelling on the fate of his family. "I'll help out."

"You don't have to—"

"I want to."

Can I get you back now?

The voice in my mind jolted me. Liam hadn't moved from where I'd left him, and although he was surrounded by his pack, his full attention was on me.

"Thank you again for"—I nodded to my fist—"this. It means more to me than I could ever tell you."

Jeb squeezed a smile onto his collapsed face.

I weaved myself between the large bodies until I reached Liam.

"Hey, sister from another mister." Matt enfolded me in a bone-crushing hug, lifting me off my feet.

"We're good again?" I asked once he'd set me down.

"As long as you're good to my man, you and I are good, Little Wolf." The warning was sugarcoated but clear.

Lucas held my gaze for a second. We didn't exchange words. Unlike what Liam had told me in the car, I could sense I was far from Lucas's favorite person. Maybe we'd grow on each other. Maybe not. We didn't need to be best friends, but we would need to be friendly, for Liam's sake.

Fingers gripped my chin and lifted my face gently.

A vein throbbed in Liam's temple. *Come home with me tonight?*

Like the feather duster I'd been carrying when we'd met after so many years of being apart, Liam's voice swept everything in the room away: the feral, rowdy men encircling us, my uncle's intractable heartache, August's strange chilliness. Even the musky male scents seemed to dim in the beam of Liam's dark gaze.

"Yes."

He smiled and then he kissed me, and whistles and cheers erupted around us. When he lifted his mouth off mine, I was completely breathless. And I could've sworn the tie that bound us together tightened a little harder.

A PACK OF VOWS AND TEARS

BOOK 2

PROLOGUE

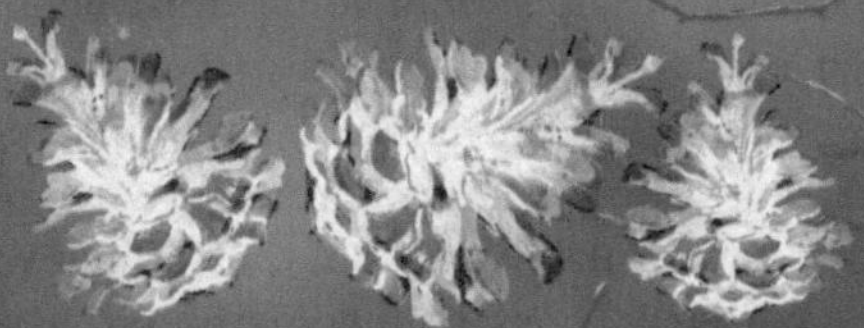

The first time I shifted, I was eleven. I still remember the matching looks of shock on my parents' faces. Where my mother's gaze had remained wide, my father's had crinkled with a smile. He'd crouched with his arms wide open to corral me. Disoriented and unsteady, catching me had been a swift affair. Dad had pinned me against his chest until my wolf quieted, until I morphed back into a naked child made of flesh and tears instead of fur and claws. And then he'd wrapped me up in a fleece blanket, whispering, "It's okay, Ness. Everything will be okay."

He was wrong.

After that day, nothing had ever been okay.

What are you thinking about, babe? Liam's voice resonated inside my skull, making me jump. I could morph into a furry beast, yet communication without sound was still bewildering.

I wasn't sure I would ever get used to hearing my Alpha speak to me through the pack's mind link.

My Alpha . . .

With blood pledges, Liam had been sworn in mere minutes ago as the Boulder Pack's new Alpha. His dream had come true. And mine along with it, because I'd gotten to swear my allegiance to him. I was now part of the pack who'd shunned me because of my gender. Take that, Heath Kolane.

How Heath had birthed a son as fair and good as Liam was almost as mystifying as an Alpha's ability to speak into minds.

Smiling up at Liam, I threaded my fingers through the soft, black swoop of hair that fell into his reddish-brown eyes and pushed it off his forehead. "Nothing. Nothing's on my mind, besides how proud I am of you."

Tonight was his night. I wouldn't spoil it with my glum thoughts.

His gaze hunted my expression. Although Alphas could speak into minds, they couldn't read what crowded them. "Ten more minutes, and we'll head out."

I looked around the large stone-walled room of Headquarters where the pledging ceremony had taken place. Outside, the world was going to sleep. Inside, the party was just beginning. The animated chatter and the tinny scent of blood drying on the pledges' wrists made my head spin.

"We can stay longer, Liam. I'm not in any rush." It wasn't as though I had anywhere to go . . . anyone to see.

No, that wasn't completely true. I'd made a friend in Colorado: Sarah Matz. She was a deejay on Thursdays and Saturdays at a place called The Den, and a Pine wolf the rest of the time. Technically, she should've been my enemy—the Boulders and the Pines despised each other—but since we'd met at her brother's engagement party, she'd been nothing but friendly. Actually, Sarah was only pleasant *after* her first cup of coffee. Before that, she was a major grouch.

Still, her personality beat the fake pertness of the Boulder wolves' girlfriends who all seemed to resent me because I possessed something they didn't—the werewolf gene—and because I'd defied Liam Kolane, the boy reared to become Alpha.

As I watched Liam talk animatedly with the pack, my stomach throbbed. Hunger, I supposed—I'd had a sandwich, but that was hours ago. Unless the throbbing was emanating from my nervousness. Liam had asked me to go home with him once the evening concluded. I'd never gone home with a man before.

I pressed my palm against my abdomen that was hardening by the second and walked toward one of the walls where drinks, cold cuts, and energy bars had been laid out on a long wooden table. I fished out a peanut butter bar from a glass salad bowl and was about to peel off the wrapper when headlights flashed over the window, blinding me in the process.

My first thoughts were that my traitorous cousin, Everest, had come to right the wrongs he'd caused by blackmailing me into believing I'd killed Liam's father.

But then the driver got out.

The energy bar slid from my fingers and toppled back into the bowl.

I could almost feel the earth shake as his boots hit the ground.

After pledging himself to Liam, August Watt had stalked out of Headquarters. And yet, here he was again, minutes later. I hoped he'd returned to apologize for his odd behavior, but his rough stride and narrowed eyes told me that was most definitely not his intent.

1

As August approached Headquarters, my entire body tightened. I felt as though someone were winding me up and up, like one of those tiny ballerinas in jewelry boxes. Crossing my arms, I watched him approach and, like those ballerinas, I whirled as he rounded the square building toward the heavy door. Had he returned to apologize for acting so distant toward me earlier or had he forgotten something?

I willed it to be the former. I willed *him* to walk toward me and say he was sorry, because I'd done nothing to deserve his aloofness. August had always been one of my favorite people in Colorado. And I wanted it to stay that way, in spite of the miles of land and ocean that would soon separate us when he returned to active duty.

The second he stepped inside, his green gaze pummeled into mine, before roving over the room toward the white-haired elder bent over my gaunt-faced uncle.

Liam intercepted August as he made his way toward Frank. Something must've been said through the mind link because August's expression became thunderous.

He brushed past Liam. "I need a word with Frank."

Liam squared his shoulders, eyes flaring with annoyance. At least I wasn't the only recipient of August's moodiness.

Frank straightened out slowly, leaving my catatonic uncle to stare at his tan loafers. Finding out his son was a traitor would haunt him for a long time.

Why did you do it, Everest? Why did you make me fight Liam? Were you hoping I would die or were you hoping he would? I yearned to get answers because a part of me couldn't believe the boy I'd grown up with could backstab me and his pack so guilelessly.

I tried to make out August's hissed whisper to Frank, but the lively banter in the glass and stone room drowned out my friend's deep timbre. Unable to leave well-enough alone, I strode through the small clusters of men chugging celebratory beers, uncrossed my arms, and poked August in the bicep. He didn't brush away my finger, but he squeezed his eyes shut a moment.

"What the hell, August? What did I do to you that merited—"

He opened his eyes, and the force of his gaze made me stop talking.

Frank sighed. "I was worried it had happened."

"That *what* had happened?" I asked, scowling at August.

"Both of you, follow me." Frank started toward the back of the building.

Neither August nor I moved.

"Now," Frank said.

August lowered his eyes.

"I don't understand," I said.

"I don't either, Ness." August's voice was infinitesimally softer, which wasn't to say soft. It was still as strained as the cream-colored Henley on his back.

"What do you mean, you don't understand?" I kept my voice low. "You're the one who snubbed me. Not the other way around."

"Ness, now." Frank's voice brooked no argument.

Stomach writhing with nerves, I started across the room that had fallen way too quiet. Lucas and Matt stared at me as I passed by them, and then they stared at August, who was a step behind me.

Ness? I felt Liam's voice inside my head, looked for him through the fence of enormous male bodies. He wasn't hard to spot. It wasn't so much that he was taller than all the others—he wasn't—but because he emitted something the others didn't, this intractable pull . . . an *Alphaness.*

"I'll be right back," I told him as August went around me.

Liam's eyes had shifted to amber, as though the wolf in him was trying to surface. He was protective and possessive of the people he liked. Since he'd climbed onto my balcony and we'd shared our first kiss, I'd become one of those people.

I pasted on a smile to reassure him that everything was all right. But was anything all right? Why did Frank want to talk to me? And why was August acting like someone had wronged him? He hadn't coveted the title of Alpha, so it couldn't be jealousy. Before he'd left Boulder, he'd even urged me not to fight Liam for it.

I walked toward one of the two small rooms in the back of the building. August was already inside. As I treaded past him, he shut the door, then planted his boot against the wood and leaned back.

I dropped down onto the black leather couch, folded one leg over the other, and laced my fingers around my knee, which had started bobbing with crackling anticipation. "Why did you need to see the both of us?"

Frank removed a wicker chair from a short stack and propped it on the stone floor. The chair groaned as he took a seat. He looked from August to me and then back at August, who'd crossed his arms, tendons pinching underneath his burnished skin. He'd never disclosed the location of where he'd been stationed these past few weeks, but I suspected he'd acquired his deeper-brown hue somewhere in the Middle East. Few regions were as contentious. Well, besides Colorado. Our state was chockfull of contention thanks to feuding packs.

At the elder's sigh, my stomach cramped again. Maybe it wasn't hunger. Maybe it *was* stress. Stress brought on by August's strange behavior.

"Your abdomen is spasming, isn't it, Ness?" Frank asked.

Blinking at Frank, I whipped my hand off my middle and clasped my knee. "It's normal."

"Normal?" I croaked.

"A symptom of what you've *contracted*."

"What I've contracted? What have I contracted?"

Frank's gaze slid toward August. "How's your stomach, son?"

"Fine," he replied gruffly.

"What did I contract, Frank?" I was scared now. I wasn't in pain but definitely in discomfort.

"A mating bond," Frank said. "That's what."

"What?" My brain felt as though it were pirouetting inside my skull. "A what?" I looked toward August.

The color had leached from his skin, and his full lips parted with an inaudible gasp. "No . . ."

"Yes," Frank said. "I'm sorry, son. I imagine this isn't what you or Ness want to hear, but your wolves decided they were meant for each other."

Our wolves?

A mating bond?

I sucked in a breath. "What?" I whispered, not because I was dumb or dense—I'd gotten what Frank had just thrown at us—but because I was shocked. Beyond shocked. I was probably experiencing what my mother had felt the night I'd barreled out of my bedroom on four paws and white fur.

While Frank explained the technicalities of a mating bond, I zoned out. I didn't want a preordained fate. I wanted the freedom to fall in love with the person of my choice. And that person wasn't August. I mean, I loved August, but as an older brother.

I didn't love him as more.

I could never love him as more.

"This has nothing to do with love," Frank said.

Had he heard my thoughts? Had I spoken them out loud?

I scrutinized the beige grout between the slabs of gray stones on the floor. The lines blurred and intersected at wrong angles. This couldn't be happening . . . I'd just become part of the pack. I'd just kissed Liam Kolane. I didn't want a mating bond.

"Mating bonds are evolutionary—"

I cut Frank off. "Like eradicating females?" I was still bitter about this. I think I would always be bitter about my pack ingesting a fossilized tree root to ensure only boys were born to the pack.

"No, Ness."

A hush fell over the room. Since Frank wasn't launching into an explanation, and August wasn't asking any questions, I deduced he'd been brought up to speed about the Boulder Wolves' selection tool.

"Not to sound pedantic, but let me give you a little history lesson. As you may already know, werewolves began existing when men and women settled around these parts. To survive, our ancestors were given the gift of claws and fur. They used their gifts to protect those who walked the earth only in skin." Frank scraped in a breath. "To make sure our species endured the test of time, each one of our ancestors was drawn to a particular mate, someone who complemented their skillset, whose genes would ensure the making of a better, stronger wolf.

"Now, with the advent of modernity, the world became less hostile to the settlers, and so our numbers dwindled, but thanks to generations of mating, we never stopped existing. Sadly, with our people being killed off by hunters—"

"Or by tree roots," I interjected, my gaze wandering over the tiny clumps of earth left behind by dirty boots, clumps that led all the way to a padlocked fridge.

What could possibly be kept in there that merited a lock and chain? The pack artifact? I hoped Liam would destroy it tonight.

"Or by tree roots," Frank conceded, "mates have become rarer. It still happens, though. Some werewolves will even experience this with humans, a rare occurrence, but still an occurrence."

"Can we . . ." I loosed a rough sigh. This situation was so unfair. "Can we break it?"

"Break it?" Frank rasped.

My navel felt as though it had been filled with gasoline and set on fire. Was that a result of our link? I didn't press my palm against my abdomen, afraid to bring attention to my duplicitous body.

"Why would you want to break it, Ness?" Frank asked.

I looked at August, who was studying the humming refrigerator in the corner with such intensity that if he'd been a warlock instead of a werewolf, I was pretty sure the fridge would've melted into a puddle of steel.

"So few of us are bequeathed such a gift—"

"Gift?" I yelped, cutting off Frank. "The theft of our freewill isn't a gift. If anything, it's a curse! Clearly, neither August or I want this."

August's gaze zipped off the fridge and landed on me.

My pulse throbbed everywhere. "Right, August?"

After a beat, he said, "Right."

Frank's bushy white eyebrows knit on his forehead. "August hasn't been back for a day. Maybe if you give yourselves some time."

I shook my head, and my long blonde hair unraveled from the knot I'd wound it in and slipped over my bare arms. "Frank, with all due respect, August and I know each other, but it's not like that between us. It can never be like that between us."

"Why not?" the elder asked.

I startled. Why was Frank being so pigheaded about this? Because pack traditions were sacred to him? Well, they weren't sacred to me.

"What if I left long enough? Will it fade?" August asked.

"Distance dims the strength of the tether, but it won't make it magically snap. This isn't like an Alpha bond, children."

"So only death will stop it?" I mused. "I'm not contemplating dying or killing August," I added, so they wouldn't lock me up. I couldn't lose all my freewill in one night.

"Good to know." August shot me a rueful smile that dimmed the insistent pounding inside my belly.

Great. My stomach was now endowed with an emotional barometer that broadcast August's mood. My gaze drifted to his stomach. He'd never once clutched it. Did my emotions not register the same way with him?

His smile waned, and his jaw hardened again. "Is there a way, besides death, to break this bond, Frank?"

"Yes." Frank leaned back in his chair and shook his head like a teacher facing two petulant children.

"How?" I asked.

"You shouldn't want to—"

"How?" August asked, voice firm.

"If mating bonds aren't consummated—"

"Consummated?" I asked.

"The bond snaps into place through sexual relations."

My cheeks lit up like brake lights. *Oh . . .*

"As I was saying, if they aren't consummated by the next solstice, the bond disintegrates."

Rolling the hem of my sky-blue camisole between my cold fingers, I said, "You'd just have to stay away for six months, August. You were planning on deploying for that long, right?"

Slow seconds passed before he answered, "Right."

Frank's features were scrunched in disapproval. "You'd be destroying something sacred."

Pounding on the door made me jump.

"Frank?" *Liam.*

Oh, crap. I wanted Liam to come in as much as I wanted to share another meal with the vile hunter who'd killed my father, Aidan Michaels.

I pressed my clammy palms against the nape of my neck, trying to lower my body temperature.

August cocked an eyebrow, as though waiting for my approval to open the door.

I reasoned that Liam deserved to hear what was happening. And yet, I abhorred the thought of him finding out. I was afraid of what it would do to him . . . *to us.*

I finger-combed my hair so that it draped around my cheeks and nodded.

August stepped away from the door at the same time as it flew open. And then Liam was standing there, crowding the entire space, slashed, bloodied T-shirt flapping. Although the cut over his heart had sealed shut, the remnants of the pledging ceremony had left behind a razor-thin pale mark and reddish smears. Like Liam's chest, my wrist had also sealed shut, yet the place I'd sliced still smarted.

He shut the door behind him with a bang. "I waited. I'm done waiting. What the hell's going on?" he demanded, a brittleness to his tone.

I rubbed the thin streaks of dried blood on the inside of my wrist, careful not to skim the knit skin.

Silence.

The sound of it was so hostile that I almost explained everything, but the words kept jamming in my throat.

Slowly, Frank said, "I was explaining to August and Ness the dynamics of mating bonds."

"Mating bonds?" Liam's eyes flared. "Is that why—why they smelled like they'd—"

I cringed. "Please don't say it. Please."

"Like we what?" August asked.

Maybe *I* would leave. Race away from Boulder until I didn't feel like I was about to die of embarrassment.

No one spoke for a long second. At least, not out loud. From the surprise rippling over August's features, I suspected Liam had finished his sentence through the mind-link.

I couldn't sit here any longer. "I need to go home," I said, shooting up.

"Home?" Liam lifted one of his dark eyebrows.

Right. He expected me to go to *his home.* "To the inn."

There was a tiny hitch in his breathing. **This doesn't change anything, Ness.** His voice stroked my harried brain.

"Doesn't it?" I whispered hoarsely.

Not to me.

Frank had gotten up too. He clapped a hand on Liam's shoulder. "It's not wise to get between mates."

Liam shrugged off Frank's hand. "With all due respect, Frank, it's not wise to tell your Alpha what to do."

Frank let his hand drop. "You're right. I apologize."

"Besides, we both know firsthand that mates don't always end up together," Liam added.

Did Frank have a mate? Or did Liam have one? No. If he'd had one, he would've known why August and I smelled like we'd . . . like we'd—*Ugh.* I couldn't even think it without growing embarrassed.

"When do you deploy, August?" Liam asked.

A vein throbbed in August's neck. Even though his expression didn't betray his annoyance, I felt the insistent pop-pop of it deep in my belly. I didn't understand the reason for it since the choice to leave was his. Liam wasn't chasing him away.

"In the morning." August's gaze hadn't moved off my overheated face.

"If you're going back to the inn, Ness," Frank said, "can you take Jeb with you? Eric got him here, but he needs to hang around a while longer."

"I don't have a car . . ." Or a license. First thing tomorrow, I'd stop by the DMV.

"I'll give you and Jeb a lift. Let me say goodnight to everyone," Liam said.

"Liam, the elders and I need to go over many things with you," Frank said.

"I'll just drop her off and then—"

"I can drive them. I was leaving anyway," August said.

Liam narrowed his eyes. The friction between the two males was so heavy that if I stuck out my finger there would probably be static.

"That'd be great. Thank you, August," Frank said.

I clasped Liam's hand, spread his fingers with mine, because his jagged expression told me he didn't find this arrangement *great*.

"And, Ness, Evelyn's at my house. Just so you don't worry when you get back to the inn."

Thinking about Evelyn, the woman who'd taken care of me during the six years I was living in LA with my mother, stole my thoughts away from Liam and August for a welcomed moment. Did that mean she and Frank were rekindling what they'd had at the time she was still married to the werewolf-hating hunter who'd shot my father? I still couldn't wrap my mind around the fact that Evelyn had once been a woman named Gloria Michaels, wife of Aidan, lover of Frank, citizen of Boulder, Colorado. I wondered if I would ever come to terms with that.

"Tell her I'll come by to see her tomorrow."

Frank nodded as he slipped between August and Liam.

Liam let go of my hand and wound his arm around my waist, pulling me against him possessively.

"I'll get Jeb and wait for you in the car." August backed out of the room.

Like a spool of thread, I felt him retreat. But then I felt something else, a hand travel up my spine, settle on the nape of my neck, tip my face up.

"It's just a car ride. And like he said, he's leaving tomorrow."

"I'm aware of all that, but I'd rather be the one taking you home."

I kissed the puckered spot between his eyebrows.

Finally he sighed and caressed my cheek, nails scraping gently over the pale scars left behind by his claws during our last trial. I could tell that, although unintentional, hurting me still tormented him.

He hovered his mouth over mine. "You are still mine."

Was he reminding me or himself? "I am."

His tongue skimmed the seam of my lips, prodding them open, while his deft fingers massaged the back of my head, eliciting a groan from me. The sound had him deepening the kiss, deepening the kneading. After a delicious minute, our mouths came apart.

"I'll stop by as soon as I'm done here. Leave your balcony door open."

"'Kay," I breathed.

He lowered his hand to the base of my spine and guided me back into the main room. Although people were still chatting boisterously, I felt gazes dart our way, saw pupils pulse with intrigue, caught nostrils flaring.

"Everything'll be okay, Ness," Liam murmured.

I glanced up at him, wishing he hadn't uttered those words, because they felt like a curse. If fated mates were real, then curses were too, right?

2

When I walked out of Headquarters, August was closing the door to the backseat of the pickup. He must've secured the seatbelt across my grief-stricken uncle's chest, because Jeb was wearing it and looked in no state to have put it on himself.

I slid into the passenger seat and clipped in my own belt. "Thanks for the ride."

August kept his gaze on the windshield, on the dark slope of pines bathed in white moonlight. Yesterday, the moon had been full and all of the wolves, young and old, had run wild through the forest. August hadn't been among them. At least not when I'd been with the pack.

After turning the key in the ignition, he drove down the dirt road, past the rusted fence and the large wooden sign emblazoned with the words *Private Property*.

"Will you go for a run before you leave?" I asked.

"Yeah."

Old August, the one who'd looked upon me like a little sister, would surely have asked me if I wanted to run with him. This new August . . . he didn't ask me to join him. Not that I would've gone. I hadn't left the party early to go for a run. Besides, what would Liam think if he showed up on my balcony and I wasn't home?

I reached over and touched August's knuckles before realizing that I probably shouldn't touch him at all. What if it somehow strengthened our bond? I removed my fingers, feeling my navel pulse as wildly as my heart.

"I'm really sorry about . . . about all this, August."

"Not your fault, Ness," he said in a rough voice. "No one's fucking fault."

I winced.

After a beat, he said, "I'll have to add a penny in Mom's curse jar now. Closer to a quarter actually."

For the first time since August had driven back to Headquarters, I smiled. "She still has it?"

"Oh, yes. She calls it her retirement fund."

I smiled wider. "I miss your mom." Preoccupied with making a place for myself in Boulder, I hadn't paid Isobel a visit yet.

"She misses you too. You should go see her once I'm gone. It'll make her happy."

I nodded. "Good thing I'm signing up to get my driver's permit tomorrow."

August glanced at me, his face much more relaxed than earlier. "You don't have your license?"

"I didn't really need one back in LA. Besides, we didn't have a car, so it wouldn't have served much of a purpose."

Jeb made a little sound, between a wheeze and a sob, which had me spinning in my seat. His lids were shut, though, and his neck craned at an awkward angle—he was asleep.

"Still can't tell me where you're going?" I asked August, turning back toward him.

"It's classified."

"But I'm your mate."

He almost swerved off the road.

"Sorry. That was supposed to be funny; it wasn't." I wrung my fingers in my lap, wondering what had gotten into me to even joke about our new bond. "I can't believe I just said that. Can you just delete it from your memory?"

August didn't say anything. Instead, he turned on the radio, tuning into a jazz station. August had always been a great fan of jazz. I used to tease him about it, telling him he had the taste of an old man. Unfortunately, I didn't consider him such an old man anymore. Would've been a heck of a lot easier if I did.

Speaking of old men . . . "Did Frank have a mate?"

"Not to my knowledge."

"Does anyone else in the pack have a mate?"

"Eric. He and his wife are going on fifty years."

"That's a long time."

"My parents are celebrating thirty next month."

I appreciated his reminder that true love existed outside of mating bonds. Not that I'd doubted it. After all, my parents had loved each other, and they hadn't been fated mates. "That's crazy."

"Yeah." He studied the dusky road ahead. "So what are your plans for the big eighteen?"

I rubbed my palms against my jeans to stop myself from fidgeting. "That's still a long time from now."

"Five weeks isn't that long."

I moistened my lips. "I'm not much of a birthday person."

"You used to love birthdays. You used to request fireworks. I almost set myself on fire lighting one up for you. Remember?"

"I remember." The bottom of his jeans were still smoking when he'd jogged back to us. "You cursed so much your mom joked she would go on a huge shopping spree thanks to all those pennies you owed her."

The memory made me smile, but it also made my eyes heat up and my lips wobble. This year would be the first birthday I'd spend without Mom.

He must've sensed my sudden sorrow, because he touched the top of my hand. "How about we don't talk about birthdays?"

"Yeah," I croaked.

"Tell me more about LA."

I discreetly wiped my wet lashes before feeding him tidbits of the years we'd spent apart.

"It wasn't all bad," I said, flipping my phone over and over. Its screen suddenly lit up with a message.

LIAM: *Don't worry, but don't leave your patio door unlocked, okay? I'll be there in an hour.*

How was I supposed to *not* worry?

ME: *You think Everest will ambush me?*

LIAM: *Just lock up OK?*

My nerves churned. *OK,* I typed back.

August glanced my way, and the car swerved a little. "What?"

I stuck my elbow on the armrest and cradled my head. "It's nothing."

"You forget I have an internal lie detector. You're scared. Why are you scared?"

"I'm not scared." I shook my head because my words didn't seem to convince him. "Annoyed, but not scared."

"Why are you annoyed?"

I sighed. "Liam seems to think Everest didn't flee Boulder."

August side-eyed me.

"You know what he did to me, right?"

"I heard pieces of the story. How about you start from the beginning?"

I glanced over at my uncle, who had drool leaking from his mouth. Even though he was asleep, I kept my voice low as I recounted how Everest convinced me I'd killed Liam's father with the three anti-shifting pills I slipped him the night I'd paid him a visit. Which led me to tell August about the escort agency, about my alliance with the Pine Pack Alpha, about Evelyn's kidnapping, and my cousin's blackmail.

I scratched a fleck of dried blood off the inside of my wrist. "I can't figure out if Everest was wishing I would die or if he was hoping I would kill Liam."

Although splashed with moonlight, August's face was too dark to read. "Your cousin was always shifty."

"The shifty shifter."

August didn't smile at my little play on words.

"I know you two never really got along, August, but he and I did. I'm holding out hope he wasn't rooting for my death. I'm holding out hope he wasn't hoping for Liam's either . . . That he did this to test my loyalty to Liam."

After a long beat, August said, "You should stay at my parents' house tonight. Every night for that matter. At least Dad can keep you safe."

I shot him a smile. "I'm not going to hide. If anything, I plan on hunting my cousin down."

He gripped the steering wheel tighter.

"I'd rather be the hunter than the hunted."

"No," August barked.

Jeb released a loud snore.

"I'm not scared," I said, dropping my voice.

"Let the pack bring him in. Liam's the Alpha now, and that's what Alphas do. They exact justice in the name of the pack."

"He'll rip out Everest's throat before hearing him out. I want answers, August. I *need* answers."

"Maybe I *should* stay . . ."

"What? No." I winced at how fast the word whipped out of my mouth. The strange tether in my stomach writhed like a snake. However petty, August couldn't stay. I had enough to contend with without our weird fated-mate connection. "Don't change your plans on my account. Everything'll be fine."

"I know you want me gone because of Liam, but do you really think I could live with myself if I left and something happened to you?"

"Nothing'll happen. I made it out of the trials alive, didn't I?"

He grunted.

"Look, I'll promise you something. If at any point I'm worried about my safety, I'll go to your parents' house."

His hazel eyes were murky with doubt.

"I promise."

"I want this in writing."

"August Watt"—I slapped a palm against my chest—"you don't trust me?"

"You've been known to backpedal on promises."

The playfulness I'd gone for withered away. "What do you mean? What promises didn't I keep?"

"When you left for LA, you said you would write."

I nibbled on my bottom lip. "Mom didn't want me to make contact with anyone from Boulder. She said cutting my ties with everyone here would help me move on, but in retrospect, I wonder if she did this so Heath wouldn't find out where we'd gone. She was scared of him . . . after what he did to her."

"What did he do to her?"

Right . . . Only a select handful of people were privy to this. Not once did I regret that Everest killed Heath. Liam's father deserved what he got.

"He raped her, August," I whispered, as though saying it softly could somehow dim the horror.

August's eyes rounded. "Shit . . ." he whispered, voice as rough as sandpaper.

We didn't talk after that.

The tight coil of mountain roads lengthened and straightened as we approached the glowing inn. I was thankful there were guests. I wouldn't have wanted to go back to a silent, dark place. I had enough silence and darkness inside of me.

After parking in front of the revolving glass doors, August draped my uncle's limp arm over his broad shoulder and heaved him into the lobby. I grabbed the master key from the small office behind the bell desk and led the way up to my uncle's private apartment on the first floor. Jeb's place wasn't as grand as Everest's attic dwelling, but it was still vast—my uncle and aunt's closet alone was the size of my entire bedroom.

After August laid my uncle in bed, I pulled off Jeb's shoes, tucked a blanket around him, and then turned off the lights. My nostrils itched with the scent of Lucy's prized potpourri. How could Jeb stand it? I'd had to put mine out on the patio, which angered my already pissy aunt.

I wondered briefly what sort of accommodations Eric had given her in his basement. Did it make me a terrible person to hope she was lying on the cold, hard floor? The image of her standing over Evelyn tied to a chair made me ball my fists. How I hated Lucy . . .

"You can talk to me, you know." August's voice made me look away from the mason jars filled with desiccated rose petals adorning the stone chimney mantle.

I wasn't going to ruin August's one night with his parents. "You should go." I started leading the way back toward the door.

"Ness—"

"Please, August. I don't want to talk anymore. I just want to watch TV until my eyes bleed."

He exited the bedroom, and I closed the door and pocketed the key. We walked back down the flight of wooden stairs decorated with an evergreen-colored runner.

At the foot of the stairs, I stood on my tiptoes and pressed a kiss against August's stubble. "Have a safe trip. And call me from time to time, okay?" I smiled at him before hurrying toward my bedroom, feeling the invisible rope thin out.

"Ness," August called out again, but I didn't stop.

The tether weakened some more, becoming as insubstantial as a spider web filament.

I took it August was gone.

A pang of sadness hit me as I realized I wouldn't see him again for months. But it was better this way. Better for everyone.

3

Liam arrived at one in the morning. I'd been just about to drift off when I heard him knock and call out my name.

The second I let him in, his arms came around me, his head dipped to the curve of my neck, and he inhaled me. "You smell like him. I hate that you smell like him."

I was startled to hear him say this considering I'd soaked in a scalding bubble bath until the water grew cold. I'd even washed my hair. I guessed soap couldn't remedy the magical mating scent. Come tomorrow, it would no longer be a problem, though. I couldn't smell like someone who was thousands of miles away.

Liam licked the spot he was nuzzling and then dragged his tongue up the column of my neck, making me shiver. Was he trying to layer his scent over August's?

He backed me into the room, lips crashing down against mine, hard and demanding. Even though I was worn out, I answered with as much fervor as I could muster.

When my calves hit the side of the bed, I pressed my hands against his chest and unglued my lips from his. "I might smell like August, but you smell like every male in our pack."

He glanced down at his bloodied shirt, tore it off, chucked it on the floor by my flannel armchair, kicked off his jeans, and finally dropped his underwear. Naked, he turned and headed toward my bathroom.

Water gushed, and the rings on my shower curtain clinked against the rod. I didn't move. Barely dared breathe. Even my heart held perfectly still. Liam was naked —not for the first time—and taking a shower in my bathroom.

I still hadn't moved when he came back out, a towel wrapped around his carved waist. He smiled brazenly as he observed my perplexed expression. And then he cradled my face in his hands and kissed me deeply, sweetly, thoroughly.

His hands left my face and raked up and down my arms that were hanging limply at my sides. I should probably have gripped his waist or clawed his back or done something with my fingers, but I couldn't get them to move. I'd never been intimate with a man and was feeling a ton of conflicting feelings from edginess to fear to excitement to guilt.

All of them made sense, except the guilt. August's face flashed through my mind, and my stomach tightened. I squeezed my lids shut, willing his face to vanish, willing the tension in my gut to recede.

"I can't do it, Liam," I said, breathless.

"Can't do what?"

My cheeks burned. "Have sex. I can't. Not tonight." My breaths were coming out in short spurts. I was having a full-fledged anxiety attack.

"Shh." He rubbed my arms. Up and down. Up and down. "We don't have to do anything, Ness. Shh."

His arms went around me, and he pulled me against him, where he held me until my chest stopped pumping with fevered breaths.

"Can I stay the night, or do you want me to leave?"

I swallowed. "You can stay." I raked my hair back. "I want you to stay."

"Good. Because I want to stay too." He kissed the tip of my nose.

I climbed into my bed and scooted over to make room for him. He clicked off the lamp on my nightstand, then molded his body around mine.

"How did it go . . . with the elders?" I asked him as he played with my hair.

"I now know everything there is to know about being an Alpha."

"I can't believe you're Alpha. *My* Alpha."

"I like the sound of that." He slid his nose down the nape of my neck.

I shivered. "Do they know where Everest went?"

"They located his car in Denver."

I turned to face Liam. "Denver? What would he be doing in Denver?"

"Don't know."

Did my cousin know someone in Denver? Maybe Megan, that last girl he'd cozied up with, the one he'd met at the music festival and then kissed at Tracy's Bar and Grille, maybe she was from Denver? She was a student at UCB—the only thing I knew about her besides that she was a shapely blonde. Maybe there was a way to check the college's directory?

Liam's eyes were smudged with exhaustion. He needed sleep, not a cross-examination, but I couldn't help but ask about the hateful gender selection tool.

"Did you destroy the stick, Liam?"

"The stick?"

"The fossilized root."

His mouth solidified into a straight line. "I'm not going to destroy it."

I added space between our bodies. "Why not?"

"Because it has value, and valuable things are worth holding on to."

"Value?" I squeaked. "It's just vile, smelly, and criminal."

"Ness"—there was an edge of exasperation to his tone—"please, let's not fight about it. Not tonight. I'll never use it, I promise." He rolled onto his back and scrubbed both his hands down the length of his face.

"But someone else might." I propped myself up.

"Ness," he growled.

"Did you ever stop to consider that if your dad's generation hadn't used it, more girls would've been born, and maybe one of them would've been your mate?"

Liam's eyes glowed as bright as a Harvest moon. "Then I'm happy it was used, because I don't want a mate. I want *you*. Temper and all, I want you."

He pushed on the elbow propping me up until I collapsed back onto the mattress. Then he threw one of his legs over my lower body and settled on top, bracing himself on his forearms. As he dipped his face toward mine, I forgot all about the Boulder relic, all about Everest, all about breathing.

"I don't have *that* much of a temper," I murmured.

He smiled as he gazed down at me. "Just like a thunderstorm doesn't have that much rain."

"I'm not sure that's a compliment."

He slanted his mouth over mine, but before breaching the distance, he whispered, "From a man who loves storms, it is the greatest compliment." And then he kissed me until our bodies became as exhausted as our minds.

4

When I awoke the following morning, Liam was already gone and the bedsheets were cold. I checked the time on my phone: six-thirty. The meager hours of sleep I'd gotten would have to do. There was an inn to run and an uncle to check up on.

I ran a brush through my hair, then applied the tiniest bit of concealer to hide the circles beneath my eyes. I had my mother's eyes—cornflower blue—but where hers had always glittered, mine seemed as dull as smudged glass these days.

After tying up my hair in a ponytail, donning jeans and a black V-neck, I fluffed my pillows, straightened my sheets with military precision, and tucked my comforter. I hoped no guests had come down for breakfast yet. I was sure we had the basics, but without Evelyn, the offerings would be modest: toast, jam, butter. Evelyn and Mom had taught me how to cook, but I wasn't especially good at it. I'd mastered the basics though.

I quickened my pace toward the kitchen, expecting it to be empty and dark, but light leaked from under the door, and the scent of caramelizing onions clung to the air. Was my uncle making himself a snack? I pushed my shoulder into the swinging door and froze at the sight of Evelyn bent over the stovetop.

Her merlot-tinted lips arched up. "Morning, *querida*."

The door smacked my back—not hard, but hard enough to make me stumble forward. I caught myself on the steel island. "I thought—"

"That I would leave you to run this place on your own? I made Frank drop me off an hour ago." She shook her head, and her bottle-black hair danced over the apron protecting her jeans and red top. She seemed happy. Happier than I'd ever seen her. Blissful. "Can you fetch the warming trays?"

As I went to retrieve them from the shelving in the back of the kitchen, I checked over my shoulder a few times to make sure Evelyn was real.

"Liam spent the night?"

I dropped one of the tray lids, and it clattered loudly against the tiled floor.

As I crouched to retrieve the fallen lid, she added, "I am not judging. I am simply enquiring."

I cleared my throat. "He—but nothing . . ."

Evelyn laid the tongs she was flipping the thick slabs of bacon with on the spoon rest and walked over to me. She grabbed both my hands. "*Querida*, you are almost eighteen. You are allowed to have sleepovers with boys. Just promise me that you will not settle for a man who is anything but kind to you. You deserve kindness and respect."

The memory of last night flashed through my mind, and then another memory, an unwelcome one settled over it like tracing paper—the night of the engagement party when I'd stopped by his place and he'd let his bestial nature override his human one. Was I being naïve to place the blame on the wolf inside him? Were our wolf natures so different from our two-legged ones?

Evelyn's black gaze tracked over my face. "Ness? You are worrying me."

I shook my head. "You don't need to worry about me."

"I will always worry about you. I love you too much not to worry."

The image of her tied to a chair flashed behind my lids. I gritted my teeth, trying to stop my canines from sharpening. I longed to visit Eric's basement and sink my teeth into Lucy's fleshy, pale throat.

My aunt hadn't hurt Evelyn, or so Evelyn had claimed, but she was the type to bear her pain in silence. She'd never complained about the arthritis that locked up her joints or the old bullet wound in her legs that still made her limp.

Breakfast went off without a hitch.

Emmy, one of the women who worked at the inn, arrived shortly after me and insisted on handling the service. She asked where Lucy was, and I mentioned she'd gone after her heartbroken son. Emmy shot me a pained smile. She'd worked long enough at the inn to be up to date on Clark family gossip. What she didn't know—or at least I didn't think she knew—was the dual nature of her employers.

While Emmy took care of the early risers, I prepped a tray of food that I brought up to my uncle. I drew his drapes open and tried to coax him out of bed to eat, but he didn't move. I checked his pulse to make sure he was alive. He was. After my third failed attempt at getting him up, I let myself out.

As I went back downstairs, it dawned on me that I'd be in charge of the inn today. The responsibility tightened my stomach so abruptly that I pressed my palm against it.

It'd be okay.

I could manage.

Besides, it was temporary. A day. Maybe two. Right?

The cramping didn't ease up. I tried spacing out my breaths, but that didn't help.

The revolving doors of the inn spun, and I realized that working on my breaths wouldn't loosen the knot in my abdomen.

What I was feeling wasn't stress; it was August.

And his mother.

"Isobel?" I exclaimed.

She hadn't changed much—her hair was still a lustrous deep brown, and her complexion pale as ever—but she seemed thinner, slighter. She opened her arms, and I descended the stairs more quickly, walking into her embrace.

"Oh, sweet girl, I've missed you." She squeezed me tight before pressing me away to look me over. "By God, you are Maggie's"—her voice caught on my mother's name—"spitting image."

I tried to smile, but Mom's name had my heart twisting. She'd died in January, yet it felt like she'd left me yesterday. Sometimes, I still reached for my phone to call her.

"What are you two doing here so early?" I asked, breathing through the ache in my heart.

Isobel gestured to the bell desk. "I've always dreamed of manning one of these."

"Um. Really?"

"I heard the position opened up." Her gaze swept back over to me, vivid green like the pines hedging the inn's driveway.

I blinked.

"I'll get myself set up . . . if that's all right with you?"

"Are you sure you want—"

"Yes."

As she walked over to the bell desk, I glanced up at August. Had he asked his mother to fill in for Lucy?

"Anything need fixing?" he asked.

"What?"

"Lightbulbs? Chipped paint?" He gestured toward the inn. When I frowned, he said, "I imagine Jeb won't be much help in the coming days, what with everything going on."

Oh. Gratitude curled through me.

"You can't do this on your own. Well, maybe you can, but you shouldn't have to." He pushed up the long sleeves of his thermal top that clung to his torso like a second skin. "I'm good at manual labor, but don't stick me in the kitchen unless you want to poison the guests." His lips quirked up.

"Aren't you supposed to be on a plane or a submarine right now?"

Gaze roaming over the lobby, he said, "I've delayed my departure."

Relief warred with worry. "You did?"

I prayed he hadn't done this because he was worried for me. I didn't dare ask.

"I need to be at a construction site in an hour, so you have me for sixty minutes."

I had him for longer than sixty minutes if he wasn't deploying. "Um, the deck might need some rearranging."

He nodded and walked toward the double-storied living room.

"Hey, sweet girl, can you walk me through a typical day here?" Isobel stood in the doorjamb between the bell desk and the back office.

Although I'd never manned the bell desk, I'd observed my aunt and uncle enough to have an idea of what they did. I explained what I knew to Isobel, then started for the stairs that led to the laundry room in the basement when Matt walked through the revolving doors arm in arm with a blonde who looked uncannily like him.

"Hey, Ness. Don't know if you remember my mom?" He tipped his head toward the woman beside him.

I didn't remember her. She must've attended the pack gathering though. Then again, Isobel hadn't been there. Maybe Matt's mother hadn't either.

I doubled back and extended my hand. "Pleasure to meet you, ma'am."

She latched onto my extended fingers. "Kasie. And the pleasure's all mine, Ness."

After she freed my hand, I slipped it into the back pocket of my jeans. When neither supplied the reason for showing up, I asked, "Did you two want some breakfast?"

"Oh, we've eaten already," Kasie chirped.

I glanced at Matt, not really understanding what else they could want. "Coffee? Tea?"

"We're here because—"

Kasie interrupted her son. "Because I love to cook. And I remember from the pack reunion that Evelyn was a fantastic chef, so I've come to train with her."

Oh.

"Why don't I show myself to the kitchen?" She stopped by the bell desk to kiss Isobel's cheek, before crossing the lobby and vanishing into the dining room.

I turned back toward Matt. Whatever he'd just told Isobel had her grinning wide.

"Such a smooth talker, that one," she told me, shaking her head at him.

The revolving doors spun again, and Lucas walked in, a gym bag slung across his chest. "I need a room," he announced, strolling up to the bell desk and sticking one forearm on the counter. "Hey, Mrs. W."

Isobel smiled. "Hi, Lucas."

I raised an eyebrow. "Why do you need a room?"

"My place got flooded. Fucking neighbors."

My eyebrow came crashing back into place. "Wow. I'm sorry about that."

He ran a hand through his shaggy black hair that curled around his ears. "Why are you sorry? Did you make them leave their tap running all night?"

I let out a small grunt. "You know what, I'm not sorry."

Lucas's light-blue eyes shone with delight. I bet he'd been crowned Boulder's Most Annoying Person back in high school. "What's your room number, Ness? 105, right?"

I crossed my arms. "Why?"

"Just want to avoid bunking in the same room." He winked at me. "Liam would have my balls in a vice. Shit. Sorry, Mrs. W."

Isobel smiled. "I've heard worse, son."

Lucas leaned forward to see the computer monitor. "Room 106 free by any chance?"

"It is. Let me get you the key." Isobel disappeared into the back office.

I crossed my arms. "Did your apartment really get flooded?"

He shot me a cocky grin.

That answered my question. "You're here to babysit me, aren't you?"

"Babysit you?" Lucas snorted. "What an idea."

"Oh my God, you are!"

He waggled his eyebrows.

"Did Liam put you up to this?"

Metal clinked in the office as Isobel sorted through the rows of keys.

"No one put me up to this. I'm doing it out of the kindness of my heart."

"Your heart isn't kind," I volleyed back.

Matt snickered whereas Lucas scowled.

I wheeled on Matt. "Your mother's not here for cooking lessons, I suppose?"

He slung a big arm around my shoulder. "The pack takes care of their own, Ness."

My wide gaze ping-ponged between the two males crowding the lobby.

"Are you crying?" Matt asked.

I touched my cheek. Sure enough, my fingertips came back damp.

"Is it that time of the month . . . *again*?" Lucas offered, sporting a smile that made me want to punch his throat.

I flipped him off a second before August's mother popped out of the office, jingling a key. I dropped my hand back to my side, praying she hadn't caught my vulgar gesture.

Lucas's lips quirked in a taunting grin as he pocketed the key, but then fell flat as his gaze landed on a spot over my head. I sensed August stood behind me, sensed it in the pit of my stomach which writhed as though the invisible rope that connected us had been cranked.

"On your way to off all the baddies?" Lucas asked.

"I've postponed my trip." August slowly wiped his palms on a pair of jeans blemished with grease smears and wood stain. "Two of the lightbulbs on the living room chandelier need changing. You know where I can find some, Ness?"

"Yeah." I ushered him toward the supply closet. The room smelled of laundry detergent, cool metal, and dusty cardboard. "Lightbulbs are over there." I pointed to the shelf that sat underneath a hatch window, and he walked over and riffled through the rows of bulbs until he located the ones he needed.

"I'll get those screwed in before I leave."

Something occurred to me then. "Does Liam know you've postponed your trip?"

He stopped in front of me. "Not yet."

"So your mom coming over to help, that was your idea?"

"Not just mine. My parents didn't want you to be alone. So Mom called Kasie. I suppose Matt called Lucas."

"Going to go unpack, roomie," Lucas said to me while staring at August, who stood inches from me.

I backed up until the base of my spine hit the doorframe. "We're not roomies, Lucas."

"Almost. Hey . . . you got an extra pair of ear plugs in there? Wouldn't want to overhear any moaning."

My body went completely rigid.

Glass broke. I shot my gaze down to the boxes of lightbulbs clutched in August's fist. Without saying a word, he went to grab new ones, staying next to the shelving a minute, surveying the piece of sky visible through the hatch window.

"Anyway, if you find me a pair, slide them under my door, will ya?" Lucas said, starting down the hallway, humming some chirpy tune. Before turning the corner, he called out, "Hey, August, you should stop by Tracy's. There's a certain waitress who's going to freak the fuck out when she learns you're single."

The muscles in August's back bunched up.

"I have to go check on"—I swallowed—"on the laundry. Thanks for all your help."

And with that, I hurried away from the supply closet, feeling my navel throb as the distance between August and me grew and grew.

5

I stayed in the laundry room a long time, sorting through dirty sheets and towels, and also through my emotions. After three loads of washing and drying, and two hours' worth of ironing, only the inn sheets were neat. My insides were still a complete mess.

I wanted to drop everything and head to the gym to punch my way to a clearer mind, but there was still too much that needed to be done before I could clock out. I returned upstairs to check on Isobel, praying I wouldn't run into anyone else.

"Everything okay up here?" I asked August's mom.

"Everything's great, sweetie. We got a couple reservations for the weekend and a birthday dinner on Friday for a party of twenty. I checked in with Evelyn and placed a grocery order, and I was just now updating the wine list. Oh, and someone left a hotel bike out front. I found it when I greeted some new arrivals. I didn't know where to put it, so I wheeled it inside the office." She gestured behind her while clicking through an excel spreadsheet—I supposed, the inn's wine list.

When I entered the office, my body went as stiff and cold as a block of marble. A nametag tied around the handlebar flapped in the cool air blasting from the revolving fan in the corner. Spit jamming up my throat, I snagged the tag and popped it off its string, hoping beyond hope Isobel had tied it.

In dark marker was written: **So you can stop by again.**

A chill crawled up my already icy spine.

"Did you see who dropped it off?" I asked, hoping my voice didn't betray my nerves.

"No. I just found it at the bottom of the driveway."

Had Aidan delivered it? Considering the injuries Lucas had inflicted to the bastard's neck the night he'd shot Liam, I doubted the hunter was strolling around Boulder, transporting bikes. He'd probably had his driver bring it over.

I crumpled the tag and tossed it into the bin.

Like hell I would pay the creep a visit.

I guided the bike out the inn doors and down the driveway toward the stockroom where Lucy and Jeb stowed the hiking gear, kayaks, fishing poles, and other paraphernalia they made available to guests.

As I walked back up, I squinted down the driveway into the bright sunlight, looking for Aidan's chauffeured limo, but if it had been here, it was long gone.

Meeting at eight tonight at the inn to discuss Everest Clark's fate. Every pack member convened.

Liam's voice was so sharp and clear I swiveled my head, expecting to see him, but not a soul stood next to me. After I got over the shock of hearing him, I focused on what he'd just said: *Everest Clark's fate.* My pulse picked up, thumping against my eardrums. I peeked at the first floor. Behind one of the windows lay my uncle. Had he heard Liam's call too, or had Liam excluded him?

I went back inside the inn, grabbed the master key, then climbed up the stairs, taking them two at a time. I knocked before entering my uncle's room.

"Jeb?" I called out. When I saw the comforter shake and heard a muted sniffle, I hurried to his side.

"Liam will . . . he will . . . *kill* my son." Jeb's voice was as thick as the syrup I'd ladled over his pancakes. "My only child."

So he had heard Liam. "He said *discuss.* Maybe—"

"You don't know the ways of the pack, Ness. You've been part of it for what? Twenty-four hours? Wolves have no mercy."

I bristled from his condescending tone. "I may not know as much as you do, Jeb, but they didn't avenge my father's death. Maybe they won't kill Everest."

"He strangled Heath and left him floating in his pool. You think Liam will forgive my son? Oh, dear girl, you have so much to learn . . ."

I pressed my lips together. Even though my urge to walk out was strong, I stifled it. "Can I get you anything, Jeb?" I asked stiffly.

Without glancing away from the Flatirons beyond his bay window, he whispered, "Why did he have to go and kill him? Did you ask him to do it?"

My vertebrae locked up. "How could you even think that?"

"Because of what he did to Maggie."

"In case you forgot, Heath also raped Becca. Maybe *she* asked Everest to kill Heath."

"She was in a coma."

My throat locked up like my spine. I swallowed. "Before she tried to take her life and fell into a coma."

My uncle's reddened gaze drifted toward me before returning to the panorama of mountains. In a way—unknowingly—I'd been an accomplice to Heath's murder, but if I'd meant to kill him, I would've done it. I would never have asked someone to do my dirty business. How could my uncle think so poorly of me?

"Call me," I whispered, backing away from his bedside. "If you need anything, call me." I wheeled around and clambered back down the stairs.

Isobel looked up from the computer monitor she was checking. "Is everything okay?"

I nodded. "Concerned about Jeb, that's all."

Isobel didn't respond, but I could feel her studying me.

I went out onto the wrap-around deck to clear my mind. Instead, the dense forest reminded me of Aidan and of the strange note he'd sent. I tried phoning Liam to tell him about it, but my call went to voicemail.

The pack meeting was in a few hours. Informing him could surely wait until then. It wasn't as though it was a threat. You didn't threaten people with invitations. Then again, Aidan Michaels was a crafty man. Maybe it was an underhanded threat. A reminder that he knew how to get to me . . . how to get under my skin.

I pushed away from the knotted wood railing my father and the Watts had crafted. I wanted someone else's opinion on the matter and since Liam wasn't answering, I decided to seek out my "roommate."

6

I knocked on Lucas's bedroom door and didn't stop until he drew it open.

"Geez. Give a man a minute." Lucas stood there barefoot, sporting a pair of low-riding sweatpants that displayed too much boxers and a wifebeater that showed off too much biceps. Although I wanted to tell him to pull up his pants, I hadn't come to police his poor taste in fashion.

I strode into the room, kicking the door shut.

"I usually don't turn down booty calls, but—"

"Oh my God, get over yourself." I rolled my eyes. "If you were the last man on Earth, I would still never get with you."

He smiled. "That's cold, Clark."

"I'm here because I got a strange delivery."

His smile vanished. "I'm listening."

"The night I went to Aidan Michaels's house, the night he shot Liam, well, I used one of the inn bikes to get there, and it was returned to me just now with a note saying, *So you can stop by again.*" I said this all in one breath.

Lucas's eyes darkened. "Who returned it?"

"I don't know. Isobel found it in the driveway."

"How do you know it was the same bike?"

"I don't, but—"

"Maybe the note was meant for someone else."

I growled in frustration. "Fine. Don't take this seriously."

His jaw ticked. "Have you called Liam?"

"I tried. He didn't answer."

For a long minute, Lucas stared at me as though trying to decide whether to trust me.

I rubbed my clammy palms against my jeans, then looked around the room that was almost identical to mine: same beige drapes, flannel-covered armchair, copper light fixtures, white sheeting. Only the landscape painting on the wall was different.

"Look, I came to you because I thought you could help me figure out if I should be worried about Aidan—"

"You should always worry about people who have too much money and influence, but we've got a bigger problem than that bed-ridden asshole right now."

My extremities turned bone-chilling cold.

Lucas dropped into the armchair, then leaned forward, elbows planted on knees, fingers slotted together. He watched me as though contemplating whether to tell me. Finally, he said, "This morning Liam found out something was stolen from HQ."

I frowned. What did the Boulders keep in Headquarters that— "The selection stick?"

Lucas snorted. "You wish."

I did wish.

"The pack's entire supply of Sillin is missing."

"Sillin? You mean the anti-shifting pills?"

He nodded.

My mother had made me ingest Sillin for three weeks when I'd moved to LA to prevent my body from shifting and to dim my scent in case other werewolves were in the area. She didn't want anyone sniffing me out. Lone wolves were deemed loose cannons and, thus, were hunted down by packs. Eventually, distance from the Boulders caused my body's werewolf gene to become dormant, and I no longer needed the drug.

"Why would someone steal them?" I asked.

"According to Greg"—it took my brain a second to remember he was the pack doctor—"they don't make them anymore."

"So?"

"So there's a market for them."

I couldn't believe I was having an actual conversation with Lucas without wanting to throttle him. "Who do you think stole them?"

"We don't think; we know. Cole checked the surveillance feed as soon as Liam called him."

"Who took them?"

"Who do you think?"

I gritted my molars. "Seriously, Lucas? You're going to make me guess?"

"Everest. Everest fucking took them. And guess when? At the exact time you showed up at the Watts' warehouse to duel Liam. And the only reason we didn't catch him earlier is because when there's a duel, the whole fucking pack has to be present, which meant the person in charge of watching the surveillance feed of the inn and of HQ was at the fucking duel."

I bristled. "Are you insinuating it was my fault?"

He let out a ragged breath, running his palms the length of his face. "You didn't know what he was up to, right?"

"How could you even ask me that, Lucas?"

"I'm sorry. We're just trying to figure out what his endgame is, that's all."

"Are they worth money?"

"You think Everest stole them for monetary gain?"

"You said they were rare. Maybe he took them to buy himself alliances with other packs."

Lucas perked up at that theory.

"Or maybe he's planning on using it on us?" Like I'd used it on Heath, which had been Everest's idea.

Lucas's pupils became pin-sized.

"You hadn't considered that?" I asked.

He slapped his hands against his knees, and the loud clap startled me. "Fuck me."

"Never." The word popped out before I even realized I'd uttered it.

Lucas smirked, but then the effect of my humor was lost as we both mulled over my suggestion.

"We have to call Liam," Lucas finally said.

And so we did, and this time our Alpha answered.

7

Liam stormed into Lucas's bedroom about fifteen minutes after our phone call, arrowing straight for me. Once he reached my side, he cupped my cheeks and swept his gaze over every inch of my face as though to ascertain I was unscathed. I wasn't sure why he imagined I was hurt, but who was I to complain someone cared enough to worry about me? One of his hands drifted down my arm to my fingers, while the other drifted over the faint white scars he'd inadvertently clawed into my cheek during the last trial.

Lucas updated him on our theories and told him about the bike. In the grand scheme of things, the bike seemed futile.

"He doesn't know about the meeting today, does he?" I asked.

"He didn't pledge himself to me, so no, he didn't hear." Liam stabbed his hand through his tousled hair as he paced the small room. "If the bastard plans on poisoning us with Sillin, he has another think coming."

"At least Sillin can't kill us," I ventured, but regretted my words when both Liam and Lucas slanted looks at me. Sure, I'd given some to Heath, but it was the silver cord Everest had wound around the Alpha's neck that had snipped his life.

"Sillin might not kill us," Liam said gently, stopping his mad prowl, "but it'll steal our edge."

I swallowed back the overwhelming guilt. Even though Liam hadn't been a fan of his father, Heath had been his only remaining parent, and I'd had a hand in his demise.

Liam ran his thumb over my furrowed brow. "Stop blaming yourself."

I whispered, "I'll never stop blaming myself."

Liam gathered me to him and stroked my hair. His minty musk scent swirled around me, soothing my fried nerves.

"What are you thinking, Liam?" Lucas asked after a beat of silence.

"I'm thinking I should pay Aidan Michaels a little visit like he asked."

I pressed away. "No. The man's a psychopath! You can't go back there."

Liam shot me a smile that was all at once rueful and dangerous. "Ness, he won't shoot me again."

"How do you know that?"

"Because one, we'll show up prepared; and two, he's at the hospital."

"Liam—no."

"What would you have me do? Sit back and wait for him to *reach out* to you again?" Liam stroked the edge of my quivering jaw. His touch just made me shiver harder. "No one threatens one of my wolves. No one."

"Then I'll go with you," I said.

"Absolutely not."

"Liam—"

"Out of the question, Ness."

"But—"

Liam shot Lucas a loaded look, probably gave him a silent order, too, because Lucas said, "On her like spandex."

Gross, and so not fair. I told them so. Not the gross part, but the not-fair one. I even squared my shoulders and gave both men my fiercest look, or what I hoped was a fierce look.

"What's not fair?" Liam asked. "Trying to keep you away from danger?"

"Isn't the pack motto to protect the Alpha at all costs?" I asked.

Liam narrowed his dark eyes. "You would be protecting my sanity by staying safe. If anything happened to you, I'd go feral, Ness. I'd go feral and maul whoever got in my way. Preserve my sanity, please." He scraped a knuckle against my cheek.

I pouted, angry to be benched. "I hope it's not because I'm a girl and you think I'm too delicate, because I'm n—"

"It's because you're *my* girl," he said.

"I'll just wait outside," Lucas mumbled.

A second later, the door snicked shut.

"Mine, Ness."

"And how do you think I'll deal if anything happened to you?"

"The pack will protect you."

My eyes heated up.

A deep emotion rushed over his face, and he pressed his mouth against my forehead, then against each one of my eyelids, my nose, my jaw, my scar. He didn't leave a single millimeter on my face untouched. No, that wasn't true. He hadn't kissed my mouth yet. But his kiss came, and along with it, waves of intense sensations. They pummeled and filled me like the Pacific Ocean had pounded and foamed against the sandy shores of Venice Beach.

Our kiss tasted of thunder and lightning and need.

So much need.

A need to keep each other safe, but also a need to hold each other, to fill each other.

As he deepened the kiss, as his hands coasted down my spine, cupped my ass, my stomach hardened like a fist. I reeled back as though someone had punched me.

Swollen lips parted and panting, Liam cast me an apologetic look. Did he think I'd detached myself from him because he was going too fast? I forced my fingers into fists to stop them from clutching my still knotted abdomen. I blamed the stupid mating link for the sudden pain. It wasn't fair.

So much wasn't fair.

Liam rubbed the back of his neck. "I'm sorry, Ness. I didn't mean to rush you—"

"You didn't."

"Then why'd you pull away from me?"

I couldn't keep this a secret from him. Not if the knee-jerk reaction happened each time Liam and I made out. I touched two fingers to my stomach. He frowned, and then he didn't. Then he understood. And the understanding steeped his face in shadows.

"But he's gone," Liam said.

"No. He's not."

The look that stained his eyes scared me. Liam backed away and exited the room. A moment later, Lucas came back inside.

I sank onto my bed and hung my head in my hands.

I hadn't thought this day could get any worse, but apparently it could.

8

"He's going to force him to leave, isn't he?" I asked Lucas.

"Hopefully he'll concentrate on Everest and Aidan and deal with your *bond* later." His cheek dimpled. Unlike me, he didn't have dimples, so I guessed he was worrying the inside of his mouth. "This makes me glad Taryn and I aren't together. You girls screw with our focus."

"You and Taryn broke up? When did that happen?"

"A couple days ago."

I didn't like Taryn, but I didn't like Lucas much either, so I'd found them well-suited. "Were you together a long time?"

A fly buzzed around my desk before landing on the landscape painting behind Lucas's head.

"Long enough for it to hurt."

I sensed she'd done the breaking up, but I didn't pry. I got up and rubbed my hands on my jeans. "I need to go work."

"You're not planning on visiting Aidan, are you now?"

"No." I snorted softy. "I'm vindictive but not suicidal."

"Then I don't have to trail your ass through the inn?"

"You can try, but I know the place better than you, so good luck with that." I shot him a smile. "If you're bored, though, I can fetch you a feather duster."

"Hard pass. I was going to hit the gym."

"Don't you have a job?"

"You are my job."

I jerked my head up so fast the pen I'd stabbed through my makeshift bun poked my skull. "You can't be serious."

"As a heart attack. Until Everest is ki—*caught*."

"Killed?" I croaked.

"Caught."

My heart held as still as the fly perched on the painted stream. "But you were going to say killed . . ."

"Does it matter?"

"It does."

"Don't you want him to die?"

"I want Aidan Michaels to die."

"Not Everest?"

"I don't know how I feel about my traitorous cousin right now. I don't understand his motivations for any of this. I thought it was Becca, but he got with this other girl while Becca was in a coma, so I don't know . . ." I toed the corner of the plush beige rug. "Speaking of the other girl: is a college directory open to the public?"

"No, but Cole can probably hack it. Why?"

"Because I wanted to see if that other girl Everest was with came from Denver."

"What's her name?"

"Megan."

"Megan what?"

"I don't know."

"How do you spell Megan?"

"I'm not sure."

"Are you fucking kidding me, Ness?"

I stuck my hands on my hips. "Don't hiss at me."

"I'm not a fucking cat."

"Fine." I huffed out a little breath. "Don't *bark* at me. Better?"

He snorted. "Do you know which college she goes to at least?"

"She's a freshman at UCB."

He typed something in his phone. "So she'll be a sophomore in the fall?"

Right . . . This was summer.

He growl-grumbled. "You don't know, do you? UCB has 24,000 undergrads." I hadn't known it was that big. "She's not Everest's Snapchat buddy by any chance? Would make things a hell of a lot easier . . ."

"I wouldn't know. I don't do social media."

Shaking his head, he brought his phone up to his ear. "Yo, Cole. I need deets on a chick called Megan, who's a freshman or sophomore at UCB . . . No, this isn't for a hookup, you tool."

I smirked.

Lucas peeled lint off the arm of the flannel armchair. His nails were ragged, chipped and roughened by stone and earth. Mine had been the same after my full-moon run with the pack. I'd filed them down to the quick after, but three days later, white crescents had already grown back.

"What color hair? Skin? Eyes?" Lucas volleyed at me.

"Fair-skinned. Blonde, shoulder-length hair. I never saw her eye color."

Lucas related the info. "Cole asks if she was fat? Thin? Any distinctive markings?"

"I saw her from afar at the music festival—she was sitting on a bench—and then again at Tracy's—sitting again. She was pretty. Does that help?"

"Girls' versions of pretty aren't usually a dude's version," Lucas muttered.

"She had a heart-shaped face."

Lucas cocked the eyebrow that was slashed with a white scar—a remnant of the car accident that snuffed out the lives of both his parents. "What does that even mean?"

I drew an air-heart with my two index fingers.

"According to Ness, she's got a massive forehead and a pointy-ass chin." While he switched his phone to the other ear, he muttered, "And you said she was pretty."

I rolled my eyes. "Her forehead wasn't freakishly wide or anything."

While Cole searched on his end, Lucas told him about the awry footage of the inn. Considering Lucas didn't break into song and dance, I imagined Matt's brother hadn't yet fixed the problem.

"Okay . . . I'll show her. Thanks, dude."

Two minutes later, Lucas's phone chirped. He tapped on the screen before passing it over to me. I scrolled through the email Cole had sent full of screenshots of Megans spelled five different ways.

I handed the phone back over, shaking my head. None of them were Everest's Megan.

Lucas scanned the screenshots. "Becca was an escort. Maybe Megan is too?"

"Everest said she wasn't."

"He also said you murdered Heath."

The fine blonde hairs on my arms stood up straight. "You're right." Then under my breath, I added, "Never thought I'd say that."

Lucas's lips quirked into a lopsided grin. "Hot men are always underestimated."

I snorted. "Oh my God. Shut. Up."

He chuckled. "What's the name of the website?"

"RedCreekEscorts.com."

"Hate the name creek," he said as he typed.

"Got something against small bodies of water?"

"I got something against large bodies of fur." He flicked his gaze up to me. "Don't tell me you've never heard of the Creek Pack?"

I frowned.

He kneaded his chin that was in dire need of a shave. "You haven't, have you? The smallest pack that became the largest . . . Ring a bell?"

I shook my head.

He leaned back in the armchair. "I'll tell you the sob story after we finish up with the escort agency." His fingers flew over his phone's screen. Without looking up, he said, "Their website's down. Do you still have a contact there?"

My skin crawled at the mere idea of calling Sandra, the pimp—or whatever running an escort service made her—Everest had introduced me to. Even though she'd always been pleasant and chirpy over the phone, I'd hoped never to speak with her after my "date" with Aidan Michaels. I shuddered from the memory.

"Give me the number."

So I did. And Lucas called the agency over loudspeaker.

An automated message for Red Creek Escorts came on, prompting us to leave a message. When the beep sounded, I shook my head so vehemently that the tendrils of hair that had escaped my bun during my earlier make-out session fluttered around my face.

"Hiya, Red Creek Escorts, I was looking for some female company for a buddy's party this weekend. I'd appreciate if you could tell me about the available girls." Lucas left his phone number before ending the call, jaw a smoky red.

"You're blushing," I said, mostly to annoy him.

He flipped me the finger, which just made me smile.

"So, tell me about the Creeks now."

He tapped his phone against the padded arm of his seat. "Four years ago, a pack we all thought was off the map seized the largest pack of the Rockies."

"That's why I didn't hear about them. Four years ago, I was in LA."

"Ever heard of the Aspens?"

"Of course. They were a pacific pack. Dad used to call them hippies."

He twirled his phone between his fingers. "Sort of. They lived in a compound—more of a small town than a compound—and barely interacted with humans. Anyway 'bout ten years back, there was a pack summit, the first in almost a century. Boulders, Pines, Aspens, and a few of the Eastern packs signed a truce of non-invasion. No Creeks came. The Aspens who were geographically closest to the Creeks reported they hadn't heard from their neighbors in years, thus we marked them as extinct."

Boulders didn't go around sticking daisies into each other's hair. And although Pines were on the civilized side, some—Justin's face flashed through my mind—were brutish and egotistical.

"How do packs become extinct?" I inquired.

"Too many of the young renege on our way of life. They move to big cities and lose touch with their true nature, and then they die sooner, because not shifting is unnatural for our bodies."

I wondered how many years of life I'd lost by being away from Boulder.

He scratched his chin. "The worst part, though, is when those who leave reproduce."

"Why is that the worst part?"

"Because, if their offspring isn't born close to the pack, the gene becomes defective and results in kids who can't fully shift. We call them *halfwolves*." His expression turned so bleak that it made me wonder if he'd ever witnessed a shifting *halfwolf*. "Creatures of nightmares." Lucas flexed his knuckles. "Anyway, turns out the Creeks weren't extinct . . . just in hiding. One winter night, the Creek Alpha walked right onto the Aspen compound with her handful of wolves and challenged the Aspen Alpha to a duel. The fight was gory as hell apparently, and the Aspens—Creeks now—mentioned foul-play, although no one was able to prove—"

"*Her?* The Creek Alpha is female?"

Lucas snorted. "Of course that's the part that sticks with you."

I crossed my arms. "Just because she won a fight doesn't mean there was foul-play, Lucas. Why would anyone jump to that conclusion? Because she was female, and females are supposed to be inferior to males?"

Lucas sandwiched his lips together. I'd obviously hit a sore nerve. "How do you explain that each high-ranking Aspen, who challenged her after the duel, lost their lives too, huh?"

I shrugged. "She's exceptionally strong."

Lucas shot me a withering look. He didn't even think this was a possibility! Sexist pig.

I squeezed my arms harder. "Have you met her?"

"No. And I never intend to meet the crazy bitch."

"You are *so* sexist."

"*Sexist*? I'd keep the judginess in check. You know nothing about me."

"Judginess isn't even a word."

Anger and something else flashed across his face. "Do you think you're superior to everyone or just me?"

I halted. "I don't think I'm superior to anyone."

"You certainly act like it."

My breastbone prickled from his comment. "I just want to be considered an equal."

He stared at the rug with such intensity I expected to see flames curl from the long fibers.

"There are forty of you. One of me, Lucas." My eyelids stung. "You try being the odd one out." I hated how my voice broke.

I spun around and left, attempting to rein in my emotions. As I tidied rooms, I thought about the Creek Alpha. Lucas might not want to meet her, but I did. Did my curiosity make me disloyal? It wasn't as though I could pledge myself to her pack—Boulder blood ran through my veins, and unless she beat our Alpha in a duel and stole his connection to us, I'd remain a Boulder.

Besides, I didn't want a new Alpha. I trusted Liam, and I didn't trust many people. But how was I supposed to prove I was their equal when he'd stuck me with a freaking guard dog?

Maybe if I found Everest first . . .

As I readied the conference room with refreshments for the meeting and tidied up the living room, I racked my brain for reasons Everest could be in Denver.

"What's in Denver, Everest?" I murmured to myself, watching the sky outside the inn's bay windows darken to a glittery periwinkle.

I felt there was something I was forgetting, but what was it?

9

At 7:45 p.m., the men started trickling into the inn. First, Nelson arrived. He embraced his wife as though he hadn't seen her in days instead of hours. I couldn't help but stare at them, remembering a time when my parents would stand that way, cheek to cheek, heart to heart, whispering to each other. Because I didn't want to pry, I averted my gaze, rearranging the green apples in the wooden bowl I'd added on the corner of the bell desk.

I heard Nelson ask Isobel if she wasn't too tired. From the corner of my eye, I caught her shaking her head no. After kissing her on the forehead, Nelson moved toward me in those fluid, long strides of his. Like his son, he was long-limbed, but where August's legs and arms teemed with muscle, Nelson was on the slender side.

He touched my shoulder, making the apple I was trying to place on top of my artful pyramid skid down.

He caught the fruit before it rolled off the counter and popped it back on top. "How are you holding up, Ness?"

"Great. Thanks to Isobel and Mrs. Rogers."

Isobel smiled at me. "By the way, I asked Skylar to man the bell desk after I go home. She said it shouldn't be a problem and that her wife could cover the dining area. I hope that's all right with you."

"It's more than all right." I hadn't even thought about finding a night manager. I would hunt Skylar down after the meeting to ask how long she could cover the night shift—hopefully, until my uncle felt "better." Would he ever feel better, though?

The revolving door spun again, carrying in the crisp, blue scent of evening and the musky smell of male bodies. Liam was among those arriving males. At the sight of him, my hearing dimmed to a faint buzzing. He walked straight to me. After greeting Nelson, Liam threaded his fingers through mine and pulled me away from August's father.

How was the rest of your day? he whispered inside my head.

I lifted my gaze to his. "Never-ending. And yours?"

What I really wanted to know was what Aidan had said.

I heard Lucas gave you a history lesson.

"He did." Had Lucas also told Liam how the lesson ended?

Passing a couple guests on their way to dinner, we turned toward the staircase that led down to the conference room. He didn't let go of my hand until we reached the head of the oval table. As he took his seat, he tipped his head at the chair next to his.

"Maybe an elder should sit here, Liam." Or someone higher up on the pack pyramid.

His dark eyes held mine. *Your place is next to me now.*

Worrying my lip, I slid into the seat. Dating the Alpha meant something; sitting next to him meant something more.

As wheels rolled over the hardwood floor and jeans whispered against the smooth leather seats, I drummed my fingers on the tabletop, studying the row of shiny glasses I'd aligned in the center of the table.

The chair next to mine stayed vacant for so long that I began to think no one would sit next to me. But Matt took pity and dropped into the seat. I exhaled a quiet breath.

A knot formed in my abdomen. *Stress . . .* I was feeling stressed. And nervous. Or was it—

I lifted my eyes to the doorway just as August strode into the room. He took a seat next to his father and scanned the room, his gaze hopping right over me.

My heart pinched from that tiny action. What had Liam said to him? I lowered my gaze back to the row of glasses, finding solace in the quiet study of inanimate objects.

"Where's Jeb?" Liam asked.

I blinked up at him, then whisked my gaze around the table. My uncle was the only person missing.

"Hasn't left his bedroom all day," Lucas said.

"He needs to be here," Liam said. "Lucas, Matt."

Both boys rose and marched out of the room.

My heart was beating double-time. I wanted to ask Liam if dragging my uncle down to this meeting was truly necessary, but bit my tongue. I didn't think it judicious to challenge the Alpha before the meeting even started.

Frank tipped his head toward Liam. Where the Alpha wasn't speaking out loud, Frank was answering with nods and *yeses*, so a conversation was happening.

Muted grunts and heavy footfalls sounded just outside the room, and then Lucas and Matt were back, my uncle wedged between them. They released him in the last free chair before returning to their respective seats.

Jeb slumped forward, complexion as gray as his salt-and-pepper scruff, and forehead as puckered as a raisin. He seemed to have aged years in the space of a couple days.

"Close the door, Little J," Liam told one of the youngest members of the pack, a boy with acne and shoulder-length copper hair.

The boy reminded me of Everest the year I left Boulder. Everest, too, had worn his red hair long, and he, too, had had a bad bout of acne. I remembered wondering how he could stand the chemical smell of the cream he'd rub into his face every day to clear it up.

"Thank you all for coming." Liam's voice rang clearly in the low-ceilinged room, echoing against the clay-colored stone walls. "We have two matters to discuss tonight. Let's begin with Everest Clark, my father's killer."

Frowns pleated foreheads, and gazes narrowed on me. My pulse spiked as I realized people still saw me as Everest's willing accomplice.

"Unless you can live without eyeballs, I urge you all to stop looking at Ness that way," Liam growled.

The men averted their gazes.

"The pack's custom has always been to avenge a death with a death."

I'd been wringing my fingers together in my lap but stopped when Liam spoke of avenging deaths. I crossed my arms and leaned against the springy backrest. *Not always*, I thought but didn't say out loud. Everyone around this table knew my father's death hadn't been avenged.

"All those in favor of Everest Clark's death, please raise your hands."

Jeb made this squeaking sound that prompted Nelson to put a hand on my uncle's slouched shoulder. Although August's dad didn't say anything, his pinched expression told me he, too, thought having Jeb sit in on this meeting was cruel.

Many hands shot up; not mine. I didn't want Everest dead; I did want him punished, though. I counted hands, looked at the faces of the men who voted for Everest's execution. Thirty-four hands out of forty. Jeb squinted at the hands too, pallid lips wobbling. Nelson hadn't raised his hand, but August had.

Liam didn't have a gavel, but he banged his fist against the table. "The majority has decided."

And just like that—a fist against a table sealed my cousin's fate. Blood beat against my skin that suddenly felt too tight for my body. I rubbed my bare arms, trying to ease the sudden strain. The dusting of hairs began to thicken underneath my palms. I was shifting! I couldn't shift here. I closed my eyes, and my nostrils flared as I pushed against my rising wolf.

I would let her out later.

Later, I promised her. *Please not now.*

I couldn't lose control in front of all these men.

I pressed harder against her. Repressed her. Slowly, like thawing ice, her hold melted away. When I felt in command of my body, I raised my lids and glanced around, praying no one had witnessed my struggle.

Thankfully, the pack was discussing some other matter. Or maybe they were still discussing Everest. Whatever they were talking about, it captivated all of their focus.

No, that wasn't true.

August was watching me, and from the concern smudging his expression, I deduced he'd witnessed my little tussle. I was about to offer him a reassuring smile but remembered his raised hand—his vote. I stared at the revolving ceiling fan, at its blades that blurred as they sliced the tension-filled air.

Liam tapped his fist against the table again to garner everyone's attention. "Now onto the second matter at hand." Liam dug an aluminum-foil tablet out of his jeans pocket and held the thing out between his middle and index fingers. "Is everyone familiar with these?"

10

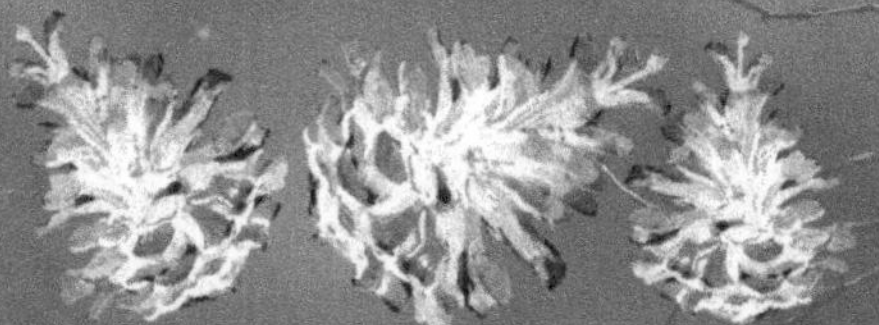

L iam wiggled the tablet, and the aluminum wrapping crinkled in the quiet conference room. "It's called Sillin. We ingest it when we need to avoid shifting. In other words, if you ever travel out of state, break a bone, or get silver poisoning, this is what we'll give you."

Silver poisoning? I didn't know Sillin countered that effect.

"Over the years, we've amassed a large stock of these. Last time my father asked Greg to procure some from the hospital, the pack doctor was told the formula had been discontinued." Liam tossed the tablet to one of the younger boys so he could take a look at it, sniff it.

Sillin didn't have an odor, which was why Heath hadn't detected it in his drink.

"Those who've taken these pills can tell you that the effect wears off fast and causes no lasting harm."

"That's the drug Ness gave Heath, isn't it?" Little J asked.

"It is," Liam said calmly, narrowing his gaze on the boy.

Little J flinched and concentrated on the tablet again before passing it along. Cheeks the color of rare beef, he leaned forward, grasped a water carafe that almost slipped out of his shaky hold, and poured himself a glass.

"This morning, the elders and I discovered the pack's entire stock of Sillin was stolen from HQ."

"Did Ness steal them?" someone asked.

"What?" I whipped toward the interlocutor.

The man was in his early thirties with a gold hoop speared through his right earlobe, and chest hair spilling out of a purple button-down shirt. For the life of me, I couldn't remember his name.

"I didn't steal anything!" I exclaimed.

"Rodrigo"—Liam's clipped tone had the man thumbing his earring—"*Everest* stole the pills."

The man next to Rodrigo placed a soothing hand on the dark shifter's forearm.

"We have footage of him cutting the lock off the fridge and taking everything inside."

The lock on the fridge . . . "It didn't look broken on Monday night," I said.

Frank sighed. "That's because he replaced it with an identical one. We realized what had happened when we tried to open it and it didn't work. When we asked Cole for the feed—"

"Bastard didn't even try to avoid the camera." Shaking his head, Cole slid the cigarette he'd wedged behind his ear and tapped it on the table.

Rodrigo lowered his fingers from his earring. "What's he planning on doing with all the Sillin he took?"

"We think he'll either try to sell it to other packs," Liam said, "or use it on us."

Rodrigo snorted. "How the hell could he swing that?"

"He could spike our drinks or mix it into our food," Liam said. "Sillin is tasteless, so it's not like any of us would notice."

When the hairy-chested wolf ogled the carafes I'd set in the middle of the table, Little J spit out the gulp of water he'd just taken, then stuck his arm in front of his face and watched his limb until the strawberry-blond hairs thickened and turned into tawny fur.

"I didn't contaminate the water," I gritted out.

"But did you stay next to it all day?" Rodrigo asked.

"Everest isn't in Boulder," I said.

"Really?" The man linked his fingers together. "And how do you know that? Did he text you?"

"Enough!" August's voice detonated like a gunshot in the room. "Ness isn't Everest's ally. He used her, made her feel guilty for something she didn't do, so cut her some fucking slack!"

Ping. A penny for his mom's jar.

Liam's lips tightened, but he didn't reprimand August for his outburst. At least not out loud. My stomach clenched from my heightened nerves, or from our bond, I wasn't sure. I laid my palm over my abdomen, hoping heat and pressure could undo the tension.

A second later, Liam stole my hand away from my stomach, laced our fingers, and tugged. My chair rolled and bumped into his.

I frowned at him, but his eyes were fixed on August. August who'd seized one of the glass carafes and poured himself water. Half of the contents sloshed over the rim. He mopped it up with the sleeve of his long-sleeved Henley, then lifted the glass to his mouth and drank long and hard. Realizing Liam was trying to make a statement, I stole my hand out of his.

The man who'd placed his palm on Rodrigo's arm earlier quirked a dark-blond eyebrow. "Maybe Lucy knows what her son is up to."

Jeb made a deep keening sound that was more animal than human.

Eric leaned his forearms on the table. "I interrogated Lucy again this morning, James. She said she didn't know."

"Then why was she helping him in the first place?" someone asked.

My uncle's Adam's apple jostled repeatedly in his unshaven throat, and his puffy eyes misted over as he shook his head from side to side.

Eric's gaze glided over to me. "Everest told her"—he rubbed his bald head—"that Ness killed Heath but was trying to frame him for it."

"He did what?" My claws came out so suddenly that I scraped the table, leaving curls of wood. No wonder my aunt hated me.

Shh. Liam's voice bounced around in my skull.

I dragged air that felt like fire into my lungs until my wolf relinquished her hold on me. Once I felt calmer, I said, "Someone had eyes on me at the warehouse."

"Lucy was monitoring you remotely," Eric said. "Everest planted a cell phone on one of the shelves and linked it to hers. We recovered the phone in question."

"She *claims* Everest put it there, and I hope she isn't lying. I hope no one else was involved in the con." Liam leaned back into his chair. "I'm feeling merciful tonight, but my mercy will be off the table come morning. So if anyone has something to confess, I strongly suggest you do it now."

No one spoke.

I highly doubted anyone would come forward, but maybe Liam wasn't seeking verbal responses . . . Maybe he was checking his pack's body language, looking for tells.

After scrutinizing his men, Liam said, "Okay then . . ."

"Do we have any leads on Everest's whereabouts?" Little J asked, his voice sounding almost squeaky.

Liam's gaze surfed over the heads of his pack members without ever settling, as though still on the lookout for a conspirator. "We do," he said slowly without offering any further details.

"Can we join the search party?" Little J asked.

Frank smoothed a hand over his thick white hair. "Your enthusiasm is commendable, Joseph, but Liam has everything under control."

"Oh, come on, Grandpa . . ."

So Little J, i.e. Joseph, was Frank's grandson? I felt a twinge more sympathy toward the boy, because like me, he'd lost his father. And I liked Frank.

"No, Joseph," Frank said. "You're too young."

Joseph crossed his freckled arms and pouted.

"The most important thing right now is that we stay united and alert. Open your own bottles and prepare your own food, and if anyone has trouble shifting, report to me immediately." Liam squared his broad shoulders, pushed away from the table, and stood. "Thank you all for coming."

Chairs rolled back, and men rose, chattering in low tones. I didn't get up. At least, not right away. Liam hadn't mentioned the bike, nor his meeting with Aidan Michaels. I wondered if it was because he didn't want to cause more alarm or because he thought there might be a mole in the pack. I glanced around me. Only

August stared back, lips alternatively parting a little and pressing tightly, as though he wanted to say something.

A hand settled on my shoulder, kneaded it. "Are you ready?" Liam asked.

I craned my neck. "Ready? To go find Everest?"

Liam shook his head as he kept massaging my shoulder. "I'm taking you home." I almost purred from how good his fingers felt against my knotted muscles. "I think you could use a full-body rubdown."

I wasn't a blusher, yet heat scalded my cheeks. I wished he hadn't said that last bit quite as loud. He could've used his Alpha link—

It hit me then. Like earlier, he was making a statement, because he felt threatened by August. I sighed and let Liam make his statement, let him claim me. When I looked around the room, only Matt and Lucas remained. I rolled my chair back, clasped Liam's fingers, and rose.

On the way out of the room, I stopped next to Lucas. Setting my annoyance aside, I asked, "Did they call you back?"

Liam frowned while Lucas's eyes turned a stormy blue. I sensed he was pissed I'd brought up the escort agency in front of his friends. What I didn't understand was why. It wasn't as though he actually wanted to hire an escort.

"Did *who* call him back?" Liam asked.

"The escort agency," I said.

Matt waggled his eyebrows. "Trying to get over Taryn, huh?"

Pink-cheeked, Lucas slugged him. "No, you douchebag. Ness thought Everest's last girlfriend might be working for Red Creek Escorts. And yeah, they phoned me back. They don't know any Megans."

My heart contracted with surprise. *So Everest hadn't lied.* I toyed with my mother's wedding band which hung from a leather cord around my neck. Slid it on my finger, then off, then on again.

"Why were you looking into her?" Liam asked.

"She thought the chick might be Everest's link to Denver," Lucas grumbled.

Liam and Matt exchanged a look. When Liam nodded toward the door, the blond giant closed it.

"We found your cousin's link to Denver," Liam said, voice low.

I let go of my ring, and it bounced over my T-shirt a few times before settling. "You did?"

"Thanks to you."

"To me?"

Liam scrubbed his thumb over my knuckles. "You know that visit we paid Aidan Michaels? It was very . . . *edifying.*"

Matt cracked his knuckles. "Don't know if you're aware of this, Little Wolf, but Michaels has a hotel in Denver."

That's why Denver sounded familiar! Sandra had sent me information about Aidan before I'd met him. He owned a hotel in Denver, Las Vegas, and . . . what was the third location again? It didn't much matter, I supposed. Unless Everest fled the Denver hotel. Then it might matter.

"So Everest traded the Sillin against shelter?" I asked.

Liam shook his head. "No."

"No?" I cocked a dubious eyebrow.

"Your cousin sold Aidan something else."

"His soul?" Lucas quipped.

Matt snorted. "I doubt he had one to sell."

"His land," Liam said. "Effective upon his death."

"His land?" What land did my cousin own?

Matt gestured to the room.

"The *inn*? He sold Aidan Michaels the inn?" I shrilled.

Liam nodded heavily.

"Good thing we never set up Headquarters here, huh?" Matt continued.

Something dawned on me. "That's why Everest struck the deal . . . Even though the inn's not Headquarters, this place is central to the pack's territory."

"Maybe that was his reasoning, but it doesn't change the outcome," Liam said.

My throat closed and opened.

Liam let go of my hand but not of my body. He cupped my cheeks and spoke to me gently. "We don't need this property, Ness. The pack has a lot of land. *I* have a lot of land."

"But it's—" I wanted to say my family's, but my dad had sold his share to buy the plot where he'd built our house. The inn and the rolling hill on which it stood wasn't *my* anything. "Can the pack really afford to part with this property?" I swallowed, blinking back the heat building behind my lids. "Your father sold Aidan Michaels so much land . . . Wasn't it enough?" I whispered. "Did he really need this place too?"

Every line on Liam's face seemed to sharpen, and his grip turned almost bruising. After a minute of complete silence, he said, "Aidan Michaels is a greedy son-of-a-bitch."

I placed my hands over his and pried his fingers off. I shouldn't have reminded Liam of the deal his father had struck with the devil.

"At least the Sillin isn't in Aidan's hands," I mused, mostly to ease Liam's lingering tension. "Can't believe that the man who hates werewolves wasn't inter-ested in buying pills that can make us weaker."

Matt crossed his arms. "My guess is he doesn't know about them."

"He hates us, Matt. Has entire files on us. The man surely knows about Sillin."

"What I meant was maybe your cousin didn't tell him about the *stolen* ones."

I raised my eyebrows. *Oh.* After a beat, I said, "Can't believe Aidan Michaels sold Everest out that quick."

Lucas grunted. "The man has no fucking scruples."

"Everest dying is in Aidan's best interest." Liam's expression had gentled again. "The quicker it happens, the quicker he gets the deed to this place. That's why he sent you the bike. He wanted to lead *you*, or one of us, back to him, so he could boast about his clever little deal."

"How are we even sure he's telling the truth? Maybe it's a trap."

Liam stroked a finger along my neck, leaving a trail of heat. "I left the bastard in the hands of Greg and two Boulders. They have orders to *slow* his healing process if he lied. So again, it's in Aidan's best interest that we find your cousin."

I sighed. This was so many shades of messed up, but at least I'd gotten answers. "We should set out tonight."

Liam frowned.

So I elaborated, "To recover Everest. We should head to Denver now."

"I already told you. You're not coming with us."

I jerked back. "But I want—"

"No."

"Liam—"

"No."

Lucas drew the door open. "I could use a beer right 'bout now. Matty?"

"Lead the way." Before trotting up the stairs, Matt glanced at me, then at Liam. Wisely, the blond giant decided to stay out of our *discussion.*

I crossed my arms. "He's my cousin, Liam."

"Which is precisely why you're not coming."

"I won't get in the way."

"Ness, unless memory fails me, your hand wasn't up earlier."

"Just because I don't want him dead doesn't mean I'd interfere with a pack decision."

"I'm still not taking you along. I don't want you to witness this. Even if the person deserves death, it isn't a pretty act."

A sour taste filled my mouth as I remembered the smell of gunpowder, the gaping black hole in my father's brown fur, the taste of metal as I tried to lick his blood away. Even though I'd thrown up the silver-laced blood, I'd had to get my stomach pumped. Had I been given Sillin then? Everything after the gunshot was such a blur.

I squeezed my eyes shut and shuddered.

Arms wound around me and reeled me in. "Let me spare you this, Ness," Liam said gently, propping his chin on the top of my head. "As a wolf, you'll see enough terrible things during your lifetime. Let me spare you one of them. Plus, I'd rather you don't watch *me* exact justice."

For a long moment, neither of us spoke. Memories of Everest crashed through me. Like the time he and I snuck around the inn, collecting pillows and comforters to construct a fort of epic proportion inside his bedroom. When Mom had found us hiding behind our fluffy cotton walls, she lay down with us and told us the story of two little wolves that went on adventures instead of going to school. I wasn't yet a wolf, so I didn't think the story was about me, but her tale had allowed me to dream that I might become one. After that day, Everest and I discussed at great lengths the adventures we'd go on if I were able to shift.

I bit my trembling lip as I realized there would be no adventures for us. A tear escaped, and then another, soaking the thin fabric of Liam's navy V-neck. He was right. I shouldn't accompany him. I might put myself between Everest and the weapon used to end his life.

"I can't believe Jeb didn't even fight to save his son's life." My words trembled like the rest of my body.

"Jeb knows the rules of the pack."

"This will *kill* him," I croaked, my voice barely louder than the whirring fan.

I waited for Liam to tell me that I was wrong, that my uncle was strong, that he'd get over it, but Liam didn't say any of these things. He just held me, stroking my spine up and down, up and down, until my body calmed.

Come home with me tonight.

I peered up at him through watery eyes and swallowed. "Okay."

11

As we drove over to his house, I realized the inn would soon belong to Aidan Michaels. Which meant I would need to find a new place to live. Maybe I could bunk with Sarah. She'd said she didn't want a roommate, but I'd make myself tiny and burrow in a corner of her palatial apartment. Or Evelyn. Maybe I could move in with her and Frank. Or would I have to continue living with Jeb, my legal guardian? What if Jeb didn't survive Everest's death? What then? Would I be entrusted to Lucy . . . if Eric ever released her from his basement? Would social services come for me, or could Evelyn finally become my guardian?

In five weeks, I'd be eighteen. Until then, my life belonged to people who were in no way fit to care for me.

"What are you thinking about?" Liam's voice made me look away from the star-strewn sky.

"Everest." I lied because I didn't want to burden him with my problems. Besides, my cousin wasn't far from my mind.

Liam squeezed the steering wheel. "I'm sorry, Ness."

"About what?"

"About the decision that was voted tonight." Starlight made his chiseled profile gleam white.

I bit my lip, then released it along with a ragged breath. "I appreciate you saying that."

After he parked in front of his modern wood-and-glass cabin, which was as dark as the sky outside the windshield, he picked up my cold hand and rubbed the pad of his thumb over my knuckles.

"Don't think for a second I'll enjoy ending his life."

I swallowed. Hard. It did nothing to dislodge the boulder-sized lump inside my throat.

He cupped my cheek and leaned over the center console of his car, ghosting a kiss across my mouth. The contact sent a shiver straight down my spine.

"Liam?"

His lips were tracing the edge of my jaw. "Yeah, babe?"

"Ask him why he did it. Before . . ." The rest of my sentence dangled silently between us.

"I will."

"And promise to make it quick. Don't torture him, okay?" I inhaled, and his potent scent swirled through me, the familiarity of it soothing.

"I promise."

Before cracking my lids open, I sighed, wondering if he'd keep his promise come morning.

He lifted my hand, flipped it over, then placed a chaste kiss against my palm. Lowering it, he asked, "Have you eaten?"

Food was the furthest thing from my mind right now. "No."

"Are you hungry?"

"Not really."

He tapped his finger against my cool skin. "Maybe once you see the contents of my fridge, it'll inspire you."

"Maybe." I doubted it, though. My stomach was one giant knot.

Clutching my crossbody bag to me, I pumped my door handle and hopped out. Once inside the house, he kicked off his boots. I followed suit, lining my sneakers up next to his shoes. As I stood back up, a nervousness—that had nothing to do with my cousin's fate—overwhelmed me. I'd never stayed at someone's house before—well, besides Evelyn's apartment.

When Mom would work late, I'd stay with Evelyn. She'd fill my belly with her delicious cooking, then fit a mug brimming with stovetop-warmed milk into my hands and read to me until I fell asleep with my head on her lap and her fingers in my hair. The month following my mother's last breath, I'd stayed with Evelyn almost every night. She'd tried to feed me, tried to make me sip milk, tried to distract me with one of her books. All I'd managed was to sleep, and even that had come in fitful bursts.

Liam propped my chin on his fingers and crooked my face up toward his. "You just checked out on me again."

"Sorry." I slid my chin off his fingers and swept my gaze over the clean, sharp décor that seemed simple but had probably cost him a small fortune.

He sighed as he wrapped his hand around mine and pulled me toward a large door. Behind it stood a bachelor's kitchen: beige-veined chocolate marble with copper fixings and smoky-mirrored cupboards that rose with the press of a finger. I'd come to his house before, but hadn't ventured into the kitchen then.

Liam seized plastic containers from the fridge and set them on the marble island, popping the lids off.

"Did you cook all of this?" I asked as I climbed onto one of the leather stools, admiring how clean and shiny the kitchen was.

"Since Dad died, Matt's mom's been sending food over religiously."

"That's really sweet of her."

"She's a good woman. I heard she came to help out at the inn." He took out two plates and silverware.

"She did. Isobel too."

"The pack takes care of their own."

A warm, fluttery feeling swept through me. I would never tire of hearing I was part of the pack.

He tipped his chin toward the offerings.

Realizing we still knew very little about each other, I asked, "What's your favorite food?"

"Steak." He spooned something that looked like polenta onto his plate before adding a bunch of green beans and a thick piece of browned meat. "Original, huh?" He shot me a brazen smile as he slid his plate into the microwave and pressed a couple buttons that filled the quiet kitchen with a soft whirring noise. "What about you?"

"I pretty much love everything. But I have a soft spot for Mexican cuisine. Evelyn" —I dragged my hand through my hair—"she made a lot of our meals back in LA."

After I prepped myself a plate, Liam set it in the microwave.

"Want anything to drink?"

"Water would be great."

He pulled open his fridge and took out a bottle of water and a beer.

"This feels like a first date," I said.

He uncapped his beer, then took a deep drink and swallowed before leaning over to kiss me. "I don't want this to be our first date. I want to take you out. Tomorrow night, you and me."

My heart rate accelerated, but then it dipped when I remembered that tomorrow night I would be deleting my cousin's contact from my phone forever. A sharp spike in my breathing had Liam tipping his head to the side.

"You don't want to be seen out with me?" he asked.

"What?" I tried to iron out my erratic pulse. "No, it's not that." I ran my index finger along the sweaty sides of my bottle. "I do want to go out with you, but not tomorrow."

His eyes shrouded with contrition. I wasn't sure—and didn't ask for fear of the answer—if the remorse was for my cousin or for postponing our dinner.

The microwave beeped then. He handed me my plate before propping himself on the stool beside mine. We didn't speak again after that, both of us tucking into our food, lost in our respective musings.

I didn't taste anything. It was just fuel for my depleted body and a means to avoid deliberating about Everest.

I took my plate over to the sink when I was done and scrubbed it clean.

"You don't have to do that, Ness. I have someone who comes over every couple days to clean."

"Been cleaning after myself and others for so long it's ingrained in my DNA." I smiled at him as I dried my hands on the kitchen towel tucked over the handle of the oven door.

"Was that really your job back in LA?"

"That, and waitressing, but I hated waitressing." I wrinkled my nose. "What's the cleaning company you use?"

Liam sipped the dregs of his beer. "Why?"

"Because I'll be out of a job soon."

"You're not seriously entertaining the idea of cleaning houses?"

I frowned. "It's what I know how to do, Liam."

"You're pack now, Ness."

"And what?" I crossed my arms in front of my chest. "Housekeeping is beneath werewolves?"

"I'll help you get a real job."

"Housekeeping *is* a real job."

"But you can do better."

"I have a high school education, Liam."

"Tomorrow, we'll stop by UCB and enroll you."

"You mean, after you off my cousin?" I snapped, voice as tight as the rest of my body.

Liam rose from his stool and rounded the island toward me. "Ness . . ."

I mashed my lips shut.

"You're angry."

I was. I was angry about Everest's fate. Angry about Liam's belittling view on my job. Angry I hadn't taken the next step in my education.

He set his palms on my sharp shoulders. "I get it, but don't be angry with me."

I glared at the dip of his midnight-colored V-neck, unwilling to look into his eyes.

"An Alpha protects his pack, Ness. Everest is a threat to you . . . to all of us." He hooked my chin and raised it until our eyes met. "As for your future, I think it would be best for you to go to college. I'm sure it's what your parents would've wanted."

My anger dissipated at the mention of my parents. In the last month of her life, Mom had hounded me to fill out college applications.

"I'll need to apply for financial aid first," I finally mumbled.

"The pack has resources. If you want to go to UCB in the fall, you'll have a spot there. All expenses paid."

"Even a dorm room?"

"Even a dorm room."

So I'd only need to figure out where to live for the next month . . . This felt too good to be true. "What's the catch?"

Liam smiled. "No catch. You're part of the pack. Education is one of the perks. We like our wolves to be equipped to conquer the world. Or at least, Boulder."

I was still going to need a job to pay back the four and a half grand I owed the bank for past rents and miscellaneous expenses, but I didn't want to bring that up again.

Liam wrapped his hands around my wrists and dragged down the bony blockade that separated our bodies. "Don't fence me out. I know you've been taking care of yourself for years, but I'm here now. And countless others are here for you too. Let us in. *Trust* us."

"I'm trying."

He pressed his mouth to mine, soft as silk, but then his kiss grew harder. It took me a few seconds to relax, but finally I sighed—more of a moan than a sigh—and hooked my hands around his waist. As though my heart had migrated into my stomach, my abdomen began to thud. I tried to squelch the offensive sensation, but it soon took over all the others.

I pulled away from Liam so quickly I half expected pieces of my lips to have stayed glued to his. His dark eyes raked over my expression, then over my body, pausing on the palm I'd pressed against my stomach. I lowered my hand, balling my fingers. The throbbing was already receding.

"Eric warned me about this, but I thought—" His Adam's apple worked in his throat. "I hoped it would be different."

"What did Eric warn you about?"

"He said your body would reject any advance that didn't come from its natural mate."

Horror filtered through me.

"The only way to void this is distance, but August isn't leaving." Liam sighed, and his muscular chest deflated the tiniest bit. "I don't know if you heard, but his mom had breast cancer a while back."

The word cancer soured my blood.

"They thought she'd beat it, but it's back. And more aggressive this time. Anyway, she's scheduled for a double mastectomy next week, and—"

I let out a shrill whimper before slamming the back of my hand against my mouth.

"Fuck." He gathered me against him. "I forgot cancer was how your mom . . ." He didn't finish his sentence. Didn't have to. He smoothed his hand over the back of my head.

I reeled from the news that hit too close to home. At least now I understood why Isobel's husband had fretted over her back at the inn, why she'd looked so wan beside her healthy son.

"August said the doctors were confident they'd get it this time, but he wants to stay until after the surgery. He promised he'd leave after."

I shook with anguish for Isobel, Nelson, and August, and with shame at how selfish I'd been. Not only had I believed that August had stayed for me, but I'd been ready to beg him to leave so I could be intimate with Liam. *Ugh.*

Liam tangled his hand in my hair. "He didn't want me to tell you, so please keep this between us."

I nodded, still pressing my knuckles against my mouth to stifle the dread brought on by Liam's news. "It's not fair," I murmured.

"Life's rarely fair." Even though I couldn't see into his mind, I sensed he was thinking of his own mother taken from him when he was only eight, by his abusive father no less.

"Speaking of unfair, I know you hate Everest, and I know you want to uphold the pack's"—I wet my lips—"*traditions*, but my cousin did you a favor. He killed your mother's murderer." I hoped phrasing it that way would sway him a little. "Won't you reconsider his sentence?"

Liam's fingers wrung my T-shirt as though it were Everest's neck. "My mother wasn't pack."

"So what?" Anger struck me in violent strokes. "Her life wasn't worth as much?"

"Don't mistake forgiveness for integrity." His eyes were so black his pupils seemed to have devoured his irises. "My father was a mean bastard, but he was still my father. If I let your cousin walk away from this, what sort of Alpha would that make me?"

"A merciful one."

"Mercy doesn't inspire respect."

"That's not true. Compassion is a laudable trait in a leader. I'd respect you for showing compassion to someone who didn't deserve it."

His gaze set on the shiny chocolate marble. "Don't, Ness."

"Don't what?"

"Don't tell me how to rule the pack. I'm the Alpha, not you."

His words grated against me, made my spine snap straight. "You might win the pack's respect with those words, but not mine." I backed away from him and walked into the living room. "Not mine."

"Where are you going?" He strode behind me.

"Outside."

He captured my wrist and wheeled me toward him. "I'm sorry. I shouldn't have said that. I'm just tired and on edge, and with all that's going on with you"—he gestured to my abdomen—"it came out wrong."

I stared at his fingers still clasping my wrist.

"I want your respect"—he tucked a piece of hair behind my ear—"but I can't change pack laws for as much. Not yet. In time—"

"You accepted me—a girl—into the pack and you didn't taint the new pledges' drinks with the stupid fossil, so you *can* change things! When you want to, you can. Which just proves you want my cousin dead or you'd have forgiven him." I flipped my hand up to loosen his grip, then yanked my arm toward me to break his hold. His fingers hadn't hurt me, yet I nursed my wrist against my chest.

His eyes widened as they fastened to the spot of skin they'd manhandled. He palmed the back of his head. And then he fell to his knees in front of me and pressed his face against my stomach, arms hooking around me.

"I'm sorry, Ness. Please don't leave."

I watched him for a long moment, watched how his apology made his big body quiver. It brought me back to the night on the inn's terrace when he'd cried in my arms. He wasn't crying now, but he was shaking.

Liam might've acted strong and brave, but so much inside him was broken, and although I was good with messes, I didn't know where to start on the one his parents had left behind. Could *I* even fix it? I was such a mess myself. Orphaned. Almost homeless. Penniless. Mated.

I rested a hand on top of his head. "I won't leave you, Liam."

He tipped his head up and inspected my face as though to make sure I was speaking the truth, and then he climbed up the length of my body. For a long minute, he just stood there, looking down at me instead of up, and I saw the solid man inside him rise again, push back the wrecked child.

Then he cupped my cheeks and tilted my head up, and he slammed his mouth against mine. Even though my stomach began to churn, I pried my lips open and tangled my tongue with his.

I didn't delude myself into thinking that this was the end of our argument, but it was a ceasefire. I wished it would last, but how could it when tomorrow he'd leave to perform a vile act? I pushed my cousin's face out of my mind while Liam demolished my mouth. I tasted blood even though none had yet been spilled.

Liam groaned and kissed me harder. The taste of blood thickened in my mouth to the point where I gagged. I dug my palms into his chest and pushed him away.

Liam's mouth and chin were smeared red.

12

"Oh my God, you're bleeding!" I yelped.

"You did bite me." There was a lilt in his tone. *Amusement?*

How could this amuse him?

I swiped my tongue against my teeth, and sure enough, my canines had lengthened. I touched my mouth. My fingertips came away red. Absolute revulsion seized me.

Liam's smile widened as he grabbed a tissue from the leather box atop the console next to the front door. He dabbed his lips, dabbed mine. Blood still trickled from the puncture wound.

"Damn if that wasn't the hottest kiss I've ever had."

I blinked at him. How could *that* have been pleasurable?

He pressed the tissue to his mouth a while longer before balling it up and tossing it on the console.

"I *hurt* you," I said, my voice as raw as his broken lip.

He frowned. "Babe, getting bitten only increases the pleasure. Or so I've been told . . . since I've never been with a she-wolf."

I momentarily forgot about having bit him. However silly, I liked the fact that I was different from his past girlfriends.

His eyes flashed yellow—wolf eyes. "Do you trust me?"

I nodded.

He nudged my jaw up with his nose, dragged his teeth that had sharpened to points down my neck, then sank them into a patch of skin right above my collarbone.

I gasped, but not in pain.

The skin he'd pierced tingled, and then shockwaves of pleasure radiated from that one spot into the rest of my body. He released my skin and laved the spot he'd bitten with his tongue.

"Fuck, you taste sweet." Once he was done lapping up all the blood, he peered into my stunned face with a satisfied smirk. "I'm happy I've found one way to pleasure you. Even though I'm not giving up on finding more."

Heat engulfed my cheeks, my entire body for that matter. "I thought only vampires did *that*."

"Vampires don't exist."

Yet we do . . .

He licked his lust-swollen lips, eyes gleaming but no longer yellow. "Have you ever heard the legend of the bite that saved a life?"

I shook my head.

"It's a good story. One of my favorites. My grandfather used to tell it to me."

I rubbed the spot Liam had bitten.

"Apparently, during a terrible forest fire, an Alpha was hit by a blazing fallen tree. The blow was so violent that while his pack worked to roll the crackling trunk off him, they felt his link to them unravel. His second-in-command"—I frowned, so he explained—"large packs have *betas*. Well, he urged the wolves to make their way home to prevent any more casualties, but the Alpha's mate, she refused to leave him. She dug a trench in the ground to reach him, and then she grabbed him by the neck and dragged his asphyxiated body out. Legend says that when her fangs pierced his skin, her love for him leaked into his bloodstream and jumpstarted his heart." He shrugged. "Story's probably embellished, but I like to think our magic has the power to save lives." He moved my fingers off the spot I was still rubbing and kissed it.

I shivered. I hadn't lost much blood, yet felt as lightheaded as when I'd extracted a whole pint from my veins to try and save my mother. She'd insisted that injecting herself with my blood wouldn't magically defeat her ovarian cancer, but I'd tried one gray afternoon. While I'd slid the needle in her catheter-bruised arm, I'd begged for a miracle.

Unlike the Alpha's mate from Liam's legend, I never got my miracle, so I didn't put much stock in our magic saving a life.

Liam tugged me out of my dreary memory by leading me into the bedroom. He flicked on the lamp on his nightstand, then let go of my hand and walked to his connecting bathroom. "Give me a sec."

He vanished into his en suite, leaving me to stand on the edge of the electric-violet rug that stretched from one wood-paneled wall to the other. Alone in the bedroom, my thoughts whirred like the microwave, continuously spinning images of my cousin.

How I wished I could save his life.

Over my shoulder, I spied my bag on the couch. My phone was in there. I could text Everest. I could warn him. He could run and stay away forever. Glancing at the bedroom door, I took my phone out and hovered my finger over the text messaging icon.

With a few little words, I could change the course of his fate. I almost went through with it, but then I thought about how he'd toyed with my life, how he'd strangled Heath, and realized I couldn't betray the pack for the sake of a blood-tie.

As I lowered my phone, it vibrated, and a message appeared on my screen.

SARAH: *Hey, friend, want to hang tomorrow?*

Even though I was feeling rather glum, Sarah's message managed to make me smile.

ME: *Would love to.*

SARAH: *Lunch at Tracy's at 3?*

ME: *No one has lunch at 3.*

SARAH: *We do.*

I shook my head. *Fine. See you tomorrow.*

The floorboards creaked, and I jumped.

Liam leaned against the doorframe of his bedroom, jeans slung low on his hips—and shirtless. My throat went a little dry at the sight of his honed chest and the indents at his waist, and the thickening trail of dark hair. Liam was so incredibly perfect. Why did I have to imprint on August?

"Who you texting?" There was a hint of something in Liam's tone—suspicion or jealousy?

"Sarah. We're meeting up tomorrow."

He uncrossed his arms and strolled over to me. "Can you be careful with her? I know she's your friend, but she's a Pine. I don't trust Pines. Same way I don't trust Creeks, or any of the Eastern packs."

"And you say I'm the one with trust issues?"

He flashed me an almost predatorial smile as he plucked the phone from my fingers and tossed it on his leather couch. "You're wearing too many clothes. Arms up."

I looked around me at the walls of glass and the night-soaked landscape beyond them.

"No one's out there," he promised. Sensing my enduring anguish, he walked over to the wall and hit a switch that brought down metal blinds before returning to me.

"Are you sure?"

"Close your eyes."

I frowned but did as I was told.

"Now, listen."

Still frowning, I strained to listen. It took a second for me to hear anything over my quick breathing and the droning of the descending metal curtain, but then I made out the steady thump of Liam's heart, the plink of insects against the windows, the rush of a breeze over the swaying wild grass, the scratch of pine needles, the hoot of owls, the flutter of insect wings, and the shallow beat of hearts too tiny to be human or wolf.

"I know you're still growing attuned to your senses, but never forget to use them. Being human allows us to live in the world. Being a wolf allows us to survive in it."

Delicately, he gathered my wrists in one hand and raised them toward the ceiling. With his other hand, he dragged my T-shirt up and over my head and arms.

Goose bumps pebbled my skin as desire spread through me. Even though my body wasn't meant for Liam's, it still desired his. After he unhooked my bra, he dipped his face to my breasts and breathed against my sensitive skin.

"Does this hurt?" His voice was low and husky.

"No," I said, a little breathily.

His fingers skimmed down my stomach, unbuttoned my jeans, and slowly rolled them off. He was on his knees again, but this time, it wasn't to implore me. His gaze turned hooded as his face leveled off on a part of me that no man had ever been near.

He hooked a finger in the side of black lace. Cold sweat slicked over my brow as he roamed nearer to my core. When a bolt of pain shot up to my navel, I batted his hand away.

"I'm sorry. I'm sorry," I croaked. "This sucks."

Liam rose to his feet, wrapped his arms around my body that had begun to tremble, and tucked my head underneath his chin. "It does, but it's just temporary."

I rested my cheek against his thumping chest, wondering why my wolf had to go and choose August as a mate.

13

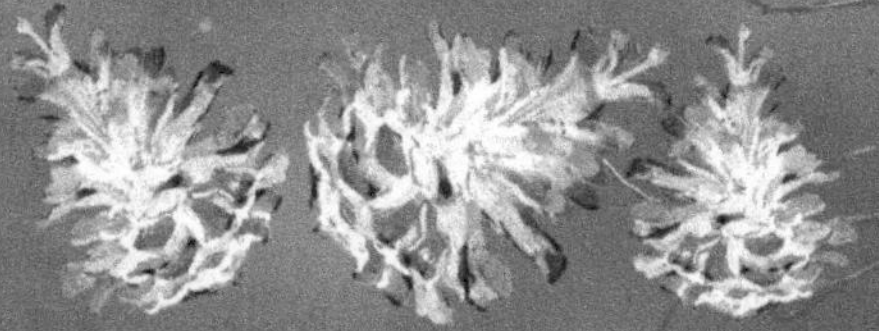

I awoke with a start. Disoriented, I took in the room that was streaked with dull sunlight. My gaze landed on the peacock feather painting over the stone fireplace. I was in Liam's room.

In his bed.

I twisted around and touched his pillow. It was cold. I tore the sheets off my legs and leaped out of bed.

"Liam," I called out, padding about the bedroom.

The door to the bathroom was cracked open, but no one was inside. I picked up my phone and checked the time, reeling when I made out the digital readout: 10:30 a.m. I couldn't remember the last time I'd slept in this late.

My phone's screen was riddled with messages from Evelyn asking me where I was and if I was okay. I dispatched a quick text to inform her I was fine and on my way to the inn.

Liam had also sent me a text message: *On the road to Denver. I already miss you.*

My heart began jackknifing my throat, making breathing a feat.

I checked the time stamp on Liam's text: 7:30 a.m. That meant he was already in Denver. Had been for more than two hours. The fact that I hadn't gotten a message from him made me queasy as hell. Did that mean they were out looking for Everest? Or did it mean they'd already gotten to him and were on their way back? Images of what they could be doing to him wafted through my mind like sticky chimney smoke.

I quieted my imagination. I needed to corral my mind, keep it from crafting scenarios. I looked for my clothes but remembered they were in the living room. In my underwear, I padded toward the door.

When I opened it, Lucas looked up from his magazine. "She finally awakens."

I shut the door with such force that the hinges rattled. *Crap. Crap. Crap.* I cupped my hands over my bare breasts as though he could somehow see them through the door.

"Would it help if I got naked too?"

Help? How did Lucas think that would help?

"I take your silence as a negative."

I hunted down a towel and wrapped it around myself. Pulling in great big gulps of air, I trudged back to the door and yanked it open.

Lucas smirked. "You do know you're pack now, Ness. You're going to have to get used to getting naked in front of us. It'll help you bond with your people."

"You and your bonding . . ." I muttered, trudging to the couch.

"Paintball was fun, eh? We should do it again."

"I'd rather eat a rotten squirrel."

He chucked his magazine on the wrought-iron coffee table before readjusting the royal-blue baseball cap he wore backward. "So cold, Clark."

"What part of paintballing was fun? Getting shot by my own teammates?" I plucked my bra off the couch before grabbing my jeans and T-shirt. "You guys were awful to me."

"It's called hazing. Everyone goes through it."

"Really? Who else in the pack got to experience the same *fun* treatment as me?"

Lucas shot me a sheepish grin.

"That's what I thought."

"Did you ever hear that holding onto resentment is like drinking poison? Only hurts you."

I gritted my teeth. "What are you doing here, anyway? Come to play guard dog again?"

He puffed air out of the corner of his lips. "First off, I'm a wolf, not a dog. Secondly, even though spending the day with you is as exciting as clipping my toenails, I take my job seriously."

Did he have to give me a visual of his feet? *Yuck.*

He got up and rubbed his hands against his black mesh shorts. "Besides, if all goes well, you'll be rid of me by tonight."

His words echoed through me. *If all goes well* . . . In other words, if Everest was found and killed.

I clamped my fingers around my clothes. "Do you have any news?"

"No." He studied me for a long second. "So, what's the plan?" His voice was a tad less cocky, as though he felt pity for me instead of annoyance. He must've figured out that my sullen mood was more due to what was happening in Denver than what was going down in Boulder.

"Do you have a car?" I asked.

"I have access to one." He gestured to the window. Even though the sky was overcast, Liam's black SUV gleamed.

However much I wanted to get rid of Lucas, I couldn't deny how practical it was that he could drive. "You have a license, right?"

He cocked the eyebrow slashed by the white scar. "Since I was sixteen. Why? You don't?"

I pressed my lips together. "No, I don't."

"Seriously?" His eyebrow seemed to rise a couple more millimeters.

"I never had time to get it. But that's what I wanted to do today. After I stop by the inn to see Evelyn and Isobel." I started for the bedroom door, holding my clothes against me, but paused and turned back to Lucas. For the first time since I'd woken up, I smiled. "Oh, and then I'm having lunch with Sarah at three at Tracy's. Or should I say, *we're* having lunch with her?"

His lips puckered as though he'd swallowed something sour. As I entered the bedroom, I heard him grumble something that sounded like, *"I'm not being paid enough for that."*

I smirked as I donned yesterday's outfit. When I returned to the living room, tying my hair up in a ponytail, Lucas was gone. I spied him outside, crouched with his nose low to the ground. Heart pounding in time with my feet, I treaded to him, surveying the dirt road and the gently swaying pines.

"Is something wrong?" My low words were snatched up by the blustery breeze.

"I got a whiff of some wolves."

"From the pack?"

"No."

"Pines?"

His nostrils flared one more time before he unfurled his long body back to standing. "No."

"Real ones, then?"

"Smell." He nodded to the grass.

I crouched and inhaled. Mixed among the earthy, green aroma of the slick blades was the woolly scent of wolf edged with the distinctive musky scent of humans.

Werewolves.

14

"How can you tell they're not Boulders?" I rose from my crouch, morning dew seeping into the fabric of my tight jeans.

"I'm a tracker, Ness."

"Meaning?"

"Meaning while you studied calc, I sniffed scraps of fabric belonging to various bodies before going after them."

"You didn't go to school?"

"Oh, I went to school." He flashed me a smug grin. "I just had more interesting after-school activities than most."

As we walked toward the car, I said, "I have a lot to learn."

"What?" He slapped a palm over his chest. "The great Ness Clark doesn't know *everything?*"

I slugged his bicep, and it was like hitting solid rock. "Shut up."

He chuckled, which was strange, because Lucas was a sulky bastard, not a chuckler. He jutted his chin toward the house. "You locked up?"

"I don't have a key."

"Liam didn't give you a key?"

I frowned. "Why would he?"

As he pulled out a keyring from the pocket of his mesh shorts, he cast me a sideways glance. I didn't ask what his look meant. While Lucas locked up, I climbed into the SUV and strapped myself in. A minute later, he sprang behind the wheel and revved up the engine.

As he pulled out of the driveway, I examined the forest again. "Is there another pack in these parts?"

"Not that I know of."

"So loners?"

"Possibly. But they're playing with fire by running around here. If they value their lives, they better have been passing through."

The landscape was cloaked in a gray light that turned everything flatter, duller. I was glad there was no sun. I didn't feel like sunshine. I checked my phone for updates on the Everest hunt. Having none, I stuffed my phone into my bag.

"Nervous?" Lucas asked as we headed up the inn's long driveway.

I chewed on my thumbnail. "Aren't you?"

"Nah. I have total faith in my Alpha." He side-eyed me. "Unless he's not the person you're nervous for."

The golden log façade of the inn rose beyond the windshield. Soon it would belong to a detestable man. Aidan would probably strip it of its hominess and transform it into another impersonal, multi-million dollar venture.

"He's my flesh and blood, Lucas."

"He used you, then tried to have you killed, yet you hope he gets away with his life? I don't get it, Clark."

I twirled the ends of my ponytail. "What if there's more to it? What if he didn't mean to do any of that? What if Aidan Michaels coerced him to do it? Or blackmailed him?"

"And what if Aidan Michaels didn't?"

My skin prickled from his sharp answer. Then that would make my cousin truly heartless. "I guess we'll never know since Everest won't get a trial."

I gripped my door handle.

"We're not animals. They'll interrogate him before putting him down."

Sucking in a sticky lungful of air, I gritted out, "He's not a dog."

"You know what I mean."

I did, but it still bothered me. "You don't have to come inside."

"Until it's over, I'm shadowing your ass."

I heaved an annoyed breath and hopped out.

While Lucas went to park, I pushed through the revolving doors. The inn was bright and warm and smelled faintly of potpourri and varnished pine, scents I'd come to associate with Boulder. It wasn't home, and it wasn't a safe haven, but for a while it had been the closest place to a home I'd had. I stopped by the bell desk where Isobel was answering a call. She raised her index finger. I waited, studying her face. She was pale, but not sickly so. And although her cheekbones pressed against her skin and her shoulders jutted through her cream blouse, she wasn't emaciated. For a moment, I superimposed the image of my mother over Isobel, and my heartbeats slowed.

After she hung up, she smiled. "Hey, sweet girl."

"Hi. How . . ." I'd been about to ask how she was feeling, but I wasn't supposed to know. "How's everything going this morning?" I jerked a hand toward the inn.

"All's fine. Quiet night. Quiet morning. I've rescheduled a couple outings for some of the guests because of the weather, and I reorganized the cleaning staff schedules."

"Thank you."

"You have nothing to thank me for." She squeezed my hand. Her skin was clammy, the same way my mother's had been on the worst of days. "I also went to check on Jeb. He's been sleeping most of the morning. I dropped off some food. Perhaps you should stop by to see him. He might appreciate some company."

I wondered if she knew what was happening. Wives weren't kept in the dark, but were they informed of the Alpha's every move?

"After I stop by to see Evelyn, I'll go sit with him."

I also needed a shower and fresh clothes. Could she smell Liam on me? She wasn't a wolf, but she'd seen me walk in, so she knew I'd spent the night somewhere other than my own bed. If she sensed where I'd been, there was no judgment on her face. Just a sweet smile. Why did disease have to attack the good people? Why couldn't it strike down people like Aidan Michaels?

I started in the direction of the kitchen when Isobel's voice stopped me. "Do you have any plans for dinner tonight?"

I turned around just as Lucas came through the doors. I longed to say no, but in what state would I be tonight? In what state would Liam be? Plus going to dinner at the Watts' probably meant August would be there, and even though I'd spent my childhood having dinner with him and his family, things were different now.

"I can't tonight," I ended up saying, at the same time as Lucas said, "Morning, Mrs. W."

"Good morning, Lucas." She smiled at him before looking back at me. "Okay. Let me know when you have a free night. I'd love to catch up."

"I . . . I will. I promise. Maybe this weekend?"

"You just let me know. Or you just show up. Our house is your house."

Her words squeezed my heart. I gave a jerky nod before resuming my walk toward the kitchen. The large space was riddled with delicious smells that had my empty stomach rumbling.

"Ness!" Evelyn handed Kasie the tongs before hobbling toward me.

The change in air pressure always made her arthritis flare up, and considering how she limped this morning, I sensed her body ached. I met her halfway. The menthol balm she religiously rubbed into her sore joints soothed my frayed nerves.

She kissed both my cheeks, surely leaving bright lipstick smears behind. "Kasie, do you have everything under control? I need to speak to Ness."

"Take your time, Evelyn. I've got our vegetables *provençal* covered."

Evelyn tucked my hand in the crook of her arm and pulled me toward the door. "Come. Let's have some tea, *querida*."

I grabbed a teapot from a high shelf in the pantry, when Skylar popped in carrying a laden breakfast tray. "Hey! How are you, hun?"

She set down the tray next to the sink, then pushed a piece of peroxided hair off her forehead and seized the teapot from me. "Here, let me do that. Black, green, herbal?"

"Earl Grey," I said. Evelyn only liked dark teas. "But I can do it—"

She shooed us away. "Out of my pantry."

"Thank you, Skylar," Evelyn said. "We will be on the terrace. It is not raining yet, is it?"

Reaching up to grab the tin box of loose-leaf tea, Skylar said, "Not yet, but I suspect it'll come down any minute."

"We will take our chances," Evelyn said, guiding me through the dining room and out onto the deck.

Only Lucas was out here. He'd taken a seat on one of the many Adirondacks and was checking out something on his phone. Had Liam sent a message? I was tempted to pull out my phone, but it could wait until after my visit with Evelyn.

The sky was tiled with mauve clouds that reminded me of the quilt Mom had sewn for me when I was a kid, the one I'd given to the army vet on our street corner one unseasonably cold winter day. While the man's dog growled at me—I assumed because I still smelled like a wolf—his master smiled, raising the bottle of liquor that seemed forever grafted to his palm, and gathered the cover around himself and his pet.

Eyeing Lucas, Evelyn walked toward the farthermost edge of the terrace. We took our seats at a square teak table.

In a low voice, she said, "Frank informed me that my ex-husband has purchased the inn from your family."

I darted a glance toward the enormous glass sliding doors, making sure that Skylar hadn't emerged from the entrails of the inn. I didn't want to alarm the loyal staff before alarm needed to be sounded. Perhaps Aidan Michaels would safeguard their jobs. I didn't know his intentions for the place. Was it simply a strategic location to keep the packs in check, or was this a business transaction to grow his real estate portfolio?

"Evelyn, do you think he bought it to insult . . . *us*?"

By us, I meant werewolves, although I didn't doubt for a second that Aidan was the type of man who'd take great pleasure in thwarting his ex-wife's happiness. Since the man was a snoop with too many connections, I didn't doubt for a second he knew she was back in Boulder.

"Or do you think he bought it as an investment?"

She scratched at a piece of citronella candlewax that had melted onto the teak. "He does not need more money or more land, *querida*."

In other words, this was no commercial endeavor.

"Here y'all go," Skylar said chirpily, depositing a wooden tray loaded with two mugs, a teapot, a bowl of sugar, a tiny pitcher of milk, and a plate of bite-sized jam cookies—one of Evelyn's specialties.

Since Evelyn had gotten access to a larger kitchen and a limitless quantity of fresh produce, she'd been making the jam herself, and the already delicious cookies had become downright sinful.

"Can I get you anything else?" Skylar asked, eyeballing the sky.

"No thank you," Evelyn said. "You have already spoiled us."

I smiled up at Skylar, who returned my smile, but her lips kept bending and straightening, as though she wanted to ask me what was wrong. Even though we'd only known each other for two months, I sensed she understood me; perhaps it was because we'd both lost our mothers. Skylar had once told me that she was a good listener in case I needed to talk.

I hadn't wanted to talk about Mom then. I still didn't want to talk about her. Her absence remained too fresh. Although I no longer cried when someone brought her up, it still abraded my heart.

"I haven't seen Emmy yet, but can you thank your wife for covering last night's shift, please? Jeb and . . . and Lucy, they really appreciate it."

She grinned. "Will do. Anyway, let me know if you need anything else."

Evelyn poured two cups of piping hot tea while I pilfered a cookie from the plate.

"Frank has an extra bedroom, which I readied for you last night. I want you to come and live with us. I know Jeb is your legal guardian, but he is incapable of caring for you, and I am not too fond of the men who prowl around you." She flicked her gaze toward Lucas, which had my nose wrinkling. I hoped she didn't assume he was a suitor, because . . . *gross*.

"Are you sure Frank won't mind?"

She placed her calloused hand over mine. "Frank does not mind. His house is . . . it is big. On weekends, his grandson Joseph visits, but otherwise, he lives there alone."

"Not anymore."

Her lips curled into a demure smile.

How I loved the glimmer Frank had put in her obsidian eyes and the rosiness he'd brought to her foundation-caked complexion. I loved that she'd gotten her happy ending. If anyone deserved happiness, it was Evelyn.

"Meet me in the kitchen tonight. We will leave together after I finish making dinner."

"Okay."

We drank our tea quietly after that, both of us enjoying each other's easy company. Almost an hour later, we both stood to leave. She leaned toward me as though to kiss my cheek, but instead she asked, "Why does the boy over there keep looking in your direction?"

"He's just helping me out with some errands today. You know, driving me around."

If I told Evelyn the truth, that Liam was afraid Everest might try to hurt me, she'd fret, and I didn't want her to fret more than she already did.

She kissed my cheeks and then rubbed them. "There. I've added some color to that pale face of yours."

In spite of my summer tan, I could feel I was pasty, the same way I could feel the first drops of rain needling my bare arms. I closed my lids and lifted my face skyward, welcoming the downpour.

15

Once I was showered and changed, I dropped by Jeb's room, Lucas in tow. It took a lot of convincing on my part, but I managed to get him to stay outside while I visited with my uncle. My intentions for stopping by weren't only selfless, though. I'd printed all the forms for my permit, for which I needed my guardian's signature.

Isobel must've drawn the curtains open, because the muted light splashed his bedroom.

"Hi, Jeb. It's Ness," I said as I approached him. I didn't want to spook him.

"Is it done?" His voice was jaded, just like his expression.

"I don't know." I pulled a chair up to the bed. "Have you eaten?" The laden tray on his nightstand told me he hadn't, but I was hoping my question might stir his interest in food.

"And Lucy?"

"Lucy?"

He fastened his pale-blue gaze flecked by burst blood vessels to my face. "I thought you might have some news."

I shook my head. "But I can call Eric. Do you want me to phone him?" I didn't have Eric's number, but Lucas probably did. I could get it from him.

"No," Jeb said quietly. For a long moment, neither of us spoke. Then my uncle's insubstantial voice gusted through the quiet bedroom. "What do I have to live for now, Ness?"

I could've lied to him and said the inn, but he didn't even have that anymore. Who was going to take him in?

"You heard Everest sold the inn to Aidan Michaels?"

His pupils contracted with surprise, and his pale lips fell open. He hadn't known.

"He sold it in exchange for his help in"—I toyed with my mother's ring, weaving my fingers in and out of it—"tampering with the pack's security monitors and getting out of Boulder."

My uncle gaped at me, confirming he hadn't known any of this. Talk about being the harbinger of crap news. I released the ring and set both my palms on my knees.

"I should never have put it in his name. Lucy, she said—" His voice broke. "Doesn't matter anymore what she said." He sealed his lips, as though to prevent himself from badmouthing the mother of his child. After another long stretch of silence, he said, "I own a few apartments in downtown Boulder."

I frowned.

"I'll have one readied for us."

I squeezed my knees. "*Us?*"

"You and me."

So he wasn't planning on ending his life. "You don't have to worry about me, Jeb. Frank said he could take me in—"

"You're my ward, not his," he snapped. That was the most energy I'd heard permeate his tone since the day of the last trial when he'd found his wife holding Evelyn hostage.

I wanted to live with Evelyn, but I couldn't abandon my uncle. "Okay."

Suddenly, he sat up in bed. "Can you hand me my cell?"

I got up to retrieve his phone from where I'd put it to charge days ago and then I stood watch as he dialed a number and barked at the unfortunate soul on the other end.

After disconnecting, he said, "Have one of the housekeepers stop by this address. The place probably needs a good cleaning." He filched a pad of paper embossed with the inn's logo and a pen from the drawer of his nightstand table, scribbled an address, then tore off the paper.

I took it reluctantly, but then pushed away my reluctance. Although my uncle had been the one to drag me back to Boulder the second he found out I was living in LA motherless, he wasn't to blame for the fiasco that had ensued. If anything, I should have been relieved that he cared enough for me that he wasn't skirting his responsibilities. I folded the note with the address, deciding I would take care of the cleaning myself.

He got out of bed so suddenly I stepped back so he wouldn't bump into me and send me flying backward. Anger flushed his features and sparked in his eyes.

"I can't believe he struck a deal with your father's killer," he muttered under his breath, grabbing the frame of a watercolor painting and tugging on it hard.

I braced for chaos by hunching a little, but Jeb didn't toss the canvas across the room. Instead, the frame folded like a book page. Behind it was a safe. He entered a six-digit number, and the safe beeped. He rifled inside, rustling papers, knocking over jewelry boxes until he found what he was looking for: an envelope. He peered inside, extracted two keys hooked to the same ring. He slid one off and tossed me the keyring. It landed at my feet.

"The key to our new home. Good thing I didn't entrust it to my son. Can't believe he sold Aidan Michaels our inn." Jeb was so red I worried he would give himself an aneurism. Not that wolves could die of aneurisms.

I crouched to retrieve the keyring. "What happens once Lucy is released?"

My uncle stopped muttering and peered up at me.

I stared at the small silver key nestled in the palm of my hand. "I don't want to live with her, Jeb. I can't," I said raising my gaze back to my uncle.

"I'm filing for divorce."

Oh.

Jeb walked over to me and gripped my shoulders. "We'll get through this, Ness."

His renewed desire to live restored my hope that we could heal from the deepest of wounds. Changed and scarred, but we survived. Even though I sensed Evelyn would put up a fight, I was touched that my uncle hadn't abandoned me.

"You know, Callum was always trying to give me pointers about how to raise my son. It drove me insane, but now, I wish I'd listened to him." He gave my shoulders a squeeze before letting go. "You're a good kid, Ness."

I pressed my lips together to drive back the emotion rising in my throat.

"Now, go pack your bags."

I nodded and started walking toward the door but remembered the papers I needed him to sign. I took them out, and he signed them, telling me not to schedule driving lessons, that he'd give them to me himself.

Another wave of emotion surged within me. Jeb could never replace my father, the same way Evelyn had never taken my mother's place, but I was glad for his support and his presence in my life, and hopeful that it would take some weight off my shoulders. I would never get to be a kid again—I didn't even desire it—but I wouldn't mind splitting some of my responsibilities with an adult.

16

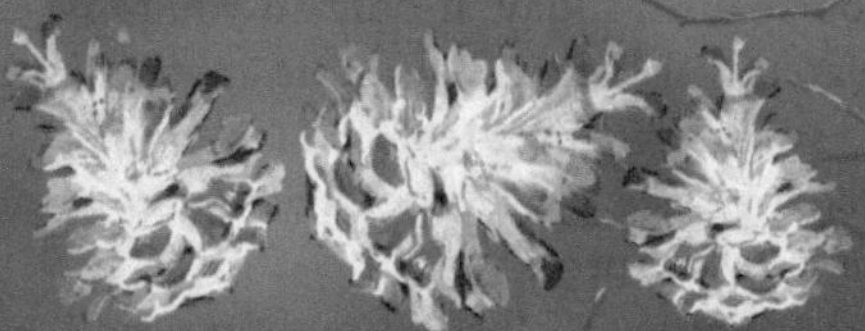

By the time Lucas and I reached Tracy's, Sarah was already there.

I'd packed my bags and swung by the new apartment to drop them off and make a list of cleaning products to purchase. Jeb's investment was on the top floor of a two-story house, about ten blocks away from Tracy's. The bedrooms were small, but they had their own bathrooms, and the living area had an open kitchen and an obstructed view of the mountains. In spite of the musty smell and the bare furnishings, I decided I didn't hate it.

What would've been the point in hating it? It was to be my new home. Besides, I'd hopefully be moving into a dorm room soon. I was glad all my stuff fit in two blue Ikea bags. If I'd owned more things, relocating would've been a much bigger hassle. Besides, I adhered to my mother's philosophy that *things* and the desire to always amass more stripped people of happiness and freedom. *"The lighter you travel, the farther you'll go,"* she used to tell me. Back then, it had frustrated me not to be able to get a new backpack at the start of the school year or the Adidas sneakers everyone else was sporting, but I'd learned to stop wanting *things*. It had taken years. To be honest, it had taken my mother falling ill. Nothing else but finding a cure to keep her alive had mattered then.

I walked past the bar toward the wooden table Sarah was sitting at, drumming her perfectly manicured fingernails in time with the rain battering the windowed façade. She smiled when she caught sight of me, but then her smile wilted when she caught sight of my *bodyguard*.

Instead of sitting at another table like he'd done at the inn, Lucas plopped down on the seat beside Sarah. "If it isn't my favorite Pine."

"You don't have a favorite Pine," Sarah shot back. Then to me, she asked, "Why is the Neanderthal here?"

Lucas smirked, twisting the cap on his head. "Still at it with the name-calling, I see."

Sarah glared at him, eyes a condemning shade of brown.

I sighed. "Long story."

"I'm listening." Sarah leaned back in her chair and folded her arms, making her extremely generous cleavage pop. I caught Lucas checking her out, and not just for a second or discreetly. He stared at her chest almost a full minute. *Sleazeball.*

Once I was done giving her the highlights, she uncrossed her arms. "Shit, Ness. That fuckin' sucks."

"Tell me about it."

"I hope they get your cousin today. If only so you're no longer stuck with this one." She tipped her head toward Lucas who stole another lengthy look at her chest. "Eyes up, Mason. Didn't your father ever teach you manners?"

Lucas's gaze slid up to her face. "My father died before I started noticing anatomical differences between girls and boys."

Sarah surely knew that Lucas had lost his parents—unlike me, she'd had a thorough werewolf and pack education. When a breathy gasp stumbled out of her mouth, I frowned.

"Forgot about that," she said, a tad more gently.

"Was a long time ago." Lucas removed his cap, dragged his fingers through his black hair, then screwed the hat back on. "Look who's staring now?" Lucas said, one corner of his mouth tilting up.

Sarah spun back toward me.

Lucas flexed his arm. "Want to cop a feel?"

"Seriously?" She wrinkled her nose, seizing the laminated menu, which I was pretty certain she knew by heart. "I'd rather pet a rattlesnake than your bicep."

"You like snakes, huh?"

"Leave her alone, Lucas," I warned.

He flashed me a cocky grin before raising his eyes to the TV broadcasting a tennis game.

A waitress with thick bangs, a perky smile, and an even perkier voice arrived to take our order. While I asked for a BLT and water, Sarah and Lucas ordered cheeseburgers and Cokes. I wondered if Miss Perky had been the girl Lucas had alluded to the day August had helped fix stuff up in the inn, the one who'd be really glad that he'd stayed in town. I was tempted to ask, but feared it would make me sound jealous instead of what I truly was: curious.

As though thinking of August activated the link, my stomach tightened. I rubbed it while Lucas and Sarah bickered about the music she'd played at The Den last Saturday, and the waitress returned with a pitcher. As she poured water into my glass, the door of Tracy's opened.

The water overflowed from my glass, spilling onto the table and dribbling onto my lap. I backed away from the table so fast my chair legs scraped against the worn wooden slats. She righted the pitcher, then apologizing profusely, she grabbed a handful of paper napkins from the dispenser on the table to clean up the mess.

"It's okay," I said, following her line of sight, which had returned to the entrance of the place.

To Cole and August.

August was absentmindedly rubbing his abdomen. When he spotted me behind the blushing waitress, his hand froze and then lowered, fingers balling into a fist.

Yep, it sucked.

For both of us.

Cole elbowed August and pointed to our table. From August's reluctant strides, I sensed he wanted to go anywhere but near me.

"Hey, Ness." Cole smiled, then nodded at Sarah and Lucas before greeting the waitress by her first name: *Kelly*.

Kelly barely registered his greeting, her entire focus on August. "I thought you'd left."

He scratched the back of his neck. "I've had to delay my departure." His face was all tensed up, which I imagined had more to do with our bothersome link than with Kelly's attention.

"Heard you and Sienna broke up." She said this very softly, so softly that if I'd been human, I would probably have missed it.

August's fingers stilled, and his eyebrows drew together. His expression, coupled with the relentless throbbing in my navel, screamed of discomfort.

I caught Sarah sniffing the air. A frown ghosted over her face. Could she smell our link? I remembered Liam saying that August had smelled like me or me like him . . . or something along those lines, but I assumed the smell had faded.

Thankfully, Sarah shattered the awkward silence. "Don't any of you have jobs?"

The three boys glanced at each other.

"Ness *is* my job," Lucas said, which made August swing the full force of his gaze from Kelly to the shaggy-haired shifter.

"And we're taking a break. Weather's way too brutal," Cole said.

Unlike my jeans that were sticking to my skin, neither his nor August's clothes were drenched, so they must've changed before coming in here. Or maybe their bodies heated at a higher temperature than mine and had already made the moisture evaporate.

Cole gestured to the pool tables in the back. "Want to join us for a game of cutthroat?"

"Thought you'd never ask." Lucas all but bounded out of his seat.

"Ness?" Cole didn't say Sarah's name, but he looked at her, which surely meant he was extending the invitation to my friend.

I shook my head. "I want to catch up with Sarah."

"We still have *so much* to catch up on," she added.

Once the boys were out of earshot and the waitress had scampered away, Sarah hissed, "Why does August Watt smell like you?"

I winced. "Do we really smell alike?" I whispered.

"Unless August and you have been swapping body lotions, then yeah. Usually dudes smell like"—she waved a hand toward the seat Lucas had just vacated—"the inside of a locker room."

"Is it really obvious?"

"To a person who knows you and your smell, yeah."

I wrinkled my nose at her wording. I figured she didn't mean it derogatively.

"Did you guys imprint on each other?"

I bit my lower lip.

"Shit." Her chair creaked as she leaned forward. "So you and Liam are already over, huh?"

"No. Why would you jump to that conclusion?"

She pressed slightly away from the table. "Babe, you do understand the purpose of mating links, right?"

"I understand their *purpose*, but I have no plans on dumping my boyfriend to jump into another man's bed."

"It's sort of unavoidable. Your body must've shut out all other males. My brother and Margaux are mates. He tried to resist her at first. He had a girlfriend. It lasted all of a week. You can't resist mating links. You just can't. It would be like trying to starve yourself and expecting to survive."

My skin prickled with annoyance. "There are lots of mates who don't end up together."

"Really? Name one pair?"

"I don't know names. I just heard about this from Frank McNamara. He mentioned someone in our pack had a mate but didn't end up with her."

Sarah tutted. "Well, I've never heard of mates who didn't end up together. It's biological or chemical or whatever. Plus, it's a good thing. It doesn't happen to everyone. I sort of wished it would happen to me." She thankfully lowered her voice to add, "Apparently, the sex is explosive." She waggled her eyebrows.

I shushed her with a forbidding look. "Besides, he's leaving soon," I added under my breath. "Distance will suppress the link."

"Why would he leave?" She glanced over at the pool table. "Is Liam making him so he can have his dirty way with you?"

Heat snaked up my neck.

She leaned in, her long, kinky blonde curls draping over her shoulders. "Oh my gosh, that's it, isn't it? That's real fucked up, Ness. No one should ever come between mates."

"I don't want a mate all right!" I unfortunately said this so loudly that even the rain pounding against the windowed façade couldn't camouflage my words.

Sure enough, the boys had stopped playing to cop a look, as well as two of the men slugging down beers at the sticky bar. Not that they knew what I was talking about, but August knew, and from the shadows that fell over his strong brow, I could tell my comment had made an impact.

I didn't think he was hurt that I didn't want to be with him, after all, he considered me like his sister . . . people didn't want to get with their sisters because that was all shades of unnatural and wrong, but he probably hadn't appreciated me voicing my disgust quite this brashly. I slid the elastic out of my hair to busy my suddenly shaky hands and to curtain off my face.

"Didn't mean to piss you off," Sarah apologized.

I rested my elbows on the table and cupped my forehead with my palms. "It's not you, Sarah. It's this whole stupid situation."

She sighed just as Kelly brought over our food. She deposited the plates a little heavily, gaze trained toward the boys.

"The other burger goes over there." Sarah pointed to Lucas.

They'd all gone back to playing. Including August. He had his back to me, as though to avoid facing me. More than ever, I hated our link because suddenly I feared it might erase our years of shared history and render us both bitter strangers.

I felt Sarah eyeing me. Whatever she was thinking, she kept it to herself.

Between greasy, ketchup-laden bites, she said, "I'm going to be an aunt soon. My brother and Margaux are expecting."

I blinked at her.

"Twins. They're having twins. A girl and a boy." She took a big bite of her burger.

"The wedding was last week. She didn't even look pregnant."

"She was. Just not showing yet. It's early though—like six weeks or something— so they're not really telling people yet."

"Six weeks! And she already knows the gender?"

Sarah cocked up one of her dark eyebrows. "We don't need ultrasounds to know these things." She wiped her fingers on her checkered paper napkin before tapping her nose with her index.

"We can smell the gender of the baby?"

"No. We can smell pregnancies. The gender's purely maternal instinct. She could be wrong, but shifter mamas are rarely wrong."

So if my mom had been a werewolf, she would've known I was a girl before I came into this world. My parents had never done an ultrasound, so convinced I would be a boy. Why would a baby born to the Boulder pack be anything else? I wondered what would have happened if someone had found out I was the wrong gender before being born. Then I stopped wondering because it was an answer I never wanted to find out.

"Did you ever date someone in your pack?" I asked.

"Yeah. Back in high school, I went out with this dude called Channing. Then I picked guys who weren't in the pack, mostly kids from UCB." She swallowed a long gulp of her soda. "My mom will probably force me to marry a wolf, so I'm getting my fix of human boys. They're less conceited than pack boys."

"UCB? Do you attend UCB?"

"Starting year two in a couple weeks. Why? Are you considering enrolling?"

"Apparently I can."

"What do you mean, *you can*?"

"Liam told me the pack sets money aside to cover tuition."

Her eyes lit up. "So you're applying?"

I nodded.

She squealed, which made everyone look our way again. "Oh my God, that's *so* exciting! I'll finally have a friend."

"Oh, come on. *You* don't have any friends there?"

"Hun, I'm opinionated. Most people don't like opinionated girls. Most people like them submissive and pleasant. Mom's always on my case about being more pleasant." She smirked. "You're, like, my first friend."

I peeled a strip of bacon off my mayo-soaked bread roll. "Does that mean I get full access to your closet?"

She tossed her head back and laughed, but then shot me a *nice-try* look.

I grinned. Even though it was thundering outside, and I was nervous as hell about what was happening within my pack, I felt momentarily happy. "You're my first *girl*-friend too."

She raised her glass and held it up, waiting for me to clink it with hers. "To firsts."

I tipped my glass into hers just as Lucas slid his empty plate onto the table and reached out between us to grab a handful of napkins.

"Didn't strike me as a virgin, Sarah," he said.

"If you're trying to get under my fur, Mason, it's not working."

He leveled his eyes on her chest, then raised them slowly. "I'm sorry, but I don't do Pines."

Her grin faltered. "That wasn't me propositioning you, you prick."

Cocking one side of his mouth up, he filched a fry from the plastic basket next to her plate, his forearm brushing against her chest. She jerked backward. His eyes flashed with undisguised amusement that heightened when Sarah glared at him.

She relocated her basket, shoving it to the farthest most edge of the table. "Hands off my fries."

"Possessive, aren't we?" Lucas wiped his fingers slowly on his wadded-up napkin, as though buying himself more time. "You deejaying tomorrow night, blondie?"

"Like every Thursday night." Her skin tone had returned to normal, but her earlier glee was gone. "Don't forget your earplugs. Or better yet, don't come at all." She turned back toward me. "Will you go, Ness?"

I was about to say maybe when the front door of Tracy's flapped open, dragging in the scent of summer rain and male perspiration. My heart stuttered when I laid eyes on Liam. His dark hair was slicked back, and his body was wound so tightly it looked like he was about to pounce on someone.

Pissed.

He looked pissed.

All the more terrifying was that he looked pissed at *me*.

17

I stood up so fast my knees bumped into the table, sending bolts of pain through my shins. The last time Liam had looked at me with so much scorn was when I'd come out of Julian Matz's maze brandishing the Boulder relic.

Aside from the low drone of the sports commentator and the unrelenting rain niggling the windows, the bar had become eerily quiet. When a cue stick hit a resin ball, I jumped.

For a long moment, Liam didn't move. Neither did Matt who flanked him.

Lucas's thick eyebrows dipped as he watched his Alpha, the slant deepening when Liam stalked over to me, boots pounding the worn flooring.

"You ratted us out?" Lucas asked, voice low. So very low.

Sarah, who'd spun around in her chair, whirled toward me.

Combined with Liam's lethal gaze, Lucas's accusation chilled the blood racing through my veins. "Wh-what?"

He ran!

Liam's voice resonated so shrilly inside my skull that I gripped my forehead, digging my fingertips into my temples. "Wh-who?" I stammered.

Your cousin! Rainwater mixed with sweat dripped from his matted hair into the collar of his black V-neck.

"Why are you screaming at me?"

"Because it's your fault," Liam growled.

Matt folded his arms in front of his huge chest. "Everest left Aidan a voicemail telling him what a prick he was to have sold him out."

I sensed two large bodies coming up behind me. I could smell August. I assumed the other one was Cole. Were they cornering me?

I squared my shoulders, trying to inject bravado into my posture. Bravado I wasn't feeling. "What does Everest's voicemail have to do with me?" I asked, voice faltering.

"He said you texted him that we were coming," Matt said.

I reeled, but then I grabbed my phone, unlocked it, and shoved it in front of Liam's face. "Check it. Check my messages. I never sent Everest a thing."

He stared at the bobbing phone.

"Check. It. Liam!"

He grabbed it, fingers moving deftly over the screen. I waited. Waited for him to see that he had it all wrong. But then . . . then his eyes blazed, and my heart stopped.

He snorted, the sound so ungentle. "Your message is right there, Ness." He flipped my phone around and leveled it in front of my face. "Right . . . fucking . . . there."

My gaze raced over the bright screen, soaked up the black letters: *Liam is coming for you. Aidan told him where you were hiding. Run!*

The words smeared together. "I didn't—" I looked over my phone at Liam. "I didn't write that. Someone—I didn't—" Tears rolled down my cheeks.

Nostrils flaring, he shook his head and thrust the phone into my numb fingers. "Don't lie to me, Ness." His labored breaths punched my throbbing forehead.

"I'm *not* lying."

"Hey, could you guys take this outside?" Kelly asked, darting wary glances at her customers.

Is that why you were with me? To get insider information? His words were ringed with a mixture of bitterness and dejection.

"No." Each one of my breaths snagged in my throat. "No! Someone hacked my phone and sent him that message." I wheeled around toward Cole. "That's easy to do, right?"

"It is," Cole said, but his narrowed eyes told me that, like the others, he believed I was trying to cover up my tracks by pinning it on a hacker.

"If I'd sent him a message, you really think I would've kept a trace of it on my phone? You really think I would've shown it to you? How dumb do you all think I am exactly?" I croaked, looking at Liam, then at Matt, then at Lucas. I didn't bother turning around to check if Cole and August, too, were glaring. I sensed the weight of their stares on my back.

"You didn't raise your hand yesterday," Lucas said.

Wariness spread over Matt's face like ink.

"So that automatically makes me a traitor?" My voice shook with tremors. My entire body shook with tremors. "Liam?" I didn't care what the others thought. As long as he—

He lowered his gaze to the floor. "You've backstabbed the pack before, Ness."

Overwhelmed by anger and disappointment, I pursed my lips and backed up but collided into a body. Hands set on my shoulders, tried to pin me in place. I brushed them off as though they were cobwebs, then grabbed my bag, dug out my wallet, and tossed a bill on the table to cover my half-eaten lunch.

"For the record, I'm glad Everest got away," I spat out as I elbowed my way past Liam and Matt.

"Ness!" Sarah called, but I didn't stop.

I dove into the crashing rain, slamming the door of Tracy's behind me, and sprinted across streets without looking for cars. Humorlessly, I felt like if a car hit me, I'd inflict more damage to it than it would to me.

You've backstabbed the pack before.

Liam's words played on a loop inside my head.

Like cement, disgust poured through me, drying between my ribs until their cage became a solid wall. My eyesight sharpened. My wolf was coming out. I raced faster down the drab streets, zigzagging through bobbing umbrellas and shoving past hooded passersby. I didn't apologize. I couldn't apologize. My teeth had extended into fangs. I was shifting, and I was still in the middle of town.

I waded through the storm-soaked streets faster, slowing only when I came upon an alley. I couldn't repress the need to shift. Didn't care to. I ran past corroded metal bins overflowing with the sour reek of food waste, relief flooding me when I noted that the alley spilled onto a parking lot edged with pines. Behind one of the bins, I pulled off my necklace and stashed it inside my bag before stripping out of my clothes. They were so waterlogged that peeling them off was a feat. Especially when my fingers began receding into stumps. I managed to kick off my jeans just as my knee joints snapped inward and forced me onto all fours.

I gritted my jaw as my wolf magic swept through me in fierce, raw waves, transforming my feeble human body into a resilient mound of white fur and taut muscles. When the change was complete, I sprang out from behind the bin, ducking behind parked cars, checking for humans.

I could hear their hearts beat in the buildings surrounding me; I could hear the timbre of their voices vibrate behind the lit windows; I could hear toilets flush, a baby wail, a young girl hum a slow tune, car tires squeal, raindrops ping off car hoods. The world turned so cacophonous and sharp it transmuted my lupine body into a livewire.

I dashed and zigzagged until my paws hit soft earth. And then I increased my speed. For a moment I was disoriented, but did it matter? I wasn't running toward something; I was running away from someone.

Away from Liam.

My fur rippled with a full-body shiver. I'd thought a Kolane could be a decent and unprejudiced man, but he'd trusted Aidan Michaels over me. Hadn't even given me the benefit of the doubt.

Thank God my body had locked Liam's out last night. If I'd lost my virginity to him— I couldn't even finish that terrible thought, so I shoved it out of my mind and focused on not losing my footing on the dicey mud and slick grass. I let the awareness of my surroundings flood me, fill me.

Alone, I ran until the sky turned the deepest shade of night, until my lungs contracted so violently I had to stop to catch my breath. I found shelter under a stone ledge. The rain fell so fiercely it curtained off the forest. Even with my heightened senses, I could barely see three feet in front of me. I didn't care, though.

I lay down with my head in between my forepaws and watched the ruined world fall apart around me.

Again . . .

18

I must've fallen asleep because the next thing I knew, something was prodding my ribs. I jerked awake and bounced onto my paws, spine snapping into alignment and teeth gnashing in a menacing growl.

A mountain of chocolate-brown fur stood inches from me. *It's me, Ness.*

The flash of green around the wolf's pin-sized pupils made my defensive stance slacken.

August?

I still kept my distance, swinging my head toward the lip of the stone ledge that had shielded my fur from the rain. Although my underbelly and legs were caked in mud, I was no longer wet. The storm had quieted while I slept. The storm outside. The one inside still raged as Liam's accusation slotted into my mind. I expected to see the black wolf materialize between the fence of trunks.

What were you thinking, going off on your own like that?

I didn't bother answering August, but I did ask, *Are you alone?*

Yes. He wrung out his body, splattering mine with warm raindrops.

Even though I wanted to trust August, I couldn't help but flick my ears around to pick up on every sound within a one-mile radius. I didn't think I had it in me to trust anyone ever again. Besides Evelyn.

Evelyn . . . She was expecting me. *What time is it?*

He tossed his head back, his slick brown fur rippling. *What time is it? That's what you're concerned about?*

I narrowed my eyes. *What else should I be concerned about? Has the pack voted for my demise?*

Your demise? What are you talking about?

What do you mean what am I talking about? You were there! Liam called me a traitor.

My words blustered out of me in a single, heated breath. *Just because I didn't put my hand up yesterday doesn't mean I would betray the pack!*

Tears tracked down my muzzle, over my rubbery lips, glided between my sharp teeth. The darkness would hide them from August. Or maybe he saw them. What did I care? I might've been a wolf, but I was also a human. Underneath the pelt and mud, I possessed a heart, and it had been broken. And broken hearts bled tears. I shouldn't be ashamed of them. What I should have been ashamed of was caring what others thought I had done. I knew I hadn't sent that message, and that was all that mattered.

Or all that should've mattered.

Do you *believe me, August?*

What do you think? He tried to approach me, but I backed up.

Yes or no?

Of course I believe you.

He said this with so little hesitation that skepticism poked through my relief. *Why?*

Green eyes steady on mine, he said, *Because I can feel you. If you'd done it, you wouldn't have been racked by anguish. You would've been racked by guilt. I told Liam, but he's a stubborn ass. He'll come around, though.*

I can't believe I pledged myself to him. I wish I could take it back. There was so much I wished I could take back: the kisses, the caresses, the trust. Again, I shuddered.

I suddenly wished I hadn't stopped running, wished I'd crossed a state line or vanished into the Rockies. I could've stayed away from Boulder until I was eighteen, until I was free of this damned place.

I stared at the woods longingly.

I felt August's muzzle push against my neck. *Don't even think about leaving.*

I turned on August. *Why not? I hate it here. I hate it so goddamn much.*

He sighed, his breath ruffling the fur around my ears. *That's how you feel tonight, but tomorrow—*

That's how I've felt almost every single day I've been back. I can count the days I've been happy on the claws of one paw.

He puffed a consolatory breath against my neck.

I'm not saying it to garner your pity. I'm just telling you because I don't want you to think I'm being hotheaded. That I feel like leaving because of what happened back at Tracy's. I twisted around and peered up at the veiled moon.

Can't let you run away.

Why not?

'Cause my mother would never forgive me for letting you go off on your own.

I let out a bitter sound that could've been a laugh, except wolves didn't laugh. We cried, but we didn't laugh. *You don't have to tell her.*

He grunted. *I wouldn't have to tell her. My mother's all-knowing.*

I drew my gaze off the sky and onto the soft ground.

Besides, have you thought about what it would do to Evelyn? From what I've heard, she cares about you a lot. How do you think she'd take your disappearance?

She has Frank now.

You think he's replaced you? People can love more than one person.

I pawed a patch of squishy earth, watching how the mud rose and molded around my claws. *I really don't want to go back.*

August leaned forward and drove his muzzle into my shoulder to get my attention. *He'll never attack you like that again. I promise.*

Don't make promises you can't keep.

Why do you think I wouldn't be able to keep it?

Because once your mom— I stopped talking abruptly. I wasn't supposed to know this.

Once my mom what?

When I didn't say anything for a full minute, he sighed. *Liam told you, didn't he?*

I nodded. *Why didn't* you *tell me?* I didn't want to sound petty, but I wished I'd heard it from him.

I didn't want to worry you any more than you already were. Especially after your own mother passed away from cancer.

My body sagged as though it was being crushed beneath tumbling rocks again. *She never had a chance. Your mom . . . her odds are good. Aren't they?*

He gave a slow nod. *If you don't stick around for anyone else, stick around for her sake.*

I eyed August, and then I eyed the dark woods. *I have no idea where I am anymore, August.* In the woods, but also in my life, I was so incredibly lost.

I'll show you the way back. He started walking but stopped when I didn't follow.

How did you even find me?

I can sense you, Ness. It's pretty much all I can sense these days. The damp breeze rushed his words to my ears.

I'm sorry. I wasn't sure why I was apologizing for something I had no control over.

He rolled one of his shoulders in a shrug, then faced away from me and started up again. *I'm sure it'll get more manageable.*

I was no longer the small pup he'd run alongside six years ago, but I still had to lengthen my strides to match his own. He must've noticed, because at some point he slowed his brisk pace. Silence grew and grew between us, but there was nothing awkward about it. If anything, it was like a balm, healing the deep cuts Liam had gouged in me.

I'm glad you're home, I whispered.

August looked at me in that quiet, all-seeing way of his. *Once you get back with Liam, you'll probably change your mind about that.*

I bristled, horrified he thought I would go back to Liam. *I might be all over the place, but I do have some self-love. Liam and I, we're not getting back together.* I thought about the time he'd sniffed me. *I forgave him once before.*

Although cloaked in fur, his limbs seemed to grow harder. *What did you forgive him for?*

August's green eyes bore into mine, but I didn't explain. I would take what had happened between Liam and me to the grave.

Even though the sky was mottled with pale puffs of clouds, I could still make out the glittery pinpricks of stars. They made me think of my father, of the night we'd star-gazed from our rooftop. He'd been such a gentle and righteous man.

A man who would *never* have lashed out at someone so bitterly and so publicly.

There were some lines that shouldn't be crossed. I'd rearranged those lines to allow Liam closer, but after today, I would paint new ones around myself and wouldn't let anyone undeserving past them.

19

August had parked his pickup in the lot where I'd morphed from human to wolf. He'd tracked my scent from Tracy's to the metal bins behind which I'd taken cover to strip.

Boulder was quiet and dark when our claws clicked onto the lot's pavement. When we reached the pickup, August's spine heaved, and then his brown fur receded into his dark, bronzed skin. When he unfurled, all his joints and muscles elongated and thickened until his backside was entirely man and no longer wolf. I noticed a line of puckered skin at the base of his spine. I wondered how he'd gotten that scar. When he began pivoting, I averted my gaze, taking great interest in the scratched rim of his back wheel.

A car door clicked, and then fabric rustled and a zipper purred shut. Only then did I let my gaze drift back to August. Lucas said I needed to get used to nudity, but it was easy for the males of the pack. They'd grown up walking naked around each other; I hadn't.

Barefoot and shirtless, August extended a cream flannel button-down to me. "Your clothes are still damp."

The shirt dangled between us. Was he expecting me to shift in front of him? When I didn't make any move to snatch the shirt, he draped it over the side of the cargo bed and turned. I was thankful he'd understood my mute plea. Closing my eyes, I arched my back and allowed the magic to pulse through my limbs and drag away the fur, the claws, the fangs, and every other part of my lupine constitution. My ears migrated back to the sides of my face, my jaw flattened, my lips reshaped.

Back in skin, I pressed my hands into the damp gravel and rose, bones clicking as I stretched to my full human height of five-seven. Glancing sideway to make sure August was still turned, I plucked the shirt from the bed and speared my arms through. I fastened the buttons quickly, leaving smudges of mud on the soft material that smelled so strongly of August it made my head spin. Or maybe it was the miles I'd traveled at breakneck speed that was making my head spin.

Pushing my stringy hair back, I said, "You can turn around now." My voice sounded raucous, as though it, too, had been dragged across the rough terrain.

As August turned, I tugged on the hem of the shirt, thankful he was an entire head taller. Otherwise, the shirt would've exposed a lot more of me.

"Thanks," I said, nodding to the shirt. I pinched the hem to prevent the material from flapping open.

He palmed his close-cropped hair. I'd never known him with any other haircut, but I remembered Isobel showing me pictures of him as a toddler where his face had been haloed by a mane of soft curls that couldn't seem to decide which way to bend. Only two things remained of the little boy from those pictures: the spray of dark freckles over his nose and cheekbones, and the penetrating green eyes flecked by sable and gold. But where the boy had had a soft jaw, the man's jaw could saw through wood.

"Feeling better, Dimples?"

The nickname startled me. I'd spent my childhood hearing it, responding to it, but I wasn't sure I liked it anymore. It made me feel juvenile. I didn't say anything, though. To August, I supposed I would always be the little pigtailed girl he'd ferry to and from school on his way to work.

"Ness?"

"Hmm." I released the lip I was reflexively sliding through my teeth.

"Are you feeling better?"

"Yeah." I wasn't.

When he cocked an eyebrow, I added a meek smile.

"I promise. Running cleared my head."

Although he still didn't seem convinced, he tipped his head to the truck. "Get in. I'll give you a lift back to the inn."

He pulled the door open. Clutching the shirt closed, I heaved myself onto the bench seat and slid all the way to the passenger side door. The scraped leather was rough and cold against the backs of my thighs.

"I need to stop by my new place first." If only I'd had the presence of mind to run toward it instead of—I looked around the lot—wherever it was I'd ended up.

"New place?"

"Yeah. Jeb and I. We're going to be living in town. In an apartment on 13th Street."

He slowed at a traffic light. "You are? Why?"

"Because my cousin sold the inn to Aidan Michaels."

August turned toward me, his stomach muscles rippling in the faint moonlight. For someone who'd sprinted through a drenched forest, he looked incredibly clean, barely flecked with mud.

Unlike myself . . .

My thighs were smeared brown, and my hair felt like dreads. A glimpse at myself in the side mirror confirmed the dreads part. I rolled my hardened hair into a larger rope, coiled it, and threaded the ends through to make it hold.

"You're kidding me?" August whispered.

"Afraid not."

August shook his head as though trying to drive the new information into it.

"Effective upon Everest's death. I bet that's why Liam believes I saved my cousin's life," I grumbled. "To make sure the inn didn't switch hands."

The word *backstab* shrilled in my brain again. I pressed my fingertips against my temple and massaged it. "Actually, can you drop me off at the inn? I need to grab a couple things. The apartment isn't exactly move-in ready."

There were mattresses, but no sheets, no pillows, no cleaning products, and no food.

"Sure."

While we drove, I took my phone out of the bag. My screen was full of messages. Mostly from Evelyn and Sarah, but one of them—a missed call and a voicemail—was from Everest. I dropped my phone onto my lap, then fumbled to grab it before August could see the name in the notification bubbles.

"Is everything okay?"

I blinked at him like a deer in headlights; I hoped I didn't look like one. "Yeah. Just Evelyn worrying. I was supposed to go sleep at Frank's place tonight."

I called her to prevent August from asking me anymore questions.

"*Querida!*" she exclaimed, ridding me of a couple decibels of hearing. "You are alive! *Dios mio*, I thought . . . I thought. Do not do this to my poor *corazón* or I will not make old bones!"

I smiled at the butchered expression, at the love that seeped out of all the Spanish interjections. "I'm so sorry. I had dinner with a friend and lost track of time. Are you still at the inn?"

"I waited forever, but Frank insisted on taking me home. He said you went out for a run with a friend. I do not like you running around the woods at night."

I tightened my hold on the hem of the flannel shirt. "I was in . . . in my other form. It's safer for us at night than during the day. Besides, like Frank said, I was not alone."

"Are you coming over now? I made your bed."

A made bed in a house with Evelyn sounded like heaven. I checked the clock on my phone and cringed when I noticed it was almost ten-thirty. I still needed to grab stuff from the inn, drop it off at my new place, shower, and change.

"I can be there in an hour. Is that too late?"

"What sort of question is that?" She sounded insulted. "You don't think I would wait all night for you?"

Her words filled me with affection. "Okay. I'll be there in an hour then." I added a whisper-soft, "I love you."

Not for the first time, I silently thanked Frank for having placed Evelyn in my life. What would I have done without her?

"Not as much as I love you," she answered.

After I disconnected, I drove the heel of my palm into one eye and then into the other. Even though I'd napped in the woods, I felt exhausted. Surely an accumulation of too many short nights and too many high-stress days.

When the pickup slowed in the inn's circular driveway, I balled up my clothes and bag.

"Thanks for coming to find me, August." I smiled at him before hopping out of the car and shutting the door.

As I started toward the entrance, another car door clicked shut.

I spun around to find August ambling toward me. "What are you doing?"

He frowned. "What do you mean, what am I doing?"

I looked at his parked car, then at him. "You can go home."

"If I go home, how will you get to your new apartment? And then to Frank's?" A gust of cool wind stole the sandalwood scent off his skin and batted it toward me.

How could he smell so good after running through the woods? I didn't dare sniff myself. I bet I reeked of dried perspiration and dank mud.

"I can cab it," I finally said.

A crooked smile turned up one corner of his mouth. "Surprisingly, I have no other engagements this evening."

"Aww. You canceled all your hot dates?"

"Wouldn't be the first time, now would it?"

I grinned. "Whatever are you talking about?"

I knew exactly what he was talking about, though. When I was still living in Boulder, I'd beg him to take me to a movie or bowling or build a campfire to grill s'mores without enquiring if he had other plans.

I hadn't wanted to share August with his girlfriends *or* friends.

I'd wanted him all to myself.

The awareness of how greedy I'd been dimmed my smile. "I'm sorry."

His eyebrows bent. "For what?"

"For having been such a demanding and selfish kid."

"You weren't."

"I took advantage of you. Of your kindness."

"Dimples—"

"Same way I'm doing right now." The heat of his half-naked body wrapped so thickly around me that I stepped away from him and then pushed through the revolving doors.

Emmy, who was manning the bell desk, clapped her chest. "Holy mother of God, you just gave me a heart attack."

I knew I looked awful, but that awful?

"Sorry," I said sheepishly.

She didn't seem to hear my apology, too fixated on the body behind mine. Her face lit up with a smirk that was almost as bright as the row of silver hoops lining the shell of her ear.

"What have you two been up to? Mud-wrestling?"

"Um. I was helping him fix a leak at the warehouse." The lie came out way too easily. To drive it home, I brandished my wet clothes. "I wasn't much help."

"Must've been a real bad leak." Her smile told me that not only did she not buy my stupid story, but that she'd also added a ton of dirty extrapolations to it.

"Her plumbing skills need some improvement," August added.

Emmy shot him a pointed look. "Never belittle a woman's *plumbing* skills."

Although I appreciated her coming to my defense, this was getting weird. "I need to shower and grab some stuff. Is everything okay here?"

"Yes. Well, except—" She flicked her gaze up to the first-floor landing. "Your uncle finally came out of his room this afternoon. He was in a strange mood. A tad manic. He must've looked through every ledger and dossier in the back office. It was like a bomb detonated in there. We tidied up with Isobel, but we weren't sure where things were supposed to be put away, so we just made a big pile."

I glanced at the staircase. "Lucy and him are . . ." I hesitated a second before adding, "divorcing." It was an easier explanation than the truth. "He and I are actually moving out."

Her mouth gaped.

"Please don't tell anyone yet. I mean you can tell Skylar, but no one else. I don't want the staff to worry how the divorce will affect the inn."

She shook her head. "I won't blab, but *wow*. I'm in shock. Poor Everest."

I clasped my phone tighter, desperate to listen to his voicemail. "I'll just head down and stick these in the wash and grab a shower. I won't be long."

August nodded even though he didn't seem too excited to be left behind with Emmy, especially when she said, "Wait. I just connected the dots. You're Isobel's boy, aren't you? She showed me a picture of you."

As she roped him into a conversation, I bounded down the stairs to the laundry room, unearthed a clean towel, tossed my clothes and August's shirt into one of the industrial machines, wrapped the towel snugly around myself, and set the washing machine to the quickest cycle. After I rinsed the rubber soles of my white sneakers, I headed to the locker rooms that connected the indoor pool to the gym.

Only then did I listen to Everest's message.

"Hey, Ness. I'm on my way back to Boulder. Thank you for having my back. I didn't deserve your help. Not after what I did. Everything's such a fucking mess. Such a fucking mess," he repeated slower, lower. I could imagine him pulling at his dark-red hair like he used to do when things didn't go his way as a kid. "In case anything happens to me, I left"—the word he uttered was garbled, as though he'd passed through a tunnel—"in your room"—static filled the receiver again—"under the fl —*Fuck!*" Air whooshed through the phone followed by a muffled thud, as though the phone had clattered out of his hand and onto the floormat. From far away, I heard him hiss, "Son-of-a-bitch found me."

The screech of metal had me yanking the phone away from my ear, and then . . . *nothing*.

Nothing.

With stiff fingers, I jabbed my screen to call him back. The dial tone sounded and sounded. And then I was prompted to leave a message.

I hung up.

I shivered but then whispered to myself, "He must've run out of battery." I prayed that was why the line had gone dead. Unless the *son-of-a-bitch* had caught up with him.

No, I couldn't go there.

Everest was all right. He was on his way back. I checked the timestamp of the voicemail. He'd phoned about an hour ago. He was probably already in Boulder.

I typed: *I'm at the inn. Where are you?*

My thumb hovered over the send icon as I read the incriminating text above the still unsent one. I searched the wording, trying to find something about it that would prove my innocence. But it sounded like me, which meant the hacker was familiar with my speech. My pulse skittered wildly at that realization.

Or maybe the hacker had perused my phone's contents. That was a possibility, right?

For a long moment, I hesitated to send Everest the message I'd just composed, afraid it would make me the traitor my Alpha already believed me to be. *Screw it.* I'd already tried phoning Everest anyway. Besides, he and I needed to talk. I deserved answers. I didn't care what that made me. I hit send, then stepped into the shower stall and turned the water on scalding to ward away the frostiness enveloping my bones.

I spent a long time lathering away the dirt from my body; I spent an even longer time trying to untangle my hair. When I accomplished both tasks, I turned off the spray and towel-dried myself, but not before checking my phone. I was hoping Everest had messaged me back.

He hadn't.

As I plucked a disposable comb from a tray of amenities and dragged the teeth through my wet hair, I wondered where he would go in Boulder. There were too many cameras here. He was probably hiding in a motel.

I listened to his message again. "In your room. Under the fl . . ." What had he left in my room? And under what? Which word started with an *fl*-sound and could be found in a bedroom?

Fl . . .

Flowers?

Did he mean his mother's desiccated flower-filled mason jar?

As I made my way back to the laundry room, I ran everything there was in my bedroom through my head, but nothing else started with a *fl*. The washing cycle had finished, so I tossed the clothes in the dryer and sat on the countertop to wait, toying with the soft terry towel as I dwelled some more on Everest's enigmatic message.

My mind kept looping back to the flower jar, but I'd gotten rid of it sometime ago because the smell of Lucy's dried roses had felt toxic.

I dialed Everest's number again. The phone rang and rang inside my ear. I was about to play back his voicemail when a dusky figure darkened the doorway. The phone slid out of my fingers and clattered against the white tiles.

20

August crouched to retrieve my phone. "Didn't mean to startle you. You just left me up there a long time." As he rose, he tendered the small apparatus, his eyes roving over the screen.

I blanched, afraid he'd see Everest's name, afraid he'd think me a traitor, afraid—

"It's not cracked," he said.

Pulse battering my neck, I tightened the towel around myself and reached an unsteady hand to retrieve my phone.

August hitched up an eyebrow. "Dimples, you're worrying me."

"I'm fine now. Just tired."

His eyes lowered to my swinging bare legs, or maybe he was looking at the machine tumbling our clothes.

There was no way they'd be dry yet, but hopefully they wouldn't be too wet. I hopped down, and he backed up, and then I leaned over and opened the front hatch.

As I stuck my hand inside the drum, he cleared his throat. "Why aren't you dressed?"

I pulled out his shirt first. "My entire wardrobe's in the new apartment."

For some reason, he flicked his gaze toward the entrance of the laundry room so fast I checked to make sure my cousin hadn't materialized there.

Empty.

"It's not completely dry yet," I said, wiggling my fingers to get his attention.

His sharp Adam's apple bobbed as he took the shirt.

I gathered up my clothes. "Give me one more second."

Back in the changing rooms, I yanked my humid jeans up my legs—horrible sensation—then clipped on my bra that was so damp my nipples pebbled. I plugged in the hairdryer and ran it for a full minute over my chest, hoping the hot air would warm me up.

It helped some.

When I returned to the laundry room, August had put on his shirt. I stuck my feet into my shoes, omitting the socks. I set them out to dry on the rack, then slung my handbag over my shoulder. I hesitated to fill a basket with sheets and towels, but since I was dressed and heading to Frank's for the night, gathering supplies could wait until morning.

"I need to stop by my bedroom before I go. If you need to—"

"I told you. There's nowhere I need to be."

"Okay." As we climbed the steps, I said, "You can wait for me in the car, if you prefer."

"Whatever you want."

What *did* I want?

I didn't even know what I was looking for . . . a flash drive, money, the stolen Sillin? *Oh my God*. What if it was the Sillin? What if Everest had planted it in my room to make me look guilty again? What if he'd popped each pill from the foil packets and hid them among the dried rose petals? My stomach began to cramp with a sudden upsurge of nerves. I was going to be sick. I reached for the banister to steady my swaying gait.

"What's going on?" August stared at my face, then at my abdomen.

Had I paled, or had he felt my jarring stress through the tether? I didn't want to carry the burden of Everest's voicemail alone, however unfair it was to push it upon someone else. I swallowed, my throat feeling as dry as Lucy's potpourri.

"Dimples?"

I closed my eyes, then opened them. "Everest left me a message."

He didn't say anything for so long that I began to tremble.

I gulped my saliva, trying to wet my throat. "He left me a message thanking me, and then he said some other things, and—"

"Why don't you play me his message?" August's eyes gleamed in the semi-obscurity of the staircase.

I nodded and dug out my phone. With shaky fingers, I located the message and pressed play. I watched August's features shift and realign, first in a frown, then in suspicion, then in shock.

"I swear I didn't warn him the pack was coming," I murmured after it ended.

His gaze hadn't moved off my phone. "What could he have left you?"

"I don't know. I don't even know what *fl-* could be. I was thinking flowers. Lucy leaves these jars filled with potpourri in the bedrooms, but I got rid of the one I had."

He dipped his chin into his neck.

"Please tell me you believe me."

He sighed.

"August, I swear—"

He finally raised his eyes back to mine. "I believe you."

Relief gushed through me.

In silence, we went to retrieve my key from the back office. I told Emmy I needed to grab something from my bedroom even though she hadn't asked for an explanation. Concern made her kind eyes crinkle.

As we made our way down the deathly quiet hallway, I asked August, "Do you have any other ideas?"

"I'm thinking."

The tether that linked us was as taut as a bowstring. I tried not to wonder why that was.

I pushed open the door and flicked on the lights, then walked down the short vestibule. I scanned my room for flowers—any flowers—but there wasn't even a jar. August knelt down and peered under the bed before lifting the mattress and checking under it. While I clanged open every drawer in my room and dismantled the flannel-covered armchair, he caught the edge of the area rug and tugged it free from the bedframe, spraying the air with flickering dust motes.

"Nothing here," he said.

I checked my closet next while he went into the bathroom and banged open the cupboards. I heard the distinct clang of porcelain—probably the toilet tank.

"Did you find any—" My skull throbbed so suddenly with a voice that I lost my balance, and my head bumped into something cold and hard, but the rest of my body landed on something warm and soft.

"Ness!" My name vibrated inside my ears.

I rolled my head back. August was gaping worriedly down at me, my limp body clutched in his arms.

Had I imagined the word *Boulders* screamed into my head? "Did you hear someone—"

"It's Liam."

The voice boomed again, and I clutched my forehead. ***Rodrigo and his team just located Everest's car in a ditch off Beek Ridge. I'm on my way there.***

August's rounded green eyes came in and out of focus.

"Oh my God," I murmured.

August's face swam back into focus. He unwound one arm from around me. Suddenly, his phone was pressed against his ear, and he was speaking into it.

"Fuck," he rumbled. "Fuck."

Two pennies for Isobel's jar, I thought.

Such a silly thought.

I stared at the small buzzing spotlight above my head. Or maybe my head was buzzing.

Everest's car was in a ditch.

Was Everest in the car?

I must've asked this out loud, because August said, "He was."

Tears curved around my cheeks, disappeared into my still-wet hair.

"Is he—" I couldn't push the last word out.

"He didn't make it." August brushed his thumbs over my cheeks, but the tears fell faster than he could wipe.

"T-Take me to . . . to *him*."

"I don't think that's a good idea."

"Please," I wheezed. "Please, August."

"Ness—"

I touched his cheek, beseeching him with my wet eyes.

He sighed and finally relented.

21

As we drove to the scene of the accident, neither of us spoke. August had turned the heater up, but that didn't stop me from trembling.

"Dimples, come closer." He patted the seat between us.

I was too numb to move, so he clicked off my seatbelt, dragged me toward him, then draped his arm around my shoulders, rubbing my pebbled skin, trying to deliver warmth into it. Tears still streamed down my cheeks and around my trembling lips, seeping into his flannel sleeve. I closed my eyes and let the scent of laundry detergent and sandalwood lull me.

Every part of my body felt anesthetized. Except my arm.

I felt my arm . . . felt the gentle strokes of August's fingers.

"We're here," he whispered after what felt like an hour. He eased the pickup to a stop dangerously close to the lip of the mountainside and clicked on his hazard lights, streaking the row of other vehicles with orange flashes.

A fire truck topped with a huge beam and two other SUVs were parked behind us. I pressed away from August, scraped the heels of my hands over my cheeks, then took a fortifying breath and got out slowly. When the balls of my feet met the ground, I teetered. I flung out my palm, catching myself on the car door. My head spun like a top. I breathed in and out slowly, each breath raking up my chest like claws.

A hand curved around my waist and another around my elbow. "Are you sure you want to go down there?"

"Yes." I inhaled again. "My bag. You have my bag?"

"It's in the car."

Everest's last message was on my phone.

My phone was in my bag.

"Can you give it to me?"

August grabbed it, then hooked the long strap over my shoulder. After closing the door, he gripped my elbow again and guided me toward the illuminated ditch. The first thing I saw was the overturned vehicle.

Everest's Jeep.

The second thing I saw was Liam's deep glare.

"What the fuck were you thinking bringing her here, Watt?" he barked.

The firefighter beside Liam peered up. The truck's beam made a small hoop gleam in his ear. In spite of his helmet, I recognized Rodrigo, the dark shifter who'd spent most of the meeting scowling at me.

"I made him bring me," I said.

Car doors slammed, and two more people approached: Frank and Eric. Frank did a double take when he spotted me. Obviously no one had expected me to come.

Eric grabbed onto the bent guardrail and hopped down the vertiginous shoulder. He slipped but didn't fall. Putting his weight in his heels, he took careful steps toward the remains of my cousin's car.

Of my cousin.

Frank exchanged a loaded look with August. The elder was probably trying to get August to keep me from going closer. Before he could heed the unspoken instruction, I shrugged him off and made my way to the ripped metal railing, brushing past it. I eased myself down the side of the rocky knoll.

Liam stepped in front of me, blocking my view of the car.

"You shouldn't be here," he growled.

"Don't tell me what to do," I snapped, my voice all at once tight and toneless.

"What happened?" Eric asked, and I thought he was asking between Liam and me, but the bald elder was staring at Rodrigo.

"Looks like he either missed the turn or went over on purpose."

He thinks Everest committed suicide? I opened my mouth wide but regretted it, because the air was laced with the acrid reek of death.

"Cause of death?" Frank asked, traipsing down the steep flank beside August. The elder almost fell, but August caught his arm and steadied him.

"A piece of metal went through his windpipe," Lucas said. He was crouched as though searching for debris among the rock and tufts of dust-flecked grass, but I saw his nostrils flare. He was trying to catch scents.

Bile lurched up my throat. I pressed my knuckles against my lips to keep them locked. Once I had my nausea under control, I said, "He didn't kill himself."

All the men looked at me.

"And you would know this how? Did you *chat* with him again?" Lucas asked.

"Bite me, Lucas," I growled at the same time as Rodrigo said, "Again?"

Liam crossed his arms. "Why do you assume it wasn't suicide?"

More car doors slammed shut, and then two beefy blonds stepped in the beam of the truck and surfed down toward us.

"Hey," Matt called out, his voice gruff. When his gaze landed on me, his honeyed eyebrows quirked in bewilderment. He quickly moved his eyes toward the Jeep. I watched his expression, waited for it to turn pained, but there was no pain. Had he not cared about Everest? Had anyone cared about my cousin?

No wonder Everest hated the pack.

No wonder he screwed them over.

Matt circled the capsized car, stopping next to the driver's side. When he winced, a fresh wave of nausea softened my bones.

Was Everest's body still in there?

"So you were telling us why Rodrigo was wrong about it being a suicide." Liam's voice blazed with cageyness.

"He left me a voicemail about an hour ago." I dug my phone out. "It sounds incriminating . . . Then again, you all think I'm a criminal already, so why am I even trying to defend myself?" I tapped on my phone's screen with my fingers that seemed to have transformed into thumbs. It took me three attempts to get my passcode right.

No one spoke.

Scraping in another breath of death-tainted air, I held out my phone and played back the voicemail over speakerphone. Hearing Everest speak and knowing that he was gone was eerie.

When the message ended, Matt said, "Someone was following him."

Lucas rose from his crouch. "It would explain the pieces of plastic we found on the road." He turned to Rodrigo. "I know you said the taillight could've come off the Jeep when it went over, but it *is* more likely another car rammed into Everest's."

Liam's jaw clenched, unclenched, clenched again. "Check the road for skid marks, Matt."

Matt climbed back, sidestepping the two firefighters who were heaving the Jaws of Life down to the scene.

"What did Everest put in your room?" Liam's voice dragged my attention off the serrated tool.

Lucas, who was still crouched, alternately scanned the tufts of dusty grass and my expression.

"I don't know. August and I turned it upside down, but didn't find anything."

Liam's already dark gaze blackened.

While Rodrigo and one of his men cut open the driver's door, the heat of a body spilled over my back, and then an arm went around my shoulders and twisted me around.

"Don't look," August said.

I didn't fight him.

"Why were you together, and why are your clothes and hair wet?" Liam growled.

"I went for a run. A long run." My words hit August's solid chest. "I wasn't planning on coming back. I might not have if August hadn't retrieved me." I wondered for a moment whether Liam would've even cared if I'd vanished forever. Keeping my eyes locked on one of the buttons on August's shirt, I added, "Frank, Evelyn called. She said I could stay with you tonight."

Frank rubbed his hands against his jeans. "Yes. She's waiting for you."

"I know you probably need to be here, but can you please take me to her?"

"Sure." He exchanged some quiet words with Eric before starting back up the steep incline.

I disentangled myself from August and went after Frank, desirous to distance myself from this dark mountain that smacked of death and distrust.

"I got something," I heard Lucas bark over the sound of an approaching siren.

Both Frank and I paused and glanced back down into the ditch. Something flat and black gleamed in his hands. A phone.

"Is it Everest's?" Frank called down.

"It's not turning on."

"Give it to Cole," Liam said, his gaze rising to mine. "If there's anything to retrieve on it, he'll find it."

His accusation was so palpable that my expression turned to stone.

Did Liam think I'd exchanged other messages with Everest? Did he think I'd colluded with him in stealing the Sillin?

I shook my head and turned away.

22

My elbow was propped on the armrest in Frank's car, and my head rested on my palm. "Was Jeb—was he informed that Everest . . ." I couldn't finish my sentence.

"He called me for news. Said he was coming, but I told him to stay put. That I'd go to him."

Jeb had been doing so much better. Granted the improvement in his mood had been fueled by anger, but still.

"You honestly didn't send Everest that text message?" Frank asked after a beat.

I hated that he didn't trust me. Then again, it seemed like no one besides August trusted me. "I swear I didn't. Whoever texted him did it remotely."

Frank sighed. "Did anyone have access to your phone last night?"

"Liam did." However angry I was with Liam, I knew he wouldn't have sent a message from my phone.

Frank knew it too. After a stretch of silence, he said, "You are your mother's daughter."

I picked my head off my palm. Well, *that* came out of nowhere.

"Maggie had so much spunk. Drove your dad crazy." He returned his gaze to the road beyond the windshield, an emotion I couldn't quite put my finger on eddying over his face. "Drove a lot of men crazy."

A lot of men? Geez, I hoped he hadn't had a crush on her.

He didn't say a word the rest of the way to his secluded, two-story log cabin a couple miles away from Headquarters. I vaguely remembered going to Frank's house with my parents when I was much younger—a lifetime ago.

Before getting out of the car, he said, "Be patient with Liam. This is an adjustment period, not only for you, but for him too. Between the stolen Sillin and learning what it means to be an Alpha, he's under a lot of stress."

I bristled. I couldn't believe he was asking *me* to be patient.

I was about to shut the door when he added, "And, Ness, be careful about pitting Liam against August. Boys, especially wolves, they're territorial *and* jealous, and well, I've seen this pattern before, and even though the mated pair didn't end up together, it caused a serious rift in the pack."

Whoa. Talk about another abrupt subject change. I took the opportunity to ask, "Who were they?"

"It doesn't matter anymore. They're all dead now."

"All of them?" And here I was certain he'd been part of the unfortunate love triangle.

Frank set his gaze on the gloomy forest dipping beyond his house. "I should head to the inn. Jeb's waiting."

Just as he said this, a voice I knew oh-so-well rang out in the night. "*Querida?*" Evelyn was standing by the front door, backlit by the soft glow of Frank's living room. Her plush robe was knotted tightly around her, and her black hair fluttered around her pale face.

I shut the car door and strode into her open arms.

When Frank drove away, she cocked an eyebrow. "Where is he going at this hour?"

I sighed. "I don't even know where to start."

She pulled me into the house, sat me at the wooden kitchen counter, and warmed water on the stovetop, but then she must've decided against making tea, because she dumped the contents, grabbed the carton of milk from the fridge door, and poured some inside the deep sauce pan. While it warmed, she wrapped her hands around my clammy ones.

"Tell me everything."

And so I did. Well, almost everything. I didn't tell her about the confrontation back at Tracy's. It would just make her resent the pack. When I was done with my account, the milk had bubbled over the sides of the pan and hit the flames, making them sizzle. She jolted toward the stove, spun off the gas, and stood there, lips mashed together. After a while, she plucked a wooden spoon from a terracotta jug and skimmed the skin off the warmed milk before dividing it between two mugs.

As she set them on the counter, she took her seat next to me again. I cupped the warm ceramic and lifted it to my mouth, singeing my lips and tongue. I plopped the mug back down, and milk splashed over the rim. Instead of cleaning it up, I dragged my fingertip through the spilled liquid and drew circles over the wood.

"You think Aidan is behind all of this?" Her black eyes glazed over as though she were remembering another time—probably the time when she was married to the man.

"He's the only one who benefits from Everest's death." Unless my cousin was wanted dead for what he'd hidden in my room.

Blinking away the haze, she got up to get a kitchen towel to clean the spilled milk. "Someone needs to put an end to that man's life."

"If he dies, his lawyers will release information about the pack to the public."

"I heard. Frank told me." She dabbed the sides of my mug until no trace of the overflow remained. "I have never hated anyone like I hate this man. He is a cancer. Do you know how many times I have dreamed of ending his life?" Her breathing increased in tempo, and her cheeks flooded with color.

I caught her hand, the one clutching the towel with which she kept wiping down the countertop even though it was clean. "Promise me you won't get involved."

She lifted her gaze to my face.

The resolve in her expression quickened my pulse. "Promise me."

After a long moment, she exhaled a slow breath. "He should not be allowed to live."

"I agree. Now agree that you will stay away from him. Because if anything happens to you . . ." My voice broke then, and in turn, it broke her doggedness.

The same way her features had hardened, they softened. And then she was pulling me against her. "I promise you, *querida*, that I will not put myself in harm's way, but you promise me the same thing."

I swallowed. I didn't want to make Evelyn a promise I had no desire to keep.

"Ness . . ."

"Fine. I'll stay away from him."

For now.

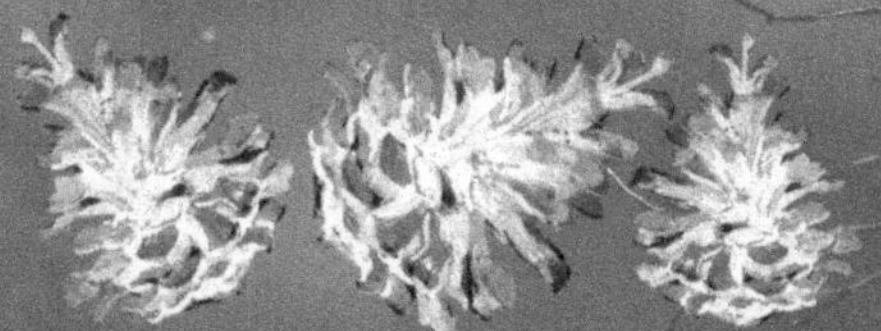

The following morning, after a brief night of sleep in one of the two twin beds set up in Frank's guest room—I suspected it was the room his grandson used when he visited because it smelled like boy and was plastered with superhero movie posters—I dressed in yesterday's clothes and went out into the kitchen for coffee.

Frank and Evelyn were already up, sitting on the couch, talking in hushed tones. The deep circles beneath Frank's eyes told me his night had been longer than mine.

"There is coffee in the kitchen, *querida*," Evelyn said.

I went to serve myself, watching as they resumed their quiet conversation.

"How's Jeb?" I ventured after a bit.

Frank rubbed his jaw that was coated in white stubble. "Not too good. Eric took your uncle back to his place last night so he and Lucy could talk. There was a lot of yelling apparently. And a lot of crying."

I took a careful sip of coffee. "What's going to happen now?"

"We'll bury Everest on pack Headquarters tonight."

I stared into the murky depths of my coffee feeling a familiar burn beneath my lids. No tears fell, though.

"They found yellow paint on one of the Jeep's side mirrors."

My gaze bounded onto the elder.

"Probably transferred from the car that pushed his off the road. It's a solid lead, because it's not a common color." He studied the vase full of wildflowers on his wooden coffee table.

"Does Aidan own a yellow car?" I asked, wending my way around the kitchen countertop toward the open living room with its peaked timber ceiling and swooping antler chandelier. I wondered if Frank had crafted the light fixture himself from collected stag horns.

"Aidan Michaels is in the hospital."

"Doesn't mean he didn't pay someone to do it."

"Perhaps, but Lucas picked up on a foreign smell out there." Frank raised his wary eyes to mine. "I think we might be dealing with Creeks."

His admission hit my ears like shattered ceramic. I actually looked down to check I hadn't dropped the mug. It was still clutched in my white-knuckled fingers. "Lucas scented foreign wolves on Liam's property yesterday. Were they Creeks too?"

"Creeks?" Evelyn asked.

Frank scraped both his hands down the length of his face and sighed, setting his gaze on the bow window across from me. For a long moment, he looked at the rolling hill dappled in long blades of sun-burnished grass and wildflowers that matched the ones in the vase.

"The Creek Pack," Frank explained, "was once the smallest pack, and then in one bloody night, they brought the largest pack to their knees."

Evelyn tightened her grip on the couch's armrest. "*Dios mío*," she murmured.

My body had turned so cold that I was afraid to move, afraid my limbs might just chip away like icicles. "Did you warn Julian?"

Frank looked back at me. "Liam's meeting with him later today. He'll try to negotiate a firm alliance."

Considering how much both packs antagonized each other, I sensed this outcome was momentous. Had the Pines and Boulders ever worked together?

"Why would the Creeks murder Everest?" I asked after a long moment.

"Liam believes it has to do with the Sillin," Frank said. "We did another sweep of your bedroom. We didn't find anything, and we're hoping no one—no Creek—got to it before us."

While Evelyn asked what Sillin was, and Frank explained it to her, I tried to puzzle out under what my cousin could've hidden the pills. If it was the pills we were talking about.

LATER IN THE MORNING, Evelyn and I stopped by the new apartment I was supposed to call home from now on. We cleaned the place, made up the beds, and unpacked my clothes. All the while she repeated that she wasn't happy about the arrangement, that my uncle was unfit to care for me, that I should stay with Frank and her. Her unhappiness increased when my uncle dropped by the apartment with a mammoth suitcase and several cardboard boxes close to bursting.

While he unpacked, he talked almost manically, never once mentioning Everest's name. It was as though he hadn't processed his son's death. I asked how Lucy was doing, which won me a pointed look followed by a sour retort.

"She killed our son by covering up for him. I don't give a rat's ass how she's doing."

When Frank drove Evelyn and me to Headquarters that evening, there were so many parked cars that they spilled onto the road. Every Boulder and their family had come. As we approached the body wrapped in a white sheet, my heart tripped. I felt like I was seeing my father's body all over again. He, also, had been enveloped in white. Werewolves weren't buried in caskets; they were placed in the ground with nothing but a sheet around them, so the earth could reclaim them.

For a moment, I wondered if the sheet that cocooned my cousin came from the inn, and then I drove that inane thought out of my mind.

A raucous whimper pierced the still air—Lucy.

I hadn't seen her since the day she'd held Evelyn hostage.

My senses sharpened at the sight of my aunt's kneeling figure. I could hear the tears tracking down her milky-white cheeks, the beats of her heart pumping blood through her organs, the sweat dripping into the waistband of her black slacks.

Evelyn squeezed my arm, which drove back my sudden urge to sink my fangs into my aunt's throat. And then Isobel and Nelson were suddenly in front of me. Where he simply nodded, face tight with grief, Isobel palmed my cheek and caught the fingers I'd balled into a fist at my side.

On the other side of the shallow hole stood Liam, flanked by Lucas and Matt. All three had their hands linked solemnly in front of them and their heads bent. I watched Liam although he didn't watch me. He stared at the hole.

Did it remind him of his father's burial?

Would he have afforded Everest a funeral had my cousin died at the Alpha's hands?

Liam must've felt the weight of my stare because he lifted his eyes to mine. They were so very dark and rimmed with red. Had he cried or was it just the mark of fatigue? Probably fatigue. Why would Liam cry over someone he'd loathed?

Ness? His unwelcome voice prickled my skull.

I lowered my gaze to my uncle, who was pressing his palm against the swathed remains of his son.

Please look at me.

I didn't.

Please, baby. Look at me.

Baby? That got my attention. I glared at him.

I deserve that.

He deserved so much worse than a glare.

I deduced from his apologetic demeanor that Cole had uncovered something from Everest's phone.

Eric started with the ritualistic singing that accompanied our people's departure from this world, so Liam didn't try to communicate with me again. I didn't shed a single tear as Everest was lowered into the dug-out hole. I didn't whimper as his remains were filmed with soil. I didn't make a single sound while the dirt rained down on the pale linen. I watched with dry eyes and a dry throat until the very last scoop fell over him, and then I watched as Jeb patted the soft mound as though tucking his son in for the very last time.

When people headed into Headquarters for the wake, I stepped away from the women holding me up and approached the one who'd always pushed me down.

"I'm sorry he died." My voice was toneless.

Lucy stopped heaving and turned her reddened hazel eyes on mine.

"I always liked Everest. Even after he double-crossed me, I wanted him to live."

She stared at me for a long moment without speaking, and then she started yelling. "It's because of you that he's dead! *You!* You ruined our lives!" She jumped to her feet and began pummeling her fists into my chest, her bangles clinking furiously. "We should've left you to rot in that foul apartment. We should *never* have brought you back!"

Her blows didn't hurt. My chest was too numb to hurt. Besides, it wasn't my fault that Everest had died; it was his own fault. I didn't bat her hands away. I didn't much care for the blows she rained on me. August and Nelson must've cared though, because they each grabbed a freckled arm. And then Jeb was shrieking at her, spittle smacking his wife's nose.

She sneered at him. "I hope you die! All of you. Your species is unnatural and should be eradicated." She spit on Jeb.

August and Nelson hauled Lucy back and then dragged her around the building. Would they lock her up underneath the silver grate? I didn't care what happened to my aunt. She was too miserable a woman.

Ness? Liam's minty scent wafted over my shoulder and snaked into me, burying deep.

Slowly, I turned and faced my Alpha. The pain on his face didn't soften my resolve to keep him away.

"What?" I asked jadedly.

I'm sorry for not believing you.

I pressed my lips tight.

Cole managed to track where the message was sent from through the Wi-Fi that was used, and it wasn't from your phone. Wasn't even from Boulder.

I was relieved to have been cleared, but the pain of the hasty condemnation remained. "Why is it, Liam, that I am I not allowed the trust you give others in the pack so freely? Because I'm new? Because I haven't *earned* it? What exactly must I do to earn it?" Breaths broke like waves around my clenched teeth. "I would never have undermined you, Liam. And not because of any exchange of blood, but because when I give my word to someone, I uphold it. I have a lot of flaws. I'm the first person to admit how stubborn and argumentative I can be, and I've spoken my fair share of lies. I'm far from being an angel."

Liam's black pupils pulsed and pulsed.

"But I've always prided myself on being a good person—a reliable and loyal one. I have *never* betrayed anyone in my entire life. And I wouldn't have started with the pack I've coveted for so long, or the boy"—my voice broke—"or the boy who . . . who . . ." I couldn't finish my sentence. It hurt too damn much.

Liam winced.

The tears that hadn't come for Everest finally surfaced. I scrubbed them away, but they wouldn't stop dripping. I took a step back, and then another. Liam didn't move. He just stayed there, legs planted like tree trunks into the earth.

I spun around. Instead of heading toward Headquarters, I headed for the road and started walking.

And walking.

Evelyn called my name, but I didn't stop.

I walked until the sky grew so dark that all the stars came out. And under this shower of light, upon blistered feet, I made my way down the miles and miles of sinuous dirt road.

I was like a hermit crab when I grieved, balled up tight within my shell. I wasn't even sure if I was grieving for my cousin or for my broken heart.

It was the first time a guy had broken it. Mom used to say that I needed my heart to be broken to know when the right man came along. She said the right one would fit all the pieces together and would fill all the fissures with his love to make sure it never cracked again.

Who's going to put your heart back together now that Daddy's gone? I'd asked her.

Her blue eyes gentled, and she gathered me against her side on our ratty denim couch that had been patched many times over. *Your dad didn't break my heart, Ness. He left with half of it.*

Car tires crunched on the road next to me, spraying tiny rocks into my ankles. "Ness, get in the car."

I stared at the luminous shapes the twin beams cast on the shrubs lining the road.

"It'll take you hours to reach town."

"I'm not in any rush, August."

For the first time in years, my agenda was empty. Sure, I'd need to look for a job, but I wouldn't have to do that tomorrow.

Tomorrow I could sleep in.

I could stare at my ceiling.

Or watch TV.

Or lunch with Sarah in the middle of the afternoon.

After the grief and stress of the last few days, I felt like I could finally breathe again. Which was strange considering Creeks might be in Boulder and a man who deserved to perish was still alive and Everest was dead.

"By God, Dimples, you're as stubborn as when you were a kid."

I smirked, flicking my gaze to August. It felt good to sport an expression that wasn't incensed or weepy. "Were you expecting me to have changed?"

August's eyes flashed in the darkness of his car. "To have matured. I'd expected you to have matured."

"If the mark of maturity is becoming biddable, then I hope I never mature, August Watt."

He shook his head. "You're really going to walk eleven more miles in the dark in heels?"

"You're right." I slid off my heels, hooking them onto my fingertips, then proceeded to the thin strip of grass edging the road to cushion my footfalls. "It's easier without heels."

He growled. "Ness, come on. I'm being serious here."

"You're always so serious. You should lighten up. Maybe take up barefoot promenades under the stars. They're very soothing." I looked at the sky and tried to find the constellations he'd taught me to find so many years ago. "Is that Andromeda or Cassiopeia? I can never tell between the two."

When he didn't answer my question, I turned toward him. Instead of looking at the sky, he was staring at me.

"Not interested in constellations anymore?" I asked.

"I'll tell you which one it is if you get in the car."

I tipped him a crooked smile. "Nice try, but it would take way more to get me off this road and into that truck."

"Ness, this isn't a joke. Creeks are running amok in our woods. They *killed* your cousin."

And he'd just *killed* my mood. "So what, August? I should live my life in fear now? I'm not invincible. I know that. If anything, Everest's death has really brought this home, but I'm also not going to hide. They killed my cousin for a reason, and I doubt that reason was because he was a Boulder wolf."

August loosed another exasperated growl. "Negotiating with terrorists is easier than with you."

And just like that, my smile was back. "So? Andromeda?"

"Yes," he huffed.

I pointed to another assortment of stars. Even though I could sense I was tugging at August's patience, he told me each one of their names. For eleven miles, he fed me information about stars and nebulas and planets.

When we reached my new home, the bottom of my feet ached, but I felt as vaporous as the stars jewelling the heavens.

I folded my arms on the open passenger window. "So this was fun."

August grunted in response.

"Okay then, Caveman Watt." I tapped the window frame. "You have yourself a good night."

I smiled at him, and it thawed some of the tightness around his eyes. As I walked toward the flight of stairs that led to my new front door, I heard him call out, "I'm glad you haven't changed, even though I sense you're going to drive me insane."

I grinned at the door. "A little insanity will do you good."

I stepped inside the tiny foyer, trailing blood and dirt across the clean oak floors, marking my new territory.

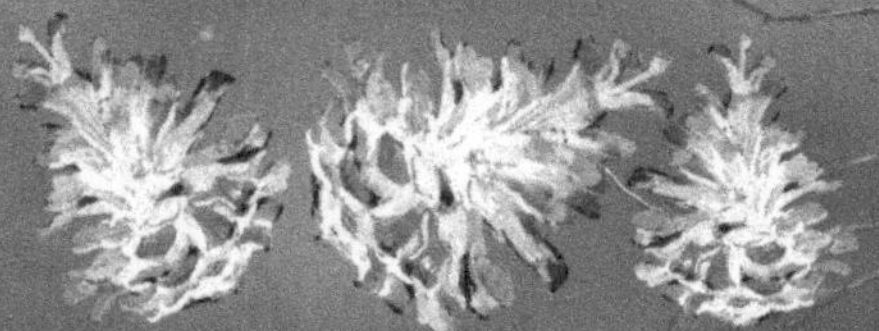

I woke up to the brightest and whitest sunshine. It streamed through my window, splashing warmth against my rumpled sheets and the bare patches of skin poking out of those sheets. I stretched, and bones cracked delightfully along my spine.

For a moment, I watched the unobstructed view of the mountains bathed in blue sky. It didn't compare to the view from the inn, but this was still a damn good view. One I could get used to.

What a dangerous thought that was.

Getting used to something.

Just because I wouldn't let myself get attached didn't mean I couldn't enjoy it until I was uprooted and tossed between another set of walls. I rolled out of bed and stood up, but the minute the soles of my feet made contact with the cool floorboards, I winced and fell back.

Maybe I'd overdone it last night.

Walking a dozen or so miles barefoot was probably not the wisest thing I'd done, and God only knew how many *unwise* things I'd already done. I could just imagine August wagging his finger at me and saying, *I told you so.* He probably wouldn't wag his finger, but he would definitely say I told you so. Good thing he wasn't here.

Keeping one hand on the bare walls of my bedroom, I limped to my bathroom. The tiles were still speckled in blood and dirt. I'd felt glad to mark my territory last night, but in the morning light, I regretted not having washed off my feet in the kitchen sink. At least I'd had the sagacity of soaking them in soap and ice-cold water before getting into bed.

After brushing my hair and teeth, I went into the living room to check on my uncle. Not only was he up, but he was having coffee with Nelson and August. I splayed my palm against the wall so I wouldn't keel over, which drove a smug smile to August's lips. How had I not heard our visitors? The apartment wasn't *that* big, and my werewolf hearing was supposed to be sharp.

I jerked my hand off the wall and took a tentative step, but grimaced. Could toes break from too much walking? Something definitely felt broken. And I wasn't even talking about the skin that had blistered and cracked in a multitude of places.

"I hope we didn't wake you," Nelson said, setting his mug down.

I took another slow, agonizing step.

"You okay, there, Ness?" August asked.

I pushed a smile onto my lips. "Yep. Great."

He leaned back in his chair and crossed his big arms like a spectator enjoying a show. Another step and I reached the small linoleum countertop that separated the living slash dining room from the kitchen.

The trail of blood I'd left behind the previous night had turned brownish, blending into the dark knots of the yellowed oak.

"Nelson and August stopped by because they were worried about our living arrangements," Jeb said, even though I hadn't asked. Not that I wasn't curious. I wondered what he thought about their concern. "And they brought us scones."

He pointed to the plate topped with golden triangles flecked with tendrils of lemon peel that scented the air, which was a feat considering how strongly August fragranced the space. I wondered if it was the mating link that intensified his aroma or if he didn't wash the soap off his skin after lathering up.

Keeping my hand on the countertop, I limped a couple inches closer to the small, round table.

"Yum," I said. About the scones. Not about August.

I mean he smelled good, but the scones smelled better. Good enough to eat. Unlike August, whom I had no desire to eat. Apparently incapable of doing two things at once, I stopped walking in order to shove away my cannibalistic deliberations.

"Are you sure you're all right?" Nelson asked.

"What?"

"You look like you're in pain." Nelson gestured to me.

Oh. "Just a Charlie horse." I looked down at my bare legs, regretting not having swapped my sleep shorts for something more concealing. I glanced toward my bedroom. *Nope.* Wasn't slogging back there. Besides I'd almost reached the free chair between Jeb and August.

One more step . . .

Cold sweat beaded on my upper lip as I finally dropped down into the chair with an audible oomph.

August, who was angled away from the table, crossed one foot over his opposite knee and grinned so wide I wanted to smack him.

"August suggested going for a hike," Jeb said. "And having a picnic."

"Nothing like sunshine and fresh air to clear the mind," August said.

I blanched a little at the idea of hiking.

"I could use a distraction." Jeb pinched the bridge of his nose. "And I wouldn't say no to physical exertion. Might help me sleep." He lifted his bruised blue eyes to me.

"What do you say?" August asked.

What do I say? Let me see . . . That you're sadistic, August Watt. Besides, I would need to be physically dragged along the trail considering the state of my body.

Obviously, I went with, "Um. I have an appointment to pass my driver's permit today." It wasn't a complete lie. If they could fit me in at the DMV, then I'd take the test. Could I just walk in?

The amused glint in August's eyes dimmed, and he grunted. "How convenient."

I lifted a scone off the plate and took a bite.

"We can leave after you're done," Nelson said. "What time's your appointment?"

The bite went down the wrong hole, and I coughed. August pushed a glass of water in front of me, and I downed it.

No rest for the injured.

What time was it now? I looked around the room for a clock. Found my answer inscribed on the cable box: 9:15. "Eleven-thirty."

"We're not in any hurry. We can leave straight after," August said.

Oh, goodie. I shot August a death glare, which put a glimmer back in his eyes.

"Great." I ripped off a large chunk of dense, flaky dough and stuffed it inside my mouth. Hopefully my werewolf gene would miraculously heal my aching bones and tattered skin within the next three hours. "Can't wait."

August cocked one of his thick eyebrows.

"I'll call Izzie to confirm the picnic." Nelson rose from his seat, cellphone already pressed to his ear.

Jeb laid his hand on my forearm and squeezed it. "Thanks for being such a good sport, Ness."

"Of course."

My uncle got up and brought his mug over to the sink. "I need to call the inn. I'll be right back."

I watched him make his way to his bedroom. Although his shoulders were hunched and his eyes puffy, he was far from the specter he'd been just a few days ago. It hadn't even been a week, I realized, yet it felt like it had been a month since the pledging ceremony. Time was a strange thing. Some days lasted seconds, and some days lasted weeks.

The heat of a hand on my knee made me look away from Jeb's closed bedroom door.

"I was just picking on you, Ness," August said quietly. "You don't have to come. Besides, you can't even walk, can you?"

August dragged his hand back to his thigh, the circumference of which equaled both my legs.

"I can hobble, and don't you dare say I told you so."

He raised both palms in the air.

"But maybe in three hours, I'll be better."

"Are you sure? You really don't have to come."

"It seemed to make Jeb happy that I was joining." I finished my scone, chewing on it thoughtfully. "If I really can't take it, I'll just sun myself until you guys are done traipsing through the woods." I wiped the crumbs off my palms. "Is your mom going to hike?"

He shook his head. "She's going to drive over. Actually, why don't you just hitch a ride with her and meet us at the lake?"

"That sounds incredibly more appealing."

Nelson came back toward us, stuffing his phone into the back pocket of his high-waisted jeans. "I need to stop by the warehouse. Christian wants to go over the blueprints of Mr. Sommerville's lodge. *Again.*"

August sighed and rose.

"Oh, you don't need to come with me, son. I can handle Christian."

"I don't mind. Besides, I'm sure Ness needs to study for her big exam."

"Why don't you help her study?"

Father and son exchanged a long look. Something passed between them. What, though, I couldn't tell, but I was most definitely going to find out the second Nelson walked out our front door.

The second it shut, I asked, "What was that about?"

"What was what about?"

"That look."

"What look?"

"Oh come on, August. I grew up with you guys."

August rubbed the back of his head sheepishly, glancing toward Jeb's door. "Dad doesn't want Jeb to be left alone. Not for the next week anyway. He's worried." August shrugged. "He's worried he might . . ." More neck rubbing. "Try to kill himself." Those last few words came out whispered.

"Oh." Goose bumps scattered all over me. "I'm here," I said finally.

"I know. *We* know."

"But you guys don't think I can handle him?"

"No. That's not it. My parents are also worried about *you.*"

My heart squeezed a little that anyone besides Evelyn cared how I was doing. "Tell them they don't have to worry."

He grunted as he sat down again and leaned back in his seat. I was a little afraid the rungs would snap right off, but the chair surprisingly held.

"Like that would ever happen," he said, picking up a knife that someone had placed on the table, probably to cut the scones in half, even though I had to wonder what self-respecting werewolf would eat only half a scone. He flipped the utensil, blade up, blade down. Over and over.

"So, does this mean we get breakfast delivered every morning? Because if that's the case, I'd like to put in some requests."

He glanced at me from underneath his dark lashes and let out a little grunt. I was starting to think grunting was August Watt's MO.

"Let me guess." He raised a finger. "Carrot cake muffins, preferably frosted." He flicked up another finger. "Chocolate-zucchini bread." A third finger came up. "Warm sourdough with salted butter." Another finger. "Cinnamon rolls with a hefty layer of icing." And then his pinkie leaped up. "Bacon—the thickly cut kind—with scrambled eggs."

I blinked at him, impressed by his memory. He'd just listed all of my favorite breakfast items. Not that I was the pickiest person, but I really did have a thing for cinnamon and fatty food. Discussing food brought me back to the meal I'd shared with Liam in his kitchen when he'd asked what I liked eating. August already knew all that about me. For some reason, this flustered me. I got up and hobbled to the kitchen to pour myself a mug of coffee.

With my back to him, I said, "Coffee. Just coffee. I don't really eat any of that stuff anymore." I wasn't sure why I was lying to August. Maybe it was because I didn't want him to think he had me all figured out. Even though he did.

I turned and leaned against the linoleum countertop. The edge bit into the sliver of skin on display between my crop top and my sleep shorts. Again, I thought about going to put on some more clothes, but I lived amongst wolves. They probably didn't even notice bare skin anymore.

August frowned at me, and then he frowned down at the white ceramic mug clutched between my fingers. I blew on the steam, watched it disperse and melt into the air.

Feeling like a jerk, I said, "If you really do have time, I'd appreciate some help with studying for my exam."

His gaze returned to my face. For a moment, I thought about confessing I'd lied, that he'd been right, that those were still all of my favorite things, but I couldn't get the words out. It was disarming to have someone know me so intimately. I hadn't eaten cinnamon rolls or carrot cake muffins in months, yet the mere mention of them made me salivate. It also brought back a whole slew of memories that included a table full of people—most of whom weren't part of this world anymore.

My mom had made the best cinnamon rolls.

And my father's usual Sunday activity—besides waltzing his wife around the house to a Roberta Flack song—was grating several pounds of carrots for her baking.

"Sure," August finally said. "Do you have the booklet?"

"No." I blew on my coffee again. No steam rose this time. "Can you pull up the questions on your phone?"

He nodded. As he quizzed me, his tone was so stiff that I knew I'd wounded him, yet I couldn't confess my deception. I might've been loyal to a fault, but I was one hell of a stubborn liar.

25

I didn't end up hiking. But I did pass my driver's permit without making so much as a single mistake, and then I celebrated at the lakeside picnic with all of my favorite people—when Isobel had pulled up in front of the DMV, Evelyn was in the car.

I'd almost cried from how happy I was that Isobel had thought to invite Evelyn. Also, I was feeling pretty emotional from getting my permit on the first try. Now I only needed fifty hours of driving experience and a vision exam, and I'd be all set to cruise around Boulder—or around the country—on my own. I was drunk on the freedom that loomed at my fingertips.

Buoyed by the thoughts of all the places I would go, I walked to the lake's edge, slid off my sandals, and waded into the crisp water that felt delicious against my blistered feet. I picked up a stone and skipped it on the glassy surface just as Isobel's contagious laughter rang through the warm summer air.

This was a perfect day.

One of the most perfect days I'd had in a long time.

"Not bad." August stared at the ripples on the water as my rock sank to the bottom.

"You think you can do better, Watt?"

He answered me with a confident smile, the first one he'd given me since I'd shot him down earlier. With that smile, all was right in the world again.

His flat pebble leaped over the surface four times before plunging to its watery grave. "That was just a warm-up shot."

I snickered. "Uh-huh."

His freckles seemed to burn a little darker. He crouched and spent almost an entire minute scouring the rocky beach for just the right stone. I remembered making fun of him once for devoting half an afternoon searching a meadow for the most faultless red poppies to give Isobel one Mother's Day. I'd ripped up the first stalks I could find and squashed them into a bouquet, which wilted on the way to my house. Mom had still complimented their beauty and displayed them in a vase on her dresser.

Slowly, August unfurled his long body, the smallest and slimmest rock nestled in his palm, and walked over to the water's edge, crouched, all of the muscles in his body purling as he frisbeed the rock in one perfect sweep.

He pumped his fist in the air. "Take that, Dimples. Nine!"

I flung my gaze toward the water, which still undulated. I'd missed his exploit. For all I knew, the pebble had skipped twice before sinking, but I couldn't admit that, because then he'd know I'd been ogling him instead of the rock, and he'd wonder why.

I wondered why.

Perhaps it was the violently hot sun.

Or maybe it was the incessant cacophony of crickets.

"You win," I conceded, wading in deeper. Water snaked up my bare thighs. I should've worn a bathing suit but hadn't thought of it. My cut-offs and tank top would have to do. "I'm going for a swim."

A dragonfly skimmed the water's surface, its green pearlescent body adding to the lake's pulsing shimmer. I swept my hand toward the insect, and it dashed off the same way bunnies ran from me when I was in my other form.

"Want to join me?" I asked, looking over my shoulder at August.

He rubbed his chin as though debating, but then he lowered his pants and yanked off his tee. I turned my prying gaze away and submerged myself completely, staying under until I felt my blood cool down. When I popped back out, August was lying on his back next to me, floating like driftwood.

He looked peaceful.

Too peaceful.

Smiling deviously, I pressed both my palms into his abdomen and drove him downward. And then I laughed so hard that when he emerged and shoved me under, I snorted in an ungodly amount of lake water.

I propelled myself away from him like a squid. "Not fair," I said, laugh-snorting.

He grinned. When I saw him cut through the water toward me, probably to dunk me under again, I raced to the middle of the lake. Only then did I stop to take a breath. From the shore, I caught Evelyn shading her eyes. I waved to her to reassure her that I was okay just before I got dunked again.

When I broke free, I tossed my hair back. "Oh. You're going to regret that!"

August shot me a challenging grin. "Am I? What are you going to do, Dimples? Stick itching powder in my bed again?"

Ha! I'd forgotten about that. "Not a bad idea . . ." I racked my brain for something worse, though. When it finally came to me, I swam up to him and started tickling his sides. August was the most ticklish person in the history of ticklish people.

He roared with laughter until he managed to cuff my wrists. Then he tried to take revenge, but I wasn't ticklish. I'd never been. He must've remembered that fact at some point because he stopped prodding my ribcage and simply rested his palm against my waist. I wasn't cold, but my skin pebbled and my heart . . . it skipped a beat.

Possibly two.

Before he could detect my weirdness, I kicked away from him. "Nice try, big guy," I said, hoping my voice sounded normal. "Race you to the shore?"

His green eyes honed into the shore with the same intensity they'd honed into me a moment ago. August had never been competitive—not ever—and yet the way he looked at that shore made me wonder if he'd changed. Maybe, in the past, when we'd played backgammon or scaled a tree, he'd let me win, because I was so much younger.

"You're going to need a head start," he finally said.

"I'm all grown up now. I don't need any more head starts."

"You sure about that?"

"Yep."

"What do I get if I win?" He submerged his chin and mouth and blew out bubbles as he treaded water next to me.

"You want a prize for beating a girl?"

He popped his head back out of the water. "That's a low blow. How am I supposed to beat you now?"

I grinned at him, my dimples feeling like they were excavating my cheeks. "Ready?"

He grunted, which I took as a yes.

I propelled my limbs, wheeling them so fast they blurred, and my pulse skyrocketed. Unlike August, I had always been competitive. Which had been one of the reasons I'd entered the Alpha trials.

His body plundered the water parallel to mine. I didn't stop to check who was in the lead though, not until I reached the embankment. The minute my fingers grazed the shore, I shot out of the water and whipped my hair off my face. August touched the shore a couple seconds after me.

"Yes!" I smacked the water triumphantly, but then I noticed he was barely out of breath, and my triumph waned. "Did you let me win, August Watt?"

He pivoted and sat facing out. "Nope."

"Liar."

He side-eyed me, and there was something in his penetrating gaze that made my grin crumble like crushed chalk. It was as though he was saying, *that makes two of us*. Maybe I was reading too much into his expression. Maybe I was only seeing what I was feeling.

Whatever it was, I got out of the lake, cool water bleeding down my legs and between my breasts. When I reached the picnic blanket, I sat down and wrung out my hair. Isobel tendered me a towel, which I wrapped around myself.

"Remember those parties we used to throw down here, Jeb?" she said to my contemplative uncle.

His gaze was fixed to the pines swaying gently around the crystalline body of water. "I remember Nelson tossing me in one night with all my clothes on because I mentioned how pretty you looked."

Nelson chuckled, a tad sheepishly, whereas Isobel flushed but smiled as big as her son.

Keeping her gaze trained on August's back, on the caterpillar-like scar that extended the length of the waistband of his black briefs, she said, "Those were the days."

I didn't ask whether my parents had attended those lake parties. I sensed they had. They'd all grown up together. They'd all splashed around the lake together. They'd all kissed and gotten married and birthed babies together.

Shifters were a community, and like all communities, they'd been rattled by tragedy, but somehow, they'd all stuck around and lifted each other up when life had weighed them down. Until my father died.

Would our generation be supportive? Would I one day picnic with August and Matt and their respective wives and laugh about the good old days?

I hoped so. I hoped I would get what Isobel, Nelson, and Jeb had. I hoped I would get a real family again.

26

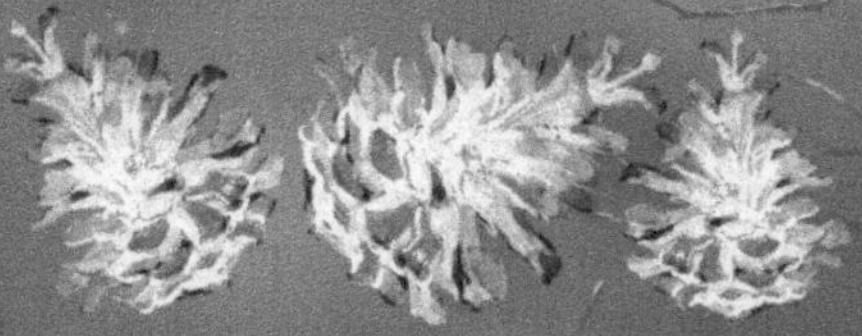

The week following Everest's burial smeared into a long blur. Every day, someone from the pack would bring us breakfast and suggest an activity—a movie, a card game, a walk. At some point, Jeb started to turn people down, and then he stopped coming out of his room altogether, which meant I got to hang out with our visitors and prove I had everything under control.

And I did.

I ached, but my sadness was tempered by the fact that Everest had dug his own grave, even though I still didn't understand why he'd done all that he'd done, or why the Creeks had silenced him. Was it for the Sillin, or was there more?

When Matt dropped by at the end of the week, brandishing a bag of homemade blueberry muffins his mom had baked, I made him sit and tell me what was going on, because I was certain *a lot* was going on.

The blond bear of a man sank down onto the couch, palming the pale stubble on his square jaw. "Julian and Liam have contacted the Creek Alpha to ask for a meeting. She hasn't gotten back to them yet, so Robbie suggested heading out there to confront her." He sighed and sat back, hooking one arm around the back of the couch and dropping the other on the armrest.

I handed him a mug of the minty tea I'd just brewed and sat on the opposite end of the couch, folding my legs beneath me. "Do you think he was killed because of the drugs?"

"It's the likeliest scenario."

"Has anyone spoken to Aidan Michaels?"

"Aidan Michaels?" Both of his honeyed eyebrows shot up on his sun-reddened forehead. I guessed he'd been working outdoors this week. "Why would he know anything?"

"Because one, he had his own business dealings with Everest. And two, he's made it his mission to know everything there is to know about werewolves. Why would his interest in packs not extend over the Boulder town limits?"

Matt thought about this so hard his large forehead puckered. "True. I'll talk to Liam." He took a sip of his tea. "Or maybe you should?"

"No way."

"Why?"

I set my mug down before I could squeeze the tea right out of it. "Seriously, Matt? You're asking me why? You were there."

"I know, Ness, but we were all under pressure, and between the text and the voicemail—"

"He should've given me the benefit of the doubt. You *all* should've."

Matt chewed on his lower lip. "He hates himself for it, but you gotta understand, that's Liam. He's always been a little . . . *impulsive*."

Impulsive? "So I'm supposed to forgive and forget?"

Matt went back to rubbing his jaw. "No. But I think you guys should talk. You don't have to get back together or anything, but he's real miserable, Ness. And his temper's gotten even shorter."

"Not my problem."

"He's your Alpha, so it sort of is your problem. It's all of our problem. If he flips a switch, he could do something that could endanger the pack."

"I'm not a shrink, Matt. Liam needs therapy. And I'm not saying that out of anger, but because his father really screwed him up. There's nothing I can say or do that can fix that sort of damage."

Matt screwed up his lips. "Tamara's sniffing around him again."

"Did she ever stop?"

"I guess not, but she's really coming on strong this time."

I stared out the window at the rolling mountains flecked with evergreens and grass. My heartbeat slowed as I pictured Liam's red-haired ex and the sneer she'd directed at me the night I'd gone out to Tracy's with the pack. The night she'd all but called me a hooker.

"She can have him," I said.

"Are you sure?"

I finally dragged my gaze back to Matt. "Yes."

He studied his dirt-flecked work boots. "Is it because of August?"

"August is like an older brother to me." One who'd stopped visiting since our lakeside picnic. Not that he'd promised to come every day, but it would've been nice to see his face or hear his voice.

"I heard you two are mates."

"Just because we're *supposed to be* mates doesn't mean we're attracted to each other."

Matt snorted, which made me bristle.

"What?" I asked.

"Nothing."

"Why did you snort?"

"Because you're hot, and August's a guy. And even if he might feel like a brother to you, the fact is, he isn't."

"So?"

"So he shot Sienna's advances down the other day. And then this waitress, who he used to hook up with before Sienna, asked if he wanted a nightcap, and he rejected her too."

I could see how him turning down girls could be misconstrued, but he was probably worried about his mother. Her surgery was on Monday. *I* was worried.

"He's got a lot going on, Matt."

"No unattached guy has *that* much going on that they turn down easy lays, Ness."

I sat up and placed my mug down on the glass coffee table. "I might have a theory."

"I'm listening."

This isn't going to be weird . . . Then again this entire conversation was weird. It was the sort of conversation I should be having with Sarah instead of Matt. Not that Sarah and I hadn't had it already. Sarah had been picking me up most afternoons to give me driving lessons in her red Mini, so the subject had come up.

Jeb said she was probably trying to squeeze information about Everest and the Creeks out of me, but I doubted it. One, she could've gone to her uncle for information, and two, we didn't discuss pack dynamics all that much. We mostly listened to music while discussing UCB and the courses I should take. I hadn't gotten my acceptance letter yet. I imagined *it*, as well as my tuition, were contingent to a talk with Liam. I hadn't been ready to face him, but I was slowly getting there.

Next week perhaps . . .

"So?" Matt's voice broke me out of my daydream. "What's your theory?"

I dragged my hand through my hair. "The mating link makes our bodies unreceptive to people who aren't our mates."

He frowned.

"We can't be . . . um"—heat eddied through me—"intimate."

"Huh?"

"Oh come on, Matt." I yanked my hand through my hair again so hard this time I plucked out a few strands. "Don't make me draw you a diagram. This is embarrassing enough." So embarrassing that I kept my gaze locked on the blank TV screen in the corner.

"Whoa. You mean you can't have sex with a random person? *Whoa* . . ." He repeated *whoa* a couple more times. "Now I get why Liam tried to get August to leave town. *Whoa.*"

"Yeah. Sucks." For August more than me. I didn't know what I was missing.

"I don't get why August isn't hauling ass out of Boulder. I mean, I do get it. His mom being sick and all, but after that"—he rubbed his hands together—"after that, Ness, if he sticks around Boulder, he's sticking around for you."

I folded my fingers together. Not in prayer. Just to do something with them. This conversation had me feeling restless. Not to mention uncomfortable. Tremendously uncomfortable. I was antsy for Matt to leave.

As though he sensed it, he stood up.

"He'll leave," I said slowly. "There's no reason for him to stay. I won't act on the link. I don't want to be with someone because of some chemical or magical connection."

"Just because it's magical doesn't mean it's not real."

I cocked an eyebrow. "That's exactly what it means. Magic isn't real, Matt."

"We're magical, and we're real." He gestured between us. "How do you explain that, huh?"

"What would you do if you suddenly had a mate, and that girl wasn't Amanda?"

His features tensed. "You can't compare us. Amanda and I, we've been together for a long time. As far as I can see, neither you nor August are attached, so there's no real reason for staying away. Unless you're holding out for Liam. In which case—"

"I'm not."

He observed me a long minute before strolling to the front door. "Life's short, Ness." He drummed his thick fingers against the wall. "Shorter for some than for others. Just make sure you get to the end of it with more satisfaction than regrets. And yeah, I know not everyone needs a relationship or love or sex to feel happy, but avoiding it on principle is a sucky reason to stay single." He turned the knob and drew open the door. "And I know I've probably overstayed my welcome and doled out too much unwanted advice, but I know August. He's like a brother to me too, and even though he's quiet 'bout his feelings, he broke up with Sienna the minute you walked back into his life. And if I'm not mistaken, you guys weren't linked yet."

"Their breakup had nothing to do with me."

"If it makes you sleep better at night."

I wanted to tell him to butt out of my personal life.

"Remember when I caught you guys sexting after the first trial?"

I rolled my eyes. "We weren't sexting."

He side-eyed me. "If you say so, Little Wolf."

"I do say so. I can show you our messages. There wasn't anything remotely sexual about any of them."

"You guys have a connection."

"*Friends*. We're just friends."

"Uh-huh. Anyway, gotta hit the road. Wouldn't want *my boss* to fire me."

"Yeah. We wouldn't want that," I grumbled. I was feeling moody now because Matt had gotten under my skin.

So much so that once he shut the door, whistling loudly on his way down the steps, I retrieved my phone from the kitchen counter and began scrolling through my past conversations with August. Although not sexual, the tone of our back-and-forth texts was pretty personal.

As I scrolled up and up, our phone conversations started coming back to me, and my heart quickened. I couldn't possibly have a crush on August, or could I?

Ugh.

I worshipped him as a kid, because he was so sweet with me, so attentive. It felt wrong to crush on him today. I barely knew him anymore.

I was so wound up about this that I went for a long, *long* run. By the time I got home, I'd come to a conclusion that sounded extremely wise: I would stay away from him until he left town.

27

I hadn't realized how nervous I was about Isobel's surgery until I woke up on Monday so early stars still blanketed the sky. I texted August, hoping he'd silenced his phone while he slept. I'd feel awful about waking him up.

ME: *Can you text me once the surgery's over so I can come and visit?*

His answer came barely a minute later. *Yes.*

ME: *Did I wake you?*

AUGUST: *No.*

From the time Mom was diagnosed till the very end, I hadn't slept through the night. I was about to ask him how he was feeling, if I could do anything, when a new text appeared on my screen.

AUGUST: *Sorry I haven't come by this week. It's been insanely busy at work. How are you and Jeb holding up?*

ME: *We're good. Don't worry about us. Besides, been busy here too. Almost everyone in the pack has dropped by.*

AUGUST: *Hope they've been bringing you good coffee.*

I bit my lip. I couldn't tell what the tone of his message was supposed to be: humorous or bitter?

ME: *No coffee. But I have enough confections to open a bakery.*

AUGUST:

Okay, so maybe August wasn't bitter. Maybe he truly was concerned about the quality of our coffee.

ME: *I should probably look into the bakery idea. I need a job. Ugh. Sorry to bore you with this.*

Dot dot dots bounced on my screen.

AUGUST: *We could use some help around the warehouse. Mom was taking care of the* *accounting, but she won't be doing that for a while. And Dad's planning on taking some time off to be with her.*

I read and reread his message, strange emotions eddying through me. I needed to say no. Being around August was not a good idea. But, hell, I really wanted to say yes. The business had been my father's, so I knew what it entailed. Although, considering the expansion, what the Watts did now probably differed from what Dad used to do.

AUGUST: *It would come with good pay of course. Anyway, think about it.*

It brought me back to one of our first conversations after my return to Boulder. He'd asked me if I wanted a job.

ME: *If I say yes, but I'm completely incompetent, do you promise not to keep me on because of guilt or pity?*

AUGUST: *Where did that come from?*

ME: *Just swear it to me.*

AUGUST: *OK. I swear it.*

It wouldn't have to be weird. It's not like we'd be working side by side. From what I'd understood, August was usually on the building sites.

AUGUST: *Why are YOU up so early?*

I looked out at the glittery expanse peeking behind my drawn curtains.

ME: *Just worried.*

AUGUST: *Everything's going to be fine.*

I sighed, wishing I could be so optimistic, but life had thrown me one too many curveballs. Still, I texted: *I know.* There was no point in infecting others with my skepticism.

AUGUST: *Get dressed.*

ME: *Why?*

AUGUST: *Because I can sense your stress all the way through the phone.*

AUGUST: *And wear comfortable shoes.*

I sat up in bed, fully awake now. After I washed my face and brushed my teeth, I tugged on black leggings, a black hoodie, and my sneakers, then went out to the kitchen and wrote Jeb a note in case he woke up and noticed my bed was empty. As I placed the paper on the dining table, I hesitated to text August that he didn't have to take care of me when he should be taking care of his mom, but a message popped onto my screen.

AUGUST: *I'm downstairs.*

I tied my hair up into a quick ponytail, grabbed my phone and keys, and left quietly so as not to wake up my uncle.

August looked pale, which was a feat considering his mixed origins. Then again, it could've been the effect of the light bouncing off his dashboard.

He smiled at me, but it didn't reach his eyes. "I think we're the two only people up in the whole of Boulder."

It was 4:30. My street was completely deserted, and every window we drove by was dark.

"Where are we going?" I asked as I strapped myself in.

"You'll see."

I wasn't the sort of person who liked to *see*, but I trusted August. As we drove, I played with the music, swapping his preferred jazz station with something a little more upbeat. And then I closed my eyes to rest them and drummed my fingers to the tempo of the music.

Up and up the mountain road we went. Finally, he pulled to a stop, grabbed a pack from the backseat, slung it over his shoulder, and we got out. We walked down a wooded trail that led to the sharp ridges of the Flatirons. The sight transported me back to the first trial, but I didn't tell August. Not even when some pebbles came loose under my feet and adrenaline spiked through my veins. I drove back my fear of the mountain raining down on me. The rockslide had been manmade—or rather *elder*made—just another part of the trials.

We came to a stop a couple yards from the lip of the steep cliff. I didn't have vertigo, but still, I didn't look down.

"You okay?" he asked as he unzipped his backpack.

"Yeah. Great."

He kept his gaze locked on mine as he tugged a blanket out of his pack, as though he didn't quite believe me. Could he sense my nerves through the link? He shook out the blanket and spread it onto the moon-bleached rock. "Want to tell me about it?"

I didn't, but at the same time I didn't want him to pin my nervousness on anything else. So I reminded him about the race, about the landslide. His entire body stiffened. He reached down and picked up the blanket, but I stepped on it.

"August, it's fine. I promise. Besides, like Mom used to say, best way to chase away a bad memory is to make a new one."

When he still hadn't let go of the blanket, I pried the edge out of his clenched fingers and let it flutter back to the stone floor. And then I sat, gathering my knees against me.

"I bet the sunrise is spectacular from here," I said, looking out at the ultraviolet darkness that stretched around us.

It took a while for August to shake off the tension in his body, but finally, he sat beside me. "Best in Boulder." He took a thermos out of his pack. "Here." When I raised an eyebrow, he said, "Coffee."

I twisted the top open, then took a sip of the scalding, bitter beverage before handing it back. "I didn't even think about bringing water. If I wasn't a shifter, and I was lost in the wilderness, I'd probably not make it out alive." I tucked my chin onto my knees. "You know, that show, *Naked and Afraid*?" I'd been watching a lot of TV recently. "They'd probably give me a survival rating of one-point-two."

August chuckled softly. "That's very specific. And incorrect, I'm sure."

"Maybe I should sign us up."

He glanced at me from the corner of his eye. "Don't we spend enough time *naked* and *afraid* as werewolves?"

"In my case, yes, but what are you afraid of?"

He passed me the thermos, gaze cast on the sky. "Helicopters."

"Helicopters? That's specific. Why helicopters?"

"Because I crashed in one."

My heart soared so high I felt it inside my throat. "When?"

"Three years ago." The darkness around us increased the shadows populating his face. "It's the reason I came back to Boulder."

I waited, not wanting to press him, but the stretch of time between that last sentence and the next lasted an eternity.

"My buddy was piloting it. I was in the backseat with two other guys from my squad when we caught enemy fire. One of them had been telling me how he planned on proposing to his girlfriend . . ." He stopped talking, and his lids came down hard. "Anyway, I made it. None of the others did. One of the medics kept saying how lucky I was. It made me so angry because how the hell was I the lucky one? I saw all of them die, Ness. All of them." He finally opened his eyes. They glinted. "And now I'm the one stuck with the memory every damn day."

I tightened my hold on my knees. I wanted to reach out to him, but then I remembered when Dad had been shot, how I'd hated the mere brush of a hand. Or the litany of *sorrys*. The only person I'd wanted to be around had been my mother. I'd even pushed August and Isobel away.

"You know what I thought when I was lying in that hospital bed?" He finally looked at me. "I thought about you. Of how brave you'd been at only eleven. I was in my twenties, and a freaking mess. It took me almost a year to stop having nightmares."

"I wasn't brave, August. I just shut myself off. I'm not even sure I've ever really turned myself back on. Not fully. A part of me died right alongside my father."

He blinked, but no tears slid out of his shiny eyes.

"How did you stomach enlisting again?" I asked after a long while.

"I thought it would help me get over what had happened." He grabbed the thermos of coffee and took a long swallow.

"Did it?"

He gave me a tight smile. "Nope. Just reminded me how much I hate helicopters."

I smiled, even though my heart bled. "You'd think that being magical creatures would give us the upper hand on death." I raised my face toward the absent moon. Although it hadn't birthed werewolves, the traction of Earth's satellite influenced our magic. "Do you still want to go back into the military?"

He sighed. "I'm not sure what I want anymore."

A strange warmth pooled inside my stomach. Relief that he might not leave?

"But I might have to." He grabbed a loose rock and flung it through the quiet air as though he were trying to skip it on the sky.

My kneecaps dug into my cheek. "Why?"

He side-eyed me. "To make things . . . *easier*."

My heart sped up.

And up . . .

"On who?" I asked so softly I wasn't sure my words would carry to his ears.

"On both of us."

"Because of the link?"

Nodding, he rolled onto his back, cushioning his head with his palms. I glanced at him over my shoulder, hoping he couldn't feel all I was feeling, but I sensed he could. Hopefully, he'd chalk it up to the stress of the coming day.

"This is your home, August. You shouldn't have to leave it because of me."

His thick eyebrows slanted over his green eyes.

"Instead of going to UCB, I could attend college in some other state. I hear New England's nice."

Would the pack pay for a school that wasn't in Boulder, or did they only foot the bill when their wolves stayed on pack territory?

I gripped the thermos of coffee and tipped it up to my lips, then set it on the blanket and lay down next to August.

He hadn't opposed my decision to go to some faraway college, and my navel wasn't pulsing with any repressed emotion on his part. Whatever I was feeling for him was one-sided.

Could he sense *my* disappointment? I hoped not.

I balled my fingers into fists, then flexed them back out, damning Matt for planting ideas inside my head and damning myself for letting them take root.

28

Isobel's surgery went smoothly, so I got to see her that very afternoon.

Although she was hooked to an EKG machine, and there were drainage tubes sticking out from underneath her powder-blue hospital gown, she was smiling and sported a way better complexion than I did. I kissed her forehead, nose prickling from the strong odor of antiseptic and infected blood, then sat in the chair August had occupied but freed up for me.

We talked about everything and nothing: the weather, college, doctors, even her work which I was supposed to take over the following day. Greg stopped by to see her at some point. Although the pack doctor hadn't been the one to operate on her, he'd been the one to choose the surgeon. Isobel laughed at something he told her, something I didn't catch because of who'd just walked into the room.

As our gazes collided, the room and all of the noise—the steady beeping of the heart monitor, Isobel's tinkling laughter, August and Nelson's quiet conversation—it all faded out for a moment. It had been eleven days since I'd seen Liam, but it felt like a month.

I jerked my gaze down to my lap, and then I jerked to my feet. "I'm going to grab something to eat from the cafeteria. Does anyone want anything?"

I was still looking at my feet when everyone answered *no*.

I walked around Isobel's bed and passed by Liam, sensing him everywhere. It was as though his *alpha-ness* had grown. Was that possible?

In the hospital hallway, I took a deep breath. The myriad of chemical smells and human diseases made my nose itch and my eyes water. Blinking repeatedly, I plucked a tissue from the box on the nurse's station to dab at the moisture.

The cafeteria was full of visitors, and the hubbub made my head throb. I needed sleep. A lot of it. Hopefully I wouldn't wake at the crack of dawn tomorrow morning. I bought an overpriced ham sandwich before returning to the wing where Isobel would spend the next two nights. As I ate my sandwich, a chill swept over my arms, and not from any AC vent; I sensed a presence. An unwelcome one. Through narrowed eyes, I took in every inch of the hallway, coming to a stop on a closed door. I strode over to it and squinted through the inset glass. The room was dark. I listened for a sound—a breath, a pulse—but was met with silence. Yet my uneasiness grew. I inhaled deeply, and layered over the unpleasant reek of the medical facility was a cloying, distinctive cologne: *Aidan Michaels's*.

I turned the doorknob and barged inside, hoping the reason I smelled him but didn't see him was because he lay dead in his hospital bed. No such luck. The bed was made with crisp, papery sheets, the adjustable overbed table wiped clean, and the blinds shut.

This must've been the room he'd recovered in.

As I turned to leave, I smacked into a large body. Heart battering, I lurched backward and flung my gaze up. Liam stared down at me, jaw set, eyes dark.

I clapped a palm over my frantic heart. "You just gave me a heart attack."

His expression softened the teeniest bit. "Good thing we're in a hospital then."

For a moment, neither of us spoke.

Then, Liam asked, "How have you been?" at the same time as I asked, "Did you find the owner of the yellow car?"

Liam pressed his lips together. "Straight to business."

He was right. That wasn't very nice. "I've been okay. And you?" The intensity with which he observed me dampened my palms. I wiped them on my leggings.

"I've been better."

Silence stretched between us.

"Cole matched it to a yellow Hummer. He saw the car on a traffic light monitor."

Cole had hacked into the city's traffic monitoring system?

Why was I surprised?

"Colorado license plates. CRK-590. Creek-owned, as I'm sure you got from the letters." He sighed. "No apology will undo how quick I was to blame you, but I'll say it again anyway." He took a step toward me. "I'll say it as many times as it takes for you to forgive me." He tilted his face down and dropped his voice to a murmur. "I. Am. Sorry."

And then he said it again through the mind link.

And again.

And with each apology, he moved closer to me, chipping at the defensive wall I'd erected around myself. He must've sensed he was getting through to me, because he didn't stop advancing until we were standing toe to toe.

I raised my hand and pressed my palm into his black T-shirt. "Stop."

I wasn't sure if he would, but he did.

He stopped.

Stopped speaking.

Stopped moving.

My hand tingled with his strong heartbeats, and my forehead prickled from his warm breaths. I lowered my gaze to his chin, smooth from a fresh shave.

His lips moved to form my name.

A slow burn traveled through my blood, concentrated in my navel, ignited there.

"I need you," he whispered.

"Don't say that. Please, don't say that."

My words had the adverse effect on him.

It untied his tongue, made him speak all the reasons he needed me—that I lent him strength, that I calmed him, that I made his life sweeter, brighter, better.

"Give me another chance, babe. Give *us* another chance. I won't screw it up this time. I understand what I stand to lose." His chocolate eyes glowed in the lines of sun spilling through the blinds. **I swear it on the pack.**

I hated his entire declaration, not because it was too little too late, but because it was too much too soon. "Don't swear on the pack," I whispered.

"On my life then. I swear it on my life."

Shaking my head, I let my palm drift off his T-shirt, off his heart. My eyes stung.

From Aidan's scent.

From Liam's.

"Liam, I can't."

For a moment, his expression shuttered up, turned into his firm Alpha mask, but a flush had risen to my cheeks. A chink in my armor. Even though he didn't lay a single finger on my body, his gaze traced the contours of my face. His earlier remorse and tentativeness were gone, replaced by something that all at once sharpened and softened all of his features.

Hope.

Even though I realized my grudge had faded, I also realized that giving Liam hope was unfair.

"Not now, Liam. Not until my mind and body clear of the mating link." Even though I appeared collected on the outside, chaos reigned inside of me. I was a mess of jumbled emotions and peculiar thoughts.

"I'll wait." He gave me a look that was so bruisingly ardent my heart fired like a rifle. "The same way your . . ."

His voice dimmed as I noticed the hulking figure darkening the open doorway. My stomach contracted. How long had August been standing there?

Liam exploited my moment of inattention to touch me. His fingers were suddenly on my face, pushing a lock of hair off my forehead.

I pranced backward.

He unhurriedly returned his hand to his side, seemingly unshaken by my reaction.

"What did you just say? The same way my what?" I repeated tersely.

"The same way your father waited for your mother."

"My father?" I frowned. "I don't understand." I glanced over his shoulder again, but the doorway was empty.

"Remember how I told you mates didn't always end up together the night of the pledging ceremony?"

Ice filled my veins. "My father had a mate?"

"No. *My* father had one."

What did Heath having a mate have to do with my father—

Oh . . .

Oh.

My hand climbed up to my mouth. "My mom was your dad's mate?"

He didn't nod. Didn't speak. Just looked at what his revelation was doing to me. At the thoughts detonating inside my skull.

My mother had been intended for Liam's father, not for my own.

Yet she'd picked my father.

She'd loved him, not her mate.

"It created quite the stir back in the day," Liam said, walking over to the bed to sit on it. The stiff mattress creased under him. "Your mom was sixteen and had already been dating your father for three years. And my father . . . Well, he wasn't looking to settle. But the mating link made tensions rise. I don't know the full story. Just bits and pieces. My father was an angry drunk, but a voluble one." Liam rubbed his hands up and down his thighs. "A month or two into the link, he decided he did want to be with your mother, so he tried to woo her away from your dad. But, Maggie, she was in love with your father." He studied one of the lines of sunshine that slashed the squeaky clean linoleum floor. "So you see, I don't put much stock in mating links, Ness."

He raised his gaze back to my face. Although I was no longer clasping my mouth, it still gaped. I wasn't sure whether it would ever close again.

My mother and Heath?

I shivered.

"Maybe the moon, or the wolf God, or whatever's up there"—he gestured noncommittally to the ceiling—"opens connections between people, but in the end, those people are still masters of their own destinies. Of their own hearts."

Dust motes spangled the air between us, coming in and out of focus.

Liam didn't speak for a long moment as though understanding that I needed time and silence to process this.

"You and August have history. And unlike my father, August is a good guy, so I understand if you're confused about how you feel about him—"

The chill that had enveloped my body was replaced by lava-hot heat. I palmed the back of my neck, hoping my cool hand would drive the heat back down.

"—but don't forget how you felt about me before he came into the picture."

How the hell did he know I felt conflicted about August?

Was it obvious?

I didn't want to have this conversation with Liam, the same way I hadn't wanted to have it with Matt.

Matt!

He must've talked to Liam. Shared our weird conversation.

I couldn't handle this right now. I blinked out of my daze and started toward the door, my strides hurried.

"And, Ness?" Liam called out.

I didn't stop. I just kept walking. I didn't want to hear anymore. I couldn't take anymore.

But his voice trailed after me, clanking inside my mind: **Remember that how you felt about me had** nothing **to do with magic.**

I clamped my hands over my ears—not that it could keep his voice out—and sped up, exiting the hospital.

THAT NIGHT, over dinner, I asked Jeb about what Liam had told me, because I'd begun to have doubts. Doubts that Liam had planted this story inside my mind to redirect me toward him. He knew how deeply I'd admired my parents' love, how deeply I wanted what they had.

Jeb raked his hand through his thinning hair. "How did you find out?"

"Liam told me."

I prodded the shrimp on my plate with the tines of my fork, just pushing it from one side to the other.

"It's true."

I whipped my gaze off the shrimp.

"Should've seen your father . . ." He got this faraway glint in his eyes. "Callum was terrified he would lose her, terrified she'd pick Heath, but Maggie never even spared Heath a glance. Your father was her first love. Her only one."

He inhaled a rickety breath and rocked onto his feet, gathering our plates without asking if I was done. He took them to the sink, scraped the rice and crustacean remnants into the bin, then hand washed both plates thoroughly.

"True love is rare, Ness. But Maggie and Callum, they had it," he added, wiping his hands on a towel.

"Did you have it too? With Lucy. Before . . . *everything*."

"I thought I did. Perhaps I did." He folded the towel, then refolded it. "To be honest, I don't know anymore." He set the plates on the drying rack before scrubbing down the sink and countertop.

My uncle was a surprisingly neat person. I wasn't sure why I'd assumed otherwise. Because he'd had a staff of cleaners?

Speaking of . . . "What's happening with the inn?"

Without removing his attention from the countertop, he said, "I'm trying to break the deal Everest—" His voice caught on his son's name. He swallowed, which made his Adam's apple joggle. "I'm trying to break the deal he struck with Aidan, trying to prove he wasn't in his right mind when he struck it. What with Becca's death . . ."

I hadn't thought of Becca in a long time. Was Everest with her now? Did people find each other again in the afterlife? *Was* there an afterlife? I scraped off a congealed splash of coconut-curry sauce from the dining table with my fingernail.

"My lawyer believes I have a real chance at dismantling the deal, but he warns me it might get pricey and could take a long time. He also warned me that he got a visit from a colleague yesterday who advised him to back off."

I felt my lids pull up real high. "He was threatened?"

"You're surprised? We *are* talking about Aidan Michaels, a man who shot his own wife."

My eyes widened further. Jeb knew about Evelyn? Had she told him or had Frank?

"Are you going to pursue it?" I asked.

"I built this inn on a parcel that's been in the family for generations. You can bet I'm going to fight for it." His tone made me jump. "Michaels has taken enough from this family, don't you think?"

I nodded. "I know Everest was probably killed by the Creeks, but do you think Aidan had a hand in it?"

"He owns a hotel on Creek territory. Is it so farfetched to think they owed him a favor, and he collected on it?"

No, it wasn't. It *absolutely* wasn't.

"Have you told Liam about your theory?" I asked, stretching my arms over my head and yawning.

"Yes. And he's looking into it."

I wondered if Liam had found out anything. Wouldn't he have called a pack gathering if he had, though?

That night, I dreamed of Liam. But suddenly, Liam morphed into another man. One who looked so much like him.

Heath.

I woke up with a scream that had Jeb crashing through my bedroom door.

"Sorry," I rasped, trembling all over. "Just a nightmare."

Jeb's eyes, which had started glowing like his wolf's, dimmed. "Got plenty of those myself." He turned to go but paused. "Want to talk about it?"

I tucked my frigid hands under the pillow. "No."

I hadn't spoken about the night I'd posed as an escort to get access to Heath with anyone but Everest. I'd hoped that not speaking about it would somehow erase the memory, but it had simply repressed it.

"Wake me if you change your mind."

I closed my eyes, willing the nightmare to vanish when the sheets rustled. Jeb pulled the comforter over my shoulders and tucked it around me. And then he placed a palm on the top of my head.

"I hope better dreams find you. You deserve better dreams. You deserve better everything." His eyes shone like freshly buffed bone.

Once he left, I watched the wall that divided our bedrooms for a long time, finally understanding why my mother had listed him as the emergency contact on my school forms. She'd known that if I ever needed saving, he would come through for me.

29

I was supposed to start at the Watts' the following day, but August texted me that it would be better if I began once his mother was released from the hospital. He'd have more time to show me the ropes.

So another day passed before I drove myself to my new job.

Jeb sat in the passenger seat. Where Sarah liked to tell me every little thing I could do better—she was annoying but thorough—he offered advice sparingly. Mostly he complimented my driving, which felt incredibly empowering, and then he told me Greg would come over that evening to give me an eye exam.

"Greg's an ophthalmologist?" I asked, sliding to a stop in front of the Watts' warehouse.

"No. But our eyes . . . our *eyesight* . . . it's not quite the same as humans."

My mouth rounded. And here I'd been ready to book an appointment with any old eye doctor. Good thing I hadn't.

Jeb got out of the Boulder Inn van and walked around the bumper. I took off my seatbelt and hopped out. As he took the seat I'd just vacated, he said, "You know, I could give you an allowance."

"And you know I would never accept it."

"Just as stubborn as Maggie."

Proud, not stubborn, although I would take any comparison to my mother.

"Call me when you're done," he said. "I'll come pick you up."

"Jeb?"

Although he clutched the handle, he didn't swing the car door shut. "Yes?"

"I'm happy I forgot to collect my high school diploma."

His forehead grooved, but then it smoothed, not entirely but a little; too much grief left indelible traces. "I'm happy you forgot too."

We smiled at each other a moment, then he tipped his head to the warehouse. "Scram, kiddo. You don't want to be late on your first day."

I backed away from the van and strode toward the warehouse. The second I set foot inside, memories of the last trial came pouring down over me. It was as though the semi-circle of men glaring down at me, the girl who'd challenged their boy, was still here. I looked away from the sawdust-covered floor and scanned the brightly lit space with its aisles upon aisles of tall metal shelving and its enormous worktables upon which carpenters were measuring slabs of wood or sanding them down.

I felt like a kid again, visiting my father at work. August would pick me up from school, then, after a pitstop at the ice cream parlor, he'd drive me over here. I wondered if the ice cream was as good as I remembered.

"Ness." A gravelly voice jerked my mind off the past.

August was standing by one of the aisles, an electronic tablet clutched beneath his arm. I walked over to him, garnering quite a few curious gazes from the employees.

"How's your mother?" I asked, tucking strands of loose hair behind my ears.

"Already on her feet when she shouldn't be." There was a startling gruffness to his tone, as though he was angry with his mother. "Let's get you set up in the office." He strode toward the glass enclosure at the back of the building without uttering a single word to me.

Once we reached the deserted office, I hooked my bag to the peg by the door.

"Dad jotted down some adjustments a client of ours requested. I need you to pull up the quote we gave that client, check what we're taking out, type in what we're adding, then look through our list of suppliers, call them up, and find us the best and timeliest deals." August handed me a stapled printout, turned on the office computer, and pulled up a file that listed all the amendments that were to be made.

I took my seat on the wheelie chair. "Do I factor in any commissions to the prices I obtain?"

"No. We charge a rate on the overall project." He stared at the huge beige printer in the corner as though it had wronged him.

"Are you okay?"

His green eyes flashed to mine, then to the computer keypad. "Just tired," he said before returning to the door. With an almost clinical detachment, he added, "Once you're done updating the quote, email it to me at August@Watt.com."

And then he was gone, and I didn't see him the rest of the day. But I did get an email from him with more things to do. Working kept me busy and kept me from thinking about his crabbiness. The warehouse grew silent as the hours ticked by, as I double-checked spreadsheet after spreadsheet to make sure the money received corresponded to the money owed.

I'd always liked numbers, so the job August had saddled me with didn't feel like work at all. I'd even have called it fun, albeit a tad disheartening. Disheartening because my access to the company's finances showed me how it had thrived. Would my father have managed to turn his carpentry business into the hundred million dollar construction company it had become?

A knock snapped my gaze off the computer monitor.

"August told me to close the place down for the night," said a man with an enlarged nose, teeming with burst blood vessels, and cheeks that were slightly purple. He had a smear of wood stain across his temple and a couple more on the top of his denim overalls.

"Oh. Okay." I saved the document before shutting down the computer and grabbing my bag. As we walked through the deserted warehouse, I sensed the man glancing my way repeatedly.

When I caught him at it, he reddened all over and said, "You look exactly like your mom, but with Callum's dimples."

I blinked at him, sifting through my memories to place him.

He hooked his thumbs under the straps of his overalls. "Tom. I'm Tom."

"*Uncle Tom?*" I said so excitedly that he shot me a toothy grin.

The nickname had been given to him by my father who'd considered him family. Especially after Tom lost his wife, daughter, son-in-law, and grandkid one blustery Christmas Eve. He'd been behind the wheel when he hit a patch of black ice. The car ended up wrapped around a tree.

"I can't believe you still work here," I said.

He grimaced. "I'm old, I know."

"Oh, that wasn't why I said that!" *Aw, crap.* Now I felt awful. I hooked my bag higher up my shoulder. "I'm just surprised to see a familiar face, that's all."

His grimace finally receded. "The Watts are good people."

I smiled at him. "They are."

"How long—" He darted a glance at his scuffed work boots before looking at me from underneath stubby blond lashes. "How long will you be helping out? Rest of the summer? Or just until Isobel gets better?"

"That's not up to me."

He held the door of the warehouse open for me to step through. As he shut the heavy door, he asked, "Still carving little figurines?"

"No." I lifted my eyes to the star-strewn immensity over our head. "Haven't had a chance to do that in a long time." My father had taught me, but I wasn't ever good at it—not like August. Everything he carved looked so lifelike.

"I still have the wolf you made me," Tom said.

I lowered my gaze back to him. "You do?" Emotion robbed my voice of volume.

"On my fireplace mantle."

The high beams of a car turning into the lot momentarily blinded me. I hadn't called Jeb yet, so it couldn't be the van. Once my eyes adjusted to the darkness again, I noticed the make—a pickup.

"I'll see you in the morning, Ness." On his way to his parked car, he stopped to greet August.

I slid my cell phone out of my bag and texted Jeb that I was done, then watched August stride over, trying to gauge his current mood through the tether. *Tense.* He was tense.

He checked the lot. "How are you getting home?"

"Jeb's coming to pick me up." When he frowned, I added, "I only have a permit, remember?"

"Right." He looked over my shoulder at the warehouse wall. "I can give you a lift."

"I'm sure he's on his way already." I pulled my bag strap over my head so the leather cut across my chest instead of digging into my shoulder. "You still have a lot of work tonight?"

"No. I'm done for the day."

"Then why are you here?"

"I live here."

"In the warehouse?"

"No." He nodded toward a small building adjacent to it. "It's temporary. I bought a plot of land on the north side of that lake we swam in but haven't had time to develop anything."

"Can I see it?"

"What? The plot?"

"No. Your current lodging."

He rubbed his jaw, as though my request necessitated profound consideration.

"Forget it," I mumbled, a little hurt. What exactly did he think I would do? Trash his place or make disparaging comments about the decor?

He peered at the still-empty road before walking in the direction of his house.

Okay, just walk away from me. That's not weird at all.

He stopped and turned a little. "Are you coming?"

"No."

"But I thought you—" He turned completely this time, shoulders straining his gray T-shirt. A galaxy of stains speckled the cotton: glue smears, white paint, grease stains. "Why not?"

I felt both my eyebrows slant on my forehead. "You clearly didn't want to show it to me, August."

He loosed an exasperated sigh. "Ness . . ."

I tapped on my phone to seem busy. He grumbled something. Because I couldn't leave well enough alone, I flung my gaze back onto him. "Did I do something?"

His jaw ticked. "I don't know. Did you?" His voice was so low that I wondered if I heard him correctly.

"You *are* mad at me!"

He just stood there, brooding and silent, cloaked in darkness, *oozing* darkness. He'd been mad at me before I came in to work, so whatever I'd *done* happened before today. But the last time we'd seen each other was at the hospital and—*Oh . . .*

Heat coursed through me as quick as the current in the Colorado River during snowmelt. Was August Watt jealous?

"Liam asked me when I was leaving," he finally said. "I'll get out of this goddamn place when I'm ready, not when someone tells me to, understood?"

My mouth fell open. *Not jealousy.*

My navel pulsed as though August's anger had somehow yanked on the tether between us. And then my heart began to pulsate in time with it. As fast as it had flooded me, the strange heat receded. I was mortified to have believed him jealous.

The darkness beyond August suddenly turned brighter, noisier. A van sped down the road, kicking up a pale cloud of dust. I kept my gaze locked on the approaching car because if I looked at August, I would either yell at him for thinking I was somehow complicit in trying to get him to leave Boulder, or I would start crying. I wasn't sure which was worse.

As I stalked toward the van, I tossed out over my shoulder, "I'll tell him to stop harassing you."

Had August concluded that Liam and I were a couple again after seeing us together in the hospital room or had Liam implied something?

As I took a seat next to Jeb and answered his questions about how my day had gone, I typed out a lengthy diatribe to Liam. In the end, I deleted all of it, sensing our Alpha would take it out on August.

So I simply sent: *I forgot to ask, do pack tuition loans extend to out-of-state colleges?*

Liam's answer came an hour later, while I was having dinner. *Why?*

ME: *Because I'm thinking of applying elsewhere.*

He called me then. Not sure I'd be able to control my tone, I declined the incoming call and texted: *Can't talk right now. But I can text.*

A couple seconds later, he sent me: *Your application's already being processed. You should be getting the welcome packet soon. And no, pack money and influence are only good on pack territory. We need to keep our wolves close.*

Then why are you trying to send August away?

I felt I knew the answer to that.

The doorbell rang then. I inhaled long and hard, expecting Liam's scent to hit me, but the smell was a mixture of antibacterial soap and ground coffee. Definitely not Liam's, unless he'd changed his soap to the hospital-grade kind and was jacked up on caffeine.

"That must be Greg," Jeb said, going to open the door.

Exhaling a relieved breath, I set my phone face down on the couch and stood up to get my eyes examined by the pack doctor, praying he wouldn't spot all the anger that brewed beneath my irises.

30

The following day, Liam stopped by the warehouse to see me, seemingly none too happy that I hadn't picked up the two calls he'd made after his last text went unanswered.

When he strode into the office, I kept my gaze fastened to the computer monitor. I felt him at my back though, felt his body thrum and his scent invade the entire room.

"Why didn't you answer any of my calls?" he exclaimed.

"Because I was mad at you." I still didn't look at him even though he'd moved to stand in front of the desk.

"I got that. But why are you mad at me? What did I do now, Ness?"

I clicked on the keyboard, then moved the cursor to the next tab.

"Goddammit, don't ice me out."

I finally leaned back in the chair, crossed my arms over my chest, and stared up into Liam's narrowed eyes. "Did you ask August to leave town again?"

His pupils pulsed and pulsed, and then his eyes turned yellow as though his wolf was about to leap to the surface.

Finally, he shook his head. "I asked him *if* he was planning on leaving soon. I didn't ask him to leave. Excuse me for wanting to know what my wolves plan to do with their lives! Especially when so much is fucking happening around Boulder. Did you hear that some Creeks pissed all over Julian's fucking hedges? Same wolves Lucas smelled around my house."

I blinked frenziedly, feeling suddenly petty for believing this had been about an amorous tryst.

"So no, I wasn't chasing your mate out of Boulder. I was trying to figure out if we could count on him if more Creeks arrived." Liam growled all of this, and his growl intensified the scudding of my heart.

"I'm—I'm sorry, Liam. I just assumed." I shivered, feeling as though someone had spun the AC to its lowest setting.

Liam didn't storm out like I was expecting him to. He just stood there, jaw clenching and unclenching, making me feel even more foolish.

I dropped my arms onto the armrests, then pushed myself up and walked toward him, laying a hand on his forearm, hoping he'd construe my gesture as a ceasefire. "What can I do to help?"

"We don't need your help," he bit out.

My hand slipped off his arm and landed on my waist. "But you need August's? You're not actually planning on making me watch from the sidelines, are you?"

"It could get dangerous." He rubbed his twitchy jaw.

"I'm not afraid."

He snorted. "You might not be, but I am."

Did he mean for me or for the pack?

"We have no clue what they're thinking, and their Alpha can't be bothered to pick up the damn phone. Robbie's dying to go to Beaver Creek to meet her, but Julian says to stay put. Like me, he's afraid it's a ploy to lure some of us to them." He stopped rubbing his face, but the hard lines of his posture didn't slacken, which told me he was still pissed. At me or at the Creeks?

"Maybe it *is* worth sending some of us to meet her."

His Adam's apple jerked in his throat. "Some of *us*? I hope you're not planning on volunteering, because my answer would be no."

"Why?" I exclaimed.

"Because you don't know the first thing about Creeks or diplomatic visits between packs."

"Then teach me."

"It can't be taught."

"Bullshit! Everything can be taught."

"I'm not sending you out there. I'm not sending any of my wolves out there. The Creeks want to talk, they come here. We are stronger on our turf than we are on theirs."

Slowly my hand slid off my waist and found purchase on the desk beside me. "What if they all come? All one thousand of them?"

"They wouldn't leave their territory unguarded."

"Even if half their pack came, they would grossly outnumber us."

"It's not always about numbers. They have many children and fe—" He stopped talking so suddenly that I sucked in a breath.

"I hope you weren't about to say females."

His pupils shrank before spreading back out.

I shook my head.

"Physically, Ness, we aren't the same, just like a child isn't built like an adult."

I fastened my gaze to the floorboards, glaring hard at the spaces between the planks.

I felt a finger crook my face up. I twisted free of Liam and stepped back. "Remind me how the Creek Alpha rose to power? Because the story I heard was that she defeated the Aspen Alpha in a duel."

"She was already an Alpha. Alphas are stronger. If she hadn't been—"

"Please just stop talking. It's making me unhappy."

"Look, I'm all for empowering females, but I'm not going to spout lies about corporeal equality when the hard facts are that we aren't built alike. How many firemen are women? They're even called fire*men*."

"No, they're called fire*fighters*."

He let out a molar-grinding growl and tossed his hands in the air. "*Ugh.* I can't win with you. I can never win!"

I crossed my arms. "Funny how illogical that is when you keep saying I have no chance of beating you."

His nostrils pulsed, and his fingers wrapped into fists. "Ness Clark, you fucking drive me crazy." And then he all but lunged toward me and cupped the back of my head, tilting my face up. "I must be one hell of a masochist for being turned on right now." His murmur skated over my lips, heightening the frantic pulse of my heart. "And just so we're clear, I don't find *you* inferior. You're too smart, persistent, and distractingly beautiful to be inferior. But that's how you'd win a battle. You might punch hard and at the right place, but your fists have nothing on"—his gaze fused to mine—"*you.*"

When I felt the brush of his lips against mine, I backed away, put the desk between us. "I have work to do, Liam." I watched the door, hoping he'd take the hint and leave. I also watched it because I was afraid of looking at him.

Afraid he'd see how deeply he rattled me.

Damn Liam Kolane. The man was such a hot-tempered beast, everything I disliked about men, and yet, he got under my skin too. He slapped and then soothed the slaps with such care and tenderness.

Without uttering another word, he crossed the office toward the door and left. Unfortunately, his retreat did little to calm my nerves.

And then it got worse when I got an email from August that read: **Please keep your personal life out of the work place.**

I would've punched the monitor, but it would break, and the replacement cost would be taken out of my salary, whatever amount that was. Since I hadn't discussed specifics, I expected minimum wage.

Liam was wrong about me being smart. Smart people didn't find themselves saddled with debt, working for men whom they were physically linked to and infatuated with others who weren't especially kind.

It was time Ness Clark sharpened up and found a way out of her pit of misery. Which led me to send Sarah a message: *Can I come with you to The Den tonight?*

Clubbing wouldn't fix anything, but it would temporarily take my mind off the hole that needed plugging.

Sarah's answer came in the afternoon. *Ness Clark wants to par-tay?*

ME: *Yes.*

SARAH: *Should I be worried?*

ME: *About what?*

SARAH: *About you wanting to go out. You haven't been in the mood to have fun since, well, since the funeral.*

ME: *I'll tell you later.*

SARAH: *Counting on it. I'll be at your place at 8 with a hot dress.*

ME: *What's wrong with my dresses?*

SARAH: *Nothing. I just have the perfect one for you. Ciao.*

I was going clubbing, or at the very least I was going to sit in a DJ booth and watch people have fun and hope it would rub off on me.

When was the last time I'd had fun?

The music festival? Nah. Everest had ditched me for this Megan chick, and then Justin Summix had all but called me a whore.

The night I'd run with the pack after the trials? Actually, that night had been more meaningful than fun.

Swimming in the lake with August? His earlier message about not mixing business with pleasure nixed that afternoon, though.

What did he think I was doing in the office anyway? And had he been there, or had one of his employees ratted me out?

I sighed, realizing I hadn't had fun in a very long time.

31

"Y̲ou want me to wear *that*? But it's . . ." I dangled the scrap of white fabric in front of me.

"Sexy."

"I was going to say slutty."

"Slutty *is* sexy." Like an impatient child, Sarah was bouncing on my bed, wearing a dress that wasn't much longer or looser than the one she'd brought me. "Besides, I was all out of denim overalls." She stopped bouncing. "Hey, you put me in charge of tonight, so put the damn dress on, Ness Clark."

Sigh-growling, I vanished into my bathroom to change into the white bandage. At least the material was opaque. I fluffed up my hair and twisted from side-to-side, checking my reflection. *Okay.* The dress was sexy and more covering than what I'd initially thought. Not that I would confess this to Sarah.

Sarah whistled when I came out. "Damn, girl. Maybe I should've dug up a pair of overalls. You're going to steal my limelight."

"No one can steal DJ Wolverine's limelight."

She leaped off the bed with the grace of a pole vaulter. "Now shoes—"

"Are we dancing?"

"Yes."

"Then flats. Heels kill me."

Sarah's lips hiked up in protest, but I slid my feet into my white sneakers before she could give me grief about it.

"I'm wearing the dress." I said this as though it were a great concession. Thank goodness I hadn't told her I liked it. I grabbed my bag, making sure I had my phone, keys, and wallet. But then I thought about my ID. "I don't have a fake ID!"

Sarah rolled her eyes so hard I didn't expect them to level back. "I work there, woman. Plus, you've got a killer bod and a *tolerably* attractive face."

I scowled, but I was smiling so my scowl lost a lot of its effect. "Tolerably attractive? Wow . . . *thanks*."

She smirked. "Oh, come on. You know you're way too hot for your own good."

I dismissed her compliment with a flick of my hand. "Shut up."

"Can we get out of here already? My shift starts in an hour." She swept her mass of blonde curls off her shoulder.

When we walked out of my bedroom, we found Jeb sitting in the living room, watching a fishing show with Derek.

"Ciao, Mr. C.," Sarah called out.

"Bye, Sar—" His eyes all but bounded out of their sockets. "Um. You girls are going out dressed like that?"

I looked down at my dress, partly amused by his reaction and partly worried he might make me change.

"That's what kids wear these days," Derek said before pointing to the screen. "Jeb, check out that monster bass."

Jeb glanced at the TV, but then his gaze returned to us. "What time will you be home?"

"I'll have her back here by one," Sarah said.

"One?" he all but sputtered.

"I'm seventeen, Jeb," I said quietly. Since when was he worried what time I got home? It wasn't as though he'd cared much back when I was living at the inn.

He rubbed his bearded chin. "Okay." He hadn't shaved since Everest's funeral, as though marking the terrible day by the length of his facial hair. "And, Sarah, if you're driving, don't drink. But if you do drink, call me, and I'll pick you girls up."

"We're wolves, Mr. C. Can't die in car crashes."

We could, though.

A flash of pain illuminated Jeb's face.

Sarah winced. "*Shit.* I'm so sorry."

He wrung his fingers together in his lap and studied them. "Just be careful, all right?" he croaked. Before we could leave, he added, "Are any of the boys going to be at The Den tonight?"

"They're *always* there."

Not that we need boys, I wanted to add, but put a lid on that thought. If the presence of males appeased my uncle, then who was I to rattle his peace of mind?

Once we were tucked inside Sarah's Mini, she said, "I really put my foot in my mouth back there."

"It's fine."

She shook her head and sighed. After a beat, she said, "It's sort of sweet how protective he's become of you."

I stabbed my seatbelt into the buckle. "It's sort of weird. He wasn't like this before." I stared at the squares of light in our downstairs neighbor's place, an ancient woman who only ever came out of her house to water the patch of grass and flowers she called a back yard. "It's as though I'm his replacement kid."

"You are. Just like he's your replacement dad. It's not a bad thing to have someone care for you like that."

"I have Evelyn."

"But she's not living with you anymore, is she?"

"That wasn't by choice."

"Hey." She tapped my knuckles. "You have two people who would lay down their lives for yours. That's a shitload more than most people."

I sighed deeply before side-eyeing her. "What you're saying is that you wouldn't lay down your life for me?"

"To salvage my dress, possibly."

I grinned and smacked her upper arm, which was firm with lean muscle. I knew she never hit the gym and ate more than the average human guy, so I imagined she shifted into her wolf form often.

At the thought of shifting, my body thrummed. "Want to run together sometime?"

"I don't own sneakers." She cast a disgruntled look at my feet as though my shoes had somehow wronged her.

I shifted them out of sight. "I meant in wolf form."

"Sure. I'll even slow my pace so you can keep up."

I snorted, even though I didn't doubt she could beat me. After all, she had years of training on me. She slowed at a red light, and a bunch of pedestrians crossed the street. Excitement that it was almost the weekend wafted off most. One girl didn't seem as thrilled as the rest. She kept darting looks around her as though worried someone was following her. I checked the sidewalks but didn't notice any stalker.

As she passed in front of the Mini our eyes locked, and recognition hit me dead-center.

Megan.

Everest's Megan.

I powered my window down and called out her name.

"You know this girl?" Sarah asked me.

Megan quickened her pace.

I unstrapped myself and leaped out just as a motorcycle swerved into the lane next to ours, almost bowling me over.

The biker yelled at me, but I didn't respond. I just took off running after Megan.

"Megan! Wait up!"

She didn't wait up. Instead she *sped* up.

So I did too. She turned a corner. Why wasn't she stopping? When I rounded the corner, I found myself face-to-face with a giant wooden cross.

"Don't come any closer!" she screeched. "Or I'll call the cops."

I backed up, frowning at the wood and the girl beyond it.

"I know what you are!" she yelled.

Obviously she didn't if she thought a wooden cross could keep me away. But I let her think she had me figured out.

"You don't go to UCB," I said, getting to the heart of the matter. "Everest told me you were a student there, but you're not. Why'd you lie about it?"

"I never claimed I was a student at UCB." She pushed her shoulder-length dirty-blonde hair behind her ear, fingers trembling. "Your cousin's a liar."

"*Was.*"

"Huh?"

"He's dead."

The cross came down an inch, then another, as though it suddenly weighed too heavily in her hand.

"Yes, and I'm sorry if I startled you back there."

A car squealed to a stop next to me. And then Sarah flung open her door and stalked toward me. "Ness?"

Megan's knuckles whitened on the wooden cross. "You're that . . . that socialite deejay."

"And you are?" Sarah sniffed the air.

"No one." Megan took a step back. "I'm no one."

Sarah cocked an eyebrow. "What's up with the giant cross?"

Megan didn't answer. She just kept backing away, gaze bouncing from me to Sarah. "I'm sorry for your loss, even though I'm not surprised. Everest was a creep."

"What do you mean?" I asked.

"He tried to recruit me for his escort agency." She made a grimace that contorted her heart-shaped face.

"*His* escort agency?"

"He said I wouldn't have to sleep with anyone, just gather information."

I must not have blinked in a while, because my eyes started to prickle.

She kept backing away. "Was he killed?" Her voice was barely above a whisper. "Wouldn't surprise me if he was."

I couldn't get my mouth to close or open. It just gaped like that striped bass Derek had been ogling.

"Anyway, leave me alone. I was serious about calling the cops." When she reached the end of the street, she spun on her heels and took off running.

"Well, that was weird," Sarah said after a beat.

A car honked so shrilly I jumped.

"Chill out, dude!"

At first I thought Sarah was saying this to me, but she was staring daggers at the driver in the car behind hers.

She grabbed my arm to unglue me from the pavement. "Come on."

The driver honked twice more. Sarah flipped him the finger.

Once inside the car, she drove out of the small street and pulled onto a delivery parking spot. "What the hell was that about?"

I told her everything. Every sordid detail.

"Your cousin was a pimp who used girls to spy? Fuckin' a. No wonder he's dead."

I realized then that perhaps it wasn't the Sillin that had gotten him killed. Perhaps it was the espionage.

"What was he up to?" Sarah asked.

"I don't know, but at least I understand *why* he's dead." Or I assumed I'd come a little closer to understanding.

He must've spied on the wrong Creek.

"But what about the Sillin? How does that fit into the equation?" she asked.

I squeezed my bare knees with my clammy hands. "Maybe it was a security measure. Maybe he needed some to give to the girls he hired." I'd used my own stock on Heath.

"Why would he drug human girls with it?"

"No. He gave it to them to use on the customers." The same way he'd told me to dose Heath's drink.

"So he was spying exclusively on the shifter community?"

Sarah and I stared at each other a long moment. And then she whispered, "Fuck," which pretty much summed up the situation.

"Sarah, I think I need to talk to my Alpha. And I think you need to talk to Julian."

32

Two cars, besides Liam's black SUV, were parked in front of the sleek cabin: Matt's Dodge silver sedan and a little blue BMW. I was sort of relieved Matt would be here. Even though I'd come to discuss a serious matter, a buffer was welcomed.

As I got out of the Mini, I tugged on the hem of my white dress. "I'm sorry about the way tonight turned out," I told Sarah.

She shook her head. "Babe, I'm just sorry for what that calculating fucker put you through."

I shivered. Ever since my run-in with Megan, I couldn't get my body to warm up.

"You want me to wait for you?" Sarah asked.

"No. I'll be okay."

"Talk tomorrow?"

I nodded, then closed the car door but heard the window power down. "By the way, why the hell did that girl have a wooden cross?"

I smirked. "Because she knew what I was apparently."

"Apparently? Where'd she get her info from? *Twilight*?"

I chuckled. "I guess." But then, as Sarah backed out of Liam's driveway, I stopped laughing. Whatever supernatural she thought I was, she deemed me dangerous. I now had my answer to how the world would react if word got out.

"Ness?"

I whirled around.

Matt was standing by the front door. "What are you doing here?"

Even though the door was only open a crack, a heady beat was pouring out through it.

I circled around the cars. "I need to speak with Liam."

"Um." He palmed his buzzed blond hair. "Yeah. Um." His skin was getting increasingly red. "Why don't you wait out here? I'll go get him."

"You're seriously going to make me wait outside?" I asked, a little peeved.

Okay, *very* peeved.

"I'm chilly. And not in the mood to wait outside." I pressed past him. Or at least, I tried to.

Matt barred my way with his forearm.

"What the hell, Hulk? I don't fucking care if you're having an orgy right now. I need to speak with Liam. This is a pack matter."

I pressed on his big arm. Matt sighed and finally let me through.

They weren't having an orgy. Just a small get-together that seemed very PG.

"Ness!" Amanda squeaked from her spot on the couch next to Sienna. "Hey."

"Hi, Ness." Sienna offered me a wispy smile that flickered off her pale face almost as quickly as it had appeared.

Lucas was here too, as well as two other guys from the pack. One was definitely named Dexter—it was the sort of name that had stuck with me—but I wasn't sure what the other one's name was. Michael, maybe? They were sitting around a table in the corner of the living room, playing a card game. I guessed poker from the stacks of chips.

"Nice dress," Dexter said, leering a little.

I wasn't sure if he was making fun of me or paying me a compliment. I didn't really care, though. "Where's Liam?"

Lucas tipped his chin into his neck and started distributing cards.

No one spoke for so long that I asked, "Did no one hear me?"

Lucas placed the deck on the table, evening it out until no card stuck out. "Matt, why don't you grab Ness a beer from the kitchen? I'll go get Liam."

"I don't want beer. I just want—"

Liam walked out of his bedroom then, buttoning up his shirt, hair tousled as though he'd just taken a nap. When his gaze landed on mine, he froze.

And so did everything and everyone in the room. Even the air seemed to congeal into one thick, unbreathable mass.

Liam shot Matt a look, and something passed between them—probably an order spoken through the mind link. Matt all but leaped toward his Alpha, skirting around him and into the bedroom. He shut the door so fast I guessed Liam had someone in there he didn't want me to see.

I pressed my lips together and swallowed. I had no right to be jealous, and yet . . . and yet I was. Or maybe I was just disappointed by how quickly I'd been replaced, especially after he'd told me he would wait for me.

That I was worth waiting for.

Apparently not.

I swallowed again, but the lump grew larger and more jagged. *Crap.* I closed my eyes and breathed in through my nose. *Crap.* Why did it have to hurt?

I didn't want back in his arms. I didn't want back in his bed.

So why did it have to hurt so damn much?

His voice crashed into my mind: *It didn't mean anything to me.*

But, to *me*, it did.

It meant that for all my insistence to the contrary, I'd still been hung up on Liam.

I felt a hand cup my shoulder and then I smelled him—mint and musk—but I also smelled her.

Whoever *her* was.

I hoped Matt would keep her inside, because I didn't want to see the girl's face.

"Ness?" This time Liam spoke out loud.

His voice was like wind. It gusted over my skin, making goose bumps rise, making my heart shudder. I stepped back and opened my eyes. I was afraid to speak. Afraid of what my voice would sound like. But I did it anyway.

"I need to—" I was right to be afraid. I sounded like I'd just spent the evening shouting at the top of my lungs. I swallowed again. "I need to talk to you about"—I glanced at the girls sitting on the couch, both of them jiggling their folded legs—"about something I found out tonight."

Liam followed my line of sight. "Hey, Amanda, can you and Sienna go into the kitchen a minute?"

Amanda's lips opened as though she were about to protest, but she must've sensed it wasn't a suggestion. She got up and, towing Sienna, vanished into Liam's kitchen.

"What is it?" he asked, tracing the shape of my face with his dark eyes.

"I ran into Everest's ex-girlfriend." I glanced at Lucas. "That Megan girl."

Lucas's blue eyes flashed in interest.

"She's not a UCB student, and she's not an escort, but Everest apparently tried to recruit her." I crossed my arms over my chest and hugged my torso tight so I would stop trembling. "She claimed *he* ran the agency. Apparently he was using the girls to spy. I think—" I gulped, and my saliva went down like a dulled knife blade. "I think he must've spied on a Creek."

Dexter speared his fingers through his spiky brown hair. "Everest was a pimp?"

Michael—or whatever his name was—placed his cards face down on the table.

"My guess is Everest stole the Sillin to use on the people . . . on the *wolves* he sent the girls to," I said.

Lucas frowned. "Aidan Michaels keeping tabs on us is one thing—he's a shifter-hater. But Everest? He's . . . he *was* one of us."

"I know. Look, I think we should try to locate the woman he was working with." I unknotted my arms to dig through my handbag for my phone. My fingers trembled so hard the slick device almost slipped out. "Uh. I'll forward the Red Creek Escort contact to you."

"You already sent it to me, remember?" Lucas reminded me.

Neither Dexter nor the other shifter asked what I was doing with the number of an escort agency, so I assumed they'd heard.

I supposed all of Boulder had heard.

It didn't matter.

Just like Liam sleeping with another girl didn't matter.

Who was I kidding? It *did* matter. So damn much.

After I'd managed the impossible task of putting away my phone, I told them about Megan's wooden cross. "I know we're not a complete secret around these parts, but I just thought you'd want a head's up."

"Were you alone when this happened?" Dexter asked, gaze running over my legs.

I wished I'd had a pair of tights on. I felt so exposed in this dress.

He winced suddenly, dropping his gaze to the poker chips. Liam was glaring at him. Had the Alpha barked at Dexter through the mind link?

"I was with Sarah Matz. We were on our way to The Den." I yanked on the hem of my dress. "She went to inform Julian about our run-in. Maybe you should call him, Liam."

Liam just stared at me, seemingly lost in thought. Was he thinking about his father? About Everest? About Julian? Or was he thinking about me?

"Um, Lucas, can you give me a ride back to my place? I don't really feel like walking."

"I'll give you a ride home," Dexter offered, already rising.

"I'll take her," Liam snapped.

"No," I said softly but firmly. I couldn't ride in a car with Liam. Not when he still smelled like *her*. Not when I was feeling so emotional. "No."

His Adam's apple joggled in his throat. "Ness, please."

"No. Lucas?" I blinked. My eyes felt so hot, but the rest of me felt cold. It was as though every ounce of heat in my body had converged into my lids.

Chair legs scraped, and then Lucas was next to me. "Let's go."

I nodded and turned away from Liam, trailing Lucas out. I prayed my tears wouldn't tumble out until I got home, but my prayers went unanswered, as my prayers usually did.

"I thought you guys were over," Lucas said after a long beat.

"We are," I whispered raucously. "Still hurts."

He touched my forearm. Briefly, but long enough to make me blink. "It sucks to walk in on someone."

My brow furrowed.

"That's what happened with Taryn. I found her with a Pine." His blue eyes flashed to mine. "Justin Summix of all people."

My mouth rounded, and for a moment, I forgot how deeply my heart ached, because Liam and I, we hadn't even been together when I caught him rolling out of bed. Lucas and Taryn though, they'd been a couple. I'd misjudged him, I realized. I'd thought he'd wronged Taryn.

"I really hate those Pines," Lucas murmured.

I didn't try to argue that they weren't all bad, didn't try to console him either. Silence grew between us, a quiet, easygoing silence that bonded us in our misery.

Once he slid the car in front of my house, I thanked him. He nodded but kept his eyes on the darkened street.

"Just remember it takes half the time you were together to get over a person," he said.

I paused with my fingers on the door. Liam and I, we'd been together for all of four days. If Lucas's logic was accurate, my grieving period should already have been over.

"How long were you with Taryn?"

Gaze sunk on the obscurity, he muttered, "Too long."

My heart went out to him. Which was crazy because I didn't think my heart would ever have gone out to Lucas Mason. Then again, I never thought my cousin was a pimp, or that Liam would lead a girl to his bed so soon after almost kissing me.

On my way up the staircase, keys jingling in my trembling fist, I worked on coming up with a good lie as to the reason I was home early. I hated deceiving my uncle, but I couldn't share what I'd just learned with him. It would shatter what little good memories he had of his son. I palmed away my tears and stepped inside.

33

The next day, I went to work and pretended everything was great when I felt completely broken on the inside. August and I didn't cross paths at least, so there was that.

I spent Saturday in bed. On Sunday though, Evelyn called and said she was expecting us for brunch. Jeb made me drive to Frank's house, and I did so without a single glitch, even though I hadn't slept well and my eyes felt gummy. I'd believed my heart couldn't possibly shatter more than it already had back at Tracy's, but I'd been wrong. The shards had simply been crushed into finer ones. Just like the vase I'd knocked over in my house one of the first times I'd shifted. The glass had fragmented on our pine floor, and then the pieces had been ground to a powder under my father's boots as he'd tried to corral me into his arms to calm me down.

"I phoned up the DMV and set an appointment for a driving test tomorrow," Jeb said, whipping me out of my thoughts.

"I thought I needed a year before I could pass it?"

"The woman who runs the place, she owed me a favor."

I glanced at Jeb.

He indulged my curiosity. "Her husband was using the inn to shack up with his mistress." He shot me a jaunty smile. "I wouldn't have tattled had the guy been an upstanding citizen, but he was a jerk, who at some point tried to get with Lucy." His glee dampened a little at the mention of his wife's—ex-wife's?—name.

"Is she still locked up in Eric's basement?"

He stared at the winding mountain road. "No. She's back at the inn."

"She's working for Aidan?"

"She's packing up and arranging the handover."

I almost swerved off the road. "I thought you were going to fight for the place!"

Jeb clutched the grab handle. "My lawyer suddenly changed his tune. He said the contract was airtight and it would be a waste of my resources to try and nullify it. And now I can't find a single lawyer in our zip code willing to represent me. Aidan Michaels's money is burning holes in too many pockets."

Not for the first time I wished the hunter dead.

I thought of Megan and her cross. Once people knew us, once they realized we weren't all out for blood, maybe their fear would subside. "Do you really think that if knowledge of us spread it would be so bad?"

Jeb scrubbed his beard, and it made a chafing sound. "That's a tough one. Some people have a romanticized idea of werewolves, but finding out we exist . . . I'm not sure their awe would outweigh their fear."

"Do you think we'd get hunted down?"

"Remember what they did to people they claimed used witchcraft back in Salem?"

I shuddered.

"And they weren't even witches. So, to answer you, Ness, I'd rather not find out." He reached over. I thought he was going to adjust my hold on the steering wheel, but instead, he laid his hand on top of mine. "Aidan Michaels is old, Ness. He'll die soon enough."

Unless he died tonight, it wouldn't be soon enough. "Did you at least recover the payment for the inn?"

"Yes. But it's being held in escrow until the divorce is finalized. Hopefully, that'll be soon." After a beat, he added, "Lucy's being a little . . . *difficult*."

I didn't ask what that was supposed to mean. If Jeb wanted to tell me more, he would.

"I like the apartment, Jeb, but I was thinking, if you have any money set aside with which you could fix up Mom and Dad's old house"—I shrugged—"at least the windows and front door, we could move in there?"

"The place needs more than new windows and a door." Jeb removed his hand from mine.

"I know, but I thought I could do the rest myself. I know how to sand and oil a floor, courtesy of Dad. I could borrow the material from the Watts. And then we'd just need to buy some paint for the walls."

"It needs an electrical overhaul and probably new plumbing."

I batted my eyelashes, trying to whisk away the disappointment that clung there.

"Derek's son is an electrician. I could ask him about rewiring the system. And we had some plumbers back at the inn. I'll get us some quotes."

I blinked at Jeb. "So yes?"

"Why not?" He smiled, but I smiled wider. "You sure you want me living there with you, kiddo? You sure you don't want to sell the parcel?"

"Sell it?" I croaked. I hadn't even considered selling it. "I just got it back. Thanks to you."

Jeb sighed. "I never should've made your mom sell it, but all our money was tied up in the inn—"

This time, I was the one who placed my hand on Jeb's. "You got it back. That's all that matters," I said just as we reached Frank's house.

There was another car parked next to Frank's—a familiar forest-green Land Rover.

"Are Nelson and Isobel here?" I asked, getting out of the car.

"Guess so." Jeb grabbed the bottle of red wine we'd bought on the way over.

A second after we rang the doorbell, I was swept into a pair of warm arms and peppered with kisses. I instinctively closed my eyes, which was smart considering some of Evelyn's kisses landed on my puffy lids.

"Oh, how I have missed you, *querida*." My ear got a loud peck, which momentarily made it ring.

"I'm glad to see you too, Evelyn."

She finally pressed me back, running her thumbs under my eyes. "You have been crying." She shot my uncle a disgruntled look that made him stick his hands in the air.

"No. Just not sleeping enough. That's all. Nothing to worry about."

She harrumphed. "I hope you are hungry. I have made all of your favorites. Cheese quesadillas, candied bacon, chocolate-zucchini bread, and Isobel is glazing the cinnamon rolls I baked this morning."

I peeked around Evelyn and caught sight of Isobel. If it wasn't for her pallor and slightly hunched shoulders, it would've been impossible to tell she'd been operated on six days ago.

Next to her, her son was wiping his hands on a kitchen towel. "Huh. I thought you weren't a fan of all that stuff anymore." He plucked one of the rolls off the cooling tray and chomped on it, while his mother chided him for not waiting until we were seated.

Evelyn cocked one of her penciled-in black eyebrows that made a flush creep up my neck.

I decided to avoid August's taunt and Evelyn's pointed gaze. "I can't believe you're already up and doing things, Isobel."

August grunted, while Evelyn said, "I do not think Isobel knows how to be still."

Isobel smiled. "I'll be still when I'm dead." But then she must've remembered we were in the presence of a man who'd just lost his son, because she bit her colorless lip. "Sorry, Jeb."

He shrugged.

She gave him a rueful smile and handed her son a dish. "Can you take those to the table?"

August scooped up the plate with one hand, and then Evelyn clapped, and we all took our seats around the table—me, between Evelyn and Jeb. August sat across from me. Unfortunately the table wasn't wide, and as he adjusted his legs, his feet knocked into mine.

Frank's grandson came out of the bedroom I'd slept in the night Everest died, bleary-eyed and messy-haired, and made his way over to the seat beside August. They fist-bumped.

The wine was uncorked and poured.

"Want some, Ness?" Nelson asked.

"She's underage," August said.

I rolled my eyes but said I was good with water.

Nelson tutted as he served Jeb. "You were drinking way before you were twenty-one, son."

"Doesn't make it legal," August said, to which I shook my head.

What was up with his hoity-toity behavior? It was so unlike him . . .

After Evelyn said grace, we all tucked in. The food was delicious, and the company, besides Mr. Broody in front of me, was delightful.

"Were you at The Den on Thursday night, August?" Jeb asked.

"No. Why? Were you?"

Jeb smirked. "Me? I'm way too old to hang out in a place like that. Ness went, but they turned her away at the door."

I took a swig from my ice-cold water, and it went down the wrong hole. I coughed so hard Evelyn rubbed me between the shoulders. The lie I'd told Jeb was that the bouncer hadn't allowed me inside, thus embarrassing me. Thus making me cry. I would never have cried about it, but Jeb ate it up.

"I told her she should've phoned one of the boys. That they would've gotten her in."

August narrowed his eyes. "That place is full of college kids. Besides, doesn't that friend of yours dee—"

I kicked his shin under the table. He couldn't blow my cover.

One of his eyebrows arched high. "I guess they're stricter in the summer."

I stabbed a piece of quesadilla. The golden shell crackled from the impact of my fork.

"Any more Creek spottings?" I asked Frank before I stuck the morsel inside my mouth. I was desperate to change the subject, but I also thought that if anyone was up to date on pack information, it would be the elder.

"It's been quiet." Frank darted a worried glance at Jeb, who was concentrated on his plate.

Perhaps me bringing up his son's murderers had been indelicate. "Is Liam going to send anyone to Beaver Creek?"

A small, vertical groove appeared between August's eyebrows.

Frank took a sip of wine. "I was thinking of going out there myself. I know Morgan. I know the way she thinks."

Evelyn went whiter than the glaze atop the cinnamon rolls. "Frank . . . *no*."

He took her hand in his and gave it a firm squeeze. "I'll be fine."

"I could go," I volunteered. "Maybe the Alpha would take well to a girl."

August's freckles darkened. "Ness, that would be completely—"

"*No, no, y no*." Evelyn squeezed my wrist so hard she cut off my blood circulation.

"Some women feel less threatened by members of the same sex," I said.

Frank scratched his wrinkled neck. "I don't think it would be wise. The Creeks are

. . . well, they're very in tune with their other nature, which doesn't make them very *civilized*."

"They killed Everest, Ness," Jeb whispered. "I won't lose you too."

I pressed my lips together. For Jeb's sake, I stopped fighting.

No one spoke of pack politics after that. They talked summer Olympics and tax reforms. When Little J left to meet up with his friends and the men started talking politics over cigars and whiskey, I cleared the table. Evelyn and Isobel tried to help, but I told them to go sit down, that I was happy to move after all the food I'd ingested.

"Honey, help Ness," Isobel told her son as she went to take a seat on the sofa.

August pushed off one the wooden beams and reluctantly made his way to the kitchen.

"I don't need your help," I said, slotting plates into the dishwasher.

But I got it anyway.

We didn't talk as we cleaned up the kitchen, didn't even look at each other.

At some point, he asked, "Why do you look like you cried all night?"

I licked my lips. There was no point in denying something that was so blatantly visible. "Because I did."

"Why?"

"A couple days ago, you send me a harsh email, and now you're concerned about why I cried?"

He frowned. "Harsh email?"

"Not to mix business with pleasure. For your information, I didn't ask Liam to come over, just like I didn't ask him to make you leave Boulder, just like I'm not *dating* Liam, okay? So there was nothing personal or remotely pleasurable about his visit." I poured in the dishwasher powder, then smacked the door shut. "Besides, you must've misunderstood him, because apparently he didn't ask you to leave. He asked *if* you'd be leaving."

August grunted.

"Can you stop grunting all the time? Seriously, you're twenty-seven. Even Little J doesn't grunt as much as you do."

He blinked at me, and then he crossed his arms and leaned his hip against the kitchen counter. "Any other compliments you want to lob my way?"

"I'm sure I can think of more if you give me a few minutes."

He had the audacity to smirk, which just infuriated me because he was obviously not taking our conversation seriously. "You get very flushed when you're angry."

"And that's funny?"

"When you were a kid, you'd get beet-red when things didn't go your way."

"Still don't see why that's funny." I washed my hands, then dried them on the kitchen towel and started covering the leftovers.

August pressed off the counter and took the Saran-wrapped dishes to the fridge. "Want to tell me why you lied about not liking zucchini bread and cinnamon rolls and all that other stuff?"

"Because I don't like people assuming they have me all figured out."

"Since when am I *people*?" There was a twinge of hurt in his tone.

I looked up from the platter topped with scraps of smoked salmon. "You think you know me because I get red when I'm angry, or because I still eat all that stuff I pretended not to like, but I'm not that little girl you ferried around in your truck and brought to the ice cream parlor for a scoop, okay?"

His frown deepened, brought out lines on other places of his face.

"You're ten years older than me. You'll always be ten years older. That's never going to change, but every time you call me Dimples, I feel like I'm six. I don't think you mean to make me feel like a kid, but that's the way it comes out. I'm tired of people thinking I'm childish. Or expendable."

"*Expendable*?" August's eyes were the vivid green of the leaves dotting the tree outside the kitchen window. "When did I make you feel expendable?"

"That wasn't—You didn't." I dragged my damp hands through my hair. "I'm really beat, August." I tried to pass by him, but he held out his arm to bar my path.

"Who made you feel expendable?"

"No one. I don't know even know why I said that."

"Ness—"

"It doesn't matter. Not anymore."

"If it didn't matter anymore, then you wouldn't look like you were about to have a meltdown." He didn't lower his arm. "You might've changed, but I haven't. I'm still a great listener."

My lips quirked into the smallest of smiles. "I appreciate the offer, but I'd rather gnaw off my arm then have a heart-to-heart with you about boys. No offense, but it would just be weird. And not because of the link, but because you're a guy."

He still didn't lower his arm.

"Fine. Want to tell me why you broke up with Sienna?" I asked, trying to prove a point, not because I wanted to discuss his ex.

The memory of the other night twisted in my gut like a dagger. Once the initial shock of finding Liam with another woman had worn off, I'd realized that something else had hurt even more: the fact that he'd done this with so many people present. It was tacky. Again, though, he hadn't cheated on me. I had to stop seeing this as a betrayal. He'd betrayed no one.

"No," August said.

It took me a second to remember what question he was answering. "See?"

He finally lowered his arm to let me through. I walked over to Evelyn and Isobel and talked exclusively with them for the next two hours. The skin on the back of my neck prickled more than once. At some point, I turned around to see if I was going crazy or if someone was watching me. I caught August staring.

At least I wasn't going crazy.

I squeezed a smile onto my lips, feeling as though our talk had somehow dismantled some of the tension between us. If only a talk could also dismantle our link.

Five more months.

What was five more months?

34

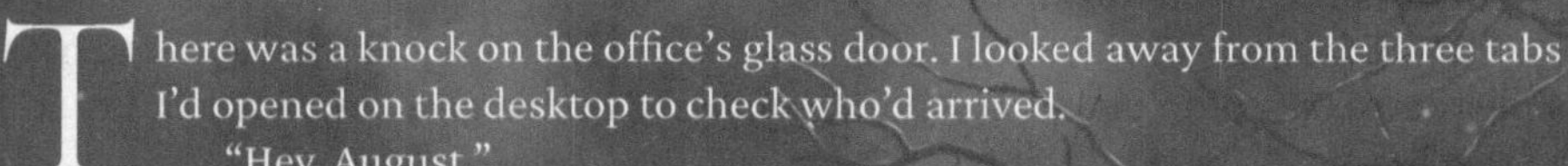

There was a knock on the office's glass door. I looked away from the three tabs I'd opened on the desktop to check who'd arrived.

"Hey, August."

He walked toward me, hands in the pockets of a pair of olive-green cargo pants that had a couple small tears in them, as though they'd gotten snagged on the construction site.

"I bought cake for one of the guys. It's his birthday. Want some?"

"Um. Sure." I started to wheel myself away from the desk when I caught the time on the upper right hand corner of the screen. "Actually, I'm going to have to take a raincheck on that cake." I gathered up my stuff and wedged it inside my bag.

"Going somewhere?"

"Driving test. I sent your dad an email that I'd be taking off for an hour."

"Oh." He thumbed the seam of his lips.

"Was I supposed to inform you, too?"

He dropped his hand from his face and shook his head. "Break a leg, or should I say a side mirror?"

I smiled. "I think that if I break a side mirror, I won't get my license."

His thick lips crooked into a smile. "Yeah. Try to avoid that."

"Will you be here when I come back?"

He nodded. "I'm working from the warehouse today."

"Good. Because I found some discrepancies on invoices from this one lumber company. Anyway I'll tell you all about it as soon as I come back." I dashed through the warehouse just as my phone started ringing.

"I'm outside," Jeb said.

I stepped through the wide-open loading dock entrance. "Me too."

I RETURNED TO THE WATTS' warehouse an hour and a half later, clutching a piece of paper so hard I'd wrinkled the crap out of it.

August and Uncle Tom were bent over a thick plank coated in a palette of stains. August must've sensed me approach through our little tether, because he looked up.

"Did you get it?" he asked.

I thought it would be obvious by my shit-eating grin, but apparently it was too subtle for August.

"Did you have any doubts I would?"

He smiled. "Well done, Dim—Ness."

"*Dimness*? That's a new one."

"I meant, Ness. Just Ness."

"I know. I was just teasing."

August scratched the base of his neck. "Hey, Tom, does your nephew still work at KPR?"

Uncle Tom tweaked the button of his overalls and gave a quick nod.

"Can you tell him to warn drivers about a blonde at the wheel of a big black van?"

I stuck my tongue out at August. "That's very mature."

Uncle Tom grinned, which made his candied-apple cheeks puff out.

I raised my chin in the air. "I'll have you know I'm an excellent driver."

August chuckled.

"The guy who gave me the exam said I was a natural." He'd then asked if I wanted to have dinner with him sometime, but I left that part out. I'd just smiled pleasantly even though I'd found it a little icky. He was a good two decades older than I was and missing a tooth, and not a molar. I wouldn't have noticed a missing molar.

"I didn't know driving instructors doled out compliments. I certainly never got one."

"Maybe because you weren't all that impressive behind the wheel of a car." I shot him a teasing smile.

"August's pretty impressive anywhere he goes," Uncle Tom said very seriously. "When I was young, even though it might seem hard to believe, I was pretty impressive myself."

That *was* hard to believe, but I said, "I don't doubt it." Yes, it was a lie, but it was a kind one. Kind lies were acceptable. Right?

The rest of Uncle Tom's face went red.

"You had something to discuss with me?" August asked.

I returned my gaze to him. "Oh. Yeah."

Together we walked to the office. I shook the computer mouse to awaken the monitor, then clicked all the tabs back open and showed him how several timber delivery slips didn't match the warehouse stocks.

"Either they're not delivering the amount listed, or someone's been stealing supplies from the warehouse." Some being a benign amount, but still noticeable. Like a missing molar. Not an incisor. I then showed him how the pattern went back almost three years.

"Shit." August perused all the highlighted numbers.

"Look, it's probably the timber company. I mean it's always the same one. If one of your employees were skimming, he'd probably do it on every order, not just on Black Timber's."

Unless the person was smart. I truly hoped it was the timber corporation and not an individual.

"How did Mom miss this? That's thousands of dollars of loss!"

"$17,533."

August blinked at me.

I shrugged. "I'll print everything out so you can double-check my number."

August stood up straighter. "I trust your calculations, but yeah, print it out so I can show Dad."

I hit control P on various documents, which made the mammoth printer roar to life in the corner.

August walked over and plucked the papers from the tray before crossing the office, but then he paused in the doorway. "Can you keep this between us? Until I find out what's going on?"

"Of course." I mimicked zipping up my lips.

He stepped out but doubled back. "And congrats again on your license. That's a heck of a milestone."

I smiled stupidly at him.

With the hand not clutching all the printouts, he tapped the doorframe. "Don't leave before I get back, okay?"

I nodded, imagining he'd want to debrief after meeting with Nelson. "I drove here, so I'm totally independent."

A butterfly performed a backflip inside my stomach.

Independent.

How I'd longed for this day.

35

The sun was setting, and everyone had left, yet August still wasn't back. I'd been done with my workload for almost an hour and had been poring over the three-dimensional elevations of a luxury lodge. I could almost smell the oiled pine floors and the tall evergreens that had been digitally added beyond the bay windows.

"What do you think?" A warm breath licked up the column of my neck.

I startled, and the 3D printouts scattered on the dusty floor. I slapped a palm across my chest, trying to ease my galloping heart. "August! You scared me."

His gaze set on my midriff. "You didn't *feel* me approach? Because I can sense you from miles away."

I lowered my palm to my stomach where the phantom thread throbbed, where it had been pulsing for a while, but I'd dismissed it as hunger pangs. "I thought I was just really hungry."

He smiled as he dropped into a crouch to gather the papers. "And? Are you hungry?"

"I don't know." August's proximity confused the heck out of my body.

He set all the papers back on the desk and nodded to them. "What do you think?"

"I'd want to live there."

"I thought your dream house was a glass cube centered around a courtyard."

"A glass cube?"

"You sketched it on a paper napkin when we went for ice cream once and made me swear I'd build it for you someday."

"Oh. I don't remember." I twisted my hair into a rope and wound it into a high bun, looping the ends through the coiled mass to make it hold. "I was quite a demanding kid, huh?"

"You even picked the sort of tree that would go in the courtyard."

I concentrated on my memories but couldn't locate the one in question. "What tree did I want?"

"A palm."

I grinned, dropping my hands from my hair. "Seriously? How *tropical* of me."

"It would thrive in Colorado."

I wrinkled my nose. "But it would probably be an eyesore."

"It'd be original, that's for sure." He tilted his head to the side. "A little like a girl in an all-male pack."

"Hmm." When he put it that way . . . Maybe a disruptive tree would do this place some good.

"You also wanted a loose floorboard in your bedroom. Like the one you had at the foot of your bed."

That, I remembered. When I was six or seven, Everest and I had pried a wooden slat loose from my floor with one of my father's work tools, and then we'd lined the shallow hollow with burlap. I stowed my diary inside, along with a treasured collection of Polaroid pictures—my Dad in his wolf form, a few silly selfies of Everest and me, one of my parents dancing in our living room, and several close-ups of August. I remembered this one shot of him, with the sun on his face and this faraway glint in his eyes. I'd labeled it *The Dreamer*.

When I'd first moved to LA, I'd look at it every night, but at some point, the sight of August just made me sad, so I'd shoved the Polaroid inside a shoe box along with the rest of my keepsakes. The next time I'd lifted the lid on that box was about three years later. A leak in our apartment had filled my box with dirty water, ruining the few mementos I'd carried from Boulder.

I blinked out of the memory. "How did the talk go with your dad?"

"I'd rather not discuss it in here."

Did he think the place was bugged? I didn't ask.

August gestured to the door of the building, and I followed him out. He turned off all the lights before setting the alarm. I thought he'd tell me about his conversation outside, but he tipped his head toward the side of the warehouse.

"Ooh." I was sure my eyes lit up. "I get to see your man cave?" I rubbed my palms together like a little kid.

"Man cave?" He grunted.

I flicked his arm.

"Ouch. What was that for?"

"Every time you grunt, I'm flicking you."

"Are you now?" he muttered.

"Uh-huh. It'll make you take notice of how often you do it."

He shook his head a little, but a smile softened his expression. "Should I remind you that inflicting bodily harm on your boss is majorly frowned upon?"

"Bodily harm?" I snorted. "I don't think I could inflict much harm on that *impressive* body of yours." I winked at him.

He flicked my ribs.

"What was that for?" I said, rubbing the spot. "It wasn't a dig. Besides, I didn't even come up with the descriptive term. That was all Uncle Tom."

"You grunted," he said matter-of-factly.

"I did not."

"You did."

I shook my head but matched his smile with one of my own.

August unlocked his front door with a digital keypad and then tapped another keypad inside, and a dozen different lights flared to life.

I tilted my head up and took in the narrow, but dizzyingly high-ceilinged space. "Wow."

The walls were brushed concrete, and the floors were gunmetal-tinged wood, and over the kitchen, there was a giant mezzanine topped with a king-sized bed.

"Total man cave," I declared.

August walked to the kitchen and tugged open the fridge that was stocked with beer, milk, and more beer.

"Don't eat here often, huh?" I ran my fingers over the knots in the giant slice of trunk that made up his kitchen island. "This is beautiful." The sides were uneven but smooth, almost like ruffles. "I want an island like this in my glass cube." I took a seat at the island as he pulled out two beers which he uncapped with his fist. I tipped an eyebrow up. "I thought I was underage."

He smiled. "I was trying to irritate you." He handed me one of the bottles, then held out his own. "To milestones."

We clinked, and then I took a small sip.

"I probably shouldn't drink and drive. Especially not on an empty stomach."

"I was going to order pizza."

My spine straightened a little. "You don't have to feed me."

"Cole's coming over soon. He requested an extra-large pie."

I took another sip. "You guys hang out often?"

"Well, we work together, but yeah, we hang out every day."

They were the same age, or maybe a year apart. "I don't remember you guys being such good friends before I left town."

"Those last few weeks you were around, we were on the outs over a girl. He hooked up with her right after I broke up with her."

"And that was a violation of the *bro-code* or something?"

He snorted.

I leaned over and flicked his wrist.

"Hey." He rubbed it, eyes glinting with a smile.

I tipped my bottle to my lips, relishing the cool fizz of the beer as it hit my tongue, as it hit my veins. "So what happened after that?"

"He ended up going out with her for four years."

"And you didn't talk the entire time?"

"Nah. We patched things up pretty quick."

I thought of the girl inside Liam's room. I still didn't know who she was, but I couldn't imagine wanting to hang out with her. Then again, Cole and August had been friends before a girl had come between them. I had no girlfriends in Boulder, besides Sarah, but Sarah had obviously not been the one behind that wall.

Would I have forgiven her if she had been?

"Ness?"

"Yeah?" I blinked out of my glum thoughts.

"Want some pizza?"

"Sure."

As he phoned up the delivery place, I went back to thinking about the girl in Liam's room. Went through my entire beer dwelling on *her*.

I really needed to get my mind off it. "So what did your dad say?" I asked once August was done placing the order.

"He said he knew. Mom caught the discrepancy."

"And?"

"And you don't need to concern yourself with it."

I crossed my legs. "You're really going to leave me hanging like that?"

He studied the label on his beer bottle, as though checking the ingredients, studied it so hard a small groove appeared between his eyebrows. Finally, he sighed. "Tom's been skimming. His nephew—the one who works at the radio station—well, his ex-wife had a shopping addiction. She emptied their bank account and left town, but she'd racked up an insane amount of debt and stuck him with it."

Debt. I knew a thing or two about that.

He peeled off a corner of his label and stripped it off the green glass. "Tom was just trying to help his nephew out."

"Why didn't he just come to you and ask for a loan?"

"I suppose he was afraid he'd be turned down, and then turned out." August leaned his forearms on the counter, folding the label up and up until it resembled a miniature accordion. "We never discussed your salary, by the way. I imagine this is just a summer job for you."

"If you need me for longer, I could temp during the fall."

He rubbed the pleated label between his fingertips, and the sticky paper disintegrated into flecks.

"But only if you find me competent—"

"We find you competent." He finished reducing the label to a mound of rice-sized pellets. "Too much so."

I blinked up at him. Was there such a thing as too competent?

"Would twenty bucks an hour be acceptable?"

"Twenty bucks?" I choked out. I'd made eleven and change back in California. "That's really generous."

He grabbed my empty beer bottle, scooped up his little mess, then dropped both in the bin underneath his sink. "Do you have money trouble?"

"Huh?" What led him to ask me that? Did I give off some starved vibe? I tried to blank out my expression. "No."

"Then why did you take that escort job?"

"To confront Heath."

"I'm not talking about that one. I'm talking about the second one."

I wrinkled my nose. "How do you know about the second one?"

"Cole was there."

Ugh. "I was promised three grand to go to dinner with Aidan. I didn't know who he was. I wouldn't have gone if I'd known."

August stared at me so long that I felt the heat seep higher than just my neck.

"Look, I'm really not proud of it, but it was three grand *just* for dinner."

"I'm not judging you, Ness."

"Everyone else did," I mumbled.

He covered one of my hands with one of his. Even though I was still a little tanned, the contrast between our skin colors was jarring—light brown against golden ivory.

"But I do want an honest answer out of you about your money situation. I know your uncle's in a bind waiting on the payment from the inn to clear, and I know what medical bills cost."

I swallowed hard, praying August couldn't feel the clamminess of my skin. "I was a minor, so after Mom . . . after she died, I wasn't responsible for her medical bills. I just needed to pay day-to-day stuff and a couple extras, you know, rent, food, her"—I slid my bottom lip between my teeth—"her funeral." I kept my gaze on our hands. "So to answer your question, I need a job, not a loan."

The doorbell rang then. The scent of melted cheese and tangy tomato had my stomach rumbling. Unhurriedly, he removed his hand and walked to the door. He relieved the delivery boy of three cardboard boxes and tipped him generously, before ferrying the food back to the island. He flipped the lids up on two of the boxes but kept the third one shut—probably Cole's extra-large pie.

"Can you give me your bank details?" he asked, taking out plates and handing me one. "So we can deposit your salary straight into it at the end of the month."

"I'll email it to you later." I eased a perfect triangle out of the box and bit off the pointy tip.

Silence fell between us as we ate. It was interrupted by a sharp knock on the door, followed by beeping.

"Yo," Cole said, walking in. He stopped when he saw me. Although Cole tried to hide his surprise, it was all over his face.

"Ness got her driver's license," August informed him. "We were celebrating with beer and pizza."

I patted my lips with a paper napkin, grabbed the bag I'd flung on the seat next to me, and hopped off the barstool. "I was just leaving. Don't want to crash your date."

As I walked toward the door, Cole squeezed my shoulder.

His fingers smelled like cigarettes. "Matt told me what happened."

Don't say it out loud. Don't say it out loud. I didn't want to relive it.

"It was a dick move," he added, lowering his hand, "but it's his loss."

I studied the floor beneath his sneakers. "He didn't do anything wrong. We weren't together," I said softly. And then I tried to smile but failed miserably. It had been five days, and yet my heart still shuddered every time someone mentioned Liam. "Good-night, boys," I mumbled, stepping out into the cobalt darkness.

I watched the stars as I made my way toward the van. And then I watched them some more while I drove myself home, wishing I could feel happier, because today had been a good day.

I thought of my dream house as I drove past the road that led to my old one, and then I rammed my foot on the brake.

Oh.

My.

God.

I blinked in the direction of my childhood home, Everest's last message trickling into my mind, then gunned the car up the drive.

36

I parked the van and raced around the house toward my old bedroom. The window that I'd busted when I'd sprang through it to rescue Evelyn was still gaping wide. I'd thought about boarding it up, but then, with everything that had happened, it had slipped my mind. Never was I gladder to be forgetful.

Shards of glass remained in the frame. I grabbed a rock from the ground, the largest I could find, and ran it around the frame, knocking out any sharp remnant. Palms and chest tingling with my rapid pulse, I heaved myself up and through the dark hole.

I must not have gotten all the glass, because beads of blood appeared on one of my palms. As I wiped them on my T-shirt, I traced the dusty floor until I located the slab. I dropped into a crouch and coaxed the floorboard up, heart rate sprinting, filling my mouth with the taste of metal. I wasn't sure what I was more afraid of: finding something or finding nothing?

Without a sound, the slat lifted.

I stared into the dark hatch but didn't reach into it. I carefully set the floorboard aside, took my phone out of my pocket, and called the one person I didn't want to speak to.

Ten minutes later, a car rumbled up my driveway. I stepped out of my bedroom and walked to the front door to unlock it. Liam and Lucas got out of the black SUV and then trailed me through my old home.

I pointed to the hatch. "I didn't touch anything."

Liam shone the light from his phone into the hole, catching the metallic glint of the stack of packages my cousin had crammed inside. With no refrigeration, was the Sillin even salvageable? I didn't ask. I didn't care. The only thing I cared about was that Liam and Lucas didn't assume I'd had a hand in hiding the Boulders' drugs.

Liam scooped the foil packets out and dropped them on the dusty floor.

"Are they all there?" Lucas asked.

Liam counted them out slowly. "There's one missing."

One out of thirty or so. Twenty-four pills to a packet.

When Liam raised his gaze to mine, I tensed up. "I didn't take it."

An emotion flared in his eyes. Pain? Regret? I averted my gaze, the ache of being in his presence still too raw.

"Ness, I wasn't insinuating that you had." He straightened up and tentatively stepped toward me. "Thank you for finding these. And for reporting them."

I nodded, gaze on the hodgepodge of Sillin.

He touched my cheek, and I jerked backward.

"I should go." I turned and started through the house, not looking at anything but the floor. I was afraid that my heart, which already felt enlarged with grief, would balloon right out of my chest if I caught sight of something that reminded me of my parents.

I got back into the car, and under the canopy of stars, with tears dripping and drying on my cheeks, I left my dark home and the stash of drugs that had caused so much harm to pass.

37

Freshly brewed coffee was waiting on my desk when I got in the next morning. I wondered if the drink was for me, and when no one came to claim it, I sipped it. I'd slept fitfully, so caffeine was extremely welcomed.

After I'd left, Liam looped in the whole pack about the recovered drugs. He didn't mention specifics, like where they'd been found and by whom, but I bet people phoned him to find out. News traveled fast through the pack.

I took another much-needed sip of the scalding beverage. It was deliciously aromatic, almost like it had been steeped with caramel and cinnamon.

Since August wasn't working from the warehouse, I sent him a text: *Do I have you to thank for the coffee?*

His answer came much later. *Was it good?*

ME: *Amazing. You'll have to tell me what brand it was.*

AUGUST: *Glad you liked it.*

AUGUST: *How are you feeling?*

I rubbed my brow.

AUGUST: *Ness?*

ME: *Fine.*

AUGUST: *. . .*

ME: *What is . . . supposed to mean?*

AUGUST: *It was me grunting.*

Smiling, I scoured my list of emojis until I found one that looked like a flick. I sent it.

AUGUST: *OK?*

ME: *That was me flicking you.*

August sent me a smiley face. Then: *Shouldn't you be working?*

Yeah. I should've been. Plus I needed to get my mind off the previous night, so I placed my phone face down on the table and didn't so much as glance its way the remainder of the day.

Just as I was getting up to go, someone filled the office's doorframe.

"Did I offend you with my last text?" August asked, leaning his broad shoulder into the door frame.

"Huh?" I strapped my bag across my body, then lifted my hair to free it from the strap.

"You never answered me after I told you that you should be working."

Oh. I smiled. "I didn't answer you because I took your advice to heart. *I worked.*" I grabbed the travel mug I'd cleaned earlier and carried it over to him. "Thanks again for the coffee."

"Same one tomorrow morning?"

"You don't need to make me coffee every morning, August."

"I live next door. Besides, I make a pot for myself. Pouring it into a mug and dropping it off isn't too hard."

"Well then, sure." I extended the mug, and he took it, our fingers brushing.

A little jolt went through my hand.

Static.

Or maybe it was the link.

I stuck both my hands into the back pockets of my jeans.

"Got any plans tonight?" His voice sounded a little rough.

The blood pounding against my eardrums probably created this distortion, because his expression was entirely normal.

"I'm having dinner with a UCB jock. What about you?"

"A UCB jock?" He straightened up, which seemed to give him an extra inch. "You're serious?"

"As a heart attack."

He grunted.

I flicked his pec. He didn't rub the spot I'd flicked.

Instead, he crossed his arms, tendons pinching underneath the skin. "What's the guy's name?"

"Why?"

"Just wondering if I know him."

I smiled a little. "You know him."

His pupils pulsed. "Really? Is it David?"

"David? Who's David?"

"Dexter's cousin. The kid with the birthmark under the eye. He plays football at UCB. He's a junior."

"Oh. No." *If David's a junior, thus two years older than I am, and you think he's a kid, what does that make me?* "My date's actually the former running back for the Colorado Buffaloes."

August's gaze narrowed.

"Might've heard of him. Jeb Clark?" I winked at him, and his eyes went wide.

Then I added, "No dating for me in the near future. I'm taking some time off men. Like a year, or a decade." I slid past August. "Anyway, I promised Jeb I'd eat with him tonight since I stood him up yesterday." I stopped halfway through the warehouse and spun around. "Want to come?"

He studied the lid of the mug. "No. I'll get some more work done."

I was a little surprised he preferred staying in the office over a warm meal with family friends. But then I realized something. "You don't have to worry about me, August. I'm not depressed or anything."

He glanced up from the mug, brow knitted as though I'd misconstrued his concern. He opened his mouth to speak just as a shrill howl pierced the night, and then another and another. My chest tightened, and my skin bristled, the fine hairs thickening. I'd never heard it before yet knew it was my Alpha's call. The insistence of it had me gaping at August.

"You're going to have to postpone that dinner of yours," he said, setting the travel mug down and yanking off his shirt.

The urgency of the moment was momentarily supplanted by the sight of August's bare chest which gave new meaning to the term washboard abs—you could most probably do laundry against his abdomen.

"Ness? Three howls means something serious has happened."

I snapped out of my daze. Had the Sillin been stolen again? Or maybe they were dummy tablets? I lowered my gaze to the swirls of sawdust beneath my feet and swallowed, my throat feeling as dry as those corn husks Evelyn filled with masa dough.

August strode over to me and cranked my chin up. "You'll be okay. I'll be there."

I nodded, fumbling to remove my bag. When the strap caught in my hair, August assisted me in hoisting it up and off. Flustered by his proximity and nakedness, I backed away. My hands trembled as I dragged off my necklace and then my T-shirt, and then my navel pulsed chaotically when August's eyes, which were on me, began to gleam brighter.

He turned away, Adam's apple working in his throat.

A howl tore through the night, seemingly nearer. Was the pack headed here? I ducked behind one of the work desks, and, keeping my back to August, I unclipped my bra and pushed down my jeans.

Claws clicked nearby, and it made my own claws jolt out of my cuticles. Making sure I wasn't in August's line of sight, I scraped off my underwear before my tail could shred it. My bones shifted and my muscles swelled, and I fell onto my knees, back arched as the rest of the change rippled through me.

When it was done, August bumped his wet muzzle into my shoulder.

Ready? he asked.

I dipped my head in assent. At least I'd face Liam in fur tonight. I felt less vulnerable in fur than I felt in skin, as though my thick white pelt could somehow shield me better than my pale hide.

Another howl stirred the air.

We trotted to the door. With his mouth, August jerked the handle, then shoved the door open with his shoulder. For a moment, I wondered how we would find the pack, but then I felt the tug of something in my chest. Like the tether that bound me to August, there was another tether inside me.

One that tied me to Liam.

One that led me straight to him.

38

In a part of the forest where the trees grew as dense as the underbrush, the pack
had assembled. Most were in wolf form, but a few had stayed in skin—the few
being the elders. The moon wouldn't be full for another week, so I imagined
they hadn't been able to shift. And yet they'd still come. They wouldn't understand
what was being said, unless Liam spoke to them through the mind link.

Could he, in wolf form?

I saw Jeb, or rather I recognized the gray-blond fur, the light-blue eyes, and the
lemony scent of his body. I walked over to him, squeezing my scrawny self between
him and Frank's grandson, who was as big as me in fur. Not in skin, though. I
wondered why that was. But then I pressed that contemplation away.

I felt Liam's glowing amber eyes on me, but I kept mine trained on the squashed
pine needles beneath his giant paws. His lupine body had grown in bulk and breadth
since he'd become Alpha.

A nose pressed against my haunches, shifting me a little more toward Jeb, and
then another large body sidled in next to me, lining up between Little J and me.
August.

Liam's gaze moved to my neighbor's. For a moment, they just observed each
other. Then August took another step forward, and his pelt bristled, ostensibly
making him seem bigger. It was an illusion. He hadn't actually grown, but he was
sending Liam a message not to look at me.

I nudged my friend's flank to tell him I was okay. That he didn't have to make
such an aggressive show. God only knew how the others would interpret it.

He didn't back down, but his fur smoothed, and Liam pivoted to face another
part of the circle.

The Creek Alpha finally made contact, he said. *She will be coming to Boulder with a
delegation of Creeks tomorrow. She says she's coming in peace and will be staying at the inn.*

Aidan Michaels is allowing that? someone asked, interrupting Liam.

He probably doesn't know they're shifters, one of the men said.

Aidan Michaels knows, Lucas growled out. *He has fucking files on the entire werewolf community, but I guess he isn't above taking money from our kind.*

I glanced at my uncle. His stare was unflinching, but I could hear his heart beating a little more strongly than the rest of the hearts around me. I rubbed his shoulder with my cheek in a show of affection and support. He turned his head and rested his own cheek against my forehead a moment.

What do they want? August's deep voice quieted the whisperings that had kindled like wildfire around us.

To meet with the Alphas and their packs. She is convening us to a meeting at the inn tomorrow night at sundown, Liam answered. *I want you all to be there.*

I peeked around the large brown wolf and met Liam's hardened gaze.

We need to present a united front, Liam said, and I swear I felt that comment was directed only at me.

Will the Pines be there? someone asked.

The Pines will be there, Liam answered.

This is a trap. We shouldn't go, someone barked.

We caught the owner of the yellow Hummer—Everest's murderer, Liam said.

I stiffened and emitted a barely audible whimper.

Liam shifted his gaze to my uncle, who stiffened next to me. *And we've identified him as Morgan's son. She knows we have him. That's one of the reasons she's coming. To retrieve him. Whether he lives or dies depends entirely on how she behaves.*

I nosed out from behind August. *He might walk away with his life? He killed Everest. Is this becoming a thing? Murderers get to kill without retribution?*

He's worth more to us alive than dead, Liam said. *Besides, Everest was dead either way. Morgan's son just spared me from exacting justice myself.*

Jeb's strangled moan made goose bumps flourish beneath my fur.

I'm sorry, Jeb, Liam said, *I understand this is still not easy for you to hear.*

Whining, Jeb folded his ears and scrambled backward and away from the pack. I started to go after him when Liam called out my name.

Ness, this meeting isn't over.

His voice held so much authority it had me lowering my head and turning around. It was as though my body and mind were two separate entities—where my mind wanted to go after my distraught uncle, my body obeyed my Alpha's command.

The Creek Alpha insisted that you come earlier with me.

Me? Why?

Apparently she's heard a lot about you.

I waited for snickers to erupt from the males whose gazes were all trained on me now. No one snickered.

So be ready at seven, Liam said.

Then he proceeded to give us orders about the night ahead, urging us not to ingest any drink or food offered at the inn in case they were doused with the missing Sillin.

I thought we recovered it all, someone said.

Almost all. But this doesn't mean the Creeks don't have their own stock, Liam barked.

He doled out more precautions, but his voice faded into white noise as I pondered why Morgan, the great and feared Alpha of the Creeks, had asked to meet *me* beforehand.

Was she looking for an ally in my pack?

39

I went in to work the next day with a mix of excitement and dread bubbling deep in the pit of my stomach. August exacerbated the dread part of my mood. His concern was so heavy that I asked him if I could leave early. Before I could drive away, he asked if I wanted him to come at seven too. When I turned down his offer—because I feared Morgan wouldn't appreciate me bringing a bodyguard—his eyes darkened like the evergreens on a moonless night.

I hadn't meant to hurt his feelings and almost backpedaled, but he'd be there shortly after me. Besides, I wasn't frightened. Well, not overly frightened.

Especially after Sarah dropped by, chattering nonstop about the meeting. She swung three dresses onto my bed. Even though I insisted on wearing something of mine, she told me this was a *soirée*. A soirée apparently called for fancy attire.

"I'm not looking to seduce any Creeks," I muttered to Sarah as I reluctantly tried dress number two.

"One of the first things Julian taught me was that the way you present yourself, the way you hold yourself, the way you speak affects the perception people will have of you. By walking in looking like a thousand dollars—I think that one was actually two—you'll stand out, because everyone, be they wolf or human, has a vested interest in beauty and riches."

She fingered the black tulle of the midi skirt while I blanched. I'd never asked how much the red dress I'd worn to her brother's wedding cost, nor the little white number that still hung in my closet.

I smoothed down the stiff bustier top that shoved my breasts together. Considering mine were way smaller than Sarah's, I asked, "Can you even fit into this thing?"

"Nope. Internet order I was too lazy to return. It's yours."

For a second, I pondered reselling it, but it would probably hurt Sarah's feelings. Plus it was really nice *and* black, so probably easy to wear to other occasions.

I finally turned away from the floor-length mirror glued to the back of my bedroom door. "You're like a fairy godmother. Except instead of little wings and a gray bun, you have sharp claws that can shred a man's throat, and a sharper attitude that can shred his ego."

She slashed through the air, manicured nails curving.

My lips quirked into a smile that tumbled off when a car honked.

Sarah lurched off the bed and peered out my window. "Liam's here. Are you gonna be okay?"

"Yeah," I lied, going into my bathroom and fishing my mascara from the glass in which I kept my toothbrush and eyeliner. Even though my hands trembled, I managed to apply a thin coat of makeup to my lashes without incident. I left the rest of my face bare. The dress was loud enough. I fluffed out my hair which had dried a bit wavy and fit my feet into my black heels.

"Let's pray tonight doesn't turn into something out of a slasher film," Sarah said, running her hand along her hair, which she'd had professionally flattened. It made her look like a different person—less wild and more refined.

I gasped. "Why would you say that?"

"I was just kidding."

"Well, it wasn't funny," I muttered.

Sarah did something very un-Sarah-like. She gave me a hug. "She has no reason to murder us. She probably came to beg for her son's life. And maybe offer us an alliance." She squeezed me tight, her flowery perfume prickling my nostrils like rose thorns. "Or maybe she wants to marry you off to her son."

I pulled away. "What?"

Sarah shrugged. "I was just speculating."

"Well don't speculate about something so . . . so awful."

"You're mated. Just use that excuse if she tries to marry you off."

As I wrenched my bedroom door open, I caught my reflection in the mirror. My face was as wraith-like as Isobel's had been back at the hospital.

Liam honked again.

"Better go before he comes upstairs and hauls your ass into his big car."

My heartbeats snagged behind my compressed ribs. "I'm not ready," I whispered, panicked.

She strode up to me and tucked a piece of hair behind my ear. "I'll come early." When I still hadn't moved, she said, "Everything'll be fine."

Oh no, no, no. Why'd she have to say that? To use those exact words?

Chilled to my bones, I finally walked out. Liam neither greeted me when I climbed into his car, nor did he spare me a passing glance. He wore his usual black V-neck and blue jeans but had added a black dinner jacket.

"Am I overdressed? I let Sarah pick my clothes . . ."

His gaze didn't budge from his windshield, but a nerve ticked in his jaw. "Are you fishing for a compliment?"

"What? No! I was just asking if I should go change before we leave."

He pressed on the gas pedal, and the car lurched forward. I hurried to strap myself in.

"Too late now," he snapped. "I'm sure August will appreciate your little princess dress."

That stunned me into silence. But only for a minute. "Don't be a jerk, Liam."

He side-eyed me. "Me? A jerk?" He barked out a dark laugh. "I think you got me and your mate mixed up." He pronounced the word *mate* as though it were something rotten.

Anger welled up behind my breastbone. "How is August the jerk? He's not the one who said I backst—"

"He challenged my authority in front of the pack! I can't even put him back in his place verbally or physically, because he's your *mate*." He narrowed his eyes. "Tell me, are you and him a thing now?"

I shook my head, not as an answer, but because he was acting crazy.

"If you and him fuck, that's it for you. You're stuck with him for life, and from what Sienna says, he's a boring lay."

I blanched, and then I flushed with anger and glared at the low buildings smearing past our window, wondering why Liam had to be so crude and petty. I wasn't the one who'd jumped into bed with someone else the second I was unattached.

He jerked the car to a stop at a red light. "The crazy thing is how much shit I'm getting from my buddies about this. It's not like I strayed, yet I'm the bad guy."

I was gripping the tulle as though it were a stress ball. Didn't do squat for my stress level. "I know you're hurt—"

"I'm not hurt! I am *fucking* furious!" He slapped his steering wheel. "You toss me to the curb at the first mistake I make. I'm not perfect. No one is! Not even you."

My knuckles whitened, and my eyesight sharpened, but I pushed back my wolf before she could rip through my *little princess* dress.

"I slept with Tammy because she stroked the ego you'd crushed." The volume of his voice had dropped, but it still rang too loudly in the car.

Tammy. Tamara. Why was I not surprised?

Had he ever stopped seeing her? Why was I torturing myself with this? It didn't matter.

She didn't matter.

What they *did* didn't matter.

"How am I supposed to be Alpha if I'm made to feel like a piece of shit?" he asked.

I didn't make a sound. I barely breathed. My spine tingled, and again, I shoved my wolf back.

The light turned green, and Liam flattened the gas pedal, weaving between cars like a Formula 1 pilot.

"She was just a means to an end," he added, so low I almost missed his words.

I still didn't say anything.

He pulled to another violent stop, this time on the side of the road that led up to the inn. "Say something," he yelled. "Shout at me! Do something! Tell me what a prick I am, slap me, tell me what a bitch Tamara is!" His violent words were limned with desperation.

Is that why he'd taken her to his bed? To test my affection? Or was it to stroke his ego like he'd said two minutes ago?

He reached over and clasped my shoulders, pivoting me toward him. "Aren't you even a little jealous? Don't you care about me?" he whispered, his powerful voice faltering.

"You broke my heart, Liam." I was incredibly calm, and it wasn't even an act. I didn't feel vindictive. "I let you in, and you wrecked me. Is that what you want to hear?" I licked my lips that felt as dry as my eyes.

His hands slid down my arms, gripped my biceps as though to keep me from falling away from him. But I'd already fallen away from him.

"Are you and August—"

"There is no me and August."

Liam's eyes flashed with something—hope. Like a lit match, it spread and made the air inside the car crackle.

"But there is also no me and you, Liam." One-by-one, I pried his fingers off my arms. "You have to let me go," I said softly. "You have to let me go."

Red handprints remained where he'd squeezed.

"I will obey you like I vowed, but don't ask me to love you."

He scrubbed a hand through his gelled hair. A hardened lock fell into his shiny eyes. "Ness . . ."

"Please, Liam, let me go," I murmured.

I touched his cheek, smooth from a fresh shave, the only soft part on his body. The rest of him was all hard lines. He swallowed, and his jaw muscles juddered under my palm. He covered my hand with his and kept both anchored to his face as we sat on the side of the road, the inn just out of reach but already in sight.

"Let's get tonight over with," I said, slipping my palm out from underneath his.

He lowered his eyelids, then lifted them back up, drawing in a long breath through his nostrils. Or maybe he was drawing in a lungful of courage. The Creeks' reputation was so dire that I worked hard on quieting my own nerves as we slowly made our way up the hill toward them.

40

Liam parked up front, behind a compact row of cars that ranged in fanciness, from gleaming Cayennes to rusted Civics. The sight of rust reassured me I wasn't out of my depths, that I'd be able to relate to some of these shifters.

We walked toward the inn side by side, the earlier tension between us diffused. We were in no way relaxed, but that had nothing to do with our row and everything to do with the den of wolves we were about to enter.

"Why do you think she asked to meet me specifically?" I asked.

"You're Everest's cousin. You worked as an escort. Maybe she thinks you spied on a Creek or two." Liam's neck was a rigid column on the unyielding mantle of his shoulders.

I must've gone slack-jawed, because Liam ran a knuckle under my chin as though to shut my mouth.

"You didn't, right?"

I removed my chin from his fingers. "Spy on Creeks? *No.*"

Car doors slammed shut, making me jump. Liam and I both turned to scan the lot. Lucas, Matt, August, and Cole were walking up from where they'd parked the pickup.

Was it eight already? Had Liam and I spent an hour in his car? The sky was streaked with oranges and pinks, which told me they were early.

"We didn't feel right about you two going in without protection," Matt said as he approached in a pair of black jeans and a long-sleeved T-shirt, both fitting snugly over his broad, ropy limbs.

He'd made even less of an effort to dress up than Liam, which confirmed my earlier worries that I was way overdressed. The boys were like evergreens, and I was like that palm tree I apparently wanted in my dream house. I gripped the tulle, wishing I could transform it into a pair of jeans and a tank top.

Lucas's blue-eyed gaze skipped between Liam and me, as though trying to gauge from our postures where we ranked on the scale of love and hate. The shaggy-haired shifter must've noticed that only billowing smoke remained from our spat, because his features relaxed. Had he been expecting to have to pry my claws out of his Alpha's skin?

August's face was a blank mask, but through the link, I felt his body thrumming with something, something that made him cross his arms, straining the fabric of the dark-olive Henley that matched his eyes.

"Shall we go see what the great Creek Alpha wants?" Lucas gestured to the inn.

Liam turned back toward the revolving doors, but Matt shoved him aside.

"I'll go in first," the blond giant said.

The doors spun, tossing the familiar scent of chimney smoke and potpourri at us, as well as the scent of musky sweat and damp fur. It smelled like the Creek delegation had traveled by paw instead of by foot and tire. Perhaps some had.

Liam went in after Matt, then Lucas. Cole gestured for me to go, so I pressed my fingertips into the cool glass and pushed. I expected noise but was greeted with silence. The place was eerily quiet. No one stood behind the bell desk. No one roamed the hallways. No footfalls echoed on the buffed pine floors.

I'd stopped just outside the revolving doors, so when Cole stepped through, I felt his hand on my back, pressing me a couple of inches to the side so he could fit into the inn without toppling me over. The tether tautened when August came in. I dropped my hand to my navel instinctively, not because it itched, but because touching it seemed to lend me strength. Unlike Cole who'd gone to stand next to his brother, August remained standing at my back, his steady heat pulsing against my bare shoulder blades, battling the goose bumps swarming over my skin.

"This doesn't feel right," Cole said.

The silence rattled my bones.

Lucas sniffed the air. "The place reeks of them."

"I sense heartbeats," Liam said. "Human and—"

There was pounding, scratching, then two wolves lurched out of the living room. Not wolves—*dogs*. Huge black and tawny ones with droopy faces. They stopped in front of the six of us, teeth bared, drool spilling over their floppy jowls.

I backed up, smacking into August's chest. His hands settled on my arms at the exact same place where Liam's had been not too long ago. Instead of bruising like Liam's, August's grip on me was gentle but firm—velvet instead of steel.

I relaxed when I noticed the dogs were hooked onto leashes, leashes that were stretched tight. Footsteps sounded on the hardwood floors, and then a silver-haired man came through the living room doors.

Aidan Michaels.

He reeled in the leashes. "I hope you'll abstain from slaying my new Blood-hounds. I only received them a week ago."

While Cole inched closer to me, Matt and Lucas positioned themselves in front of Liam. August didn't move. Didn't let go of my arms that had started to shake. Not with fear but with pure, unadulterated hatred.

I had no interest in killing the dogs, but their owner . . . I was sure interested in sectioning off one of his arteries and watching him bleed out.

"He can't hurt you," August murmured.

I wasn't afraid of him hurting me. Quite the opposite.

"What are you doing here?" Liam's tone was as cutting as a chainsaw.

"I was just visiting my new acquisition. It's a tad shabby, but the view is splendid. Best thing about the place." His bespectacled navy eyes sought mine through the wall of male bodies.

"Where are your *guests*?" Lucas bit out.

"They went out for a little exercise. Lovely bunch. Very educated and forward-thinking. A nice change from the citizens of Boulder."

"All of them?" Liam asked.

"They're not all sharp as tacks, but—"

Matt cut in. "Liam meant, are all of them out running?"

"Oh, yes. They all went. Even the young'uns." Aidan scratched one of his hounds between the ears. "If you'll follow me, I'll lead you to the festivities."

"You're staying?" Lucas asked.

"Why not? This place is mine now, isn't it?" Aidan swept his gaze over the high-ceilinged foyer.

Tendons shifted in the back of Liam's neck. "Does Mrs. Morgan know you'll be staying?"

Mrs. Morgan? Wasn't Morgan her first name?

Aidan smiled that oily smile of his. "Oh, she does. Now come this way." He gestured toward the living room. "After you."

"You go on ahead, Aidan," Liam said. It was the first time I'd heard him address the old man by his first name. "*We'll* follow *you*."

The hunter's lips curled higher. "I've no rifle on me, Kolane."

"Unless you want me to snap your dogs' necks, you'll walk in front of us," Liam said.

Aidan tapped the flank of the bigger of the two Bloodhounds affectionately. "These two boys could be your cousins."

"We aren't related to dogs," Liam gritted out.

Liam's rising anger was fueling Aidan Michaels's perverted glee.

The old man yanked on the leashes and then turned, leading the way into the living room. Liam turned toward me as though about to say something. His eyes glowed amber with bloodlust, the color intensifying when he caught August's hands on me.

I'd been so absorbed by the sight of Aidan that I'd forgotten August was even holding on to me. I eased out of his grip. No one spoke, making the already uncomfortable moment all the more awkward.

"I can't believe the bastards are out running," Matt finally said.

"It's nothing more than a negotiating technique," Liam muttered. His eyes were slowly shifting back to their normal human hue. Only the rings around his irises remained lit like flames.

I crossed my arms, rubbing my pebbled skin. They'd turned the AC units to their full power.

"Is turning this place into an icebox also a negotiating technique?" I asked.

"Anything that creates discomfort is a technique." He unbuttoned his jacket, as though to offer it to me.

Before he could, I walked off, heels clicking on the hardwood floors. "We'll wait for them on the terrace then."

Matt caught up to me, matching my brusque pace. "Don't separate yourself from the group, Ness."

A new chill swept up my spine at his warning, and then another locked my knees when I stepped into the two-storied living room. Standing right beside the entrance was Lucy, flaming hair coiffed in neat waves, pert smile slicked with red lipstick. She was dressed in a black shift that accentuated all of her curves and the milky paleness of her freckled skin. She proffered a silver platter topped with shot glasses.

"Welcome," she said, the ashen stink of her breath grating me almost as much as her presence.

"Mrs. Clark," Matt said.

"Oh. Just Lucy now. Haven't you heard? As of this afternoon, I am no longer a Clark. The dirt over my son's grave has barely settled, and already, I'm cast out of the family I gave twenty years of my life to." She turned the full power of her icy smile on me. "The Clarks are a fickle bunch."

"Why are you serving at this party, Lucy?" Liam's question shifted my aunt's attention on him.

"Aidan Michaels has just made me director of the inn."

"You accepted a job from your son's killer?" Lucas said. "That's sick."

Aidan, who'd stepped onto the terrace, came back inside, dog-free. Had he set them loose or tied them to the balustrade?

"Now now, Lucas, I didn't kill Everest. But you know that since the killer's in your custody, is he not?"

Aidan Michaels's knowledge of us was truly chilling.

"Just because you didn't get your hands dirty, old man, doesn't mean they aren't filthy as fuck," Lucas shot back.

"It's a real shame you were raised by a pack of wolves, Lucas. An education would've done your speech wonders."

Lucas reeled his arm back, but Cole caught it before Lucas could let his fist fly into Aidan's jaw.

"Jumpy tonight, aren't we?" Aidan nodded to the platter before lifting one of the diminutive glasses. "Why don't you try our welcome drink? It's lovely. Lucy made it herself with rose water distilled from her prized roses."

Just the scent wafting from the glasses had my eyes stinging.

"And what else did you put in there again, my dear?" Aidan asked, tapping his index finger to the flared rim of his shot glass.

"Sillin?" Matt supplied under his breath.

"Vodka and sugar syrup," Lucy said brightly.

"Sillin?" Aidan's eyebrows rose, crinkling his forehead. "Now why would she have used Sillin? It wouldn't have added any flavor to this exquisite drink."

"How do you know the flavor of Sillin?" Liam asked, narrowing his gaze on the hunter.

Aidan thumbed his ear, then pressed his wire-rimmed glasses back up the bridge of his nose even though they hadn't slid down. "When I research something, Liam, I do so thoroughly," he finally said. He raised his glass and waited, but none of us followed his lead. "Your loss." He knocked the clear drink back, then smacked his lips. "Absolutely delightful, just like the woman who concocted it."

Was Aidan Michaels hitting on my aunt—*former* aunt? *Yuck.*

When two spots of color rose to her cheeks, I gagged. I must've done so audibly, because she glared at me, smile gone.

Voices suddenly rose in the foyer.

"I believe more guests have arrived. Shall we go out to greet them, Lucy?"

Aidan took the platter from her hands and offered Lucy his arm. And she took it.

"More guests, and still no host," Matt said, gaze sunk on the darkening forest that swayed beyond the overhanging porch like wet paintbrushes.

Liam tipped his chin toward the terrace, and the boys followed him out. I was still too stunned by what I'd just witnessed to move.

"Ness?" August's voice pierced the gray fog of my thoughts.

I released my elbows, letting my hands drop into the fluffy, itchy tulle. "Jeb can't come. He'll—He'll . . ." I patted my skirt as though to locate a pocket, but I had no pocket just like I had no bag. I hadn't thought I would need to bring anything since my uncle was coming. "Can you call him, August? Tell him not to come." My voice was shrill with nerves. "I don't want him to . . . to see what we just witnessed."

August fished his phone out of his pants pocket and pressed on the screen before lifting it to his ear. As he spoke, I caught sight of a familiar blonde and expelled a breath of relief.

Sarah walked over to me in a shimmery gown that made her look more goddess than wolf. "I heard the Creeks were late."

"You didn't drink the shots, did you?" I whispered urgently.

She nocked a crooked grin onto her glossy lips. "Wouldn't dream of ingesting anything Creep-made." Winking, she threaded her arm through mine and pulled me toward the terrace, but I dug my heels in.

"Did you get him on the phone?" I asked August.

"I did. He'll stay home."

A trickle of relief dripped through me, too little to do away with my gnawing anxiety. "I have such a bad feeling," I murmured to Sarah as we joined the others on the deck.

She squeezed my arm. "It'll be fine."

Even though her voice didn't waver, her optimism did little to reassure me. Perhaps it was because Liam looked as though he was about to snap someone's head off and Lucas hadn't taken a jab at Sarah's appearance as he usually did, even though he'd stared her up and down a couple times. Or perhaps it was because of the matching grim expressions August and the two Rogers brothers wore.

Whatever it was, I braced myself for utter chaos. Better to be pleasantly surprised than surprisingly disappointed.

41

Julian Matz strolled through the living room as though he owned the place, his sister, Nora, hanging from his arm.

"Is your father here?" I asked Sarah.

Surprise, or was it shock, puckered her brow. "My father had a falling-out with my uncle some years ago. He's no longer welcomed to pack gatherings."

"Your parents are divorced?"

"No, but they lead separate lives."

"Oh."

Julian advanced toward us. "Miss Clark, it has been too long." He let go of his sister and picked up my hand, bringing it to his pouty lips, the diamond on his pinky ring glittering wildly. "Much too long." His breath, like his kiss, skated over my knuckles.

I snatched my hand away. I wasn't afraid of Julian, but he still unsettled me. "Good evening, Mr. Matz. Mrs . . ." What was I supposed to call her?

"Matz," Nora supplied. She offered me a smile that gleamed as brightly as the sapphire hoops speared through her earlobes. "Ooh, Robbie and Margaux have arrived. I'll be right back."

She tottered in her sky-high heels toward her son and his wife. Both were dapperly dressed. Unlike my pack. I resembled a Pine more than a Boulder tonight, and that didn't feel right, but it wasn't Sarah's fault. She couldn't have guessed my pack would make no effort.

Once Julian had gone off to greet some more arrivals, I asked, "Why is your mom's last name Matz?"

"Because Dad's not a wolf," Sarah said, as though it were obvious. "Last names are pack names. If you ever married outside the pack, you keep your wolf name, and your kids get your last name. It makes tracing bloodlines easier."

I raised a brow. "Huh."

She rolled her kohl-lined eyes. "Babe, you're such a newb."

Lucas, who was standing beside us, smirked.

"What are you smirking about, Mason?" Sarah shot him a little glare. It was more playful than vicious though. She was probably stockpiling the vicious ones for when the Creeks arrived.

"Your hair. What's wrong with it?"

Color rose to her cheeks. "I straightened it."

I became distracted by Julian and Liam walking toward one end of the terrace, heads bent in conversation, two burly Pines in tow. Matt and Cole strode closer too, dividing their attention between Liam and Julian's bodyguards. I watched the two Alphas for a long moment, wondering what they could be discussing, hoping they had a strategy to get us out of here safely if the Creeks attacked or set fire to the inn.

My heart juddered. Where had that contemplation even come from? From the logs burning in the massive stone fireplace beyond the sliding glass doors? I glanced toward the staircase at the side of the terrace. It was wide, but if everyone suddenly started running for it, it would clog up. I peered over the railing. I'd survive the two-story fall, but it would surely break some of my bones.

"What are you thinking about?" August asked, stealing me out of my dire musings.

He'd gone over to see his father and the elders but had come back without my noticing and was now standing with his hip propped against the wooden handrail and his arms crossed. I needed to be more aware of my surroundings.

"Fire," I whispered, gripping the smooth log.

He cocked up a dark brow.

"What if they're not here because they want to set fire to the inn?" I murmured.

I wanted August to tell me that was crazy-talk, that they'd come in peace, but he didn't.

"We'll jump and make a run for it," he said.

I swallowed.

"I won't let anything happen to you, kid." He tendered me a strained smile.

Kid? I'd take Dimples over kid any day. I clutched my elbows and turned to face the forest.

"Ness?" August asked.

Why did it even bother me that he thought of me as a kid? I made no sense to myself. It was the link. The link was screwing with my emotions.

I didn't say anything, just concentrated on the woods.

And that's when I heard them.

The distant sound of hearts pounding in unison, of paws stamping the earth.

August had sensed them, too. "They're here," he whispered.

Every single Pine and Boulder had sensed them because every face turned toward the woods.

42

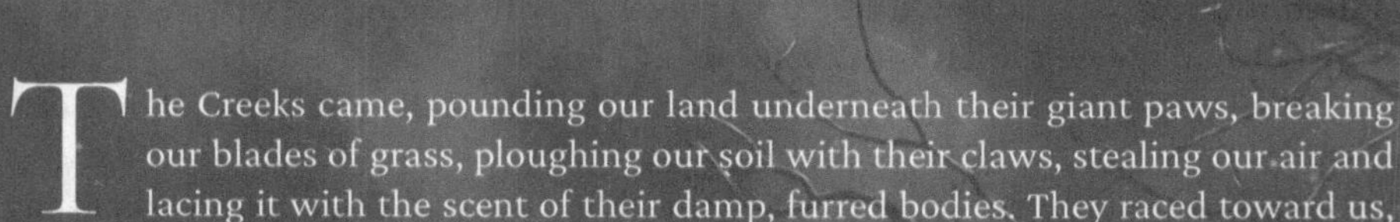

The Creeks came, pounding our land underneath their giant paws, breaking our blades of grass, ploughing our soil with their claws, stealing our air and lacing it with the scent of their damp, furred bodies. They raced toward us, moving like columns of soldiers with a wolf larger than all the others up front.

Their Alpha.

Morgan.

The light-brown wolf led her wolves toward us with a determination that made me step back from the railing, that made many of us retreat from the balustrade.

Silly since there was no way her shifters could leap onto it.

When she stopped and let out a long howl, the fine hair on my arms thickened.

No one shift, Liam ordered.

My skin felt uncomfortably tight, but I reined my wolf back.

Julian must've given the same order to his pack, because everyone stayed in skin.

On the great expanse of grass below us, the Creeks began to rise onto two legs, their fur vanishing into human pores, their pointed ears migrating to the sides of their faces, their muzzles shrinking into noses. Breasts developed on certain bodies, and chest hair on others. The smaller bodies had no body hair and no breasts.

I moved my attention off the sea of naked bodies and onto the woman at the helm. Her hair was short like a man's, but her face was thin and feminine, just like the rest of her body. She had muscle, but nothing like the bulk of some of the wolves crowding her. I kept my gaze fixed to their faces, or attempted to. It was a feat when appendages swung each time someone so much as twitched. Clearly, the Creeks weren't prudes . . .

I wondered if anyone else was bothered by their nudity. Some Pines were grimacing, but I didn't think it was for the same reason. I checked Liam's face. What was he thinking? How I wished he would speak to us through the mind link, because I wasn't sure how to take the display beneath the balustrade. His features were hard-set, his gaze amber and glowing, his shoulders pulled tight.

Julian spoke, breaking the thick silence, "You have accomplished a great feat tonight, dearest Cassandra."

So Morgan was her last name.

Small wrinkles bracketed the Alpha's pale eyes as she carefully examined the rows of faces looking down at her.

"You have accomplished the feat of making me feel overdressed." Julian guffawed, and so did many other Pines.

With bated breath, I scrutinized Cassandra's face, waiting on her reaction to Julian's comments. When her lips bent with a smile, a collective exhale of breaths whooshed around me.

"I apologize, Julian," she said, her voice making me blink and blink.

She skimmed the row of faces again until she found mine.

Until her eyes settled on *mine*.

"I've heard great things about the woods in these parts." She smiled, baring shiny teeth that overlapped.

Heart hurtling against my ribs, I backed up, and one of my heels caught. I wind-milled my arms. Lucas caught me before I could fall.

After steadying me, he muttered, "Can you let a Pine wipe out first?"

Don't show fear, Ness, Liam said through our mind link.

How could I not show fear?

I gaped at him, and then I gaped at all of the Pines and Boulders who'd turned to look at me, and then finally I gaped back down at the Creek Alpha.

Aidan Michaels crossed the lawn, coming to a stop next to her, and then, like her, he smiled up at me.

43

"What is it?" August asked, the only person who was still staring at me. Everyone else was peering downward as Cassandra pressed her cheek into Aidan Michaels's, as though marking him, as though he were a wolf instead of a hunter.

August stepped in front of me, blocking my view of the Creeks so I would focus on him. "Ness? Why are you so freaked out?"

I blinked up at him. "Cassandra . . . she's . . . I . . ."

He placed a hand on my shoulder, leaking warmth into my frozen skin, not enough to thaw me out of my stupor though. "What is Cassandra?"

"Her voice," I whispered.

"What about her voice?"

"*IknowitIknowher.*" I whipped the words out so fast they blended into one another.

He frowned. "How?"

"She's . . . she's the woman who . . . who operates . . . Red Creek Escorts. Called herself . . . Sandra." I slammed the back of my hand over my mouth. "Oh my God. I'm going to be sick."

"Shh." He pulled me into his chest while I dry-heaved.

Thankfully my lunch didn't come up. Just my anxieties. They rose and rose like steam from a pressure cooker. I was going to blow. I pressed away from August and rushed back to the guardrail.

"You!" I yelled at her, at Aidan, my voice ringing through the night, quieting all the others.

Gasps arose.

"Hi, Candy."

"Candy?" Sarah echoed.

"Probably some Creek-way of saying sweetie," the girl next to her said.

For a long moment, the woman I'd come to know as Sandra stared at me, and I stared back at her, and the rest of the world faded around us.

Had she manipulated Everest into working for her the same way she'd manipulated me into going on a date with Aidan? I turned my searing gaze onto Aidan, who was thumbing his ear. What connection existed between the hunter and the Alpha?

"Get dressed!" the Creek Alpha bellowed, shattering the silence.

"What was that about?" Liam asked me.

I was still too rattled to talk, so I let August explain.

The Creeks poured past her, trickling into the inn by the doors beneath the terrace, the ones that led to the pool. A moment later, the first clothed ones reemerged. One of them, a young girl with hair the color of Cassandra's fur, returned toward the Creek Alpha, brandishing a light-blue shift, which Cassandra pulled over her head. It settled shapelessly above the Alpha's ankles.

"Thank you, Lori."

Lori craned her neck to look at us. Her face was thin like Cassandra's, eyebrows thick and curved like the Alpha's. I bet they were related. Mother and daughter perhaps? I wished I'd studied the Creeks. It would've spared me the shock of finding out that I'd been casually conversing with their Alpha.

Cassandra Morgan. I shivered.

She'd barely even bothered to disguise her identity. Had she wanted me to figure it out? Both women and Aidan started toward the terrace stairs, making their unhurried way onto the deck.

Liam and Julian waded through the throng of Pines and Boulders, positioning themselves in front of their packs.

"Cassandra," Julian said.

"Julian." She didn't smile at him. She turned toward Liam, looked him up and down as though sizing him up. She was slightly shorter than he was, but that could've been because she was barefoot, whereas he wore boots. "Your resemblance to Heath is simply alarming." She didn't smile at him either.

Tendons shifted like windblown branches in the back of Liam's neck, the only part of him I could see from my vantage point.

Lori, who was standing just behind her Alpha, regarded Liam, but unlike her Alpha, she seemed to like what she saw because her pink lips lilted into a seductive smile.

"Aidan Michaels abhors wolves, Cassandra," Julian said, just as more of her pack walked up the porch steps, creating a thick wall behind Cassandra.

"You must be mistaken," she said, wrapping one of her hands around Aidan's wrist. "Aidan's a great animal lover."

"He might love dogs and his fellow rats, but he has no love for wolves," Liam said.

"Aidan!" She released his wrist to clap a hand over her chest. "What am I hearin'?"

A smile tugged at Aidan's thin lips. A matching one clung to the lips of many a Creek.

I stepped around Sarah and the girl from her pack to better see the Alphas, but something tugged on me, stopping me from moving any closer. I looked around me, wondering who'd grabbed onto my dress, but no one had. When I met August's green gaze, I realized it wasn't a hand that had held me back, but a tether. He shook his head, as though warning me from going closer. I bit my lip, turning back toward the Alphas.

"Grandma's bones must be rattlin' around in her grave," Cassandra said.

I frowned.

"Why would your grandmother's bones be *rattlin'*?" Julian asked, accenting the last word to match her diction.

Cassandra smiled. "'Cause Grandma was staunchly opposed to wolves hatin' their own."

I inhaled so fast white dots danced on the edge of my vision. Was she saying Aidan Michaels was a . . . a—

Julian gasped. "Aidan Michaels is a wolf?"

"Yes." Cassandra cast Aidan an affectionate glance. "My cousin."

No one spoke, but a couple of the Creeks snickered.

"He doesn't smell like a wolf," Liam said.

She stuck her nose in the crook of Aidan's neck. "It's slight, I'll admit. The Sillin he's been ingestin' during all the years he's lived amongst you has weakened his scent."

Aidan Michaels is one of us.

It made absolutely no sense. Why would he threaten to reveal the existence of werewolves to the public if he was one himself?

Everyone turned to me, and I realized I'd spoken this out loud. I was so shocked I didn't even flinch from the onslaught of attention.

"It enhanced my cover story," Aidan said.

"So you don't have files on us?" I asked.

"Oh, I have files on each one of you, or rather Sandy does."

"But not your lawyers?"

He took off his wire-rimmed glasses and cleaned them on the hem of his blue dress shirt, then placed them back on his nose and peered at me through them. "I know what you're getting at, Miss Clark. You're thinking nothing's standing in your way of killing me."

I held his gaze. "Isn't *a life for a life* the law of all packs? Or do the Creeks play by different rules?"

Cassandra was the one to answer me. "We play by the same rules, Ness, but I strongly discourage you from killin' my cousin."

"Why is that, Mrs. Morgan?"

"'Cause then this whole terrace would turn into a bloodbath, and we honest to goodness came in peace."

"But he killed my father."

"And Julian Matz killed mine!" Her voice rang out shrilly over the terrace. "Yet you don't see me lungin' for his neck. We've all lost people, Ness. Which is the reason

I'm here. Because I think it's time we unite instead of fight. But first, I'd really appreciate seein' my son."

"He's indisposed tonight, but you'll see him in the morning," Liam said.

She glared at him a long moment. "He better be alive and well, Kolane."

"He's alive." Liam said nothing about his condition.

She turned her attention to her cousin. "Aidan, you said there would be food."

Aidan clapped, looking through the crowd until his gaze set on Lucy's. He nodded to her, and she scurried inside. I didn't have time to see her expression, see if she shared my shock in learning that the hunter was a wolf. Did anyone have suspicions about him, or had he really flown underneath every single Boulder and Pine's radar?

44

Servers spilled onto the terrace, as well as music. I recognized Emmy and Skylar but not the others. They weaved through the mismatched crowd, platters bobbing from their fingertips. Had they heard anything that had been said? Did they know what we were? Emmy caught my eye, but then her gaze lowered to the tray of mini sandwiches in her hands, her face uncharacteristically pale.

She'd heard.

She knew.

Would they tell more people? Or had Aidan Michaels somehow bought their silence?

"What a fucking fuck-fest," Lucas muttered behind me.

"Couldn't agree with you more, Mason," Sarah said.

"*You're* agreeing with *me*? Shit, can I get that in writing?"

"Shut the hell up."

Their banter unfortunately didn't ease my stress. I wondered if it eased theirs?

When Cassandra started toward me, I stood my ground even though I wanted to leap over the railing and run far away from the inn, from Boulder, from this woman who was a stranger, and yet who wasn't.

But I wanted answers. And I sensed she had many of them.

Stay calm, Liam whispered through the mind link, making his way back to me. **Whatever she says, stay calm.**

That was easy for him to say, harder for me to do. She'd *manipulated* me. I liked being manipulated as much as I liked slicing my finger on a kitchen knife.

Suddenly, Cassandra was standing right in front of me. She was so tall that even in my heels I had to tip my head up. I hated having to tip my head up to her.

"I understand why your pack's been going through such an upheaval since your return."

I disregarded her bizarre compliment. If that's what it was. "Was it you who hacked my phone?"

"Not me personally."

"But someone from your pack?"

"We tried to warn Everest ourselves, but he didn't believe us. We were just trying to help him."

"You mean, get him off your land before the Boulders arrived and realized your connection to him."

When her gaze grinded into mine, I realized I'd struck a nerve. Well, I was about to strike a whole bunch more, because I wasn't done with her.

"Whose idea was the escort agency, *Sandra*?" My voice was as tight as my spine. "Everest's or yours?"

She cocked her head to the side, lips pursed. She was older than I'd assumed. Fifty, sixty perhaps. Tiny wrinkles ringed her mouth. What held my attention, though, was the odd bluish tinge to her lips—a recent bruise or a strange birthmark? Or maybe she was chilly. The nippiness in the air definitely made me regret not having taken a jacket.

"It was my idea," she said.

I blew out a relieved breath. "Why?"

"To get insight into other packs."

"To spy, then?"

She wrinkled her pert nose. "I'm not a fan of the word *spy*."

"Would you rather I say *snoop*?" My voice crackled with animosity.

She snapped her head straight. "Aren't you a little spitfire?"

"How did you reel Everest into your opportunistic scheme?"

"I didn't. Becca did. The silly girl fell in love." She took the glass of water someone tendered her way—Lori.

I gave the tall woman beside Cassandra a cursory once-over. All of her was thin and narrow, from her face to her body.

"Thank you, sweet thing." Cassandra wrapped fingers topped with lacquered burgundy nails filed to a dull point around the glass and tipped it to her bluish lips. "Where was I?"

"Becca and Everest fell in love," I supplied curtly.

"Right. Becca convinced me Everest was unhappy with the Boulders." She slanted her eyes to Liam. "That he could be an asset. So we talked, and I brought him on."

Liam's body had hardened next to mine as though he were made entirely of bones.

"Everest wanted to have Heath demoted and asked if I had anythin' on him he could use. Even though Aidan had supplied me with somethin' your cousin could've used"—her gaze slid back to me—"my goal wasn't to instigate a war between the packs. I told him I'd let him use the girls to dig up his own dirt."

Even though Liam didn't react verbally or physically, I sensed the frenzied beat of his heart inside of mine. All of the pack seemed to sense it, because suddenly Frank was wrapping his fingers around Liam's wrist, and Lucas had squeezed in between Liam and me.

Lori handed Cassandra a plate laden with food and took away her glass of water.

"And whose idea was it to use me as an escort?" I asked.

Cassandra devoured a pig-in-a-blanket in a single bite, then made another vanish just as swiftly. "His. But I seconded it. You were vengeful and desirous of closure. I believed meetin' with Heath would bring you closure."

In a way, it had, but I would never ever admit this. I kept my expression blank. The air was so rife with tension that I expected some of the Boulders to shift, but everyone remained in skin.

"Why did you send me to meet Aidan?" He wasn't by her side and he wasn't in the crowd. "So I could get closure for my father's death?"

"No. I did that so that *he* could get closure. Killing your father was a mistake. A terrible one. He'd been aimin' for Heath, but I believe you already know that."

"Doesn't erase what he did."

"No, it doesn't. Except he was tryin' to help your father, Ness."

"What are you talking about?"

"I'm talkin' about something your Alpha should explain."

She started to turn away, but I called her back. "Mrs. Morgan, why did you have Everest killed?"

"I didn't have Everest killed. I had him followed."

"Having him followed got him killed."

"Extorting money from my pack got him killed," she lobbed back. "Your cousin was a thief. He said he had access to Sillin, made us pay a substantial deposit for it, and then he never delivered."

My heart was beating double-time. "What did you need Sillin for?"

She made a sort of guttural sound, halfway between a growl and a sigh. "For injuries. For travel. For my cousin—although now he won't be needin' it anymore. And before you go on assumin' anything, we had *no* intention of using it as a weapon."

Like I'd ever believe that . . .

She shook her head. "An Alpha's responsibility is to protect the pack at any costs. At least, that's what an Alpha *should* do. May I suggest that before you go judgin' me and mine, you take a good look at your own Alpha."

Liam's eyes glowed as bright as the flames I'd imagined licking up the sides of the inn.

With a skein of Creeks trailing her, she finally took off toward the living room but paused by the sliding door, her blue sheath flapping in the gentle breeze. "Oh, and, Candy, I'll be here for several days. We still have so much to discuss, you and I, so don't be a stranger." She flicked her fingers in a little wave, then went to take a seat on one of the couches inside.

Her wolves milled around her, quietly ferrying plates to and from the buffet, gazes roving over us in both curiosity and caution.

The hush that draped over all three packs raised the hairs on the nape of my neck.

"Liam?" I whispered.

He looked everywhere but at my face.

My stomach felt as though a swarm of moths were flapping their little wings against its lining.

"What was Morgan talking about, Kolane?" August asked.

"None of your fucking business, Watt," Liam snapped.

"If it has to do with Ness, it is my fucking business."

Without turning around, I said, "No, August. I know you consider me like a sister, but I'm not. So it's not your business. This is between Liam and me."

My words stung August. I sensed it in the tremor that crossed through the tether. As he backed away, it vibrated like a flicked clothes string. He didn't leave the inn, just put distance between us. A lot of it.

I accorded Liam my full attention. "I'm listening."

A nerve ticked in his temple and another in his jaw.

When he still didn't speak, I asked, "Would you rather I ask Aidan Michaels to enlighten me?"

"A couple days before he was shot, your father challenged mine for Alpha," Liam said roughly. "My father said he would kill him, and Aidan caught it with one of the many bugs he'd planted in our homes. After Callum died, when we came for Aidan, the bastard played back the recording. Said he'd play it for the entire pack. Even though Dad didn't shoot Callum, it made him look guilty. That's why your father's death wasn't avenged."

The music stopped, replaced by a screechy recording. A voice risen from the dead boomed across the terrace.

"The nerve of Clark! He already stole my mate. And now he wants my pack?" Heath sounded crazed. *"The fucking nerve of him."*

Something shattered. Heath had probably lobbed one of his crystal highballs into a wall. I could just imagine the whiskey dripping down the wooden pillar in his cushy home.

"Why do you think he challenged you?" Liam's fifteen-year-old voice rang across the deathly quiet porch.

"To bring his bastard child into the pack. He doesn't get that she's not his kid. That she can't fucking be his kid. Boulders don't have girls!" Heath bellowed a couple expletives that had Frank shutting his eyes. *"The Clarks are parasites, Liam. They suck up the resources of the pack and bring nothing but fucking problems in return."*

For a moment, no sound came out of the speakers, and I thought Aidan or whoever was broadcasting the recording had pressed pause. I looked at Liam, but he stared at the weathered teak slats beneath our feet.

"I just had a fucking fantastic idea." Heath's voice exploded over the terrace. *"I'll kill him before he publicly challenges me."*

A pause, then: *"If you make it look like a hunting accident"*—Liam sounded so cool and collected, the complete antithesis of his dad—*"you can blame that creepy-ass hunter so we can finally get rid of him."*

There was a click. It was probably the recording, but it felt like my heart. Like an explosion had detonated in the marrow of my bones, surged into my muscles, and vibrated through my flesh, coating every inch of me in goose bumps. They cascaded over my skin in icy waves.

"I didn't even know my father wanted to be Alpha," I whispered, even though that was far *far* from the worst part of what I'd just heard. Of what everyone had just heard.

Liam lifted his face, pain etched inside each one of his features.

I rolled my fingers into such tight fists that my nails carved up my palms. I had a strong urge to hit him. In the heart. Instead, I wiped my mouth on my forearm in an attempt to erase every kiss we'd ever shared.

He dragged a hand through his dark hair, and a lock flopped into his eyes. "I was fifteen, Ness. A kid. I had no idea what I was saying."

"Is that really your excuse?" My voice rang inside my ears.

"I just wanted Aidan gone. Not your father—"

"And yet you didn't tell your father not to kill mine."

Sarah tried to touch my arm, but I whipped it out of her reach and stepped back until my tailbone smacked into the guardrail.

"Ness . . ." Liam started.

I'd pledged myself to a man who'd been on board with eliminating my father. "You are Heath's son."

Liam shut his eyes as though I'd taken a swing at him.

"I don't want you as my Alpha." I gripped the handrail behind my back for support. "How do I break our link?"

His eyes snapped open, then grew wide.

"You can't break the Alpha link," Frank said, forehead grooved with so many wrinkles that it seemed as though the evening had added years to his face. "The only thing you can do is move away until you don't feel the pull of the pack."

I stared at the elder, then at the shifters surrounding us, at the Creek Alpha who was sitting with her wolves in the living room, watching me through the open glass doors, at Sarah whose mouth gaped, at Lucas and Matt and Cole who all wore matching looks of regret, and finally at August. He was the only one who didn't stare back. His eyes were like twin rifles set on the back of Liam's head.

"I'll leave, then." I pressed off the balustrade and walked past Liam, who put his hand on my arm. "Don't you *dare* touch me." I snatched my arm away, my icy shock replaced by a searing wrath.

"I'm sorry," he murmured as I passed by him.

I whirled. "No, you're not. You're just sorry I found out."

Liam shook his head. "They were just words. We never ended up hurting him. Aidan pulled that trigger. We didn't."

"Lucky for you, huh? Lucky for you he made a mistake!" I backed away before stalking off, speeding through the living room in my stupid heels, clutching my stupid dress. I walked toward the bell desk to phone my uncle.

As I dialed his number, Aidan strolled out of the back office, a USB key in his hand

—probably the vessel containing the malicious conversation. I dropped the phone, and it clattered at my feet, the battery flying out of the handheld device.

"Should've heeded my note," he said.

"What note?" I pressed a hand against my chest as though to keep my heart from dropping like the phone.

"The one I tied to the bicycle, which I had delivered to the inn."

"You shot my father and your ex-wife. You really thought I would stop by for tea?"

"I'm not a fan of tea. I'd have served something fizzy."

I arced my hand in the air in frustration. "Oh, you know what I mean!"

He squeezed an oily smile onto his lips.

I crouched to grab the phone and then attempted to fit the battery back inside, but my hands were shaking.

"Want some help?" He extended his hand.

"No." After several botched attempts, I jammed the battery back in. While the phone powered up, I said, "I know killing my father was a mistake, that you were aiming for Heath. Why?"

"I had my own vendetta toward him. He took something I loved."

I hadn't considered Aidan Michaels capable of love, but I also hadn't considered he could be a werewolf.

"The recording came in handy when Heath came to avenge your father's death. Should've seen how astonished he was when I played it back for him." He flashed me a smile that made my skin crawl.

Aidan Michaels was a monster. Just like Heath Kolane. Where Heath raped women, Aidan shot them.

"Even though you didn't mean to kill my father, it was still your finger on that trigger."

"Is that a threat, little girl?"

"Maybe it is."

"I'd be very careful doling out threats. You might be an orphan, but there are still people you care about . . ."

My stomach curled onto itself at his menace. I backed away from him, clutching the phone to my chest. Keeping one eye on the Creek wolf, I tried to dial Jeb's number from memory, but an automated message kept telling me I'd entered the wrong number. *Ugh.*

"Need a ride home, Ness?" Aidan asked.

"Like I'd ever let you drive me anywhere."

"Oh, I would've phoned up my driver. I have better things to do with my evening. Better yet, you could use the bicycle I sent back. Here, let me get you the key to the garage."

Footsteps pounded the foyer floor, and then a gruff voice said, "She won't be needing that key."

45

"You don't need to take me home, August," I said.

"You're right. I don't, but I was leaving. If you don't want a ride, by all means, make your own way home." He paused by the entrance of the inn, waiting for me to decide.

I all but flung the phone at Aidan Michaels and raced to the revolving doors As soon as we were outside, I said, "I'll kill that man someday."

August glanced at me, eyes bathed in shadows, shadows I'd put there. Not all of them, perhaps, but some. We didn't talk as we walked to his pickup, and we didn't talk as he drove me back home. When we reached my street, August finally spoke.

"You're not serious about leaving Boulder, are you?"

"I am."

"You're still a minor."

I stared up at the darkened apartment. Was my uncle already sleeping?

"Jeb will understand that I can't stay in Boulder. He'll understand that I can't obey a man I . . . I can't trust."

"You don't have to leave. Liam won't harm you."

"I know Liam isn't that spiteful fifteen-year-old boy, but every time I'll look at him, I'll remember that he was complicit in killing my father." I touched the door handle. "Besides, my leaving will benefit you."

"How?" he asked sharply. "How will it benefit me?"

I quirked an eyebrow. "Um. Did tonight's gathering make you forget about the mating link?"

"The mating link doesn't bother me, Ness."

"How can it not?"

"Does it bother you?"

"No, but I've sworn off men." I raised a smile I wasn't really feeling. Mom used to say that if you smiled in spite of being down, your emotions would eventually catch up with your face. "Anyway, August Watt, I promise I'll write this time."

He stared fixedly ahead of him. I was tempted to lean over and plant a kiss on his cheek but chickened out. I got out of the car and shut the door, then climbed the steps. The pickup didn't pull away. August was probably waiting for me to go inside. A gentleman till the very end . . .

I rang the doorbell. Seconds passed. When a minute went by, I rang the doorbell again but heard no footsteps. Was my uncle not home?

Frowning, I went back down the stairs and knuckled the passenger window. August powered it down. His phone was already ringing, and then my uncle's voice came on the speakerphone.

"Yes, August?"

"Ness was trying to get home, but she doesn't have her keys."

"I'm at Headquarters, watching over our asset with Derek and his son. If you swing by, I can give you the key."

I bit my lip. "What time will you be home?"

"I won't. I don't want to risk those bastard Creeks freeing Everest's murderer." His desire for vengeance palpitated through the phone.

"Okay, we'll figure something out," August said.

When he hung up, I said, "I can—" I had been about to say drive myself there and back, but Jeb had taken the van. *Shoot*. I was stranded. "Actually, do you mind giving me a ride?"

He nodded, and I got back inside.

Pulling away from the curb, he said, "I don't like the idea of you sleeping here all by yourself. Not with the Creeks in town."

"I lived six months on my own in a real crappy neighborhood."

"You weren't on my watch then."

"I'm not on your watch now either."

"Ness," he sighed. "Please give me a break tonight."

I nibbled on my lip and relented. "What did you have in mind?"

"You can stay with me tonight."

"Um." The seatbelt felt like it was cutting off my breath. I hooked my thumbs underneath the taut fabric and tugged.

"I'll sleep on the couch," he said.

Yeah. But his place was one big open space. Taking the couch wouldn't give either of us much privacy. "I could go to Frank's—"

"He might not get home until late." He'd already started driving toward the warehouse.

I sensed reminding him that Evelyn would be there would do little to change the course of my evening. "Fine, but I'll take the couch."

"The bed's more comfortable."

"It's your bed."

"It's also my couch."

A ghost of a smile made its way to my lips.

"Do you know how many girls would love to be in your shoes right now?"

"My shoes are starting to hurt my feet, so I don't think many."

He side-eyed me, and although there wasn't much light, his eyes seemed greener. "There's the Ness Clark I know and adore."

"Shut up."

He chuckled softly, and it smoothed the spiny ridges of this strange night.

46

After feasting on leftover lasagna, I showered and changed into one of his T-shirts that smelled so strongly of him it made my head spin. Did I also smell like sandalwood and sawdust now? Or did August smell like me? Or maybe our scents had mixed and created a completely different aroma.

I asked him as I helped him pull a sheet over the couch.

His freckles seemed to darken at my question, which of course prompted me to ask, "What?"

He spent an extra-long time tucking the sheet under the seat cushions before straightening up and rubbing the back of his neck. "They meant that we smelled like we"—he snatched the coverlet from the coffee table and unfolded it—"like we'd had sex."

"Oh." I wrinkled my nose. "So . . . sweaty?"

A bark of laughter burst out of him.

I tossed the pillow I'd been stuffing in a pillowcase at him. He caught it and finished my half-ass job.

"What did I say now?" I asked, arching an eyebrow.

"What sort of strenuous sex have you been having?" He was still grinning.

I dragged my hand through my hair. "I, um . . . haven't."

"Never?" His grin settled into a faint smile.

I was certain I was beet-red.

He simply said, "Huh," which was really worse than not saying anything at all. "I didn't mean to make you feel embarrassed."

"You didn't. It's just a really weird conversation to be having." I straightened the coverlet he'd tossed over the couch. "On the upside, I don't know what I'm missing." I sat down, the T-shirt with the small Watt logo riding up. I tugged on the hem. "I know you said you got used to the mating link, but you know what you're missing, so it must suck."

His Adam's apple bobbed. "I've had so much on my mind lately between Mom and the pack and work that I haven't had much time to dwell on it."

"Apparently men think about sex every seven seconds."

He snorted. "Is that so?"

I leaned over and flicked his arm.

He shook his head, but his grin increased. "You're really going to keep that up?"

"Until I leave."

That zapped the smile right off his face. He sat down next to me, his weight dipping the couch. "You shouldn't have to leave again. It's not good for your body."

"It wouldn't be good for my mind to stick around. The day Liam's no longer Alpha—"

"Could be decades from now."

"—I'll come back." I stuck my hands between my knees and squeezed them.

"Ness . . ."

"Let's not talk about it anymore, okay? I'm really tired."

Sighing, he wrapped an arm around my shoulders, dragged me into his body, and kissed my temple. I closed my eyes, enjoying the proximity of him, the smell of him. Enjoying it too much.

Another reason I needed to leave . . .

I had feelings that weren't sisterly at all toward August, and that would just make things weird between us in the coming months.

I ducked out from underneath his arm. "Mind if I turn off the lights?"

"Go right ahead."

I got up from the couch and walked over to his front door. I touched the little panel and then returned to the couch. Moonlight filtered in through the open window, but even without moonlight, I could see well in the dark. Probably not as sharply as a real wolf, but more sharply than a human. This was how I saw the great lump sprawled on the couch.

"Take the bed, Ness."

"But it's your bed."

"Didn't we just have this conversation?"

"Fine." I padded toward the ladder and climbed up to the mezzanine, then crawled over the giant bed and slipped underneath the thick comforter. I wasn't sure I'd be able to sleep. Every time I closed my eyes, I heard the recording again.

And again.

If you make it look like a hunting accident, you can blame the hunter.

I kept my eyes open until the darkness turned a bit brighter.

A bit greener.

A bit bluer.

And I was running.

Next to a big black wolf with smiling silver eyes. *You think you can catch that squirrel, baby girl?*

I darted after the fluffy rodent that spiraled up the trunk of a pine and snatched it right off the tree. *Too easy, Dad.*

Snap his neck quick. You don't want it to suffer.

A second later, the squirrel stopped moving. We feasted on the squirrel, blood and gore dripping from our noses. Well, mostly from mine.

My father was watching on, eyes shining with pride. Suddenly, he whipped his head to the side, ears pricked up, and whirled around, muscles coiled to leap. *Ness, run!*

We didn't have time to run.

A bullet whizzed through the inert air and buried itself into his pelt with a pop. He faltered and tumbled, and blood sprayed out of him, covering my face, mixing with the squirrel's blood.

I whimpered and whimpered, my lament disseminating through the woods like torn dandelion florets.

Suddenly, a heavy weight pinned me to the supple ground, and I flailed, clawing my attacker, trying to get him off me, snarling.

"Ness, wake up! It's just me."

My lids flew open. August was straddling me, my wrists cuffed in his hands. A line of blood seeped out of a thin gash right beneath his eye.

I gasped. "Your face!"

"My face is fine."

"You're bleeding." I struggled to free my wrists from the vice of his hands. He let go, and I hovered my fingertips over the strip of skin I'd removed. I didn't think touching the cut would staunch the reddened flow, so I wiggled out from underneath him, and then once I was sitting up, I tugged the hem of my T-shirt up to the wound.

"Shoot. I'm so sorry."

"It's okay." He shut his eye as I applied pressure.

The blood reminded me of my father's. Except there had been so much more in that forest.

I shuddered and shut my lids.

Large, warm hands clamped my cold cheeks. "Look at me."

I did.

"It was a nightmare. You're awake now. You're safe."

I pulled my bottom lip into my mouth as I lowered the fabric to peer at the torn flesh. The hairline cut was already sealing. "I didn't get you anywhere else, did I?"

He smiled. "Not for lack of trying." He sat back on his heels, his smile flickering as his gaze dropped to the inches of bare skin between the band of my black underwear and the bunched-up cotton T-shirt I was still holding.

I released the hem, and it fluttered back down.

Palming his cropped hair, August turned to get off the bed, but I reached out and caught his elbow.

"Can you stay with me? Please?" I felt incredibly childish for asking. "Just until I fall back asleep?"

Several seconds slipped by before he gave a nod so heavy it almost made me regret asking. I lay back down and tucked my hands underneath the pillow.

"I'll try not to attack you again," I said, pressing my cheek into the creased fabric that was damp with tears or sweat—perhaps both.

I watched as August attempted to get comfortable beside me. He didn't venture under the comforter. His long legs ensconced in a pair of gray sweats spanned the entire length of the mattress.

"Did I steal your side of the bed?" I asked as he threw one of his arms over his head.

He was sprawled on his back, his T-shirt riding up, revealing taut brown skin dusted with a trail of dark hair. I snapped my eyes closed, but the image was already seared behind my retinas and was doing strange things to my stomach . . . And lower. I squeezed my thighs and flipped over.

"I usually take up the entire thing," he said.

I slid to the edge of the mattress to make myself smaller.

"What are you doing?"

"Trying to give you more space."

And myself.

I needed more space.

He grunted.

I didn't flick him; I didn't dare touch him. But he touched me. He dragged me back toward the center of the bed. Except his hands were nowhere near my body.

"How did you do that?" I asked, part enthralled, part freaked out. Controlling another person's movements without touching them resided in a realm of magic I just couldn't wrap my mind around. *And yes, I know . . . I could transform into a werewolf.*

"I pulled on the rope connecting us."

My navel still pulsated. "Can you teach me how to do it?" Not that I'd have much use for the ability once I was gone . . .

"You have to focus your mind on that rope. Visualize it. For me it's blue and shiny. Once you can *see* it, you contract your stomach, and it reels it in. That's how I do it, anyway. Maybe for you it's different."

"Can I try?"

He nodded.

My brow puckered as I concentrated. I saw the rope. It wasn't blue but it was shiny. I wrapped my mind around it and sucked in my stomach. I felt a tightening, but August's body didn't even budge an inch.

"I'm bigger and heavier than you."

I tried again. Failed again. "Can you feel it at least?"

"Yes." He smiled. "It tickles."

"You can haul my body over several feet, but when I do it, it tickles? Damn. That's unfair."

He turned up the force of his smile but winced when it tugged on the flesh I'd clawed. I reached out and ran my thumb over the cut, and his breath caught.

"Does it sting?" I asked.

"I'm fine, Ness." He dragged my hand away from his face.

Our heads were so close I could see the shape of each one of his freckles. I remembered trying to map out constellations on his skin when I was a kid. I remembered succeeding, although I didn't remember the names of the ones I'd found.

"What are you thinking about?" His voice was a gravelly whisper.

"I was trying to remember which constellations I'd matched to your freckles."

"Cassiopeia. You were convinced this"—he took the index finger of the hand he was still holding, set the tip of it on his injured cheek, and dragged it down, then straight, then down again, and finally up—"was Cassiopeia."

His warm breaths hit my nose, and yet it was my stomach that felt warmer, not my face. I dropped my eyes to his mouth, wondering what it would feel like to kiss him. His breathing hitched as though he could read my train of thoughts, as though he could sense it through our link. Perhaps he could.

I slid the finger he still gripped out of his hold and glided the tip across the hard plane of his cheek, over the dark stubble of his jaw, down the side of his strong neck. I watched my index's path as I traced the edge of his body, as my finger rounded his broad shoulder and dipped along his carved bicep. When my finger met bare skin, his flesh pebbled.

I kept waiting for him to put a stop to my exploration. I kept waiting for him to ask me what had gotten into me, but he stayed silent, allowing me access to his sinful form. I outlined the sharp edge of his elbow, then drew a straight line down the inside of his forearm, where the skin was the softest, stopping when I reached the center of his palm.

Only then did I dare look up into those mossy eyes that had enchanted me my entire childhood. His pupils pulsed, devoured his irises. I inched closer to him until my lips were aligned with the trail of dried blood on his cheek. I pressed my mouth to his skin and darted my tongue out to lick away the coppery smear. Never in a million years would I have imagined licking August's face. Perhaps in fur, but not in skin. In fur, the act would've been deemed playful, affectionate. In skin, it was intimate.

August, who'd lain perfectly still, finally stirred to life. The hand I was still touching clamped over mine, cocooning my fingers, and his other hand snaked underneath my head and threaded through my hair. Gently, he tugged on it to unfasten my mouth from his cheek.

"Ness . . ." My name felt like a gust of night wind, the sort that made fir needles shiver and sway. "If you kiss me, then you can't leave," he murmured.

It took me a moment to make sense of his words. "Why not?"

"Because you can't feed a starving man, then take away his food." If his voice hadn't been so low and raucous, I might've poked fun at him for that metaphor, but his timbre told me he was serious.

"You'll find better food," I finally said, heart fluttering the gray cotton that had coiled around my torso.

The fingers cupping the back of my head relaxed, slid to the nape of my neck, then back up. "How long?"

I thought he was asking me how long I was planning on staying, and I said until the morning.

"No, Ness. How long have you felt this way about me?"

Oh.

Oh . . .

I lowered my eyelashes, heat snaking up my chest like a warm current. "For a while now. Since the lake. But this link . . . it confuses me. Every time you touch me . . . even when you do it by mistake—"

"I never do anything by mistake."

I jerked my attention back to his face, the warm current spreading and heating up *every* part of me. "Well, when it happens, it does things to me, August. Things I don't think I should be feeling. Things I don't think I should be telling you about."

But here I was, confessing my deepest, darkest secrets.

"Is that why you got mad at me for calling you Dimples or kid? Because you thought it meant I only saw you as a little girl?"

I nodded, and the audacity that had taken ahold of me began to slip through my fingers like crumbling rock.

He stayed quiet so long that I said, "If you don't say something soon, I'm going to die of embarrassment."

His fingers spiraled up the column of my neck and stilled on the back of my scalp again, tipping it infinitesimally upward. "What would you like me to say?"

I twisted up my lips before mumbling, "That you feel a little bit of the same things I do."

"But if I said that, I'd be lying."

My heart squeezed in humiliation, and then my lids clinched.

"I'd be lying because whatever you feel, I feel it tenfold. But I've been feeling this way since you walked into that living room with that chin held so high. Since before this link snapped into place between us, which makes me reticent of letting this kiss happen at all."

I opened my eyes, humiliation replaced by something else entirely. Something that made the tether between us thrum. "Why?"

"Because once you're far from Boulder, far from me and our link, you'll stop wanting me, but I won't stop wanting you."

"You don't know that."

"That I won't stop wanting you? Yeah. I do. I was in—" He licked his lush lips, making them glisten. "There was an ocean separating us, and I couldn't get you out of my mind, Ness. And it screwed me up real bad. I wasn't focused on the team, on the mission. All I could think of was you and what the pack was putting you through, and what you were feeling. And then when Cole told me Liam—"

He rolled onto his back, releasing my hand but curling the other around my shoulders. I laid my head in the crook of his shoulder, my hair fanning over his arm. He wove his fingers through it, making my scalp tingle, making all of me tingle.

"When Cole told me Liam made a move on you, I was blinded by such jealousy that I made a grave tactical error that put one of my buddies at risk. It was bad, Ness." He shuddered and closed his eyes a long second.

I placed my palm over his beating heart, trapping its brisk rhythm with my fingertips. "I'm sorry."

"It's not your fault, sweetheart. I left you. Not the other way around."

And now I was the one talking about leaving. What if he did find *better food*? The mere thought of that waitress or Sienna resting where I lay had me gritting my teeth.

"I lied," I said, trying to ease the tension in my jaw. I kept my gaze on the palm flattened against his chest. "I've had a crush on you since I was a kid. A *real* kid. Which I know is disturbing. But you were everything to me. You *meant* everything to me. Remember the day you let me tag along on that movie date of yours with Betsy, or whatever her name was?" Her face flashed behind my lids. "I hated that she had curves and brown hair, and that I was as flat as a board and blonde. I hated that you kept touching her hair. Her hand. I hated it so much that I faked a stomachache so you'd take me home. So that you'd stay with *me*. So that you'd touch *my* hair."

He didn't say anything for a little while, as though trying to locate the memory. Or maybe he was rethinking what he'd told me, about liking me after my declaration.

"Her name was Carrie."

Oh, goodie. He remembered her. Worse, he smiled as he reminisced. A punch in the ribs would've hurt less.

He looped the ends of my hair around his fingers. "She broke up with me that night, because I chose you over her." His smile grew a little broader. "I knew you had a crush on me, but—"

"It really wasn't a crush; it was an infatuation." I grimaced. "And I honestly have no idea why I'm telling you all this."

"I think I know."

"Really?"

He rolled onto his side. "Because you're trying to test my willpower." He stared into my eyes. "Or break it . . ."

"Is it working?"

"When have you ever failed at anything?"

I smiled, but then I didn't. Then, in a rush of boldness—or foolishness—I closed the distance between our mouths, fitting mine on top of his.

A groan rumbled out of his chest, and he skated his mouth off mine. "Are you staying?" His chest rose and fell.

"I don't think I can—"

He winced.

"Let me finish my sentence. You didn't let me finish my sentence."

His gaze tripped over my face. "Finish your sentence."

Heart palpitating against my jaw, my lips, my chin, my forehead, I repeated what I'd said, but added the final word, the one that would change everything.

For him.

For me.

For us.

"I don't think I can *leave*."

I didn't want to answer to Liam, and I wasn't sure how I would get around this if I stayed, but I wasn't ready to abandon August, Evelyn, or Jeb. I didn't want to lose the ability to transform into a powerful beast, nor leave the home I'd just gotten back.

August clasped my chin with heartbreaking tenderness. "I need you to be perfectly certain about this."

"*This?*"

"Staying. Being with me." He ran his thumb over my lower lip. "I want you as my mate, Ness. Not tonight. Not tomorrow, but before the Winter Solstice. I need to know if you want this too. Because this isn't a simple crush. At least, not for me."

He was talking about *forever*. Forever scared the hell out of me. "I've never even been in a relationship, August."

"So you're not ready?"

"Because you are?"

"I've been with other people. I know what's out there, and I understand how precious what I've been given is. How precious *you* are." He caressed my cheek.

"I want to be with you, August—only you—and I *have* seen what's out there. I'm not settling for you because you happen to be around and magically connected to me. But I don't want to promise you forever, because that scares me." I moistened my dry lips with the tip of my tongue. "If that's not enough for you—"

His hand scooped up the back of my head and pressed my face closer to his, interrupting the flow of my thoughts and words. Against my lips, he whispered, "*Only me.*"

"Only you," I murmured to the man lying beside me, so familiar and yet a complete stranger.

He crushed his mouth to mine, and the rope that bound us drew me nearer and nearer. I didn't know if he'd reeled me in or if I'd done that. All I knew was that each one of our bones aligned; each inch of our flesh molded together to the point where it was impossible to distinguish where one of us began and the other ended.

And that—fitting so perfectly with someone—scared me more than anything, because if we ended, it would tear up more than just our hearts. It would tear up our very bodies.

47

Sleep fell over me as quietly as dawn crept over the horizon and kept me in its arms the same way August kept me in his. I felt safe and calm and sated in a way I hadn't felt in a long time. All we'd done was kiss, our fingers not venturing across the acres of skin that were now ours to explore. I sensed August was worried of frightening me by going too fast.

I appreciated the slowness. Everything with Liam had been rushed. We'd kissed as though we were out of time, and in a way, we had been, even though neither of us had known it then.

As the sun crested higher into the sky, I stroked August's long fingers splayed on my stomach, keeping me pinned to him, thinking of the awful recording, dwelling on how low men could sink to keep what they believed was theirs, and then I thought of my father wanting to be Alpha.

I found it strange that he'd coveted leadership. Had he desired this to bring me into the pack like Heath insinuated, or had it been a life goal? Had my mother known his intentions?

My mother who'd been another man's mate . . .

As I lay with the one who was supposed to be mine, I wondered if resisting the pull had been difficult. Perhaps it hadn't been such a feat considering her mate was neither gentle nor sweet. The fact that she'd managed, though, reassured me that I hadn't ended up in August's bed because of any magic. If August had been a violent narcissist, I would've kept my distance.

As though he'd felt me thinking of him, he stirred behind me, and the fingers I was caressing crimped my T-shirt and hoisted me a little higher up his body. I smiled, knowing the reason he'd readjusted me . . . having *felt* the reason against my tailbone. His lips connected with my shoulder blade and laid the warmest and softest kiss that penetrated through the barrier of cotton and skin, and then those lips moved to the slope of my neck and pressed a tantalizing kiss there, and then he nipped his way higher, to the sensitive place right behind my earlobe.

Still smiling, I spun in his arms to face him.

He returned my smile, a hesitant version of it, though, that had my heart beating double-time.

"No regrets?" he finally asked.

"No."

He ran a knuckle down my cheek, dipping it into my dimple before curving it around my jaw.

"What about you?" I asked.

"My only regret is that morning has come."

"Are you worried I'll turn into a pumpkin?"

He laughed, and then he pressed that beautiful, laughing mouth of his against mine and spilled the deep notes of his joy inside me. As the kiss deepened, the shape of his mouth changed, uncurled, opened. He pulled me into him, all of me, from my tongue to my body. When the bulge that strained his sweatpants pushed against my thighs, he disconnected our mouths and pressed me slightly away as though afraid to bruise me.

He studied my face, tucking a piece of hair behind my ear. "I'm going to be saving lots on water heating."

I studied him back. From his pupils ringed with brown that melted into the brightest green flecked with gold, to the scattering of chocolate freckles on his light-brown skin, to the dark auburn stubble on his oblong jaw, to the faint scar left over from my nighttime attack.

"I'll make up for your cold showers by taking extra hot ones," I said.

His pupils dilated, and his nose flicked mine. "Planning on showering here again, huh?"

Heat engulfed me. What in the world had prompted me to say that? "No. Um. Only if I get stranded—"

"I hope you'll get stranded often then." He smiled while I tried to rein back the rising heat. "I might even arrange for it to happen." He deposited a brief and searing kiss on my mouth that did absolutely nothing to cool me off.

"I'm going to need a cold shower too," I mumbled.

"I'd suggest taking one together, but that would defeat the purpose."

"It really would."

He combed another lock off my face, lifted my hair, then released it, watching as each strand fluttered down. "Do you think it might be real gold?"

I gave a very unladylike snort. "I wouldn't be riddled with debt if it were."

His gaze turned guarded. "You said you didn't—"

"It's nothing." I bit my lower lip. "Nothing I can't handle."

"How much?"

"Not telling you."

"Why not?"

"Because, it's personal."

"So are we. How much?"

"Please, leave it alone."

He rolled into a sitting position. "Fine. I'll leave it alone."

My lips fell open at how swiftly he'd relented. "Thank you."

"Mm-hmm." He scooted to the foot of the bed, then swung himself around and latched onto the ladder. "Going to take that much needed shower now. And I'll put a pot of coffee on."

I propped myself onto my elbows. "Hey, can you text Jeb to find out if he's home? I need to get back into the apartment."

"Will do."

I lay back down for a moment and watched the play of light and shadows on the concrete ceiling, wondering what I was supposed to do with myself now that I was staying—not professionally-speaking, but pack-speaking. Would I have to attend gatherings? How had yesterday's ended? If only I had my phone, I'd call Sarah. I was never leaving the house without *it* or my keys from now on, or my wallet for that matter. I prided myself on being street smart, but if I truly had been, I'd have taken my bag with me last night. I pressed my fingers into the still-warm duvet, watching the indent they left behind. Then again, if I'd taken my bag, I wouldn't have slept on this cloud of a bed, cocooned against a sexy shifter. The mere thought of the night had my body murring—the wolf's version of a purr.

When the percolator began gurgling, I got out of bed and stretched, before climbing down the ladder. The hardwood floor was cool beneath my feet, but the air was delightfully warm. I spied my dress on one of the kitchen barstools and debated whether to put the itchy thing back on but elected to keep August's T-shirt. It was comfier than tulle and long enough to cover my ass.

I padded into the kitchen and looked through cupboards until I found the one with mugs. No two recipients were alike. I shuffled them around, smiling at some of the slogans printed on them. I sucked in a breath when my gaze settled on a thick muck-green mug. I took it out and just stared at it.

Ceramic wasn't magical—unlike stinky wooden fossils—and yet this particular mug held magic. It made time reverse. I was sitting behind a pottery wheel, my hair in two long braids. Unlike most of the other kids who were making something for their parents, I'd decided to craft something for August. I stroked the glazed handle, the same way August had touched it when I'd given it to him seven years ago.

I set the mug down reverently, then filled it with coffee, the first sip of which had me moaning softly.

Something beeped, and then a door swept open. I froze, mug clutched in midair.

"Auggie, I brought—" Cole stopped talking when he spotted me.

We blinked at each other, and then another door groaned, and August strolled into the kitchen, a towel wrapped casually around his hips, the scent of his sandal-wood soap almost choking me. Or maybe my increased heartbeats were choking me.

As August banged around behind me, probably getting himself a mug for the coffee, I considered ducking behind the island in the hopes that Cole would *unsee* me.

"It's not what it looks like," I blurted out.

But then I felt the heat of August's still damp body against my back. "It's exactly what it looks like."

Oh . . . God, strike me down. Because *He* didn't, I elbowed August gently and stepped to the side so that he wasn't glued so conspicuously to my backside.

A shit-eating grin rose to Cole's lips as he walked over to us. "Damn."

I tried to reason it could've been worse. It could've been Nelson or Isobel who'd come through that door instead of Cole.

"Mom sends muffins." He dropped a plastic container on the island. "I send my congratulations."

Had someone turned up the heat? Because I was pretty certain I'd started perspiring. I set my mug down. Holding hot coffee wasn't helping my sweating situation. Self-consciously, I tugged on the hem of my T-shirt. Not that Cole could see my legs with an island between us. I really wished it were a real island—palm trees and sand dunes and all.

Holy crap. I really did have a thing for palm trees apparently.

"Um." I pivoted around. "August, can we talk a second?" *In private,* I mouthed.

His gaze left Cole's and set back on me. The power of it, combined with the smug smile gracing his lips, sent me into cardiac arrest zone.

"Sure thing." He tipped his head toward the bathroom door.

I all but raced toward it.

"I can leave if you guys want," Cole said while taking a seat on one of the barstools.

"We'll only be a minute," I reassured him.

"One minute?" Cole gave an amused snort. "All those weeks of sexual frustration taking a toll, huh?"

August flipped him off as he trailed me. I shut the door and locked it, even though it was ridiculous. It wasn't as though Cole would barge in. I unlocked it.

"Let me guess, you want me to change the door code?"

"What? No. I mean . . . maybe." I dragged my hand through my hair. "But that's not what I wanted to discuss."

He crossed his arms in front of his broad, broad chest. I tweaked the inside of my wrist to refocus myself, but a glimpse into the foggy mirror nulled the effect of the pinch. The glass was clearing, so I could see August's V-shaped back which was frankly just as alluring as his front.

"You okay, sweetheart?"

I twisted my hair into a long rope to lift it from my neck before my skin could scorch it right off. "Um. Yes, but . . ."

"You don't want people finding out about us?"

I nodded a little maniacally.

"Why?"

"Because. Liam and I, we just broke up—"

"Happened three weeks ago."

Had it already been three weeks? Okay, good. At least I wasn't a total tramp. "Can we still keep it on the down-low for now? Just a couple weeks."

August leaned back against the white enamel sink top, one eyebrow cocked up. "Why?"

"Because . . ."

"Because what?"

Ugh. Why couldn't he just go with it? "Because I'm afraid to hurt Liam's feelings."

"He wasn't afraid to hurt yours."

"I walked in on him. It wasn't like he flaunted his hookup in my face."

"I wasn't talking about the *hookup.* I was talking about what went down at Tracy's." There was a jagged edge to his deep voice. "Ness, do you still have feelings for him?"

"What?" I blinked. "No."

"You sure?"

"Of course I'm sure."

His Adam's apple bobbed once, twice. Then he sighed, pushed off the sink top, and took a step toward me. His arms came loose before wrapping around my waist.

I tipped my head up. "Why would you think that?"

"Because I'm jealous, and it'll probably get worse, although I'm not sure how that would work considering I already want to wring the neck of anyone who so much as looks your way." He tipped his head to the door. "Cole included."

"You don't have to be jealous. I promise. I'm just nervous. What if your parents are horrified?"

"My parents already love you like a daughter."

"Exactly."

"Exactly what?"

"They might find it weird that you and I, you know . . ."

He smiled down at me.

"You're enjoying how nervous this is making me?"

"A little. You're cute when you blush."

"Puppies are cute. And I don't blush."

"You do. And fine, you're drop-dead gorgeous, and I'm the luckiest bastard in the entire world."

I rolled my eyes. "You don't have to overdo it."

"That was me stating a hard fact, Ness. You *are* the most beautiful girl, and I *am* the luckiest guy." He leaned in and stole a kiss. "But I don't think we'll be able to hide this for weeks. Days, possibly."

I nodded. "Days are good."

He kissed me again, dragging my mouth open, deepening the kiss until the tiles beneath my feet vanished. And they really did, because he lifted me and pressed me into the warm wall. Before I could fall, I wrapped my legs around his waist and got so carried away with our make-out session that my brain turned blissfully blank.

But then a phone rang, and Cole's voice resonated outside the door, and I landed with a thump back into the present. August set me down gently, the stiff swell tenting his towel brushing along the insides of my thighs. Dizzy with lust, I leaned back against the wall to even out my scattered heartbeats.

August bracketed my head with his palms, breathing in the air I panted out. "I might have to take another shower." His gravelly voice intensified my lust-induced daze.

There was a knock on the door. "Guys, sorry to interrupt, but there's been a development, so if you two don't mind taking a little break from—"

I opened the door so fast Cole almost stumbled inside the bathroom. "What development?"

"Julian just challenged Cassandra Morgan."

I frowned. "Challenged her to do what?"

"A potato-sack race," Cole said, just as August whispered, "No way."

"Yes, way." Cole spun his phone between his fingers. "And I was kidding about the race."

"He challenged her for leadership of the Creeks?" I blurted out. "What did she say?"

He inhaled a long breath. "When an Alpha challenges another Alpha, Ness, there are two solutions. You either relinquish your territory and scram, or you accept to duel and hope you'll catch the challenger on a bad day."

"She'd have to give up Beaver Creek?" I asked.

"And the inn. And any other land that belongs to them. It's the law of the packs . . . the law of the fittest."

"That's a ballsy move on Julian's part," August said.

Cole stopped twirling his phone. "He'll either go down a legend or an imbecile, that's for sure."

"Do you think he'll challenge Liam next?" I asked.

"Julian would've done it before now if he'd wanted our pack's land," August said.

"Julian was probably frightened of doing it before," Cole said, "what with the whisperings of the pack being so *evolutionary*."

"Evolutionary?" I asked.

"All-male," Cole said. "And before you rip me a new one, I neither came up with the term, nor did I believe we were more evolved. I was simply guessing at a reason Julian never challenged Heath."

"But what if he *does* challenge Liam?" I asked. "Or *she* . . . ?" Dismissing Cassandra was foolish, considering she'd already defeated an Alpha.

"If either of them challenge Liam to a duel, my guess is he'll fight them," Cole said.

My heart skipped into my throat and expanded there until I had so much trouble breathing that August sketched small circles on my lower back.

"We'll be okay," he said.

Black dots danced at the edge of my vision.

"*He'll* be okay," he added in a weighty whisper, sensing I needed reassurance that Liam's life wasn't in peril. August stopped circling his palm, drawing me into his side instead, and then he kissed my forehead and repeated, "He'll be okay."

I clutched the hand wrapped around my waist as though it were the only thing keeping me from tipping over.

"Hey, Cole," August said, heart thudding steadily against my shoulder blade, "keep what you saw this morning to yourself."

Cole nodded. "Course, man." He pressed off the doorjamb. "Anyone want a muffin?"

My throat had closed up so tight that I didn't even think coffee would go down. "I need . . . clothes. I need clothes. Jeb—" I whispered raucously.

"He's home. Let me get dressed, and I'll take you."

"Okay," I breathed.

August unwrapped his arm from around me but threaded his fingers through mine and towed me back into the kitchen. I climbed onto a barstool, while he went through a passageway next to his bathroom—I assumed his closet.

After pouring himself a cup of coffee, Cole watched me from beneath his blond eyelashes. "I'm surprised you still care about him after last night. You looked angry enough to murder him."

Huh? Him? Oh . . . Liam. "The only person I wish dead is Aidan Michaels."

Cole leaned his forearms into the island. "Can I ask you something?"

I pressed my lips together warily.

"What are your intentions?" he asked.

"That's really none of your business, Cole."

"I just want to know if you're serious about him. That's all. He's been through a lot. And before you growl at me, I know you have too, but he's . . . well, he's—" He ping-ponged his phone between his hands. His fingers were as thick as Matt's and dotted with the same blond hairs. "I guess what I'm trying to say is I hope this isn't a rebound."

Even though I didn't appreciate his mistrust, I couldn't help but admire the consideration he had for August, which was the only reason I answered, "It's not a rebound."

"Cole," August said sharply, emerging from the closet dressed in army fatigues and a cream thermal tee molded to his torso.

Cole straightened up, raising both palms in the air. "Just watching out for you, man."

"Thanks, but stay out of it."

Cole's jaw set tightly. "Sorry."

As August leaned over me and nuzzled my neck, I said, "August?"

"Yeah, sweetheart?"

I pivoted to face him, forcing him to stop making my skin tingle. "This right here" —I pointed to Cole—"what he just asked . . . That's the reason why I don't want people to find out. The others will have the same reaction. It doesn't matter that Liam and I broke up three weeks ago, or that he's already slept with someone else; I'll be seen as *that* girl."

August's gaze tightened before glowing greener. "If anyone so much as insinuates—"

I pressed my finger against his mouth to calm his rising wolf. His hair had begun to lengthen and thicken. "Let's not discuss this anymore. Not with everything that's happening."

He dragged in a long, long breath, and I lowered my hand. "Fine. But if anyone says something—"

"I'll clock him over the head with the hammer from that state-of-the-art toolbox you got me last Christmas," Cole offered.

"Thank you," August said, rising up to his full height.

"You'd do the same for me."

"I would." August grabbed a muffin, bit into it, swallowed, bit into it again, swallowed again. Two more bites, and he was rubbing his hands together to get the clingy crumbs off. "Ready to go?"

I got down from the barstool. "If you don't mind me keeping the shirt, then yes. If not, I can put the dress—"

"Keep the shirt."

He pocketed his car keys, wallet, and phone from a hand-carved wooden bowl on the island, while I stuck my feet back into my heels and grabbed my dress. When I drew the front door open, brightness flooded the loft-like space.

Sunny days heralded good things.

Today would be a good day.

Julian would take out Cassandra.

It struck me that he would inherit her pack. Would all of them move to Boulder? I hoped not because a thousand more werewolves in the area would not only clutter our woods but also instigate territorial skirmishes. I turned away from the bright sky to see what was holding up August. I imagined it was Cole, but both of them were staring at me.

I shifted a little. "Are you coming?"

August smacked his buddy's chest, tossed him a murderous look, then walked over to me. He wrapped his arm around my waist and ushered me out. The warehouse parking lot was full of cars and trucks, so I stepped out of his reach.

His eyes, that hadn't lost their homicidal glint, swept over me. He didn't say anything, but I felt a tug deep in my stomach, and the tug had me sidling back up to him.

"August—" I gasped, tripping on my heels.

He reached out to steady me. "What?" His tone was innocent, but his expression wasn't.

"You know exactly what," I grumbled, quickly scanning the lot.

Thankfully no one was outside.

When we reached the pickup, he opened the door. "Ness, I have a physical need to keep you close to me. It's beyond my control."

I shook my head. "Says the man with the greatest amount of self-control."

"Not when it comes to you."

He dipped his chin into his neck, and then the hand that wasn't holding the door brushed my waist before opening like a flower in front of me. Sighing, I slipped my hand into his proffered one and climbed into the truck.

Once he was settled behind the wheel, and we'd pulled out of the lot, I scooted closer to him and rested my head on his shoulder. His arm came around my waist and held me against him.

"Do you think Julian will win?" I asked.

August sighed, and his sigh fluttered pieces of my uncombed hair. "We'll know soon enough."

"This fight-to-the-death tradition is so barbaric."

August pulled away to look down at me. "Says the girl who signed up for the Alpha trials."

"I didn't know that was going to be the ultimate test. The elders just said I would have to leave if I lost. They didn't mention dying."

He stopped in the middle of the road. Thankfully there were two lanes, so although we got honked at, the cars went around us.

"I thought you were aware of the final trial."

"No."

"Would you have signed up had you known?"

Before I could answer, Liam's voice filled my mind. *The fight will take place at noon on the lawn of the inn. I hope to see you all there to support our allies, the Pines.*

I checked the time on the car's dashboard. "That's in—in one hour."

August's fingers cinched around the steering wheel. "I don't want you to go, Ness. These fights . . . they can escalate. Spark other fights."

"And you don't think I can hold my own?"

"Of course I think you can, but do I want to risk it? No."

"I appreciate your desire to keep me safe, but I'm never going to be the girl who'll stay at home and wait by the phone. That's not in my DNA."

A couple different emotions slotted over his face—surprise, frustration, alarm. "Fine," he finally said, "but you'll be at my side the entire time. Hope you'll be okay with that."

"August . . ."

"Not up for discussion."

I growled a little.

"Indulge me, sweetheart. You've never attended a duel. These things are ugly. Even if the wolf you're rooting for wins, they're ugly."

I *had* attended one, but not as a spectator. I didn't think bringing up my own trials again would help ease August's mood, so I kept quiet. Besides, I didn't hate the idea of being at his side.

48

We drove to the inn in August's truck. I let Jeb sit up front, content to have the backseat to myself. As we rolled up the road to the inn, I intermittently texted Sarah and stared out the window at the sun-soaked mountains. She was confident her uncle would demolish the Creek Alpha. I hoped she was right.

"I've never seen so many cars." Jeb stared at the ocean of parked cars unfurling like a multi-colored wave down the sloping driveway.

Even though he was hyper—probably jacked-up on coffee and stress—I worried coming here would be tough on him. Especially if his ex-wife was in the vicinity, fawning over Aidan Michaels. I really hoped Lucy wouldn't show her face. For Jeb's sake, and for mine. Could she not see what a vile man Aidan was? Could she not spy the dried blood of her son underneath the hunter's—the Creek's—buffed fingernails? Sure, he hadn't confessed to Everest's murder, but I sensed with every fiber of my being that Aidan had had a hand in it. After all, the inn would still be Clark-owned if Everest were alive. Which would've been a heck of lot less convenient to host Aidan's extended family.

"You heard Aidan Michaels is a wolf," I told Jeb as I got out of the car.

"I heard. I still can't believe it. The quantity of Sillin he must've ingested to keep his scent in check . . ." He shook his head, which ruffled his already mussed-up blond-gray hair. I'd never seen him so unkempt.

August came around the car, hands in his pockets, probably to keep them off my body. Even though I'd promised to stay close, I'd begged him not to touch me. Touching would give us away. Maybe our scents already did.

My uncle's red-tinged gaze kept flitting from place to place without ever settling. "He probably can't shift anymore. Or if he can, he must be one hell of an ugly bastard.

One of those *halfwolves*. The only good part about him being a wolf is that now you can end him."

August came to an abrupt halt. "End him?"

One of Jeb's eyebrows shot up while the other slanted downward. "Don't you want Callum's murder avenged, August?"

"Of course I do."

My uncle dropped his voice to a mere whisper. "Ness should use the duel as a diversion to slit his throat."

"Do you care about your niece?" August barked, jerking on the tether to bring me closer to him.

"Excuse me?" Jeb asked.

"If you cared about her, you wouldn't incite her to do something so incredibly reckless."

"Reckless?" Jeb blurted out. "Blood killings are allowed! Encouraged, even."

"Perhaps, but advising her to attack the man during an Alpha duel? You and I both know how that could finish." August was growling now.

"It could finish with my brother getting peace, that's how it could finish." A vein ticked hectically in my uncle's temple.

"Why don't you slit the asshole's throat yourself, then?" August bit out.

Ping.

"Because I plan on slitting another man's throat today."

"Whose?" I asked.

"Alex Morgan's."

"Cassandra's son?" I asked.

He nodded. "I spent the better half of last night contemplating the little shifter's face through the silver grate. If Eric hadn't kept me in check, the boy would be dead this morning." On top of looking like he was hopped-up on drugs, my uncle sounded like it.

"Is Alex here?" I gestured to the inn.

"He'll be here later." Jeb dropped his voice and took a step closer to us. "Liam's bringing him to barter in case . . . in case Julian isn't successful."

"Barter against what?" August asked.

"The Creeks's immediate departure from Boulder," he whispered loudly. "If she doesn't accept Liam's terms, then I get to kill the son-of-a-bitch." Waves of anger and bloodlust pulsed off my uncle.

I glanced up at August, worried today would turn into absolute carnage, and his expression mirrored mine.

Jeb checked his wristwatch. "Twenty minutes to go." His eyes sparked. "Twenty minutes." He rubbed his palms together gleefully before prancing ahead of us. "I'm going to go find myself a front row seat."

For a while, neither August nor I spoke. We just watched my uncle's form vanish into the entrails of his former inn.

"Well, well, well. What do we have here?" came a voice I hadn't heard in a long time. A voice I hadn't missed at all.

August inspected my face slowly before he turned around even slower. He stepped in front of me, barring me from Justin Summix's view.

"If it isn't G.I. Watt." Justin was chewing on a piece of gum, which made him look more bovine than lupine. Like at the music festival, he was flanked by his two cronies. "Heard you were dishonorably discharged."

"Is there a reason you're trying to provoke me, Justin, or do you simply get a kick out of being a world-class prick?" August asked, his voice stretched as taut as a rubber band.

Justin smiled before starting back up on his loud mastication. He craned his neck to the side to look at me. I wasn't hiding behind August. I just had no desire to look at the sleazy Pine.

"Guess I had you pegged right the first time we met, huh?" Justin blew out a bubble that smacked against his crooked mouth.

"Choke on your gum, Justin," I spat out.

He smirked, and so did his two friends. One of them cracked his knuckles while the other just leered at me.

"How does it work?" Justin continued. "Do you take them one at time or all at once?"

That was it. I lunged around August, but he tugged so hard on the tether I flailed backward, whacking against his chest. A second later, Justin was dangling in midair, sputtering. Either August was squeezing his neck too tight or the gum had gone down the wrong hole.

"Apologize. Now," August growled.

"Landon," Justin wheezed, his face beginning to turn purple.

Did that mean *I'm sorry* in some weird werewolf tongue?

His friend, the one with the matching wifebeater and buzz cut, shot his arm out. I guessed Landon was a name.

August dodged the fist flying at his face, then backhanded Landon in the jaw so suddenly that he blinked and stumbled backward before toppling onto the ground. I charged the other friend just as he raised his foot to kick August between the legs. August would've probably blocked the hit, but I didn't wait to find out. I slammed my foot against the boy's rising leg, flinging it away, then grabbed his shoulders and kneed him so hard in the groin he let out a high-pitched shriek before bending over and panting in pain.

Adrenaline coursed through me, sharpening all of my senses. I could feel the cluster of raw energy on the lawn of the inn and the din of voices. I could hear the whisper of the smile growing on August's lips and the steady thumps of his heart as he gazed down at me.

"Fuck . . . you . . . both," Justin hissed, snapping August's attention back onto him.

"That didn't sound like an apology," August said.

Justin's nails curved and sharpened, and then he clawed at August's hand.

August tossed him almost as far as the rock he'd skipped on the lake. "If any of you so much as look at Ness again, I will shred you like the vermin you are."

I grabbed onto his hand. Blood trickled out of the puncture wounds, ribboning down his wrist and soaking the cuff of his cream cotton shirt. I pushed his sleeve up, then dug a tissue from my handbag and pressed it against the four small wounds.

"You're a fucking lunatic, Watt, just like all the Boulders. All fucking inbred degenerates," Justin rasped, rubbing his reddened throat. "First thing Julian'll do when he wins the duel is kick your pack off our land for good."

"We aren't on your land," I said, still tending to August's wounds.

"He'd have to win first," August added matter-of-factly. I didn't think for a second he hoped for another outcome, but the taunt made Justin purple with rage.

"Like that bitch has a chance in hell," Landon muttered.

"She beat the Aspen Alpha," I reminded him.

"I see where your loyalties lie." Justin tugged on the hem of his white wifebeater to lower it over his baggy jeans. "Is it because she's a bitch like you?"

"Stop referring to my gender like that." I lifted the bloodied tissue and balled it up in my fist. The torn flesh had stopped bleeding and was already knitting together.

The fight begins in five minutes.

Both August and I craned our necks in the direction of the lawn at the sound of Liam's call.

"Let's go." August snaked his arm around my waist and towed me up the driveway.

No one was inside the inn—no housekeepers, no perfidious aunt. I stretched my hearing to check if I sensed human heartbeats, but all the hearts that pounded were not the least bit human.

Before we walked into the living room, August said, "You were remarkable out there."

I rolled my eyes.

He stopped and pulled me against him, stroking my cheek. "I'm serious. In case you forgot, I was at the receiving end of a punch once."

I frowned.

"The day I startled you at the gym . . ."

The day I'd decided to enter the trials. That day felt like eons ago.

He dipped his head. Before he could kiss me, I pulled out of his arms.

"August . . ." I whispered.

Thankfully no one was around. Justin and his friends must've circled the inn walls.

August rubbed his mouth. "Right."

I knew it was silly to worry about being caught, considering what was happening outside the inn walls, but I couldn't help it. I was a ball of nerves—because of August, but also because of the impending duel.

We crossed the living room toward the wall of bodies lining the deck's railing. I slid in next to Cole, scanning the grounds for Sarah. She stood between her brother and another girl—a short redhead.

Although the Matzs were too far below for me to gauge their expressions, the set of their shoulders told me Julian's family was on edge. The rest of his pack seemed slightly more relaxed. They formed a loose web behind Julian, who was discarding his clothes. He was down to a white undershirt and a pair of tight white briefs.

His sister was circling Cassandra, whose body was already bared, shoulders held back, large breasts hanging low. Did the Creeks walk around naked all the time? Nudity was really the last thing I should be wondering about at this moment.

"What is Nora Matz doing?" I asked.

"She's Julian's Second," August said, just as Lori broke away from the Creek Pack and crossed the field toward Julian.

"What's a Second?" I asked.

Cole leaned his hip against the railing, one eyebrow raised.

"Don't look at me like that, Cole. My werewolf education was cut short when my dad died, and although I've learned a couple things recently, I know there are still a lot of gaps in my shifter knowledge."

"Alphas can't duel without Seconds. It's a human tradition that the packs adopted and have used since the first recorded Alpha duel in the Appalachians." It was August who answered. "Like in human duels, Seconds are in charge of making sure there's no foul play. They'll also watch the duel up close—like referees of sorts. If any rules are broken, they can separate the parties. The duel is then either postponed if both parties desire a rematch or canceled altogether. If that happens, then each pack has an obligation to return to their territories and the Alphas are no longer allowed to challenge each other during the rest of their lifetime. However, if one of the packs sees a new Alpha rise, then that new Alpha may challenge the reigning Alpha of the enemy pack."

"What if the Seconds can't stop the duel in time and one of the challengers dies as a result of a broken rule?"

"Then the Second of the fallen Alpha can challenge the victor instantly, without waiting a full moon cycle." August was focused on Lori who was circling Julian's now entirely naked form, stopping to grab his hand and look beneath his fingernails. She then tilted his head up and stuck her finger inside his mouth.

"She's checking for concealed weapons and illegal substances implanted in the enamel," Cole explained, angling his big body back toward the lawn.

If anything, I was more confused now. "I don't understand how fighting right away benefits the Seconds," I said, returning to the rules of dueling.

"The victor expends a lot of energy during a fight. Especially in an Alpha battle. Considering the Second isn't an Alpha, their odds of winning against one are usually nil." August's eyes were on me now. "Let's say Julian beats Cassandra, but somehow Lori notices that he used foul play to do so—a trap on the ground, or a staged commotion in his ranks, or he somehow turned a stick into a weapon—Lori has the right to challenge him on the spot. She'll have the advantage of being fresh *and* her body won't go through an inspection, so technically she could have a concealed weapon. You can bet both Lori and Nora are prepped to counteract. Of course, it doesn't mean they can beat an Alpha. They won't have the body mass or training of an Alpha. Most of the times, Seconds forfeit to save their hides."

"I've never heard of a Second challenging a victorious Alpha," Cole said.

The Creek Pack shaped a compact arc behind Cassandra. I guessed from the sheer swell of unfamiliar faces that all the Creeks had arrived for the event. The mass of bodies made the hundred Pines standing behind Julian seem measly. The Seconds met in the center of the field. After they exchanged quiet words, they both nodded and traipsed back toward their respective families, ridding their bodies of clothes before shifting into fur.

You stayed. Liam's voice inside my mind was so jarring that my heart leaped.

I placed a palm against my chest before looking for him in the row of Boulders lining the railing. I'd imagined he was standing somewhere below, holding Cassandra's son in some death vice, but Liam was right there amongst his men and me, no Alex in sight.

I'm truly sorry, Ness. And not that you found out. I'm sorry for having wanted your father dead. I'm sorry that I kept it from you, that I hurt you . . . that I disappointed you . . . again. I hope in time you'll be able to forgive me.

I bit my lip, whisking my lashes down to counter the surging slickness. I darted my gaze back to the field, Julian's and Cassandra's naked forms coming in and out of focus. Next to me, I felt August's fingers graze my hip. I moved away from him, bumping into Cole.

From the corner of my eye, I caught Cole exchanging a look with August. Sadly, I knew what that look was about. Cole oozed wariness. It wafted off him like the stench of his cigarettes. He was wrong to be wary. Not wanting August to touch me had nothing to do with harboring secret romantic feelings for Liam. I simply didn't want attention from the pack—be it from Liam or from any other Boulder.

August gripped the railing as though ready to splinter the wood he and our fathers had sanded down years ago, tendons pinching in his hands, making the dried blood that still stained his skin crackle.

A low howl pierced the bright-blue sky, and then a second howl answered.

"And so it begins," Cole whispered under his breath.

49

My hands joined the many other sets gripping the deck railing. The fight had started about ten minutes ago, and although the light-brown fur on Cassandra's back was tinged red from where Julian had sank his teeth into her, she was still on all fours. She moved slowly, as though the pain in her rear was taking a toll on her body. Considering he'd bit her at the start of the fight, she should've begun to heal.

Julian waited for Cassandra to creep closer before jumping on her. She flattened against the grass, then rolled over onto her back. I expected she'd keep rolling, but no . . . she stopped moving, as though waiting for Julian to land on her. The second his body came within limb-length of hers, she slashed his belly with her claws, then whirled around beneath him and bucked him off her injured back.

Julian landed with a heavy thump a couple feet away from her. For a moment, he didn't move.

I held my breath.

Everyone held their breath.

Cole said, "He's going to end her."

Julian pressed back onto his paws like a mountain rising from tectonic plates and lunged toward Cassandra again, dark muzzle wet with her blood, fangs bared. He gripped her thigh in his mouth and shook his head as though trying to dismember her. Her leg stayed attached, but she toppled over. He dragged her a couple feet, but then she bucked, and Julian sputtered, emitting a great choking sound as though he'd gotten a mouthful of fur. The moment he let her go, she crawled away from him, belly to the ground.

But he was still wheezing, batting one of his legs across his muzzle as though trying to brush off Cassandra's blood. He retched.

Voices began to rise, shouts, jeers, cheers. Like spectators at a sports match, the crowd was becoming boisterous. Although they kept a safe distance from the wolves, Nora and Lori orbited around their Alphas.

At the sound of Julian vomiting, Cassandra flipped around, positioned herself in a crouch, and, with a keening moan, heaved herself up. Her momentum was so sluggish it looked as though she were moving in slow-motion and yet she managed to tip Julian over. Both wolves crashed down in a mix of bloodied brown fur, bodies writhing and jerking.

A snarl echoed against the tawny trunks of the swaying pine trees and ricocheted like the blaring sunlight on the tall glass façade of the inn.

A whimper ensued.

And then the wet snap of an overextended vein.

My skin broke out in goose bumps as one Alpha stole the life of another.

50

Julian had fallen.

The upset created a ripple of cries and outbursts down below but also on the deck. Every Boulder body tightened and straightened, every set of eyes strained, and every mouth pursed. No one spoke beside me, not even Liam through the mind link. We all just stood shoulder to shoulder, solemn in our shock and grief.

Yes, *grief* . . .

Even though I hadn't much liked the Pine Alpha, I liked Cassandra even less.

A sharp cry tore through the field as Nora rushed to Julian's mangled, inert form. Robbie sprang away from his pack and caught his mother before she could throw herself atop her brother. She whimpered and whined and snarled at her son, while he spoke quietly into her ear. After a long moment, she stopped snarling and slid back into skin. Shaking with sobs that were so shrill they could probably be heard in the middle of town, she burrowed her head against Robbie's chest.

My gaze skated over the strange scene below. People had begun pouring onto the field to felicitate their Alpha, who was still in fur. On the other side of the field, Sarah had crumpled to her knees. I started to go toward her when August caught my wrist and shook his head.

"No," he said, his tone brooking no argument.

"But Sarah—"

"Sarah will be taken care of." His grip was all at once loose but firm, as though he was fighting his urge to hold me tighter. "Stay up here."

Margaux and a redheaded girl had kneeled next to Sarah, but still I itched to go to her. What decided me to stay away was the pulse of terror throbbing through the link. My already clenching stomach roiled and contracted with August's fear.

I returned to the railing, and he let go of my wrist. Although he didn't put his hands on me again, he held on to me through the tether as though he didn't trust me not to sprint down those stairs.

"I won't go," I reassured him, but it did little to loosen his invisible grip.

I turned my attention back to the ground below. For the final time, the fur receded into Julian's pores, his muzzle retracted, and his limbs twisted back into his human ones.

"Do you wish to contest the fairness of the fight and challenge the Alpha today?" Lori hollered, back in skin and clothes, her voice thundering over all the others.

Along with every shifter present, I watched Nora. Watched as she turned in her son's arm. Watched as her lips trembled. Watched as her head shook, first with a shudder, then with an answer.

No.

"Do you wish to challenge the Alpha in one moon cycle from now?" Lori asked, voice loud and clear.

Again, Julian's sister shook her head. Robbie plucked the blonde hair sticking to his mother's pale forehead and cheeks. Margaux tossed a sort of cape over her mother-in-law's shoulders, and then Robbie wrapped an arm around her and helped her off the field. A cry ripped from her throat, and then another, her grief echoing against the Flatirons and the farthest and tallest mountain peaks.

"Alpha of the Creeks!" Lori turned to her mother who was still in fur. "The fallen's heart is yours for the taking, and with it, the fallen's pack."

The fallen's heart?

I wasn't sure if I asked this out loud or if August read the confusion etched on my face, but he said, "The victor eats the heart of the loser, thus acquiring a link to the dead Alpha's pack."

A lump of bile shot up my throat.

August stepped in front of me and tucked me into his chest. "I told you it was brutal."

I didn't look, but I heard the watery tear of flesh, the placid crunch of bones, and the bloody squelch of what had once fueled life into a man and would now fuel magic into a woman.

Even though I was probably imagining it, I felt as though I heard the blood drip off Cassandra's muzzle and mix into the tear-and-vomit-soaked soil.

At long last, triumphant howls ripped through the summer sky, announcing that an Alpha had fallen and another had taken its place.

I thought back to the last trial I'd had to endure against Liam—the test of strength. Was what I'd just witnessed what the elders had in mind? Had they hoped Liam would tear open my breastbone and eat my heart?

I shuddered, which made August squeeze me tighter, and I let him. I didn't care who spotted me in his arms. I still had a heart beating inside my chest. I wouldn't force it to be quiet to avoid criticism or stares, just like I wouldn't force August to keep his distance. I needed him. I wanted him.

If today had taught me anything, it was that life was too short to worry about what others thought. I wrapped my arms around August's waist and burrowed closer, hoping that his scent and warmth would help dull the terrible images and sounds that kept replaying in my skull.

51

Voices grew louder around us. Ambient conversations began to penetrate my buzzing mind.

"What do you think he swallowed that made him throw up?" Matt was asking his brother.

"Fur, or maybe a chunk of flesh. That'll make anyone gag."

At the mention of gagging, bile rose anew in my throat. "You were right. I shouldn't have come," I murmured against August's chest.

He tucked a strand of hair behind my ear. "At least now you know." His mouth brushed the top of my head while his fingers brushed down my spine. If anyone had lingering suspicions as to whether he and I had crossed the line between friendship and more, I imagined our present proximity obliterated them.

"You should take her away from here, son," I heard Nelson say.

I peeled myself off August so fast I must've left a couple eyelashes behind.

Nelson's mouth was pressed into a grim line. "That was awful, wasn't it?"

"Y-yes," I stammered.

I forced myself to meet Nelson's deep-brown eyes, dreading the disgust I expected, but there was no disgust. Just wariness. I tried not to wonder if his wariness stemmed from what had unfolded down below or from what had unfolded up on the deck between August and me.

I pushed the bra strap that had slipped down my arm back under my tank top. "What's going to happen now?"

Several Boulders were speaking in hushed tones behind Nelson. I heard the words: *Cassandra, duel, Liam.* I feared that those words might belong in the same sentence.

"Now"—August's father inhaled a grave breath—"the Creeks will probably extend their trip in Boulder. The time it takes to acclimate the newest members of their pack."

James, the blond with impeccably coiffed hair, came up behind August. "It'll be good for business."

"You can cut and style their hair all you want, but we won't be doing business with the Creeks," August said.

"We lived alongside the Pines for almost a century and we did business with *them*. Why wouldn't we take Creek money?"

August's jaw hardened, as though he were holding back a biting retort.

Nelson touched his son's forearm. "Let's see what happens. There's no point forecasting what we will and will not do until we understand what it is they want."

"What they want is to take our land," Rodrigo said, coming to stand by James's side, "and our men."

I didn't even bother sticking my hand up to remind him that I wasn't a man. It was really beside the point.

"How do you know that, Rodrigo? Did you have yourself a little chat with Cassandra before the duel?" Nelson asked. I'd never heard him be so short with anyone. I didn't even know he was capable of such curtness.

"No, Nelson, I didn't," Rodrigo bit out. "But why else would they have all come? Why else did they have Aidan observe us for so many years? Liam said there was a missing packet of Sillin. I bet they got some pills in Julian—"

"He wouldn't have been able to shift. Besides, he didn't drink or eat anything last night," James said.

"How do you know? Were you with him all night, Jamie?" Under his breath, he added, "*Again*."

James backed away, shaking his head. "You can be a real ass sometimes." He turned and headed toward another group of Boulders.

"Liam told Robbie they should have Julian's blood analyzed for Sillin." The dark-haired, dark-tempered firefighter tipped his head toward the lawn where Liam was talking with Robbie. "But Julian's body belongs to the Creeks now that Nora refused to fight. If they so much as allow him a burial, I'd be surprised."

"Will Robbie challenge Cassandra now?"

"Possibly," Rodrigo said, "but his odds of winning against an Alpha would be shit." He slanted his dark eyes on me. "You have to have a screw loose to challenge an Alpha."

I recoiled, because that last part felt personal.

Nelson's fingers tightened around August's arm. "That was out of line, Rodrigo."

"My father could've won," I murmured.

"Odds are—"

"Enough!" Nelson said, still gripping August's arm. "That's enough."

Rodrigo pinched his thick pink lips closed.

"It takes courage to fight for what you want," Nelson said. "What takes no courage is denigrating others."

Rodrigo lowered his eyes, chastised by Nelson, but too proud to apologize for having insulted my family.

"August, we need your help with something." Cole cocked his head toward Matt and Dexter.

When Nelson released his son's arm, August turned toward me as though worried to leave me alone.

I flexed my lips into a smile I wasn't feeling. "Go."

Reluctantly, he left with the three other Boulders.

I stepped a little farther from Nelson, who was still giving Rodrigo a tongue-lashing. I tried to glimpse Sarah down below. If Liam was down there, it was probably safe—

"You and August a thing now?" Lucas asked.

He stood next to me, forearms propped on the railing, gaze sunk on the field below, or rather on the crumpled girl with the lustrous blonde hair. Margaux placed a kiss on the top of Sarah's head, then, cradling her abdomen, she stood and walked over to an older man—her father perhaps.

"Yes," I finally said.

Lucas pivoted toward me, leaning against the balustrade. "Is it serious?"

Margaux made her way over to Robbie next. Although he was still deep in conversation with Liam, Robbie tugged his pregnant mate against him.

I sighed. "I stayed."

"You were really going to skip town?"

"Yeah."

"Where would you have gone?"

I shrugged. "Maybe back to LA. I couldn't feel the pack's pull out there." The idea of returning to Los Angeles made my stomach churn. LA reminded me too much of Mom. "Or maybe I would've tried my luck on the East Coast."

"You know he feels like shit about everything, don't you? The recording. Tammy."

I returned my gaze to Sarah, who was alone now. "I'm sure he does, but it's not really my problem anymore, is it?"

"He's our Alpha, Ness."

"What are you saying?"

"A conflicted Alpha can get sloppy, and that can impact the entire pack."

I crossed my arms. "So what? Are you suggesting I go down there and give him a big old hug and tell him I forgive him for breaking my heart?"

"Did he?"

"Break my heart? Yeah, he did."

Although the tinny scent of death stained the air, most of the bloody patches on the lawn were hidden behind clusters of shifters—some in mourning, some in celebration. Someone had covered Julian with a white sheet from which only his feet and head protruded. Blood bloomed on the white, so much of it that I didn't think any amount of meat tenderizer would be able to get it out.

"You cared that much about him?"

"I did."

"He still cares about you."

"He'll get over it."

"What if he doesn't?"

"Did you get over Taryn?"

He watched Sarah as she rose and craned her neck to stare into the sun. Maybe she was hoping its blazing heat would dry her tears.

"I don't miss her anymore," he said.

She squinted toward the inn. When she caught sight of us, she headed for the porch steps, treading fast, as though in a hurry to get away from her new pack, ironed hair glinting like a swath of gold. When she reached the deck, she lurched toward me. I just had time to open my arms before she sprang into them.

"We told him not to challenge her." Her tears soaked the collar of my tank. "We begged him not to do it."

I rubbed the top of her spine.

"He's gone. And now we're . . . we're . . . Creeks." Her voice cracked on that last word. "It's her voice I'll hear in my mind. She'll be the one to tell us what to do." She pulled away from me, fixing me with her shiny brown eyes. "I. Hate. Her," she bit out, trembling all over. "I hate all of them." She glared at a small group of Creeks passing below us.

There were five of them, not much older than us. Where two of the boys and one of the girls stared at us with restraint, the other two—a boy and girl, who looked so much alike I assumed they were siblings—watched us with unabashed interest.

"They can't all be bad," I whispered to her, trying to soothe her.

"I still hate them," she muttered.

"I know." I smoothed her hair back.

She pressed away from me and shot her red-tinged gaze toward Lucas. "Liam has to challenge her. He has to take the packs back. You guys have to tell him to challenge her."

The blood drained from Lucas's face, turning his complexion as white as the scar that slashed his black eyebrow. "No way. If she doesn't challenge him, then we're advising him to stay out of it."

"I'm sure she cheated, Lucas. I don't know how she did it, but I'm sure of it. Julian wasn't throwing up *fur balls* out there. I bet she poisoned him."

"If she had"—I wrinkled my nose for what I was about to say—"she couldn't have eaten his *heart* without it poisoning her."

"Ness is right, Sarah."

Sarah scrubbed her eyes with the heels of her hands. "But she did something. She must've. Maybe she managed to slip him Sillin. It would've weakened him."

My brow puckered. "How would she have done that?"

"I don't know, but—"

Lucas interrupted Sarah. "Wouldn't Sillin have made him shift back into his human form?"

Would it? "It keeps us from shifting when we're in skin," I said, remembering what it had done to me, "but I'm not sure what it does when we're in fur."

"It'll show up on his tox screen," Lucas said.

The same way it had shown up on Heath's . . .

"If we're even allowed to run one," Sarah muttered.

"If she doesn't allow you to run one, it'll be as much of an answer. It'll prove she has something to hide."

Cassandra had finally shifted back. Her body was bruised and bloodied, yet pride squared her shoulders and her jaw. A man was wrapping a bandage around her thigh that was still weeping blood.

"What if it's in her blood?" I whispered.

"What if what's in her blood?"

"The Sillin. What if it's in her blood?" I kept my voice so low that both Lucas and Sarah strained toward me. "Her wound should've sealed up by now."

"But she managed to shift into a wolf," Sarah said.

"She must've swallowed it while in wolf form," I said, scanning the makeshift dueling ring for what—white pills, a crushed foil packet?

"Mom would've seen her eat something and signaled it."

"Maybe your mom missed it?" I suggested.

Sarah inhaled a swift breath. "You know what this means, though? That she's weaker now. That if Liam challenged her, he might very well win."

"Unless she poisons him, too," I murmured.

Color had returned to Lucas's face. "If the Sillin's in her system, there's no way she can shift back into fur. Not for a couple hours. Possibly days, depending on the dose."

"Could they duel in skin?" I asked.

"Would be atypical, but why the hell not?" Lucas sounded pumped.

I didn't like his enthusiasm. *Feared* it. Feared it might incite Liam to act recklessly. Before I could quiet him, Lucas shouted, "Great Alpha Morgan, shift back!"

Everyone turned to stare at him, and I mean, *everyone*.

"Excuse me?" Cassandra said.

Lucas had his arms crossed in front of his chest. "Shift. Back."

"Why, Mr. Mason?" I was impressed she knew his name. Then again, she must've spent decades studying all the files her cousin had sent her.

Her cousin, who was standing next to her, looking like the cat who ate the canary. How I despised Aidan Michaels.

"To satisfy my curiosity," he said.

"I bet you, she won't do it," Sarah whispered.

"Very well," Cassandra said.

Keeping her gaze locked on Lucas, brown fur poured from her pores, and then her eyes flashed with an inhuman glow, and she landed on all fours, trampling our Sillin-theory the same way she trampled the broken blades of grass underneath her paws.

52

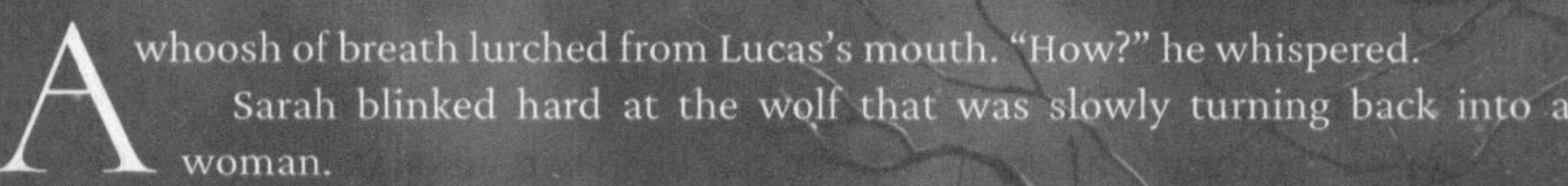

A whoosh of breath lurched from Lucas's mouth. "How?" he whispered.

Sarah blinked hard at the wolf that was slowly turning back into a woman.

Once Cassandra was in skin, she craned her neck to look up at us, pulling the bandage that had slid down her thigh back up. "Have I satisfied your curiosity, Mr. Mason?"

Lucas's lips were still parted, but no sound came out of him.

Could she have applied a cream to her body that would've made Julian sick?

"Was Julian allergic to anything?" I asked Sarah.

She shook her head, eyes so wide there was white around her irises.

"Fuck," Lucas finally said, just as heavy footsteps pounded the terrace floor.

We all turned toward the disturbance.

Gripped between August and Cole stood a boy no older than I was. Was this the infamous Alex Morgan? Everest's killer?

Alex had the blond curls of a cherub, a boyish jaw that had yet to be chiseled by life even though it was riddled with fading bruises that matched the violet shade of his eyes. He was more pretty-boy than cold-blooded killer.

"Damn, she's way hotter in real," he said, gaze raking over me.

August smacked his elbow into the side of Alex's head.

"Ow. What was that for?" Alex carped, trying to raise his hand to cradle his head, but both Cole and August clamped down on his wrists, pinning them behind his lanky body.

Alex really didn't look like he needed two mammoth shifters to keep him in check. Then again, there was something slippery about him, as though he were more eel than wolf.

"*He* killed Everest?" Sarah asked.

"I know, right," Lucas grumbled.

Alex smirked at Sarah, or rather at her rack. "The region's good to its females."

"Shut the fuck up," Lucas growled.

Alex grinned, seemingly getting off on irritating everyone. He stared beyond us then, at the lawn. "Hey, Ma, I'm home!"

A couple muffled laughs rose from the Creek pack.

"You said you wouldn't hurt him," Cassandra snarled at Liam.

"No. We said we wouldn't kill him. And we didn't." Liam sounded chillingly calm.

Cassandra gave him a hard stare. "Your terms. What are they?"

"You take your pack and leave Boulder immediately."

Sarah gasped.

I put a hand on her arm. "He surely doesn't mean you," I murmured reassuringly.

"I doubt my new pledges—" Cassandra began.

"Pledges?" Sarah's fingers curled into fists. "We didn't pledge ourselves to you. We would *never!*"

Cassandra flicked her gray gaze onto my friend. "My new *compatriots*. Does the term suit you better, Miss Matz?"

Sarah scowled.

"I doubt they want to abandon their land," Cassandra continued, returning her attention to Liam. "Technically, *my* land."

"So you don't accept my terms?"

"I do not accept your terms," Cassandra said calmly.

I snuck a glance over my shoulder at Alex. He was no longer grinning, but he was also not peeing his pants.

"Technically, Kolane, Everest was already a dead man, was he not?" she continued.

"We're not in a court of law. Your son isn't getting off on a technicality. This is pack law, and pack law forbids inter-pack murders," Liam said, a pointed edge to his voice. "We have proof your son deliberately ran him off the road. We found yellow paint on Everest's Jeep. Yellow paint that rubbed off from your son's Hummer."

"Paint? That's your proof?" Cassandra's lips puckered. "When Everest took off from our property, he back-ended my son's car. That's why—"

"Just before the crash, he called me!" My voice fired across the field, leaving a trail of billowing silence. "He said he was being chased." I swallowed hard. "So don't you *dare* claim he crashed into that ditch by accident!"

Cassandra's eyebrows quirked in surprise. She licked the blood off her lips that seemed bluer in the sunlight.

Fingers twined with my own. Slender fingers. Sarah's. She squeezed my palm tight.

"Look, Kolane," Cassandra said, "if you give me back my son, I swear in front of every Creek and Boulder that I'll *never* challenge you to a duel." She tapped the spot over her heart as though to prove her sincerity. "I'll let your pack go on. I'm willin' to sign a treaty with you this very minute."

A spark of hope ignited within me . . . within Liam. I felt the speeding up of his heart inside my own chest.

"I didn't come here to challenge Alphas," Cassandra said. "I came here to create alliances."

"Says the wolf who just murdered a man," Robbie interjected.

"I didn't challenge your uncle!" Cassandra's temper exploded all over her haggard face. She took a few steps back, a noticeable limp in her right leg. "He challenged me! And he *lost*." She stopped backing up and jerked her arm toward Julian's remains. "That's what hubris does to men. It makes them feel like gods but act like fools."

Liam studied her for a long moment. I prayed he was considering her terms.

"Take her deal," I whispered, not that he could hear me. "Take it."

Sarah glanced at me, conflict written all over her face.

"No!" Liam's answer was like an explosion—terrifying. "You fight me right here. Right now."

My blood became ice.

"Liam!" Lucas rushed the handrail so fast I worried he would break right through it.

Cassandra scrutinized Liam. "Trying to take advantage of my injuries, Kolane?"

"Do you accept?" Liam asked.

"Liam, no!" I yelled.

"Do. You. Accept?"

"Didn't you listen to a word I just said about *hubris*?" she asked calmly.

"Are you afraid to face me?" Liam asked.

I willed her not to accept.

"You'll need a Second," she finally said.

Liam wheeled around and craned his neck. "Lucas—"

"Don't fucking ask me to do this, man." Lucas shook his head so fiercely his black hair flogged his sheet-white jaw. Liam must've said something else to him, this time through the mind link, because Lucas growled a loud, unflinching, "Absolutely not!"

Liam flung his gaze on Matt.

Matt jerked, and then, like Lucas, shook his head. "No."

Liam's eyes narrowed.

A smile lilted Lori's lips. "Your pack doesn't seem very confident in your abilities—"

"Rodrigo?" Annoyance chafed Liam's tone.

Rodrigo's face glistened with perspiration. "Take her deal, Liam."

Have faith in me! His voice raged inside my skull.

I clapped my hands against my ears. I wasn't alone in doing this.

I can defeat her! She is weak. I can do this! But I have to do it NOW.

A whimper escaped me.

Liam fastened his eyes on mine for a long moment. So much passed between us then. Regret, resentment, disappointment, affection.

Don't do it, I mouthed.

Finally he spun back around. "I challenge you without a Second."

EPILOGUE

Cassandra drummed her fingers against the bloodied bandage on her thigh. "Dueling without a Second is unheard of."

"Unheard of but not unlawful," Liam said, his voice taut with determination. "Besides, it puts me at a disadvantage. You should be jumping at the opportunity."

Cassandra studied Liam. "I don't *jump*. I calculate risks."

I frantically scanned the faces of the Boulders surrounding me. Some had gone ghostly pale.

August's gaze struck mine. "Liam—"

"Don't even think about giving me advice, Watt," Liam barked.

I sucked in air, but it seemed devoid of oxygen. I pulled in another breath, and it went down the wrong pipe. I began to cough so hard I thought I would hack out one of my lungs.

Perhaps Liam could defeat Cassandra, but what if he couldn't?

Then . . . then she'd . . . she'd eat his heart.

Not for the first time today, bile shot up my throat. I was about to spin back around when my gaze landed on Alex's. He was smiling as though he could taste his freedom, as though he sensed his mother wouldn't walk away from the challenge, as though he knew she'd be victorious.

I flipped back around. Cassandra was stroking her narrow, bloody chin. Next to her, Lori and Aidan stood side by side, both relaxed and smiling as easily as Alex.

"I volunteer," I shouted suddenly. "I'll be his Second!"

"What?" Lucas roared, at the same time as August yelled, "Out of the question!"

Before anyone could stop me, I flew down the stairs and raced toward Liam.

His dark eyes were wide with shock.

"But since I'm the Second, I get a say in when the duel happens."

"Ness—" Liam started.

"Right?" I all but screeched, my throat on fire.

"No. Only the challenged party gets a say in when and where it happens," Lori said. "And we'd—"

"Release my son, and you'll get to decide when and where the duel takes place."

"Like hell we're setting him loose," Liam said.

"My son won't harm anyone. I'll give you my word."

"Your word means shit."

"Then let's fight now." She was limping and bleeding, and yet she was willing to go back into the ring?

"Liam." I jutted my head toward the indoor pool.

Jaw set tight, he headed for the inn, slid open the glass door, and after we'd both stepped inside, he shut it so hard the glass rattled in its frame. Before I could talk, he exclaimed, "Are you trying to screw me over?"

"Screw you over? No, Liam. I wouldn't have signed up for this if I were trying to *screw you over*."

His pupils pulsed and pulsed.

I glanced through the glass at Cassandra, who was rubbing her body down with a wet towel to get rid of the blood and gore, and then around the pool room to check for surveillance equipment.

I didn't see any cameras, but it didn't mean the place wasn't bugged, so I dropped my voice to a hissing whisper. "She did something to Julian, and I plan on figuring out what that is, so it isn't your heart she eats next."

"Why do you care what happens to my heart?"

I dragged my hand through my hair, my fingers snagging on some strands. "Beats me. I just do."

"You chose August."

I squashed my lips together. This was so not the moment to have this discussion. Then again, there would never be a good time to have this discussion.

"You spent the night with him." It wasn't a question.

"It's none of your business."

"You're my wolves. It is my—"

"No, Liam. What happens between August and me only concerns *him* and *me*."

A nerve ticked in his clenched jaw. For a long moment, he simply stared at me.

"Look, I know you don't want to release Alex, but it'll buy us time. We *need* time." When that didn't extinguish the bloodlust lighting up his irises, I tossed my hands in the air. "You know what, if you don't give a shit about dying, then by all means, be your usual hotheaded self and go fight her now, but you'll be doing it alone, because I won't stand by to see you get gutted!"

Doubt finally smudged his eyes. "Fine. *Fine*, I'll wait."

"Good."

"But I'll only take you on as a Second on one condition."

"No conditions. You either take me on or you don't. But if you don't, you'll lose."

"Maybe I won't lose."

I growled with annoyance. "Liam. Come on. This isn't some joke. This is your life! Don't you care about seeing another night? Another year?"

"My condition is simple. All I'm asking is—"

"I said I wasn't negotiating with you."

"—that you don't date August until after the duel."

"What?"

"I want you focused on *me*. If you're consolidating a mating link, your mind and body will be too preoccupied with him to worry about me."

"Liam . . ." I breathed. "That's ridiculous."

"If I'm going to put my life in your hands, I need your hands not to be busy rubbing down some other man's body."

Heat smacked my cheeks. "Liam!"

"I don't see the problem with what I'm asking. The guy's so infatuated with you, he'll wait. It's not like I'm asking you to stay unmated until the Winter Solstice. Just until my duel."

I blinked at him in disbelief. "Which we haven't even set a date for. It could take months."

"Better find out quick how she cheated then."

This was ridiculous. *He* was being ridiculous.

"Look, my condition isn't a way to win you back. It's just a ground rule to avoid distractions that could cost me my life."

"A life you were willing to sacrifice a moment ago."

He stared long and hard at me. "Do you accept?"

He was being completely unfair. Dating August wouldn't impair my focus. Sure we were mates, but I'd be able to concentrate on other things . . . on other people.

My nostrils flared with annoyed breaths. "What if something happens?"

"If *something happens*, then *I'll* pick the duel date."

"You do realize how stupid that is, right? You're blackmailing me with your own fate."

"By accepting you as my Second, I'm putting my fate in your hands. I'm choosing to give you the benefit of the doubt. Truthfully, I still think I should go fight her right this second." His gaze shifted to Cassandra's before settling back on me. "So? Do you accept?"

I hated what he was asking of me. "I'll still work for him and his dad."

"No. I'll pay you from now on."

I opened my mouth to object.

"Prepping me for the duel will become your job."

I still hadn't shut my mouth.

"Your *only* job. Understood?"

August would be pissed. I could already sense through the pulsating tautness in the tether that my volunteering to be Liam's Second was eating at him.

"You reeked of him this morning, so don't think for a second I won't know if you spend *time* with him."

"I'm not even allowed to spend time with him now?"

"Not alone, and not in close quarters."

"What about college? Do I get to go to college, or is that off the table too?"

"You can attend classes, but as soon as they let out, you're with me." He extended his hand. "Do we have a deal?"

"I hate you," I said, giving him my hand.

"If you hated me, then you would've let me fight today." His smile grew, not wider, just wickeder. "We're going to have fun working together."

"Fun? This'll be a lot of things, but not fun."

Our hearts were both on the line; our lives both suspended.

He lifted my fingers to his lips and kissed my knuckles.

I snatched my hand away and rubbed it against my cut-offs. "This is just some game to you, isn't it?"

"In a way, it is. If I play my hand well, I stand to win *everything* I've ever coveted." His gaze stroked my face. "What do you say we become the characters of the bedtime stories shifters will tell their children for generations to come, Ness Clark?"

"I say, let's save your damn life so I can go back to living mine."

His eyes gleamed with the same stealthy smile that adorned his lips. He nodded toward the lawn, slid the door open, and ushered me out of the shadows and back into the sunshine.

A PACK OF LOVE AND HATE

BOOK 3

PROLOGUE

Minutes ago, I volunteered to be my ex's Second in his duel against the ruthless Creek Alpha. In other words, I signed up to referee a fight-to-the-death between the two most powerful werewolves in Colorado.

Both my heart and stomach were a mess of nerves, but not for the same reasons. Where my heart pounded with dread, my stomach clenched from my mate's heightened pulse.

I craned my neck and squinted into the bright midday sun until I located August standing on the deck overlooking the lawn, light-brown skin a shade paler than usual, and the spray of freckles across his nose and cheekbones a shade darker.

I bit my lower lip. He was about to get a lot angrier once he learned the extent of my deal with Liam. Even though I itched to touch my navel that was fluttering with August's fury, I didn't want to draw attention to our bond, so I clenched my fingers into fists and locked them against the frayed hem of my cut-offs.

Liam strode ahead of me onto the sun-soaked lawn of the inn. "Set Alex Morgan free!" he bellowed to the males of my pack holding Everest's murderer.

Blue eyes flashing with confusion, my uncle leaned over the wooden railing of the inn's deck. "Free? He murdered my son, Liam!"

Releasing the enemy Alpha's son was a risky move, but it was the only one that gave us leverage on this godforsaken duel. By cutting Alex loose, Liam and I were buying time to figure out how Cassandra Morgan defeated the Pine Pack Alpha. Even though Liam wasn't convinced she'd cheated, I was. Julian had thrown up after biting her. A throatful of fur and blood shouldn't have upset a werewolf's stomach. My theory was that she'd rubbed a toxic but odorless lotion into her skin, odorless because Julian's Second inspected the Creek Alpha's body before the duel and didn't notice anything amiss.

Cole freed Alex's arm and stepped aside.

"Watt, let Alex go!" Liam repeated, voice clapping the air.

Color darkening his jaw, August all but tossed Alex's arm, making the Creek shifter stumble. The boy steadied himself against the railing, then pushed his blond hair off his bruised face—the Boulders who'd held him captive had done on a number on him—and started down the deck's staircase, a small limp in his gait, probably a result of my pack's roughness. The limp didn't damage his self-assurance, though. His confidence was as potent as the scent of day-old sweat and caked blood that wafted from his body. I backed away as he passed me, then backed away some more when his gaze zipped over me.

The boy might've resembled a Renaissance cherub with his golden curls and arresting violet eyes, but as far as I was concerned, he was the devil.

Liam stepped in front of me. "Eyes off my wolf."

I cringed. Technically, Liam *was* my Alpha, so I *was* his wolf, but I sensed that wasn't how he'd meant it. And from the heightened pounding inside my abdomen, I took it August sensed the insinuation too.

I looked over my shoulder, imploring him with my eyes to calm down. After a moment, the pulsing quieted. Not to say it became quiet. Oh no. My navel still ticked like a time bomb, but the sensation stopped overwhelming all my other senses. I returned my attention to Cassandra Morgan, who'd finally cloaked her naked body in a white sheath that made her look more wraith than werewolf.

"Alexander Morgan." Tipping her face down toward her son, Cassandra ran her knuckles over his cheek.

Alex wasn't short—he had a good three or four inches on my five-seven stature—yet the top of his head only reached Cassandra's chin.

Suddenly, the same hand that had caressed him slapped him. Hard.

Alex jerked in surprise. "What was that for?"

"Scarin' your poor old ma. Now"—she turned the full force of her tapered blue eyes on Liam—"state your terms, Kolane."

I sidled up to Liam. What sort of message did cowering behind my Alpha like a frightened pup send? Definitely not the right one. I didn't think I could ever inspire fear in someone, but I hoped to come across as a worthy enemy.

I was so close to Liam that I could feel the steady beat of his heart. Would it still be drumming had I not raised my hand to be his Second? The memory of Cassandra eating Julian Matz's heart to acquire his link to the Pine Pack had my gaze drifting over the field, toward the sheet-shrouded body of the fallen Alpha. Bile surged up my throat at the sight of the ruby stains that had bloomed over the white cotton. I gritted my teeth.

"As discussed, Ness and I will set the date and location for the venue, and we don't need to give you more than a half-day's notice," Liam said.

"I'm not at your beck-and-call."

"Then we don't have a deal."

Cassandra pursed her lips. "I agree to the twelve-hour notice, but we duel before summer's end."

"We duel when my Second and I decide," Liam answered.

"Be sensible, Kolane. We have packs to govern and care for. It's not fair to them to drag it out. Let's get this over with as soon as possible. I'm sure it's in your best interest, too."

Was it in our best interest, or simply in hers?

Liam peered down at me. "Ness?"

Summer would end in a little over a month. Would that be long enough?

Even though I hated giving Cassandra an inch, I nodded.

Liam focused on the Creek Alpha again. "Before summer ends it is. But, Morgan, if your son, or any other Creek for that matter"—Liam's brown gaze surfed over the field dotted with shifters in skin before returning to Cassandra—"if any of them so much as harm my wolves or their families, your son *and* cousin will be executed without trial and without contest."

Cassandra's cousin, who'd posed as a werewolf-hating hunter for decades in order to gather information on our pack, eyed Liam and me through the wire-rimmed bifocals propped on the bridge of his nose while thumbing his earlobe.

"Alex will behave, just like I said he would." Cassandra wrapped a hand around her son's wrist.

The duel had blunted her nails that, last night, had looked sharp enough to gouge out an eye, but somehow hadn't chipped her burgundy polish. Or had it? As I squinted at her fingers, she released her son's wrist and curled them into her palm.

"This goes both ways, though, Kolane. If any harm comes to my son or to Aidan before the duel, the choice of time and date reverts back to us."

A warm breeze blew tendrils of my blonde hair into my eyes. I wrenched the strands back, but they escaped a moment later. "Alex and Aidan are living on borrowed time, so you have no right to make demands."

"Ness is right," Liam said. "You're lucky they're even alive, and that we've returned Alex."

A crooked smile touched her blood-stained lips. "Careful, Kolane," she said, taking a step closer to Liam, "you're grossly outnumbered."

The Creek pack had swelled by a hundred today, making my pack, with its forty wolves, an even tinier blip on the shifter map.

"Is that a threat?" Liam growled.

"It's a warning."

"I thought you came in peace," I said.

"We offered peace," she snapped. "Your Alpha turned it down."

My jaw set tight. She was right. She had offered, but Liam insisted on dueling her.

"My request that you not harm my son or my cousin is far from outrageous."

"They won't be killed," Liam said after a beat. "Satisfied?"

"Or tortured," she added.

Liam crossed his arms.

As she waited for Liam's answer, Morgan's eyes became incandescent, as though her wolf were fighting to surge out.

"My people will stay away from them," Liam finally relented.

Her eyes lost their inhuman glow. "Good. Do you have any more demands, Kolane?"

Should I ask her to take her pack and leave Boulder until the duel? Liam's voice tickled my mind.

Since I couldn't communicate the same way my Alpha could, I shook my head.

As much as I didn't want Creeks wandering our woods, I also didn't want to banish my best friend and her family from their hometown. I couldn't do that to Sarah. She might be a Creek now that her uncle had been defeated, but at heart, she'd always be a Pine.

Besides, there was a reason the saying *keep your friends close and your enemies closer* had endured through the ages. We'd have an easier time of finding out how Cassandra had cheated by observing her and her pack.

"We have no further demands," Liam finally announced.

"Then it's settled." Morgan started to lift her hand, probably to shake on their deal.

"Who will you choose as your Second, Mrs. Morgan?"

Cassandra's hand halted in midair. I still had trouble reconciling that this woman was the same one who'd set me up on dates through a fake escort agency. The same way I had trouble coming to terms that my cousin had allied himself with her and pinned Liam's father's murder on me.

"I was gonna pick my daughter Lori . . ."

The thin woman, who bore the same narrow facial structure as Cassandra, seemed to stand a little taller.

"But I'm tempted to go with one of my new wolves." The Creek Alpha raised her gaze to the deck where Sarah stood, her straightened blonde hair gusting around her taut shoulders.

As much as I wanted to spare Sarah the perils of being involved in a duel, if she became Cassandra's Second—

"Better not pick me," my friend yelled. "I'd let them kill you."

Hand coming back down to her side, Cassandra grinned. "Dear Miss Matz, I don't believe you'd let them kill me. I believe you'd do it yourself."

"You're right. I would."

Liam's best friend loomed closer to Sarah. I wasn't sure when it had happened, but Lucas, who'd always abhorred the pack that shared our land, had decided Sarah wasn't hateful, or at least, not *as* hateful as non-Boulders.

"Are there any volunteers who'd care to duel at my side?" Was this her way of testing her new wolves' allegiance?

For a long moment, no one spoke.

But then, a voice I despised more than the Creek Alpha's rang across the blue summer air. "I'll do it, Alpha Morgan." Justin Summix stepped away from his two buddies, his white wifebeater and the skin around his nostrils still speckled with blood from the beating August had delivered after the creep insulted me.

As he approached, Cassandra sized him up. "And you are?"

And here I thought she'd done her homework on all foreign packs . . . Justin Summix must not have been of much interest to her. He *was* a petty and vile shifter who'd insinuated more than once that being the pack's only "bitch"—however biologically correct, I hated the term—meant I was a Boulder slut. He'd touted this barely an hour ago when I strolled up to the inn in August's company.

"Justin Summix, ma'am." He palmed his brown scruff that was the same length and shade as his buzzed hair.

Her gaze halted on the blood splatter before rising to his pulsing nostrils. "Why do you want to duel at my side, Justin?"

"'Cause I know how the Boulders operate." One side of his mouth curled in a sneer. "And I'd really enjoy bringing these two to their knees."

All three Morgans surveyed Justin.

I glanced up at my Alpha, whose lips had arched into a smile. I sensed the turn of events pleased him. Was it because he felt like he knew how Justin operated?

"What happened to your nose?" Cassandra asked.

Justin locked eyes with me. "Like I said, I know how the Boulders operate."

Did you do that?

I didn't answer Liam's question, busy pondering what Justin was hinting at. Was he saying he knew about the mating link? That he would go after August to get to me? My navel tightened from this conclusion, or maybe my navel tightened because August was contemplating wringing Justin's thick neck.

Cassandra licked her lips, removing some of Julian Matz's blood. "Mr. Summix, a duel isn't a settlin' of scores."

I blinked. Was she turning him down?

Justin's yellow-brown eyes widened.

"However," she continued, "I'm willin' to accept your candidature."

Of course she was.

"Are we good, Kolane?"

Liam nodded.

She extended her hand again.

Liam looked at it, then looked back up at her.

"Keep your phone on, Morgan." And then he whirled around and yelled into our minds with such authority that my forehead spasmed. ***We're done here!*** On our way back toward the deck's staircase, he added, ***Ness, you're coming home with me.***

I stumbled, just managing to catch myself on the handrail. He'd said those exact words to me a month ago.

Our work starts today.

I swallowed.

August started down the stairs, but Liam stepped into his path and said, "I said we were done here."

"Get out of my way, Liam."

Liam must've spoken directly into August's mind, because my intended's jaw turned as hard as bark, and then his gaze fell on me, *narrowed* on me. He backed away, before stalking into the inn, stretching the tether so violently that, for a second, I feared it would snap.

But it didn't.

It simply thinned and weakened until all that was left behind was a dull hollowness.

To spare Liam's heart, I'd maimed August's.

1

I didn't speak to Liam during the ride over to his house, because I was angry at how he'd dealt with August. I was also mad at myself for not having put up more of a fight. Then again, I'd been trying to get Liam to calm down and leave the inn with his heart still locked in his chest.

I propped my elbow on the door handle and my forehead on my fingertips. A headache was blooming against my temples. Too much stress and too little sleep. I didn't regret the too little sleep part, though.

Spending the night with August had been . . . well, it had been something I would never regret. My lips still tingled from the heat of his mouth, and my heart still pounded from the memory of his beating against mine.

Would I ever get another night with him? What if he left Boulder until the Winter Solstice? Or what if he stayed but shunned my existence?

That made my heart start twisting.

Before being my intended mate, he was my friend, the boy who'd taught me to climb trees and read stars, the boy who'd picked me up from school when my parents couldn't, the boy who'd sat in my darkened room so the monsters under my bed couldn't reach out and harm me.

When the mating link clicked into place between us on the night of Liam's swearing-in as Alpha, I'd been desperate to break it. After all, Liam was still my boyfriend then. But that relationship lasted a whopping four days. The rain-soaked afternoon Liam called me a traitor was the end of him and me. However much he'd groveled once he figured out I hadn't backstabbed my own pack, I couldn't bring myself to forgive him for his rushed and erroneous judgment. And then last week, he'd slept with his gorgeous, red-headed ex, Tamara, which hurt, but the pain of losing him was nothing compared to the fear of losing August.

The black Mercedes SUV bumped along the short dirt driveway, jostling me out of my morose deliberations. Once we were parked, I reached for the door handle.

"I know you hate my guts right now, but I didn't force you and August apart to annoy you, Ness. My life's on the line, and I need a hundred percent of your attention."

I side-eyed my Alpha. Like I would believe that. He'd been willing to give up his life minutes ago.

"Do you have any food?" I asked, forcing the topic away from August.

Liam's tense expression stuttered. "Yeah. Matt's mom sent me lots of stuff a couple days ago."

"Good. Because I'm starving."

I got out of the car and walked to the front door of his sleek one-storied cabin with the glassed-in living room. I didn't tap my foot as I waited for him, even though he was taking his grand old time. He checked his phone and typed out a message before finally making his way to me. He unlocked the door and gestured for me to go ahead of him. My nostrils flared at the scent of mint lacing the air, which had once felt like silk against my senses, but now felt like sandpaper.

"Why don't you take a seat? I'll get the food."

I crossed over the cowhide rug and sank into his brown leather couch. As he banged around in his kitchen, I checked my phone for messages. I had plenty, but none from August.

I opened one of Sarah's. The first read: *WTF?*

The second: *You volunteered to be his Second! Are you insane?!*

The third: *Why did you leave with Liam?*

The third: *Call me.*

The fourth: *I'm worried. Please call.*

I was touched she was concerned considering she'd lost her uncle today. I should've been the furthest thing from her mind. I pressed on her phone number, then held the phone to my ear.

Big mistake.

Her voice poured out of the receiver so shrilly I winced. "What the hell, Ness? You're going to duel Cassandra Morgan? *And* Justin? Did you see how he was looking at you? Like he wants to kill you, that's how he was looking at you! And knowing him, he'll try! I know I said I wanted Liam to take over the packs, but—"

"Sarah!" I spoke her name sharply to make her stop yelling. "Your mom was Julian's Second, and she's fine."

"But Julian's not! He's not fine! He's . . ." A sob lurched out of her. "He's dead. Julian is dead." Another sob. "Oh, God . . . I think I'm going to puke again." Her words were muffled, as though she'd clapped a hand over her mouth.

"Is someone with you?"

"Yeah. Robbie and Margaux. We're going to the . . ." She sniffled. "To our old headquarters." She blew her nose. "We're holding a vigil for Julian."

"Oh, sweetie."

"I can't believe he's dead. I can't—"

A thought occurred to me. "Sarah, did your pack have a stock of Sillin?" The word tasted bitter, because the anti-shifting drug had caused so much harm.

First at the Alpha trials, when Everest blackmailed me into entering the last duel so he could steal the Boulder's stock from HQ. Then, when he'd reneged on his deal to sell the pills to the Creeks, and Alex Morgan drove my cousin's Jeep off the road.

The night I decrypted his last voicemail and found the Boulder's stock—minus one packet—under the loose floorboard of my childhood home, I hadn't felt any pride or relief. Just despondency, because it had been too late . . . my cousin was already gone forever.

Werewolves possessed magic, but resurrecting the dead wasn't part of our arsenal.

Unless the fable Liam had told me of the wolf resurrecting her mate with a love bite was true, but I doubted fangs sinking into flesh could do much else than stop a heart. It was a pretty legend, nonetheless.

"Robbie says we have some," Sarah answered just as Liam walked out of his kitchen, toting two plates and silverware.

He set everything down on his wrought-iron coffee table, then took the two bottles of water he'd secured underneath his arm and placed them on top of a huge glossy tome.

"Before you go to the wake, can you grab them and hide them?" I asked Sarah.

As he sat in the armchair across from me, he lifted an eyebrow.

"We'll go get them now," Sarah said.

"Thank you."

"If you need anything else, Ness, anything at all, call me."

I smiled in spite of the hellish day I'd had. In spite of the hellish days to come. "Is the wake open to other packs?"

"If Cassandra shows up—" Sarah started.

"I was asking because *I'd* like to come."

"Oh." She paused. "You don't need to, Ness."

"I never do anything I don't want to do."

"You signed up to be Liam's Second," she said.

The tendons in Liam's neck strained against his tanned throat. Even though Sarah wasn't on speakerphone, his hearing was sharp enough to hear her.

"As crazy as it may sound, I wasn't ready to see him die," I replied softly.

Liam rested his forearms on his knees, linked his fingers, and stared so hard at his knuckles that a vertical groove appeared between his eyebrows.

After hanging up, I placed my phone face down on the coffee table. "I think it would be in good form for you to attend Julian's wake, too."

His gaze jerked to mine. "You do realize they're all Creeks now."

"They're also human. *Part* human. Anyway, it was just a suggestion. Not an order."

Slowly, he nodded. "You're right. I'll accompany you."

"Good."

"So, Sillin, huh? You're really convinced that's how she defeated Julian?"

I looked around the bright, clean room with all of its sharp angles and muted colors. Dust motes sparkled in a streak of sunlight. "Any chance your house is bugged?"

"Cole did a sweep of it the other day. No listening devices or hidden cameras."

"I'm not convinced of *how* she cheated, just that she did."

"Then why didn't Nora Matz signal foul play?"

"Sillin is odorless. If Sandra ground it up into her body lotion—"

"Cassandra." When I frowned, he added, "You just called her Sandra."

Right. "Sandra's what she called herself when she posed as a Red Creek Escort pimp." I ran my lower lip between my teeth. Three little letters that had hidden her identity from me. I couldn't figure out if she'd chosen the moniker for lack of creativity or in the hopes that I'd figure out who she was.

"Your theory?"

I picked at the frayed hem of my cutoffs. "She rubbed it into her skin, and when Julian bit her, it made him weaker."

"But Sillin doesn't make us throw up."

He was right, but maybe mixed with lotion . . .

"Besides, wouldn't it have penetrated her bloodstream?"

"Eventually." I sighed. "I'd like to test my theory. Is the Sillin here?"

"No."

"Where did you put it?"

"Somewhere safe."

"Which is?"

"Somewhere safe," he repeated as though I hadn't heard him the first time.

I crossed my arms. "Which you're going to keep me in the dark about?"

"It's better that I do."

"Because you still don't trust me?"

"I trust you."

"Then why won't you tell me?"

"Because the Creeks killed Everest over this drug."

"They killed him because he defaulted on his deal to sell it to them."

"The Creeks have more money than they could ever use. Especially if you factor in Aidan's real estate contribution. I may hate the man, but he's smart at business and has built an empire." Liam unlinked his fingers and set his palms on his denim-clad knees. "They didn't off your cousin because of a monetary loss."

A chill swept over me. *So they really need Sillin . . .* "And yet you were willing to fight her."

"I was ready to fight her because I know how the drug works."

"And I don't?"

He made a growly sound that had my shoulders squaring.

"I took it for weeks, Liam. When I moved to LA, Mom forced me to ingest it every day to make my werewolf gene dormant."

"Then you know that once the pills are popped out of their packaging and exposed to air and heat, their effect wears off. That's why we kept ours in a padlocked fridge."

I raised an eyebrow.

"So *if*—and this is a huge if—Sillin was in Morgan's bloodstream or on her skin, its effect would've diminished by the time I got around to fighting her."

I took in this information, filed it away.

He tilted his head to the side. "You know what baffles me most about all of this? You're always the first to proclaim that women are equal to men, yet a female Alpha defeats a male, and you're convinced she cheated? Why is that?"

My arms went lax, but since they were still knotted in front of my chest, they didn't plummet against the couch. "Julian threw up."

"Yet his Second—who has absolutely no love for the Creek Alpha—didn't signal foul play? Either Nora Matz is dumb as shit or you're smart as fuck."

I watched his expression, watched it closely to know what his conclusion was.

"Don't look at me like that."

"Like what?" I asked.

"Like you don't know what I'm thinking."

"I don't know what you're thinking."

His haggard face softened. "You always know what I'm thinking." He looked down at his long fingers as he rubbed his knees. Back and forth. Back and forth. When he raised his gaze back to mine, he said, "If you were dumb as shit, I wouldn't have accepted you as my Second . . . however enthralling you might be." A heavy breath puffed out of him. "I know I suggested killing your father, Ness, but I'm the first person to admit how wrong it was. I sincerely hope that, someday, I'll be half the man he was."

Liam hadn't moved off the armchair, yet it felt as though he were kneeling beside me, repeatedly flicking my heart.

"If *you* think I'm worth fighting for, then fuck, I'll fight. Alongside you, I'll fight. I'll become a worthy Alpha. One that you will never"—his eyes bore into mine—"want to run from again. One who would never let you run again."

Silence settled between us.

"I want your admiration, Ness. I might never get anything else from you, but I hope I'll earn that much back."

Tears slickened my eyes.

Because he'd brought up my father, I told myself. That was the reason for my tears. The *only* reason for them.

Big fat lie. If that had been the only reason, I would've been able to keep my gaze on his, and I couldn't.

I studied the cowhide rug, discreetly running a knuckle along my cheeks, then took a fortifying breath and lifted my gaze. "How much are you going to pay me?"

His piercing stare swept over my face. For a moment, he neither answered nor moved. Then he leaned back in the chair, crossed one foot over the other, and bounced his legs as though annoyed I'd brought up payment. "How much do you want?"

"Five grand."

"Per week?"

I blinked, whipping my gaze to his. "No. In total."

He stilled his legs. "I'll give you five grand today and the sum of *my* choice when we win the duel."

"Liam, I don't need—"

"Without wanting to sound cocky, I have more money than I could ever spend already. If I win, well those zeroes are going to add up."

"Good for you and for the pack, but that's not why I'm doing this."

The steadiness of his gaze was unnerving. "Why are you doing this?"

"I already told you why."

"Tell me again."

I raked my hand through my hair. "Because I don't want you to die."

"Why don't you want me to die? Don't I deserve it?"

"Don't worry. I've tortured you plenty in my thoughts for calling me a traitor."

He snorted, and crazy as it sounded, I smiled.

How far we'd come, him and me.

How far we still had to go, though.

I took my plate of food and balanced it on my knees. "Can we be clear about one thing? This isn't a game to me. I want to save your life, and the reason I want to save it is because you don't seem to care what happens to it."

That sobered him up.

I bit into a chunk of cheese. "I have some leftover Sillin from LA. I haven't refrigerated it, but it's still in the packaging. You think it's still effective?"

He picked up his plate and cut into his steak. "If it's from the same batch you slipped my father, then yes, it's still effective."

Guilt spread through me. Heath hadn't deserved to live, yet I regretted having a hand in his death. "You think Morgan will release Julian's body to his family?"

"Not if she poisoned him." He uncapped his water bottle and took a swig. "Unless she was certain the Sillin was no longer in his blood."

"How long would that take?"

"Depends on the dose."

"I guess it doesn't actually matter," I ended up saying. "Once we test the Sillin out ourselves, we'll know whether she used it or not."

2

After discussing other ways Cassandra Morgan might've won the duel—Sillin-free ways—Liam dropped me off in front of the apartment I shared with Jeb on the top floor of a two-story house.

Before I could shut the car door, Liam said, "Matt will be over in the morning. Probably around 6:30."

I frowned.

"I want you to start building muscle and stamina."

"Why do I need Matt for that?"

Liam draped his hand over the back of the seat I'd just vacated. "He's going to take you running."

"I can take myself running."

He smirked. "I'm sure you can. But in case you've forgotten, we have a lot more wolves in town."

"You think they might attack me?"

His eyes blackened. "No. I don't think they'd risk such a *tactless* move, but you're not running around in the woods alone. Come to think of it, Lucas should move back in with you, or you could"—he ran his hand through his hair—"stay at my place."

However much Lucas had grown on me, he was not moving into my two-bedroom apartment. "I have Jeb. Besides, what sort of message would me needing a babysitter send out?" I didn't even bother bringing up Liam's other suggestion. "They already don't take me very seriously. Don't add to it."

"Who's *they*?"

"Pretty much everyone." When he opened his mouth, I tossed in, "I'll be going to Pine HQ around seven."

He scrutinized my face a long moment before saying, "Okay. I'll pick you up at six."

"I have my license now." I flashed him a smile that he didn't reciprocate. "I'll get myself there."

His eyes clouded, as though he wasn't pleased with my budding independence. Or was my arrangement of getting there on my own not to his liking?

THE LAST AND only time I'd gone to the Pines' headquarters was for Margaux and Robbie Matz's engagement, and it hadn't been to celebrate them. I'd gone to secure an alliance with Julian because my cousin had convinced me I'd killed Heath and that the pack would avenge their Alpha's death by ending my life.

I'd gotten so much more than Julian's help that day. I'd gotten a confession which had overturned my world: the name of the man who'd murdered my father . . . a man who was still very much alive even though my pack had claimed otherwise.

My heels clicked on the stone staircase that was bare of rose petals and votive candles tonight. Steeling my spine, I stepped past the open doors. The high-ceilinged atrium lined with French windows on one end and dark, wainscoted walls on the other was filled with black-clad grievers. Even the orchid arrangement by the propped picture of Julian was a shade of purple so dark it looked black.

I tried to replace the last image I had of Julian with the blown-up tanned and expressive face staring back at me from within the gilt frame. He would've loved that frame, so golden and ornately carved. The man had such a weakness for expensive things.

My gaze surfed over the room until I spotted Sarah. She was opening one of the French windows overlooking the labyrinthian hedges that separated HQ from the deceased's pale-stone mansion.

As I forded through the copse of wary wolves, I offered condolences to the mourners. From the scrunched brows and skeptic looks, I surmised few believed I was being genuine.

Oh well. I wasn't here to convince them; I was here for Sarah.

When I finally reached her, I tapped her shoulder, and she spun around, puffy brown eyes growing wide in surprise. Apparently, she hadn't put much stock into me coming. She hooked her arms around my neck and hugged me tight.

"Twice in a day. What's the world coming to?" I said into her blonde mane.

She pressed away from me. "Wh-what?"

"You hugging me. That's twice."

Her lips quirked up in a smile. "Don't get used to it."

"I wouldn't dream of getting used to anything around here. Everything's always shifting: alliances, hearts, Alphas . . . people."

She cocked an eyebrow. "Did you just make a joke?"

"Maybe. But don't get used to it," I said, using her own words. "I'm not a very funny person."

Her smile grew a little wider, and then it froze as her gaze locked on a place over my shoulder. She tilted her head toward the entrance.

I turned and saw Lucas and Liam making their way toward us. Both wore black—where Liam had donned a button-down over dark slacks, Lucas sported a T-shirt over jeans.

"Are a lot more of you coming?" Sarah asked after they reached us.

"Why?" Lucas waggled his eyebrow, the one slashed by a white scar. "Afraid of running out of finger food, blondie?"

Liam coughed, probably trying to signal that Lucas's joke was in poor taste, but Sarah laughed, which won her many scowls.

"I don't know if more of us are coming." Liam scanned the room, which from his vantage point, was way easier than from mine. Not quite as tall as August's six-and-a-half foot frame, Liam was still up there. "Did they release Julian's body?"

Sarah shook her head. "I doubt they will." She took a small step toward me, almost as though she were about to drop a kiss on my cheek. "I got all the packets out."

I squeezed her wrist in gratitude.

"What packets?" Lucas asked, ever so subtle.

Liam must've answered Lucas through the mind-link, because the latter blinked. Sarah nodded. "I put them somewhere safe and cool."

"Not in your house, I hope," Lucas said.

Her cheeks pinked. "No."

"Remind me to play poker with you. You're a shit liar."

She flushed a little more.

"Lucas . . ." Liam started, a warning in his voice.

"She shouldn't keep that shit anywhere near her," Lucas growled.

Panic tightened my throat. "He's right, Sarah. Look at what they did to my cousin."

"Oh." Even though Sarah's lids were bloated with tears, they lifted a little higher. "Where should I put them then?"

"You could give them to us," Lucas offered.

I could tell from the way her head jerked back that she wasn't fond of the idea. "I don't think Robbie will go for that."

Lucas puffed out a breath. "Your brother knows?"

"He helped me get them out," she murmured.

A nerve ticked in his jaw. "And he let you keep the stash?"

Sarah splayed her hands on her hips. "He trusts me, Lucas."

I didn't think trust was the issue.

Before I could say anything, a hush fell over the room, disturbed only by the swish of fabric and the clink of jewelry.

"Don't stop talkin' on our account," came a voice that was becoming familiar all too quickly.

I whirled toward the sweeping staircase. At the top of it stood Cassandra Morgan, barefoot and sheathed in a tunic that resembled a burlap sack.

Sarah hissed before clapping her hands over her ears.

"What did she say?" I whispered.

"She called us her little Creeks," Sarah muttered.

Cassandra gestured behind her. "I've come barin' a gift."

Two men with bulging muscles entered the room, hefting a stretcher. On top rested Julian's naked body. No sheet covered it. No blood or dirt either. The Creeks had cleaned him up and sewed his thorax shut with thick black thread. Considering how waxen his flesh was, I assumed they'd syphoned away his blood. Unless they'd left him in the field until he'd bled out completely.

Gasps thundered through the crowd, and then a jarring sob ripped across the room, louder than all the gasps.

"Justin urged me to return your fallen Alpha. So here I am, returning' him. Consider it a peace offerin'."

The men behind her crouched, depositing the stretcher beside the framed picture; then they backed up and remained standing shoulder to shoulder by the front door.

A raucous voice swam through the bewildered crowd. "Cover. Cover," it said, and then heels clicked on the stone stairs as a gray-haired woman tottered up to the landing. She vanished through a small door, before returning with an armful of lavender hand towels monogrammed with golden Ps. Complexion almost as pallid as her dead Alpha's, she kneeled and gently covered him, strip by cottony strip.

Once Julian was mummified in terrycloth, Casandra started down the stairs. "Aidan said Boulders weren't empathetic, but I see my cousin was wrong. I thank you"—she inclined her head toward us—"for showin' my people such kindness."

"We are *not* your people!" Sarah's voice pinged against the buffed stone floors.

Cassandra narrowed her eyes, and Sarah clutched her head, shrinking into herself.

"You can hear my voice in your head, can you not, Miss Matz?" the Creek Alpha asked pleasantly.

Sarah didn't say anything, but her spine tautened.

"If you can hear me, then you are mine." As Cassandra strolled through the room, shadows played across her features, staining her eyes. "Just as I am yours." She stopped when she reached Sarah's brother, who'd gathered his shoulder-length blond hair into a ponytail. "You were next in line if I'm not mistaken."

Robbie nodded cautiously, his hair glinting gold in the dim lighting.

"I'd like you to tell me about your pack so that I may lead it well. Shall we take a walk in the gardens?"

Before he acquiesced, Robbie's eyes flashed to his sister's. I moved in front of Sarah as though I could somehow deflect his glance, but Cassandra trailed his line of sight, and although her gaze paused on me, she tilted her face, which told me she hadn't missed the true object of Robbie's attention.

Dread pooled in my stomach. Robbie probably hadn't considered the repercussion of looking his sister's way, but I did, and I didn't like it one bit, the same way I didn't like that he'd left the Sillin in her care. If he didn't have all the answers

Cassandra wanted, she'd come looking for Sarah, and I didn't want the Creek Alpha sniffing around my friend.

Cassandra claimed she'd come in peace, but if that were true, she wouldn't have brought her shifter army with her . . . she wouldn't have created an escort agency to spy on other packs.

We should leave. Liam's silent command startled the air out of my lungs.

I sucked in a breath before nodding and turning toward my friend. "Ready to go?"

Sarah's dark eyebrows quirked. "Go?"

I spread open my eyes to drive my intent home; I wasn't leaving without her. "My car's right outside."

Maybe Cassandra wasn't after the Pine's stock of Sillin, but what if she was?

As understanding crept over Sarah, color leached from her skin. "Let me say goodbye to Mom."

"Of course."

She wound around her pack toward her mother, who was slumped on a couch, pallid cheeks shiny with tears.

"Ness?" Liam nodded to the entrance.

I set off alongside him and Lucas. As we took the stairs, my gaze wandered to the lavender shroud atop Julian's still form.

"If anyone ever buries me in fucking tea towels, I'm going to haunt their ass," Lucas huffed under his breath.

Laughter burst out of me. Even Liam's lips quirked up. I pressed the back of my hand against my mouth to stifle the sound that was so incredibly inappropriate that even Cassandra's bodyguards gave me a hard stare, and I doubted they had any love for Julian and his pack.

I elbowed Lucas as we exited. "They're all going to think I'm heartless now."

Lucas dragged his hand through his shaggy black hair, grinning. "You should always keep your enemies guessing."

"The Pines aren't my enemies."

"They're no longer Pines," Lucas said just as Sarah surged out of the building.

She must not have heard him, because she didn't react to his comment. She hooked her arm through mine and all but dragged me down the stairs. "I've changed my mind. I'd like you guys to take the stuff."

It took me a second to compute what *the stuff* was. When I did, I turned and exchanged a quick glance with Liam.

"Lucas"—he tossed him the car keys—"take Sarah home."

Lucas frowned at first, but Liam must've elaborated, because he nodded. "How're you getting home? Running?"

"Ness has a car."

I clutched my keys tight enough to leave an imprint. "I think it's better if you go with them, Liam."

A dark lock of hair fell into his eyes.

"I'd feel better if Sarah had both of you with her," I added.

A half-truth.

The other half of that truth was that the drive took a little more than a half hour, and I felt like Liam and I had spent enough time together for one day.

And I might not have trusted his intentions concerning me yet.

It took a couple minutes—maybe seconds—for Liam to unglue the soles of his black boots from the flagstone path. Shoulders wrenched back, he strode to his car.

Lucas looked between us before going after our Alpha.

Sarah bit her lip. "I'll call you tomorrow, hun." And then she was gone too.

And I was finally alone.

The drive home took me straight past the Watts' warehouse. Even though it wasn't late, August's apartment, which flanked the warehouse, was pitch-black.

I tried to feel him through the tether, but my stomach was a giant jumble of emotions. I parked on the side of the road, grabbed my phone, and typed out a text: *Don't leave Boulder, ok?*

In the starlit darkness, under a moon that was almost full, I waited for August to reply.

No reply came.

3

At 6:15 a.m. the following day, I peeled my body out of my warm bedsheets and got ready for my early morning run with Matt. I was lacing my sneakers when he messaged me that he was downstairs. Stuffing my key and phone in the zippered pocket of my track jacket, I tiptoed past my sleeping uncle's room, opened and shut our front door discreetly, then bounded down the porch stairs.

"Sorry you got saddled with me."

He pushed away from his silver Dodge sedan, palming his cropped blond hair. "Don't sweat it, Little Wolf. I owe you."

"What do you owe me for?"

"Stopping Liam from dueling Morgan without backup."

I tightened my ponytail, sighing. "If only he'd taken her deal."

"You're telling me." Matt Rogers was a big guy but as gentle as a puppy. "Should we get going? I need to be at work in an hour."

I stretched out my calves. "I'm ready."

Thirty minutes into our ridiculously strenuous workout—Matt had picked a trail that wound up the flank of the mountain—I wheezed, "I don't get . . . why I have to train. Your brother said . . . Seconds rarely get . . . dragged into the fight." I gulped in some much needed oxygen, then puffed it out. "Look at Nora . . ." My heart rate became so frenzied I had to take a minute off from speaking.

"If Julian's sister had gotten involved, he might still be alive today." Perspiration beaded on Matt's forehead, but unlike me, he wasn't panting like a bull in a pen.

I came to an abrupt halt, which forced Matt to stop, then bent at the waist and pressed my palms into my thighs. "The poison was already . . . in his system."

His gaze swept over the fence of evergreens on our left, as though he were expecting to see furred creatures with perked ears and glowing eyes. "I heard about your theory, but Morgan could shift. If she'd been jacked up on Sillin, there's no way she could've transformed."

"I don't think it was . . . in her blood." I sucked in a lungful of hot, dry air. The sun was peaking, brightening the pink hue of the mountain lupines lining the steep path. "I think it was . . . on her skin."

"Stuff on your skin penetrates your bloodstream."

I straightened, crossing my arms in front of my still-heaving chest. "Don't tell me you think . . . she won fair and square."

"Nora Matz seems to think so."

I wasn't in wolf form, yet I growled at my friend. "That's impossible."

A slow smile lit up his ruddy face. "I agree. I mean, she *is* female—"

"Prick." I slugged his huge bicep, which just increased his smirking.

"You know I don't actually think your gender is feeble, right?" His smirk turned back into a smile.

"Yeah. I know." It had taken me months to prove that a female could hold her own in a pack of all-male wolves. Did I regret entering the Alpha trials at the start of summer?

No.

Okay . . . Maybe a little.

After all, I'd almost lost my life during a landslide and then again during the final duel, which thankfully had been aborted when my crafty cousin had his mother kidnap Evelyn.

As Matt and I started down the mountain, I asked him about work, which was merely a roundabout way of getting to August since he was Matt's boss.

He told me they were putting up the walls on some luxury lodge on Valmont Road. "Place is wicked."

"Is August . . . Does he help with the building part?"

"Yeah. He gets his hands dirty."

"Is he on site every day?"

Matt cast me a sideways glance. "What exactly do you want to know?"

I bit my lip but released it to gather some oxygen. "Did he stay?"

"You seriously think he up and left? He got the girl. He's never going to leave. At least not without you."

A flush creeped up my neck. Hopefully Matt would attribute it to our strenuous exercising. "Liam's making me keep away from him."

"What do you mean, *making you keep away*?"

"He told me that since he's entrusting me with his life, he wants my entire focus to be on him. He said that until the duel, I couldn't hang out with August. That if I did, he'd duel Cassandra on his own terms."

Matt didn't say anything, just focused on the dust puffing under his sneakers.

"You think he's really worried about August being a distraction, or do you think it's his way of getting me back?"

Without breaking stride, he said, "What do you think?"

"I don't know what to think, Matt. I don't know Liam like you do."

"He's not over you, Ness."

Even though my limbs felt on fire from running, a chill crept into my bones. "You think he'd really face Cassandra without my help if something happened between August and me?"

"I'd hope he wouldn't do something so dumb, but he was ready to challenge her without a Second, so yeah, I think he'd really schedule a showdown without you. Men will do stupid shit to impress girls."

"It wouldn't impress me, though. It would just piss me off."

"It'll get your attention."

I sighed.

"Look, I'm not sure I'd take my own advice, but if you can rein in your urges, then do it."

I snorted. "Rein in my urges? I'm not some animal."

Matt grinned. "Beg to differ, Little Wolf." After a beat, he added, "At least, try to repress your lustfulness."

The flush, which had started on my neck, engulfed my entire face.

"Did I just make Ness Clark blush?"

"Shut up," I grumbled, breathing hard again. "And I'm not blushing . . . I'm just overheated from this stupid . . . run."

"Uh-huh." He simpered all the way to his car. "Look, if anyone can tame their urges, it's you."

Hand pressed on the hood of his car, I pulled my ankle into my hamstring to loosen my thigh.

"Besides, we're talking days, right? Not weeks?" Matt asked, muscles bunching in his arms and thighs as he stretched.

"I don't know how long it'll take." I kicked a stray cigarette butt off the sidewalk and into the gutter. "Perhaps it'll take the full five weeks we have."

As he got into his car, he said, "Well, I'm sure August'll understand."

Yeah, I wasn't sure about that at all. He still hadn't answered the text I'd sent him last night.

"Same time tomorrow?"

I whipped my gaze off the squashed death-stick. "We're running tomorrow?"

"Every day until the duel. I'll plan a different route, though."

"What the hell did I sign up for?" I grumbled.

"You signed up to save your Alpha's ass."

"I don't need muscle for that, Matt; I need a working brain and time to think."

"Little Wolf, if the fighting gets dirty, you'll want the muscle."

Matt's comment eclipsed all my residual annoyance.

Before taking off, he added, "We can't make you unbreakable, but we can make you strong enough to break Justin Summix."

When he put it that way . . .

He shot me a quick grin and a wave as he drove off.

I watched his taillights become mere pinpricks and then vanish altogether. Before heading inside, I checked my phone, hoping I'd gotten a text message.

I sighed when I saw that I had, but not from the right wolf.

Liam had sent me the address of a gym I was to meet him at after lunch. At least I had the morning off. It would give me time to deposit his check and pay Evelyn a visit. Two things that made me happy.

I'd have to find a lot more to keep myself sane in the coming weeks.

4

After a delicious homemade breakfast at Evelyn's and plenty of bone-crushing hugs to last me throughout the day, Frank McNamara insisted on walking me out to the Boulder Inn minivan.

"I didn't tell her about the duel," he said as I set the container filled with cinnamon rolls on the passenger seat. "I suggest you don't either."

"I don't plan to, Frank. She's already so worried about . . . *everything*." Evelyn had only recently learned of the existence of werewolves. I'd been so afraid she would stop loving me and start fearing me, but she hadn't. "Did you tell her about Aidan? About what he is?"

"I did." He rubbed the white stubble coating his jaw. "Said she wasn't surprised."

"Really?"

"Apparently he had this room in the basement that locks from the inside. A bunker of sorts. And it had all these scratch marks on the walls. When she asked him about it, he said it was where he kept the dogs that weren't housebroken yet. She didn't believe him of course—I mean the lock was on the inside of the room—but back then, she thought he used it as a torture chamber."

My heart clenched with horror. "You think"—I lowered my voice—"he tortures people?"

Frank shook his head, and his mass of white hair fluttered around his face. "I think he used that room when he needed to shift. Even with Sillin in his system, in his prime, the full moon would've brought on a change. Perhaps not a complete shift, but parts of his body would've taken on a different form or texture."

"When I was in LA, full moons didn't affect me."

"You were a thousand miles away. His pack was only a hundred miles away. He'd have felt their influence. Anyway"—he tapped the hood of the car—"I'm sure you have places to be."

I drew my door open, but before climbing in, I asked, "You think I'm right, Frank? About Cassandra cheating?"

"I hope you are. But if you aren't, I hope Liam will have the strength to defeat her, because the alternative—" He shuddered. "I'd rather not consider the alternative."

AFTER LIAM CHALLENGED CASSANDRA, I'd told him he was impulsive and insane, but wasn't I the same? Thinking I could save him was insane. Truth was, I didn't even wish Cassandra Morgan dead, but since only one leader could walk out of the duel with their heart intact, I'd do everything in my power for that person to be Liam.

I turned the volume of the car stereo louder to drown out the incessant chatter in my brain. Not to mention my stomach was cramping from the stress of all the thinking I was doing.

I pressed a hand against my navel as I stopped at a red traffic light, then scanned the street for a parking spot, but then I forgot all about parking and all about the cramping and all about Cassandra Morgan. Stopped opposite me at the intersection was a black pickup, and at its wheel was the man who still hadn't answered my text message.

His gaze banged into mine. The impact was so tremendous it knocked the breath from my lungs and made my heart rattle.

Only a day had gone by since I'd seen him, and yet the hours we'd spent apart stretched further than all the years we'd been separated.

I watched him watch me, wondering what he was thinking, wondering if he'd pull over so we could talk. I imagined myself getting out of the van and striding over to his car. I imagined myself knocking on his window—

A loud honk had me jerking on the gas pedal. I lurched into the intersection before even checking if the light had turned green, and then I was driving past him, and he wasn't looking at me anymore. He was staring straight ahead as though I wasn't even there. I swerved a little, and the car behind August's honked. I spun my steering wheel and gunned the van back into its rightful lane before turning on my blinker and sidling in next to the curb to catch my breath.

Breaths tinted with the fragrance of Old Spice and sawdust that always clung to his skin.

Surely I was imagining his smell—my windows were shut. Nonetheless, I inhaled long and deep, as though if I managed to pull his scent into my lungs, I could reel in the man.

Didn't work like that unfortunately.

The only thing I could potentially reel in was the tether, but the last and only time I'd tried, it had tickled August's abdomen. When he'd done it to me, though, he'd moved my entire body.

Some things simply weren't fair.

Matt said August would understand, but Matt was wrong.

I clutched my phone and typed: *Turn back. Let me explain.*

My thumb hovered over the send icon. Before I could chicken out, I stamped the screen. Phone rattling in my hands, I waited for August to answer, but he sent no words back. How was I supposed to make him understand if he wouldn't give me the time of day? I slapped my steering wheel so hard I blasted the horn.

"Goddammit, August, I didn't do it to spite you!"

At least Liam has nothing to worry about, I thought morosely.

I gripped my head between both hands until my skull stopped throbbing and my eyesight cleared. My track record with boys was so pitiful—four days with Liam, one night with August. Was there something wrong with me? Before pulling back into the light morning traffic, I picked up my phone and texted my question to Sarah on the off-chance she'd gotten out of bed before noon.

By the time I found a parking spot, my hands were still shaking. I thought of Mom's silver-lining theory, that if you looked long enough at one, it would outshine everything else. The silver lining of today: solicitors would stop hounding me to inform me of rising interest fees.

As I entered the bank, I took the check out of my wallet and smoothed the crinkles to make sure the ink hadn't faded overnight, but all three zeroes were still there. I got in line behind an old woman hunched over a walker, the knobs of her curved spine pressing against her flowered blouse. She glanced over her sunken shoulder at me and smiled. I smiled but then wondered if she'd meant to smile at someone else.

"You're the girl from the inn, aren't you?"

The trembling subsided then, replaced by surprise that made me go rigid. And mute . . .

"You served me a lovely brunch a couple weeks ago. I called to make a reservation, but they told me the inn was closing indefinitely. Is that right?"

"It changed"—I cleared my voice—"ownership."

"What a shame. What a shame. And just when the food was getting good. You wouldn't happen to know what happened to the chef?"

I cocked an eyebrow. "She's still in Boulder."

"Oh. How wonderful. My son and his wife run a restaurant in town. You might've heard about it? The Silver Bowl?"

"I don't go out much."

"Next," a bank teller called.

The hunched woman paid her no mind. "Anyway, she used to do the cooking, but she came down with something called algeria or agora, and it made her very fatigued. So they're on the market for a new chef. You wouldn't happen to know if the one from the inn would be interested?"

"I could ask her."

"Next!" the teller called out louder.

"Great. Let me get you my phone number." As she dug through her bag, its contents spilled onto the floor.

I gathered everything up for her, then hooked it on the walker.

"Ladies, I don't have all day," the teller said, exasperated.

"You know what, why don't I just tell her to call the restaurant?" I asked.

The old woman nodded, and her wispy gray hair frolicked around her face. "Tell her to say Charlotte sent her."

The teller cleared her throat.

"The young are always in such a hurry," Charlotte huffed as she hobbled forward, her walker scraping the floor.

For a second, I thought she was talking about me because the teller was well past her prime, but Charlotte didn't know me, so she couldn't know at what speed I lived my life.

But it was true. I was in a hurry.

In a hurry to get to the bottom of Cassandra Morgan's feat.

In a hurry for the duel to be over.

In a hurry to get back in August's good graces.

A moment later, another teller called out, "Next."

I smoothed out the check again before handing it over, along with my debit card and a picture ID.

The employee squinted at my ID, then at my card, then flipped the check over. "Sign at the back, please." She tapped a long acrylic nail against the check.

I signed it nervously, my name looping off the faint line. This felt too good to be true. I expected the check to bounce and security guards to escort me away for questioning. I moistened my lips with the tip of my tongue and waited as the teller clicked and clicked her computer keypad with those long nails of hers.

Finally, she printed out a sheet of paper and handed it over. "Your balance."

I snatched it, and my heart stuttered to a stop when I saw the new number. "Um. I think there's a mistake."

"A mistake?"

"Are you sure this is my account?"

"Are you Ness Marianne Clark?"

"Yes."

She leveled her gaze on her monitor, clicked on her keyboard again. "Then there's no mistake."

My heart hurtled around my ribcage now.

"Were you expecting a higher balance?" she asked when I still hadn't moved. As I read the number over—and over—she added, "We have some great investment opportunities. I'd be more than happy to set up an appointment."

I licked my lips again. Was there any other way of depositing money into someone's account? "Can you give me a printout of the latest activity? Wire transfers or checks or . . ."

"Sure thing."

Her printer burst to life and spat out another sheet of paper, which I all but ripped from her fingers this time. When I saw the name on the check that had been deposited into my account barely an hour ago, my hands started shaking anew. Or maybe they'd never stopped shaking.

"Thank you," I whispered hoarsely.

"Everything all right, honey?" Charlotte asked from her teller's window.

I nodded even though nothing was really all right. It was all wrong. "I'll . . . I'll—Um. I'll tell Evelyn to call." I waved, then slipped my phone out of my bag and, fingers stumbling over the slick screen, I dialed August.

It went to voicemail.

Ugh!

ME: *I just stopped by the bank. What did you do?*

I tried calling him again. Again, he didn't pick up.

ME: *If you don't answer me, I'm going to hunt you down.*

A dropped pin on a map appeared in my messages.

5

The address August sent me took me to the construction site Matt had mentioned during our run.

I shut the car door so hard it lifted the hem of my white eyelet dress. So many emotions whirred inside me as I stomped toward the site that I didn't feel the ground beneath my feet or the sun in my hair. I felt like a livewire, jumpy and ready to electrocute anyone who came in between me and my target: August Watt.

I walked around the work site until I located him.

The man who'd looked at a traffic light instead of at me and yet who'd deposited an ungodly amount of money into my bank account.

The man who hadn't taken any of my calls and yet had sent me his location.

The man who was wearing a hard hat even though he'd crashed in a helicopter and survived.

The man who made my heart sprint and my navel burn and yet who was no longer mine to hold.

"August Watt!" I yelled.

I must've called out his name *really* loudly because every single worker swiveled around.

August looked up from a blueprint stretched over a work table. Unhurriedly, he exchanged a few words with one of his men before strolling toward me, hands in the pockets of a pair of faded jeans.

His body ate up the sun and the land and the sky and all of the ambient noise.

Once he stood in front of me, I craned my neck.

"Yes?" His husky voice brushed over the tip of my nose.

I swallowed because my mind had gone blank, and I couldn't remember why I'd come. And why I was mad. Was I even mad?

Oh, yes. I was *livid*.

I narrowed my eyes. "What the hell's gotten into you?"

"Funny." He crossed his arms, making all of his muscles pop. "I could ask you the same thing."

"I didn't deposit"—I dropped my voice to a hiss—"*five hundred thousand* dollars into your account."

"No, you put your life on the line for your ex. Your fucking ex who then proceeded to tell me to fuck off. So let me turn that question on you; what the hell's gotten into *you*?" His jaw clenched so hard it sapped all the curves from his face. Even his full lips looked etched in steel instead of skin.

"I hope you didn't give me all your money, because you're going to owe your mom a whole bunch for all the cursing."

His mouth didn't even twitch, which alerted me to the fact that he was well and truly mad.

I sighed. "Why?"

"Why did I give you that money? Because it was owed to you."

"Owed to me? What are you talking about?"

"When we bought your family's business, we got it at a bargain price. Dad never felt right for paying your mother such a pittance."

My jaw slackened but then snapped shut. "Mom never thought you guys underpaid, August."

"But the fact is we did."

"No you didn't. You paid the amount it was worth at the time."

"Why does it matter?"

"Because it's half a million dollars," I whisper-shouted. "You can't just go around gifting that much money to people."

"You're not people," he said, a tad more softly.

"What am I?"

"I was hoping you could help me define that."

Even though I stood in his shadow, heat still pricked my skin. I suspected it had little to do with the sun and everything to do with the looming male.

"Why did Liam tell me to fuck off, Ness? What exactly happened back at the inn? What did you promise him?"

I pushed my hair off my face. "I promised him that I would stop . . . whatever it is we'd started . . . to prep him for his duel."

His dark eyebrows dipped. "Why would you have to stop seeing me to prep him for his duel?"

I averted my gaze, studied a dusty clump of grass next to August's heavy-duty work boots. "He wants a hundred percent of my attention."

August snorted. After a stretch of silence, he muttered, "You forgot to flick me."

I returned my gaze to his. Every time he'd grunted in the past, I'd flicked him to show him how often he resorted to making that caveman noise instead of using words. "If I touch you, your scent"—spice, wood, earth, heat, home—"it'll rub off on me, and he'll know I saw you."

A muscle flexed in his forearm. "So what?"

"So he'll fight Cassandra without my input." I rolled the hem of my dress between my fingers.

"I'm not sure whether to be offended or fucking jealous that he wants you back so badly he'd lure you away with blackmail." His warm breath fanned against my forehead. "Look at me, Dimples."

I raised my gaze to his, but not because he'd asked. Because he'd called me that nickname that made me feel knee-high to a ladybug. "August, you know I can't stand that nickname."

"And I can't stand that my girlfriend is breaking up with me over her ex's bruised ego. So I'll call you what I want to from now on, the same way you did what you wanted yesterday."

I sucked in a breath that burst right back out of my mouth. "August, I didn't *want* this. His confidence was going to get him killed!"

His green gaze flared so brightly it became almost phosphorescent. And then my stomach acted up, performed a slow roll that had me pressing my palm against it. The warm wind blew August's intoxicating scent into me. Instead of easing the tension, it increased it, made my skin desire the long fingers that gripped his bent elbows to brush over *my* elbows, *my* arms, *my* wrists.

This was *so* not the right time to concoct racy scenarios.

I shifted from one foot to the other, hoping he couldn't guess all that was going through my mind.

"I need to know something." His voice was so rough it spurred my smutty contemplations. "Am I going to lose you?"

"Lose me?" I snapped out of my trance.

"To him? Am I going to lose you to him?" His words whispered over my nose. "You're worth fighting for, but I need to know if it's a fight I have a chance of winning."

My heart climbed into my throat.

"I'll step back, Dimples"—the nickname didn't sound very childish suddenly—"even if it goes against everything I want, I'll step back, but you have to ask me. Do you want me to step back?"

"No," I blurted.

His stance softened, which wasn't to say he slumped or unwound his arms. He was just more timber than steel. "But I can't step forward, can I?"

I gulped and shook my head.

He bobbed his head as though he was filing the rules away. After a beat, he said, "I don't share what's mine."

Those words were like lighter fluid poured right into my core, igniting something fierce and deep. "Good, because I don't share either."

A smile ghosted over his lips, bumped straight into my heart, made it beat faster.

"I've got some terms of my own."

"Oh?" I swallowed, trying to moisten my throat that felt as dry as plaster. "I'm listening."

"I won't touch you, but there's no way I'm not seeing you every day, and *not* from the nosebleed section."

"Okay."

"I want to know what you're up to, and where, and not through the mating link. This isn't me being a stalker, but there are Creeks in Boulder, and I trust those bastards even less than I trust Liam, which is saying a fucking lot."

I'd never heard August curse so much. Then again, he was no longer the soft boy I'd had a crush on but a man weathered by human wars and pack skirmishes.

"And before you make a comment about my unhinged swearing, know that I'll drop a hundred dollar bill in Mom's curse jar, and you're going to witness me doing it, because I'll deposit it tomorrow night during dinner at their place, dinner to which you are coming. And to which you can bring Jeb."

I jutted my hip to one side and planted my hand on it. "What if I don't want to go to dinner at your parents' house tomorrow night?" I did, but I didn't appreciate the form of his invitation.

His gaze turned challenging. "You don't have to come, but that'll break Mom's heart."

My hand skidded off my hip. "That's a low-blow. How am I supposed to *not come* now?"

His smile grew a little wider and a little more roguish too. He was enjoying riling me up.

"You know, if you'd just asked me, I would've said yes."

"Just wanted to see your face light up, Dimples. Just wanted to see your eyes turn that spectacular shade of blue they get when you're emotional. Even though I'd much rather make them bluer using . . . *other* methods."

I was pretty certain my eyes had just gotten a *lot* bluer.

He raised his hand to my face, but before he could touch me, he curled his fingers into his palm. "Fuck the convalescence period after the helicopter crash. This is going to be so much worse." His hand plummeted to his side.

"Maybe"—I wet my lips—"maybe we shouldn't spend too much time together. It'll make it harder."

He snorted. "That part's not negotiable."

I flicked him, then snatched my hand away, shocked I'd broken the rule first.

He stared at my hand. "Never thought I'd crave getting flicked, but if that's the extent of our physical contact, then flick away."

"I shouldn't even have done that," I said, tugging my lip into my mouth.

"That thing you're doing to your lips. Try not to do that when we're together." He took a step back as though it would somehow ease the tension jostling the tether between us.

I freed my lip. "Sorry."

"Don't be sorry, sweetheart. It's not your fault I'm so darn attracted to you."

A thrill shot up the entire length of my body. "I should probably go, huh?"

He palmed his dark, cropped hair, then looked over his shoulder at the construction site. We were far enough away that our conversation hadn't carried but close enough for the men to watch us. When he looked at me again, his eyelids had thinned. "Yeah. You probably should because I'm about to fire a whole bunch of people."

I frowned.

"And if you ever come back to visit, wear a muumuu or something *bigger*."

He wanted to fire people because they'd looked at me a little too long? "A muumuu? I don't even know what that is."

"A shapeless dress. Grams used to wear them."

I smirked. "I don't own any *muumuus*."

"Well, buy some."

"With your money?"

"It's *your* money. All of it. I've already paid taxes on it."

"August, I can't accept—"

"If you don't want it, give it to charity."

"August . . ." I all but growled.

"Dimples . . ."

Ugh.

He smiled.

"You're impossible," I muttered.

"Pot calling the kettle black, sweetheart."

I shook my head, but a smile made its way to my lips. "Shouldn't you be working?"

"Shouldn't you be leaving?"

My smiled increased; his, too.

I started toward the van, glancing over my shoulder as I left. His posture had straightened again, and his eyes blazed with renewed assurance.

The future was uncertain, and not just because we were werewolves fighting for our land and pack, but because we weren't diviners. Yet I sensed August would stand by me even if he couldn't hold my hand.

The only certainty I possessed in this uncertain world.

6

I remembered feeling beat-up after the first contest in my pack's Alpha trials, but two hours into training with Liam and I felt like I'd been fed through a trash compactor and dumped in a landfill.

When my back hit the sweat-slicked mats for the hundredth time, I didn't get up. I just lay there, gaping at the exposed metal tubing on the ceiling with great fascination until Liam's barely perspiring face appeared in my line of sight.

I closed my eyes so that maybe he'd leave me alone, but no such luck.

"Up, Ness. We're not done."

"You might not be, but I am," I muttered.

"Is that what you'll tell Justin if you end up having to fight? Up!"

I snapped my lids open and glared, even though I wasn't truly mad at him. I knew he was pushing me because he had my best interests at heart.

"Chicks are so fragile." Lucas's voice made me lurch up.

I sent him a chilling look that made him simper. He winked at me at the same time as Sarah smacked his chest so hard the sound echoed against the brick walls.

"Geez, blondie, I was just motivating her," he said.

I'd invited Sarah along for moral support. At least, that's how I'd presented the invite. In truth, I was worried about leaving her alone after the phone call I'd had with her on my way back from August's construction site.

Last night, her brother called her to tell her that, sure enough, Cassandra inquired about the Pine's stock of Sillin. After he told her they'd run out of the drug a couple months back, the Alpha apparently lapped it up. I doubted Cassandra Morgan *lapped* anything up.

On the plus side, it assured me the Sillin was important to her.

Now if I could just fig—

Liam swiped my ankle with his foot, sending me flailing backward. Air whooshed out of my lungs with an audible, "Oomphf," and little stars spangled my vision.

I blinked. The stars glittered less fiercely, but they were still there, brightening the maze of metal tubes crisscrossing the ceiling.

I was *never* getting back up.

Ever.

Liam brushed his brow with his forearm, pushing back the locks of dark-brown hair plastered to his forehead, before extending his arm. Even though my hand felt attached to a massive dumbbell, I heaved my fingers off the mats and latched onto Liam's. He hauled me up so fast I stumbled against him. The contact had me pitching backward. Thankfully I stayed upright, but that had little to do with my footwork and everything to do with his solid grip.

Averting my gaze from his piercing one, I slid my hand out of his and rubbed the back of my hot neck. "I'm beat, Liam. I'm not even sure I'll be able to run tomorrow morning with Matt."

He observed me slowly and silently, his musky, minty scent ribboning off his gleaming skin and filling the air, stirring many conflicting emotions within me.

After an entire minute, he nodded. "Okay."

"Okay, we're done?"

When he nodded, I contemplated fist-pumping the air, but the effort that would take felt remarkable.

"And okay to canceling your run. You'll do enough running on Sunday night."

It took my frazzled brain a second to remember that Sunday night was the full moon—the entire pack's night out in fur. After a certain age, werewolves could only shift during the full moon.

Last month, I'd run with the pack for the first time in my life. I'd experienced another first that night too. I wondered if Liam was also remembering our kiss. Even though so much had happened since then, I'd forever cherish that night.

As we walked over to the bench where Sarah was trying to convince Lucas to cut his hair or jump on the manbun-trend wagon, I said, "Shouldn't we be training in fur?"

"We'll get to that," Liam said.

"And shouldn't we be practicing with Sillin?"

"We'll get to that too."

"When?"

"You visit the Watts' construction site, and suddenly, you're in a hurry?"

So he knew . . . Had he smelled August on my fingertip, or had Matt informed him?

"Why are you suddenly so *un*hurried?" I volleyed back.

His expression, which had been far from open, shuttered up. He snatched a bottle of water from the bench and tipped the rim to his lips, squashing the plastic between his fingers.

Concern edged Sarah's features.

"You told me I wasn't allowed to date him or hang out alone with him. I wasn't alone, and we're not sneaking around, so I don't get why you're giving me attitude about this." Suddenly, I wasn't exhausted anymore.

"Hey, Lucas, can you show me where the water fountain is again?" Sarah asked, springing off the bench.

Lucas pointed to the back of the gigantic room. Rolling her eyes, she grabbed his outstretched finger and heaved him up, letting go as soon as he was on his feet. If I wasn't seething, I might've laughed at his stunned expression.

She jutted her head, and he followed suit, even though he seemed reluctant to leave Liam and me alone. What did Lucas think I would do? Claw up Liam's pretty face?

"Subtlety's not your forte, huh?" I heard Sarah ask. Whatever Lucas answered made her bellow, "Oh my God, get over yourself."

I uncapped another bottle of water and downed half of it in one gulp. "I'll be going to dinner at his parents' house tomorrow night. He'll be there too, as well as Jeb. I'm telling you this so you don't get your information from another source and misconstrue a family dinner for a hot date." I screwed the cap back onto my bottle slowly.

Liam's gaze narrowed on the steel bench. "Family? Did you get engaged?"

"No. I did not get engaged. I'm seventeen." I squared my shoulders and crossed my arms. "The Watts have always been like a second family to me. When I was growing up, I spent almost as much time with them as I spent with my own parents."

Liam still didn't say anything.

"And just so you stop assuming this, I'm not going to let a mating link drive me into a marriage. No amount of magic will dictate the course of my life. August and I go way back, but maybe we're all wrong for each other." We hadn't felt all wrong for each other the night at his place, but Liam hadn't felt wrong for me either.

Liam glanced at me, and even though his gaze was still hardened, it sparked, and that spark felt dangerous. I hadn't planned on giving him hope . . . I'd planned on setting him straight.

"But I won't know that until I actually date him, which I plan on doing once this duel is over." My words dimmed the spark but didn't extinguish it.

"You know, it would've been in your best interest to let me duel Morgan yesterday," Liam said.

"Why?"

"If I'd lost, I would've been gone. For good."

My arms fell alongside my body, the half-empty bottle clapping against my thigh. "Don't say stupid shit like that."

He balked at my sharp words.

"I'll see you tomorrow. Bring Sillin. Or I'll bring what I have left." I turned to go, but Liam's voice stopped me.

"I have to take care of some things tomorrow, so I won't have time to meet you. But I'll pick you up on Sunday morning at seven. Pack an overnight bag."

"Overnight? What about the pack run?"

"We'll be running, but not with the Boulders."

My pulse picked up speed. "Who will we be running with?"

"The Rivers."

"The Rivers? One of the Eastern packs?"

Liam nodded, then tipped his head to the side, his gaze hunting mine.

I wasn't sure if it was the sweat drying on my skin or the idea of running with lots of foreign wolves or traveling out of state with Liam, but I suddenly felt incredibly cold. "And it'll be just the two of us going out there?"

An emotion crossed his face. Hurt, maybe? He shrugged his shoulders that seemed to have gotten a little broader since he'd become Alpha. "I can ask Matt to fly out with us if it makes you feel more comfortable."

I didn't need a chaperone, or did I? "I trust you to keep this professional, Liam."

This would be the first time I would be physically far enough from August for it to affect the link. What if . . . what if my attraction to him faded? Why was I scared of this? I'd told Liam that wasn't the reason I wanted August in the first place. I stretched my neck from side to side, finding a little solace when it cracked.

"You seem nervous?"

Instead of confessing the true reason I was jumpy, I said, "I've never flown before. What should I pack?"

"Nothing fancy. The Rivers are denim-and-tees sort of people."

"Okay." I rubbed one clammy palm against my workout leggings.

"The Rivers, huh?" Sarah said. I hadn't even noticed her return. "I heard they hate the Creeks because Morgan killed the Alpha's daughter. The girl was visiting the Aspens the night Morgan demanded to duel the Alpha." I supposed she added that last part for my benefit, since I imagined Liam and Lucas were well-versed in pack facts.

Liam stared at her as though her presence had slipped his mind. "If my trip gets back to Morgan, I'll know where she got her information."

Sarah's gaze turned incendiary. "You should stop confusing allies for traitors. Didn't work out so well for you last time," she added under her breath.

Liam's posture locked up.

"Anyway, I need to get home. Ness, you done here?"

"I'm done," I said, lifting my bag off the bench.

I didn't look back at the boys as I left the gym with Sarah. The second we stepped out of the brick loft-like building that housed the gym, she muttered, "I can't believe he thinks I'd tell Morgan anything." Her blonde hair was starting to frizz, as though her kinky curls were desperate to bend her straightened locks into their original shape.

"I don't think he fully trusts *me*, Sarah."

She side-eyed me as she unlocked the door of her red Mini. "Do *you* trust him?

"What do you mean?"

"You're going on an overnight trip with him. Do you trust he's not going to try anything on you?"

I bit my lip, which made Sarah raise an eyebrow.

"I don't think he'll try anything," I said a little hoarsely.

She gave a me a tight-lipped smile. "I wish I could come along."

"I wish you could, too."

But Sarah was a Creek. There was no way she could come with us. First, because Liam wouldn't allow it, and second, because then Cassandra, who was able to track her wolves through her Alpha blood-link, would know Sarah was double-crossing her pack.

7

J eb couldn't make dinner at the Watts, so I ended up going alone. Since he'd needed the car, I took a cab. During the entire ride, I alternated between crinkling the brown paper wrapped around the bouquet of black parrot tulips resting on the seat next to me and smoothing the fabric of my red silk dress—the one that had belonged to Mom and that I'd worn only once before, for my "date" with Aidan Michaels. If it had been any other dress, I would've burned it, but it had belonged to Mom.

"That's a mighty nice house," the cab driver said as he pulled up in front of the Watts' high-ceilinged log cabin.

The wood façade glowed amber in the setting sun, and the beveled windows gleamed like diamonds.

August's pickup was parked up front, which meant he was already here.

"Nine dollars, please," the driver said.

I dug through my wallet for a ten dollar bill, handed it to the man, then touched the door handle but couldn't bring myself to pump it. This felt like a meet-the-parents, even though I'd met the parents at the same time I'd met August—in the hospital room where Mom birthed me. In one of their photo albums, there was a picture of me cradled in August's arms. My stomach churned and churned like the cinnamon chocolate ice-cream Evelyn made this summer in the inn's fancy ice-cream maker.

God, this was wrong.

How could I want someone a decade older?

Someone who'd felt like a brother my entire childhood?

Maybe Liam's ban was a good thing.

Maybe I should wait for the Winter Solstice to arrive so the mating link vanished and put an end to my scandalous attraction.

Would it put an end to it, though?

"Is this not the right address?" The cabby spun around in his seat.

"No, it's . . . um . . . I think I forgot—"

The Watts' front door opened and filled with August's hulking shape.

My heart beat bruisingly hard.

When I still hadn't gotten out of the cab, August strode over. He opened the car door, and since I hadn't released the handle, drew me right out of the taxi. I stumbled, my bouquet toppling onto the black pebbles lining the driveway.

He caught one of my wrists and steadied me. I think he asked the cabby if I'd paid, and I think the cabby answered, but maybe I was imagining them having a conversation. All I could hear was my thundering pulse. All I could feel was August's thumb pressing lightly into my vein.

Was I too young to have a heart attack?

August smiled a little wider. "Shifters don't get those, sweetheart."

Shoot . . . I'd voiced my pathetic deliberation out loud.

His thumb stroked the inside of my wrist, and my skin broke out in goose bumps.

Remembering I wasn't supposed to make contact with any part of August, I wrenched my arm out of his grip. Where he'd touched tingled and burned. A lot like my navel. Did his navel feel as though it was forever tumbling through a dryer set on the fastest and hottest setting? I would've asked but then thought better of it. If his abdomen didn't feel that way, then I'd just be confessing to being one intensely hormonal girl.

August crouched to retrieve my fallen bouquet. I took it without touching his fingers and nestled it against my heaving chest. As he straightened, he returned his hands to the pockets of his gray jeans.

"I'm sorry." He tipped his head to my wrist. "I didn't mean to break the rule."

I tucked the bouquet closer, probably injuring the petals. "It's okay."

"You look beautiful tonight," he said huskily. "But if you could avoid wearing dresses and the color red while I'm banned to touch you, I'd be really appreciative."

My lips bent with what I hoped looked like a smirk and not an *I'm-about-to-melt-at-your-scuffed-boots* look. "We're back to discussing muumuus, huh?" A gentle breeze twisted the hair I'd spent a long time blow-drying straight. "I haven't forgotten your advice."

A firefly buzzed around August's stubble-coated jaw. "It wasn't advice."

The vibrations of his deep voice had the goose bumps, which had started receding, make a brusque second appearance. I seriously needed to calm down before entering his parents' home. Which reminded me . . .

"How much do your parents know about . . . *everything*?"

"Everything."

I almost choked on my own saliva. "They know I spent the night at your place?" I whispered, praying my voice wouldn't carry to Nelson's lupine eardrums.

"No. But they know about the mating link, and they know how I feel about it."

Heat wrapped around my collarbone and neck like a rampant vine. "Are they horrified?"

He stared at the sprinting pulse point in my neck. "Why would they be horrified?"

"Because I'm so much younger, and like a little sister to you, and you held me in the maternity ward." I said all of this in one breath.

"Hey . . ." He stepped closer, and his heady heat scent enveloped me. "First off, age doesn't matter. You're not a kid anymore, Ness. You're a woman and I'm a man, and that's all that matters. All that *should* matter. And if anyone ever makes a derogatory comment to you about our age gap, then send them my way, and I'll set them straight. Secondly, you are *not* related to me, therefore you *aren't* my little sister. And yeah, I held you in the maternity ward, and yeah, back then I didn't think I was holding my mate, but apparently I was. How many people can claim they saw the person meant for them come into this world? Not many. So I'll always cherish that, and no, it doesn't color the way I think of you today." His words were so quiet they tangled with his exhale.

His exhale which I tasted on my parted lips.

"*Fuck*." His pupils bled into his gold-green irises. "How long are we supposed to stay away from each other?"

I smiled, even though my pulse felt like it had hitched a ride on a fighter jet. "You give your mom that hundred dollar bill yet?"

His pupils retracted. "Not yet. I was waiting for you to witness the donation." He tipped his head to the house. "We better go inside before I break all the rules and take you back to *my* house."

A breathy gasp escaped me, and that little sound made August's gaze flick to my mouth.

He shook his head as though trying to clear it of any dirty thoughts. I assumed that's what his jerky movement was about since I had my fair share of brand-new steamy scenarios scrolling through my mind.

We didn't speak the whole way up the path. He gestured for me to go ahead of him inside the house. The scent of simmering tomato sauce and caramelized onions hit my nostrils, awakening my hunger for something other than August.

Isobel smiled at me from where she stood at the stove top. "We finally managed to get you to come over." She set down the wooden spoon and approached me, arms extended. I wasn't sure if she wanted to hug me or take the flowers from my arms, so I remained statue-still.

Her arms wrapped around me and pulled me in.

"It smells so good in here," I said into Isobel's dark-brown hair.

Even though the strands were real, they weren't hers. They had this chemical keratin smell to them like all wigs. I remembered visiting a shop for one with Mom before she'd decided she wouldn't need a wig. The reminder of her cancer had me pressing away and inspecting Isobel's face for signs of the disease.

"How are you feeling?" I asked.

"Alive. Very much alive." She smiled that bright smile of hers that could burn away the densest of fogs.

I gave her the bouquet, examining her for a noticeable slump or another mark of fatigue. She ran a knuckle over my cheek. "Don't you start worrying now, too, sweet girl. I promise I'm fine."

I nodded.

"August, honey, can you get one of the vases down from the shelf?"

August strode past me and opened one of the kitchen cabinets. Barely straining, he reached the top shelf and took down a fluted crystal recipient just as his father came in through the open doors that gave onto the paved terrace.

"Hi, Ness."

"Hi, Nelson."

Holding a pair of tongs out so that the charred greasy bits didn't transfer onto my dress, he leaned in for a one-armed hug. I suddenly wished August hadn't told them anything. Then they'd just be Nelson and Isobel, my parents' best friends instead of a set of parents whom I felt like I needed to impress. My nervousness was so violent that the air probably shimmied with it.

"We probably shouldn't be offering you alcohol, but would you like a glass of wine?" Nelson asked. "I opened one of the bottles from our wedding. It's matured as beautifully as my bride."

Smiling, Isobel shook her head. "I've matured, huh?"

"You've gotten more ravishing, which was a feat considering how beautiful you were thirty years ago."

When he dropped a kiss on his wife's glowing cheek, I became misty-eyed. They reminded me so much of my parents. My parents who'd loved each other so fiercely and completely that they'd resisted a mating link to stay together.

My eyes bumped into August's worried ones, before vaulting to the serrated egg-shaped heads of the purple tulips.

"So, wine?" Nelson asked me, even though his gaze was on August. "Or is my son going to give you a hard time about underage drinking again?"

August raised his palms. "She didn't drive here, so I'm not passing any judgment."

I suspected that even if I *had* driven here, he wouldn't have objected to me imbibing alcohol since the one and only time he'd made a fuss about it was back at Frank's when August had been annoyed with me over Liam.

Nelson gestured to the terrace.

Before I walked out, I put my bag down on the speckled granite. "Can I bring anything out?"

"You can grab the pitcher of water from the fridge," Isobel said, stirring her tomato sauce before removing the pan from the burner.

I pulled the water from the fridge and headed to the terrace where I set the pitcher between two giant candles flickering in glass hurricane holders.

I gazed around the paved veranda where nothing had changed: the stacked firepit was still surrounded by five burgundy Adirondacks; and the low stone wall, from which sprouted little purple blooms, still girdled the deck.

When I was younger, I used to skip atop the wall with my arms stretched out like a tightrope walker picturing a pit of hungry alligators beneath me. I had a vivid imagination back then. Not that it had changed. My imagination was still plenty vivid, except it ran on a very different frequency these days.

"You okay?" August asked, coming up behind me.

"Your parents . . . They just remind me so much of Mom and Dad."

He draped his arm around my shoulders and tucked me into his side, and although we weren't supposed to touch, I didn't fight his embrace. Even though his fingers only connected to my bicep, it felt like they were resting on my heart, towing one ripped segment toward the other.

After a while, he whispered a quick, "Sorry," against my hairline before releasing me.

I wasn't sorry.

That hand might've left a trace on my body, but it had also left one on my heart.

I thought of Mom again, of her claim that the right man could fix a broken heart. August could touch mine, and this was as thrilling as it was terrifying because that meant he could mend it just as he could break it.

8

Dinner was delicious and laid-back. Neither Isobel nor Nelson brought up the mating link, and neither of them asked questions about my intentions toward their son or his intentions toward me.

But after dinner . . . Well, after dinner was a different story.

While the men cleaned up the vestiges of our meal, Isobel brewed a pot of chamomile tea before leading me to the firepit. Flames snapped in between the circle of stones and warmed the cooling night air, casting shadows over her haggard face.

She'd promised me she was well, but the deep creases around her eyes and lips worried me nonetheless. As she reclined in the burgundy Adirondack, I prayed her fatigue wasn't a symptom that her double-mastectomy had failed its purpose.

"August spoke to us before you arrived," she said, jouncing me out of my pessimistic musings.

Clutching my mug, I focused on the dancing blaze.

"Nelson and I, we don't want to meddle, but your parents are no longer here, and well, we feel a responsibility toward them to discuss it with you. This . . . *link*, it's momentous and not without consequence, for you and for our son."

How I wished the fire could leap out of the pit and incinerate something, anything, just to drag the focus away from me.

"I don't know if you're aware of this, but your mother, she was intended for—"

"Heath. I heard."

"Oh." There was a pregnant pause, then, "The reason I'm bringing up your mom is because I want to remind you that you have a choice in the matter. You and my son might have a connection—you always had a connection—but I guess, what I'm trying to say, is that this connection has grown into something . . . *more*."

At this point, if the flames decided to incinerate me, I wouldn't have truly minded.

"August feels strongly toward you, but you're so young, so if you don't reciprocate his feelings, he'll understand. Maybe not right away, but in time, he will."

She touched my forearm, and I jumped, spilling tea all over my lap.

"Oh, I'm sorry."

"It's okay." The tea seeped into the red silk, darkening it.

"A mother wants only one thing in life, and that's her child's happiness. You've always contributed to August's, but now you've become the pivotal object of it. And although he claims it's not because of the link, the link doubtlessly enhances what he feels. Doubtlessly enhances what you feel, too."

Although I wanted to melt through the planks of my chair, I finally looked at Isobel. Her green eyes were gentle instead of reproachful like I'd feared.

"I want what's best for *both* of you, and maybe that's each other. But you're only seventeen."

I'd be eighteen in two weeks, but then August would be twenty-eight in March, so we'd always have this nine-years-and-some-months gap.

Over the husky notes of the jazz song pouring from the outdoor speakers, Isobel said, "Nelson and I, we met when I was sixteen and he was twenty-two. And Maggie, she was—"

"Thirteen. And Dad was three years older, which had made a lot of people balk."

She smiled. "How I remember. But Maggie was so spirited and strong-willed that whenever anyone mentioned the age difference, she'd get all up in their faces." Isobel turned her gaze to the flames and sighed. "I guess age doesn't really matter in the end." She removed her hand from my arm. "What does matter, though, is making an informed decision. You have options. August is one of them, but the Winter Solstice is another."

I cast a glance over my shoulder to make sure the men were still out of earshot. August was drying a plate by the sink while Nelson was stacking the glasses inside a cupboard. They seemed deep into their own conversation.

"Isobel, would you and Nelson be disgusted if I chose August?"

She whipped her gaze to me. "Disgusted? No! Absolutely not. Ness, we love you. We've always loved you and we will *always* love you. *Whatever* you decide. The only reason I brought this up is because we care so much about you, and we don't want you to feel pressured into something you're not ready for."

I twirled my mug, wishing it could leak warmth into more than just my fingers. "I understand my options, and I'm not going to rush into anything that's indelible."

"Good."

"What's good?"

I glanced up at August. "The tea," I lied, raising it to my lips.

He eyed me suspiciously. *Yeah . . .* he hadn't bought that.

"I brought you girls some covers." He handed one to his mother, who draped it over her lap, then gave me the other folded rectangle that felt like spun clouds. I set my mug on the rim of the firepit to tuck the soft blanket around my shoulders.

August sank into the chair beside mine, and then Nelson arrived with a glass brimming with wine and sat next to him.

"Look at that sky," he mused.

We all raised our gazes to the glittering darkness overhead. Magical. Simply magical.

August leaned a little toward me. "Did you find Cassiopeia?"

I stared at the dark freckles beneath his left eye where a thin pale scar lingered—a remnant of when my wolf claw had scraped across his face. How I longed to drag my finger over the freckles shaped like the constellation. Instead, I burrowed my fingers into the cashmere wrap. "I always find Cassiopeia."

His gaze blazed as bright as the fire.

But then the heat in his eyes turned cold as a voice entered our minds.

There will be no full moon run this month. I apologize to the elders, but I urge you all to stay in skin.

Liam's voice dragged me away from the starlit evening that had been a welcomed parenthesis in my tumultuous life.

I will be leaving to meet with the Rivers tomorrow morning, and I'll return the following day. Please clear Monday evening for a debriefing.

I waited for him to mention I would be accompanying him. When a full minute passed and nothing more was uttered, I let out a quiet breath.

"The Rivers, huh?" Nelson said.

"What about the Rivers?" Isobel asked.

August studied my face as he said, "Liam's going to meet with them."

"The pack that commissioned you to build their meeting hall?" Isobel said. "I thought Heath had given you grief for working with them."

Nelson swirled his wine. "He did. Liam must be desperate for a new ally now that we lost the Pines."

"Did you know he was traveling East?" August asked me.

I nodded. Informing him that I was accompanying Liam hung on the tip of my tongue, but I couldn't propel the words out of my mouth. I was afraid my confession would stoke August's jealousy.

Besides, if Liam hadn't mentioned me, then maybe he wasn't taking me with him in the end. I held on to that possibility as the night wore on. But of course, right as I was about to call a cab, Liam's voice resonated inside my head: *I'll be at your place at 7:00 a.m.*

August nodded to my phone. "You weren't actually going to call a cab, were you?"

I forced my features to smooth out. "I don't want to get you in trouble."

Sitting together in a confined space was against Liam's rules.

"You don't want to get *me* in trouble, or *him*?" he asked slowly.

I swallowed. "Both of you. *Either* of you. I don't want to get either of you in trouble."

Nelson and Isobel were still outside on the patio, speaking quietly. Was it about us? Even though she'd given me her blessing, her anguish was palpable.

"It's a short ride."

I sighed and put my phone away. "Okay."

I prayed Liam wouldn't find out and challenge Cassandra to punish me for disobeying.

As we made our way to the pickup, August kept casting concerned glances my way.

Only when I was settled in the car did he ask, "What did my mother say? Did she try to talk you out of being with me?"

I fingered the hem of my dress, not quite daring to look at him. "She reminded me that I had options."

"Options?" His voice was low and rough.

"She told me I could let the Winter Solstice go by before deciding." I raised my gaze back to his. "That you'd understand."

Would he, though?

His lips parted a little, then pressed tight. I sensed he didn't want me to choose that option. I sensed he feared that the disappearance of the bond would lead to the disappearance of my feelings for him.

I guessed neither of us could be sure it wouldn't.

Perhaps tomorrow's trip wouldn't be so unwelcomed after all. At least it would shed light on how I really felt about him since the bond would vanish.

When we arrived in front of my apartment, I didn't linger in the car, afraid someone would spot us and report to Liam.

"What are you doing tomorrow?" August asked after I'd hopped out.

My heart, which had been beating double-time since we'd left his parents' place, stilled.

Should I tell him?

"I wanted to show you something," he said.

I opened my mouth.

To lie.

Or at least that had been my intent, but he would sense I was out of Boulder. Besides, I didn't want to lie to him. "I'm going with Liam."

His Adam's apple seemed suddenly spikier. "If I hadn't asked, would you have told me?"

"No."

He dropped his gaze to his illuminated dashboard, features tightening.

"I was afraid you'd torture yourself with what I could be doing with him in a place where the bond doesn't affect my body."

His wolf must've been close to the surface because his eyes shone like emeralds. Jaw barely budging, he muttered something that sounded like, *If Cassandra doesn't kill him, I might.* "I know the Rivers. I'll come too, then."

My heart twitched back to life. "August—"

"Unless you don't want me there."

I pressed my lips together. I wanted him there, but I also wanted him to trust me. Besides, I needed to know what distance did to us. If not now, then later, but later might hurt more.

His pupils gushed darkness into his irises. "You don't want me there."

"What I want is for you to trust me."

"You, I trust."

I gripped the edge of the car door. "Then trust that I can handle Liam."

"Sweetheart"—his nostrils flared—"you're asking a very human man to be superhuman. I'm not sure I'm capable of that."

My lips bent with a smile. "Says a werewolf."

My humor defused some of his anger. Not all of it, though. The tether was so stiff it seemed made of metal instead of magic.

"Let's hope the Rivers know something we don't," he said.

It took my hazy mind a second to understand he was talking about Morgan's tricks. "Yeah. Let's hope they do."

We stared at each other for another endless beat. I sensed him tugging on the tether, trying to reel me to him. I had to clutch the door harder to avoid stumbling.

"August," I chided gently.

"What?"

"You're going to make me fall."

The pressure on my abdomen decreased so suddenly I almost tumbled backward.

"I'm sorry," he said.

It was late, and Liam would be here early, and the longer I remained next to August, the more chances we had of being caught. "I should really go. . ."

As I rounded the bumper, August powered his window down. "Come back to me, okay?"

Pleasure and trepidation dripped in equal parts inside my veins. Because his affection for me was so absolute that I was suddenly afraid of what tomorrow would bring.

Turning away, I said, "I'll come back." I climbed up my stairs fast, then went inside my home even faster.

The tether vibrated with his hurt.

Hurt I'd put there by not telling him I would come back *to him*.

Because what if the absence of magic affected the strength of my attraction?

I was already sitting on the bottom step when Liam arrived the next morning. I slung the backpack I'd borrowed from Jeb, and which I'd filled with the bare necessities, over my shoulder, then walked to the passenger side.

After I settled in, Liam asked, "Had a fun night?" He wore dark sunglasses that made it impossible to read his expression.

"I did."

He started driving. "I have a half a mind to cancel the trip and phone up Morgan. You reek of him."

Trying to keep as calm as lycanthropically possible, I said, "He gave me a ride back from his parents. Nothing happened."

He didn't pick up his phone or do a U-turn to drop me back off. I wasn't sure if it was because he realized the only one who would get hurt would be him or because my tone had been so flat. I wore my emotions on my vocal cords. Guilt would've heightened my pitch. I didn't feel guilty about last night. At least not in the way Liam was insinuating.

But I did feel guilt. I'd been so torn up I'd barely slept. I rested my elbow on the armrest, cradled my throbbing forehead, and shut my eyes.

A brassy whooshing sound jerked me awake. I'd meant to rest, not sleep. How long had I been out?

I rubbed my lids and stared at the gated airstrip. "We're flying private?"

Nodding, Liam lowered his window to press on an intercom. The gate clanged open, and we glided right through toward a gleaming silver jet.

I gaped at it.

"It was Dad's, but it's at the disposal of the entire pack. If you ever need to use it, all you have to do is ask."

My enchantment withered. I'd despised Liam's father so much that my hatred extended to anything he'd touched or owned.

A man in a navy suit drew open my car door. "Morning, Miss."

"Good morning," I said, grabbing my backpack and scooting out of the SUV.

"Morning, Captain," Liam said, rounding the bumper of his car.

He sported jeans—like me—and a black V-neck, which reassured me that my white tank and zip-up hoodie weren't too dire.

The man in the suit nodded at Liam. "Morning, Mr. Kolane. We're ready to go when you are."

Liam gestured to the staircase that led into the belly of the sleek, winged beast. I moved toward it, my wolf bristling under my skin, as though trying to stick her claws into the tarmac to avoid taking to the skies.

We were land animals after all.

I battled through her reluctance and climbed the stairs. The air smelled of leather and flowery air freshener, which did little to appease my pacing wolf. My nails began to lengthen. I stopped in the narrow hallway, focusing on pushing her back. I doubted the captain or the flight attendant smiling at me from the galley in the back of the plane knew what we were.

"It's safe," Liam whispered behind me, his words blowing through the hairs thickening on the nape of my neck.

He set his hand on the small of my back and guided me onto one of the buttery beige armchairs.

After taking the seat across from me, he said, "I've never much enjoyed flying either."

We weren't even airborne yet. How would I react then? The pilot pulled in the retractable staircase, and the door shut with a suction noise.

"Let me know if you feel like you're losing control," Liam said, studying my face.

I nodded and swallowed.

The air hostess strutted over toward us, her lips a shade of fuchsia so bright they were almost blinding. "I'll set out breakfast after takeoff. Would you like coffee or tea?"

"Coffee," I said.

She didn't wait for Liam's answer. She must've known his order already.

She flitted back to the galley, leaving behind a pungent cloud of rose-scented perfume that reminded me of my aunt and her prized rosebushes.

"Do you have any news about Lucy?"

"Lucy?" Liam frowned.

"You know, my two-timing aunt?"

Liam's lips curved into a crooked smile. "Oh . . . *that* Lucy."

I rolled my eyes.

The engine turned on, and the entire plane began to rattle. Or maybe I was the one rattling. I gripped the armrests.

Breathe. Liam's command shocked the tremor right out of me. Then, out loud, he said, "Last I heard she's still working at the inn."

"Why would she work for Aidan? After what she said at Everest's funeral—about hating what we were—why would she willingly work for the Creeks?"

"Grieving people say and do uncharacteristic things. It might be a way of getting back at us."

"But we didn't kill Everest."

Liam was supposed to, but Alex beat him to it.

"She still believes it's our fault. Like I said, grief screws with people's minds."

The plane started to roll past other shiny aircrafts varying in size. I wondered if one of them belonged to the Creeks. Maybe more than one. And then I wondered if the Watts owned a plane too.

"I heard August and his father did business with the Rivers two years ago," I said, mostly to distract myself from the long dotted strip in front of us. The plane bumped to a stop, and then it made a U-turn and hurtled so fast it pinned my heart to my spine.

Shh.

When my claws dented the buttery leather, I ripped my hands off the armrests and cinched my thighs. I pulled in a long breath, then let it out. I did this over and over until the plane's nose lifted and the wheels left the ground.

"You're okay, Ness. Everything's going to be okay."

"*Don't* say that," I snapped, "because nothing ever goes right when people say that."

His head jerked back a little. "Where did that come from?"

I shut my eyes, air pulsing through my nostrils. "Dad said that to me, and then he was shot. You said that to me, and then you turned on me. I hate that sentence."

After a beat, he said, "I'm sorry."

I laid my head back, eyes still clenched.

"I have something that'll cheer you up."

When paper rustled, I raised my lids. A large white envelope dropped into my lap. On the top left corner was an intertwined C and U.

"Your college packet," Liam explained, mistaking my surprise for confusion. "Classes start in a week. Do you know what you're going to study?"

"Business."

"Practical."

I stared at the envelope, feeling both fraudulent and lucky. The pack's money and connections had gotten me in, not my exceptional transcript.

"There's a course catalogue in there. I was a business major too, so I can help you figure out the best classes to take."

The flight attendant came back then, a white tablecloth draped over her arm. She pulled out a hidden table from the wall between our seats, then smoothed the crisp cloth before returning to the galley. As she set up breakfast in real porcelain and silverware, I opened the envelope and read over my welcome letter, then flipped through the catalogue while Liam told me stories of his college days, about his initiation into the frat house run by generations of Boulder wolves. Even though it was open to all male students —human or supernatural—a shifter was always in charge, and that shifter made sure the hazing was "eventful."

"What did they make you do?" I asked.

He got this far away smile. "Fight in a ring lined with dog excrement. Loser got tossed in the shit."

"Bet you didn't lose."

He turned that smile on me. "I didn't lose."

Gratitude and excitement drifted up in me. As I ate flaky pastries and drank bitter coffee, I pored over every sheet of material on my lap. "Thank you so much for this."

Liam raised a palm. "Please. It's nothing."

"It's *not* nothing. It's my future."

"No, your future is saving my ass, remember?"

A smile tugged at my lips, and I closed the catalogue. "So tell me about the Rivers."

I learned they were the largest of the Eastern packs and the most influential. They'd done their share of dueling in the East but weren't interested in expanding to the West or to the North—the territory of the igloo-dwelling Glacier Pack, descendants of the Inuits.

"I'm surprised August didn't tell you about them. He knew the Alpha's daughter quite intimately." My sudden intake of air had Liam dip his chin into his neck. "You didn't think he was a choir boy, now did you?"

"Of course not," I said a little too abruptly. And I truly hadn't, but that didn't mean I wanted to know about all the beds August had warmed and all the bodies he'd stroked.

Jealousy reared its petty head, and I turned my attention to the ocean of sky surrounding us. Just as brusquely as the jealousy appeared, the realization that my navel didn't tingle—not even a little—hit me.

The link was gone.

Between talk of the Rivers and petty jealous musings, I barely realized the plane had started its descent toward an airstrip at the base of the Smoky Mountains. When the wheels jounced against the tarmac, though, I became wholly centered on the aircraft. And then the pilot braked, and the lap belt dug into my stomach, sending what I'd eaten back up my throat. I mashed my lips together and swallowed so hard I almost choked on my spit, but that beat hurling all over Liam.

Liam, whose eyes glinted as though amused by my predicament.

The pilot's voice crackled over a loudspeaker, announcing we'd touched down, as if we'd somehow missed it.

"You can leave the college packet on board," Liam said, getting up. "We're taking the same plane home."

As I unbuckled myself, the door with the retractable staircase popped open, letting in a burst of hot, humid air. I followed Liam out of the jet, and when my white sneakers met solid earth, I almost purred. Liam tossed me another amused look, but then his features hardened into his Alpha mask.

Two open-roofed SUVs fit for a safari were snaking past the few parked private aircrafts. Laughter and chatter floated from the bodies crowding the vehicles.

"Did the entire pack come to greet us?" I murmured over the drone of the approaching cars.

"They're close to three hundred, so no."

I'd been joking, but Liam was too concentrated to pick up on my intended humor. When the fenders all but butted against our thighs, the vehicles stopped and the passengers jumped over the sides. A man with a thick auburn-brown beard pushed through the tight web of shifters circling us.

"Liam!" he boomed, clapping my Alpha on the back as though they were old pals.

Even though Liam was as stiff as an ironing board, he offered the large male a tense smile.

And then the man moved toward me and extended his hand. "Zachary. But everyone calls me Zack."

I shook his gargantuan palm.

"So you're the Boulder female everyone's been yappin' about, huh?" He hadn't released me yet.

"The one and only," I said, eyeing him and his pack.

"Well, welcome to the East," he boomed again.

I tugged my fingers loose. "Thank you."

He nodded before turning to Liam. "Shall we run for the hills?" A slash of white teeth appeared between the coarse brown hairs of his beard.

Some of his wolves chuckled, stances slack, exhibiting no signs of aggression.

"I'm kidding. We'll do enough running tonight. Liam, you're ridin' with me, son," Zack barked.

Liam nodded, but before going off, he signaled for me to follow.

"My son Samuel can give her a lift," the River Alpha offered.

A man, who had the same sturdy build as Zack and the same reddish-brown hair, lifted his hand in a wave.

"My Second rides with us," Liam said.

I sensed from the weighted look father and son exchanged that they weren't too pleased with Liam interfering in their plans.

"All right," Zack said, his voice a little less loud, which wasn't to say it was at a normal pitch. It was most definitely louder than any voice I'd ever heard.

Although they all climbed in the way they'd poured out of the vehicles, Liam opened the door. He gestured for me to go ahead of him before hopping in, and then we were off, warm wind scraping through my hair and pounding against my eardrums.

At some point during the drive, the girl sitting beside me introduced herself. "Jane." She looked to be around my age, perhaps a year or two younger, with a round face dusted in freckles and sweeping lashes that looked red in the sunlight.

"Ness."

"I know." She pushed a bluntly cut piece of auburn hair out of her dark-blue eyes. "Are you and your Alpha a thing?"

When I shook my head, she scrutinized Liam a little more boldly.

"Why the heck not?" she asked after a long beat.

"It's a long story." One I didn't see myself sharing with her.

"It's a long ride."

Was she really expecting me to confide in her? I didn't know her, plus Liam was sitting right there. Not that I would've felt comfortable had he been in the other car.

"The males in your pack are so hot," she said with a breathy sigh. "Makes me want to visit Colorado."

I frowned. "How do you know if you've never been to Colorado?"

"I attended the pack summit a couple years ago."

Oh. Right.

"After what happened to my older sister, though, Daddy doesn't want us straying too far off our land."

I was glad Sarah had told me about the Alpha's daughter, the one who'd been killed by Morgan. "You're Zack's daughter then?"

"One of them. We're seven. Two boys, five girls. Well, only four now." Her gaze turned a little misty, but she blinked, and her eyes dried.

I wondered which of her sisters had been the one to sleep with August, because Jane was far too young to be the girl in question.

Thinking about August made me acutely aware of his absence.

And of the emptiness inside my stomach.

I pressed my hand to my navel as though my touch could somehow reactivate the link.

Liam's gaze drifted to my hand. Thankfully, he didn't ask me how I was feeling . . . or rather *what* I was feeling.

As we drove over miles of concrete roads that turned into rough terrain, I wondered what August was doing.

What he was feeling.

My blood turned to ice as a thought collided into me. What if August had been wrong about liking me before the link formed? What if he felt relieved by its absence?

I dug my phone out of the front pocket of my backpack and powered it on to send him a message that I'd arrived safely.

That I was thinking of him.

As my carrier searched for network, Jane said, "You won't get any reception 'round these parts. Dad put up a bunch of jammers. He's not a fan of technology."

And suddenly my concern of what August was feeling was superseded by a new one—that of being disconnected from the entire world. The Rivers suddenly felt more oppressing than welcoming.

Liam leaned over me. "Will you have Wi-Fi at the compound?"

"We have a computer connected to dial-up."

I gaped at Liam.

They hate the Creeks, not us, he said through the mind-link.

I tried to let his words reassure me, but I wasn't reassured.

What had we gotten ourselves into?

11

August and Nelson had come out to Tennessee and returned to tell the tale.

The Rivers weren't going to make Liam and me vanish.

I repeated this to myself as we drove down a dusty road lined with identical one-storied stone and log cabins. The only building that was different was the one at the very end. It was built in the same style—rough gray stone, tawny slats, grids of windows—but it was long like horse stables with a thatched roof.

The car came to an abrupt halt right in front of it.

"Lunchtime," Zack bellowed, stretching himself up to his full height before vaulting over the side of the car.

This time, Liam jumped over too, then held out his hand to me. When in Tennessee, do as the Tennesseans, I supposed. I sat on the edge, swung my legs over, then placed my hand in his and hopped down. As soon as my feet touched the ground, I let go.

This trip wouldn't change the fact that I was Liam's Second and not his girlfriend. Not even his friend for that matter.

Business partners.

A petite and shapely woman with crinkly blue eyes was stationed by the entrance of the thatched structure. As we approached, she extended both her hands. First to me, then to Liam, and then she stepped close to Zack.

"My mate, Eileen."

The word *mate* made my heart pinch. Even though werewolves called their spouses this way, I couldn't help but think of August.

"Nice to meet y'all," she said.

Zack pointed to the two women standing around a young boy. "Three more of my flesh and blood: Poppy, Penny, and Jack."

I committed all of their names to memory. Where Jack waved to us, his sisters—

who looked identical—observed me and Liam with quiet caution. They had the same auburn hair as Jane, but their eyes were different, dark, almost black, like the bitter coffee I'd drunk on the plane.

Zack rubbed his palms. "Lunch ready?"

Eileen nodded.

He kissed the top of her head before striding through the open doorway.

Eileen tipped her head for us to go ahead of her inside the giant structure. Clutching the strap of my backpack, I walked alongside Liam, gaze zipping over every inch of the building. I'd expected it to be dark, but the entire back wall was made of glass. A river rushed beyond the picture window, and beyond that stretched a copse of evergreens so dense the trees looked welded together.

"A Watt original," Zack bellowed. "Ain't it strikin'?"

I pulled Mom's ring out of my tank top and speared my finger through the warmed band, twirling it at the same time as I rotated to take in my surroundings. The building *was* spectacular. When I stopped spinning, I came face to face with one of the twins. I wasn't sure which one she was.

The girl observed me quietly, like most of her pack.

I stood my ground even though I wanted to back up a little. "Poppy or Penny?"

"Poppy. Penny's the ugly one."

Her twin sister smacked her arm. "Bitch."

Poppy grinned.

"You're twins, right?" I asked, even though it seemed obvious.

"Yup."

I wondered how old they were. Nineteen, maybe?

"Just call them Pee. They both answer to that," their older brother said, ruffling Penny's hair.

"So not funny, Sam," she said.

Their familiarity slackened some of the tension in my body.

"We don't respond to Pee. Or Pee-wee. Or any derivative of that nickname," Poppy added.

"Yeah, they do." A girl with brown hair down to her waist came up to us. "I'm the last Burley child. Or rather the first. Ingrid." She extended her hand, and I shook it.

"Now that you've met the whole clan, it's time to take your seats and dig in." Zack gestured to the table that stretched the length of the structure and that was heaped with bowls of creamed corn, crisp salads, barbecued meat, and pitchers of fresh juice.

In a rush of excessive affability, Jane hooked her arm through mine and towed me toward one of the benches propped under the table, chattering on about how hungry she always was. I looked over my shoulder toward Liam, wondering where he would be sitting.

You okay? he asked.

I didn't need him to hold my hand, or want him to, for that matter, so I nodded.

"So, how come you're the only female in your pack?" Ingrid asked, taking a seat across the table from me.

Lowering my backpack to the ground, I bit my lip, wondering if I was allowed to disclose this. I supposed it was no longer a secret. "Because of a fossilized tree root concoction they had the males in my pack ingest. It destroyed female sperm."

Her eyes grew as round as the burger patty she'd put on her plate. Her sisters' gazes widened too.

"Whoa," Samuel said, ladling some creamed corn onto his plate and then onto mine without asking if I wanted any.

"We're not going to have any females for another decade or so, since Liam's generation took it," I added.

"Unless you absorb the Creeks," Ingrid pointed out.

"Unless that."

"I hate those bastards," Samuel said, adding three skewers of cubed meat to his plate. He deposited one on my plate too. "Well, not the whole pack. Just the OCs. You eat meat, right?"

"Yes." I cocked an eyebrow. "Who are the OCs?"

"The Original Creeks," Jane said.

"What about the Aspens?" I asked, spearing some corn onto my fork tines.

"The Aspens are chill—*were* chill," one of the twins said.

I still couldn't believe the Burleys were seven kids. No family in my pack had more than two sons. Was that because Boulder wives were all human? As I pondered this, I studied the other Rivers seated at the long table. Most of the people I looked at looked right back with just as much unabashed curiosity.

"But who knows what they've become. No one's impervious to a bad influence," Ingrid was saying.

"Do all of you live on the compound?" I asked.

"Yep, but we're not all here," Jane said.

"We'll all be here tonight though. The Wolf Moon brings all the pack together." Ingrid chewed on a bite of salad, then chased it down with a sip of something that smelled like sweet tea.

Samuel, who couldn't seem to help himself from taking care of me, had poured me a tall glass of the iced brown beverage.

"Too bad more of you couldn't make it down here," Ingrid said.

One of the twins smiled brashly. "She's just sorry *August* couldn't make it down here."

My vertebrae jammed together.

Ingrid shoved her shoulder into her sister's. "Shut up, Poppy. Besides, he's probably off in Iraq. I heard he enlisted again."

August had never told me where he'd been stationed, but he'd told her?

I was clutching my fork so hard that I was probably bending it. I set it down before anyone could notice. "He did, but he came back early."

Jane plopped both her elbows on the table. "Daddy wants to commission another building from them, so you'll see him soon enough."

"She's totes whipped," the youngest brother, Jack, said.

Jealousy sharpened my senses, or maybe it was the approach of the full moon.

"He probably has a girlfriend," the other twin told Ingrid. "Dudes like him don't stay single for long. Dudes in general. Seriously, men are like incapable of bein' alone. Why is that, Sam?"

Samuel set down the skewer he'd picked clean. "Why you asking me? I'm on a break."

"Since last week, and you're already fillin' up *her* plate."

Sam flushed. "I'm bein' a good host, is all," he muttered around a bite of meat.

"So? Does August have a girlfriend?" Jane asked.

"Yeah," I said slowly, hoping my voice wasn't giving away all I was feeling.

Ingrid blinked in surprise. "It's that girl Sienna, isn't it?"

Had he cheated on Sienna with Ingrid, or had he slept with Ingrid before hooking up with Sienna? The chronology of August's girlfriends was foreign to me, not that I had any desire to familiarize myself with his string of conquests.

"You guys know Sienna?" I asked in a wooden voice.

"We know *of* her. He mentioned her. They were casually seein' each other the summer he came to install this building." Ingrid tipped her head to the roof. "They weren't serious or nothing." After a beat, she asked, "Are they serious now?"

"No."

"Is he dating anyone else?"

I wasn't sure why, but instead of setting her straight, I said, "No." And then I focused on my food even though my appetite had vanished.

12

After lunch, Jane led Liam and me to a cottage. She gave us a tour of the simply decorated space: one leather couch, two armchairs, a wooden coffee table, a stone chimney blackened by use.

In the bedroom, there was a queen-sized bed and a gray-tiled bathroom. Everything was clean and functional. There were no paintings on the wall, no books atop the mantle, no pictures on any of the side tables, no chemical smells, just the scent of sun-warmed animal hide and scrubbed pine.

"You guys can rest up." She pulled open the front door. "We'll come fetch you before the run."

I spun around. "Wait, where's the second bedroom?"

"We were told you'd be sharing . . ."

Did she honestly think I'd share a bed with a guy I wasn't dating? "By whom?"

Liam placed a hand on my forearm. "We are sharing. Thanks, Jane."

She gave him a dazzlingly bright smile.

Once she'd shut the door, I muttered, "I suppose you could stay with *her*. I bet she wouldn't mind."

"I suppose I could, but unlike some people, I didn't come here to screw girls. Plus she's a little young for my taste."

I inhaled sharply. "You shouldn't attack people when they aren't here to defend themselves, Liam."

"That wasn't an attack. It was a remark."

"It was a very judgmental remark for someone who had sex with a girl while his buddies were playing poker in his living room."

A beat of silence descended over us.

After almost a full minute, Liam asked, "Why didn't you tell Ingrid she had it wrong about Sienna?"

I'd been sitting halfway across the dining hall, yet he'd heard the conversation? I wasn't sure whether to be impressed or annoyed. "Because it's none of her business. None of anyone's business. Besides, thanks to you, I'm not his girlfriend, am I?"

"If I'm supposed to feel bad about that—"

"It was just a remark," I said.

"Uh-huh."

"Anyway, we're not sharing a bed."

His eyebrows lowered, darkening his chocolate eyes. "Don't worry. I'll take the couch. But I'll have to go through the bedroom to use the bathroom. Just in case you were planning on sleeping in the buff." His gaze locked on mine.

I hoisted my backpack higher on my shoulder and then headed toward the bedroom. "If you need the toilet, it's now or never."

A crooked grin settled over his lips. "Anyone ever tell you that you have a bossy streak?"

"I've heard it said, but usually behind my back."

Liam chuckled. "Might be because we'd like to keep our balls attached to the rest of our bodies."

As I entered the bedroom, my anger dissipated a little. I set down my bag on a wicker chair propped in the corner of the small room, underneath a window that gave right onto the living room of the cottage next to ours. I closed the blinds, then pulled out my phone, but like Jane had said, there was no reception, so I put it away and took out the rest of my clothes, setting everything neatly atop the dresser.

The toilet flushed and then water ran, and then it shut off and Liam strode out of the bathroom, running his wet hand through his dark locks. "Have a nice nap." He offered me a smile before shutting the bedroom door.

I contemplated locking it, but there was no lock. Hoping he wouldn't barge inside, I stripped down to my underwear and tank top and slid underneath the comforter.

I woke up to loud banging. "Ness!"

I blinked, disoriented for a moment. When the room swam into focus, I all but lurched out of bed. "I'm awake!" I said before Liam could enter.

I tugged on my jeans, then alternately dragged my hand through my hair and rubbed sleep out of my eyes.

I opened the door. Liam stood there barefoot in an unbuttoned plaid shirt and a pair of unbelted, low-slung jeans. "Moon's up."

The mention of Earth's satellite had my skin strumming.

When we reached the door, I bent to put on my sneakers.

He drew the front door open. "You won't be needing shoes."

Right...

"Stay close to me during the run, okay?"

I nodded. Outside, a steady stream of Rivers were exiting their respective cabins and making their way toward a field filled with long, swaying grass that tickled my calves.

"My Rivers. May the Wolf Moon light up your paths tonight and for the rest of your lives. Be wild. Be free. Be merry," Zack hollered, yanking off his T-shirt before tugging down his jeans.

I averted my gaze as the sound of zippers and rustling fabric filled the air.

"Consider this training," Liam said, chucking his shirt on the ground.

"Training?"

"For the duel. You'll have to strip in front of everyone."

I bit the inside of my cheek.

He pulled down his jeans in one quick swoop. When I realized he wasn't sporting anything underneath them, I looked down at my toes poking through the long grass.

"I'd offer my assistance, but you'd probably bite my head off."

Ugh. I really didn't want to get naked in front of Liam, or anyone else for that matter.

Sighing, I pulled off my tank top and then rolled my jeans down. Liam's gaze struck my bare collarbone and the swell of my breasts. I turned so I had my back to him, and then I crouched, unclipped my bra and shimmied out of my underwear. Finally, I removed the leather strand speared through with my mother's wedding band, which I always wore around my neck, and stuffed it inside the pocket of my jeans.

Screened off by the long grass, I let the change sweep through me.

13

We ran long and hard, trampling miles and miles of moonlit grass, clay-rich soil, and fresh mountain streams. My tight muscles stretched and coiled as I raced parallel to Liam and Zack through the Rivers' domain.

It dawned on me that, for all my talk of leaving Boulder, I was unwilling to give up my ability to travel the earth as a wolf.

Twigs cracked, and leaves drifted over me like fuzzy down. I halted and raised my head. Hanging mere feet above me was a black beast with gleaming eyes. At first I thought it was another wolf, but wolves didn't climb trees. I eyed the creature, and it eyed me back. A black bear.

Liam's muzzle bumped into my haunch. **He won't come down. Too many wolves,** he said through the mind-link.

Some Rivers had stopped beside me and were pawing the ground, alternatively snarling and yapping at the creature hanging for dear life on a branch that seemed too flimsy for its massive weight.

One of the Rivers got on his hind paws and batted the branch with his front leg. The bear bobbed and then let out a blood-curling sound of his own. Emboldened, other wolves lurched up and punched the branch, howling at the bear that skittered backward toward the trunk.

A sharp crack sounded over the pack's garish attack, and then the smell of warm blood wafted through the air, tantalizing, intoxicating. Stiff, horizontal tails poked out of frenzied bodies. My own tail came up in anticipation.

Ness, move! Liam yelled.

Even though I wanted to leap onto the bowed branch and help bring our prey down, Liam's order had me backing up. I whimpered, not understanding why he was making me step back from the kill. I tried to poke back toward the tree, but Liam growled, and my body sank lower to the ground.

I'm hungry, I yelped.

And you'll eat, but let them do the kill. We're on their land. That bear's theirs to kill.

His explanation didn't smother my hunger, but at least I understood why he was making me recede. I shot my gaze up to the creature that had reached the trunk. One of the wolves leaped and latched onto the bear's back paw. The bear released a guttural yap and kicked at the wolf's head, sending the ball of brown fur tumbling and rolling. Another brown wolf scampered toward the collapsed wolf, licking at a weeping gash on her packmate's head.

The wolf whined, and even though the growls and howls had grown in volume in the forest, I heard the wolf tending to the fallen one whimper, *Poppy.*

Poppy didn't stir.

The other wolf—I imagined one of her sisters . . . her twin perhaps?—yelped, and Zack snapped his attention off his ravenous pack.

The River Alpha bounded toward his daughter, and then he headbutted the thin brown wolf aside to have access to the immobile one. I strained to catch the beat of her pulse over the thundering hearts surrounding me.

She had to be alive. Werewolves didn't die so easily. When she still hadn't moved, I peered into Liam's alarmed face.

That could've been you, he said through the mind-link.

My stomach contracted with a mix of dread and hunger brought on by the bear's fatty flesh.

After releasing a raspy bark, Zack whipped his face toward his pack. He must've spoken into their minds, because his wolves halted their attack, reluctantly turning away from the cornered bear.

The animal huffed warily as it scrambled higher.

It wasn't my place to go to Poppy, so I stayed shoulder to shoulder—or rather shoulder to belly—with Liam.

Zack nudged the lump of brown fur at his paws.

Can we die of an animal attack? I enquired.

If the bear sectioned her artery, yes, he answered.

After a minute of terrible stillness, the brown lump emitted a whimper as faint as the patter of rain, so faint I wondered if I'd made it up, but then, through the trellis of furred legs, I saw Poppy lift her head. It glistened with dark blood which Zack and another wolf began to lick animatedly.

The River Alpha let out a keening howl, which every wolf in his pack reciprocated. A branch snapped overhead. I craned my neck and locked eyes on the creature that had almost stolen another daughter from the Rivers. My wolf longed to lunge up at it and devour its flesh for the pain it had caused my kind, but the human in me rooted for it to climb higher, because we'd lashed out first.

I'd never considered myself a predator before tonight, but the combination of wolf and human made us the most lethal kind.

Poppy rose to her feet like a newborn foal, struggling to stay upright.

I'll take her back, the wolf who'd cleaned her said. I recognized her mother's voice.

My heart pinched at the sight of the two females. Not only did Poppy still have her mother, but her mother was a shifter. I envied what they shared. How I wished my mother had been a wolf too. Cancer wouldn't have taken her from me if she had been.

As I stared at them, I imagined myself standing protectively next to my own pup someday, and a maternal instinct I didn't even know I possessed rose within me.

Looming larger than the other wolves in his pack, Zack waded toward Liam and me. *Alpha, you desire an alliance? Kill the bear that attacked my daughter, and for as long as you lead your pack, the Rivers will be your allies.*

You want Liam to bring down the bear? I yelped, wanting to add that the bear hadn't even attacked his daughter, that *she'd* attacked *it*, but I bit back my observation.

You may help him. You are his Second after all.

No. I'll do it alone, Liam said.

Liam—

He fixed me with his glowing yellow eyes, and through the mind-link, he added, **Not risking your life over a bear.** To Zack, he said, *Order your shifters back.*

While Zack bellowed for his pack to retreat, I turned on Liam and hissed, *You're not a squirrel, Liam. You can't climb trees.*

He snorted in amusement, or maybe it was annoyance, then flicked his ears. *Get back, too.*

Like I was going to let him face off with a bear on his own.

When I still hadn't moved, he growled at me and shoved his head into my belly.

Don't you dare growl at me, you overgrown furball. I'm your Second, so I'm staying. Now, tell me your plan.

He blinked at me.

What's your plan? Besides biting my head off for trying to help you? When he still hadn't said anything, I added, *You do have a plan, don't you?*

He looked at me, then at the bear, then back at me. **My plan was not involving you**.

Then you need a new plan.

He blew out a long, annoyed breath that ruffled the fur atop my ears. *Squirrel . . .*

I smirked, even though the situation was far from funny. Zack's test may not have been an impossible one, but it held its fair share of risk.

Liam's eyes flashed with an idea. *When the bear hits the ground, corral him, okay?*

My brow felt as though it was puckering—maybe it was. *Are you planning on gnawing on the trunk until it tips the bear out?*

He smiled, and then his rubbery lips retracted and his teeth shortened and the fur on his body became fine hair.

I yipped, *Are you crazy?* He wouldn't understand me now that he was back in skin. I shoved my head into his shins to make him back up.

He was going to face off with a bear in skin?

I shouldered him again.

Ness! Stop.

I froze, momentarily baffled by the fact that he could speak into my mind even though we were in different forms. Taking advantage of my bewilderment, he stalked around me toward the trunk under the watchful gaze of the River pack, which had retreated so far back all I could see were lambent eyes and moonlit forms.

The sound of bark scraping had me gaping back at the tree. Muscles twisted underneath Liam's dirt-flecked thighs. He proved agile, and soon, he'd reached the first large branch. He balanced on it, then reached over and broke off a smaller one. The bear barked.

Because he'd apparently not read the same nature guides I had, Liam decided it would be a good idea to poke the massive animal. The bear's bark turned into a blood-curdling growl. Liam poked him again. This time the bear flipped around and caught the branch between his fangs before shaking his head until he'd ripped the stick from Liam's grasp.

Liam reached for another branch at the same time as the bear unhooked his paws from the trunk and launched himself on Liam, sharp teeth bared.

Liam swung down to the ground just as the bear hit the branch. It broke free, and the bear fell, hitting the forest floor with a heavy thump. Instead of stunning him, the creature sprang up. Liam started to shift back into fur, but the bear charged. I blinked out of my daze and raced toward the bear before it could jump my Alpha.

Heart pinioned to my spine, I crouched and leaped, my claws finding purchase in the bear's back. The animal growled and climbed onto its hind paws, swiping at me as though I was a pesky flea. I ducked my head and slid down the long expanse of black fur, gouging his flesh.

He let out a feral bellow and landed on his front paws so hard it knocked my claws right out of his skin and sent me flailing to the ground. I blinked up at the sky that seemed brighter and whiter, as though the moon had bloated and spread.

The sound of battle had me blinking again.

Liam!

I rolled onto my stomach and jolted onto all fours, the world spinning and fragmenting. I shook my head to clear my vision. Two black shapes collided right in front of me. I backed up, and they crashed in a heap right at my paws. For a terrible moment, I thought the bear had Liam pinned underneath him, but then my eyesight finally cleared, and I saw the distinctive yellow eyes of my Alpha staring down at the bulky beast.

Heaving with rushed breaths, Liam sank his fangs into the bear's neck. A wet pop sounded, followed by the thump of the bear's lifeless head banging against the rich soil. Muzzle dripping with blood, Liam picked his head up, leveled his victorious gaze on me, then jutted his neck heavenward and howled his triumph.

14

"I still can't believe you poked a bear," I told Liam after I'd wormed myself into my clothes.

Dried bear blood was smeared on one corner of his tipped mouth. The kill, or maybe the fight, had buoyed my Alpha. His neck was straighter, his shoulders broader, and his gaze brighter. He radiated adrenaline and pride.

It had been thrilling and terrifying. I was actually slightly terrified of how thrilling it had felt to bring down the beast.

"Says the girl who threw herself on his back."

"He was charging you!"

Liam's eyes sparked as he lifted his thumb to my jaw. When I jerked, his smile blunted. "You had blood."

I rubbed at the spot he'd touched to get rid of the blood, and to get rid of the tingling left behind by his fingers. August's face flashed behind my pupils. I backed up a step, not trusting myself to be so close to a man who'd once held the same gravitational pull over me as the moon held over the magic in our blood.

Two Rivers in skin passed next to us. "Nice hunt, Alpha." They inclined their heads toward Liam and then toward me.

My fingers stilled on my jaw. Had they just bowed to me?

More Rivers trickled past, chattering excitedly and dipping their heads when they caught our eye.

Zack and one of his twin girls approached. Considering she didn't have a claw mark anywhere on her body, I assumed it was Penny.

"Kolane"—the River Alpha extended his hand that was streaked in dirt and blood—"in fur and in skin, you have our backin'."

Liam clasped the extended hand. "Thank you."

Zack seemed to wait for Liam to reciprocate his declaration, but what had the

Rivers done for us? If they helped us defeat Cassandra, then they'd earn Boulder backing.

After a pregnant pause, Zack nodded toward the meeting house. "Beverages and dessert will be served in the meetin' house shortly. Shall we? I believe we still got much to discuss."

Liam nodded.

Zack let go of Liam's hand, then grabbed a hold of my shoulder and squeezed it so hard I thought the bone might pop out of the socket. "For a little thing, you did good out there."

"Thank you."

"I get why you picked her as your Second," Zack said, lowering his hand. "She's brave and easily underestimated."

The Alpha's compliment warmed my blood even though I wasn't sure what I'd done to deserve it. I didn't think leaping on a bear was brave; in my opinion, my actions had been a little impulsive and a lot reckless.

"Ness picked me, actually," Liam said.

I fixed my gaze on the long blades of grass swaying against my jean-clad thighs. I stroked the dried tips with my palm.

I *had* picked him, and yet, I also hadn't.

Not in the way he'd wanted.

"Is your sister okay?" I asked to change the subject.

"Yeah," Penny said.

"Thank the God of all wolves," Zack added. And then he gestured to the meeting house, and we all started toward it.

Liam fell in step with his fellow Alpha, and I fell in step with his daughter, not walking nearly as fast as both pack leaders. How were they not exhausted? My muscles spasmed with fatigue. If it hadn't been for Zack's mention of having much to discuss, I would've backpedaled straight to my cottage, sloughed my skin clean in a hot shower, and stuffed my bruised body between the crisp sheets.

Nostrils working the air, Penny said, "He's not your mate, and he's not your boyfriend."

Even though they weren't quite questions, I answered, "Just my Alpha."

"But he wants more."

Again, it wasn't a question. "We had a brief . . . *fling*. It didn't end so well."

"And yet, you're his Second."

"And yet, I'm his Second," I repeated. "What about you? Do you have a boyfriend?"

"I have a fated mate. Dad expects us to get together before the Winter Solstice, but I don't know"—she tugged a lock of hair behind her ear—"he's two years younger and *real* immature. I'm havin' trouble wrapping my head around the fact that I'm going to be spending the rest of my life with him." She smiled. "But it could be worse. My sister, the one who died, her fated mate was almost Daddy's age. It was real weird for everyone at first."

I peered at her through my lashes.

She shrugged. "But then people got used to it."

"So she consolidated the link?"

"No. She chose not to. She had a crush on an Aspen. She was trying to get Daddy to allow her to marry him. That's why she was in their territory when"—she bit her lip—"when the Creeks came."

"But . . . We can't change packs."

"Technically, we can't, 'cause we can never be looped into another pack's mind-link without the same blood. Unless there's a duel, but I guess you know that considerin' what happened to the Pines."

I nodded.

"But we can marry into another pack. Usually though, it causes a rift at some point, that point being when we pop out kids. Mixed pups have to pledge themselves to an Alpha. They can't pledge themselves to two. And once they pick one, they can never pick the other."

We'd arrived in front of the meeting house that was vibrating with animated conversations and the clink of utensils. She pushed open the door, revealing a dining hall dripping in candlelight and moonlight.

Penny's smile increased. "Want to meet my mate?" She tipped her head toward a boy with a mop of black hair and lashes so long I could see them clear across the room. "Hey, Isaac!"

The boy looked up from the long table topped with plates heaped with fruit—cut and whole—and bottles of every drink imaginable. A giant smile overtook his fuzzy jaw.

Penny leaned in toward me and whispered, "I told him that if he managed to catch me a squirrel, we'd be doin' the dirty tonight." With a grin, she added, "He caught five."

I smiled, but then I frowned. "You're consolidating the link tonight?"

"Are you crazy? I'm not ready for that."

"But I thought—if you have sex, doesn't it—"

She grinned. "Um, hello. Ever heard of condoms? Got to test the goods before you buy them."

"Oh."

Before she could lead me toward Isaac, Liam spoke in my mind, *I didn't bring you along for a sex ed class.*

Hackles raised, I scanned the room, spotting him standing with Zack by the picture window. I bet that if my mate had been Liam instead of August, my Alpha wouldn't have had such a problem with my conversation.

Please come. We're about to discuss Morgan.

For a moment, I didn't move, didn't *want* to move. At least not toward him. When I took a step back, he repeated my name through the mind-link, and it halted my retreat. He was using his alpha*ness* to manipulate my body.

How I wished *I* could speak into his mind. I'd tell him exactly what I was thinking.

Unless you don't care to find out what the Rivers know about the Creeks.

"Ness, you all right?" Penny asked.

"I need to"—*punch Liam*—"talk with the Alphas."

Liam had his back to me, so I glared at his shoulder blades as I wound my way around the boisterous shifters.

"Nice of you to join us," Liam said out loud.

I squeezed my fingers into fists that knocked against my thighs.

"So, let me recap what I've just learned," Liam said. "Morgan's never lost a fight nor a duel before, and the Aspen werewolves who tried to run after their Alpha lost were picked off one by one."

"Picked off?" I asked, setting aside my annoyance. *For now.*

"Killed," Zack said. "My daughter . . . the one who was . . ." His voice trailed off as he cast his gaze on the glimmering river beyond the window.

My heart pitched because I recognized the look of loss all too well.

He returned his attention to us. "She and Will were trying to get back here. They were caught before they crossed the Colorado state line." Pain deepened the network of fine wrinkles over his sunbaked face. "Stupid blood-link made tracking them so friggin' easy. If my baby hadn't traveled with Will . . ." His voice caught.

Because she wasn't linked to Morgan, but he was.

He cleared his throat. "But she wouldn't leave him behind." His deep-seated hatred told me we would've gotten his alliance had we slain the bear or not.

"Being noble comes at a cost." Liam's voice was soft yet carried over the rumble of talk around us. ***I'm sorry for snapping at you,*** he added.

I kept my gaze riveted to Zack. Liam and I would discuss his mood swings later, in the privacy of our shared hut. If he wanted to keep me at his side, he needed to change his attitude. He pushed as hard as he pulled. At some point, he'd shove too hard, and there would be no luring me back in.

He'd be on his own against Cassandra.

I thought of August then, of how calm he was, how he contained his temper even in moments of great stress. Thinking of him deepened the hollowness behind my navel. A hollowness that had annexed my entire chest.

". . . all taken Sillin," Zack was saying.

I shook my head to dispel the fog of my thoughts. I needed to focus.

"And I never heard of anyone able to shift with Sillin in their blood. It nulls our werewolf power."

"Ness was thinking Morgan could've rubbed it into her skin," Liam said.

"Like an ointment?" Zack hiked a thick eyebrow. "Hey, Sam, come over here a sec." As Samuel made his way over, the Creek Alpha explained that his son was studying to be the pack doctor. "We got a question for you. What would happen if we applied Sillin to our skin? Would it get into our bloodstream?"

"Apply Sillin?"

"If it's mixed into a cream," I clarified.

"As soon as it's exposed to air and heat, it loses most of its effect."

"Most is not all," I said.

He took a swig of the drink in his hand—a fizzy transparent concoction that smelled incredibly bitter. "If there *is* a residual effect, it would penetrate the blood-stream. Not to depress y'all, but I wouldn't put too much stock in that theory."

"She had nail polish," I blurted out.

All three men's foreheads grooved.

"She doesn't seem the type to wear nail polish. I mean, she wears no other makeup."

The men were still doling out confused stares.

"Maybe she puts the Sillin in her nail polish. If she brushes it on her nails right before a fight, then manages to claw through a wolf's body, perhaps some of it gets into her opponent's bloodstream." When still no one spoke, I added, "Is my theory that inane?"

Sam sighed, swirling the ice cubes in his glass. "Not inane, Ness."

"It's an interesting theory," Zack said. "But the effect would still wear off fast."

"Maybe nail polish locks in the drug's properties," Liam said.

"Maybe." Sam's hesitant tone trampled most of my hope.

"Could she"—I swallowed—"could she have won without cheating?"

I didn't dare look at Liam as I said this, too afraid of the *I-told-you-so* expression that was surely written all over his face. If she had won without help from any substance, then I'd ruined his chances of defeating her by forcing him to wait.

"Everything's possible with that woman. The best advice I can give you two is to watch your backs around Morgan. Watch your fronts and sides too for that matter. I wouldn't it put it past her to strike from any direction."

I felt my eyes widening. "You think she'd attack us before the duel?"

"If she senses her chances of winning aren't that great, then yeah. She wouldn't do it herself, of course. She'd get someone else to do her dirty work."

"Like she sent her son to kill my cousin," I said.

"We heard." Zack exchanged a look with Sam. "Got anyone in the Creek Pack you trust, Ness? Nothin' like an insider to get a clearer picture."

"I do, but she was a Pine before, so I doubt the Creeks will trust her with anything."

"Yeah." Zack rubbed his beard, picking a twig out of it. "I doubt her new wolves will be given any classified information."

Sam's eyes widened. "Will's brother. He could help 'em. I can email him tonight."

Zack's dirt-and-blood flecked hand stilled on his beard. "Avery hates Morgan, son. I doubt he's privy to pack intel."

"It's been four years. He must've learned something in four years."

"Have you two kept in contact?" Zack asked.

"I think Ingrid did."

"Ask her to message him to see what his thoughts are on his Alpha."

Samuel turned and scanned the room.

"I believe she's with Poppy and your ma."

Once his son stalked away, Zack said, "Hopefully he'll be able to help us."

It was strange to hear him say us and not you. Strange, but oddly comforting. I liked that our small pack wasn't quite as alone, that we had allies. Sure, they were halfway across the country, but that didn't mean their influence and backing couldn't stretch over the thousands of miles.

"Ness, you mind if I take Liam aside for a bit? He and I need to discuss some personal matters."

"Of course not." My gaze skipped between the two Alphas. "I'll see you back at the cabin, Liam."

"I'm not kicking you out of the grub hall, Ness."

"I know, but it's been a long and eventful night. Plus, I'm pretty sure I'm still covered in bear gore."

Zack grinned. "'Kay then. See you in a couple hours for brunch."

As I strode through the long building, I wondered what he and Liam were going to discuss—the selection stick, perhaps? I couldn't imagine Zack, father of so many girls, wanted that thing anywhere near his pack.

A brief moonlit walk later, I was back at the guest cottage. I took a long shower, then put on my sleep shorts and a clean tank top. Before getting into bed, I checked my phone for a signal, but found none. I went into the living room and held up the device; I wasn't sure why I thought elevating it could help snag a network.

The front door opened then, and Liam came in.

I yanked my arm back, hoping he hadn't seen me acting like a human antenna. "What did Zack want?"

He eyed my phone. "He wanted to know my stance on inter-pack marriage."

I frowned. "He wanted to marry you off to one of his daughters?"

"Not exactly."

"Who then?"

Liam's gaze climbed up to my face.

"Me?" I squawked.

"No. Not you either, Ness."

Relief crept over me, but then it crept away, because Liam's expression remained serious.

"He'd only be interested if we won the duel, though."

"Just spit it out, Liam."

"He said Ingrid expressed interest in seeing August again."

The missing tether felt like a phantom limb—absent but forever there. "Did you tell him August wasn't on the market?"

"I didn't tell him anything."

"Why not?"

"Because I don't think it's a good idea that people know my Second has a fated mate. I wouldn't want anyone to use him against you."

"Oh." I dragged the fingers that weren't clutching my cell phone through my damp hair.

"And because a lot can change between now and the Winter Solstice. Look at how fast it changed between us."

"Whose fault was that?"

"Mine. It was entirely *my* fault. I let Aidan Michaels put doubt in my head. I regret every second of what happened, but werewolves can't time-travel, so besides apologizing, there isn't much else I can do to fix the past." Several breaths later, he added, "Do you miss him?"

I bit my lower lip. I did, but I didn't want to discuss August with Liam, so I kept quiet.

"Forget it. I don't want to know." He walked toward the bedroom. "I'll grab a shower, and then I'll be out of your hair for the night."

"Will you tell August about the proposal?"

He stopped in the doorway and turned sideways but kept his gaze on the fireplace mantle. "I promised Zack I'd pass on the message, but I won't force August to marry someone." His gaze scaled up the bare wall. "You two have a history, I get that, but he's a decade older than you. Doesn't it bother you?"

My fingers squeezed around my phone. "Does it bother you?"

His mouth pressed into a sullen line. "You kept telling me he was like a brother to you, so yeah, I find your attraction . . . *incongruous*, but you guys have a mating link, and apparently, they blind people to what's wrong or right."

"So you think it's wrong?"

"Does it matter what I think?"

I assumed that what Liam thought was shared by the rest of the pack. Perhaps not the entire pack. Frank had been all for it. "I didn't ask for this mating link."

Before stepping inside the bedroom, Liam sighed. "I don't know if you remember, but August thought I killed my own father, so he's not really up there on the list of people I trust or like. Plus, he got you. And I'd be lying if I said that didn't play into what I thought of the guy. But I'll also admit that from an outside perspective, a twenty-seven-year-old guy preying on an eighteen-year-old will raise some eyebrows. No one will judge *you*, but August will definitely incur judgment. Anyway, thanks to me"—he tapped the doorway—"you have some time to think about it."

The implications of what he was saying hit me.

Really hit me.

I didn't want August to be crucified because of me. And yes, in a week from now, I would no longer be a minor, but I'd still be nine years younger.

I'd *always* be nine years younger.

In my twenties, that difference wouldn't be so horrendous, but until then, what he and I had was taboo.

Perhaps Liam's condition was a blessing in disguise.

15

P ounding.

It echoed around me, driving needles of adrenaline through my legs.

I twisted around to find a black bear on my heels. I pushed my breathless body harder until every footfall felt like I was shattering a bone.

The beast jumped and sank its claws inside my human spine, and I screamed.

"Ness!" a voice yelled.

Two paws slammed into my shoulders, and I lurched into a sitting position, shoving the creature's paws off me.

Not a creature, and not paws.

Just Liam.

Blood battered my veins as I scrubbed my hands along the sides of my face to dispel the nightmarish chase.

"Bad dream?" he asked.

"Yeah."

"Want to tell me about it?"

I shuddered at the memory. "The bear we killed, it was running after me. And it caught me."

Concern pinched his brow. "My first big kill haunted me for weeks."

"It's not my first big kill, Liam."

He frowned.

"*You* killed it, not me." I scooted higher on the bed. "But it was definitely the largest animal I've ever gone up against."

"*Our* first big kill together." He smiled wistfully. "We made a good tag team out there." His expression undid more of our snarled past.

"Hope we make as good of a tag team during the duel."

"I have no doubt we will." His gaze lingered on my face a moment, but then he shook his head, got off my tangled bedsheets, and rubbed his palms over his jean-clad thighs. "Pack your bag. We'll stop by the dining hall for brunch, and then we'll head straight to the airport."

After he closed the door, I exchanged my sleep shorts and tank top for a pair of white denim shorts and a black T-shirt. I made a pit stop at the bathroom and attempted to smooth out my long tresses. Sleeping on wet hair had created movement and volume. Too much of both. I brushed my teeth, then packed everything away in my backpack. As I shouldered it, excitement at returning home steamed away the remnants of the sticky nightmare.

I would see August and Evelyn and—

My breaths spiked as I remembered last night's conversation. In the light of day, being with the ex-marine didn't seem as sinister. Just thinking of him had my navel pulsing, even though he was hundreds of miles away.

I looked out the window at the long grass that shivered in a light breeze. *What would you have done, Mom?*

I would ask Evelyn. If anyone was going to be a hundred percent unbiased about this, it would be her.

When I left the bedroom, Liam was already gone, and so were his things. I walked to the dining hall, passing a couple Rivers on the way. They waved, and I waved back.

Our allies . . .

At least, the trip proved a success for the Boulder Pack.

When I entered the gussied-up barn, I beelined straight for the head of the table where Zack sat surrounded by Liam, Ingrid, and Samuel.

"Mornin'. How'd you sleep?" Zack asked as I took my seat next to Liam.

"Great. Thank you. How's Poppy?" I asked.

"She's recuperating with her mother. I reckon it'll take both my girls a couple days to recover from the attack." The crumbs of bread caught in his beard peppered the table as he spoke. "I was telling Liam 'bout the experiment Sam carried out last night—he mixed crushed Sillin into Ingrid's body lotion and rubbed it into her skin, and then he shifted into fur and licked her arm."

I grabbed a pitcher of orange juice and poured myself a glass.

"He changed back into skin a couple minutes later."

"Which was what happened to Julian," I said excitedly.

"Except I didn't throw up," Sam said.

Julian had thrown up. A lot.

"*And* although Ingrid was able to shift into fur, she was incapable of keeping her form. When she tried to shift again an hour later, she wasn't able to."

"I tried again this mornin', and I still can't shift," Ingrid said. "So it does penetrate the bloodstream, and perhaps it's still on my skin, but if Cassandra Morgan could shift from fur to skin and back to fur, then she didn't slather herself in Sillin-lotion."

I wondered if we could trust their experimenting or if we should carry out our own.

Ingrid pushed her thick, waist-length braid behind her shoulder. "I got an email from Avery this morning. He said he didn't want to get involved, because he's about to become a father and worries for the safety of his child and mate. He hopes you understand that it isn't to spite you guys but to protect his loved ones. He wishes Liam luck, though. Says many, *many* Creeks are hoping for Liam to win." She eyed her father. When he nodded, she added, "He did tell us one thing that might help. 'Parently, Morgan's often bedridden. Word circulating around the Creek Pack is that she's got a sensitive constitution."

Liam set his half-drunk glass of juice on the thick wooden table. "Werewolves can eat carrion without getting sick."

"Exactly," Sam said, buttering a slice of sourdough. "We think it might be a symptom of whatever she's doing to keep up her edge."

I rubbed the satiny finish of the wooden tabletop. "Would taking tiny doses of Sillin for years create a habituation? Meaning, could her body shift in spite of having a minimal amount of the drug in her system?"

"I highly doubt it," Sam said.

"She doesn't heal fast," I interjected. "I forgot to mention that last night, but for a shifter, her wounds bleed longer than they should. You noticed that too, Liam, right?"

"I did, but wounds caused by an Alpha take longer to heal, so I didn't think it was particularly odd."

"Oh. I didn't know that." I bit my lip, feeling a little foolish, but then I thought of her lips, and the bluish tinge. "Does extended use of Sillin cause skin discoloration?"

Sam frowned.

"Her lips are a bit . . . *blue*." I grabbed a berry muffin from the basket in front of me and bit into the cakey treat, the tart sweetness of the fruit bursting on my tongue.

"They've always been like that," Zack said. "It's a birthmark or nevus or somethin'."

"Samuel, you mind if I put you in contact with our pack doctor? He's not a shifter but has been taking care of the Boulders for years now. We trust him completely," Liam said.

"Sure. I'll communicate my findings."

Liam stood up. "I need to get back to my wolves. Are you coming with us to the airport, Zack?"

"No. I need to be with my little girl, but Ingrid and Sam will accompany you."

"And me!" came a chirpy voice: Jane's. "Sorry I'm late. I was with Poppy."

"That's all right, darlin'," Zack said, getting up. He shook my hand. "Pleasure to make your acquaintance, Ness. We wish you great strength for the coming duel." Then he shook Liam's. "We'll be in touch. And don't forget about . . ." He flicked his gaze toward Ingrid whose cheeks instantly turned crimson.

"Dad," she muttered.

He gave her a wolfish grin before heading out of the dining hall, patting backs and leaning in to wish his shifters a good morning. From the laughter and smiles, I took it that Zack was a well-liked leader. Nostalgia for something I'd never had, a pack where everyone belonged, hit me square in the chest.

Liam touched my forearm. "Let's go."

Flanked by Zack's kids, we left the compound.

Liam sat up front with Sam, and I sat in the back with the sisters. While the men talked about setting up a lab to create a new type of Sillin, I zoned out.

"Did he answer you?" Jane asked her sister at some point. Her voice was hushed, but the urgency made it carry to me.

"He did."

"And?"

Were they talking about August? *He* could really be anyone. I was just being paranoid.

"I didn't talk to him about *that*," Ingrid murmured. "I just asked how he was doing and told him we might have a new project for him."

Jane giggled and chirped, "Project *marry-Ingrid*," but then she blurted out, "Ouch. What was that for?"

Ingrid must've made her reason clear with a look, because there was a long stretch of silence.

"I bet Ness would love not being the only she-wolf in her pack," Jane said. "Right, Ness?"

I untaped my gaze from the landscape and turned to look at the two Burley sisters. I almost told them that August wasn't on the market for a wife but bit my tongue. When their expectant gazes turned to frowns, I said, "It would be nice to have other females."

But not Ingrid.

At least, not as August's mate.

There were about ten other eligible guys to pick from within the Boulder pack. "You should meet the other Boulder bachelors before you settle."

The back of Liam's neck clenched. Of course he was listening.

"I did meet the others at the pack summit," Ingrid said. "They were . . . *nice*. But I can't picture myself with any of them. August, though"—her dreamy expression made me want to stab her eyeballs with toothpicks—"I can totally picture myself with him."

Well, stop doing it. I jerked my gaze to the road before she could pick up on my rampant jealousy.

If I wasn't able to let him go when the mating link was absent, how was I supposed to let him go once the link clicked back into place?

16

The plane ride back was nerve-wracking. I spent most of it gouging new scratches into the poor leather armrest. Liam didn't make me feel bad about the damage. He barely seemed to notice, contemplative as he was. He alternated between staring out the hatch window and studying his phone screen.

I'd looked at mine and found a message from August that dated to the previous night: *I wish you were sleeping next to me.* The words created a resonating pang inside my chest that echoed in my heart.

"What did you take away from our trip?" Liam asked, dragging me out of my reveries.

"That I should start taking micro-doses of Sillin."

"What?" Clearly not what he was expecting.

"Greg can figure out a dose that doesn't affect me more than a couple hours at a time, right?"

Liam's lips thinned in disapproval. "Not you. I'll get Matt or someone else—"

"You're paying me to help you, Liam. Let me be worth what you're paying."

His nostrils flared a few times before he finally conceded. "Fine." He bobbed his head. "Fine. What's your height and weight?"

"Five-seven. I haven't weighed myself in months, though."

"Approximately? One-forty?" he asked, typing out an email.

"Last time I checked, one-thirty." I contemplated the cottony clouds fraying and assembling into new shapes outside the window. "You think Aidan Michaels can still shift? He must've taken more than Morgan to hide in plain sight."

Liam looked up from the screen, amber eyes shaded by a swooping curl of black hair.

His cheek dimpled as though he were worrying the inside of it. "It'd be interesting to know."

"Maybe we can invite him for a run? Like a ceasefire before the war."

"Ceasefires happen after wars, Ness."

I wasn't trying to be literal. "Like the calm before the storm then."

"Even though I'd rather fight another bear than extend an invitation to run with that man, you might be onto something."

After the flight attendant removed our empty glasses to prepare for landing, I asked, "I've been thinking a lot about something recently. Why didn't you tell me your father wanted to kill mine?"

Liam's head jerked in surprise. Had he thought I wouldn't pick at the scab? That I'd just let the truth of my father's death slide into the tide of things past and unchangeable? "What made you think of that?"

"Aidan."

He bobbed his head twice. Then, "Telling you meant confessing I knew your father was going to die . . . that I'd done nothing to stop it."

That he'd been all for it.

"I didn't know Callum well, Ness, but Mom used to say he was a good man. She would tell my father that she wished he would be more like yours." He stopped talking and directed his gaze to the tiny rooftops and blue spots that were swimming pools gleaming below us. "You can imagine what that did to him." He pressed his lips together for a long, *long* moment. "To me."

"I'm sorry you suffered because you didn't have the right role model, Liam. I'm sorry Heath gave you all these inner demons. That he made you lose faith in people. But I've also seen what sort of man you can be when you fight those demons, and that's the sort of man I want as my Alpha."

He swept his gaze back to me. "But just as your Alpha?"

"Liam, you only want me"—my eyes drifted to his black V-neck that quivered with breaths—"because you can't have me."

"That's not true."

"I'm the girl who got away."

He crossed one ankle over his opposite knee. "You challenge me. You're the only girl who's ever dared challenge me. How am I supposed to become a better man if all I get are pats on the back and strokes to my ego?"

I raised a small smile. "I don't need to date you in order to challenge you."

"But it would make the challenges and criticism a lot more palatable," he said, just as the wheels of the plane bumped into the tarmac.

The lap belt dug into my waist, slamming my navel into my spine. "How about we try to be friends? According to Sarah, I'm pretty good at friendship."

The vein in his neck throbbed and throbbed. "Fine. But I draw the line at mani-pedis."

I snorted. "Is that really what you think we do?"

"I also think you discuss shoes and tampon sizes."

"Tampon sizes?"

He smirked.

I took the balled napkin in my cupholder and lobbed it at him. "Ass."

He batted it away, then picked it up and stuffed it inside his cupholder.

"Besides, according to you, dating and sex interfere with concentration, so you should really swear both off until after the duel." I smiled, finding a little pleasure in tossing his words back at him.

"Done."

The smile skittered off my lips.

"How about we grab dinner this week?"

"Liam . . ."

"Friends have dinner together, don't they?"

"They do, but—"

"But we can't?" He got up, gripping his overnight bag so tight his knuckles whitened.

"I'll have dinner, but not just with you." I stood and swung my backpack onto my shoulder. "We can go out as a group."

"Does that group include August?"

"I would hope so."

His pupils pulsed with annoyance. "Fine, but don't expect me to make small talk with him."

"I'm not expecting you to talk to him at all."

"I'll ask Matt and Lucas. Some of the girls might come too then. Hope that's okay."

"As long as I'm not expected to discuss tampon sizes with them, the more the merrier."

He smiled, but it didn't reach his eyes. It barely creased the corners of his mouth.

17

After landing, I asked Liam to drop me off at Frank's.

I realized I hadn't even phoned ahead to know if Evelyn was home. I assumed she'd be there. I always assumed Evelyn would be there when I needed her.

Sure enough, when I rang the doorbell a little after three, she was the one to sweep the door open, dispersing her familiar scent of menthol and cooking oil.

"*Querida!*" Her solid arms came around me, and she drew me into her soft chest. "What a beautiful surprise."

After thoroughly kissing my forehead and cheeks, surely smearing her red lipstick all over my face, she pressed me away and looked me over. Seemed like since we'd moved to Colorado, she was always checking for new bruises or cuts or other signs that I'd been hurt.

When her gaze alighted on my backpack, she asked, "What did Jeb do now?"

"Jeb?"

"You have a backpack."

"Oh." She thought I was coming to stay the night. I smiled. "I'm actually just returning from an overnight trip."

"Overnight?" She cocked one of her thin black eyebrows. "Do I need to sit down for this story?"

My smile increased. "Probably." The bear hunt returned to me. "Actually, yes. Unless you want me to spare you certain details."

She paled.

Yeah. She probably didn't need to hear about the bear.

I took her hand and led her to the couch, and we both took a seat.

"Before you begin telling me, have you had lunch?"

"I'm not hungry."

"I am not asking you if you are hungry. I am asking if you had lunch."

"I ate a sandwich on the plane."

"The plane? You took *un avión*? Where did you go?"

Clasping her lotion-softened hands in between mine, I started from the beginning but left out the midnight battle. Just as I was about to speak to her about August, the front door opened, and Frank traipsed in, forehead glossy with sweat, which he mopped with his forearm.

"Hi, Ness. Heard the trip went well."

Evelyn spun in her seat. "You knew about the trip and did not tell me?"

"Evelyn, you know I can't share all the happenings in the pack. And not because I don't trust you, but because I don't trust that someone won't try to get that information out of you."

Her intake of breath was so turbulent I squeezed her hands.

Frank walked over to the sink and poured himself a glass of water before returning to the living room. "Heard about that hunt of yours," he said, sinking into one of the armchairs. "Proud of you, kid."

"What hunt?" Evelyn asked.

I shot Frank a look, which made his gaze widen before dropping to his glass. "Um. The deer. Ness caught a deer."

"I have never seen you so fascinated by a glass of water, Frank," Evelyn said.

He tipped up his face, shooting her a rueful look from beneath his bushy white eyebrows.

"It was no *ciervo* that she hunted, was it?"

Frank tugged at the collar of his sweat-soaked undershirt. "It's mighty hot out today. I'm going to go shower. You girls probably don't even want me around."

Oh, I wanted him around.

I sent tiny imaginary daggers into his back as he walked away.

"Why do I feel like I am going to have an attack to the heart?"

I clutched her fingers a little tighter. "Let me preface this by saying that I'm a hundred percent fine."

"What. Did. You. Hunt?"

I winced from the brittleness of her tone. "A bear." I said this really fast and really quietly.

Her black eyes went so wide they looked like eight-balls. "A bear? You hunted *un oso*?"

"Not all by myself."

"Is that supposed to reduce my worries?" she asked. "Why?"

"To secure the Rivers' backing."

Her lips thinned, vanished. "They made you hunt down a bear? Please tell me you were sitting in a vehicle with a very big *pistola*."

I grimaced.

She clapped a hand over her heart. "As *un lobo*?" she whispered.

"Yes."

"I believe even the dye I put on my hair will turn white."

I grinned, but then realized she wasn't joking, so I swallowed back my smile. "Evelyn, I completely forgot to tell you this, but I ran into a woman at the bank the other day. She asked me if you were looking for work."

"I do not think I have the energy to clean—"

"Not a housekeeping job. She asked if you'd be interested in becoming the chef in her son's restaurant."

Evelyn's dark eyes grew wider, rounder. "A chef? Me? I am no chef."

"Are you kidding? You're the best cook I know."

A smile played on her red lips. "Do you know many cooks, *querida*?"

"I know enough of them to appreciate how talented you are."

Her hand rose to my face and cupped my cheek affectionately.

"Will you at least interview for them?"

"Perhaps." She lowered her hand. "I will talk about it with Frank. What is the name of the restaurant?"

After I gave her all the details, I steeled my spine and said, "Oh, and I need to talk to you about something else." I eyed the bedroom door that Frank had closed behind him. "It's nothing dangerous or worrisome. I just need advice. About boys."

"Oh." Surprise drove the fear off her face, and then her reddened lips bent into a smile. "What would you like to know about boys?" she asked, settling against one of the flowered throw pillows.

"I, um . . . I don't know if you heard but, uh . . ." I loosed a deep breath. "Our kind sometimes develop something called a mating link."

When the smile drifted off her lips, I understood Frank hadn't touched upon the subject.

I dragged my hands through my hair. "It's basically some sort of link that pushes two people to be together. For the continuation of our . . . species." Her slowly thinning gaze made me suck in a breath. "It doesn't mean the two people end up together. Mom had one, but she resisted its pull until it vanished. Anyway, I have a link, which will vanish after the Winter Solstice as long as I don't act upon it."

Her brow wrinkled. "Act upon it?"

My face became exceedingly warm. "Have sex with the person."

Her neck seemed to grow a little longer. "Go on."

I dragged a pillow into my lap and hugged it to me as though it could somehow prevent my navel from pulsing. Because, God, was it pulsing. Was August on his way here? Or was he angry I hadn't returned his call yet? Or was it just nerves from discussing boys with Evelyn?

"Who are you linked to?"

"August Watt."

"Isobel's son?" Her voice went a little high-pitched.

I clutched the pillow tighter.

"But he is almost thirty."

"Twenty-seven," I blurted out.

"And you are not even eighteen."

"I'll be eighteen next week."

"Do not get me wrong, August is a fine young man, but you cannot entertain thoughts about dating him, *querida*. You two are not at all at the same place in your life. You are starting college next week. He has been out of college for years. He has traveled the world. Fought for his country. He surely has had many girlfriends, which means he will expect things from you. He will pressure you—"

"He hasn't pressured me into anything," I mumbled,

"Yet. But it will come." She patted one of my hands. "If you came to ask for my blessing, I cannot give it to you. And it is not because I want to hurt you, but because I want to protect you."

My bottom lip started wobbling.

"Oh, Ness. Love is not an easy thing, and I cannot imagine a magical link makes it any easier, but you are still so young. The link will fade this winter, and then you will be free."

The heat in my cheeks filtered into my eyes.

She sighed. "You like him very deeply, don't you?"

I swallowed. "I do. I've always liked him."

"Then wait a few years. If you still feel this strongly about him once you are done with college, you two will reconnect."

"That's in four years. He'll be thirty-one. What if he gets married?" Ingrid's face flashed in front of my eyes. I blinked her away.

"If he feels the same way for you as you do for him, he will wait. The same way I waited for Frank, and Frank waited for me after his wife passed away." She dipped her chin into her neck. "Besides, have you considered what reputation he will have?"

There it was again . . . his reputation.

When a tiny whimper broke out of me, she leaned forward, tugged the pillow out of my hands, and gathered me against her, her palm stroking my hair.

"Think of what people will say about him when they learn he seduced an underage girl. That is not a reputation any man wants to have. He will be judged harshly, and that judgment will cause both of you pain." As I attempted to stifle my sobs against her slowly rising chest, she added, "Please, Ness, do not be mad at me," she said this softly, as though her tone might mitigate my pain. "I cannot encourage this relationship—however magical—because you are too precious to me."

Moment after moment passed in interminable silence.

Hands coasting over my hair, she finally added, "But in the end, it is your decision, not mine. I can only advise you. And whatever you decide, you will always have my love."

And here I'd come for her blessing.

As I shed tears against her shoulder, I rehashed all that she'd just said.

I'd never much cared about what people thought of me, but I didn't want the world to turn against August.

Which left me with only one thing to do.

Wade back toward shore before I got in too deep.

18

I got home a little before dinnertime, having moped away the afternoon with Evelyn who tried her best to cheer me up with episodes of her favorite TV show and homemade brownies.

An uncharacteristically quiet Frank drove me home. Not that I felt very chatty myself, so the silence was welcomed. I didn't ask if he'd heard our conversation, because it wouldn't change much if he had.

I did a load of laundry, then turned on the oven and set the casserole Evelyn had prepared for me and Jeb inside. As I waited for it to bake, I took out my college course catalogue and circled the classes that held my interest, but my mind kept wandering back to August.

I needed to call him, but I didn't want to break up with him over the phone.

Maybe I would stop by after dinner.

I took out my phone to read the message he'd sent me when I was at Frank's: *Heard you were back. Want to grab dinner? Cole will be there. So no rule-breaking.* :)

I'd answered him that I was with Evelyn and that I'd call as soon as I left her house. I hadn't called yet, and I'd left over an hour ago. Guilt was making my stomach throb and pulse. I massaged it as I tried to focus on the catalogue.

A knock on the door made me jerk.

"Ness?" a deep voice called out.

Well, there went sticking my head in the sand. Sighing, I strode over to the door and opened it.

August was leaning against the wall, sporting a black beanie, a dark waffle-knit Henley, and fitted stonewashed jeans. His jaw was smooth from a fresh shave, and he smelled like he'd just stepped from his shower right onto my doormat.

Why oh why did he have to be so handsome?

His gaze trekked over my face. "You weren't answering your phone."

"I must have left the ringer off."

He pushed off the wall and rounded me. "Something's wrong," he said quietly.

The throbbing in my navel turned thunderous. I wasn't sure if I was feeling his stress or my own. "Why don't we sit down?"

He dropped down onto the couch and placed his forearms on his spread thighs.

I tugged on the hem of my crop top, trying to extend it beyond my navel, but the pale turquoise cotton just sprang right back up. I folded my knees beneath me and perched on the opposite side of the couch, hoping physical distance would make this easier.

"Something happened between you and Liam, didn't it?" There was a tremor in his gravelly voice.

"No." I shook my head, and my loose hair fluttered around my shoulders. "Nothing happened between us. When I was away, I . . ." I forced my eyes to stay locked on his, knowing that if I looked anywhere else, he would sense the lie before it even left my lips. "I didn't miss you, August. Not in *that* way."

Shadows rushed over his features. "Really?"

"I'm sorry for leading you on. I feel terrible right now. But I'm hoping we can move past this and stay friends?" My voice was so steady I sounded both convinced and convincing.

August didn't speak. He just stared as though waiting for me to say: *gotcha, didn't I?*

When I didn't utter those words, or any others for that matter, he got up. "Well, I . . ." He cleared his throat, gaze on the dining table and the open course catalogue. "I'll just show myself out." His tone was so heavy I almost leaped off the couch, but Evelyn's words held me in place.

He'd understand in time.

"Will you leave Boulder now?" I asked.

"I don't know." He glanced over his shoulder at me, eyebrows almost touching from how deeply his brow was furrowed. "You probably want me gone, don't you?"

"No," I replied so quickly his eyebrows jolted up. "Don't leave on my account, August." I gripped my bottom lip between my teeth. My heart was beating so fast I tasted metal.

He didn't move for a long moment, neither toward me nor toward the door. Did he sense my lie? Finally, his hand curled around the handle.

Before he stepped out, I said, "If you want me to return the money you put in my bank account, I'll—"

"Don't add insult to injury." Tendons strained against the bronzed skin of his neck.

My teeth elongated into fangs that sank into my lip, drawing blood. I swallowed down the salty taste of it, battling back my wolf before she could rise and take control of my human body.

August's nostrils flared. Could he scent my blood? Was he wondering why I'd lost control? Maybe he assumed I was anxious for him to get out of my house.

He shut his eyes and squeezed the bridge of his nose. "I guess I'll see you around."

The tether that linked us swung like a jump rope. "Good luck with college," he added tonelessly.

"Thank you."

When he opened his eyes again, they shone as brightly as the bloated moon hanging over Boulder. He looked at me one last heartbreaking time, and then he left, the door snicking shut behind him. I held my breath as his heavy footfalls pounded the stairs, and then held it some more as his car engine rumbled.

Only when it had petered out and the world had turned silent did I unbolt my bloodied lips and let my pain pour out of me in great heaving sobs.

19

I spent all of Tuesday in bed. I told Liam I'd suffered from food poisoning, and he let me take the day off. The following day, though, I got up and drove to the gym at the crack of dawn. When I reached the building, Liam, Lucas, and Greg were already there, waiting for me.

Lucas dragged his blue gaze up and then down my body. "What the fuck did you eat, Clark? You look like hell."

"Thanks, Lucas. Exactly what I rolled out of bed to hear."

Lucas smirked, but then his smirk vanished when he turned toward our Alpha. I didn't meet Liam's gaze, afraid he would see that it wasn't my stomach that had made me sick but my heart. I bet he knew—wouldn't be long before the entire pack knew. I just hoped he wouldn't see it as an overture to make a move on me.

Why couldn't I have stuck to my plan about not dating any man for at least a year?

"So the Sillin . . . How much am I taking, Greg? And how long before we can test the results?"

Greg handed me an insulated pouch containing two pill packs. "Take two pills every day at exactly the same time. From the minute you stop taking them, you'll need about ten hours for your werewolf gene to reactivate, give or take an hour. Oh, and store them in the fridge when you get home." He unzipped a leather satchel and took out a syringe. "I'm going to take some of your blood now, and then again in two weeks to check for traces of Sillin."

"Okay."

"Not afraid of needles, are you?"

"No." Still, as he took my wrist in his dry hand and brought the syringe to the inside of my arm, I looked away.

When the pointed tip slid beneath my skin, I cinched my eyes shut. The uncomfortable pinch soon subsided, and then it was done, and Greg said, "Call me if you notice any side effects. There shouldn't be any, but just in case, you can reach me at any time, day or night."

I nodded and took the business card he extended my way.

"I guess you won't be needing a bandage," he said.

Sure enough, my skin had already patched up. Only a bead of blood remained. I swiped it away with my thumb. "Should I take the Sillin now or after my torture session?"

"After," Liam said, shrugging off his black hoodie. He wore nothing underneath. "Since we won't have another opportunity to train in fur once you start taking those pills, we're fighting as wolves today."

As Greg left, the heavy door clanging shut behind him, I looked around for a place to change. The loft space didn't have locker rooms, but it did have a questionably clean bathroom stall.

As I started toward it, Liam called me back. "Ness, you'll be shifting out here. You need to get used to it."

I must have gone ghostly pale, because Lucas chuckled. "In the other packs, females and males shift together. Didn't Sarah tell you?"

"She did, but—"

"I'm not trying to make you uncomfortable," Liam added, hooking his thumbs in the elastic waistband of his sweatpants.

"I promise that on the day of the duel, I'll shed my clothes in front of everyone, but please don't ask me to do it today."

My desperation must've rang out loud and clear, because he relented. I scurried into the bathroom that stank of dried piss, leaving the door ajar so I could get out after the change. I kicked off my sneakers, yanked off my leggings and exercise top, and piled everything neatly on the sink top even though it wasn't much cleaner than the beige-tiled floor.

Once I'd morphed, I padded out into the gym on four legs. Liam was already in fur, three full hands taller than I was. Only Lucas remained in skin. He was sitting on a bench, curling massive dumbbells.

Justin's the one you're going to have to keep in your line of sight at all times, Liam said.

My ears perked up. *You think he'll attack me?*

He's not supposed to, but it's Justin we're talking about. He might attack you to distract me.

But that wouldn't be fair . . .

If you're expecting fairness, you signed up for the wrong duel.

But am I not allowed to stop the duel if he doesn't play by the rules?

By the time you manage to stop the duel, it might be too late.

What do you mean too late?

Cassandra will have delivered a blow I won't be able to recover from.

The skin beneath my fur broke out in goose bumps. *How do I stop the fight?*

You'd need to howl three times.

Liam, when we're out there, don't watch my back, okay? I can take care of myself.

He looked at me long and hard. *You're risking your life for mine, so don't think for a single moment that I'll let you out of my sight.*

Liam—

He cut my whine off with a sharp bark that made my muscles jam together.

We're going to work on your defensive game. I'm going to come at you from all angles, and you're going to have to get away. It'll teach you to think fast and act faster. Ready?

I said yes, but that was before I got my ass handed to me. If I'd known I would be trampled and shoved and flattened against the jockstrap-smelling mats, I probably would've said no.

Then again, I didn't want Liam to take it easy on me, because leniency wouldn't serve me.

Two hours later, pancaked against the gym floor, Liam took pity on me and called it a day. Before leaving, I swallowed my first dose of Sillin, then entered a daily reminder into my phone.

"Dinner tomorrow night at Tracy's?" Liam asked just before I pushed through the doors.

Lucas looked at Liam, then at me.

Before the invitation was misconstrued as a date, I said, "Can I invite Sarah?"

"I'm not sure that's a great idea."

"She's not spying on us, Liam."

"That's not why. I just think it's not a great idea for her. I'm not sure the Creeks would appreciate one of theirs sitting at a table of Boulders."

"She's not a Creek."

Liam's jaw twitched. "At the present moment, she is."

"So, is that a no?" I asked.

He dragged his hand through his damp hair. "Fine. Bring her along." He looked over his shoulder at Lucas. "Free for dinner tomorrow night, Lucas?"

Lucas's frown grew. "Why are we all going to dinner?"

"Why, to bond obviously." I shot Lucas a taunting smile. "The paintball arena was already booked."

A corner of his lips sloped up. "I knew you'd enjoyed that activity."

"Yeah. Top ten best moments of my life."

That earned me a grin from Liam and a chuckle from Lucas.

"Who else will be at this dinner?" Lucas asked.

"Matt and Amanda." Liam turned back toward me, the smile gone from his lips. "Did you want to bring anyone besides Sarah?"

What he was really asking me was if I planned on inviting August. "No."

Liam's umber eyes glittered like topaz in the sunlight streaming through the loft windows set high enough that no one could look into the gym, a good thing considering our morning activity.

Not August? he asked through the mind-link.

Before he could get his hopes up, I said, "He's busy. Anyway, I need to go. Tomorrow, I'm running with Matt at six-thirty and then?"

"That's it for tomorrow. Wouldn't want to tire you too much before our big night out."

Snorting, I waved and unbolted the heavy doors. Before heading to my car, I made a pit stop at the drug store on the corner. I grabbed a basket and went aisle to aisle, tossing in energy bars and ultra-moisturizing conditioners and lotions, because my skin and hair felt brittle from all my shifting. As I turned a corner, I bumped into someone I hadn't seen in a long time.

Tamara let out a little *oomph,* and what she clutched fell on the ground. I crouched and picked it up. She snatched it from me, her cheeks going as red as her hair.

"It's not for me," she said.

I sniffed the air, remembering Sarah telling me shifters could scent pregnancies. My sense of smell was definitely not as sharp as Sarah's or Lucas's, and would probably dull further because of my Sillin intake, but over Tamara's flowery scent, I smelled something else—loamy earth. Since I wasn't standing in the gardening aisle of Home Depot, I assumed she was giving off that scent.

And there was this tiny fluttering vibration in the air between us.

A heartbeat?

Tamara was halfway down the aisle before I said, "It's going to be positive."

She froze and then slowly spun around, green feline eyes narrowing. "I told you, it's not for me."

As she whirled back around, wavy hair bouncing against her shoulders, the enormity of her news hit me. Even though I could be wrong—but I doubted it—Tamara was carrying a werewolf baby.

Liam's.

20

After showering, I met Evelyn at The Silver Bowl where she was interviewing for the position of head cook. The establishment was extremely fancy, which intimidated Evelyn. Before she could choke herself from tightening the red silk scarf tied around her neck, I grabbed both her hands and towed them off the scarf Mom left her in the will she'd scrawled on a legal pad.

"You do realize you already have the job, don't you?"

"If I had the job, I would not be passing an interview."

I smiled. "This isn't an interview. It's a meeting to discuss your salary and hours."

"I should have made them my *polvorones*," she said, completely disregarding my comment. "Or my *taquitos*."

I squeezed her hands. "You don't need to woo them. They need to woo you."

Her black eyes bolted to mine. "*Bueno.*"

Feeling her composure strengthening, I let go of her hands. "Want me to come inside with you?"

"No. I will be all right."

"*Te quiero*, Evelyn." I rarely spoke Spanish but understood it perfectly.

Her eyes got all misty.

"Go." I tipped my head to the restaurant. "I'll wait out here."

As she hobbled to the door, dragging her bad leg, she checked over her shoulder a few times as though to make sure I was really staying put. And I'd planned to, but when fifteen minutes had gone by and the scent of charred coffee beans and chilled milk ribboned toward me, I headed toward the coffee house next door.

As I waited in line for my order, I kept my gaze on the entrance of the restaurant. Which was probably the reason I didn't see August until he stepped right into my line of vision.

"Hey."

I tipped my head up, my heart whipping into gear. "Hi."

His gaze was soft and bright, devoid of the darkness and tension from two nights ago. For some reason, that stumped me. Not that August needed to pine for me or harbor resentment, but he seemed almost . . . *happy* to see me. I mean, I was happy to see him too, but if the tables were turned and he'd done the breaking up, I'd probably not have been all too glad to run into him.

Which highlighted my lack of maturity.

Which highlighted his surplus of it.

His lips moved, and I'm pretty sure he uttered words, but I was so lost in thought I failed to hear them.

"What?" I asked.

"I was asking what you were doing?"

"Oh. Uh."

The barista called out my name.

"Buying coffee," I finally answered.

He smiled, and I swear it dimmed the noise level around me. "I can see you're buying coffee. I guess I was wondering why you were in this neighborhood."

"Oh." I really had a way with words today. "Um. I was—*Shoot!*" I peeked around him just as the door to the restaurant opened and Evelyn limped out.

Shoot. Shoot. Shoot.

Not only was I not where I promised I would be, but I was with August. "I'm sorry, but I have to go."

"Okay." He frowned. "See you around, Dimples."

The fact that he was calling me Dimples again made me feel like he didn't detest me.

Right before pushing my back into the door of the shop, I asked him, "By the way, could I borrow some equipment from the warehouse? I wanted to sand down the floors of my old house."

He shook his head a little. "I'm offended you feel the need to ask me whether you can borrow stuff from me. What's mine is yours."

What was his wasn't mine, even if once upon a time, it had been my father's.

"I'm headed back to the warehouse after I deliver coffee to the crew. Stop by whenever you want," he said.

"Thanks?" I didn't mean for it come out as a question, but his genial attitude stumped me. Had he already gotten over me?

I turned away before he could spot my anguish and joined Evelyn on the sidewalk where she was chatting with a man who looked to be around Jeb's age. I pasted on my widest smile as I approached them.

"Sorry. Just went to grab us some coffees." I extended her cup, then shot out my hand to the man and smiled. "Hi, I'm Ness. Evelyn's granddaughter."

I didn't usually introduce myself this way, but seeing the breadth of Evelyn's smile, I decided I should start doing it more often.

"Nice to meet you, Ness. I'm Trent." His grip was firm and his expression friendly.

"Grams told me we have you to thank for getting in touch with Evelyn," he said, letting go of my hand.

"Glad to have been at the right place at the right time. Is your wife feeling better?"

"She's feeling fine, thank you for asking. Anyway, I should get back to my accounting. I'll see you tomorrow, Evelyn."

"*Sí*. Tomorrow."

After Trent was gone, I squealed and hugged her. "Told you so."

She ran her enlarged knuckle down my cheek. "*Mi nieta*." My granddaughter.

"You think your *nieta* can get a free meal in your new restaurant?"

She smiled, but then her tender expression warped as her eyes settled on a spot over my shoulder.

"Hi, Mrs. Lopez." August was carrying two cardboard trays filled with iced beverages. "You're looking mighty lovely this morning."

"August." As she said his name—none too congenially—her gaze traveled to me.

She probably assumed I'd rendezvoused with him in the coffee house, disregarding her advice.

"I should get this to my guys. Have a pleasant afternoon, ladies."

Thankfully he didn't say, *see you later, Ness*. If he had, Evelyn wouldn't have believed our run-in had been random.

After he got into his car, I whispered, "Before you jump to any conclusions, there's nothing going on between us."

She took a sip of her milky beverage, wrinkles deepening around her eyes.

"You believe me, right?"

"I believe you." She offered me her arm. "Now come and walk with me. It is so beautiful out."

I hooked my arm through hers and, chatting about her new job, we walked slowly down the street, bypassing the playground where my parents used to bring me. I told her stories of Dad, whom she'd never gotten to meet, and life in Boulder before I was uprooted. August came up in many of my stories, which earned me repeated chary glances.

"He was a big part of my life," I said as we took a seat on a bench shaded by a glossy-leafed magnolia.

"Did he . . . ever behave indecently?"

Horror had me gasping, "No! Never."

She folded one leg over the other and massaged her bad calf—the one her ex-husband had put a bullet through.

Just as I thought of Aidan Michaels, a yellow Hummer drove down the street. I didn't have to squint through the tinted window at the boy sitting behind the wheel to grasp whom the car belonged to: Alex Morgan. Another detestable Creek.

A violent desire to slash his tires, and his chest while I was at it, animated me. I balled my fingers into fists.

As though he sensed my glare, Alex turned his face toward me. He had the audacity to toss me a wink before taking off, tires screeching.

"Who was that, *querida*?"

Evelyn's voice zapped me out of my violent musings. "A Creek."

She wrapped her fingers around my fists, easing my hands open. "And what has he done to make you abhor him so? Besides being a *Creek*."

"He's the reason Everest is dead."

A long beat of silence passed between us.

Then, "Have many Creeks remained in Boulder?"

"Yes."

"Why?"

"Because of the—" I smacked my lips shut. Had I really been about to tell her about the duel? She *absolutely* couldn't know about it. She'd kidnap me and fly me out of Colorado. "Because of the inn. Because Aidan bought it, and Aidan's a Creek. So they feel at home here."

Nothing worked quite as well as burying a big truth under a smaller one.

She tapped my knuckles with her fingers. "*El diablo*."

Another reason I needed to help Liam win this duel . . . so that nothing and no one stood in my way to send the devil to Hell.

21

After dropping Evelyn off at Frank's, I drove over to the warehouse. I called Sarah on the way. I preluded my invitation to dine with a bunch of Boulders with a, "Are you busy tomorrow night?"

"You mean, am I deejaying at The Den?"

Right. It was Thursday night. "I meant earlier, for dinner."

"I'm free for dinner, and even afterward. I'm taking some time off deejaying."

I didn't ask why, but I suspected it was because she was still grieving for her uncle and for her pack's annexation.

"Meet me at Tracy's at eight?"

"Is it just the two of us?"

"Um. No."

"Who else will be there?"

"Some people."

"Which people?"

"Um. Liam, Lucas, Matt and his girlfriend."

Would Tamara come? If she did, the guys would surely pick up on her pregnancy . . . How would Liam react?

"Why are you having dinner with all these people?" Sarah asked.

"*We.* You said you were free."

"Not sure if I am anymore."

"*Please.*"

"What about August? Is he coming?"

I sighed. "What are you doing tonight, actually?"

"Hanging out with you to find out what the heck's going on in your life. Plus, I'm dying to know how your weekend went."

As I made plans to head to her place later, the warehouse materialized like an oasis, which made my pulse skip. I parked the van next to August's pickup, then made my way toward the wide-open loading dock. As I approached, the tether solidified like concrete. Standing beside Uncle Tom at one of the worktables, August looked up at me.

I tried to smile, but I was so jittery the simple process proved tremendously arduous. When I was close enough, I said, "Hi, Uncle Tom."

"Ness!" Tom grinned wide, which made his purplish-red cheeks rise and round, and the faint scent of cold whiskey clout my nose.

It was just after lunch, and yet he was hitting the bottle? I knew he needed the job, but I hoped August was monitoring him so he didn't hurt himself—or anyone else for that matter.

"We miss you around here!" Uncle Tom's strident voice made me glance worriedly at August.

"I miss it here too." And I did, even though the warehouse brought me equal parts pain and pleasure.

Pain, because it reminded me of Dad.

Pleasure, because it reminded me of Dad.

I could almost hear my five-year-old self squeal with delight when Dad would suggest a game of hide-and-seek in the stacks.

"Ness?" August tipped his head toward one of the aisles.

I snapped out of my daze. "Sorry. What?"

"The sanders are down there."

As I trailed after him, I whispered, "He's drunk, isn't he?"

After a beat, August nodded.

"Isn't it . . . dangerous?" I gestured to all the heavy-duty machinery around us.

"I got one of my guys keeping an eye on him."

"Is he often like this?"

"Liquored up? Yeah. But not usually while he's at work. Today's his wife's birthday. Every year, Dad tells him to take the day off, but he says it's easier to spend his day here than in his home where everything reminds him of her."

August's words made my heart hurt. "I'm not sure I could keep living if everyone I loved died."

"You'd find new people to love," he said.

"I don't love very easily."

One corner of his mouth tipped up. "You're telling me."

Realizing what he was saying, I added, "I still love you."

"It's okay."

"No, it's not. Not if you think otherwise."

"Ness . . ." He sighed.

Why couldn't I have returned to Boulder at twenty-one? I dragged my ponytail over my shoulder and toyed with the ends. "You're one of my two favorite people in Boulder."

A small groove appeared between his brows. "Who's the second one?"

"Evelyn."

As August watched my coiling blonde locks, I wondered where I stood in his favorites list. Had I been relegated to the bottom? Was I even still on the list?

Even though the warehouse was alive with noise, in the shade of the tall metal shelves, away from everyone else, it felt as though August and I were enclosed in our own little world, a world as fragile as a soap bubble.

He closed his eyes and took a step back, bursting the bubble. When he lifted his lids, he was staring at something behind me. He cleared his throat. "You'll need a big drum and an edging sander. And a vacuum."

"If I can borrow all of the above, it would be really helpful."

He nodded and stepped toward the rack, his arm brushing mine. Even though he seemed absolutely unaffected, I jerked from the contact. As he grabbed both tools, I thought of what he'd told me . . . that he never did anything by mistake. Which led me to wonder if he'd meant to touch me and test the durability of my nerves.

"The vacuum's at the end of the aisle." He canted his head in the direction.

As I spun, my sneakers' rubber soles squeaked on the concrete. I hurried to grab the vacuum; then together, we walked out of the warehouse and back toward the van. I shifted my hold on the contraption in order to pop the trunk open, but August loaded everything in the bed of his pickup.

As he eased the vacuum from my arms, he said, "You need a generator, or do you have electricity?"

"Jeb said we have electricity."

"And windows?"

"And windows." I smiled at his observance and thoroughness, and then I gestured to his truck. "Why did you put the stuff in your car? It'll fit in the van."

"I was going to help you set up the equipment."

"Jeb's at the house."

"And he's familiar with sanders?"

"Probably not, but I sort of remember how to use them."

"I'll give you a refresher course."

"You surely have better things to do with your time . . ."

"It's my lunchbreak."

"Well then, eat lunch."

"Not hungry."

Okay . . . I started toward the driver's side of the van. "Remember the way?"

Sadness glinted in his eyes. "I remember."

He was probably wondering why I'd want to move back into a house filled with ghosts. Or maybe *I* was wondering this and just projecting my qualms on him. Should I have sold it and moved on?

I shook my head.

I'd make new memories in it.

Fill it with new laughter and new scratch marks.

Besides, this was a good project for my uncle, who would've gone stir-crazy sitting at home, plotting his revenge on Alex Morgan. It was keeping him sane and safe.

22

Jeb came out of the house when I drove up, white wifebeater stained and damp with sweat. "We should be done with the plumbing by next week," he said as I hopped out of the van.

The overhaul had gone fast. It helped that one the elders' sons was an electrician. It also helped that Jeb was so hands-on.

August parked next to me, then got out and went to gather the equipment. "Hey, Jeb."

As Jeb wiped his hands on a rag that looked dirtier than his palms, he narrowed his eyes. "We got everything under control here, August."

I frowned.

"Oh, I'm not here on behalf of Watt Enterprises," August said. "Just came to get Ness set up."

Jeb thought I'd hired August?

My uncle was still wiping his hands, arms a little tense, as though he felt threatened by August. I rolled my eyes. Even though Jeb wasn't in wolf form, he was acting mighty territorial.

"Ness, can I grab the car keys? I wanted to go get some supplies."

I dug them out of my bag and handed them over.

Once he'd driven away, I said, "Sorry about that."

"'Bout what?"

"Jeb's strange behavior."

August smiled as he lugged the sanders past the wisteria vines wrapped around the porch's beams. "I'm used to people reacting that way. They see us coming and think we're either going to steal their job or present them with a hefty bill."

We carried the tools into the house that looked larger now that the furniture had been disposed of—Jeb had gotten some Boulders together over the weekend to clear the space. He'd asked me what I wanted to keep, and I said nothing. Not that there had been much left over from Mom and Dad; the previous owners had stripped the house.

As August set everything down, he stared around the bare space. "Never thought I'd come back here."

"You and me both."

He turned his attention to me. "You sure you want to live here?"

"I'm not really sure of much these days, but I don't see myself staying in Jeb's apartment forever. Besides, I want the forest on my doorstep. I want to be able to shift and come home without running into any humans."

I gazed out at the woods cinching the property and at the grayed picnic table buried in overgrown grass. I could still picture the boisterous meals we'd shared, could still hear my mother debating the merits of medicinal plants with Isobel, and my dad discussing inventions that would revolutionize the timber industry with Nelson while I swung on the tire swing August had fashioned for me.

God . . . he really had been such an integral part of my life.

August touched my arm. "Dimples?"

I swallowed and pushed away the memory before it slicked my eyes. "When are you starting construction on *your* home?"

"When I have time."

"Do you have a design in mind?"

He lowered his eyes to a dark knot in a floorboard. "I did. I'm not sure of it anymore."

"If you need input, I'll gladly offer my consulting services."

He nodded as though filing my offer away in a drawer he was never planning on opening. I supposed he didn't need the input of a girl with no experience or skill.

"Ready for your Parquet 101 class?" he asked after a moment.

I smiled. "I am."

After quickly vacuuming a corner of the living room, he showed me how to work both sanders. Even though there shouldn't have been anything remotely sexy about sanders, watching him operate the machines was mesmerizing.

"How old is Sienna?" The question popped out of my mouth before I could think better of bringing up his ex.

He flicked the big drum sander off. "What made you think of her?"

"*You* made me think of her."

"I'd rather if I didn't make you think of her." He straightened and rubbed his palms against his jeans. "She turned twenty-one back in January. Why?"

I shrugged. "Just wondering."

He eyed me. "You're never just wondering anything." He came a little closer, still skimming his hands over his jeans. "Age is just a number, Ness. I know some thirty-year-olds who act like teenagers and some teenagers who act like adults. What you've lived through, it made you mature faster." In a voice so low goose bumps flourished on my bare arms, he added, "Not that it matters anymore, considering how you feel about me."

For a moment, he didn't move, and neither did I, but then his gaze dropped to my mouth, and he inclined his head, and I thought that if he bridged the distance, I'd toss Liam's ban and Evelyn's opinion to the wind and confess my lie.

A ringing erupted between us. He shut his eyes and took a step back.

Palming the nape of his neck, he slid his phone out of his pocket. "I'll be right back," he said, returning outside.

I glanced at him through the window, watched his tendons and muscles shift beneath his caramel skin, watched the perfect Vee of his back. If only I hadn't missed him when the link had faded.

Sighing, I crouched and checked the floorboards for nails that would need to be removed. As I pried one loose, August's heavy boots reappeared before me. I trailed my gaze up his legs that were set stiffly apart, at his knees that were locked as tight as his jaw.

"You told me nothing happened between you and Liam when you were out in the Rivers' territory." There was a sharpness to his tone that made me rock back onto my heels. "You two shared a cabin. A *one*-bedroom cabin."

As I stood, I folded my arms. "Liam was worried about leaving me on my own in the enemy camp."

"The Rivers aren't our enemy," August said through gritted teeth.

"I figured as much when Ingrid's father asked Liam to arrange a wedding between you and his daughter."

His face jerked back. "What? What are you talking about?"

"Ingrid wants to marry you, August. If you remain a Boulder, that is. If Liam and I fail, and you become a Creek, the proposal will be off the table."

His eyebrows lost some of their slant.

"And I didn't tell you about sharing a cabin with Liam, because I knew it would annoy you."

"If nothing happened, why would it annoy me?"

"Nothing happened, and it's bothering you now. And we're not even . . . *together*."

Silence stretched out like the ocean that had separated us after he'd reenlisted.

"Will you consider it?"

His chest rose and fell bumpily. "Consider what?"

"Marrying her?"

"Of course not," he snapped.

It shouldn't have brought me any relief, but hearing him say this filled me with hope that he might just wait for me to grow up. "How did you find out anyway?"

"Same way I find out about everything . . ." He tossed me a hurt look as he stalked away. "Through other people."

His words sliced past my ribcage, cutting deep. What else had he found out about? Was he talking about the dinner tomorrow night?

"So you don't find out about this *through other people*, I'm going to dinner at Tracy's tomorrow with a couple Boulders and their girlfriends."

He paused on the threshold of the house. "Are you telling me or inviting me?
I folded my arms in front of me. "Do you want to come?"
He looked at me long and hard before saying, "No."
And then he was trampling the unkempt front yard and climbing into his car. I felt his anger agitate the tether long after he'd gone.

23

"Hey, bitch," Sarah said, flinging her front door wide. "Hope you like Chinese food, 'cause we're having Chinese food."

"I like Chinese food," I mumbled as I entered her marble-and-stainless-steel palace.

"Do contain your enthusiasm."

"Sorry. I've just had a crappy few days."

"Crappy? Try my life right now. I had the pleasure of being convened to a Creek assembly yesterday. Lori, who's apparently her mother's spokesperson, commanded us to fraternize with our new packmates and learn the fifty or so rules of the Creek way of life."

"I broke up with August on Monday," I blurted out.

Sarah's brown eyes broadened. "Okay, your crappy trumps mine. But only by a fraction . . ." She followed me over to the couch and sat daintily while I just dropped onto the seat cushion. "Spill."

"Both Liam and Evelyn think I shouldn't date a guy who's a decade older."

"Liam's your ex, and Evelyn isn't a shifter."

I glanced at Sarah, at the wild blonde corkscrews framing her delicate face. "What does that have to do with anything?"

"*He's* totally biased, and *she* doesn't understand the importance of mating links."

"What she doesn't understand is what a twenty-seven-year-old man sees in an eighteen-year-old girl."

"Did you tell her about the link?"

"I did, but that's not why I'm with . . . *was* with August in the first place." *Ugh.*

"I know, but maybe you could've used it to convince her that you're incapable of *not* being with him."

I snorted. The sound reminded me of August, which made my heart feel black and blue. "Like she would ever have fallen for that."

"She's not a werewolf. She doesn't know how it works."

"I don't want her to think I'm with him because I'm incapable of being without him." I burrowed deeper into the couch. "Doesn't even matter. I got in a fight with him this afternoon because he found out I shared a cabin with Liam when I was out East, and he's convinced something happened."

"Did something happen?"

"No!"

She raised both her palms in the air. "I was just fact-checking. I like to get all my info before doling out advice."

I leaned back into the couch and threw one arm over my eyes a tad dramatically.

"Just explain something. If you broke up with him on Monday, why are you having a jealous row two days later?"

"Because something almost happened between us this afternoon."

"I think I might be more confused now than a couple seconds ago. Start from the beginning."

And so I did. I told her everything in such detail that when I was done, the food in the little white takeaway cartons was cold.

"You do realize *you're* ridiculous, and *he's* ridiculous. Just fucking call him and tell him you lied, and tell Evelyn that you love August, graying hair and all."

"His hair isn't graying."

She smirked. "Life's too short, hun. You know this better than anyone else. You're here today, but you might be gone tomorrow, so just focus on making yourself happy instead of pleasing everyone else around you." She toyed with a diamond ring that looked a lot like the one which used to grace her uncle's pinkie.

"But I don't want people to pass judgment on August."

"He's a big boy. I'm sure he can handle it. I'm sure he'll be *happy* to handle it if it means getting you back."

I wasn't so sure he wanted me back after this afternoon. "I asked him to dinner tomorrow night, and he said he wasn't interested." I didn't clarify that I told him about it before inviting him because that would've won me an eye-roll, and I didn't want an eye-roll.

I wanted a hug.

I settled on dumplings and fried rice.

A lot of dumplings and a lot of fried rice.

While I ate, we talked about the Creeks, because one, I was done talking about myself, and two, I was hoping Sarah had uncovered something we could use.

"Cassandra didn't run with us during the Full Moon."

Alphas always ran with their packs during the Full Moon. "Why not?"

"Lori said her mother was feeling under the weather."

"Did Aidan Michaels run?"

"Nope. I doubt he can even shift what with all that Sillin still in his system."

I stuck my chopsticks into the carton of rice. "Sillin changes a werewolf's smell, correct?"

"Yeah, in substantial quantities, it dims it."

"Does Sandra still smell like a wolf?"

Sarah frowned.

"I mean, Cassandra."

"I got who you meant. I'm trying to remember."

I stuck my wrist in her face. "Do I still smell like a wolf?"

She sniffed my skin, then pushed my arm away. "Yeah, you do. You'd have to be away from your pack and taking *a lot* of Sillin to stop smelling like a wolf, Ness."

I sighed. "Do you think we're wrong in considering Sillin's how she defeated Julian?"

"Gosh, if I had the answer to that question, you'd be the first to know."

"I bet her family knows. The day of the duel, when Liam said he wanted to fight her straight away, Alex didn't look concerned at all. It was as though he knew his mother couldn't lose. Which is why I'm convinced it wasn't just skill and luck."

Sarah sat up a little straighter. "You just gave me a brilliant idea."

"I did?"

She nodded, her springy corkscrews popping out from behind her ears. "I'm going to flirt with Alex Morgan."

I hissed. "Sarah—no. He drove Everest off the road! He's insane."

She stared at the crystal chandelier dangling over her leather coffee table without really looking at it. I prayed she was reevaluating the soundness of her decision.

I leaned over and trapped her fingers. "Sarah, I'm serious. Don't do this."

"I'll be careful."

A smile, which I imagined was supposed to be reassuring, graced her mouth. "I can't go out to dinner with you tomorrow night, though. Alex will see right through me if I dine with a bunch of Boulders. And you and I can't hang out for the duration of my stint."

"Sarah—"

"Why didn't I think about this sooner?"

"Because it's crazy, not to mention dangerous."

"And fighting in a duel is *oh-so*-safe?" She pried my fingers off hers. "I'll be fine. I promise." She rose and walked over to the island to root through her handbag. She came up with a cell phone. "I'm going to tell him about your visit out East to win his trust. Don't tell Liam or Lucas or anyone else the reason I'm betraying your pack, though. It's better they all think I'm trying to be a good Creek."

"I hate this."

"Well, I hate your lack of style, but you don't see me making a fuss about it."

"My lack of style? Seriously?"

She raised a wolfish grin. "All you wear is denim and tank tops—in a variety of blues and whites and blacks. Granted your clothes are skintight, so they're not horribly unsexy, but you could have so much more fun gussying up your hot self." She tossed her phone on her bag, then went into her bedroom.

Doors slid on rails, metal hangers clinked, heavy things thumped.

She returned a couple minutes later, lugging a huge bag filled to the brim with clothes. "Since you and I won't be hanging out for a while, here's some stuff. Most of it's too small for me—"

"We're the same size."

"—on top. Or no longer my style."

"Sarah . . ."

"Stop saying my name all breathily. You sound blonde."

"I *am* blonde. And so are you. And the only reason I'm saying your name like that is because you're not letting me finish any of my sentences, and you're behaving like you just broke out of the loony bin."

"I want Cassandra Morgan dead, Ness. And so do you. And unless you want me to creep up on her in her sleep and murder her, which would just make her heart useless for the taking—if I even manage to make it stop beating—I'm going to seduce her son to help you guys." She forced the bag into my arms. "Now go. I need to fumigate my apartment to get rid of your smell."

I got up, clutching the bag. "Why would her heart be useless for the taking?"

"Because only Alphas can take another's heart." When I frowned, she added, "Their hearts are already open to connections."

"So Liam could sneak up on her and kill her in her sleep?"

"He could, but there'd be no honor in doing it. He'd just be considered a coward and a thief. No self-respecting Alpha would resort to murder in order to steal a foreign pack."

I mulled this over as I walked toward her front door. Before letting myself out, I said, "If Alex tries anything, you let me know straight away, and I'll get you out."

She nodded, but excitement glimmered in her eyes. I understood her desire to help—if the tables had been turned, I would've been the first to volunteer—but I feared what the Creeks would do to her if they discovered her duplicity. Even though Morgan claimed she wasn't out for blood, she'd punished her defectors—Everest, disloyal Aspens, the River Alpha's daughter—with murder.

24

Matt decided to test my endurance and friendship the following morning. Instead of a one-hour trek, he took me on a two-hour tour of Boulder's rockiest mountain roads and most treacherous hiking trails.

"Heard we're all doing dinner tonight," he said as he hydrated in my kitchen, his big forehead flushed and sweaty.

At least the exercise hadn't been too easy on him either.

"Not sure I'll be able to peel myself out of bed after what you just made me do. Did Liam ask you to torture me, or was it all your idea?"

"All my idea, Little Wolf. Glad you enjoyed it."

I stuck out my tongue as I refilled my glass with cold tap water. "Not to pry, but what's going on between you and August?"

"Nothing's going on between us."

Matt cocked one of his very blond eyebrows. "He almost ripped me a new one for hammering the wrong baseboard into a wall yesterday when just last week he was discussing bonuses, so I don't buy that nothing's going on."

"I'm telling the truth. Nothing's going on between us. I broke up with him for good."

"What? Why?"

"Because."

"Because what?"

I set my glass down on the counter, then turned on the tap and scooped some water up to splash my face. "Because I didn't miss him when I was out there, which means our attraction is caused by the bond." I hoped that between the sound of running water and having my back turned, Matt wouldn't detect the glaring lie.

"For real?"

I let the water run a couple seconds more, then shut it off. It trailed down my neck and bled into my running bra, cooling down my warm body. When I turned around, Matt's entire forehead was pleated.

"That's brutal."

"He'll get over it."

"I remember you saying the exact same thing about Liam." Matt shook his head. "He didn't get over it."

"He's about to get over me, considering—" I snapped my lips shut. Had I really been about to blurt out Tamara's baby news to Matt?

"Considering what?"

"Considering something I'm not at liberty to discuss."

"Ness . . ."

"Can't tell you, Matt."

"Why not?"

"Because it doesn't involve me."

"Who does it involve?"

"Liam. I think."

"I got that, but—"

"Please, Matt. Forget I said anything."

He pushed away from my kitchen counter. "You do realize that's like telling my wolf to forget about a deer? Once I spot it, I want it."

"Look at that. It's eight o'clock."

"Don't change the subject."

"You're late for work."

"And you're being amazingly annoying, which is quite the feat for you."

I shot him a brazen smile. "I can't be *that* annoying. After all, you hang out with me when you don't need to."

That won me a big-ass grin. "I have a thing for annoying people."

"I won't tell Amanda."

He chuckled. "I wasn't talking about my girlfriend."

I winked at him as he opened the door.

"Take an ice bath, Little Wolf. It helps with sore muscles."

I didn't take an ice bath, but I did take a cold shower that felt like standing underneath falling needles, and then I headed to the house and worked on the floors until I'd scraped off every last speck of the past. My bedroom took the longest, but that was mostly because I spent a bunch of minutes staring at the loose floorboard. For a moment, I thought of nailing it shut so it could never again be used to conceal secrets, but finally decided to leave it be.

Before being a depository for stolen Sillin, it had been a place where I'd stowed away my treasures and dreams.

THAT NIGHT, exhausted, I almost bailed on dinner but ended up going because I felt like I should make an effort to spend time with the pack outside of training.

When I got to Tracy's, Amanda and Matt were already seated at a table along the wall which was decorated with vintage movie posters in cheap frames that were smudged with greasy handprints. The former housekeeper in me cringed at the cleanliness of this place. I didn't even want to think about the state of the kitchen. Thankfully, I was endowed with a wolf stomach; in other words, I could digest questionable meat and not hurl.

As I sat in front of Amanda, Matt all but yelled over the music playing in the background and the continuous plink of cue sticks against pool balls, "You made it!"

"I almost didn't. Everywhere hurts."

"I heard my baby's been working you out," Amanda said, pushing her wavy, brown hair behind her ear.

"Torturing me's more like it."

Matt grinned, and so did Amanda, which was a nice change from her usual hot and cold attitude toward me.

She took a sip of her beer. "Heard you were starting at UCB. Did Matt tell you I'm going there too?"

"No!" Even though Amanda and I weren't besties, it was neat to know another person at UCB. Especially if I was to have no interaction with Sarah.

A waitress with heavy bangs came up behind me and asked what I wanted to drink. I recognized her right away: Kelly.

Another one of August's hookups . . .

"I'll have the same as them," I said. Thankfully, she didn't card me.

"Coming right up." She pushed her hair out of her eyes with her pinky finger, then poured me some iced water before leaving to grab my beer.

Amanda set her elbows on the table and steepled her fingers under her chin. "What are you thinking of majoring in?"

"Business."

Her already large eyes went a little larger. "Me too! So we'll probably be in all the same classes. Sienna and Matty already told me all the professors to stay away from and all the awesome ones."

"Liam's also filled me in."

"Yeah?" She cranked one eyebrow up and flicked her gaze to Matt as though to ask him what the deal was between Liam and me.

"Sorry we're late," Lucas chirped. "Liam had trouble deciding whether to wear his black T-shirt or his black T-shirt."

I turned and craned my neck in time to catch Liam smack Lucas's chest.

"Where's blondie?" Lucas asked, scanning the crowd by the pool tables. Why he thought Sarah would be playing pool instead of sitting with us was beyond me.

"She couldn't make it."

I caught Amanda mouthing *blondie* and Matt whispering Sarah Matz's name.

"So it's just the five of us?" Lucas asked.

"Seems like it," Liam said.

Lucas eyed the bar as though he were contemplating heading over there, but Liam must've spoken into Lucas's mind, because he cringed and dropped into a free chair. Unfortunately, not the one next to me. Liam took that one. And then he draped his arm over the top of my chair.

I leaned forward so that my shoulders didn't touch his arm.

Kelly came back with my drink and beers for the boys. She apparently knew them so well she'd preempted their order.

I bet she also knew what August drank.

After we'd ordered food, Liam said, "Heard Matt made you run twelve miles this morning."

"Twelve? Felt closer to forty."

Liam chuckled.

Even though the music was getting progressively louder, making conversation was surprisingly easy. This could've been due to the number of beers we'd put away. Kelly seemed way nicer toward the end of the meal. Especially when she delivered three extra orders of fries.

I probably overindulged, because my stomach was as hard as a pool ball. I caught Liam looking at the hand I held against my abdomen, before twisting around and scowling.

I turned.

It wasn't the hedonistic meal that was causing the stomach cramps.

Sitting at the bar with Cole was August.

And taking his order was Kelly, who suddenly didn't look especially pleasant anymore.

25

"Hey, Cole's here!" Amanda bellowed loudly. She waved to get his attention. I spun my almost empty beer bottle between my index and middle fingers, contemplating ordering another drink.

If they came over to the table, I'd definitely need another.

They didn't come over, but a couple minutes later, two girls showed up: Tamara and Sienna. Lucas grabbed some chairs from a neighboring table and scooted them around ours. Where Sienna smiled at me, Tamara didn't even glance my way.

I caught Lucas sniffing the air. Even though Tracy's was riddled with smells that ranged from bacon grease and tangy barbecue sauce, to perspiration and pungent perfumes, I felt like Lucas, who was a tracker, would detect the baby growing in Tamara's womb. When his black eyebrows jotted up and his gaze narrowed on Tamara's midsection, I took it he'd figured it out. He cast a glance in Liam's direction, but our Alpha was busy laughing at something Sienna was saying. I stared at Lucas steadily until his gaze met mine. Blinking, he shot to his feet and came around the table.

"We'll be right back," Lucas said as I got up.

We walked toward the pool tables where the noise level had grown almost deafening.

"What the fuck?" Lucas snapped.

"You're going to have to give me some more to go on, because I'm not sure how to answer that question. Was it even a question?"

He growled a little. "You knew?"

"I . . . *inadvertently* found out."

He scraped his hand through his chin-length black hair. "Fuck."

"We shouldn't be making a scene, Lucas."

"Not making a scene? She's fucking pregnant!" he whisper-hissed.

"Keep your voice down. Besides, maybe it's not his baby."

"Tamara hasn't *been* with anyone else."

I didn't ask how he knew that.

Concern, anger, and disbelief contorted all of his features. I wasn't sure what warranted the anger. "He's going to be furious."

He was speaking as though it was all Tamara's fault.

"It takes two people to make a baby, Lucas."

"No shit." Then in a low voice, he grumbled, "The last thing he needs or wants right now is to be a daddy."

I folded my arms in front of the leather tank top I'd dug out of Sarah's bag. It was pretty bad-ass and also pretty tight. "He should've thought about that before forgoing using a condom."

"He would never have forgotten to suit up. And why the fuck are we discussing Liam and condoms?" Lucas's jaw twitched. "He's about to fucking duel an Alpha . . . *Trust* me, he doesn't want to discuss diaper rashes and formula."

"Well, it's not like he has a choice." I glanced over Lucas's shoulder at our table. Thankfully, everyone was chatting again, even though the banter felt stilted.

Lucas grumbled something unintelligible, then looked over his shoulder at Liam. "I'm surprised he hasn't picked up on it yet."

Of course, the instant he said that, Liam's shoulders tensed. Had he heard our discussion or the stirring of life in Tamara's womb? He rocketed up so fast his chair skidded and toppled over. After setting it back on its legs, he looked toward us, froze, but then shook himself out of his stupor. Tamara's face paled as he leaned over and whispered something in her ear. Even though I stood at a distance from them, the tremors going through her body as she rose didn't elude me.

I chewed on my pinky's nail, worried he was angry, but from what I could see of his face, it wasn't anger . . . more like shock. He placed his hand on her elbow and steered her through the rowdy bar and then out onto the street.

Lucas started going after them, but I clapped his forearm. "Let them be."

"But—" He looked at me, then at the glass door, then back at me.

"They need to talk. Let them talk."

Matt had gotten up now, too. Instead of traipsing after Liam, he came to us. "What the hell's happening?"

Since Lucas's mouth was gaping, but not moving otherwise, I said, "Tamara's pregnant."

Matt's green eyes rounded like frisbees. "No . . ."

"Yeah," I said.

"Was that your—"

"Big secret? Yeah."

"*Whoa.*"

"Yeah."

Cole made his way to us, but August didn't. As Matt filled in his brother, I weaved myself through the thickening crowd toward the shifter who had his back to me and climbed onto the barstool Cole had vacated.

"You're still angry with me, aren't you?" I asked.

August's gaze skimmed over my face, then over the black leather encasing my upper body, before returning to one of the TVs over the bar. Instead of answering my question, he asked, "Had a nice dinner?"

His tone made me smile. "You sound like you hope it was awful." This won me a piercing side-eye. "What about you?"

"We haven't had our food yet."

"I'm sure Kelly's working extra hard to fix that, or maybe she hasn't brought it over to extend your visit."

"What's that supposed to mean?"

I crossed my legs and spun on the barstool so that I was facing the TV too. "Didn't you have a fling with her?"

I felt his gaze trace my profile, linger on my chin . . . or was it my mouth? "I'm surprised this bothers you considering . . ."

"Considering?"

"Considering how you're not interested in me."

Ouch. I could've lied at that point, told him that it didn't bother me, that he could have flings with every girl in this bar for all I cared, but truth was, I did care and absolutely didn't want to drive him into the arms of another girl. "I finished sanding the floors. I'll bring all the equipment back tomorrow."

August watched me, then watched the boys who were still discussing the new development behind us, then moved his gaze back to the television displaying a live baseball game. He didn't ask me what all the excitement was about. Had he figured it out on his own, or was he simply uninterested?

"I was thinking of oiling the wood like Dad used to," I continued. "Which brand would you recommend?"

"The one we have at the warehouse. I'll put some aside for you tomorrow. You can grab it from the office when you drop off the sanders."

"I can also go to the store and buy it."

He angled himself fully toward me now, his broad chest eclipsing everyone behind him. "You could, but then you wouldn't get the quality stuff we stock."

I sighed. "Will you at least let me pay for it?"

Instead of answering me—or maybe his pointed look was the answer—he raised his hand to get the bartender's attention. "Hey, Tommy, can I get a Coors and another Michelob?"

The bartender nodded. Seconds later, two bottles appeared in front of us on the sticky bar.

August pushed the Coors my way. "That's what you were drinking, right?"

I wasn't sure why he was asking me, since he was well aware of the answer—August was the most attentive person in the Northern hemisphere.

I wasn't sure whether I should be drinking another beer. Then again, I was walking home, not driving, and I had a werewolf metabolism, so one more couldn't hurt. "I'll only drink it if I can pay for this round."

He smiled, as though amused. "Same way you're going to pay me for the hard-wood finishing?"

"You do know I wasn't fake-offering, right?"

"I know."

"Then why won't you let me? I'd be using your money to pay anyway."

His smile vanished. "Stop thinking of it as my money. It isn't. It's money that was owed to your family—"

"Stop saying it was owed. Nothing was owed. You just gave me a handout because you pity me."

His eyebrows shot up. "That wasn't pity."

"I'm not mad; I'm just stating a fact."

"Don't state incorrect facts because that makes *me* mad." He lifted his bottle to his lips and drank a long, hard gulp that made his Adam's apple judder.

"I didn't come over here to fight with you."

His freckles darkened. "We're not fighting; we're talking."

"Well, let's talk about something else, then."

The spicy scent of his skin seemed to have gotten stronger. Perhaps because he was flushed from the heat of our *talk*. "What are you doing for your birthday next week?"

"Haven't planned anything. Probably just dinner with Evelyn after her shift at The Silver Bowl." Even though he hadn't asked, I explained why we'd been there the other day. "Actually, how about we all go to dinner there?"

He cocked up an eyebrow. "All?"

"Your parents, Jeb, Frank, you? We could go late so Evelyn can get out of the kitchen." I scrunched up my nose. Had I really just suggested his family join me? Just because they'd been to most of my birthdays, didn't mean they cared to sit through yet another one. Especially after everything that had transpired between me and their son. "Unless—unless you have other plans."

"I have no other plans."

"You really don't have to come if—"

"I'm honored to have been invited. And I can already tell you Mom and Dad will be there." A smile finally fractured his tension-filled face.

"Okay," I whispered.

He turned in his seat, and his knee knocked into mine. The contact made me jump, which in turn made him lay a big palm on my thigh. I wasn't sure if he was trying to pin me in place or calm me.

It wasn't calming in the least . . .

"Sorry about that. Not much room in between these barstools."

I wondered why he was passing it off as an accident when it was blatantly not. My gaze dropped to his hand, which he hadn't removed.

"You're not supposed to touch me," I said, my voice coming out a little choked.

"We're no longer dating, so I don't really see how I'm breaking Liam's rules."

August was so close that I could hear the steady cadence of his heart through his tight Henley, which meant he could hear the frenzied tempo of mine.

"Right?" he asked in a voice so rough it sounded like he'd used the big drum sander on his throat.

I swallowed, and I swear everyone in the bar heard my saliva go down. I grabbed the beer and chugged some down to cool off and calm down just as Kelly bustled over with August's and Cole's order. August slipped his hand off my leg and thanked her.

Before jetting off toward another table, she studied me, then August.

"I should probably give Cole his seat back." I started to get off the barstool when August caught the edge of the seat to cage me in. "He can find another seat."

"August . . ."

"He's not even back yet."

Cole stood with Matt and Lucas. Were those three still discussing Tamara and Liam? Hadn't they exhausted the subject yet?

As I turned my attention back toward the plate topped with ribs and barbecue sauce, my gaze stumbled on Sienna and Amanda, also huddled together.

Long feather earrings fluttered against Sienna's bare freckled shoulders, tangling with her pale, wispy hair. She was nibbling on her lip as though nervous. Were they also discussing Tamara? She must've sensed my stare, because she looked up. For a second, she froze, but then she offered me a tentative smile. Instead of reassuring me that I wasn't the most detestable person in Tracy's, it filled me with guilt.

Technically, I hadn't stolen August away; he'd broken up with her because he was reenlisting, which had nothing to do with me. But sitting next to him, letting him buy me a drink so publicly, letting him brand me with his hand . . .

How could she *not* hate me?

I thought of Tamara then and realized I didn't hate her because I was no longer hung up on Liam. Was that why Sienna wasn't sticking pins inside a voodoo doll version of me? Because she'd moved on?

"Ness?" August's voice made my attention jounce back to him.

"Did you say something?"

"Only your name a half dozen times." He placed his elbow on the bar and rubbed the back of his neck. "I'm sorry about yesterday. I had no right to be jealous or mad. I think I haven't gotten it through my head that I have no claim on you anymore." He sighed. "Might take me a while to accept it, so bear with me, okay?"

I bit down on my lip, thinking of my conversation with Sarah. I valued Evelyn's opinion, but I also cared deeply for the man sitting beside me. I glanced around the room, wondering if anyone was looking at the two of us in disgust.

No one was looking at us, period.

No one seemed to care.

I was drinking a beer so they probably assumed I was twenty-one. Maybe if they knew the truth, they'd gawk and wrinkle their noses.

"You have nothing to apologize for, August." I filched a fry and swirled it in the little heap of ketchup next to his burger. God only knew why I ate it since my stomach was jam-packed with food, beer, and nerves.

Cole returned then, blasting us with the charred scent of tobacco. "Just gonna grab my food. Don't want to interrupt anything."

I hopped down from the stool. "I was leaving."

Cole's blue-gray eyes zipped to August. "Don't leave on my account."

"I'm not." I smiled at both of them. "Matt made me run two hours this morning, so it's a miracle I even made it out."

"I heard about your little half-marathon. Apparently I'll be joining you two on Saturday. Matty's on my case about getting in better shape." Cole was already in amazing shape, so I wasn't sure how running could better it.

Werewolves had a couple advantages over humans—one of those being our metabolisms. Once the shifting process slowed though, around forty, shifter bodies didn't burn off calories as quickly, but even then, most remained in athletic form.

"I could use a run, too," August said. "If you don't mind the added company."

"Gosh, I'd love the added company. Especially Matt. After the third mile, I pretty much turn mute, whereas he can talk the whole way through."

Cole chuckled. "Sounds like Matty. Don't you know his full name?"

I cocked an eyebrow.

"Matty-the-Motormouth-Rogers."

I smiled. "I'm sure he loves that. Anyway, see you guys on Saturday." I went back to my table to grab my stuff. "I'm gonna head home."

"So soon?" Lucas asked. "The evening's young."

"If I'm expected at the gym tomorrow morning, I need to get myself to bed." I rooted around my bag for my wallet. "Am I expected tomorrow morning?"

His expression sobered. "I'll text you."

"Okay." I plucked out two twenties and put them on the table. "If I owe anymore, just tell me in the morning."

"Sure thing, Clark."

"It was nice seeing you, Amanda. And I guess we're going to be hanging out a lot more come Monday, huh?"

She bobbed her head, which she'd nestled in the crook of Matt's arms, and shot me a disarmingly nice smile. "Yep."

"What's happening on Monday?" Sienna asked in that silken voice of hers.

"Ness is starting UCB."

"Ooh, that's fantastic! You're going to love it." She smiled, and again, I wondered *why?* "I'll try to meet up with you two at lunch if we break at the same period. Can't believe I'm graduating in nine months. It went by so fast."

As she discussed the passage of time with Amanda, my mind stuck to the nine months part.

In nine months, she'd graduate and Tamara would have a baby.

I was so lost in thought that I bumped into someone by the entrance of the bar.

26

"Well if it isn't my favorite Boulder bitch."

I glared at Justin, my knee itching to make contact with his crotch. "Get out of my way, Justin."

He grinned, nice and wide, putting all of his teeth on display. He looked like he had an abnormal amount of them, or maybe they were just all bigger than normal.

"Or what? You'll call all those boyfriends of yours to the rescue?"

"Do you have the shortest memory in the history of *shifter*kind, or are you missing a brain completely?"

He smirked.

"I don't need anyone to rescue me, asshole. Now get out of my way." I tried to shoulder my way past him, but he blocked me.

I shoved my elbow into his jaw, but he anticipated my move because he bent backward and swiped at my arm. A burn erupted over my skin. The bastard had clawed me!

"Gosh, dueling you's going to be so fun," he slurred.

Out of the corner of my eye, I caught a flurry of movement. Cole seized Justin's two buddies by the neck and clapped their heads together, and then Matt was jumping another large guy.

A hand dragged me back. Not a hand.

August yanked on the tether to get me out of the way, then stepped in front of me. "You just never learn," he growled right before delivering a mean right hook to Justin's ear that had the hateful Creek swaying a little.

Unfortunately, it didn't make him stumble or fall.

"Fucking mutt." Justin's lips flapped, and spittle hit August's forehead.

I drew my bleeding arm closer.

"What did you just call me?" August asked in a deadly whisper.

Lucas shoved past August, rubbing his palms together. "Justin, my man, I've been meaning to pay you a visit for some time now."

Justin rubbed his temple. "That reminds me . . . Taryn's no longer wrapped around my cock. But she's going around the Creeks. If you get my drift." He tossed Lucas a wink that made him pounce, but the shifter fell into a crouch, managing to get out of the way. When he lurched up, he headbutted Lucas in the chin.

I gasped at the sound of cracking. Lucas seemed stunned for a second, but then he narrowed his eyes and barreled into Justin so hard he backed him into the door of Tracy's and right out into the street. I stood frozen for a second, but then I moved, heading out onto the street after them.

August hooked his finger into one of my beltloops and held me back. "Lucas can handle him, sweetheart."

"But—"

"But nothing. You stay away from that asshole." He pulled me to the side, along the windowed façade and then farther down the sidewalk, but then he stopped walking and cinched my wrist, slowly tugging it away from my leather top. As he took in my wounds, his eyes flashed with bloodlust. "He did this?"

As he started to turn, I grabbed a handful of his T-shirt. "Don't bother."

He listened to me—even though it seemed to take everything in him to do so.

A car alarm made us both look back at the scene unfolding outside Tracy's. Lucas had tossed Justin onto the hood of a car, cracking the windshield. A police siren layered itself over the sound of the wrecked car. Matt and Cole gripped Lucas's shoulders and peeled him off Justin, and then they shoved Lucas down the street in the opposite direction from where I stood with August.

"We have to go. The cops in Boulder are all dirty," August hissed.

I remembered someone telling me they worked for Aidan Michaels. Did they know what he was? Would they still be loyal to him if they knew?

August gripped my fingers hard, as though afraid they'd slip out of his hold, and towed me down the road just as police strobe lights painted the pavement and the gathered crowd blue. Even though my arm hurt and my legs felt like a solid bruise, I lengthened my strides to match August's. In minutes, we'd reached my apartment.

I dug through my bag for my key, but my fingers shook from a mixture of adrenaline and fear. My bag toppled, and everything inside spilled onto the sidewalk.

August crouched to retrieve my things. When he noticed how hard I trembled, he stood and cupped my jaw. "Sweetheart, it's okay. You're okay. Everything's okay."

That miserable phrase again. All those words ever did was herald chaos into my life.

Sensing I wasn't reassured, he wrapped one hand around the base of my neck and pulled me to him. I let out a dismal whimper, because nothing was okay.

"I couldn't even . . . I didn't even manage—" My voice caught on a sob. "How am I supposed to . . . block Justin in fur when I can't even . . . do that in skin?"

"Seconds don't usually fight."

"He said . . . he said"—I pulled in a shuddering breath—"that dueling me . . . would be fun." I'd always suspected Justin was planning on doing more than standing guard over his new Alpha, but the realization that my suspicions might become true felt like salt in my veins.

August pressed me away and tipped my head up. "You think I'd let that happen?"

"You won't be in the ring," I murmured.

My navel pulsed and heated. And then my body slammed into August's, and it felt like hugging a rock, except this rock hugged back.

He dropped his mouth to my earlobe. "Of course, I'll be there," he whispered.

My navel thrummed again. He was talking about using the tether to cheat.

"They must know what we are, August, which means they'll keep you away from the fight."

His gaze crowded with shadows. I gathered he hadn't considered that.

"How about we discuss this off the street?" he asked.

Because my boots had become one with the sidewalk, he steered me up the stairs, and then he unlocked the door and pushed it open. After shutting it behind us, I dropped down in one of the dining room chairs while he went into the kitchen. He grabbed a dish cloth and wet it, then returned to tend to my arm. I tried not to wince, but failed.

August's jaw slackened and tensed, as though he were working out a kink in his cheek. "Why are you still bleeding?"

I stared at the grooves Justin had etched into my skin. "Probably because I'm taking Sillin."

August's green gaze jerked to my face. "Why are you taking Sillin?"

I pulled my bottom lip between my teeth before releasing it and sighing. "Because we're experimenting with it."

"Experimenting?"

"I volunteered to take Sillin to test its long-term effects."

"You what?" he choked out.

I was pretty certain he'd heard me.

His eyes gleamed with anger. "And Liam okayed this?"

I got those two had baggage, but that didn't give August a right to blame Liam for this. "I didn't give him a choice."

"He should've picked someone else to experiment on. You can't be taking Sillin and doing all that training!" He clapped the table, which made me jump. "You shouldn't even be doing all that training in the first place. You shouldn't have signed up for another duel!"

"Why don't you tell me how you really feel?" I muttered.

His nostrils pulsed. "I hate this. *All of this.*" He carved the air with his hand. "Ness, I lost you once before"—his voice shook with anger, but also with something else— "and I don't want to lose you again."

I leaned over and placed my hands over his. "That's why I'm experimenting with the Sillin. We suspect Morgan's taking it, and *she* fought a duel."

"She's an Alpha, Ness. The way things affect her body isn't comparable to the way things affect yours."

I slid my hand off his and curled my fingers into my lap.

He leaned back in his chair, making the rungs creak, then looked toward my uncle's closed bedroom door. There was no other heartbeat in the apartment—Jeb wasn't home.

August crossed his arms. "Besides, she wouldn't have been able to shift if she were taking Sillin."

"I'm trying to see if a habituation to the drug modifies the body's response to it."

"Habituation? How long are you planning on taking it?"

I studied the bloodied tracks on my forearm. Unspoken words saturated the air between us. He wasn't pleased, but was it with me or with our theory? Or was it with something else altogether?

"Maybe the happy news will knock some sense into Liam and make him cancel the duel," he grumbled.

So he'd heard about Tamara.

I peeked up at him through my lashes. "You think Morgan would accept canceling the duel?"

August sighed. "She didn't seem overly keen on dueling the day Liam challenged her. And she *did* offer Liam a peace treaty. Maybe it's still on the table."

"That was to save her son. Alex is free now."

"He could become *un*free."

"You're not actually entertaining thoughts of kidnapping him?"

"If it saves your life, I'm entertaining many thoughts. Killing Justin's another. In case you were wondering."

I leaned forward and touched his arm. His tendons twitched under my fingertips. "It'll turn this town into a bloodbath."

"So it's okay if your blood's spilled, but no one else's?"

I'd signed up for this, so yes, I supposed it was. I refrained from pointing this out to August.

It dawned on me that instead of resolving this with violence, we could resolve it with words. Morgan was a smart woman. Surely wise, too. She'd understand that things had changed for our pack.

Besides, she'd told me to pay her a visit. I decided it was time I took her up on it.

The front door opened then, and Jeb walked in. He blinked as he took us in, bloodied towel and all.

"What the hell happened?" he asked.

While I was trying to decide what to tell my uncle, so as not to worry him, August said, "Bar brawl with some Creeks."

So much for not worrying Jeb. His light-blue eyes went as wide as doorknobs. "Creeks?"

I got up. "August will fill you in. I'm going to bed."

As I stepped past August, he caught my hand, then flipped my arm around and inspected the wound. "Still not healed."

"It'll heal during the night." I added a smile to reassure him, but it seemed to miss its mark, so I leaned over and placed a kiss on his forehead. "Don't frown so much. You'll get premature wrinkles."

His forehead didn't smooth out as I freed my hand from his grip and walked to my room. If anything, the grooves seemed to deepen. After washing my arm with soap and wrapping gauze around it, I pulled on my sleep shorts and a long sleeved tee to keep my bandage in place, then slid under the covers.

August and Jeb were still talking in the living room. I tried to stretch my hearing to grasp what they were saying, but however hard I tried, their words sounded like gibberish. Was the Sillin to blame for this too?

I pressed my hand against my abdomen. Would the tether also fade if I kept ingesting the drug?

My heart held still, then skittered, making my skin prickle from the release of rapid beats. I didn't want it to fade.

I pressed the pillow against my face and let out a muffled cry of frustration, because I was so damn confused about everything.

If only *one* thing made sense . . . If only *one* thing could go right . . .

Mom would tell me to count my blessings, so I did. Evelyn was alive and happy. August was sticking around Boulder. My house was almost in livable condition. I was starting college on Monday. I was turning eighteen on Friday. Isobel had beat cancer.

I counted my blessings until sleep zippered over me.

27

Even though I'd dressed for the gym, Lucas texted me that there would be no working out this morning, which suited me perfectly. My arm had stopped bleeding but was in no shape to swing or block a punch. After a cup of bitter black coffee, I knuckled my uncle's door and asked if I could borrow the van.

"Sure." The word was garbled. He popped open his door, a toothbrush dangling from his mouth. "I'll get Eric to pick me up. He was planning on helping me out at the house this morning anyway."

"Thanks."

"How's the arm?"

"Still attached to my elbow, so there's that."

He took his toothbrush out, and pasty-foam dribbled out. "Is it still bleeding?"

"No." I pushed off the wall I'd been leaning on and displayed my knitted skin. "All healed. Anyway, I'll see you at the house later. I was going to oil the floors today."

"Eric and I can do that."

"You're already doing so much."

He let out a little snort. "Honey, I'm loving this project."

I smiled. "I'm glad."

As I headed for the front door, he asked, "Where *are* you going?"

"To campus. To pick up books I need for Monday."

He nodded. "I keep forgetting you're starting college. For some reason, I feel like you're so much older."

I felt way older too.

"Hey, it's your birthday next week!"

I jumped from the intensity of his voice.

"Eighteen." He wiped his mouth with the back of his hand. "That's . . . that's it. You won't need me anymore." Sadness mangled my uncle's tone.

"Aw, Jeb. Just because I'll no longer be a minor doesn't mean I won't need you."

His lips bent but then fell, and then his eyes became all glossy.

I strode back over and hugged him. "I'm not going anywhere. At least nowhere without you, okay?"

He didn't speak but squeezed me hard. When he released me, I repeated that I wasn't leaving, because he wore a look I recognized; it was the look of people who'd been repeatedly abandoned . . . who didn't believe people stuck around.

"Love you," he said right before I exited the house. I was pretty certain it was the first time he'd said those words to me.

"Love you too." I was pretty certain it was the first time I'd said them back.

As I drove down the roads I knew only-too-well, I itched to phone Sarah and find out how her evening had gone, but what if she was hanging out with the Creeks and they saw my name appear on her phone?

Maybe she'd be at the inn.

When I started up the sinuous drive, my heart grew weighty with dread and something else . . . anticipation? Call me crazy, but I was looking forward to speaking with Sandra. *Cas*sandra. I wondered why I hadn't gone sooner.

I parked in the far corner of the employee lot; then, fully alert, I walked up to the revolving doors. The land had once belonged to my family, but not anymore. Now I was in enemy territory. When I pushed through the glass doors, I expected shifters to pounce on me, but no one pounced. No one was even here. I had to remind myself that this was no longer a public inn.

Nothing had changed. Except the smell.

The air still carried the odor of wood smoke, but it was barely distinguishable under the aroma of damp fur and warm musk. It was as though the Creeks spent more time in fur than in skin. Perhaps they did. I realized I knew more about the Rivers than I did about the wolves in my own town.

Heartbeats pounded behind the wooden walls. I heard them above me, below me, in front of me.

"Hello?" I called out, not wanting to spook anyone.

The shuffle of rubber soles had me jerking my face toward the back office. Emmy, one of the women who worked at the inn before it was annexed, froze on the threshold.

"You're still here?"

I'd imagined she'd handed in her letter of resignation after the night the Creeks arrived.

She crossed her arms nice and tight. "Are you expected?" Her tone was so sharp that both my eyebrows jolted up.

"You're mad at me?"

"I'm mad at a lot of people and things right now." We stared at each other in silence for a long beat. Then, "Are you one, too?"

The desire to shake my head almost won over my desire to confess the truth. "Yes."

She shuddered, and the row of tiny silver hoops adorning the shell of one of her ears glittered.

I moved toward her, and her body seized. She even took a step back. She was afraid of *me*?

"Why are you still working here?"

"Because I signed a contract." Her gaze snapped to the entrance of the living room.

We were still alone.

"Emmy, you're not trapped, are you?"

Her eyes gleamed with unshed tears.

"Are you?" I repeated a little more insistently.

"Michaels offered me twice what your uncle and aunt were paying, so I signed on the dotted line. Skylar, she said the new management gave her the creeps, so she didn't renew her contract. After I found out—" Her voice cracked and then tapered off. "After I found out what you all were, I told Mr. Michaels I didn't feel comfortable working here anymore. I told him I wouldn't talk, but he said it was too late. He said I should've read the fine print better." She sniffed. "You know what the fine print says? It says that if I leave my place of employment or speak about my new employers' nature, I would be taken into the woods. And *not* for a nature hike."

Without even realizing it, I'd moved closer to the bell desk, closer to her. "They threatened your life?"

She nodded. "Along with the lives of everyone I hold dear." She snorted. "Serves me right for not listening to my wife."

"Have they hurt you?"

"No. As long as I make up their rooms and clean their clothes and pick up their dirty dishes, no one bothers me."

I rounded the bell desk.

She uncrossed her arms and shot out her palm. "Don't come any closer."

"Emmy! I'm not like them. You don't have to be scared of me."

"You just said you were one of them."

"Just because I can shift doesn't mean I'm like them."

"That's exactly what it means."

I sensed there was no reasoning with her. "How many humans work here?"

"Four. But the other three are thrilled. I don't think they've gone home once since the *pack* arrived. You should hear them talk. They're all so freaking dazzled. Even your aunt. I swear. It's disgusting how attentive she is to her new employer."

"Emmy!" The snap of a familiar nasal voice had me whirling around. "If you're done gossiping, Linda could use some help setting out breakfast."

Emmy scurried past my aunt without a backward glance at me.

Lucy had slimmed down considerably, or perhaps it was an illusion cast by her choice of attire—a simple black sheath belted at the waist. As I kept staring at her, I realized it wasn't an illusion. Her milky-pale cheeks had lost their roundness, and her freckled arms seemed too narrow for her column of bangles. Even her eyes had gone through a transformation. They carried haunted shadows, as though grief had absorbed into the fragile skin of her lids and swelled her orbits.

"What are you doing here, Ness?" she asked.

"I came to see Mrs. Morgan."

"Mrs. Morgan doesn't care for visitors. *Especially* Boulders."

She spoke the word as though we were something glued to the bottom of her shoe. Granted, she wasn't a werewolf, but being the wife of a wolf and the mother of another had made her just as much of a Boulder as I was.

"She told me to stop by."

"I very much doubt that." I started advancing, but she blocked the entrance of the living room. "You are no longer welcomed here. *Leave.*"

I reined in my annoyance by tightening my hold on my bag's crossbody strap. "Lucy, I *have* to talk to her."

"I'll let her know you stopped by. Now, go."

"Lucy?" came another voice that always made my hackles rise.

Her hazel eyes widened, and she mouthed, "Go," again, but I didn't heed her command.

Surely Aidan would allow me to meet with his cousin. He appeared behind my aunt and then slowly brushed past her. "Miss Clark, to what do we owe the pleasure of your visit?"

"I came to see Sandra."

"Huh." His lips twitched, and then his fingers rose to his earlobe, and he rubbed it —one of his weird little ticks. He did it when he was nervous, but he also did it when he was intrigued. His stealthy smile told me it was the latter. "Right this way."

My aunt—former aunt—went as rigid as marble. "Aidan, I—I don't think it's a good idea. We don't know what her intentions are."

"My intentions?" I said. "You think I came to burn down the inn?"

Her nostrils flared.

"My rose"—Aidan ran a knuckle along the pillar that was Lucy's neck—"do not fear for our safety. You know we could snap her like a twig before she'd even have time to strike a match."

I let out a low hiss.

Leering at me, Aidan started toward the living room but stopped and patted his thigh. "Come along now."

"I'm not a dog," I snapped.

"Oh, I know. I'm fond of dogs; I'm not particularly fond of you."

The feeling was mutual.

Lucy didn't even blink as I passed by her, didn't even twitch, but I caught the spike of her pulse and the aroma of something cold and tinny wafting over her heavy rose-and-tobacco scent: fear. Was Lucy truly scared I'd set the inn on fire? My aunt had never been a very caring person—at least not toward me—but believing me capable of arson was a whole new level.

The leather couches in the living room had been arranged in a semi-circle around the massive stone fireplace blackened by a recent fire, and the Native-American patterned rugs had been dragged in the middle. They overlapped and were strewn with throw pillows as though the yellow-stuccoed living room had become a hippy campsite.

"You like our new décor?" Aidan asked.

I eyed him.

"I think it's much more convivial."

"Do the rest of your hotels look like this?"

"No. But this isn't a hotel. It's a family home."

From what I could see through the glass wall of windows separating the living room from the deck was that the Adirondacks and charming teak tables had been removed and replaced by plain picnic tables, the sort with attached benches. Dozens of them from the looks of it. They were lined up in two neat rows and topped with pitchers of drinks, thermoses of tea and coffee, and platters of breakfast offerings.

A handful of Creeks were already seated, digging into the food. As I stepped out, the loud chewing noises subsided and hunched backs straightened. And then heads perked up.

Only two were familiar—the Alpha's and her daughter's.

"Sandy, look who stopped by to see you," Aidan said.

28

Cassandra's narrow jaw moved as she chewed on whatever was in her mouth. After swallowing, she wiped her lips with a napkin. "I was expectin' you sooner."

My heart began to stampede inside my chest. Was walking into this den of wolves alone a poor idea? Would I leave here alive and in one piece?

I lifted my chin a notch to show I wasn't scared, hoping they wouldn't associate the pounding behind my ribs with fear. What else would they associate it with, though?

"Can we speak in private, Sandra?"

She smiled at me. "You may call me Sandy. All my wolves do."

"I'm not your wolf."

Her smile strengthened, and although she didn't utter the word, *yet*, I could see its shape take form on her bluish lips. She rose and stepped over the bench. A shapeless tunic that seemed made of tarp dropped to just below her knees. "Would you like to take a stroll or sit in the living room?"

As she stepped closer, I cranked my face up. I didn't like how small she made me feel, even though being a full head taller than me wasn't her fault. She wasn't even wearing shoes. Her toenails, like her fingernails, were lacquered in dark polish, and her toes were stained with dried mud and crushed grass.

"I'm not a fan of shoes. I'm not much of a fan of clothes either, but I was told walkin' around these populated parts naked was frowned upon."

"Where you live in Beaver Creek is that remote?"

"Even more so than the Rivers' compound. Was your trip to their domain enjoyable?"

Sarah had shared the info I surmised. I found myself gaping up at the small balconies in front of each room, wondering if my friend was standing on one of them.

When Cassandra raised her head to study the log façade, I shot my gaze away. I couldn't have her wondering what or who I was looking for.

"A walk sounds good, but not in the woods. Right here in the clearing."

The Creek Alpha turned the full force of her blue gaze to me. "I got no plans on murderin' you, Candy."

"My name's not Candy."

"Sorry. Must've slipped my mind."

I doubted it had. As we walked side by side toward the stairs built into the porch, I heard footsteps behind us and glanced over my shoulder. "Tell your cousin not to follow us."

"Aidan. You heard the girl. Leave us be."

After a beat, I asked, "Where's the rest of your pack?"

"Some are runnin'. Some are sleepin'."

"They're all still here?"

"Not all of them, but most stayed. They like how fresh the air is here." She tipped her face toward the sun and inhaled slow breaths. "What's the nature of your visit, Ness?"

"I wanted to know if your offer to sign a peace treaty is still on the table."

She closed her eyes and pulled in another breath. "Is Liam gettin' cold feet?"

"Liam doesn't even know I'm here."

Her eyes opened and set on me again.

"But my uncle knows I'm here," I lied so she didn't do away with me. "So . . . is your offer still available?"

Her light-brown hair, which was cut within two inches of her scalp, appeared grayer in the sunlight. "Why didn't you become Alpha? Everest all but handed it to you."

"Handed it to me? How did he *all-but-hand* it to me?"

"Liam cares for you. He wouldn't have fought you."

"If we hadn't dueled, Lucas would've been Alpha, not me."

"What I meant was if you'd actually fought, Liam would've let you win."

I blinked as I understood what she was insinuating. "Winning would've meant killing him."

"Your pack's soft, Ness. They surely wouldn't have required death."

I didn't think the Boulders were soft. Unless by soft, she meant civilized, which hadn't been my first impression, but now that I'd met the Creeks . . .

"You don't know that," I ended up saying.

She clasped her hands behind her back. "Did it even cross your mind to fight for what you wanted?"

"I didn't want to become Alpha."

"Then why did you enter the trials?"

"Because I didn't want a Kolane to become Alpha."

"And yet a Kolane became Alpha."

"Look, I'm not here to discuss the past. I'm here to discuss the future. Is your offer still available?" I asked for the third time.

"We agreed to duel."

"Agreements change all the time."

"You're obviously not well-versed in pack politics."

Her condescension stung.

"When duels are agreed upon, they can no longer be annulled."

"Why not? No one's forcing you to fight another shifter to the death."

"I offered him peace, and he didn't want it, so—"

"That's why I'm here."

"Listen," she hissed, which made my wolf bristle. Not that she could get out from her Sillin-cage. "Alex is always cuttin' me off before I can finish explaining things."

"Don't compare me to your son."

"When an Alpha expresses a desire to kill another, it's never taken lightly. If Liam had accepted my treaty, I would've spent my life lookin' over my shoulder, which would not have been ideal, but would've been worth it, because it would've meant saving my son's hide and my own."

Niggling guilt filled me . . . We should've kept Alex locked away.

"It wouldn't have been the first threat I'd have had to learn to live with, but that's neither here nor there. Anyway, Liam wasn't content with my offer. Your Alpha thirsts for more, which is a dangerous trait in a leader."

"You thirsted for more. You took over the Aspens."

"You think the Aspens were innocent? They killed off most of my pack."

"No, they didn't. You're the one who walked into their camp and challenged their Alpha."

"Your truncated comprehension of my pack's history is alarming. I can't tell if you've been fed wrong information or if you're lacking information."

I bristled again. "Why don't you tell me your version?"

"My version?" Her tone turned a notch shriller. "You mean, the truth?"

Although we hadn't penetrated the forest, we were following the tree line fencing the great lawn from the wilderness beyond.

"Yes." There was no point debating whether her truth was the same as everyone else's.

"Something in the mountains made us sick, and when we came to the Aspens for Sillin, which is one of the only drugs that work on wolves—"

"I thought it only helped us if our blood came in contact with silver?"

Her eyes thinned a little. "It has lots more properties than voiding our magic."

"I didn't know."

"You don't seem to know much about werewolves."

I bristled. "That was uncalled for."

She didn't apologize. "Do you want to hear the rest of it?"

What I wanted was for her to stop disparaging me. Fearing how childish it would sound to voice this, I grumbled, "Go on."

Cassandra observed me a protracted instant before pursuing her tale. "When we went to the Aspens for help, they turned us away. They had stocks of Sillin yet wouldn't share a meager amount. We'd even offered to pay an exorbitant amount for the drug. A month went by, and so many of us died that my grandfather, who was Alpha at the time, attempted a new negotiation with the Aspen Alpha. Again, they told us we should've taken better care of our supplies and offered us nothing. My little sister and I, we snuck onto their property and into their stock. We took only what we needed. She was caught and executed instantly. I got away, and then we ran and hid. Only five of us survived. Well, six . . . Aidan never lived among us, so he wasn't subjected to the poisoning.

"Four years ago, when I took over the Aspen pack, Julian Matz visited the compound to meet with me. At least, he claimed that was the nature of his visit. My father, who was so sickly he could no longer shift, was found dead the following morning. The pack doctor said he'd stopped breathing. I believed he'd been asphyxiated, but for the sake of diplomacy, I let it go. I let *Julian* go . . ."

A chill skated over my skin, which had nothing to do with the tall shadows that stretched like fingers over Cassandra and me. "What poisoned you?"

She watched the loamy earth squish between her bare toes. "There was a toxic waste site on our land. It polluted our main water source." Her gaze scraped over my face with such intensity that her eyes felt like claws. "Do you understand now why Sillin is so near and dear to me? I liken it to my security blanket; I may never need it again, but I can no longer live without it. I learned the hard way what lack of foresight brings about, and I will not let this happen to my wolves."

I wasn't going about getting what I wanted from Sandra the right way. "Thank you for sharing your pack's history with me."

She dipped her chin into her swan-like neck and scrutinized me from underneath her stubby lashes.

"I've always felt you were smart, but now I see you're a sensible woman." The words burned on their way out. "So I have to wonder why you won't offer us the deal again. I swear I'd make Liam keep away from you."

Her lips twitched, and then a bark of laughter burst out. "You'd *make* him? Oh, honey," she tittered, "Liam may appreciate your looks, but he doesn't *respect* you. Men like him—so conceited and chauvinistic—they don't take advice from a gender they deem inferior."

"You have a skewed vision of Liam. He's nothing like his father. Besides, he listened to me when I told him not to duel you the day you killed Julian."

Her smile turned broader. "He listened to get you into his bed."

Heat splashed my face. Why did I have to go and blush now? "That's not true."

"Ness, let me tell you a little something about myself that very few people know. My sister, she was mute, so I learned to read lips at the same time I learned to talk." Her shoulders were pulled back as straight as a rake. "That day beside the pool, I saw what Liam asked you . . . to break up with your new boyfriend. August, correct?"

The shock of her revelation made my footing falter. Cassandra shot out her arm to steady me, and it felt like a wooden bat against my sternum.

"I also know y'all think I cheated to win and you're desperately tryin' to figure out what I did. One of the reasons for your trip to meet with the Rivers, if I'm not mistaken?"

I kept silent.

"Let me save you some time and headaches. I did not inject Julian Matz with any substance." She glanced at the deck where more Creeks had arrived. Although most were busy eating, many gawked at us. She returned her attention to me and canted her head to the side. "So, have you picked a date yet?"

"You didn't even want to fight before. Why so adamant about it now?"

"'Cause I want to go home, *and* you have nothin' I need or want anymore."

"We have Sillin. A lot of it." I had no clue if the amount we had constituted a lot.

"I have enough to tide me over for a couple years. Besides, if I beat Liam, I get your pack's stock, and the Pines', for that matter."

Icy fingers climbed up my spine. *She knows it's hidden . . .*

"So it's a win-win for me."

"If you lose, you get nothing."

"If I lose, my pack still gets the Sillin."

"You mean to tell me, you're doing this for your pack?"

"Everything I do is for my pack." Her gaze tightened on me. "I didn't ascend to the highest tier for a title; I did it to better the lives of shifters." She gestured to the terrace. "Please, be my guest, Ness. Go around and ask my people what they think of me."

I was most definitely not going to ask a bunch of shifters what they thought of their Alpha in front of said Alpha. No one would *ever* tell me the truth. I thought of the Rivers' contact then—Avery—about how he'd said many were rooting for Liam, which meant Cassandra was either delusional or lying.

"No one visits us for a week, and now two Boulders in a day."

Her voice made me follow her line of sight. Lucas was glaring at me while descending the stairs two at a time.

Shit. Shit. Shit.

"That one's particularly insufferable, isn't he?"

I didn't answer her, just started striding toward Lucas before he could cause a bigger scene than I had.

29

"What the fuck are you doing here, Clark?" he spat out as I joined him in the middle of the lawn.

Cassandra was still standing in the shadows of the evergreens, and the rest of her pack had remained on the terrace.

I pursed my lips. "How did you even know where I was?"

"Liam wanted to speak with you, so we drove over to your house. Jeb said you were at the campus bookstore, but the campus bookstore doesn't open at the ass crack of dawn, so I'm not sure how he fell for that. He probably assumed you went to see your boyfriend."

"August isn't my boyfriend," I said, making sure my mouth was visible to Morgan. I wanted her to know this. Even though she hadn't threatened August, it couldn't hurt to get him off her radar. "And I'm here because I was trying to get her to put the peace treaty back on the table."

"You think Liam's changed his mind because of the—" I stepped on his foot so hard that he grumble-shouted, "What the hell's wrong with you?"

"I'm his Second. I should get to make these calls without being undermined by someone who has no rank in the pack."

His jaw unhinged.

"Now let's get out of here. We're making a scene. I bet Liam would hate that even more than his Second coming to negotiate on his behalf. And even though you didn't ask, the duel's still on."

I started walking around the inn. There was no need to go through the deck where more wolves had come out to eat breakfast.

Lucas fell in step beside me. "Wasn't sure if we'd get you back in one—" A soundless snarl contorted his lips.

I followed the direction of his stare. Sitting at one of the picnic tables was Sarah, and next to her was another blond: Alex Morgan.

"When did that fucking happen?" Lucas said through gritted teeth.

"Sarah eating breakfast with her pack?" I knew that wasn't what had gotten his boxers in a twist.

"He's playing with her fucking hair," he hissed.

Alex caught us looking his way and smiled wide, and inside, I cringed, but outside, I glared. Sarah said something that made the Creek in front of her chuckle, and that deepened Lucas's scowl.

I touched his arm that felt like steel rigging. "She's a Creek now. It's only normal that she tries to fit in."

"Fit in?" He sounded like he was choking.

I pulled him around the building, straight into the employee parking lot where I'd left the van.

"How come you're so chill about this, Clark? Isn't she your bestie?"

"She's nineteen. She knows what she's doing."

Lucas's lips curled in disgust.

I scanned the parking lot for Liam's car. When I didn't see it, I asked, "You have a ride or do you need one?"

Barely opening his lips, he said, "Liam dropped me off but was worried what he'd do if he stuck around."

To me or to Cassandra?

I beeped the doors open. "Well, get in then."

During the drive into town, he didn't say a word. Just simmered quietly. I almost confessed that Sarah was putting on an act, that she hadn't turned on us . . . on *him* . . . like Taryn had. But I clamped down on the truth. Lucas was trustworthy, sure, but the more incensed my pack seemed with Sarah, the more believable she'd be to the Creeks.

At a traffic light, I asked, "Where am I dropping you off?"

"The gym. But you're coming in with me."

"I thought we weren't working out."

"We aren't."

I raised an eyebrow.

When we arrived, Lucas texted Liam. A moment later, the heavy doors were unbolted. The vast space was as dark as a cave, and it took my eyes a moment to adjust.

Liam's face sheened with sweat, and his knuckles bled from pummeling the punching bag that still swayed in the back of the room. "Do you have a death wish, Ness?"

I squared my shoulders. "No more than you do."

"Do you know what they could've done to you?" Even though his voice was still loud, it had lost some of its venom.

The realization that he'd been afraid for me softened my stance. "I wanted to see if she'd agree to cancel the duel."

"Cancel the duel?" Liam sputtered. "What makes you think I'd want to cancel the duel?"

Had the thought *not* crossed his mind? "I thought that after—"

"Yesterday changes nothing!"

"You're going to be a father, Liam. Don't you want to be there for your kid?"

His eyebrows hugged closer to his eyes. "You know what the odds of shifter babies making it to the end of the first trimester in a human womb? Fifteen percent. But even if it were a hundred percent, it wouldn't change anything. I still want to destroy that woman, so you had no right to make this call without consulting me! I'm not interested in a treaty."

I crossed my arms. "She said no anyway."

His chest heaved. "Good."

"You could lose."

"I could also win."

A beat of silence echoed like an ominous drumroll between us. I was angry about his reaction. I glanced at Lucas, wishing he'd weigh in and tell Liam he was being a stubborn ass, but Lucas was too busy sulking and glaring at the weight rack.

"There are more important things in life than winning or losing, Liam."

"Not for an Alpha. Besides, I already have a family, Ness. The pack is my family. And I need to protect them." His voice had quieted. "You all think I'm doing this to prove something. I'm not. Sure, I could've taken that treaty, but once Cassandra gets replaced or dies, her successor would've challenged us. We'd only be pushing back the inevitable. I'm young now and in way better shape than she is; Julian was old and slow." His breathing deepened, his chest growing calmer with each passing minute.

Even though I was disappointed, a part of me also understood his reasoning.

"Did you learn anything interesting at least?"

Sighing, I let my arms fall back along my sides. "She can read lips."

"She can read lips?" Lucas asked, finally popping out of his daze.

"Yeah. Her sister was mute. So start watching what you say around her."

Liam dragged his fingers through his sweat-matted hair. "We don't need to watch what we say around her, because the next time we see her will be at the duel. Am I making myself clear?"

"Crystal," I said a tad frostily because I sensed that was directed only at me. "I also learned she took an extremely high dose of Sillin when she was younger to cure herself of toxic waste poisoning. Which might mean traces of Sillin remain in her body." I tucked a strand of hair behind my ear. "So maybe taking tiny doses of the stuff is pointless. Maybe I should take a huge dose and see what it does."

Liam went as still as the punching bag behind him.

"Morgan can still shift, so it wouldn't impair Ness's magic completely," Lucas said.

For a moment, I wondered if we'd be dueling Morgan if Liam and I had still been together. But then I wondered why I was even contemplating this and shook my head.

"I'll speak to Greg to see what a high dose would be," he finally said.

As he took out his cell phone, a twinge of panic crept up my spine . . . What if it irreparably impaired my werewolf gene? What if that was the reason she was often bedridden and healed slower? I swallowed back my panic, reminding myself that Morgan had still risen to the top of shifter hierarchy.

Liam disconnected the call I'd heard no word of. "He's going to figure out the dosage based on your weight and age, then phone you this afternoon to administer it intravenously." He flipped his phone over and over in his hand, shadows devouring his eyes. "Even though I want you to consult me in the future, it was good work."

"Thank you." I nibbled on my bottom lip. "Can I leave now?"

"You can leave."

I started to go, but before reaching the door, I glanced at him over my shoulder. "Are you happy at least? About Tamara?"

Although his lips didn't move, inside my head I heard, *I didn't want a kid, and I didn't want Tamara.*

Pain carved his forehead. I hoped it was the shock of the news and the worry of the first trimester that was to blame. Perhaps he'd never love Tamara, but I hoped he'd grow to want and love his child.

I hoped he'd be the man his father never was.

30

I spent the rest of the morning buying college supplies and paint cans and brushes for the house. The only thing I ended up not buying was a laptop. I needed one, and technically, I could afford one, but the money on my account didn't feel like my own. Since August wasn't going to take it back, I'd decided to go speak with Nelson and Isobel about it. I was sort of dreading the conversation, especially if they didn't know about their son's generous donation.

After stopping by The Silver Bowl to check up on Evelyn, whose cheeks were high in color from the heat of all the simmering pots around her and the excitement of her new job, I went home fed and relaxed, ready for Greg to arrive.

He got to my place around four, a cooler swinging from his fingers. "Sorry I'm late. I went to check on Isobel."

My blood turned to ice. "Why? Is she—Is the cancer back?"

"The cancer's gone." Greg smiled. "Sorry. I didn't mean to worry you."

I nodded and watched as he set a syringe, a vial filled with clear liquid, and some gauze on the kitchen table.

Concern deepened the wrinkles bracketing his eyes and mouth. "Are you sure you want to do this?"

"Someone has to."

"But does that someone have to be you?"

I frowned. "There's no chance of it killing me, is there?"

He took a seat and scooted closer to the table. "No, but . . ."

Fear tiptoed into my veins and navel as I sat down beside him. "But what?"

"But I've never administered such a high dose, so I can't even tell you what the side effects might be. Besides not shifting, that is."

"How long will it block my wolf?"

"From my calculations, if all goes well, you should be back in fur before the next full moon."

Considering we had to fight Cassandra then, that was good.

I licked my chapped lips. "And if all *doesn't* go well?"

"The Sillin could stay in your system longer."

"Like another month?" I couldn't be Liam's Second if that happened . . . Someone else would have to be. Could another Boulder take my place? Were we allowed to switch Seconds? Perhaps Lucas—

"It could affect your magic forever," Greg said in such a low voice I almost missed his words.

"You mean, turn me into a *halfwolf?*"

He nodded.

"I thought that could only happen after prolonged use?"

Greg twirled the vial, squinting at the liquid sloshing inside as though seeking an answer within its clear depths. "I don't know. I've never administered so much Sillin." He fisted the vial before placing it carefully back on the table. "Your parents would be so angry with me right now."

I was certain they'd be mad at a whole bunch of people if they'd been alive, the first one being me, but they weren't here. Besides, if it meant saving Liam's life, I'd endure being a *halfwolf* for a while.

"I'm surprised Jeb's letting you do this," Greg added.

"Jeb doesn't know, and I'd like it to stay that way. He's got plenty enough to worry about."

Greg studied me for a beat. "Any way I can talk you out of this?"

I shook my head. "We need to understand."

"But why you? Why don't I call the River medic and see if his pack can test it out—"

"They might be our allies, Greg, but I don't trust the Rivers. Besides, if this experiment could potentially harm one of their wolves, why would they agree?"

"Because they hate Morgan."

I worried the inside of my cheek. "They'll ask for something in return." Ingrid wanting to marry August came to mind. "Favors never come for free."

"You're right. Favors are never free." He sighed. "What about another Boulder?"

"I'd never forgive myself if this had a lasting effect on someone from my pack." I tapped my fingernail against the tabletop. "So just lay it all out there. How else do you think this injection can affect me?"

"It'll dim your senses. And, possibly, it'll affect your mating link."

I suddenly felt a lot warmer. I gathered my hair and rolled the strands up into a bun. "You know everything that goes on in the pack, huh?"

"Pretty much."

"How come you work with us?"

"Why wouldn't I work with you?"

"Because we're not . . . *human.*"

He leaned back in the chair. "My father was the pack physician before me, and my grandfather before him. So I grew up right alongside the Boulders. They never treated me differently because of what I wasn't."

"Lucky you."

"I'm sorry they were hard on you, Ness."

"Not your fault."

Greg's gaze roamed over my face. "Do you know that Maggie was one of my favorite people?"

"My mother? Really?"

"We were in the same grade in school. And I was, well, a bit of a nerd, which got me bullied a lot. Maggie, she was always really quick at thinking up the best comebacks, and she was popular, so no one ever messed with her. Back in third grade and until the end of high school, she took it upon herself to be my protector."

I frowned. "I didn't know that." I dug through my memories for Greg, but he didn't feature in any. "I don't remember you from before I left Boulder."

"Because I went to study in Boston and then practiced there until my father died. When Heath called and asked if I'd come home, you'd been gone a year with your mom." He steepled his fingers. "I was heartbroken when I heard . . . that she'd passed."

My throat felt like a drawbridge was being yanked shut. "Yeah." I whisked my lids closed a moment, breathed in slowly, then, when I felt like I'd gotten myself under control again, I opened my eyes. "Can we get this over with?"

"Yes. Of course. Sorry."

"Don't be sorry. I'm always glad to hear stories about her. To know that little pieces of her live on in other people's hearts and minds. It's the closest thing to getting her back." My voice cracked. "It gets easier, right?" I fit a smile onto my lips to make them stop quivering and to make Greg stop looking at me as though I were about to break apart.

"It does." He slid his hand over mine and squeezed my fingers before picking up the syringe. As he popped the solution into it, pounding that threatened to bring down my door had Greg turning.

I didn't turn because I knew who was behind the pounding. My navel had tightened like a fishing knot.

I got up to let August in. When his hands gripped my shoulders, I thought he was going to shake me, but he just stood there, gaze running over my body and nostrils flaring as though to pull in my scent . . . make sure I still had one.

"You didn't take it yet." He was so completely out of breath that I suspected he'd run from his house to mine. His crazed eyes scanned the apartment, landed on the paraphernalia laid out on the table. He removed his fingers from my shoulders so suddenly I almost stumbled. "Greg, you can put all of it away. Ness isn't *experimenting*."

"August!" Surprise made me speak his name louder than intended.

"What?" he snapped.

"You can't just barge in here and make decisions for me."

He took a step nearer, even though not much distance separated us. "You are not injecting yourself with fucking poison to test out a theory."

I planted my hands on my hips. "Sillin isn't poison."

"It messes with our werewolf gene, Ness. It's poison! Ask Greg if you don't believe me."

"August is right," Greg said. "It's not lethal, but it's not *good* for you."

"I'm aware of the risks—"

"Are you?" August's tone was so sharp that it made me blink. "Because I'm not aware of them. And I doubt Greg's aware of them since no one's ever taken such a high dose."

"Morgan has, and she's still alive. *And* she became an Alpha."

A nerve ticked in his jaw. "What if she lied to you?"

"Lied to me?"

"So you'd poison yourself."

"She doesn't want me dead."

"How do you know that?"

"August, you're being completely irrational right now."

"Because I *care*! I care what happens to you even though no one else in this stupid pack seems to."

Silence settled as thickly as snow, making the air lose several degrees of warmth.

"Greg said the worst case scenario is impairing my gene for an undetermined length of time." I didn't want to be a *halfwolf*, but it beat Liam being a dead one, because even though no one was speaking about it, if Morgan had an unfair advantage over us, and we didn't figure out what it was, she'd win the duel.

"Not exactly, Ness. I said I didn't know. It could *irreparably* damage your gene, your senses, your mating link."

Pain streaked over August's face at that last part. He tried to disguise it by turning away from me, but I saw it.

"That *halfwolf* complication could become permanent," Greg added.

"I understand," I said at the same time as August said, "I'll do it." Then, "Is it the same dosage?"

My hands slipped off my hipbones. "August, no."

"Not exactly, but frankly," Greg said, "I'd rather give you this dose than her. It'll still affect you, but you should burn it off quicker."

"No!" When August started for the chair, I wrapped my fingers around his forearm. "I am *not* okay with this! I don't want you to experiment on yourself." My voice sounded so thin.

His lips flexed but didn't produce words for ten whole heartbeats. "Everyone has to do their part for the pack. This is me doing my part." He pried my fingers off his arm one at a time, then took a seat, pushed the sleeves of his sweat-stained navy Henley up, and laid his arm flat on the table.

"Ready?" Greg asked.

August looked at the window. "Hit me."

I crossed my arms to make them stop trembling. When that didn't work, I went to draw myself a glass of water. As I brought it up to my lips, water sloshed over the rim and trickled down my wrist.

There was a hollow suctioning noise—probably the cooler—and then chair legs scraped against the floor.

"Try to shift every day," Greg said. "Once you manage, call me, and I'll come and take a blood sample to see if any traces remain." I heard him walk to the door, but I kept my back to him. "It shouldn't give you any fever or seizures, but I'd feel better if someone was with you tonight. Maybe go sleep at your parents."

Chills zigzagged through my body, icing my already frigid limbs.

"And, Ness, I left you some salve for your arm. It'll help with the scars."

When the door snicked shut, more water spilled out of my glass. I set it down, then ripped paper towels off the roll to blot my skin, the countertop, and the floor.

"Ness—"

"I'm so mad at you," I hissed.

"I got that, but it's done now, and I didn't drop dead, so—"

"So that's supposed to make me feel better?" I yelled, spinning around. "Greg just mentioned seizures. Seizures!"

He snorted. "You do realize this could've been you?"

"I *do* realize!" I breathed hard. "But if this hurt me, it would've been my fault. If this hurts you . . ." My voice broke. "I'll never forgive myself if this hurts you."

"Shh. It'll be all right. I'll phone up Cole. Get him to spend the night at my place."

"No, I'll do it. There's no need to drag yet another person into my harebrained schemes." After the ice, I now felt filled with fire. I bet smoke was wafting from my nostrils.

"You don't have to—"

"After what you just did, you don't get to tell me what to do. I'm spending the night at your place or you'll spend the night at my place. Your choice."

One side of his mouth tipped up with a smile. "If I'd known that was all it took to get you to spend another night with me, I might've injected myself sooner."

I glared at him. Not because I was mad at what he'd just said, but because I was furious with what he'd just done.

His smile vanished. "Pack a bag. I'll call a cab."

31

"Have you seen this movie?"

"What's the title?" Since leaving my apartment, I hadn't taken my eyes off August, not even to glance at his enormous television screen.

He sighed and set the remote control on the arm of the couch. We were sitting on either end of it—me with my legs curled beneath me, and him with his ankle perched on his opposite knee.

"Please stop looking at me as though you want to throttle me." His leg had been bobbing restlessly since he'd sat down. "It's done. Let it go."

"Let it go? Really?" I narrowed my eyes. "Until you shift—*fully* shift—I'm not going to let this go."

He wrapped his arm around the back of the couch. "You're going to stay mad at me for weeks?"

"Possibly even months."

He winced so suddenly that my heart all but stopped.

When his fingers came up to his temples, I sprang toward him, almost landing in his lap, and palmed his forehead. "What is it? What's wrong?"

His forehead smoothed out, and a smile overtook his lush lips. "You were sitting too far away."

I blinked, and then I smacked his chest hard. "That was *so* not funny, August Watt."

When I tried to crawl back to my side, he wrapped his fingers around my wrist and held me in place. His expression was gentle but serious. "I don't want you to be mad at me even another minute."

"I'm not mad. I'm scared."

"I know, Dimples, but put your anger on hold for a second and look at me. I'm fine."

I scanned him from forehead to chest. Even though I wasn't on his lap, I was close. The side of my bent leg was flush against his thigh, and I could see every single dab of green and sable in his irises, every freckle dotting his nose and cheekbones.

I was way too close.

Heat snaking up my neck, I averted my gaze and wriggled away. "I'm hungry. Are you hungry?" I asked, getting to my feet.

August stared at me fixedly, and then I felt a tug behind my navel that had my shins hitting the frame of the couch. I bent at the knees to absorb the listing.

"I wanted to check if it had affected the link," he said.

Relief surged within me, washing away the awkwardness that had made me shoot to my feet. "It hasn't!"

His eyebrows rose. "Why do you look happy about this? Don't you want it gone?"

I froze like a robber caught mid-theft. From the intensity with which he studied my face, I thought August was going to see right through me.

"I do," I lied, dragging my hair back, "but the fact that it's still there means the Sillin's not wreaking havoc on your system." I hoped the excuse sounded believable. "How's your sense of smell?"

Eyebrows still raised, he pulled in a lungful of air. "Still there, too."

"But is it as strong as before?"

He lowered his gaze to the pulse point in my neck. "It's hard to tell with you standing so close."

I didn't ask him why that was because I understood. I had the same "problem." When I was close to him, little else penetrated my senses over his woodsy, spicy scent, and the steady drumbeat of his heart, and the sight of his remarkable body.

I hadn't taken my dose of Sillin this morning, so my senses were sharpening again. Afraid my frenzied pulse would give away all I was feeling, I took a step back, then rounded the couch and ambled to the kitchen. "What do you feel like eating?"

August twisted around. "I'm not sure I have much back there."

"I found some dried pasta and a jar of tomato sauce."

"You don't have to cook. We can order in."

"Don't underestimate my water-boiling skills."

A smile ghosted over his lips.

"Why are you smiling?"

"Am I not allowed to smile now?"

"I was just wondering if it was a *she's-going-to-burn-down-my-kitchen* smile, or a polite *is-she-going-to-make-me-eat-undercooked-pasta* smile?"

He snorted, and my fingers itched to flick him. "It's an *I'm-relieved-she-doesn't-hate-my-guts* smile."

My hands faltered on the jar, and it dropped onto the wooden countertop. Thankfully, the glass didn't shatter. "I never hated your guts, August. I was scared. I still am. Because, like you, I care."

His eyes didn't turn a brighter shade of green like they usually did, but his gaze scraped across my face with an intensity that made me crouch and pull open one of his cupboards to get out of his line of sight.

"Now where do you keep your pots and pans?"

32

I sat up so fast my head spun, and August's apartment swam out of focus. A coverlet slid off my shoulders and pooled onto the floor. I clicked my lids open and shut a few times to clear my eyesight, then looked around for August.

He wasn't on the couch. Maybe he was in his bed?

The sound of running water had me leaping to my feet, plodding to the bathroom, and knuckling the door. "August?"

"Be out in a minute!" His voice was strong and steady. He was all right.

Pulse decelerating, I dragged the heels of my hands into my eyes. Something buzzed. I shot my gaze to my bag which I'd set on one of his barstools. I plodded over and dug my cell phone out.

There was a message from Matt: *In front of your door. Ready?*

I checked the time, then mumbled, "Shoot, shoot, shoot," just as the door of the bathroom opened and steam billowed out, thickening the air with August's scent.

ME: *I'm not at my place. Can you pick me up at the warehouse? And it's NOT what you think.*

MATT: *I'll be right over. And the fact that you're telling me that it's not what I think means it's exactly what I think.*

ME: *Your logic is illogical.*

MATT: *Apparently that's what you told Cole last time he was over at August's place.*

MATT: *Be there in a sec. We like our coffees with lots of milk.*

"What's going on?" August asked.

"Matt and Cole are on their way over here. They think . . ." I set my phone down on the smooth slab of ruffled wood. "I'm sure you can guess what they think."

"Are you worried they're going to tell Liam?"

"No. Why—*oh!*" My eyes went wide. With everything going on, I'd completely forgotten about his ban. But then I reasoned that I hadn't broken any rules, because August and I weren't together, *together*.

"Might want to inform him so he doesn't schedule your duel for today."

I worried the inside of my mouth, surely deepening my dimples. "I'll call him later. Right now, I have to get ready. May I use the bathroom?"

"Go right ahead."

I carried my bag inside and quickly changed into my exercise bra and running shorts, then put yesterday's tank top on and brushed my teeth. Tying up my hair, I returned into the kitchen where August was brewing coffee. He'd pulled on a pair of mesh shorts and a short sleeved T-shirt.

"You're feeling up to running?" I asked, grabbing a glass and filling it with tap water.

"Yeah."

"Nothing hurts?"

"Just my neck." He rubbed the back of it. "But that's probably from falling asleep sitting up."

"Can't believe I slept. I'd suck as a nurse."

He smiled. "I'm sure plenty of bedridden men would disagree with you."

Leaning back against the island, I shook my head and drank my fill. "Thanks for trying to make me feel better about my lousy job."

"I survived the night. And I feel absolutely fine. I promise. You can stop worrying about me."

"Can you shift?"

He held out his arm and concentrated. When brown fur didn't sprout from his pores, he shook his head.

"Then I'm not done worrying."

The coffee maker behind him began to gurgle and dribble dark, sweetly charred liquid into the glass carafe.

"Dimples . . ."

"Don't Dimples-me, August Watt. You're my best friend. I'll worry if I want to worry."

His lips tightened as though he found my reasoning maddening. Or maybe it was my sticking him in the friend-zone which he found maddening. Little did he know that he featured in many more zones than that one.

Loud knocking redirected our attention toward the front door. A keypad beeped, but it wasn't followed by a click.

"You changed the code?" I asked as he strode over to open up for Matt and Cole.

"I did."

I clutched my glass of water tighter. Had August changed it for me? So that people—his parents and Cole—didn't walk in on us?

If there had been an *us* . . .

"Yo." Cole slugged August's shoulder.

Although Matt's brother was the same height as my mate, he wasn't half as ripped. August had been away from the Marines for over a month now and was still in formidable shape—slimmer than Matt but carved like a Greek God.

I really had to stop ogling August if I wanted to convince the two Rogers my sleepover had been platonic.

"Morning, Little Wolf," Matt belted out, moss-green eyes way too shiny.

I decided not to bother convincing him or his brother of anything. I didn't have anything to feel ashamed of. Besides—as I took a sip of my water, I sniffed my hand discreetly—I didn't think I smelled of August or of our mating link. Sure, I'd slept on his couch, but apart from when I'd all but jumped onto his lap to check if he had a fever, I'd kept my distance from him.

Giant smile pasted on his lips, Matt rubbed his hands together. "You got our coffees ready?"

I tipped my head toward the coffee machine, and he dug through the cupboard of mismatched mugs to grab two.

I wasn't sure why he was Mr. Smiley this morning. He was one of Liam's friends. Shouldn't Matt have been rooting against me and August? Unless he thought my presence in August's life would get him work benefits.

"Milk?" Matt asked.

"In the fridge," August said.

I noticed he'd put on his sneakers while I was still barefoot. I curled my unpolished toes, feeling, however superficial, that a coat of nail polish might've made my feet more attractive. Not that anyone was staring at them. I set down my glass and grabbed a pair of socks from my bag. After lacing up my sneakers, I went back for some coffee.

"So . . .?" Matt started as I elbowed past him to grab the carafe.

"So . . .?" I volleyed back. I knew exactly what he was hunting for.

"You guys have something to tell us?" Cole asked.

I looked at August, who proceeded to rub his neck. I wasn't sure if he was still trying to get the kink out of it or if he was nervous.

Taking in a deep breath, I said, "August decided to get injected with a massive dose of Sillin so I wouldn't do it myself. I stayed over to make sure he didn't have a seizure during the night."

The brothers blinked at me, smiles fading.

I sipped my coffee, letting the information settle. "Let me guess . . . that wasn't where your minds had gone?"

"Nope. Not even close," Cole said.

"Why?" Matt asked, watching August as though to spot the effect of the drug.

"Morgan told me that when she was younger, she had to take a big dose of it to heal from a toxic waste poisoning. This led me to wonder if taking an enormous dose somehow left traces in our system—not enough to impair our magic, but enough to impair our enemies. Once August manages to shift, Greg will test his blood."

The atmosphere, which had bordered on lighthearted when the Rogers had arrived, turned downright somber.

"How long before we know the result?" Matt asked.

"Greg said it could take weeks before I can shift," August said, which skewered me with renewed guilt. August must've spotted the guilt, because he added, "But I feel good. Great, even."

I sensed he was overplaying how *great* he felt to reassure me, but I also sensed, through the link, that he wasn't in any pain.

"As you both can see, though, Dimples doesn't believe me."

I pursed my lips.

"You sure you feel up for a run, man?" Matt asked.

August shook his head. "Don't you start babying me too, Matty."

Cole smirked. "Ness's babying you, Auggie? I'm sure that's really awful."

August smacked his friend, which just made Cole chuckle.

I rolled my eyes. "If you guys are done acting like girls, can we go?"

"Acting like girls?" Cole howled a laugh. "I'll have you know, we Rogers are extremely manly. Watt, though—"

"Don't bother coming into work on Monday. You're fired."

"August!" I yelled.

"Don't worry, Ness. That's the twentieth time he's fake-fired me."

"Nothing fake about it this time," August grumbled.

"Temperature's supposed to be scorching today," Matt said, setting his mug in the sink. "We should head out soon."

33

"Yo, Matty, can we stop?" Cole wheezed. "My lungs are on fire . . . and I feel like I'm gonna hurl." He was running beside me while Matt and August were ahead of us.

Way ahead of us.

Even though my lungs felt vacuum-packed, at least I didn't sound as though I was about to drop dead.

Matt whirled and jogged backward. "If you quit smoking, you'd feel a lot better."

August glanced over his shoulder at us. Like Matt, he'd barely broken a sweat. "Maybe we should take a breather. Don't want to have to explain to Kasie how she lost her oldest son to physical exertion."

Cole flipped him off before coming to a stop. He bent over and clutched his thighs, panting hard. "Why are we running . . . on a Saturday morning . . . again?"

"Because Ness needs endurance training," Matt said, finally halting too.

"Let me rephrase. Why am *I* running? Liam should be the one up here murdering his lungs."

A shadow crossed August's face at the mention of Liam.

"Liam's Alpha," Matt said. "He's magically in better shape than all of us put together. You know that."

I raised an eyebrow. "Magically?"

"The blood oath acts like natural steroids," August explained.

So why had he asked me to prep him for the duel when he didn't need any training?

My gaze snagged on August.

Of course . . .

Cole and Matt suddenly snapped their heads toward the evergreens behind them. Glowing eyes stared back at us from the cover of the forest. I squinted to make out any distinctive markings on the wolves' pelts, but they stood at a distance. I sniffed the air. Sure enough, these wolves weren't Boulders. In case I hadn't come to this realization on my own, the sweaty T-shirt smacking my bare thigh followed by the sight of the two Rogers' naked backsides would've alerted me to the fact that we weren't in the presence of friends.

August stepped closer to me, the lines of his face and body as taut as the spines of the two giant blond wolves now standing guard next to us. The six Creeks trotted out of the shadows but kept their distance from us. One of them—a lemon-yellow wolf—whined. Matt barked.

How I wish my human ears could've grasped wolf speech...

The only thing I could tell from Matt's raised hackles was that they weren't exchanging pleasantries.

"Do you recognize any of them?" I whispered to August.

"No, but the yellow one with the violet eyes could be Alex." He tipped his chin up and smelled the air, and a rumble of frustration ripped up his corded throat. "I can't fucking smell anything."

A penny for his Mom's curse jar and a punch to my already guilt-ridden gut.

The yellow wolf—Alex?—craned his long neck and peered at us over one of his companion's pelts. Had they picked up on what August had just said?

I sidled closer until my hipbone hit the side of August's thigh, feeling my wolf scratching against my envelope of skin, desirous to come out. I bridled her back, because one, I didn't want to get naked—yes, I know . . . incredibly silly—and two, because I wanted to offer August some solidarity. His anger at not being able to morph agitated the tether.

The Creeks made more whiny noises. When one took a step closer, Cole charged her, bumping her back a couple steps with his shoulder. The brown wolf yelped and stuck her tail between her legs.

The fair-colored wolf growled at Cole but didn't attack. Even though Matt's fangs were bared, he didn't lunge forward.

Cole gnashed his pointy teeth, and the wolf in front of him soared back. The yellow wolf emitted a shrill howl, which got the attention of the five others. He swung around and sprinted into the copse of trees, and his packmates followed.

Matt and Cole waited a good five minutes before shifting back into skin. Once their fur had receded, they straightened, eyes wild with energy and ferocity.

Keeping my gaze on their torsos, I asked, "What did they want?"

"They said we were trespassing on their property!" Cole exclaimed.

"Put your clothes on." August plucked dark mesh from the grass and lobbed it at Cole, before stepping in front of me.

"You do know I have to get used to nudity?" I whispered against his shoulder blades that were pulled in like metal wings.

He grunted, so I flicked the base of his spine. He tossed me a hooded glance over his shoulder.

"What?" I asked all innocently.

He didn't say anything, just slowly returned his attention to the Rogers.

After a few seconds, I walked around my muscular blockade. "*Were* we trespassing?"

"No. This is neutral territory," Cole said, spearing his arms through his muscle tee. "The Boulders and the Pines signed an agreement a long time ago about boundaries. This part of the forest belongs to no one."

If the land was for sale, Aidan Michaels would surely snatch it up with a briefcase of cash.

"Who was here?" August asked.

"Alex Morgan, his sister Lori . . . She's the one Cole knocked back. The other four were Creeks I'm not familiar with."

"Why did you leap at her?" I asked Cole.

"'Cause she was trying to sniff you guys."

My head jerked back. "Sniff us?"

"She said you had an odd smell."

"The mating link," August murmured, barely shifting his lips.

I twisted toward him so fast my ponytail flogged my cheek. "You think they don't know about it?"

"If they didn't, they probably do now," Matt said.

"Or not," Cole said, straightening up. "It's pretty faint."

"It is?" I asked. "You think that's because of the Sillin?"

"Either that, or it's because you've been keeping your hands off each other. You have, right?"

My cheeks burned. "Yes," I hissed.

Cole raised his palms in the air. "Don't bite my head off."

"We should head back," Matt said, studying the woods as though expecting more wolves to show up.

"Did they say anything else?" I asked.

Matt flicked his gaze to the grass at my feet. "Nothing worth repeating."

I folded my arms. "What else did they say?"

The Rogers exchanged a look.

"What. Else?"

"Alex said something about Sarah." Cole spoke really fast, as though speed might lessen the sting. "About how *fun* she was and asked if you'd be interested in a threesome."

My navel pulsed so hard I half expected it to pop right off my abdomen. August hadn't said a word nor let out a sound, but his already rigid body became as still as the trunks of the evergreens in front of us.

"Classy," I said.

"*Classy*?" Matt raised a blond eyebrow. "That's what you got from that?"

"What else was I supposed to get from that?"

"Your best friend's screwing him," Cole said. "Doesn't that repulse you?"

My forearms tightened in front of my chest. "It does, but I'm not her keeper."

Cole exchanged another look with his brother, and then both of them looked at me again, and for a second, I thought they would see the truth behind Sarah's actions, but then they shook their heads, and Matt said, "I hope you didn't share too much sensitive information with her, because if she's willing to screw them, she's probably willing to screw you over."

"She doesn't know anything damning."

"She knows we're mates," August said.

"But she won't tell them." I said this way too quickly and confidently.

"How do you know that?" Matt asked.

In truth, I didn't know. I'd never told her it was a secret. I could only hope she would keep it to herself. "What'll it change if she does tell them?"

"They'll keep me away during the duel," August said softly.

I stared up into the hazel depths of his eyes.

"Yeah," Cole said. "They're always worried about the reaction of mates. Some turn feral if their partners get hurt."

"Eric told me," Matt spoke slowly, "that some mates—when both are wolves—can control the other's body. Apparently, that ability's linked to how much they crave the other as a mate."

Whoa . . . I averted my gaze and rubbed my palms against my running shorts.

"Can you guys do that?" he asked.

"No," August said.

I frowned at him, then at the grass, wondering why he was lying. Was he afraid Matt and Cole would tell others about our ability, or was he embarrassed by it? But then it hit me . . . it wasn't *our* ability.

It was *his*.

I wasn't able to move his body. We'd assumed it was because he was so much bigger than me, but the true reason had nothing to do with size.

He backed away from me, his large sneakers crushing the earth beneath him. "We should get back. I promised my parents I was going to have lunch at their place."

I sensed his desire to get down from the mountain had nothing to do with being on time for his meal and everything to do with what Matt had just told us. Was August ashamed by how much he wanted me, or was he angry by how little he thought I wanted him?

I hadn't tried to pull on the tether since the night I'd slept in his bed, but considering how my feelings for him had grown and solidified, I was pretty certain I could drag him all the way down the mountain if I tried.

I didn't try, though, because if I moved his body, it would destroy all the work I'd put into keeping my hands off it.

Off him.

34

I sent August several text messages during the weekend to ask how he was feeling. His answer to all of them was the four-letter word: *Fine*. He wasn't fine, but I didn't think that had to do with the Sillin.

Throughout Sunday night dinner at Frank's, Evelyn kept asking me what was wrong, and I kept telling her I was nervous about starting college. While Jeb told stories about his college days, especially about what a formidable running back he'd been, Frank kept casting glances my way. He probably thought my mood was sullen because of the imminent duel.

During the ride back to the apartment, Jeb was acting so uncharacteristically giddy that I worried something could be wrong. My uncle wasn't a giddy person.

"Are you all right, Jeb?" I asked after he'd parked the van on our street and we'd gotten out.

He grinned so wide his teeth gleamed in his gray-blond beard. There was definitely something up with him.

"I know your birthday isn't until Friday"—he dug into his pocket—"but I'm going to give you your present early."

"You don't need to give me any presents."

He *tsk*ed and plucked my hand from my side, then dropped a car key into it. "The payment for the inn came in, so I got you something. It's not brand new, but it doesn't have lots of mileage."

"You got me"—my voice caught—"a car?" I finished quietly.

He pointed at a compact silver SUV with a big red bow on the back fender. "Here she is."

I let out a breath that sounded a lot like a whimper, and Jeb grinned, eyes all glittery. I flung my arms around his neck and hugged him tight.

"Thank you thank you thank you," I whispered.

"You're very welcome." He patted my back. "How about we take it out for a spin?"

"Yes! Absolutely yes!" I detached myself from my uncle and strode over to the car, running my fingertips along its shiny, smooth body.

Mine.

It was mine.

Jeb was still grinning. "Let's get ice-cream. I noticed our freezer was depressingly empty."

I didn't think I could eat anything more after Evelyn's meal, but I nodded excitedly. I climbed behind the wheel and adjusted the seat and the mirrors, my heart feeling exactly like my stomach—close to bursting.

The following morning, pumped up on caffeine and excitement, I slipped into my car and turned up the music to match my mood.

I rolled down the window and took my time getting to the campus, relishing the purr of the engine and the feel of the warm breeze twisting my hair. After I parked in the student lot, I took a map of the campus and my schedule out from my college packet. I studied both a moment before setting out toward my Introduction to Statistics course.

I dragged my hand through my snarled hair, realizing I hadn't even checked my reflection in the rearview mirror. I hoped I didn't look like I had an addiction to hairspray. I arrived in the lecture hall with a few minutes to spare and sat up front. As I dug out my notebook, the scent of apricot flecked the air, overpowering the smell of chalky deodorant, milky coffees, and synthetic perfumes.

"Hey, Amanda," I said without even looking up.

She flounced into the seat next to mine. "Did you sleep last night? I didn't. I couldn't. I just drank my weight in coffee."

I smiled at her exuberance.

She peered at me through her thick lashes, brown eyes narrowed. "This might be one of the first times I've seen you smile since you got to Boulder."

My smiled faltered.

"It's a nice change. Makes you more . . . *approachable.*"

An older man walked in then, plaid shirt neatly tucked into pressed pants. He set a leather briefcase down on the desk up front.

What Amanda said troubled me. I'd never realized that not being a high-spirited person made me aloof.

In a low voice, I said, "I thought you girls didn't like me because I was . . . *you know* . . . different."

"Ness, we never *disliked* you, per se. You're just very reserved and a little prickly. But I think we'd all be if we were in your position."

"Tamara and Taryn definitely don't like me."

She pursed her lips. "Taryn's a ho, so whatever. As for Tamara, you sort of stole her boyfriend."

"He said they weren't dating," I whispered a little louder.

She gave me a look that said: *and you believed that?*

"I didn't know."

For a long while, Amanda studied my expression. A couple minutes into the lecture, she said, "She'd really like to sort things out with him." Even though she didn't add, *stay away*, I heard her warning loud and clear.

"What about Sienna?"

"What about her?"

"Does *she* hate me?"

Propping her mouth to my ear so no one else overheard our conversation, she said, "Sienna had a tough time right after the breakup, but the girl's got the biggest heart in the world. Plus, like she told me, there's no point in trying to keep a man who's in love with someone else." She pulled away to inspect my face. "This isn't news to you, right?"

My heart began to batter my ribs so loudly I thought Amanda's human ears might hear it. Hell, I thought our professor, who was busy singling out students and asking them what they hoped to learn during the semester, would hear it.

"I know you're not together because of Liam—Matt told me—but if you ask me, maybe you should get with August. That way, Liam would go back to Tammy."

My spine drew straight.

"What?" Amanda asked.

I didn't know much about dating but sensed entering a relationship to better someone else's wasn't smart. "Tamara shouldn't be Liam's backup plan; she should be his only plan."

Amanda puckered her lips.

"As for August, he's my friend."

"I thought . . . never mind."

"What did you think?"

"That you and him already crossed that line," she said, just as the professor called upon her to introduce herself.

I was surprised that Amanda, a notoriously critical person, didn't seem disgusted by the age gap. If anything, she seemed confused as to why we weren't together anymore. Or perhaps, she was acting cool as a cucumber in the hopes of driving Liam back into Tamara's arms.

35

The first week was almost over before I crossed paths with Sarah. She was standing with two guys from her pack beside the entrance of the Roser Atlas Center. I almost waved when I spotted her—a kneejerk reaction—but thankfully, I stuffed my hands in the back pocket of my shorts.

She didn't acknowledge me either. It had been more than a week since we'd started acting like strangers, and it had left a huge gap in my life which I'd been filling up with work on my house and learning new fighting techniques from Lucas. Liam had stopped by the gym only once since the day he'd yelled at me for going to visit Cassandra alone. Lucas was vague as to our Alpha's whereabouts. I hoped he was off learning something we could use during the duel, but maybe he was spending time getting reacquainted with Tamara.

This afternoon was no different; Lucas trained me. We fought in fur, and although I felt like I was getting better, he wasn't doling out any compliments. Honestly, I didn't need praise, but getting some verbal encouragement would've been nice. Not that Lucas had seemed in any mood to be overly kind. Since the inn episode, he'd been acting downright testy.

I imagined his crabby mood was due to Sarah but didn't broach the subject, because one, I didn't want to meddle, and two, I was afraid I might let the truth slip out to comfort him.

As I left the gym, he called out, "Happy birthday, Clark. Hope you have a fun evening planned." He raised a smile that didn't reach his eyes.

I paused with my fingers on the heavy door. "Thanks." I almost invited him to come, but it would be a little weird. Lucas and I weren't really friends.

If Sarah had come, though . . . I let that thought drift away before it could bum me out. Soon, I'd get my friend back.

"You did good today," Lucas said.

I blinked. "Did you just compliment me?"

His plastic smile turned into a real smirk. "Only because it's your birthday."

"Uh-huh." I winked at him and turned to go, but before heading home, I patted the door and said, "Sometimes, things aren't what they seem, Lucas."

His black eyebrows listed toward his nose.

Hoping I hadn't said too much, I left him to ponder my cryptic declaration.

When I got home, there was a shopping bag on the kitchen counter with crinkly pink silk paper spilling over the top like cotton candy.

"Came for you after you left this morning," Jeb said, flipping through channels. He was already dressed for dinner in a crisp linen button-down and khaki pants.

I opened the little card tied around the fabric handles. It wasn't signed, but it said: *So you don't wear sneakers to your b-day dinner. Miss you. XX*

I grinned. Only one person had an issue with my sneakers, and that person was Sarah.

I pulled the paper out and extricated a shoe box. Inside was a pair of sky-high nude heels. I stared at the shoes before kicking off my sneakers to try my gift on.

"Who got you shoes?" Jeb asked.

"A friend."

"Which friend?"

"Just a friend." My left foot jammed against a piece of balled paper. I removed the shoe and fished the paper out.

"A *boy*-friend?"

I looked at my uncle. "I don't have a boyfriend, Jeb."

"You don't?"

I shook my head, still clutching the piece of paper.

"What about Liam?"

"Liam?" I almost choked on his name. "He and I broke up a while ago."

The day your son died . . . Like paddles, the memory of Everest delivered an electrical jab inside my chest.

I slid my feet out of the pretty heels and tossed the piece of paper in the box, but lines of black ink caught my eye. I picked it back up and smoothed it out. As I read the words on it, my breath snagged.

Hoping my face didn't betray my emotions, I said, "I should get ready." I hurried to my bedroom, already dialing Liam. The second he answered, I blurted out, "Liam, the Creeks are coming after the Pines' stash of Sillin. They know where you hid it."

"How do you know that?" His voice was hushed, as though he was somewhere he couldn't talk.

"I can't tell you, but you have to move it."

He was so silent I thought the line went dead. "Okay. I'll call Lucas." I was about to say bye, when he added, "Happy birthday, by the way."

"Thank you."

Hinges groaned, and then air rushed through the receiver. "Got any plans?" he asked, louder this time.

"Just dinner with Evelyn, Frank, and Jeb." I didn't mention the Watts would be there.

There was another beat of silence. Was he waiting for me to invite him?

He sighed and said, "I'll call you later," before hanging up.

I thought Tamara's pregnancy would lessen his feelings for me, but what if it hadn't? Perhaps it was a matter of time. Or perhaps it was a matter of me being single.

Maybe Amanda was right. Maybe if I was in a relationship, Liam would stop seeing me as an option.

FRANK, Nelson, and Isobel were already seated at a table in the back of the restaurant when I arrived with Jeb. All three got up. Where Frank and Nelson offered me one-armed hugs and whispered happy birthdays, Isobel kissed my cheeks and then held me in a hug that was almost as fierce as my mother's used to be.

As my heart pinched, I was dragged into a set of new arms.

"*Feliz cumpleaños, querida.*" Evelyn pecked my forehead. "You are sitting here. Next to me."

After lowering herself into her seat, which Frank gallantly held out for her, she leaned over and scrubbed her thumb over my forehead. "I am always leaving marks on you."

I didn't mind the marks she left on me. I let her wipe away the kiss, even though I was certain I'd get more before the evening was over.

The vacant seat at the end of the table had me glancing at Isobel. "Is August coming?"

"He said he was on his way. You look beautiful tonight. Doesn't she, Evelyn?"

"She always looks beautiful," Evelyn answered, her tone a little gruff.

Isobel's lips flexed into a wide smile as she leaned over and whispered, "Remind me never to get on her bad side."

Trent, The Silver Bowl's owner, arrived then, and I got up to shake his hand and thank him for hosting us. "It's my pleasure." He uncorked a bottle of champagne from my year of birth. Which meant he knew I was underage, and yet he filled the champagne flute on the table. He winked at me. "A little gift from my wife and myself. Enjoy."

Just as he was finishing pouring champagne into everyone's flutes, the door of the restaurant opened. I didn't have to look up to know who'd arrived, but I looked anyway, because the tether thrummed. August smiled at the hostess at the door, who smiled right back. He spoke a couple words to her, and she tittered, fingers dropping to the V-collar of her dress. Was she trying to drag August's eyes down to her breasts?

Subtle.

Finally, she turned sideways and pointed to our table. His eyes locked with mine as she led the way toward us. I should've probably looked away, and I sort of did. I looked down, first at his white dress shirt which he'd left unbuttoned at the top, and then lower, at his dark-gray slacks that hugged his long, muscular legs.

I realized I was being as unsubtle as the hostess, so I finally tore my gaze off him and set it on the champagne popping in the glass I'd unconsciously plucked off the table.

"Sorry I'm late." Before taking his seat, he kissed his mother's cheek, then his hand gripped my shoulder gently, and my heart jumped high, as though trying to reach his palm. "Happy birthday, Dimples." He handed me a little pouch.

Heart still suspended, I set my champagne down. "You didn't have to get me anything."

"It's nothing really." He smiled, and I sensed we were okay again. It had just taken him a week of one-word text messages to come around.

I undid the ties on the pouch, then dipped my fingers inside the velvet until I came away with something warm and smooth: an intricate carving of a palm tree on a metal keyring. A grin broke over my lips as I stroked the perfect little piece of wood.

"I heard you got a car. I thought you might need something to put your new key on."

"Is that a palm tree?" Isobel asked, leaning in closer to look at it.

I nodded, the hair I'd blow-dried straight fluttering over one of the dresses from Sarah's reject pile. The frock was as red as Evelyn's lipstick and draped off one of my shoulders before tapering at the waist and flaring out. It had this vintage flair that made me think of something a Hollywood star would wear.

"They're my favorite trees," I explained, then added, "Apparently."

"Apparently?" Isobel quirked a painted-on eyebrow. Like her hair, which was covered by a wig, her real eyebrows were growing back, but the process was slow.

"Apparently I sketched my dream house when I was a kid, and it had a palm tree in the middle. August reminded me of it."

"Can I see the carving?" Jeb asked.

I handed it over, and he *ooh*ed and *aah*ed at the detail before passing it along to Frank.

I mouthed a *thank you* to August, and it won me a devastating smile, which made my navel tingle behind my cinched waistband.

Nelson lifted his champagne. "Before the food arrives, we wanted to say a little something. Ness, you're like a daughter to Isobel and me, and although we know we can never replace Maggie and Callum, I hope you know you can come to us with anything you might need."

My bottom lip wobbled.

"We will always be here for you, sweet girl," Isobel said, making my attempt at keeping it together worse.

"Nelson, you just stole my entire toast," Jeb chided, humor lilting his tone. Directing his attention on me, he said, "Ness, I know you're eighteen now, and *legally* not mine to keep, but I hope you'll choose to stay with me a couple more years. I really enjoy having someone to take care of, even though"—his Adam's apple bobbed underneath his gray-blond scruff—"even though you take better care of me than—" He stopped talking abruptly, his eyes growing red and shiny with emotion.

As Frank patted my uncle's back, tears trickled down my cheeks. I palmed them away, hoping they weren't dragging down the mascara I'd applied.

"I'm not going anywhere, Jeb," I managed to whisper. "At least not without you."

He smiled, and my heart squeezed because in that moment, he looked so much like Dad. He didn't have his dimples, but he had the same smile.

"Six years ago, I met a sweet little girl with blonde pigtails who would not let me into her apartment," Evelyn said, "and yet, the same little girl ended up letting me into her heart. *Querida*, I never had the chance to become a mother, so I never imagined I would have the chance to become a grandmother, but you made this dream of mine come true."

So much for staying stoic and well made-up. I lifted my napkin from my lap and blotted the corners of my eyes, leaving behind little black smudges on the pale linen.

"I do not know if I am any good at it, though." She lowered her gaze to her ornate plate and added quietly, "I want what is best for you, but maybe I have been wrong about what is best for you."

A beat of silence descended upon the table.

I nibbled on my lip, my heart accelerating. I prayed I was the only one who knew what she was referring to.

Whom she was referring to.

"I'm happy your father didn't take well to the pledge drink, Ness," Frank blurted out, which made Evelyn's gaze jerk off her plate.

I laughed, which was a nice change from all the crying.

"What about you, son?" Nelson said.

"I'm still thinking," August said, but something in the intensity with which he stared at my face told me he knew exactly what he wanted to say but didn't want to utter it in front of everyone. Which was fine by me, because I was also certain that whatever he'd say would be heartfelt and make me cry . . . *again*. "But don't let my thinking keep you from your drinking." He raised his glass. "To you, Ness."

Without breaking eye contact, he took a long sip of champagne.

36

We had three incredible courses followed by the most decadent flourless chocolate birthday cake. When it was brought out, ablaze with candles, everyone in the restaurant sang and clapped. By the time coffees and teas were served, the waistband of my dress felt like steel wire.

I was listening to one of Evelyn's kitchen nightmare stories when I caught Nelson asking August at what time he was flying out to Tennessee to meet with the Rivers.

He was going to meet the Rivers?

I was so disconcerted by the news of his impending trip that I didn't realize I'd spoken out loud until both Watts turned toward me.

"They want us to build them an indoor recreation center for the winter months." Nelson beamed proudly.

"That's . . . that's"—I flipped the tiny spoon on my teacup saucer over and over— "*wonderful*."

It wasn't, though. Not in the least. Even though I knew firsthand that the Rivers genuinely liked what August and Nelson had crafted, I also knew the River Alpha's daughter had a thing—more than a thing . . . *ugh*—for August. And if he went, the distance would cancel out our bond, and since he assumed my feelings for him were entirely platonic, nothing would stand in his way to hook up with her again. Trying to rein in my glumness, I swallowed the tepid and over-infused dregs of my tea that tasted way better than the jealousy basting my palate.

At the end of dinner, after everyone had thanked Trent and filed out of the restaurant, Nelson said, "We have a birthday present for you. It's for your new house. Let me know when you're done redoing it, and I'll bring it over."

"You didn't have to—"

"Will you just let us spoil you without putting up a fight?" Isobel asked, flicking the tip of my nose.

"Okay."

Nelson pulled open her car door, and she climbed into the passenger seat. Before shutting the door, she said, "Thank you for sharing your special night, sweet girl," and then she blew me another kiss.

They couldn't replace Mom and Dad—no one could—but I was fortunate to have them in my life. Whoever August ended up with would be one lucky girl.

That thought just crushed me. Where had it even come from?

Evelyn hugged me tight and told me she loved me a great many times before finally letting Frank tug her away. Only Jeb, August, and I remained on the glittery pavement.

Digging the van's key out of his jacket pocket, my uncle congratulated August on landing another deal with the Rivers, then to me, he said, "I'll bring the car around."

We hadn't parked far, but I was glad not to have to walk in the heels that were so high I was only half a head shorter than August.

Keeping my gaze on the stubble coating his jaw, I said, "Thanks for my palm tree."

"You're welcome."

His scent and heat eddied in the air between us, tempting me to step in closer. "I love it."

His lips arched. "I'm glad."

I inhaled a long breath that just tortured my heart. "How are you feeling?"

"I still can't shift. But otherwise, I feel good."

For a moment, neither of us spoke, and then we both spoke at the same time. He said, "How was your first week of school?" while I asked, "When are you leaving?"

"You first," he said.

"My first week was really good."

"It's a big milestone. We should celebrate. If you have time next week, we could go for ice-cream at the Creamery."

His suggestion had me wincing. I loved that parlor and I loved the idea of going with him, but it was a place he'd bring me to when I was a kid, and that made me feel so young, like I'd blown out thirteen candles instead of eighteen.

"Sure," I said, just as the van turned the corner. I started heading toward it, but paused. "You didn't answer *my* question."

"I'm leaving tomorrow morning."

I clenched the pouch that held my little palm tree. "For how long?"

"Two nights."

I swallowed and eased my grip before I could break the creation like I'd broken us. "Huh," I ended up saying. Not very eloquent, but it beat the wounded sound forming at the back of my throat.

As I staggered the few feet that separated me from the van, I attempted not to topple from the weight of the war raging within me. I paused by the car door, the desire to admit my lie burning on my tongue. I glanced over my shoulder. August was reading something on his phone's screen.

Something that made him smile.
Had the River Alpha's daughter sent him a text message?
"Ness?" My uncle's voice made me jump. "I'm holding up traffic, sweetie."
"Sorry," I mumbled, getting into the car.
I didn't look at August as we drove away, afraid he was still smiling at his phone.

37

"Last coat of paint goes on tomorrow," Jeb said before heading into his bedroom. "If we start early, we could be done with everything by nightfall and move in on Sunday."

"Only if you take the bigger room."

"Ness—"

"Please, Jeb. I can't live in their room." Already moving into my old home, however different it would look with fresh paint and new furniture, was going to be difficult.

"You're sure?"

"Two hundred percent."

He looked at me a long time before saying, "Okay," then drummed his fingers against the doorframe. "Have a good night, sweetie. And again, happy birthday."

Once his door clicked shut, I reached for my zipper and started easing it down, but then the memory of August smiling at his phone had me tugging it back up and grabbing my keys.

Maybe it hadn't been the River Alpha's daughter on the other end of his *pleasant* conversation, but either way, I wasn't letting him leave without understanding my reasons for shutting him out.

I wrote Jeb a note that I was going over to a friend's house and left the paper on the dining table. Ten minutes later, I was standing in front of August's front door. I lifted my finger to the ringer, but before I could press it, the door opened.

August stood on the threshold, shirt flapping open, as though I'd caught him in the middle of undressing.

"How—how did you know I was here?" My voice tripped in time with my pulse.

He tapped his bare midriff. "I have this nifty, built-in mate-detector. I believe you possess the same one."

My stomach was tied in too many knots to sense much over my heightened nerves. "Can I . . . can I come in?"

He drew the door wider.

My heels clicked on the gray floorboards, echoing through the dimly lit loft. A slowly moving image of our planet seen from space ebbed on his TV screen, splashing one end of the apartment in a rich-blue glow. The only other source of light came from the glass fixture suspended over the kitchen island, dimmed to its lowest setting.

I closed my eyes to center myself and silence the voice of reason that was telling me to get back into my car and drive away. When I lifted my lids, August was standing before me.

"Don't—" I swallowed thickly.

"Don't what?"

"Don't go tomorrow."

He frowned. "Why?"

"Because . . ." I tucked a lock of hair behind my ear. I was being selfish; I had no right to ask this of him.

"Because what, Dimples?"

"Because I don't want to lose you."

His gaze turned so dusky his bright irises became barely distinguishable from his pupils. "Why would you lose me?"

"Because"—I wet my lips—"the Alpha's daughter. She wants to marry you. And the link—"

"You think I'm going there to get engaged to Ingrid?"

Ingrid . . . I'd conveniently forgotten her name, but August hadn't.

He never forgot anything.

"It's just work." He tilted his face to the side. "But I do have to wonder why it would bother you since you don't have feelings for me."

Evelyn's warning beat against my temples, but then the words she'd spoken tonight trickled over them, blurring the line between right and wrong.

I steeled my spine. "August, I lied."

A beat of silence passed before he said, "I know."

"When I was away, I—wait. What do you mean, *you know*?"

His expression gentled but stayed guarded. "Frank called me a couple nights ago."

"Frank?" I frowned. "I don't understand."

"He overheard you and Evelyn talk the day you came back from your trip. He didn't want to get involved, but you know Frank, and how sacred he finds mating links."

My eyes widened.

"And he might've mentioned that you looked miserable and that I was obtuse if I actually believed you didn't want me."

I didn't think my eyes could get wider, but my lids stretched higher.

August raised his hand to the nape of his neck and cradled it. "What is it you want from me?" His voice was so raw it had me shivering. "To wait a couple years for you to grow *readier*?"

"No."

His brow furrowed. "Then what?"

"I want you to forgive me."

"For what?"

"For lying. I know I hurt you, and I hate myself for it."

He let his hand drop back to his side. "You think I can stay mad at you?"

"Not staying mad at me and forgiving me are two separate things."

His jaw tensed. And then, in a voice that scattered goose bumps over my skin, he said, "I forgive you."

My heart was pounding so hard the fabric of my red dress vibrated. The tether too, probably. For a second, I considered tugging it to pull August toward me, but what if . . . what if it *didn't* work?

Or what if he didn't want me like that anymore?

My arms started shaking, so I clutched my elbows. "I'd understand if you say no, but would you give me a second chance?"

He didn't answer me for so long that I wondered if I'd spoken too quietly, but then he took a tentative step toward me and crooked my chin up on his finger. "Only if you promise not to let anyone, and I mean *anyone*—not Evelyn, not Liam—come between us again, because I'm not interested in our Alpha's rules or societal propriety. It's *you* and *me*. No one else. And even though I could never hate you, if you break my heart again—"

"When I break yours, it breaks mine," I whispered in a tenuous voice. I hadn't realized I'd started crying until his thumbs swiped my cheeks. And here I thought I'd exhausted my tear ducts earlier, but apparently they were bottomless. "I'm so sorry, August."

He pressed his mouth to mine and stroked away my apology with his tongue. And then his hands trailed down my arms, loosening them, before lacing around my waist.

His scent would be all over me, but I no longer cared. Besides, I was pretty confident that Tamara's pregnancy would make Liam think twice before jumping into a duel now.

I pushed up on my tiptoes and gripped the back of August's neck to deepen the kiss and to erase any remaining space between our bodies. His mouth slid off mine but didn't leave my body. It traveled across my jaw and down my neck, traced the slope of my shoulder, tracking wet heat over my sensitive skin.

I shivered. Shuddered. Shook.

When he lifted his head to look at me, I thumbed the back of his neck. "As far as birthday presents go, that kiss might've beat the palm tree. Which is a feat, considering how much I love that palm tree."

He smiled quietly, his fingertips sketching unhurried circles at the base of my spine. "Ness, I have to ask, what made you change your mind?"

I worried the inside of my cheek. "I didn't want you going somewhere the link didn't work thinking I wasn't attracted to you." I dragged my hand through my straightened hair. "I'm really jealous of Ingrid. Of pretty much every girl you've dated."

"You have nothing to be jealous about."

"Are you kidding? They're all still hung up on you. And they're all older, and way more experienced, and—"

He kissed me before saying, "And none of them are you."

"Are *you* sure it's not just the link that makes you want me?"

He pulled away, the tendons in his neck pinching beneath my fingertips. "When you went off to Tennessee with Liam, I considered boarding a plane and coming after you, but Mom told me the best way to scare a girl off was to do just that, so I stayed here and sulked and imagined the worst things. And then when you came back and said you hadn't missed me"—he grimaced—"it felt like I'd taken a bullet to the heart."

"I'm sorry," I said again.

"I'm just sorry we lost all this time, sweetheart." He nudged my nose with his before kissing me so tenderly it made my toes curl. After a deliciously long while, he said, "I have a confession of my own."

"You do?"

"I went to speak with Evelyn this week."

I blanched.

"I told her about my intentions toward you."

I stared at him in mute horror. "Your intentions?"

"I told her that when I returned from my trip, I would ask you out. On a proper date."

"Did she threaten to murder you?"

His lips quirked. "No. She thanked me for my honesty and then she left the room." His mouth straightened into a contemplative expression. "I didn't mean to upset her; I only meant to show her that I was serious about you. I hope that, in time, she'll accept me."

"I think she's already starting to."

He stared so intently into my eyes that I shivered again.

"What *are* your intentions toward me?"

He leaned in to nuzzle the base of my neck again. "Long term, making you mine, but you already know that."

My heartbeat detonated.

"Short term, showing you how right we are for each other." He licked a line up to my earlobe, making a fierce wave of desire break against my skin. "How well we *fit* together."

The word *fitting* had my mind concocting all sorts of scenarios that involved a lot less clothes. None at all for that matter. "If we use protection, we can have sex without consolidating the mating link," I blurted out, before slapping my hand over my mouth.

Had I really said this out loud?

He pulled away from me, eyebrows writhing in amusement.

"I learned that in Tennessee," I mumbled, cheeks flaming.

He studied me a long beat before dragging my hand off my mouth. "Is that what you want?"

My throat went dry so fast I had to swallow several times before I could speak again. "Isn't it what you want?"

"What I want is you." He crooked my face up. "And I'm not going to lie . . . I most definitely want to make love to you, but I don't want to rush into something you're not ready for."

"I'm ready."

His gaze turned hooded.

"I don't want to feel like a kid anymore, August."

He frowned. "You're not." His hands tracked up my ribcage and cupped my breasts. "I'm not sure why you don't seem to believe this, but you're already very much a woman."

"Maybe I feel this way because I'm still a virgin." I strained against his palms. "Please?"

Letting out a husky growl, he dropped his hands to my ass and lifted me up. I gasped, my legs reflexively coming around his waist. He carried me over to the kitchen island and sat me down on the satiny wood, the dim glow over our heads casting luminous ripples over his face.

As he stood between my legs, he said, "I won't have sex with you to make you feel like more of a woman."

My heart stumbled around in my chest. Everything about his body echoed my own desire. Had I read him wrong?

He traced the contour of my lips with his fingertip. "I'll have sex with you to show you that you already are."

He dipped his finger down my neck, then kissed the hollow at the base of my neck where his finger had been, before trawling his tongue lower. His hands came around my back and eased my zipper open.

Air rushed out of my mouth at the sensation of the fabric falling away from my skin, baring my upper body.

He straightened and drank me in. "God, you're beautiful."

I wanted to roll my eyes or say, *have you looked in a mirror?* Instead, I forced his already open shirt off his shoulders and rolled it down his arms. I knew this wasn't a comparison, but my upper body had nothing on his. I trailed my fingers over his copper skin, over his dark nipples, over the perfect grid of his abs, stilling on the sharp indents at his waist.

Looking back into his eyes that flashed with the same lust heating my blood, I lowered my hands to the button of his pants and popped it open, then got off the island so that my dress pooled around my feet.

August's pupils swelled, blotting out all the green around them, and then his calloused hands grazed my skin. After an agonizingly quiet moment, his face slanted to one of my breasts. He tugged me into his mouth, licking the pebbling skin. As he moved to the other, he raked his deft hands down my spine, hooking the waistband of my black thong and sliding it down my legs.

He lifted me back to the island, his breathing growing so ragged that the mere sound of him exhaling on me sent daggers of heat into my core. When he took a step back, I squeezed my thighs together and covered my breasts.

"Please don't hide yourself from me, sweetheart."

Biting my lip, I whispered, "Can you also—I don't want to be the only one . . . naked." I felt silly asking him to take off his clothes, but the weight of his stare made me terribly self-conscious.

He pushed his pants and briefs down in one swift stroke. The sight of him springing out, thick and ready, made my entire body blaze warmer. I inched my hand closer to his silky flesh, closed my fingers around him, then dragged them up to the tip.

He cuffed my wrist and towed it off his body.

"You have a . . . condom?"

A corner of his mouth tipped up. "I do, but we won't be needing one for a while still." He eased me onto my back until my spine was flush against the cool wood, and then he parted my legs and draped them over his shoulders.

When his tongue flicked against me, I picked my head off and gasped, "August! You don't have to do that."

I could only see his eyes, and they glowed with amusement and with a bunch of other things, but mostly amusement.

"Don't have to do that?" He spoke the words so close to my delicate flesh that I shivered and writhed. He clamped his hands around my thighs to pin them to his shoulders. "Oh, I've been wanting to do this"—he gave me a long, slow lick—"since the day you walked back into my life." He skated a kiss over my pulsing center. "Fuck, you taste so good," he growled.

He was relentless and made me shatter so many times that my body felt made of clouds and stars instead of flesh and blood.

At some point, he came up for air, lips swollen and slick. He scooped my boneless body up, grabbed his wallet, then carried me over to the couch. He laid me out before pulling a condom from his wallet. The casing crinkled as he tore it open. With unabashed curiosity, I watched him roll it on.

"Ness," he whispered raucously, climbing over me and bracing himself on his arms as his length settled against my abdomen, "condoms . . . they can break. It's never happened to me before, but they can. Are you sure you want to do this?"

I traced the shape of Cassiopeia on his cheek, connecting each freckle to the next. "I have never wanted anything more."

"But you understand the risks?"

"I understand the risks." When he still hadn't moved, I said, "Are you going to make me sign a disclaimer?"

A laugh burst from him. "Maybe I should." He moved down my body to position himself at my entrance. "Next time."

Next time . . . My heart felt like it had melted and little pieces of it were beating everywhere in me.

His hips shifted, and then he was stretching me open, and a gasp tore up my throat. When he pulled out, eyes stained with concern, I clamped my hands on his backside, over his scar, and pressed him back in.

Pleasure warred with pain. Neither sensation won. They battled till the very end, till his body stilled and shuddered over mine . . . *into* mine.

Stroking his scar, I whispered, "You had a toast ready for me tonight, didn't you?"

A smile touched his mouth that smelled like a mix of him and me. "I did."

"Can I hear it?"

"You can." He nosed my jaw.

When he didn't say anything more for a prolonged stretch of time, I asked, "Tonight?"

He lifted his head, tucked a lock of hair behind my ear, and then in that raw-honeyed voice of his, he said, "I may not have been your first choice for a mate, but I hope I'll be your last."

Emotion gripped my throat so hard I couldn't respond with words, so instead, I picked my neck off the couch pillow and aligned my lips and heartbeats with his.

38

I woke up to the scent of coffee.

As I stretched, every second of our love-making replayed in my mind. I twisted around, but August was no longer on the couch next to me. Last night, he removed the back pillows to make room for our two bodies, and then he dragged me against his chest, and we fell asleep skin to skin.

"August?" I called out.

When he didn't answer me, I sat up but regretted the sudden movement that awakened a dull throbbing between my legs.

Pale sunlight fanned over the loft, tinting everything lavender and gray.

"August?" I repeated, my throat feeling as raw as the rest of me. Had he left for Tennessee?

I pushed my senses out, trying to pick up on another heartbeat, but only mine resounded.

He left.

He'd gone and left, and he hadn't even woken me to say goodbye. The most over-whelming devastation crushed my lungs, made it impossible to breathe. Hands shak-ing, I took the cover and wrapped it around myself, then struggled to a standing position that intensified the throbbing.

The front door snicked open, and my heart all but short-circuited.

I clutched the cover tighter.

August walked in, a brown paper bag dangling from his fingers. When he caught sight of my expression, he kicked the door shut, tossed the paper bag on the kitchen island, and rushed over. "What is it?"

My bottom lip wobbled. "I thought you . . . I thought you'd left."

His forehead puckered, but then he smiled, cupped both my cheeks, and tipped my face up. "Just to get breakfast."

When had I become this needy girl ready to cry for having been left alone? I averted my gaze from his. "I feel so stupid right now."

"Why?"

"For flipping out."

"I like that you flipped out." He pushed a lock of tangled hair off my face. "I was worried you might have regrets and run away from me again."

I looked up at him. "Run away? It was the best night of my life."

His hazel eyes blazed. "That's a dangerous thing to say."

"Why?"

"Because I want to hear you say that every morning you wake up"—his hands settled on the base of my spine and pressed me against him—"which means I'll have to outdo myself each and every night." He bumped his nose into mine.

My pulse fluttered against my neck and then lower, until it had all but soothed the shallow ache and replaced it with fierce want.

"I'm on board with that," I murmured.

His eyes twinkled a tad wickedly. "On a scale of one to ten, how much pain are you in right now?"

"Pain?"

"Down there."

"Not much."

"Not much isn't a number."

"Two."

His brows slanted. "Really?"

"Okay, maybe three. And a half." My body was supposed to heal fast. Why was I even still in pain?

Yes, he was *big*, but—

"When you get to zero, you let me know." And then he walked back to the kitchen, pulled a bread basket from a cupboard, and poured out the flaky pastries that smelled like warmed butter and spicy cinnamon. My stomach clenched and let out an embarrassingly loud rumble.

"Someone's hungry," he said, smiling.

"Ravenous." Still mummified in the cover, I shuffled over to the island. "Aren't you?"

He ran his palm over the wood that had absorbed the waves of my pleasure. "Oh, I'm starving."

Sandwiching my face between two hot irons would probably have scorched my cheeks less.

"Did I just make you blush?" he asked, smirking.

I broke off a piece from the cinnamon roll and lobbed it at him.

"How very mature, Dimples. I thought you were a real woman, now."

"Shut up," I muttered, breaking off another piece of the sweet pastry, but this time to eat it.

August came around the island and sat on the stool beside mine. Still laughing, he leaned over and kissed me. It started out as a peck but escalated quickly.

"Two," I whispered against his mouth.

"What?" he asked, voice all raspy.

"On a scale of one to ten, I'm down to a two. Kiss me again, and I might get to zero faster."

He sucked in a ragged breath before clearing his throat. "Your body needs to heal."

"My body needs yours."

"It's all yours."

"But you're leaving in a couple hours."

His eyes, which encompassed every color of the forest beyond these walls, turned very serious. "Ness, I'm not going anywhere."

"You canceled your trip?"

"Dad's gonna go."

The silliest relief filled me. Even though I'd rather have gnawed off my own leg than let him go into River territory, I said, "If you need to go with him, you can."

"The only place I need to be is here with you."

And here I'd up and gone on my trip without considering how my absence would make *him* feel. "I don't deserve you."

"What are you talking about?"

My eyes heated. Oh my God, was I about to cry? *Again?* What was wrong with me? Was I getting my period?

"Hey, hey, hey." He kissed my lids.

"I don't know what's happening to me," I whispered. "I've never been like this."

"Like what?"

"So needy."

He stroked the edge of my face.

Had we somehow consolidated the bond, and now I couldn't physically be away from him? "You think the condom broke?" It would explain—

"The condom didn't break."

Then how come I felt like I couldn't breathe if he wasn't around?

How come I wanted to duct-tape my body to his?

"You look a little pale," he said.

I lifted my hair and twisted it into a rope. "However clingy I get, don't run from me, okay?"

He leaned over again and gripped the back of my neck. "Why would I run from the one thing I want?"

As he kissed me, the tether between us solidified into a thick and shiny rope, which I itched to pluck but still feared to touch. In the end, I set the temptation aside for another time, a time when August would be so certain of my feelings for him that he wouldn't worry if I couldn't move his body with my mind.

39

I was glad it was Saturday. At least none of August's employees would witness my walk of shame.

August flicked his gaze toward me as we ambled hand-in-hand toward my car. "I know some very capable house painters who work weekends."

I powered open my car doors. "I'm sure you do."

"Let me call—"

I kissed his still moving mouth, then pulled away and said, "I like painting walls."

"If memory serves me, you also like what I did to you last night . . ."

Heat smacked my cheeks. "I did also like that."

"And swimming in lakes." He gestured to the sky. "I mean, look at this weather. It's perfect for what I had planned."

Maybe I could let Jeb—*No.* I needed to help out. Especially if we wanted to move in tomorrow.

"You know what I also really like?" I asked. "Sunset swims. Less people around."

His eyes flashed. "You make a convincing argument. What time should I pick you up?"

"Six. At the apartment, so I have time to change."

He looked up at the sky before returning his gaze to my face. "That's in too many hours."

I smiled. "Want to bring us lunch?"

His lips curved. "I can most definitely do that." As he leaned in for a kiss, my phone vibrated inside my bag. I disregarded the call, giving August's addictive mouth my full attention.

A while later, he drew open my car door, and I settled behind the wheel. And then he backed away and watched me leave, the rope between us stretching like spun sugar. At a traffic light, I dug my phone out of my bag to call Sarah, but then remembered I couldn't make contact with her.

My disappointment was quickly superseded by apprehension when I noticed Liam's three missed calls.

Bracing myself, I dialed him back.

It was Lucas who answered. "We're waiting for you in the gym."

"I thought you said I had the day off."

He sighed, then dropped his voice, "Just get here quick, Clark."

"Did the Creeks—"

"Not over the phone."

"Okay. I'll be there in twenty." Pulse skittering like claws on pavement, I tightened my grip on the steering wheel and tore down the streets toward my apartment.

SHOWERED AND CHANGED, I banged on the gym doors. I hadn't been convened to train, so I'd donned a plain crop top and a pair of overalls I'd purchased to work on the house. A small part of me was hoping the burned-plastic smell of the paint primer dappling the denim would conceal August's scent.

But I quieted that small part of me.

I wasn't here to hide what I'd done; I was here to defend my actions. If this meeting was even about August.

Lucas opened the door, and I strode in, muttering a quick hello, but then I did a doubletake when I caught sight of a bruise purpling his jaw.

"What happened to your face?" I asked. "Did you get in a fight?"

His blue eyes shone like lapis. "No. I walked into Alex Morgan's fist for the fun of it."

I stiffened. "Alex Morgan?" My gaze jumped to Liam to see if he, too, had gotten hit. His face was shiny with sweat but unblemished.

As he set down the weights he'd been curling, he speared me with a look that had my heart banging harder. "Thanks to your little message, the Creeks followed Lucas and Matt to where we'd stashed the Sillin, and ambushed them."

I gasped. "Ambushed?"

"It was a fucking set-up, Ness! They had no clue where we'd hidden it," Lucas hissed.

"Sarah sent you the message, didn't she?" Liam asked.

My lips trembled too hard to answer.

He rose from the weight bench and strode over to me, his gait so brutal I took a step back. "I told you she was using us, and you *didn't* listen."

"Sarah wouldn't have done that . . ." I whispered.

"How can you still defend her?" Liam hollered.

I pressed my palms against my ears. "I can hear you fine. Don't shout."

"You didn't hear me fine the first time I said it. Maybe this time, if I say it loud enough, you'll listen!" Spittle smacked my nose.

I gritted my teeth. "Stop it, Liam!"

Would Sarah have set me up to gain the Creeks' trust? I couldn't imagine her doing such a thing.

I prayed she hadn't.

"I trust Sarah. She wouldn't have betrayed us, not willingly anyway. Maybe *they* set her up. Maybe—"

Liam's eyes flashed like hammered copper. "Funny you should mention trust."

I sucked in a breath. "What's that supposed to mean?"

"You broke your promise." His voice was chillingly flat, but his expression wasn't. His expression was a medley of sharp angles. "I can smell him all over you."

My lungs contracted, but then I crossed my arms. "Don't you think we have more important—"

"We had a deal," he snapped.

"That deal went both ways." Underneath the hot musk and fresh mint of Liam lay another scent, a feminine one. "I'm not the only one who spent the night with someone, so don't you dare tell me off. You don't get to tell me off!"

His Adam's apple jostled in his throat. He hadn't shaved in days, which made him look older, more severe.

"How's Matt?" I asked, his wellbeing mattering more than this stupid feud over who we'd spent our night with.

"What?" Liam blinked.

I turned toward Lucas. "How is he? Did he also get banged up?"

"He looks better than I do. Fucking Alex Morgan. I was this close"—his index finger hovered a breath away from his thumb—"to killing him. This. Close."

"I'm really sorry you guys got jumped," I said, "but I stand by my conviction. Sarah cozied up to Alex Morgan to get *us* information. Not to give them any."

Lucas narrowed his eyes at first, but then he shook his head, tossing his shaggy black hair. "I don't buy that, Clark. She's a Creek through and through."

Tension whirred as loud as the AC vents blowing cold air into the high-ceilinged room. It was interrupted by the ringing of a cell phone.

Lucas pulled it out of the pocket of his black mesh shorts. "It's Frank."

"Pick it up," Liam said, "and tell him what happened."

"He probably wants to speak with y—"

"Just take the call, Lucas. And tell him I'll call him back when I'm done here."

Meaning, when he was done hauling me over the coals.

Once Lucas had walked to the other end of the gym, busy recounting the Creeks' trap, Liam said, "You didn't tell me the Watts would be at your birthday dinner."

"Why are we still talking about that, Liam? And how do you know?"

"After Lucas and Matt got jumped, you weren't answering your phone, so I tracked you through the blood-link to tell you what happened. Led me straight to that fancy restaurant."

"I didn't see you," I said.

"I didn't go inside. I thought better of interrupting your cozy celebration." After a beat, he added, "You've found another family, and there's no place in it for me."

And here I thought he was about to admonish me again. My throat squeezed tight.

"I hate how it ended, Ness. I hate that August came back. I hate that you and him have all this history. I hate that whatever fucking God up there decided to link the two of you! Why not *us*? Why the hell not us?" he whispered hoarsely.

After the heat of his anger, Liam's anguished outburst softened my stance. "I didn't choose him because of a magical link."

"You chose him because I failed you."

Like my throat, my heart tightened. "Your distrust broke me . . . broke *us* . . . but it didn't drive me into someone else's arms."

"Then what did?"

"When you slept with Tamara—"

"It was a mistake."

"Don't say that," I said gently but firmly. "She's the mother of your baby, Liam. Besides, she's not a random girl you picked up in a club. You guys have history, just like August and me."

Pain crinkled Liam's face. "If I could go back—"

"But you can't." A beat of silence filled the cavernous space, disrupted only by Lucas's animated conversation. "We have to learn to live with our choices. And in the end, even if your intention was to test my affection, maybe what happened is a blessing in disguise. You're an Alpha, Liam. An Alpha with a strong, *strong* personality." I made my tone light to sweeten my assertion. "You need a woman who's willing to bend without breaking. I'm not that woman. When someone bends me too hard, I splinter."

He snorted. "You obviously haven't spent much time with Tamara. She's not submissive."

I smiled. "Perhaps not, but from what I've seen, she worships you."

He loosed a ragged sigh. "The night I found out, I lost it. I asked her if she'd done it on purpose. To trap me."

"Liam!"

"I know. Not my finest hour, but I was scared, Ness. A baby? Do you see me with a baby? I can barely take care of a pack of grown men. *And* a woman." He added that last part with a wry smile that dismantled some more of the tension between us. "Know what she said? She said that if I didn't want the baby, then she would raise him on her own, that she wouldn't even ask me for handouts, that she wouldn't ask me for anything until our son reached puberty and would need to be brought into the pack. And even then, she would turn to Matt or someone else if I didn't want to be involved." He shook his head. "Can you imagine that she thought I'd want nothing to do with my own son?"

"I don't think she thought you wanted nothing to do with your son. I think she was giving you a way out." Cornering a man, who was part wild animal, was never a good idea, and Tamara knew this. "Which leads me to think she'll make a good mother."

"I know."

"And you'll make a good father."

He let out a brusque exhale. "I'm not so sure about that."

"Well, I'm sure for the both of us. You're protective and generous, but you do have to work on your fuse. It's a little short."

A streak of sunlight cut across his face, illuminating his brown eyes, making them glow more amber than brown. "I can't believe we just had a heart-to-heart."

"That's what friends do," I said.

"Is that what we are?"

"I think we're getting there." My lips flexed into a smile that he returned. "You're not going to phone up Cassandra and schedule the duel for tomorrow, are you?"

"I'm not."

"Good. Now about that Sillin. They took their stock. But we still have ours, right?"

His features hardened again. "We stored it in the same place."

"Shit." The word popped out of my mouth.

"Yeah." He stabbed his fingers through his hair. "Not my brightest decision."

"Well, I still have some." In truth, I hadn't checked, but since I hadn't spotted any breaking-and-entering, I assumed as much. "Thirty-two pills."

Liam nodded. "Can you shift yet?"

I frowned but then realized he was talking about the injection. "Greg didn't tell you?"

"Tell me what?"

"I'm not the one he inoculated."

Liam's eyebrows tipped toward his nose.

"August volunteered. And no, he can't shift yet."

My news thinned Liam's mouth. "You should've run this by me."

"August didn't give me a choice. Besides, I didn't want to bother you. I knew you had other stuff to deal with."

"The pack always comes first, Ness. No matter what."

I felt a twinge of regret for Tamara, because she would always come second to the pack. Perhaps it would be enough for her, but for me, it would never have been enough. And this made me appreciate August more, because I knew with complete certainty that he'd always put me first.

40

As promised, August arrived with lunch. But he didn't leave afterward. He rolled up his sleeves and stayed through the afternoon, lending the walls of our house his time and expertise and sneaking me kisses when my uncle wasn't looking.

While I painted my bedroom, the ambush ran on a loop inside my mind. I wanted to discuss it with August; I wanted to get his opinion on the matter but was worried about what it might be. What if he aligned with Lucas and Liam and insisted Sarah was a traitor?

Could someone else have sent me the message?

No, it had been her handwriting.

Had they forced her to write the message? My fingers itched to call her, but what if they'd forced her to con us? Then getting a message from me would only seal her fate . . .

Dusk was falling when I emerged from my bedroom, dizzy with worry and paint fumes. "I'm done."

August glanced away from the baseboard to which he was adding a final coat of white paint. "I'm almost finished here."

"Me too," Jeb said, dragging the lambs-wool roller over the ceiling in the hallway. Paint dribbled down his arm and onto the plastic tarp blanketing our lustrous floors. "How does Chinese takeout sound to you guys? I could go get some while this last coat dries."

August caught my eye.

"Um." I bit my lip. "I, uh . . . already have plans."

Jeb nodded even though disappointment was written all over his face.

August rose from his crouch and dunked the brush into the almost empty paint bucket. "Maybe you could change your plans, Ness?"

I tipped my gaze up to meet his and mouthed a *thank you*. "Yeah. Maybe I could meet my friend *after* dinner."

"Or maybe your friend can join you for dinner," August said, and my heart performed a little backbend because inviting said friend would reveal who said friend was.

"It's okay, Ness," Jeb said. "Derek's always up for getting out of his house. Let me call him."

"You sure?"

"Yeah." He rolled the brush one last time before setting it down and going to grab his phone from the kitchen counter that was also covered in plastic. He dialed Derek, exchanged a couple words, then gave me a thumbs up. After they disconnected, Jeb grabbed his car keys. "I'll be back in an hour. Don't lock up, okay?"

"'Kay."

As soon as the van vanished down the short driveway, August came at me with a predatorial gleam in his eyes that made him look more wolf than man. "You have some paint"—he dipped his fingers inside a bucket, then raked them down my side, over the patch of bare skin beneath my crop top—"right here."

Goose bumps rose beneath the white paint dripping down my ribs. "Huh. Clumsy me. I must've brushed up against a wall."

He smiled, then brought that smile closer to my mouth.

"A very big one," I added.

"Very big," he echoed. "We should clean you up, and I know just the place."

I rolled my eyes but smiled nonetheless, and it dispersed some of my clinging stress.

When car beams splashed the window, I sprang away from August.

Jeb blustered back in, face so white it looked as though he'd dunked it in the bucket of paint. "Ness! Ness, you . . . she . . . Lucy . . ."

My spine snapped into alignment. "Lucy what? What happened, Jeb?"

"Lucy is . . . at Aidan's." He was breathing so hard I had trouble understanding the next words out of his mouth. I caught the last, though. "Dead."

"*Dead?* Lucy's dead?" I asked.

My uncle shook his head from side to side. "No. Maybe Aidan. She doesn't know."

Color leached from August's skin. "What do you mean, she doesn't know?"

"Aidan's house. I need to get to Aidan's house," Jeb whispered.

My skin bristled, and white fur spouted from my pores. I was shifting. I pushed my wolf back before she could rip through my clothes and race across the forest toward the hateful Creek's estate.

"Give me your car key," August said, taking charge. "I'll drive."

"August, you can't shift. I'll go with Jeb—"

He shot me a glare that shut me up. "Like hell I'm letting you go without me. Get in the van."

We all sprinted outside and into the car. My uncle was muttering to himself. I tried to make out what he was saying, but his words were all garbled.

I leaned between the front seats and said, "We should call Liam."

August's gaze was narrowed on the road he was hurtling down at breakneck speed. "I texted Cole."

When, I wondered? I hadn't even seen him use his phone.

He tore his gaze off the road to look at me. "When we get there—"

"Don't tell me to stay in the car."

He slammed his gaze back on the windshield and took a turn so fast I had to dig my nails into his headrest to stay upright. He veered again and then the van lurched up the long driveway toward Aidan's glass and wood mansion. My aunt stood on the threshold, shivering like a strip of cut-out paper dolls.

Jeb flung open the passenger door and leaped out before the car had come to a full stop. He ran to his ex-wife and hugged her.

August spun around in his seat. "Ness—"

"Together. We go in together." I jumped into the passenger seat and out the door that was still open.

August rounded the front bumper, long strides devouring the flagstones.

Amidst chest-wracking sobs, my aunt said, "He's downstairs. With a knife in his throat."

"Lucy!" Jeb said, gaping at her in terror.

"He helped Alex murder our son, Jeb. I heard them joking about it. *Joking.*"

My uncle made a pained sound as he gathered his ex-wife against him again.

"I went to the police," she said. "They asked me for proof. I told them Aidan put a tracking device in the Jeep. They called me back saying they'd gone to the impound lot and checked the car. They told me they didn't find anything."

"Oh, Lucy," Jeb said. "The police . . . they're corrupt. You should've come to us."

"You hate me." Her voice trembled. "You all hate me."

"Lucy . . ." He squeezed her tighter to him.

"Stay out here with her," August told my uncle whose face had gone as pale as his beard.

I started toward the door when Lucy called out my name.

Her lids were so puffy her eyes were mere pinholes. "I'm sorry for . . . for everything." Tears ran down her cheeks, mixing with the blood splatter. "Everest, he was my baby. He could do no wrong."

My uncle's lips wobbled.

"But he did do a lot of wrong." Lucy's body shook anew, jangling all her bracelets. "And I helped him. And now he's gone."

My aunt's apology was so unexpected that it rooted me in place.

"Ness . . ." The urgency in August's voice broke the spell.

"Get her out of here, Jeb," I said. "In case—"

"We'll wait for you."

"Jeb, if she killed him, the Creeks will hunt her down."

Lucy released a whimper that had my uncle's face contorting with indecision.

"Go!" I hissed.

He jolted, then latched onto her arm and guided his ex-wife to the car. After he shut the door, he sprinted back toward me and crushed me against his chest.

In a rushed whisper, he said, "I'll come back for you. I promise."

I nodded. "Just keep her safe. Keep *yourself* safe."

He broke away and jogged to the car. As the van rumbled to life, I sent a silent prayer up into the heavens that someone would watch over them so they didn't end up in a ditch like their son.

I watched the car turn before drifting into the house behind August. As soon as I stepped into the foyer, I pushed out my senses for sounds other than my gunning pulse. A faint thump hit my eardrums.

"Did you hear that?" I whispered.

August nodded, narrowed gaze sweeping the house.

Canine whines and scratches ensued.

"Just his dogs," August murmured, but he nonetheless raised the umbrella he'd grabbed from beside the front door, positioning it over his head like a baseball bat, before stalking toward an open doorway.

When I realized he was following a trail of bloody footprints, my stomach contracted.

"Stay behind me, Ness," he said as we crept through the kitchen that was white and black like a checkered board, and glaringly bright.

The only color in the room was an abstract neon-yellow painting on the far wall and crimson droplets on the shiny floor. As we passed the knife rack, I grabbed a small paring blade that almost slipped out of my clammy fingers. The damp scent of blood wafted through the air, made my lungs cramp.

August was calm, his pulse barely speeding, a person used to the sight of carnage, a person used to storming into homes and seeking out criminals and corpses. He tipped his head toward a door smeared with red handprints, gaping like an open wound.

Were those Lucy's handprints?

Nausea made monochromatic dots dance in front of my eyes. I'd wanted the man dead, yet the idea of finding him swimming in a pool of blood had my stomach roiling. I flung my hand out to clutch the black marble island before I blacked out. The knife clattered from my fingers, and I heaved, but nothing came out.

August hissed my name.

"I'm okay," I murmured, blinking to clear my eyesight.

His concerned and lengthy gaze told me he didn't believe me.

"I promise," I added.

Another long second passed before he raised his hand to the door and drew it open. The hinges creaked like in a horror movie. He touched his ear, and I understood he was asking me to listen. I closed my eyes and concentrated.

A faint but steady thud had my eyes flying open.

Either there was someone else in the house or Aidan Michaels wasn't dead.

August nodded once in understanding, and then he started down the stairs just as an arm hooked my throat. I screamed as I was hauled backward.

August spun and lunged back up the stairs but froze on the landing.

A wet voice rasped against my temple, "I called Sandy . . . She's on her way."

Aidan's speech was slurred, as though he were gurgling on mouthwash. "So you go on . . . and leave now, Watt."

Something sharp prodded the skin on my neck. Without moving a muscle, I glanced down and caught sight of a glinting blade soaked in blood. I thought of my own knife and flexed my fingers, but then remembered I'd dropped it.

"Let Ness go, and we'll leave," August said calmly.

Aidan didn't let me go. The blade even nicked my skin.

For a brief second, I wondered if Lucy had set us up, but the pain in her eyes . . . her apology . . . *No*, she'd really tried to put an end to this man's life.

"Who do you . . . take me for?" Aidan's voice was jagged and slow. "The village idiot? Ness will be staying with me . . . until my pack arrives . . . to make sure no other . . . Boulder attacks me."

Something hot dripped down my neck, over my collarbone.

I needed to get out of Aidan's chokehold. I concentrated hard, trying to force magic into my extremities to sprout claws and fangs. As my neck thickened and lined with fur, the knife burrowed deeper into my flesh, and I yelped.

"Don't you shift," Aidan warned, his tinny breath reeking of death.

Howls sounded outside, and Aidan flicked his gaze to the doorway.

If his pack was here . . .

I stared at August, my eyes misting with tears.

If the Creeks were here . . . they would . . .

I shuddered, unable to bring myself to envision what they might do to us.

41

"This is your last chance, Michaels. Let her go or die." My navel pulsed with August's barely contained fury.

When claws clicked in the foyer, Aidan pulled me back, tightening his hold on my neck that was long and thin again, delicate . . . human.

Three furred beasts erupted into the kitchen, eyes aglow, thick bodies tensed, tails horizontal.

Boulders. Not Creeks!

The black wolf's lambent yellow eyes met mine, and relief careened up my spine.

Our wolves had come. Not Aidan's.

I used the distraction to my advantage.

Willing my nails to transform into claws, I shifted my hips to the side and swiped my paw between Aidan's legs. When my sharp claws pierced the fabric of his pants and met skin, he let out a shrill shriek, and the knife popped away from my skin. I whirled, and remembering what Liam had taught me, shoved Aidan's flailing limb under my armpit, clamping down on his elbow with both my palms to immobilize him.

Aidan's face had become a patchwork of whites and reds glossed over by sweat. He puffed out his cheeks and agitated his wrist. The blade scraped my shoulder before clattering onto the floor.

Suddenly, his body was torn out of my grip and airlifted. Even though he was still in skin, August snarled as loudly as the wolves circling us. He flipped Aidan around, squashed him against his chest, then wound his arm around the Creek's shoulder and cupped his chin.

Aidan's eyes bulged behind his glasses that sat askew on the bridge of his nose.

Our Alpha barked and then shouted into our minds: ***STOP! Don't kill him!***

August stared fixedly at Liam, and then at my neck, absorbed the cut that must've been deep because it was still dribbling blood. With a flick of his wrist, my mate snapped Aidan's neck.

NO! Liam's voice exploded inside my skull.

August unwrapped his bicep from around Aidan's shoulders, and the limp body of the man who'd destroyed my family crumpled, his cheek smacking the floor like a dead fish, his glasses tinkling against the stone like a Christmas ornament.

I squinted at his chest to see if it still rose and fell. Weren't we more difficult to kill?

In a croaky whisper that barely carried over Liam's barking, I asked, "Is he . . .?"

Ignoring our Alpha, August stepped over the prostrate body. And then his arms were around me and his face burrowed into my hair. "Yes. He's gone. He can never hurt you again. He's gone."

Both my neck and navel burned, one with blood and the other with fear and fury. The dregs of adrenaline made me shiver so hard my teeth rattled. All of my bones felt as though they were rattling.

"Are you sure?" I murmured.

"Sweetheart, I severed his windpipe. Even we can't—" A guttural *oomph* surged out of August as we rocketed forward, hitting the yellow painting on the wall. He cushioned the back of my skull with his palm, his knuckles getting the brunt of the blow.

What the? I peeked over his shoulder and found Liam back in skin, his incendiary gaze burning a hole into August's back.

"Liam!" I gasped at the same time August wheeled around, muscles twisting beneath his skin.

Our Alpha punched August in the jaw. "What part of *no* didn't you understand, Watt?"

August growled, "Aidan was a threat to the pack, and to Ness. He didn't deserve to live. He should've been killed six years ago!"

Liam snarled. "You don't realize what you've just done, do you?"

"I neutralized a threat."

"Neutralized a threat?" Liam snorted. "This isn't the fucking Marines, Watt!"

"Liam, calm down," I said

"*Calm down?*" He yanked on the roots of his hair as though trying to tear it off his scalp. "Do you not remember what we promised Morgan, Ness?"

What we'd promised Morgan?

What *had* we promised Morgan?

Oh . . .

Realization hit me as hard as a kick to the gut.

"Yeah." Liam bobbed his head a tad maniacally. "I hope you're ready to duel, because now, it'll be on their terms."

"What are you talking about?" August asked.

"I'm talking about the fact that we promised Morgan no harm would come to her son or her cousin until after the duel! I'm talking about the fact that if one of them died at our hands, then the choice of time reverted back to them! That's what

I'm talking about!" Spittle flew out of Liam's mouth and smacked August's grinding jaw.

"Lucy . . ." I whispered, my fingers coming up to my neck. Wetness slicked my shaky fingertips. "She's the one who attacked him. She's not a Boulder. We can pin the murder on her."

Liam's nostrils pulsed, and his shoulders still heaved, but his heart rate was slowing. I could feel the echo of it in my own chest. "Our smells are all over Aidan."

"We could burn him and his house down." The new voice had me peering past August's rigid arm.

Cole was crouched over Aidan's lifeless form, fully clothed, which told me he'd come by car. Matt and Lucas, though, prowled beside him, both in fur.

"Aidan said he called the Creeks," I said. "That they were on their way."

"He was bluffing." August's voice was alarmingly flat.

"How do you know?" I stepped around August whose temper had bled into his eyes, stamping out their natural brilliance.

"I've been around enough people like him."

The tether trembled between us as he hunted my expression. I realized he was trying to gauge my reaction to the chain of events Aidan's death would set in motion. I was scared—we weren't ready to face the Creeks—but I was also grateful that justice had finally been served. I caught the balled fist resting against his thigh and spread his stiff fingers with my own.

"August is right. They'd already be here if he'd called them," Cole added.

Liam backed away. "Burn the place down," he said before shifting back into fur.

He craned his neck and watched me through his yellow eyes. *Let's hope they'll believe Lucy did all this on her own. Cole, phone Rodrigo. Tell him to stall the firetrucks as long as he can.* He swung around. *Keep your phone on, Ness. I'm going to try and do some damage control. In case I can't . . .*

He let his voice trail off, but I heard all the absent words.

In case he couldn't talk sense into the Creeks, we'd be at their mercy.

42

I tugged on August's hand, trying to dislodge him from where he stood beside Cole, watching the fire devour Aidan's mansion. They'd splashed a variety of chemicals throughout the house, over the expensive drapes framing his large windows, over the wooden furniture. The flames skipped around the trails of flammable liquids, growing rabid.

I heard Aidan's hounds howl. I'd broken the window of the study in which he or Lucy had locked them, hoping they'd find their way out. I hadn't dared open the door, afraid their master had trained them to scent Boulder blood and attack.

"We need to go," Cole said, heading to his navy sedan.

August got in the back with me, his arm wound tight around my shoulders.

"I'm glad he's dead," I whispered so he'd stop torturing himself.

"It was the right call," Cole said as he sped down the darkened roads toward the warehouse.

Grunting, August set his attention on the moonless sky. Even the stars seemed darker tonight. At some point, he squeezed the bridge of his nose and closed his eyes, so I cupped his jaw.

"Look at me," I said.

He did.

"My aunt fled. After cozying up to him, she fled. They'll connect the dots and blame her."

"What if they don't, Dimples? What if they don't?"

"We were going to duel them anyway. It was a matter of days."

He made a low growly sound in the back of his throat and punched the headrest of the empty passenger seat. "We don't even know the outcome of the Sillin injection. What if that's not Morgan's *trick*?"

"Maybe Sarah found out something."

"Sarah?" Cole asked. "I thought she'd turned to the dark side."

Of course he'd think this. "I know that's what Liam and Lucas think, but I don't."

Cole's gaze flashed to mine in the rearview mirror. "She set us up to help her new pack steal the Sillin."

When August frowned, I recapped all that had happened, from the concealed missive inside my birthday present to the theft.

"Why didn't you tell me before?" he asked.

"Because I didn't want to worry you," I mumbled.

He twisted around on the seat to peer down at me. "It wouldn't have worried me. What worries me is you carrying the weight of this on your own." He pushed a lock of hair off my face. "I'm here for you."

He'd always been there for me.

I attempted a smile but failed miserably. He settled back against the seat and pulled me into him.

"Cole, can you get in touch with her?" I asked, my voice cracking around each word, as though the knife had damaged my vocal cords.

He scrutinized me a long minute before offering, "I can message her from a remote number when I get home. What do you want to know?"

"If she's all right." I wish I'd thought of asking Lucy.

I took my phone out of my pocket and dialed Jeb. His phone didn't even ring, which made me think he'd turned it off. Or maybe he'd tossed it so he couldn't be tracked.

"And if maybe"—I flipped my phone around, then flipped it again—"if maybe she found out how they're planning on using the Sillin."

He nodded.

Everything had gone from bad to shit so quickly, and yet, I feared we hadn't reached rock bottom.

Soon, Cole was pulling in next to the warehouse. "I'll call you if I get news."

"Okay," I said, scooting out after August. As Cole drove off, August wrapped his arm around my waist, and together, we walked toward his front door.

He punched in his code, and the door beeped open. After he entered, he let go of me and paced while I turned the lights on.

"Let's go away. You and me," he said suddenly. "We can leave tonight."

"August, I can't leave."

"So you want to see Liam die?"

I swallowed. "Liam won't die."

"Ness—"

"He won't. He's stronger than you give him credit for."

"Strength won't help him if she's cheating!"

"Don't yell, August."

He dropped into his armchair and cradled his head between his large, blood-soaked hands. "I'm sorry," he whispered. "I'm sorry."

I went over to him and placed my palm on his hunched spine. He sighed, long and hard, and then he pulled me into his lap and hugged me, burying his face against my collarbone. After several quiet minutes, he pulled away and leveled his gaze on my injured neck. I probably looked like I'd escaped from the set of a slasher film.

"Bet this wasn't quite how you pictured our romantic lakeside evening going," I said, curling my fingers around the nape of his neck.

He grunted, and I flicked him. Although it brought a little light to his eyes, it wasn't nearly enough to disperse the shadows teeming in them.

I stood up and extended my hand. "Come on. Let's go wash away all this blood."

Exhaling raggedly, he took my hand and rose. On the way to the bathroom, he said, "We need to burn our clothes."

Right. Aidan's blood was all over them.

August yanked off his shirt, jeans, and briefs, and dumped everything in the kitchen sink. While I unclipped my overalls and pulled off my crop top, he walked over to the wall and used a pole to open two of the hopper windows.

Even though it was probably not the time to appreciate his naked body, I couldn't help myself from taking him in.

"Your underwear too," he said, coming back toward me.

"My underwear?"

"It'll smell like smoke."

Nibbling my lip, I lowered my thong to the ground, then scooped it up and added it to the soiled pile. He grabbed a bottle of vodka from his freezer, doused the fabric, then struck a match and tossed it in. Flames burst to life and spread, consuming the last pieces of the terrible night.

"Go," he said. "I'll keep an eye on the fire until it burns out."

Hoping the spectacle would rid him of his lingering anguish, I went into the bathroom and stepped inside the enormous shower.

Hot water spurted out of the rain-shower nozzle, raced down my hair and over my skin, dragging away the blood and smoke. I closed my eyes and didn't move for a long moment. How had we gone from playing with paint to arson?

I touched my sides, felt the white paint that had dried there. Large fingers pressed mine away and curved around my ribs. I opened my eyes but didn't turn. August reached around me for a bar of green soap that he dragged over my body. He worked the woodsy sandalwood into a lather over my collarbone and shoulders. When his palm coasted up my neck, I cringed, and he gentled his touch. Without saying a single word, he dragged the slick bar over my breasts, then over my stomach, and circled his calloused palm over my soapy skin.

When his hands drifted lower, I rested my cheek against his shoulder and closed my eyes again. Sensations rose like steam, curling through my veins, warming my blood, billowing through my stomach, and expanding in my chest. I relaxed against August's solid chest, my breathing slowing as his fingers moved against me. When his mouth nipped mine, I dragged my heavy lids up and crooked my neck.

The sable and green eddied as he stared at me, watching . . . waiting.

Pressure built and swelled everywhere, and then I was soaring over a cliff into a lake full of moon and stars, the wondrous sensation buffing away the horror of my strange world.

As my body softened, as my moans quieted, he spun me in his arms, my wet skin sliding like silk against his. I hooked my hands around his bent neck and pushed onto my tiptoes, guiding his mouth to mine.

Our kiss was gentle at first, but soon his lips crushed mine, devouring me the same way the flames had devoured one monstrous Creek.

43

The shower had rid August of a layer of stress, which wasn't to say he was calm. He was anything but. His upheaval worsened when my phone rang, and Liam's name appeared on the screen.

I answered the call on speakerphone and sat down on the couch. August wound his arm around me and pulled me close.

There was rustling, as though Liam were taking off his jacket. "I just came back from the inn."

"And?" I asked.

"And the duel will take place tomorrow evening."

August's fingers flexed on my waist. "She didn't believe it was Lucy?"

For a moment, Liam didn't answer, as though he hadn't expected me to have company. "Oh, no. She believed it, Watt. Apparently Lori repeatedly warned her mom that Lucy was ill-intentioned."

I blinked. "Then why are we fighting them tomorrow?"

"Because she asked me to call Jeb so he would bring Lucy in, and I refused to sacrifice your aunt."

I didn't say anything.

Something thumped on his end of the line. A shoe, maybe. "Would you rather I make Jeb bring her in?"

"No." Lucy was far from my favorite person, but her courage to avenge her son had changed my opinion of her. Besides, I couldn't do that to Jeb. A divorce surely hadn't erased years of tenderness and love.

Liam sighed. "That's what I thought. Come over in the morning so we can figure out how to win this damn fight."

"Want me to come over now?" Trepidation distorted the sound of my voice.

"No. I need to think."

"Try to sleep," I whispered.

"You, too."

I didn't think I could sleep. I didn't think Liam could either.

"I'm sorry it took so long for your dad to be avenged, Ness," Liam said. "I'm sorry I was too much of a coward to do it myself."

I swallowed down the ball of emotion rising in my throat. "You're not a coward."

He let out a rattling breath.

"Liam, when you were at the inn, did you see Sarah?" I asked.

"No."

Worry suspended my breaths for a few heartbeats. "Did you ask them about our Sillin?"

"I did. They said they took what was theirs."

"They took more—"

"I was in no position to negotiate!"

His tone made guilt well up inside me.

"I'll see you tomorrow," he said, a tad less gruffly, and then he hung up.

August pressed his mouth against my temple. Then, suddenly, he rose and pulled me up. "Go into the kitchen."

I frowned. "What? Why?"

"Because I have an idea."

I sniffled. "Okay."

While I walked toward one end of the apartment, he went to stand by the other.

"I'm going to test my reach," he said.

My eyebrows jolted up, and then I gasped as my body jerked forward. I caught myself on the island. "That was really . . . *strong*."

His eyes gleamed as he strode toward the front door and extended his hand. "Let's try it in the warehouse."

The T-shirt I'd borrowed from his closet twisted against the tops of my bare thighs as I followed him into the night and into the cavernous building that smelled of sawdust and wood varnish and home.

After turning on a row of industrial lights, he said, "Stay here," then padded down one of the aisles. When he reached the farthest shelving unit, he turned and concentrated on me.

A moment later, I felt a hard tug that had my bare feet shuffling over the cool concrete. Unlike in the apartment, he didn't let go of his hold. He reeled me in.

"Dig your heels in, Ness. I want to see how much strength I can exert."

"I *am* digging my heels in," I called out.

He pulled my body halfway across the warehouse before slackening his magical grip, and then he strode toward me, a new spring in his step.

"At least I can keep you safe tomorrow." He locked his arms around my waist and rested his forehead against mine. "This way, you can concentrate on keeping Liam safe."

My thundering pulse beat against the delicate, knitted skin of my neck as his hope enveloped me.

"Good thing I desire you so much, huh?" Even though his tone was light and no blame limned his words, I couldn't help but sense his underlying sadness.

He still believed I didn't reciprocate the intensity of his feelings.

After the duel . . . once my mind was clear and my heart didn't beat with trepidation . . . I'd show him just how much *I* desired him.

44

August and I spent the night lying in his bed, talking about the past, about the present, but not about the future. Whenever he'd venture into the unknown territory of the days ahead, I'd steer the conversation back to the here and now.

I feared what the next few hours would bring.

I feared all it might change.

At some point, I drifted, but a nightmare had me springing awake with a gasp.

August's heavy arm anchored me to the warm mattress. When I shivered, he pulled me closer and whispered, "You're safe, Dimples."

Dimples . . . I no longer minded when he called me by his favorite nickname. Perhaps it was the alluring tone with which he spoke the word, or perhaps it was because I no longer doubted how deeply he craved me.

I turned in his arms. "I should get up. I need clothes. And my car."

August combed a lock of hair off my forehead.

"Your truck's at my house, too." *Shoot.*

"How about you relax here while I go get one of our cars?"

"*Relax?*" I snorted.

He flicked the tip of my nose.

"Hey," I chided him.

Smiling, he kissed the spot he'd flicked. "You grunted."

"You did just tell me to relax."

Meaning to be reassuring, he said, "It'll be over soon."

It was the absolute opposite of comforting. His words made my stomach writhe with more nerves; they made my heart thump with more anguish.

"We should really get going," I said, scooting out from underneath his arm to crawl off the bed and down the ladder. "Can I borrow a pair of boxers? I feel a little naked."

He climbed down the ladder slowly, every muscle in his back roiling alluringly. I'd put on muscle in the past two and a half weeks, but I had nothing on August. Not that I wanted his body. Well, I did, just not—What was I rambling on about?

I added a pair of boxers underneath the T-shirt that tented around my body, then gathered my phone and bag while he got dressed in his fatigues and an oatmeal Henley that hugged his upper body.

He leaned over and kissed me. I savored the sweet interlude, sensing that once I walked out August's front door, there would be no more sweetness to this day.

He called a cab, which took us back to my house. As the cab bumped up my cracked driveway, I thought about how I needed to get the road fixed, and then I stopped thinking about asphalt and seized up. I must've gasped because August's attention jerked off the wad of cash he'd taken out of his pocket to pay for our ride. He trailed my line of sight, his jaw hardening when he saw what I was looking at.

"Whoa. Wild party?" the cabby asked.

Stuffing a bill into the driver's hand, August kicked the door open and got out. "Yeah," he answered gruffly.

When I still hadn't moved, he leaned over to pluck the fingers I'd balled into a hard fist and towed me out. I stumbled, because my joints had locked as tight as my knuckles.

Last night, in our haste, we'd left the front door wide open, and someone—more than one person from the looks of it—had let themselves in.

Anger fired through me. I ripped my hand from August's and stalked inside my home. Smells assaulted me—sweet metal, charred dust, sour urine. The white walls had been smeared in blood—deer blood, from the loamy odor of it—and acrid black ash. Puddles of ochre piss glistened on the plastic tarp and browned the baseboards August had so painstakingly painted.

This was payback for Aidan's death. The Creeks must've seen my uncle working on the house and assumed it was his and Lucy's.

"I will *kill* whoever did this," I whispered.

I started down the hallway to inspect the extent of the destruction, but August caught my arm and held me back. "Let's go."

"I want to see—"

"You've seen enough. Let's go." When I didn't move, he added, "Now."

Gritting my teeth, I turned around and headed back out of my stinking kingdom. *How. Dare. They.*

"I'll follow you in my—" He froze by the truck's bed.

Two eviscerated deer carcasses haloed by black flies had been heaped inside. A slew of words that would make his mother's curse jar overflow spewed from his mouth. He unlatched the tailgate, then seized the hooves of one creature and yanked hard. The animal landed on the grass with an awful thud. As he wrenched the second one out, I peered through the windows of his car.

"August!" I gasped.

Something viscous oozed down the backrest and dripped on the seat that was covered in animal intestines.

His eyes turned a murderous shade of black. "Check your car," he said, his voice as sharp as the knife blade Aidan had held against my throat yesterday.

I sprang toward my silver SUV. Thankfully the doors were all locked, and the vandals hadn't shattered any windows, but they'd raked their claws through the silver paint, leaving grooves *everywhere*.

"Those fucking Creeks," August growled from behind me.

We stared at the destruction a moment longer, and then he snatched my palm tree keychain and opened the passenger door for me.

He didn't say anything as he drove too quickly down the quiet Boulder streets toward my apartment. Fear that it, too, had been defaced made me wring the life out of the grab handle.

The second I stepped over the threshold, I exhaled the breath I'd been holding since leaving my house. August walked to the sink and lathered his hands with dish detergent, scrubbing his skin until it turned pink. After almost a minute, he shut the water off and tore the dish cloth hanging on the oven handle.

"I'll fix your house." His eyes were animated with the same ferocity I'd spied last night when Aidan held me hostage.

I wanted to tell August he didn't need to do that, that I'd do it myself, but nausea roiled in my stomach at the memory of the blood and piss, so I clamped my lips shut. As he lifted his cell phone to his ear, I went to change into shorts, a tank top, and my black hoodie. I took off my necklace and buried it in my underwear drawer, then stuffed my feet inside my scuffed boots. Even though we'd sprayed our shoes with air freshener last night to camouflage any lingering smells, I thought it safer to wear some that hadn't been in contact with blood and smoke.

Suddenly, a horrific thought speared my mind, and I sprinted out of my bedroom. "August!"

He dropped the phone, and it clattered against the floor but didn't break. "What?"

"You need to get out of Boulder!"

His eyes, which had widened with panic, now crimped with confusion.

"They sabotaged your pickup, which means they know you were involved." The words rushed out of my mouth.

His eyebrows pinched closer together, darkening his already murky gaze. "I don't care."

"What if they try to hurt you during the duel? Or after the duel? Or—"

"Sweetheart"—he gripped the back of my neck—"I'm angry but I'm not scared. If anyone should be scared, it should be the people who did this, because, mark my words, I'll find out who was involved." His fingers were hot and unyielding. "Besides, how can you even think I'd run away without you?"

I bit my lip. "Fine, but tonight, during the duel, you need to look out for yourself, or I'm not letting you come."

Smirking, he chucked me under the chin.

"What?" I asked.

"Not letting me come . . ." He *tsk*ed and shook his head. "I respect the hell out of you, Dimples, and I know you're strong, but don't *ever* ask me to stay away or flee. It's insulting."

I crossed my arms. "I didn't mean it as an insult."

He nodded, smirk gone. "I know."

"I'm scared, August."

"I know." Sighing, he pried my arms out of their tight knot. "But don't worry about me. I'll be fine. Everything will be—"

"*Don't!*" My heart jolted into my throat and beat there. "Don't finish that sentence!"

He frowned.

"It never comes true."

Dipping his chin into his neck, he gathered my stiff body in his arms and held me.

Just held me.

And I held him.

Until my heart settled back behind my ribs. Until my pulse quieted. Until my temper appeased and my muscles stopped spasming. Until I was ready to take on the outside world again.

45

Before going over to Liam's, I called Evelyn because I wanted to see her.

I *needed* to see her.

She told me she was already at the restaurant, prepping for their popular Sunday brunch, so we drove there. While August parked the car, I went inside and straight into the kitchen. I hugged her before even saying *hi*, which wasn't smart of me. Instantly, her pleasure at my visit wilted into concern.

Her all-seeing eyes skipped over all my haggard features. I hadn't bothered improving my appearance with makeup this morning, so I knew I looked part ghost, part zombie, possibly worse than when I'd gone "rock-climbing" on my own, which had been the story fed to Evelyn when I'd been returned to her after the first Alpha trial.

"*Querida*, what is wrong?"

I shrugged. "I didn't sleep well. That's all."

She hunted my face some more, seeking the truth I was holding back.

Did she know about Aidan? Did she know that my uncle was gone? Did she know there would be a duel tonight?

"You do not fool me, Ness Clark. That is *not* all."

From the worry tightening her crimson lips, I guessed Frank hadn't imparted any of those things. I was glad he'd protected her. I hoped he would shield her from the world for the rest of her life in case I wasn't there to do it myself.

The thought made my heart drop to somewhere below my ankles.

Seconds rarely engage, I reminded myself, but then I also reminded myself that I would be facing Justin.

Justin delighted in hurting people.

"It is. I promise." I smiled but then followed the arc of her gaze as it moved to a place above my shoulder.

I glanced over my shoulder. Biting my lip, I turned back toward Evelyn. I hadn't even considered how it would look arriving with August so early on a Sunday morning.

On any morning, for that matter.

I hesitated to lie and tell her we were on our way to work on my house, but I didn't want to risk her coming there after her shift.

"Morning, Mrs. Lopez." He didn't touch me, but his body heated my taut spine.

Without taking her eyes off mine, she said, "Good morning, August."

Her sous-chef glanced our way, a giant knife rocking rhythmically against a white onion, dicing the slimy flesh into tiny little squares that flecked the air with stinging fumes.

Even though Evelyn had given me her blessing two nights ago, I sensed it would take her a little more time to accept August and me together. "There is a waitlist for the brunch, but I am sure I could find you two a table."

I smiled. "We can't do brunch today. I just came by to say hi."

Her thin eyebrows writhed a few times. "Dinner then? Tonight. At the house. I would like"—she fixed her eyes on August again—"I would like to get to know the man my baby girl has decided to let into her heart."

God only knew in what state we'd be tonight. I slipped my pinky's fingernail between my lips and chewed on the edge of it. "Tomorrow would be better. The restaurant's closed on Monday nights too, right?"

She nodded. "Before you leave, Trent's wife wanted very much to meet you. She is in the dining room. Will you go out there and introduce yourself, please?"

I took my pinky out of my mouth. "Sure." I kissed her cheek and then turned to leave.

When August started after me, Evelyn called him back. "Can I speak to you a moment longer, August?"

I cringed, but August squeezed my arm in reassurance. I mouthed, *good luck*, which kicked up one side of his mouth.

There were three women in the dining room. One of them had served us the night of my birthday, so I assumed she wasn't Trent's wife.

"Hi, I'm looking for—" I racked my brain for the family name but wasn't sure if I even knew it, so I went with: "Trent's wife?"

The waitress tipped her head toward a woman clipping the stems of poppies on the mirrored bar.

"Thank you," I whispered as I traipsed toward the blonde with a sharp bob cut. "Hi. I'm Ness. Evelyn's granddaughter."

The woman twirled away from her flowery spread and extended her hand. "Ness!"

I blinked as she smiled at me.

When I still hadn't taken her outstretched hand—because shock had made me forget my manners—she said, "It's not contagious. I promise."

I jolted my hand into hers and shook it. "I'm sorry. It's not—What, *um* . . . how come . . . ?"

"My lips are blue and my nails purple?" Her smile was still intact. "I have something called Argyria, which is sort of ironic considering the name of my restaurant."

I slipped my hand out of hers and gripped the crossbody strap of my bag.

"Anyway, it's my dentist's fault. He put all these silver fillings in my molars . . . I won't bore you with the details, but know that it looks way worse than it is. I'm Molly, by the way."

I tried to snap my jaw shut, but it wouldn't close. "*I'msorryI'mstaring*," I said in a single breath.

"It's okay, honey. A lot of people do. Besides, if it truly bothered me, I'd wear makeup."

"I know this woman who has the same thing," I blurted out. "At least, I think it's the same thing. She told me it was a birthmark."

"Yeah, some people are a little embarrassed by the condition." She fingered one of the poppies' fuzzy stems. "Tell her that if she needs someone to talk to, she can find me here most days. Especially now that the kids are back in school." She gave me one last smile. "I should get these flowers into water before they wilt. It was a pleasure to make your acquaintance, and thank you again for lending us your grandmother. She is a godsend."

"Thank *you*," I said. And I didn't mean for employing Evelyn—even though I *was* grateful for that—but for giving me the answer to a question which had tormented me for the past two and a half weeks.

My speculations were accurate—Cassandra Morgan *had* poisoned Julian. But not with Sillin. With silver! I wasn't sure yet how her blood could contain the toxic metal without killing her, but it didn't matter.

We could call the duel off now that I had proof she was cheating.

As Molly turned back toward her flowers, August came out of the kitchen.

I rushed to him and threw my arms around his neck, waves of relief coursing through me, breaking the stress that had devoured me since Liam's phone call.

"Were you worried I wouldn't survive?" August asked, a lilt to his voice. "It *was* a close call."

Smiling, I pressed away from him, crooked my head up, and whispered, "I know how she did it."

A groove appeared between his eyebrows. "We're not talking about Evelyn now, are we?"

I shook my head. "I'll explain everything on the drive over to Liam's."

<h1 style="text-align:center">46</h1>

* * *

August whipped his eyes off the road to stare at me. "Silver? In her blood?"

"It's called Argyria." I gasped as a memory collided into my brain. "Trent's mother told me about it. The day I met her in the bank."

To think I'd known all along . . .

I watched the dashboard without seeing it. Thank God I wasn't at the wheel of the car; I would've been incapable of staying on the road.

"How can she have silver in her blood, yet still be alive?" he asked.

Something niggled at me. What was it?

I spun toward him as my synapses fired off a hypothesis. "After Dad was shot, I was given Sillin because I'd licked his gunshot wound." Bile rose in the back of my throat. "What if that's why she needs Sillin? To neutralize the silver."

His brows rose. "Still doesn't explain how she can shift."

"Does silver impair shifting?"

"No, but Sillin does."

"You don't think that she's somehow figured out a dose that cancels each substance out?"

"We'd have to ask Greg. Although I'm not sure he'd even know."

I rested my head back and expelled a sigh, which made August reach over the center console and pluck my restless fingers off the latch on my bag.

To think of something else for a short while, I asked, "What did Evelyn want?"

"She asked me the real reason you'd stopped by."

"You didn't tell her, did you?"

"No. I told her you came to check whether she was truly okay with *us* being together."

"I'm sorry you had to lie."

He squeezed my fingers. "Some lies are kinder than some truths."

As we turned down Liam's driveway, I asked, "Is your dad home?"

"Not yet. He's coming back today."

Through the picture window, I spotted Liam sitting on his couch. Cole, Matt, and Lucas were there too. I was glad Liam wasn't alone. I didn't hear any human heartbeats, so I guessed Tamara wasn't around.

I started to disengage my fingers from August's, but he held on to them.

I smiled at him. "Can't get out of the car if I'm holding your hand."

"I'm worried what'll happen once I let go."

"Once you let go?"

His gaze shifted toward Liam.

Oh. "I'm yours, August."

"Say it again," he whispered, his tone an octave deeper.

"I'm yours." I leaned over and kissed him, sensing several sets of eyes on us.

My promise combined with the kiss loosened his fingers but didn't do much to ease the tension in his shoulders.

Liam's front door was open. As I strutted inside, all eyes turned to me. Probably because I was giving off *way-too-cheery* vibes.

Lucas's scarred eyebrow hiked up. "How many bowls of Lucky Charms did you ingest this morning?"

I rolled my eyes and then announced, "I know how Cassandra killed Julian!" I said it so loudly Morgan herself probably heard me all the way back at the inn.

Liam, who'd been sitting a little hunched, straightened.

"She's been poisoning herself with silver."

The silence that ensued was deafening.

"Forget the Lucky Charms, what the fuck have you been smoking?" Lucas asked.

I shot him a genial scowl. "What she has on her mouth isn't a birthmark. Silver poisoning causes lips and nails to turn blue." They all stared at me as though I'd morphed into a squirrel.

"That's impossible, Clark," Lucas said. "Silver kills us."

"Not if you take Sillin to balance it out," I countered, feeling more and more certain about my theory.

"If she's ingesting Sillin, then there's no way she can shift," Cole said.

Their mood was seriously starting to put a damper on mine. "Liam, remember her story about the toxic waste poisoning? What if the toxin was silver? What if she somehow built an immunity to it? Would that be possible?"

"What toxic waste poisoning?" August asked. The first words he'd uttered since stepping inside Liam's house. He was leaning against a wall, long sleeves pushed up to his elbows, arms crossed in front of his chest.

Lucas tipped his head in my direction. "The day she went to have tea at the inn with Morgan—"

August's expression darkened. "You went to the inn?"

"Yes, but not for a tea party." This time, there was nothing amiable about the scowl I shot Lucas. "I went to talk to her about canceling the duel, which she refused. And then she filled me in on her pack's history. She told me that what decimated the original Creeks was their water source. Apparently, it was polluted." I perked up again as an idea materialized. "Is there a way to see the topography of their old territory? Maybe there's a mine, or a news article."

"Cole?" Liam said. "Can you look it up?"

Cole nodded and went to take a seat at the game table where a laptop was already powered on. As he clicked away on the keypad, I walked over to him.

"Can you shift?" Liam's voice was taut and low.

I glanced over my shoulder.

"No," August said.

"When did you do the injection again?"

"Nine days ago."

"Have you tried shifting this morning?"

"Yes. It didn't work."

"Show me."

"Why?" Tendons writhed beneath the skin of his forearms. "You think I'm lying?"

A nerve ticked in Liam's jaw. "Greg will be over soon. He can test your blood to see how much Sillin's left."

Wishing those two could bury the hatchet, I sighed and returned my attention to Cole's computer screen.

"So . . . anything?" Matt asked, slinking toward me as though to move as far away as possible from Liam and August.

Windows were popping open on the computer, one over the other, and then a map appeared. Cole zoomed in, then clicked on something that turned the flat map 3-dimensional.

He squinted at the screen before leaning back in his chair and clucking his tongue. "So Ness is a little genius."

My skin prickled. "There's a mine?"

"There's a mine. A silver mine. And a bunch of class action suits filed to have it shut down by a certain Henry Morgan."

"Was that Cassandra's father?"

"Uncle." Liam's breath burst against my temple.

So concentrated on the screen, I hadn't heard him come up behind me.

"He was the Creek Alpha at the time," Lucas explained.

I turned toward my Alpha, goose bumps scattering over my arms from the thrill of our discovery. "Liam, you realize this means we can call the duel off?"

His eyes gleamed as brightly as his teeth, which were on full display.

His smile unsettled me. "What?"

"Babe, we're not calling it off. Thanks to you, we now know how to defeat her."

My stomach hardened like a fist. "Thanks to me, we know how she cheated. We have no clue how to beat her."

"Of course we do. By not getting any of her silver-tainted blood in us." Liam backed up and started pacing the cowhide rug. "Julian bit her. That was the beginning of his end. I won't bite her."

I gasped, not okay at all with the turn of events. "How are you going to kill her if you don't bite her?"

"Claws. I'll use my claws."

"What if she wounds you and rubs her blood into your wound?"

"I heal fast."

"You said wounds inflicted by Alphas take longer to heal," I sputtered.

"I'll make sure to keep away until my skin seals shut. Besides, you saw her. She's slow and not particularly strong." He stopped pacing, beelined toward me, and then scooped me up and spun me. "Fuck, Ness, we got this."

When he set me down, my head spun, but not only from the sudden movement. It spun from dread. There were still so many risks . . . And then, because having a headache wasn't bad enough, my navel began to burn as though someone were jabbing it with a fiery poker.

August pushed off the wall and shot toward Liam. "You're a selfish prick, Kolane."

Liam wrenched his shoulders back and got into August's face. "A selfish prick?"

"You think you got this, but what if you don't? You won't be the only one in that ring tonight."

"Seconds don't engage," Liam spat out.

"Have you fucking met Morgan's Second?" August snapped.

I squeezed myself between both males and pushed them away from each other. "Stop it. Both of you."

"August is right, Liam," Matt said. "Justin's a sick fuck."

"We know what their edge is," Liam exclaimed. "We're going to beat them at their own game."

I slid my hands off their battering chests and whirled to face Liam. "Stop calling it a game. It's not!"

His excitement dimmed. *Finally!*

"It was a manner of speaking, Ness."

"Was it? Because if memory serves me, you called it a game the day we signed up."

His voice lowered, and more light left his eyes. "I hadn't been referring to the duel then."

August's chest brushed up against my shoulder blades.

I stared long and hard at Liam. "None of it was ever a game to me, all right?"

"I'll take her place," August said. "I'll be your Second."

"No!" I spun around.

"Don't believe she can hold her own out there, Watt?" Liam asked.

August's gaze sharpened on Liam. "This has nothing to do with what I think of Ness," he said in a chillingly low voice, "and everything to do with what I think of Justin."

"*I* signed up for this. *I'll* see it through." I turned back around. "If I have to," I added. "I still think we should call them up on their cheating and chase them off our land."

"They own the inn and all the Pine territory," Liam said, eyes locked on August's, "so chasing them off our land won't get them out of Boulder."

Pine territory! "Cole, did you get in touch with Sarah?"

"No, but Liam received a message from Avery."

"Avery?" I asked.

"The Rivers' contact," Cole said.

"I remember who he is," I said. "I meant, why did he send us a message?"

"Because he heard Alex Morgan talk about *having put the two-timing Pine bitch in her place*, and he believes Alex is talking about Sarah since he's seen them together," Liam said.

Dread curled through me. "In her place?"

"I don't know what that means," Liam said. "He doesn't either, but he's trying to find out."

Fear for Sarah superseded everything else in that moment. I pressed a fist against my mouth. "Oh my God."

Lucas careened toward the door. "I can track her smell."

"No," Liam said. "We stay put. Avery's there. He said he's working on it, and I trust he is."

My head jerked back. "He didn't even want to get involved, yet you trust he's helping us?"

"People change their minds all the time." When his eyes lifted to August, I wondered if Liam was talking about Avery or about me.

A thought struck me. However much I wanted to call this duel off, I couldn't abandon Sarah to the Morgans. But Liam couldn't turn the Creeks into Boulders without ingesting Cassandra's heart. "Let's say we go through with the duel, and you win—"

"I will win."

His conviction made me purse my lips. It also made August's pulse spike and hammer my tight spine.

"Have a little faith in me, Ness."

"Okay. Fine. What happens after you win? How exactly are you planning on eating her heart?"

A corner of his mouth curled. "With my teeth."

I rolled my eyes. "Don't be dense. If her blood's full of silver, then her heart is too."

"Little Wolf's right," Matt said.

"I'll have it injected with Sillin. Or I'll inject myself with Sillin. Greg would know. You brought it?"

I pulled the tablets out of my bag just as the front door opened and Greg stepped in.

Liam smirked. "Look at that. I speak his name and he appears. We were just talking about you."

Surprise crinkled the fine lines around the doctor's eyes. Or maybe it was concern. "And what were you discussing?"

"We were discussing how you're going to purge a heart of silver without purging it of blood. You know, so I can eat it."

47

Greg scrutinized the screen of the portable device in which he'd just inserted a drop of August's blood. "Down by a little more than a half. You should be Sillin-free by the next full moon."

Considering the duel was tonight, it was a good thing I hadn't been the guinea-pig in the experiment.

"Can you shift at all?" Greg asked, putting away the handheld machine.

August, who was sitting at the game table between Cole and the doctor, palmed his cropped hair. "No."

"Can you get your claws to come out?"

Studying the ball of cotton he held to the puncture wound on the inside of his elbow, he said, "No."

"Did it affect the mating link?"

August raised his gaze to me. "No."

I was standing by the windowed wall, alternately watching the males behind me and the ones on the other side of the glass. Ever since Greg told Liam that injecting him with a hefty dose of Sillin at the end of the duel—not as hefty as what he'd given August, because we didn't have enough pills left for that—would counteract the silver in Cassandra's blood, Liam was mentally and physically psyching himself up for the duel.

Both he and Matt had shed their clothes and morphed into fur. For the past half hour, they'd been battling relentlessly. Liam wasn't immune to Matt's blows—he tumbled and winced—but he'd hop back on his paws and give as good as he got.

Better.

But then, they were play-acting.

However violent the fight, it wasn't real.

I lifted my gaze to the miles of swaying pines that separated Liam's property from the Inn, wondering what the Creeks were doing at this exact moment. Vandalizing more of our homes, burying Aidan's ashes, or preparing to face-off with us?

As Lucas came to stand next to me, I hugged my torso. "Sarah got with Alex to help us. She hates him."

He watched Matt catch Liam's hind leg and flip him onto his back.

"How do you feel, by the way?" I asked.

"Fucking relieved."

I couldn't help smiling a little at his answer. "Not about Sarah."

"Oh." A blush streaked his cheeks.

"I meant, since you ran into Alex Morgan's fist."

"Murderous, but otherwise, good."

"For what he did to you or what he might've done to her?"

His eyebrows slanted behind his shaggy, black hair. "Both."

We went back to our silent but companionable observation of Liam and Matt.

At some point, Lucas said, "I know you're worried, but Liam's skilled and quick. Have you ever noticed how fast he moves? Like those vampires in the shows chicks love to watch."

I side-eyed him. "I'm not sure I'm familiar with those shows. Why don't you tell me more about them?"

He started to walk me through the plot of one, but then he caught my dimples excavating my cheeks and stopped.

"Don't worry. I won't tell Sarah about your secret obsession with vampires."

A brighter blush slashed his cheeks. "You're a real pain in my furry ass."

"But surprisingly endearing, right?"

He shot me a look, which was probably supposed to be scathing, if it weren't for his crooked smile. "Surprisingly so."

I knocked my shoulder into his, and his mouth curved a little more.

"You know what's crazy?" I asked after a while.

"I think you should rephrase your question to: do you know what *isn't* crazy?"

"Probably." I bobbed my head. "Anyway, if we win tonight, I'll go from being the only female in my pack to being one of many females."

"Oh, the horror."

I shoved him again. "Watch it, Mason."

He chuckled quietly.

Ness, get out here and shift.

I jumped at Liam's command.

And no getting naked behind closed doors. When I still hadn't moved, he pawed the ground. ***Now.***

Heat spiraled through my body.

"What?" Lucas asked.

"Liam wants me to"—I uncrossed my arms, because coupled with the hoodie and Liam's order, I was getting hot—"join them."

Lucas frowned. "Can't hurt to train a little more."

"That's not—*um* . . ." I pulled on the collar of the hoodie but still couldn't get myself to peel it off.

The black wolf barked, which made me jump, and then he pawed the earth again.

"Go on," Lucas said.

Pressing my palms, which were thankfully a little cold, against my neck, I unglued my soles from the hardwood floors and stalked out the front door. "I said I'd do it tonight, and I will."

Now.

My body felt as though it were impaled on a spit hung over an open fire. "Why?"

The shimmering blue rope that connected me to August tightened as he stepped out of the house, Lucas at his side. At least Cole and Greg hadn't come to watch, not that they couldn't see me through the window.

"Please, Liam—"

You're a werewolf, Ness. Act like one.

I bristled. "Fine." I pulled off the hoodie and tossed it on the ground, then unlaced my boots and kicked them off.

When I reached for the hem of my tank top, August trampled the grass until he stood in front of me. "What are you doing?"

"Acting like a werewolf, apparently," I gritted out, yanking off the top, exposing my bare chest.

August's nostrils flared, and he snapped his head toward Liam. "If I want to stand in front of her, I'll stand in front of her." I guessed Liam had told August to move through the mind-link. "I get that tonight she'll be on her own." He returned his attention to me, his chest all but squashing my bare breasts.

I'd rather have been waxed from muzzle to paw than strip in front of an audience, but Liam was right, I was a shifter, and nudity wasn't taboo in our circle. It was a way of life.

I sighed and splayed my palms on August's pecs to press him away, but it was like trying to displace a block of cement.

"I can do this," I told him.

The green around his irises seemed to glow brighter, as though his wolf was somehow rising to the surface in spite of the Sillin.

I took a step back as I popped the button of my shorts and dropped them. When my thumbs hooked into my underwear, August turned his attention to the others and stared them all down until they looked away.

I shut my eyes, willing the transformation to come quick, realizing full well that tonight I would be expected to stand out there—wherever out there was—in the buff way longer than mere seconds.

It was silly, but when I dropped onto my paws, I felt a little braver by what I'd just accomplished.

A little more ready to face off against Justin.

I trotted toward August and rubbed my cheek on his stiff thigh before glancing into his human face, finding that his features had softened. His fingers slid through my white fur. Once I sensed he was calm, I darted toward my Alpha.

"Nice ass," Lucas said, tossing me a wink. "A little on the skinny side for my taste, but—"

August cast Lucas such a barbed glare that he shut up and raised his palms.

"Calm down there, Watt. No one's stealing your girl. I mean, with that temper . . . *yeesh*. She's all yours."

I smiled on the inside because my rubbery lupine lips weren't engineered for smiles. But then I gasped as I was knocked onto my ass.

Hey, I growled at Liam. *Was that really necessary?*

The minute you're in fur, your attention needs to be on me, Justin, and Morgan. Not on your mate.

My attention wasn't on my mate. It was on Lucas.

Get up, Liam barked.

Huffing, I stood. *You want me to attack you? Or—*

My body skidded sideways as though my black pads had sprouted tiny wheels.

What the hell? Matt yelped, sliding right past me. *How'd you do that, Little Wolf?*

For a moment, both wolves observed me in silence, and then Matt craned his long neck and peered over his shoulder at August who was still planted on the lawn, fingers tapping his thighs.

Fuck . . . Matt said at the same time as Liam asked, *Can one of you please enlighten me as to what just happened?*

As Matt filled Liam in on the mysterious mechanism of mating links, August tugged on the tether again, but not to move my body, just to remind me he was there, watching over me.

That he had my back.

The shimmery blue rope tautened between us. I wrapped an invisible hand around it and prepared to pull back to prove to August it went both ways, but then Liam barked.

I jumped, losing sight of the elusive rope.

How far is his reach? he asked.

Far.

How far?

As long as I'm in his line of sight.

Good. Although his massive body was coiled tight, he sounded genuinely pleased by what he'd just learned.

He must've spoken through the mind-link, because August nodded before returning to the open front door and sidling in next to Lucas.

He's not going to help you out until tonight, Liam said. *In case anyone's watching . . .*

Heart skidding to a halt, my gaze swept over the wooded expanse surrounding us, seeking lambent eyes in the shadows of the great evergreens. I saw none, but did it mean they weren't watching?

Where will the fight take place? I asked Liam, skirting his lunge.

On the lawn of the former Pines' headquarters.

In the maze?

Not in the maze, but next to it.

I didn't like the idea of fighting next to a maze. There was no telling what could leap from the dense shrubs.

Liam pounced on top of my back. *Concentrate, Ness.*

I shoved him off.

As he circled me, surely calculating at which angle to come at me, he added through the mind-link: ***Don't ever rely on another person to keep you safe.***

Was he insinuating that I wouldn't be able to keep him safe or that August wouldn't be able to keep me safe?

I'll try to keep track of you the entire time, but I might not be able to.

His words stilled me. *I* was supposed to keep track of him, not the other way around.

Of course, Matt took advantage of my lapse of attention to barrel straight into me, and none too gently. He apologized, but the impact still stung.

As I straightened and wrung myself out, I pinned Liam with an inflexible stare. *Don't you dare take your eyes off Morgan tonight. Not for a second.*

His yellow irises seemed to ignite at my concern, but then he chuffed and wheeled around. *Matt, again!*

48

We spent the remainder of the afternoon sitting around Liam's house, discussing everything but the duel. Even Greg stayed. Under Matt's curious gaze, the pack doctor distilled Sillin into three little vials, then aligned and realigned them in his cooler.

After I'd shifted back into skin, Liam made me take a shower in his house, and then he told me to stay away from August. "In case the Creeks aren't aware he's your mate."

When he suggested August leave and meet us at the former Pine HQ, my mate glared and muttered, "Like hell."

So he'd stayed too, alternately clutching the armrest of the couch, glowering at the woods outside, and pacing the lawn while barking on his phone.

About an hour before we had to leave, Liam got a message that made him speak my name very loudly even though I was sitting a couple feet away from him. "Avery."

He pushed his phone into my hands.

AVERY: *Sarah just arrived at her family's former HQ with Alex Morgan. I haven't been able to get her alone, but thought you'd want to know she was here. She looks a little spooked. Hope Alex hasn't hurt her.*

Spooked? Sarah wasn't the type of girl who spooked easily, so Avery stating this had my hackles rising. "She's alive," I said, handing the phone to Lucas who'd stiffened at the mention of Avery's name, "but if you don't kill Alex Morgan tonight, I will."

Either Lucas read the message slowly, or he read it a few times, because he scrutinized the screen a long time.

My hatred fueled my mounting adrenaline. By the time Liam rose from the couch and announced that it was time, I was extremely ready to get out there.

"Ready when you are, boss," Lucas said, jingling Liam's car keys.

Liam nodded to his black SUV. "Ness, you ride with us."

I didn't care who I rode with as long as they got me there fast so I could ascertain that my friend was truly all right. I opened the door to the backseat and got in. Instead of getting in the front, Liam climbed in the back with me.

When August opened the passenger side door, Liam said, "Not a good idea, Watt."

"I won't touch her."

Liam narrowed his eyes. "Do you want the Creeks to make you leave the dueling ring?"

Heat erupted behind my navel as August's gaze found mine. Even though it seemed to take everything within him to back away, he heeded Liam's words and headed to Cole's car with Greg.

Matt hopped up front, and then Lucas careened down the driveway. I watched the dark world unfurl past my window. At some point, I asked Matt to shut off the AC. My bones were so cold I thought they might not thaw out in time for the duel.

"Did you speak to Tamara today?" I asked Liam as a beat-heavy song came to an end and another began.

He glanced away from his window. "I sent her a message."

"Does she know what's happening tonight?"

"I told her I'd call her later. And that if I didn't, the pack would take care of her."

My breathing stuttered.

Liam leaned over and patted my knee. "I'll be calling her later."

I tried to return his smile but couldn't. I went back to staring at the stars blooming like baby's-breath in the purpling sky. I wondered if my parents were somewhere among them, watching over me, but that line of thinking turned even more painful than contemplating the duel.

As we drove, Liam went through the rules again. They'd been drilled so many times inside my skull that I knew them by heart. Still, I paid attention.

"Your main purpose is to referee the fight, not to get involved. When you inspect Cassandra tonight, don't linger on her lips or nails. We're not looking at calling her out on foul play. If Justin attacks you *or* me, you're allowed to strike back."

"And if Cassandra attacks me?"

His expression became more cutting than a knife point. "If Cassandra attacks you, she'll regret it for the rest of her very short life."

"I'm serious. What happens if she does? Can I kill her, or does it have to be you?"

"If she attacks first, then you're allowed to retaliate." He reached across the backseat, collected my hand, and squeezed it reassuringly. "But it won't come to that."

For three entire songs, he was quiet. We were all quiet.

When the ten-foot metal fence that screened off the Pines' former property came into view, I shivered. And then I shivered harder when Lucas slid the car through the open gate. The white stone headquarters appeared like a mirage at the end of the cedar-lined alley, its staircase darkened by bodies. It seemed like every man and boy in our pack had come.

My heart began to beat a rhythm more hectic than the one blaring out of the SUV's speakers.

Liam squeezed my hand to garner my attention. "Ness, if I fall tonight, you are not to challenge her, understood?"

I blinked as emotion rushed into my eyes. And then I squeezed his fingers back. "The day I signed up to be your Second, you said you wanted my admiration. Well, you'll get it, but not if you don't get back up."

A gentle smile settled over his lips, and then he squeezed my hand one last time before letting go and exiting the car. The pack swarmed him, whispering words of encouragement. I hopped out after Liam, and Matt and Lucas came to stand at my sides like two giant bookends.

I looked for August, but Cole's car hadn't pulled up yet. Hadn't they been right behind us? Had they stopped at a red light? Or missed a turn?

"You look a bit green, Little Wolf."

I tried to feel out the distance using the tether, but my stomach was in shambles. "Can you call your brother, Matt?"

I wasn't looking to stress him out, but my quiet plea had him craning his neck toward the long driveway.

He all but tore the seams off his shorts pocket in search of his phone as we climbed up the stairs and entered the buffed stone atrium. "He's not answering."

"I'll try August," Lucas said, taking out his own phone. "Matt, call Greg."

As we descended the staircase, I watched the crowd milling beyond the French doors along the sharp hedges of the maze. The slender moon crescent cast an eerie glow over the land and the dueling ring that stretched from the maze to the stone terrace.

"Did you reach them?" I asked, returning my gaze to Matt.

He shook his head.

Liam had gone down the terrace steps, but one look at my pallid cheeks had him lumbering back up. "What's going on?"

"We can't reach Greg, Cole, *or* August," Lucas said quietly, darting a glance at the assembled Creeks below who were all—and I mean, *all*—staring at us.

"Can you sense them?" I asked Liam hopefully.

He closed his eyes. After a while, he said, "They're a couple miles out but approaching fast."

A breath whispered through my lips just as someone spoke my name. I turned around to find Frank.

He hugged me, cinching my rigid body. "You go on out there and show them what Boulder females are made of, okay?" He rubbed his bristly jaw against my temple, marking me with his scent in a show of affection.

Heels resonated in the quiet headquarters. I pulled away and peered past Frank, praying I'd see August or Sarah, but found my friend's mother and sister-in-law instead. They strode toward the terrace, arms locked together.

"We believe," Margaux whispered.

They believed what? In us? That we'd win?

No other footfalls disrupted the silence; no car tires crunched the pebbled driveway.

"Boulders, it's mighty impolite to keep your hosts waitin'." Cassandra's voice bellowed from the center of the torch-lit field.

Liam lifted his gaze to mine. *They're coming, Ness.*

I hoped he was saying this because he felt them approach through the blood-link and not as some inane reassurance.

He tipped his head toward the garden. In perfect synchronicity, we walked down the stairs. Memories of another time flashed through my mind—Liam, lip bleeding, yelling for me to come home with him while two Pines shackled his wrists.

I didn't like that memory. There'd been too much hurt in Liam's eyes that night, hurt I'd put there.

I realized then that what had broken Liam and me wasn't Tamara or my mating link. What had broken us was that we'd spent more time fighting each other than fighting alongside one another.

They're getting closer.

The words whispered into my mind made my skin buzz with renewed hope. I became acutely aware of the tether which swelled and effervesced with something dark and sour.

"Something's wrong," I whispered to Liam.

Liam frowned, zeroing in on the ring of shifters and then on Cassandra, whose blue lips twitched with a smile.

Remembering her confession, I placed my palm in front of my mouth before murmuring, "With August. He's angry. Really angry."

A mane of wild blonde curls caught my attention in the first line of shifters. Sarah stood directly ahead of us, her hand clutched in Alex's, her eyes glistening as though she were crying. Was he hurting her, or were her tears for us? Had she found out something else but not found a way to relay the information?

Suddenly, she gasped, and her eyes rounded as they set on a spot over my head.

I whirled around.

August, Cole, and Greg burst through the open veranda doors, sweat glossing their flushed cheeks and bruises marbling their jaws. Blood had seeped into the collar of Cole's gray T-shirt and speckled the oatmeal fabric of August's torn Henley.

I started in their direction, but Liam clapped his hand over my forearm.

Don't. They're fine. They're here.

"They're not fine," I growled. Then to Cassandra, I yelled, "What did you do to them?"

"Me? I'm a werewolf, honey, not a magician. I've been here waitin' the whole time. I didn't do nothin' to these men."

But someone had.

I caught Justin exchanging a loaded glance with Alex Morgan. *Of course . . .*

I searched my intended's gaze for a hint of what had happened, but all of his features were ironed too tight to read anything besides absolute fury.

I noticed Greg's empty fingers balling and uncurling at his sides at the same time as Liam.

They took our Sillin, his voice sputtered inside my skull.

That was why they'd been attacked . . . Not to keep August away, but to keep the drug away.

Doesn't matter.

Didn't it? Could he eat her heart without a Sillin injection?

"For the love of the Wolf God, could we please begin?" Cassandra asked.

"By all means"—Liam yanked off his black V-neck and tossed it to the ground—"let's get this over with."

49

Liam and Cassandra stood naked, shoulders squared, spines taut, muscles twitching. Justin had already shed his clothes, but I hadn't. I'd take them off at the last minute.

As I circled the giant Creek Alpha, pretending to inspect her body, she said, "You're a ruthless little thing, aren't you?"

"Wanting what's right doesn't make me ruthless."

"*What's right?*" Her glacial blue eyes, mere slits behind her gummy lids, thinned even more. "Righteous people possess virtue. You lost yours this weekend."

Alarm straightened my vertebrae. Had she spied on August and me? Or could she smell him—

"And don't you bother convincin' me it was all your aunt's doing. I know she had help, and who better than a girl famished for revenge?"

She was talking about Aidan, not August. I tried not to let my relief show, repressing it as best I could.

"Or maybe it was my cousin's ex-wife who aided your aunt?"

That snapped something in me. "Evelyn had *nothing* to do with Aidan's death."

"And how would you know, since you weren't *there*?"

She's trying to get under your skin. The intensity of Liam's voice had me flinching. **Finish the inspection and return to me.**

Cassandra raised a stealthy smile. "I believe it's her night off from that fancy new job of hers . . . Too bad Frank decided to attend the duel."

My breaths congealed inside my lungs. "Are you trying to get me to kill you before the duel begins?"

Ness!

I started to turn, but spun right back to face the black-hearted woman. "The first time I heard about the female Alpha who brought the largest pack to their knees, I was awestruck. Proud that a woman had risen so high. But now that I've met you and understand how you got to the top, I'm ashamed."

Her blue lips writhed as though she were chewing on something particularly unsavory. Even though I wasn't the only one who'd fallen for her birthmark lie, it incensed me to have been so naïve.

"How I got to the top? You mean by fightin'? We all got our techniques, but seducin' men to get to the top wasn't for me." Her eyes glinted maliciously. "To each her own."

Anger bolted my bones. What man had I seduced? Was she talking about when she'd sent me to Heath, posing as an escort? Or did her barb have to do with Liam? Did she think he and I were—

"Ness!" This time, Liam roared my name out loud.

I jerked around. "She passes my inspection," I muttered, my voice crackling through the starlit expanse.

"And Kolane passes my inspection," Justin said, crossing back over toward his Alpha, leering at me. "Time to take those clothes off, Ness."

I glowered at Justin as I stalked to the perimeter of the ring, yanking off my hoodie and lobbing it at Matt. He caught it.

As I closed in on him, fingers trembling on the bottom of my tank top, I whispered, "Tell Frank to go home."

Matt's pale eyebrows pinched together.

"Evelyn . . ." Her name came out hushed but clear.

As I handed him my top, he nodded. "I'll tell him."

A howl pierced the night. I looked over my shoulder to find Cassandra's light-brown wolf edged in pale moonlight.

"I'll take care of it. Now, go on out there, Little Wolf, and crush them, 'cause that's what Boulders do. We roll and we crush."

I could feel the sting of eyes on my spine as I dropped my shorts and underwear, but I didn't care. I was too infuriated to care. I kicked both beyond the dueling ring, then padded back out toward Liam, who was still in skin and waiting for me.

Behind me, Matt repeated, "Roll and crush."

"Ready?" Liam asked.

I nodded without hesitation. I'd never been this ready for anything.

50

When Liam released a howl to signal the beginning of the duel, everything and everyone outside the ring melted into the darkness.

My breaths were loud in my ears, like the whoosh of waves on sand, frothing into my veins, slowly filling them with grit.

Unless I call you, Ness, you stay as far back as you can, you hear me?

I hear you. But just because I'd heard him didn't mean I'd heed his command. If I felt I could help, I would.

Justin was larger than I remembered, more bulky than tall. I estimated he weighed twice what I did and bet he planned on using those extra pounds on me if push came to shove.

His golden eyes slid from Liam to me, lighting up with a smirk.

I wasn't scrawny, but I was small.

Unimpressive.

Easily overlooked, like the River Alpha said after Liam and I slayed the bear.

A breeze picked up, blowing clouds over the sliver of moon and smattering of stars, darkening the already dusky expanse. My lupine eyesight sharpened, adjusting to the dim luminosity. Cassandra was waiting for Liam to make the first move, the same way she'd waited for Julian to attack.

Exactly like he'd predicted.

Now! His word cracked like a whip against my hide

I took off alongside him as he raced toward Cassandra.

She waited and waited, and then, just as his hind legs bent in preparation to fling himself upward, she pressed her belly low to the ground, limbs coiled tight against her long body. She didn't move, expecting him to pounce on her, but he arched high, overtaking her flattened form.

She blinked, ears perked up in surprise that he hadn't landed on her. His front paws hit the earth with a thud that shook the ground. When his hind paws crushed the blades of grass, Cassandra lurched back onto all fours and swung around.

Liam turned fluidly and then held still, fixing the Creek Alpha with his yellow eyes.

For a moment, neither moved. And then she lurched forward.

Liam hopped back, his big body stirring with a grace that shouldn't have belonged to a creature so colossal. She stopped her attack, which wasn't so much an attack as a taunt. She wanted him to sink his fangs into her. Not into her neck of course, or into her chest where dwelled that soft organ that had miraculously kept her alive all these years, but in a chunk of flesh irrigated by her silver-tainted blood.

Justin, who was standing opposite me, jerked, and then his muzzle scrunched up as though Cassandra had assaulted his skull with silent words. She snarled and launched herself at Liam, and he crouched and opened his maw wide.

Which was exactly what Cassandra wanted.

Her speed decreased, and she stumbled, her performance impeccable. If I'd been standing on the sidelines, I would've assumed she'd tripped.

I wouldn't have seen the eagerness to feed the waiting wolf flare in her blue eyes.

A heartbeat before she landed on Liam, he flipped over and scraped his claws into her belly, yanking a shrill whine from the Creek Alpha. Blood sprayed out of her wound. Liam twisted his face, shutting his eyes and mouth so that none of the crimson liquid landed in him. Droplets dotted his fur though, wetting the black mass.

Just as Cassandra toppled, he sprang onto his paws and pounced, swiping her withers with his claws, slicing her flesh. A sound between a yowl and a snarl pitched out of her.

If Liam could've bitten her, this would already have been the end of the duel.

He had her on the ground, neck exposed. But claws, however sharp, didn't have the impact of teeth, and paws didn't have the pressure of jaws.

She tried to rise, but he slammed his two front legs into her spine, and she sprawled back onto her belly. Low growl rumbling out of her, she bared her teeth and wrenched her neck to nip at his pastern.

She must've sunk her fangs in, because Liam jolted off her body. Even though licking his wound would've made it heal faster, the injury was too near his claws that were wet with her blood.

As Cassandra heaved herself up, pale fur mottled by maroon patches, her eyes burned with murder and fury.

Did she understand that we'd figured out her technique for eliminating the greatest Alphas?

A flutter erupted deep in my belly, not strong enough to move me, more of a quiet reminder that August was watching. A shadow crept into my peripheral vision, and then the oily musk scent of Justin snaked into my nose. I skipped away, never taking my gaze off Liam who remained still as a boulder while his leg healed.

Cassandra snarled, ripping the heavy silence. She took off running, her strokes slow but powerful. Liam dashed, sketching a wide arc around the dueling ring, making her run after him, making her expend precious energy.

When I noticed he was favoring his left leg, worry enveloped me. Was her saliva laced with silver the same way as her blood?

Justin bumped into me, and I staggered but stayed upright and growled at him. *Didn't see you there, bitch.*

My white fur made me stand out in pitch blackness . . . I practically glowed.

I growled at him before snapping my attention back toward Liam. He was still running but had slowed down considerably. Again, I worried it was from pain, but then I noticed Cassandra had stopped chasing him and imagined he was evaluating her next move.

I liked what you did to your new house, but you gotta admit, it was a little . . . sterile.

My skin prickled at Justin's implied admission. Of course he'd been among the Creeks who'd vandalized my home. He'd probably led the whole damn team.

After this duel, I'll kill you, Justin, I muttered between clenched teeth.

He made a noise that sounded like a chuckle. *'Cause you think Cassandra will let you out of this ring alive? She knows you're a bitch that can't be tamed. Which makes you a liability. She doesn't keep liabilities.*

Good thing she's not going to win this fight.

Oh . . . she's not gonna lose. She can't *lose.*

As the clouds shuffled off the moon, I could see every twitching muscle in my Alpha's body, every sweep of eyelashes, every pulse of air. He lifted his tail high in the air.

Get away from Justin, Ness. Liam spoke into my mind without breaking eye contact with Cassandra.

I loped off toward the other side of the ring.

Cassandra dipped her muzzle, and then she burst toward Liam. His muscles coiled like springs as he exploded forward, running straight at her. Just before their bodies connected, he executed the sharpest turn I'd ever seen a wolf make.

Cassandra dug her claws into the ground, spraying the faces of the shifters on the cusp of the dueling ring with grass and dirt. Flicking her ears, she turned and dashed after Liam, neck extended, snout inches from Liam's tail. Jaw wide, she seized it. Liam growled, and then his back paw came up and scraped Cassandra's cheek, shoving her face away, inflicting another deep gash.

She grunted as she released his tail and hacked up black fur, cheek weeping blood. How was he going to end her with just his claws? None of her injuries had healed yet, and if he added any more, not making contact with her blood would become near impossible.

Stashing his tail between his legs, Liam pranced away. I didn't know how deep she'd chomped down, but he would need several minutes for his skin to zipper shut.

Cassandra's nostrils flared, and then her head canted toward me. For numerous heartbeats, she stared my way, blue eyes thin and calculating.

My navel heated up to scorching as something wet bumped my rump. I whipped around and growled. *Did you just sniff me, you prick?*

What if I did? What are you going to do?

Justin was looking for me to attack, because if I made the first move, I'd become fair game for Cassandra to kill.

The dark-brown wolf leered at me. *You smell awfully sweet for something that isn't.*

You touch me again, and I will rip your testicles off and toss them to the coyotes. My breaths came in violent spurts. *And then I'll kill you.*

Will you be ripping them off with your mouth? 'Cause I've been fantasizing about your head between my legs.

A shrill bark erupted from the field, and I spun to find Liam standing over Cassandra. He swiped at her neck, and she swiped back, the dark tips of her claws sinking into his belly.

He let out a cry that had me pitching toward him, but before I could get close, Justin planted teeth that felt like twin saws into my hip and dragged me to the ground. I spun and batted him away, the pain so violent it blanched my eyesight.

Up . . . I needed to get up.

I needed to get to Liam.

51

After managing to dislodge Justin's jaw with my kicks, I crawled away, belly to the ground, limbs trembling like the tiny leaves of Julian Matz's hedges. Suddenly, my body skidded several feet to the side.

What the fuck? Justin growled, standing at the exact spot I'd been.

Using his astonishment to my advantage, I hoisted myself up, my backside ablaze from his bite.

Ness? Are you okay? Liam's voice pinged inside my skull.

I nodded, backing away from Justin when he started advancing. Thankfully, he moved slowly as though afraid that if he progressed any faster, I'd slip away from him again.

A black form materialized between us: Liam. *You stay the fuck away from her, Justin.*

She attacked me first, Justin said.

I did not! I bellowed, the pain in my rump forgotten.

Cassandra stepped in next to Justin. *Seems like our referees can't agree.*

I saw what happened. Justin bit her; Ness did nothing, Liam growled.

He wouldn't have bitten her if she'd done nothin'. Besides, you aren't a referee, Kolane. Cassandra peered at me behind Liam. *Good thing you prepared her so well, 'cause rules are rules.* She licked the blood coating her rubbery lips.

This fight stays between you and me, Liam barked.

Too late for that.

Liam's body seemed to expand like an afternoon shadow, blackening the over-wrought air. **Ness, can you run?**

Yes, I answered out loud because he had his back to me.

Remember our bear hunt?

My ears peaked. Was Liam about to shift back into skin to distract the Creeks?

I'm going to create a diversion.

The Creek Alpha's furry brow wrinkled. *What are you two cookin' up?*

Energy crackled through my body.

Our audience should be told what's happening, Liam said.

They'll understand, Morgan said.

I'd rather explain it. I'll switch into skin. And since we're sticking so closely to the rule book, unless you get into skin, you can't attack me until I'm back in fur. Right, Morgan?

Her blue gaze glowed like a flame atop a wick. *Right.*

Even though the air was rife with rapid heartbeats, I caught the pace of hers accelerating. Was that excitement?

Don't keep us waitin' too long, Morgan said, her voice syrupy, borderline gleeful.

I backed up a few paces, agitated by the intensity of her focus.

Keeping his back to me, Liam said through the mind-link, **She thinks I've forgotten that you're fair game to attack since you're in fur.**

I jerked to a stop.

They're going to go after you. Just keep running, and don't stop. Run in circles; run around the ring. August will adjust your trajectory. Got it?

I didn't say anything, afraid of spoiling our plan, and afraid Liam would hear the tremor building inside me at the idea of being chased by not one, but *two* giant wolves.

Like he'd done in the Smoky Mountains, Liam slid into skin. His muscled form was outlined in moonlight. He turned a little, and I blinked at the amount of blood coating his stomach. Scabs and seeping gashes crisscrossed all over his abdomen. "Shifters, Justin attacked my Second."

People frowned. I didn't think it was in surprise—after all, they'd seen it happen —but in confusion—they probably didn't understand why Liam felt the need to interrupt the show to explain it to them.

The tether tautened . . . I glanced over my shoulder at August. His green eyes were steady, his arms crossed in front of his chest, his shoulders pulled in a line. He was ready and concentrated.

As I twisted around, my gaze collided into Alex's. His hand was no longer wrapped around Sarah's, but she still stood next to him, concern glittering in her dark eyes.

"Ness! Watch out!" she screamed.

Just as Liam predicted, Cassandra and Justin raced in opposite directions, drawing a V around my Alpha, a V that converged on me. I took off at breakneck speed along the edge of the ring, thanking Matt when my lungs didn't explode and my muscles didn't give out. Then again, I couldn't feel any of my limbs, only the wind brushing my fur, whooshing inside my ears. In that moment, I became more bird than wolf.

Suddenly, my body was hauled almost to the center of the ring, blades of grass ripping beneath my claws, the only things keeping me from toppling over. I whipped my neck toward where I'd stood, and found Cassandra shaking Justin off of her. They must've collided, which might've amused me had her gaze not locked like a double-barreled shotgun on me.

She must've yelled through the mind-link, because Justin squirmed and then vaulted in my direction.

I took off again, my back paws almost reaching my ears as I ran. A roar sounded at my left, and then a shadow shot out from behind me. Was it Cassandra? I pushed myself harder, sprinting faster than when the rocks rained down the mountain during the first trial. Bodies crashed behind me, and then snarls. Without decreasing my pace, I swung my head toward the ruckus, found a mountain of black fur atop a mountain of dark brown.

A sharp wince punctured the night, followed by a wet rip.

I was so shocked by the sight of Justin's blood dripping from Liam's muzzle that I didn't see the shape arrowing for me.

Ness! he screeched into my skull.

I froze. A heartbeat before Cassandra crashed into me, August yanked on the tether. This time, I fell as he drew my body toward the center of the ring, mere feet away from Justin's slack form.

Cassandra yowled in frustration.

My pulse seemed to have penetrated my eyes, because the world beat and bobbed.

Liam trotted out in front of me, head and tail held high, shoulders relaxed, a wall of pure, unadulterated confidence.

She's cheatin'! Morgan yelled.

Too bad your referee's no longer alive to call the duel off, Liam barked.

Wheezing, I climbed back onto my paws, ribs feeling bruised and displaced. The smell of warm blood and wet earth penetrated my nostrils. I kept expecting Justin to twitch, but only his fur rustled.

He was gone.

I could hardly believe how rapidly his life had been snuffed out.

There one minute and gone the next.

A disturbance in the ring of shifters behind Justin had my gaze springing up. Alex Morgan was elbowing his way toward my pack. I let out a shrill bark, but my mate's attention didn't veer off me. I barked again, and still he didn't look around him, but a groove appeared between his eyebrows. Did no one see Alex approach? He wasn't freaking transparent!

Then again, he hadn't breeched the first line of Boulders yet.

A snarl had my attention jumping back to the ring where Cassandra was hurtling toward Liam.

I needed to focus on Liam.

Someone in my pack would surely spot Alex and bar his path.

I tried to keep my eyes on the two Alphas, but I peeked past their bodies. Alex had disappeared, but August was still there.

Where had Alex gone?

A burst of yellow materialized in the darkness behind the thin row of Boulders.

Alex had shifted.

I barked.

Still, August didn't understand. The groove simply deepened.

No Boulder looked over their shoulder. All of them too focused on what was happening in the dueling ring.

The yellow shape loomed larger so terrifyingly fast that I locked my gaze on the shimmery blue cord that connected me to August and pulled so hard my belly button almost burst open.

August jerked.

His arms fell out of their bind and extended to steady his teetering body.

I'd moved him, but only by inches.

August finally looked away from me, but only to stare at his abdomen.

Over your shoulder, I barked. *Behind you!*

When he looked back at me, wonder lit up his entire demeanor.

He didn't understand.

I raced toward him, hoping Liam had Cassandra under control, hoping that by choosing one wolf, I wasn't sacrificing the other.

When Alex dropped into a crouch, I was still too far away.

I don't know if it was the panic lighting up my pupils or my mad dash toward him, but August finally spun around.

Too late.

Too late.

Alex was already airborne.

5²

I clutched the blue rope with my mind and poured all of my hatred for the boy who'd driven my cousin off the road and into his grave into my grip.

August lurched forward, several feet this time. He fell, hands smacking the ground before his head could make contact. Alex's lids hitched up as he landed on grass instead of flesh, and the shock made him stumble.

As he righted himself, his narrowed violet gaze locked on August's kneeling form. Before my mate could stand, Alex galloped toward him. The rope escaped my invisible grip and swung so chaotically it blurred, thwarting my attempt to latch onto it.

I came to a screeching halt, and the rope stabilized some. I clutched it, and this time, closed my ghostly fingers hard around it. I pulled just as another wolf barreled out from behind the blockade of human legs and jumped on top of Alex. At first, I thought it was a Boulder, but the wolf was small and slender, not male. And its fur was wavy.

Sarah.

Alex flung her off, and her small body arched through the air, slamming hard into the ground.

Alex growled and darted toward her just as another wolf appeared, this one gray and large.

Larger than Alex.

Lucas.

Snarling like a wild animal, my packmate sank his fangs into Alex's spine. I watched in morbid fascination as Lucas's muzzle and teeth came away drenched in blood.

Ness.

The thin sound of my Alpha calling my name jerked my attention off the sidelines.

I pitched around so fast my vision swam, but then it honed in on the heap of fur at the far side of the ring. Cassandra was standing over Liam, front paws on his shoulders.

He wrung his body to shake her off, but her paws stayed put as though welded to his fur. When he heaved a cry that detonated against my eardrums and echoed in my chest, I understood it wasn't her weight keeping her anchored to him but her purple claws.

As her mouth lowered to his neck, I shot forward, adrenaline zipping through my bones and electrifying my muscles.

He twisted sideways, and her mouth missed its mark, but she remained fastened to him. When another violent holler hit my ears, I sensed her claws had cleaved open more of his back.

I was almost there.

Almost beside them.

Cassandra snarled, and her moonlit fangs approached the mound of thrashing black fur beneath her.

I'd sworn to protect him, but I'd gone off and left him on his own.

I'd let my mate distract me.

I'd failed Liam.

He bucked, interrupting Cassandra's momentum but failing to dislodge her.

Another blood-curdling yowl erupted from my Alpha just as I slammed into Morgan's side. It was like hitting a brick wall, but the wall toppled. Her claws popping out plucked another guttural moan from Liam.

Runnels of split flesh wept blood onto his black fur, but his heart still beat.

It still beat . . .

Praying she hadn't bled into him, I hopped over him, creating a shield with my scrawny body.

Before Cassandra was fully upright, I jumped on top of her and forced her back down. She landed on her spine, teeth flashing. I batted her face with my paws, but all that served was to anger her further.

Like the punching bag Liam had obliged me to train on until my knuckles bled, I hit her, over and over and over, dragging my claws across her cheek, across her forehead, across any pliant surface I could make contact with. Howling and snarling, she smacked my cheek, trailing fire over my temple, my left eye, my muzzle.

I blinked wildly, but I couldn't clear my vision. And then I was yanked off her.

NO! I cried as August pulled on the tether, reeling me in.

I dug my claws into the ground, my muscles screaming, my bones spasming. I fought against the invisible bit hauling me away from Cassandra and Liam.

Liam who still hadn't gotten up but whose chest continued to rise and fall.

As Cassandra bounded onto all fours, I crawled toward her, stretching the tether so tight it almost snapped. And then, praying that for once I'd be stronger than August, I vaulted onto the Creek Alpha's back and did the only thing I could think of to save Liam's life.

I sank my teeth into her neck. As the taste of metal and salt filled my mouth, I worked on not swallowing a drop of it.

"No!" I heard someone scream. I couldn't tell if the voice was inside my head or outside.

I whipped my face from side to side to tear through her sinews and veins, and didn't stop until her body slackened . . . until her giant body collapsed beneath mine.

53

I gagged on the mouthful of Morgan's blood. Forcing my throat closed so that none of her tainted fluids entered my throat, I spit and heaved. A jet of vomit spurted out of me and sprayed Cassandra's blotchy fur, which was already receding into her pores.

I blinked as my eyes filled with heat and more slickness. My vision became even blurrier, but not blurry enough to miss her slipping back into skin for the very last time.

Cassandra was dead, and I was still alive.

We did it, Liam, I whispered.

I inched closer to my Alpha, reveling in the sound of his heart pounding against his injured flesh. If her poison had penetrated him, his heart would've already stopped. His neck lifted, and his luminous yellow gaze fell over me.

We did it, I said again, swiping my paw over my cheek, trying to see through the sticky veil of blood.

His entire body moved this time. He rose like a billow of smoke, darkening the sapphire air and the emerald grass, advancing in slow-motion toward me.

The ground trembled, rife with footfalls. I tried to turn my head, but it felt so heavy, as though Lucas had attached a set of those enormous dumbbells he so enjoyed curling when he watched me train.

The world blurred, colors and sounds swimming and blending like murky watercolors.

When I blinked, I found myself staring at a sheet of brilliant stars.

Even though I was a creature made for land, I loved the sky, the beauty of its forever shifting colors, of its distant luminaries that had inspired so many of my father's stories, of its clouds that drifted like windblown dandelion florets, of its brilliant moon that had found me worthy of its magic.

A face as magnificent as the sky loomed over me, obscuring the sight of constellations and yet presenting me with another made of freckles instead of stars.

The low, raspy timbre of August's voice soothed the sting streaking through my veins and drew my lids down. How many times had I fallen asleep listening to that rough silken voice?

My chin dropped against my collarbone and then lolled backward.

The earth shook again, or perhaps it was the arms clasped around me that quaked.

"Dimples!"

I heaved my heavy lids up, caught a glint of green and gold, like sunlight threading through the leaves of the tree August had taught me to climb.

My heart jerked as though hit by a shot of pure adrenaline, and my skin bristled, my muscles seizing and my bones clinking as they realigned.

Large fingers swept over my cheek, through my hair, curled around my human neck, lifting my limp form, cradling it.

The world spun, as though toppling off its axis, and the green and gold melted into black, then gray, and then pure white as though the night had been shot through with fireworks.

Had August lit up the sky for me again?

I so loved fireworks.

I looked for him, but he'd gone.

All was quiet.

All was bright.

54

Fire singed my veins.

55

Noise crashed against my eardrums.

56

Heat charred my skin, and then a chill slid down my throat, and my lungs expanded like bellows, ripping a cry that reverberated against my palate and pulsed my cheeks, awakening a ferocious ache.

Thump.

Thump.

57

Metal clinked.
Wild battering inside my chest.
Strips of glaring light.
Flashes of blinding pain.
Smears of color.
Light blue.
Peach.
Green.
Brown.
Then white.
So much white.

58

Beep . . . Beep . . . Beep.

"She died but she came back, Mom."

Who'd died? *Sandra?*

"Wait. I have to—I'll call you back."

A loud, shrill scrape.

Then five dots of heat on my cheek.

And green.

Two green orbs.

Not orbs.

Eyes.

"Dimples?"

The green blurred, faded.

Not into white but into black.

59

*B*eep ... *Beep* ... *Beep.*

The warm scent of skin.

Spice and sawdust.

The steady beat of a heart against my spine.

Ba-bump ... Ba-bump ... Ba-bump ...

Rhythmic and solid.

The sharp spike of beeps echoing around me jolted the body cocooning mine.

"Dimples?"

Beep. Beep. Beep.

I blinked, but everything was dark. So dark.

"I want ..."

"What do you want, sweetheart?"

"Colors."

Something clicked, and then hands gently eased me onto my back.

Against the cream ceiling, green, sable, and gold churned. Heat stung my eyes; then something wet rolled along my cheek: a tear.

The beats of my heart lengthened. Slowed. *Beep ... Beep ... Beep ...*

"What is it?" the deep voice trembled in the air between our faces.

I lifted my hand to touch August's jaw. He turned his face until his lips connected with my palm. "It was so dark and then so white," I murmured. "What happened to me?"

His breaths faltered.

"What?" I asked as I lifted my other hand to push the hair obscuring my left eye.

Found it wasn't hair but gauze.

Thick gauze.

I prodded it until I found the edge and then started peeling it away when August caught my fingers. "Don't take it off."

"Why not? Am I bleeding?"

"No. Maybe. Just don't take it off yet. Greg said he'd be here in the morning. He'll do it."

"O-okay." Something about his expression had my heart thump a little quicker, which filled the hospital room with nippy, harsh *beeps*. "Is Cassandra . . . is she . . .?"

"Dead? Yes. She's dead. You killed her. Which killed you." His voice broke. "It . . . killed . . . you."

I ran my palm along his jaw, pressing a little harder to make sure he was real, and that I was too. "I died?"

The quiet white void had been death.

"How . . . how did I come back?"

His lids swept down over his eyes as though to clear them of the memory. "I bit you."

I frowned. "You bit—*oh* . . ." My unbandaged eye widened. "Like in the legend?"

He nodded, his dense stubble scraping my palm.

"You brought me back to life," I said in wonder. As I remembered who told me the story, his name burst through my lips. "*Liam!* What about Liam? Is he alive?"

"He's alive."

Beep. Beep. Beep.

"We won then?"

August closed his eyes. "Oh . . . Ness."

"What? We didn't win?"

"No. We won. But—"

"But what?"

He removed his cheek from my hand and laced his fingers through mine, careful not to shift the heart monitor clamped to the tip of my index.

"What is it, August?"

His silence intensified my pulse. The beeps pinged against my eardrums, against the fawn-colored walls, against the closed hospital door. He lowered our twined hands to my abdomen.

"It's gone," he whispered raucously.

My brow furrowed. "What is?"

"The link," he murmured. "It's gone."

And that was when I felt it.

Or rather . . . when I didn't feel it. "Oh."

He watched my face as the revelation settled like silt on the bottom of a river.

"Death severed it," I said matter-of-factly.

He pressed his forehead against my collarbone, his body heaving, first with ragged breaths and then with quiet sobs.

Was he mourning its absence, or had its absence made him realize that the link was the reason he'd been attracted to me?

Probably the latter.

He wouldn't be crying over a broken link.

Not if it hadn't altered his feelings toward me.

He was probably worried confessing his change of heart would send me into a tailspin of intractable pain. Or back into the white void.

I shuddered just remembering.

I lifted my free hand to his hunched spine and stroked the hard knobs of his vertebrae. "It's okay," I whispered, trying to act strong even though I felt the loss inside the marrow of my very bones. "You don't need to feel guilty, August. I won't break, I promise."

I was too broken to break, right?

"Wh-what?" He picked his head off my chest and dug the heel of his palm into his reddened eyes.

"We'll go back to being . . ." I shrugged to buy myself time to clear my throat. "Friends." I tried to smile, but my lips wobbled too much for it to stick.

His strong brow grooved. "What are you talking about?"

"I . . . you . . . I thought . . ." My eyebrows pulled together. "Why *are* you crying?"

"Because I lost you." He said this with an anger that made me shrink deeper into the tough pillow propping my head up. "Because when Liam told me to bite you, I thought it was some sick joke, that he'd gone soft in the head. Ness, you died in my arms. And then for the past week, you've been in and out of consciousness. I apologize for being emotional, but until a few minutes ago, I was terrified you might never wake up. Or that when you did, you wouldn't remember my name. Or that you might not want me now that nothing binds us."

"The past week?" I whispered. "The duel was last week?"

He nodded carefully, as though waiting for me to touch upon the rest of what he'd said.

"You think I forgot you?" I dragged my thumb across his palm. "How could I forget the boy who picked me up from school to buy me ice-cream? Who taught me to climb my first tree and who sat by my bed to make sure all the monsters stayed underneath it?" I kept stroking his palm. "I remember everything about you, August. I remember when you came to talk to me the day of the pack gathering, when you shot Lucas at the paintball arena, when you collected me in the woods the night Liam called me a traitor. I remember our swim in the lake when you tried to tickle me, and the feel of your palm on my skin. It was the day I realized my feelings for you weren't all that platonic." While I kept caressing his palm with my thumb, I raised my other hand to touch the faint-white line where I'd carved his cheek the night I'd had a nightmare, and he'd woken me up. "I remember giving you this scar, and then licking the blood away."

A full-body shiver went through him.

"I remember our first kiss. Each one of our kisses, for that matter. I remember my birthday dinner and all that happened after."

His lips parted a little, as though he were trying to catch his breath.

"I remember you, August." I cupped his chiseled jaw.

Those glorious emerald eyes bore down on mine.

"And concerning the link, it's not the first time the bond between us has been absent, now is it?"

His eyes seemed to shine a little harder.

"What about you?" I asked.

"What about me, what?"

"Have your feelings for me *changed*? I know you love me, but do you still"—I shrugged—"*want* me?"

Shaking his head, he captured my wrist and brought it up to his lips. "Want is a mighty feeble word for what I feel for you, Ness Clark."

When he kissed the delicate skin, the room filled with the melody of my heartbeats.

He peppered the inside of my arm with kisses before carefully laying my hand down on the twisted sheets, wrapping his fingers around the back rung of the bed to keep his weight off me, and leaning over until his mouth was parallel to mine. I tried to reach around his back, but the cord of the heart monitor fumbled my first attempt.

"Can you turn off that machine so I can get my finger back? I don't want to remove the clip and give all the nurses strokes when they hear me flatline."

Would it still alert them? Probably . . .

August winced.

I wrinkled my nose. "I didn't mean to remind you."

"I don't think it's something I'll ever be able to forget, sweetheart. Those were the worst minutes of my life. On par with crashing in the helicopter and having a heart-to-heart with Evelyn."

"Evelyn! Does she know?" I asked as he studied the machine monitoring my heartbeats to figure out how to turn it off.

In the end, he simply unplugged it.

"She knows." He slipped the clamp off my fingertip. "The first two days, she didn't leave the chair next to your bed, but then Frank forced her to go home at night so she could rest. She made me swear not to leave your side, then muttered a couple things in Spanish, but I didn't quite catch their meaning. She was probably hexing me."

I grinned, but it tugged on my injured cheek, so I uncurled my lips.

As I raised my hand to feel what was underneath the gauze, August caught my fingers and towed them away. "Tomorrow. You'll get the bandage off tomorrow. Now, where were we again? Right . . . I was just about to do this." He kissed me gently, and it made me forget all about my injury.

It made me forget about a lot of things . . .

Suddenly, a lightbulb went off in my head, and I skated my mouth off his. "You could've died!"

"What?" His voice was all raspy.

"When you bit me! I had silver in my blood. You could've died. How come you didn't?"

"That Sillin injection Greg gave me counteracted the silver I ingested. Counteracted the metal in your blood, too."

I was about to go off on him when the door of my room flew open and a nurse burst in, cheeks puffing and red.

"You . . . the machine . . ." She couldn't seem to catch her breath.

"Sorry. We unplugged it," I said. "But I'm fine." When she started bustling toward me, I raised my palm to stop her. "I promise."

"I'm going to have to call your doctor."

"Sure." I doubted he'd ask her to clip me back onto the monitor. Once the door shut, I focused on August again. "Liam should *never* have told you about—"

He pressed a finger against my lips. "When I bit you, I understood the risks, and I would take them a thousand times over to get you back."

Tears welled up.

"Oh, sweetheart. Don't cry. There's been too much crying around here."

I inhaled a breath, trying to rein in my emotions.

"Between Mom, Evelyn, Matt, Sarah—"

I smiled, even though my cheek turned wet. "Sarah cried?" I scrubbed the tears away with the back of my hand. I could believe Matt had gotten teary-eyed; he had the gentlest heart. But Sarah?

"Don't tell her I told you. She swore me to secrecy." August tucked a piece of hair behind my ear. "You're the most popular girl in this hospital. Every single Boulder has come to visit you, to the greatest pleasure of the nurses."

I laughed, and again it tugged on whatever awaited me behind the gauze.

"I have more questions."

He sighed. "Let me get comfortable." He scooted me to the side of the narrow bed so he could lie down beside me.

"I know Evelyn visited me here, so I imagine she's okay, but did Cassandra—did she send someone?"

"Are you sure you want to know everything tonight?"

I nodded.

He splayed his hand against my ribcage. "After you warned Matt, Frank left with Derek. They found Morgan's daughter lurking on his property."

I blanched.

"Little J.—Frank made him stay behind—he managed to put a bullet in her leg with his dad's old shotgun."

Dread creeped up my veins. "He's only fourteen."

August smiled. "Stood his ground like a grown man."

"What about the girls? Were they okay?"

"The girls?"

"Tamara, Amanda . . ." I didn't add Sienna's name to the list, since, to my knowledge, she wasn't dating a Boulder, which meant she probably wouldn't have been targeted.

"Liam ordered two of our guys to stay with them before the fight began. They're all fine."

I was glad to hear Liam had guarded Tamara.

"Any more questions?"

I nibbled on my bottom lip. "Do you think they'll discharge me tomorrow?"

"Greg will decide. If it was up to me, you'd be recuperating at my place."

His place . . . Thankfully, I was no longer connected to the machine, because I was pretty certain my heart rate had just shot through the roof.

"Is that where I'm going after this?"

His freckles darkened. "I'd like that, but I'd understand if that's too much for you. Your new house is also ready."

The memory of the blood and urine made the walls of my hospital room squeeze in around me. "It was Justin. He confessed to the vandalism. He probably had help, though."

August's head dipped. "Don't worry. I already took care of it."

It being my house or the rest of the perpetrators? I didn't ask. "What about Alex? What happened to him?"

"He's gone too."

"Gone?"

"Dead. Lucas."

"And Lori? Did Frank kill her when he got to his house?"

"No. She's in captivity back at HQ. Liam wanted to keep her for questioning. He's trying to find out who Morgan's biggest supporters are."

A yawn popped out of my mouth.

August's eyes softened. "You need to rest."

"I've been sleeping for a week."

"You've been *mending* for a week. You had three cracked ribs and several other . . . *injuries*."

I inhaled deeply. Nothing hurt, which told me my ribs must have already set.

"Nothing feels broken anymore," I said. Except my face.

"I'm relieved to hear that."

"Did Liam . . . Did he"—I wrinkled my nose—"*eat* Morgan's heart?"

"He did."

"How? Did your blood also—"

"Remember how Dad was with the Rivers? The afternoon of the duel, Greg was worried about how little Sillin we had left, so I told Dad to purchase some from the Rivers. They ended up giving it to us for free."

"Oh. That's . . . *kind* of them." Since nothing was ever free in this world, I assumed it was given in the hopes of getting something in return. Was August that something?

"They arrived at the duel right after . . ." He shuddered.

"Right after?"

"Right after you made it back to us." His words lingered in the air. "But he got the whole story, which made his hair go a lot grayer."

"He must hate me for having put you at risk."

August's body went a tad rigid. "*Hate you?* First off, Dimples, my dad loves you. Both my parents do. Secondly, you didn't put me at risk, so don't ever say that again. Don't even think it, all right?"

I said, "All right," even though I knew I would always think it. How could I not?

When August reached over me to click off the light shining over the bed, I said, "Can you leave it on?"

"Of course."

He played with my hair, and the gentle movement lulled me.

"I didn't see them," I murmured.

"Didn't see who, sweetheart?"

"Mom and Dad." My throat narrowed. "When I died, I didn't see them." A beat passed. "You think I wasn't dead long enough, or do you think there's nothing waiting for us *after*?"

Although his chest rose and fell steadily, his pulse picked up speed. "I don't know."

I appreciated his honesty, even though it made my throat close up some more. "Thank you."

"For what?"

"For bringing me back." At least people had waited for me on this side.

He dropped my hair and tucked me closer, stamping a kiss on my temple, which I felt even through the gauze. "I'll always bring you back."

And I knew he would. Every time I'd gotten lost, he'd been the one to bring me back.

60

I woke up to a brightness so white I snapped my lids up—*lid*. The other one was still mummified by the gauze. The tan wall came into focus first. I'd never been particularly fond of that color, but as I gazed at it, I thought it was quite marvelous.

The low drone of voices outside my hospital room made me turn onto my other side. Chair legs scraped, and a tremulous whispered, "*Querida*," rose in time with Evelyn.

With trembling hands, she cupped my cheeks, careful not to apply too much pressure to my bandaged one, and then pressed her uncharacteristically pale lips to my forehead, then to my nose, and then to my forehead again. "I will not make old bones if you keep doing things like this to me."

"I'm sorry, Evelyn."

Moisture clumped her black lashes together. "Oh, *querida*. Please, no more danger. Please."

"I promise I'm done with duels and contests for the rest of my life."

"*Bueno*. Now tell me, how do you feel? Frank said you heal fast, but I worry."

When did she not? "I feel fine."

Her dark eyes inspected my covered face, making me wonder if the gauze was soaked in blood. As I raised my fingers to feel it, there was a knock on the door.

"Can we come in?" Frank called.

Evelyn looked over her shoulder, then back at me.

"Who's we?" I asked her quietly.

"The men you call the elders."

"All five of them?"

She nodded.

I hoisted myself into a sitting position and finger-combed my hair. Not that they'd notice my rat's nest when half my face was swathed up. "C-come in!"

The door opened, and they entered, one after the other, August closing ranks.

Last night, I hadn't noticed the violet shadows beneath his eyes or his ashen complexion. I wanted to tell him to go home and rest, but Eric stepped in front of him and started speaking to me, saying what a spectacular fight Liam and I had led, and then Derek mentioned how I'd go down in the Hall of Fame of Boulder Wolves, which made me wonder if my pack had an actual Hall of Fame. And then Frank, placing his hand on Evelyn's shoulder, said that my courage changed the course of pack history.

Even though tears were probably out of character for the warrior they were painting me as, emotion rose and overflowed.

Evelyn knitted her warm fingers through my chilled ones.

"We are so proud of you, Ness. You will forever have our gratitude," Frank added.

I swiped my palm against my wet cheek just as another knock sounded. The person didn't ask to be allowed inside.

He just barged in.

This was so like Liam that it made me smile. He walked over to my bed, winding through the picket fence of elders. For a moment, he didn't say anything, neither out loud nor in my mind.

Could he still speak into my mind, or was that bond broken too?

He cleared his throat. "Could you all give me a moment with the girl who saved my life?"

The girl who'd saved his life . . . "I didn't save your life, Liam."

He didn't answer, but his jaw worked.

The elders patted my arm before leaving. Frank kissed my cheek, and then he tugged on Evelyn's hand.

"I will be back this afternoon. Or earlier if you need me," she said.

After she left, Liam said, "You too, Watt."

August stiffened. Even though no tether connected us anymore, I could feel his reticence at leaving me alone in a room with my ex.

"I'll go get us some coffees," he finally said.

I nodded. "I'd like that."

Rigidly, he walked to the door.

When the door snicked shut, Liam said, "I can't believe you bit her!"

I winced from the shrillness of his voice but then squared my shoulders. "It got you what you wanted."

"You died, Ness! You. Died!"

"I know. I was there," I said drily.

He shook his head, not appreciating my morbid humor. His shoulders seemed broader, his arms ropier. Even his height seemed to have changed. Although his face was unscathed, I couldn't help but wonder what his abdomen looked like. Had he healed, or was his stomach crisscrossed with scars?

After heaving a sigh, he dropped onto the foot of my bed and ran his hands through his hair. A wayward lock fell into his amber eyes. He shoved it away, but it just tumbled back down.

"How are you doing?" I asked.

He grunted. "How do you think I'm doing? You died," he repeated. The morning sun slanting through the blinds made his eyes seem shinier, as though he were about to cry.

I captured the hand with which he was wringing the scratchy bedsheet. "You didn't think I'd let you become the only living legend?" I fit a smile onto my lips and winked. "Way neater than being a dead one."

He grunted, but his fingers softened in my grip.

My smile grew, but so did the ache in my face, so I leveled my lips. "I'm getting inducted into the Boulder Hall of Fame apparently."

"Didn't know we had one of those . . ."

"And you call yourself Alpha?" I rolled my eyes—well, my *eye*. I hoped Greg would come soon . . . "Aren't Alphas supposed to be all-knowing?"

Something I said destroyed Liam's fragile tranquility. "About that."

I frowned.

"I ate Morgan's heart."

I wrinkled my nose. "I heard. Did it taste black and bitter?"

"I'd rather not recall what it tasted like. The point is, if I hadn't ingested it right after the duel, I wouldn't have been able to connect our two packs."

"Okay . . ."

"But it wasn't mine for the taking."

I cocked my unbandaged eyebrow up.

"Ness, *you* defeated Morgan. That heart belonged to *you*. Our pack . . . it belongs to *you*."

"What? What are you talking about?"

"You deserve to be Alpha, and I'm here to make that happen."

I dropped his hand as though the mere contact of his fingers could somehow transfer the link. "Um. No." I clasped my fingers in my lap. "I most definitely don't want to be Alpha."

"Why not?"

"Because that was never my ambition. I signed up to be your Second to help you. Now that that's done, I want to go back to college and"—I shrugged—"*live*. Like, really live. Without having to scheme and run half-marathons and watch over my shoulder."

He glanced at me through his long lashes. "Are you certain?"

"I've never been more certain of anything."

"I owe you. So much. I owe you *everything*."

"You owe me nothing, Liam."

"I do. Money, for starters."

"I don't need any money."

He raised a quizzical brow.

"At least, not right now." Maybe once I spoke to Isobel and Nelson to return what their crazy son had given me.

"You tell me as soon as that changes, all right?"

"I will."

"And if you need anything else—and I mean, *anything*—come to me, and I'll make it happen."

I nodded.

"I mean it, Ness."

"I know you do."

A beat of companionable silence ensued.

"Feels strange," I finally said.

"What does?"

"That it's over."

"Over? It's just beginning. The pack's so big now. Speaking of"—his eyes practically glowed—"I'm going to need Betas. Would you consider being one of them?"

"Me?" I squeaked. "Why? Did Lucas turn you down?"

The smirk was slow to come, but it made an appearance on Liam's hard-edged face. "Haven't asked him yet."

"Well, you should."

"I'm going to need at least two or three."

"I'm no politician, Liam, but maybe you shouldn't designate only Original Boulders for the job."

"I was thinking of making Sarah a Beta."

I smiled. "She'll make a great Beta. And so would Lucas. Now you just need a Creek, and you'll have a holy trinity."

His expression gentled. "You're right. So wise, Miss Clark."

"Why thank you, Mr. Kolane."

We smiled at each other a moment, and then his gaze dropped to my abdomen.

Worried he might mention the tether, I said, "Morgan mentioned they were six. Well, five, because Aidan wasn't living with his pack back then."

He raised his gaze back to my face. "Huh?"

"Original Creeks." When he frowned, I added, "Did the others have tainted blood too, or was she the only one?"

"Oh." His nostrils flared. "Funny you should ask. I just had a long chat with Lori about that."

"You trust her?"

"I trust she wants to live." He rubbed his palms against his thighs. "One of them was Cassandra's father—the one supposedly murdered by Julian. The other was her grandmother; she died of old age two years back. And then there was Lori and Alex, but they were never exposed to the toxic spring since they were born years later. However"—he rested his hands on the bed—"they were exposed to something else."

I frowned.

"The heavy dose of Sillin Cassandra ingested after the poisoning, it transferred to them during the pregnancy, which gave them a very high tolerance to silver."

How interesting . . . "Like a new and improved race of shifters."

"Exactly."

"So the only OC left is Lori?" I asked.

"Yes."

"And you're sure she has no silver in her blood?"

"I had Greg run tests on her. No silver showed up. Besides, Lucas killed Alex, and his blood didn't poison him, so it's safe to assume Lori's silver-free."

I chewed on my bottom lip. "How did Cassandra survive when the rest of her pack died?"

"Because she was the Alpha's niece. He reserved the highest doses for his surviving relatives. Him and his mother never shifted again, but Cassandra somehow managed to tap into her werewolf magic. Took her years, according to Lori."

"So it *is* possible to shift with Sillin in our blood?"

"Lori thinks it was the combination of silver and Sillin. Cassandra never got rid of either."

I frowned. "It stayed in her system? So she wasn't still taking it?"

"No."

"Then why did they steal our Sillin?"

"Because they didn't want *us* to have it."

My frown deepened.

"As long as we had it, we could heal from her silver blood."

My eyebrows shot up so fast it tugged on my left cheek.

"Cassandra's plan was to annex us because we had a good foothold in the region. That's why she had Everest take our stock."

"So she didn't come in peace?"

"No."

I stared a long minute at Liam, trying to arrange all this information inside my slow-firing brain. I didn't know if it was the medication they'd given me or my week-long coma, but my head felt wadded up with cotton. "Why did they go after ours instead of the Pines?"

"Apparently it was next up on their to-do list. Lori said her mother wanted to start with ours because we were more dissipated, and therefore, *easier* to take over."

I fingered a crease in my bedsheet, trying desperately to smooth it out. To think I'd once longed to meet this woman. To think I'd once been impressed with her. I'd sink my fangs into her neck all over again if I had to.

Liam reached over and trapped my hand in his. "I can't do this without you, Ness."

"*This?*"

"Reorganize three packs and make them one."

"Of course you can."

"I don't *want* to do it without you."

"I'm not going anywhere," I promised him, easing my fingers out of his grip.

He made a fist, his knuckles turning paler then redder as he tightened and released them. "I heard the mating link's gone."

My heart stilled a moment. After several breaths, I said softly, "Doesn't change how I feel about August, though."

He shut his eyes. "Maybe, in time, it will."

"Liam," I whispered, "you have a pack to take care of, a son on the way, a woman who adores you, friends who would do anything for you. You don't need me."

His lids flew up, and his amber gaze flared. "You're wrong!"

I let the intensity of the emotions rolling off him settle before adding, "Guilt and gratitude are coloring the way you think of me."

"Guilt and gratitude?" he scoffed.

"Yes. Guilt because, for some reason, you feel like you took this position from me. And gratitude for saving your ass. 'Cause I sort of did save it, didn't I?" A corner of my mouth tugged up, in turn yanking on my injured cheek. "Could you call Greg? I'd really like to get this bandage off."

Adam's apple bobbing, Liam stood to extract his phone from the pocket of his jeans. As he phoned the doctor, the door to my room flew open.

61

"Ness!" Sarah raced to me. Her arms went around my shoulders and pulled me into the fiercest hug. After a couple long seconds, she pressed me away. "I'll have you know, I'm really pissed at you! You can't go playing hero and dying on me like that."

"Says the girl who dated Alex Morgan to gather info." I inspected what I could see of her body. "Did he hurt you? Are you okay?"

"I'm fine, hun." She shuddered as she said this, which made me sit up straighter.

"What happened?"

"I'll tell you everything some other time. I think you have enough to deal with right now."

"I have nothing to deal with right now besides getting this bandage off."

"Greg's on his way," Liam said.

"Thank you, Liam." Then to Sarah, I said, "I hope he's going to take this thing off. And discharge me."

Sarah and Liam exchanged a glance that made my stomach tighten. Had they seen what lay beneath the bandage?

"Did I lose my eye or something?" I thought I still felt its presence, but perhaps it was like a phantom limb.

"Your eye's still there," Liam said.

"Then why does everyone keep blanching when I bring it up?"

"The reason I sent you that message in the shoe is because I overheard Alex and Justin talk about how they'd found out the location of the Sillin stash." Even though I was glad for an explanation, I sensed Sarah was feeding it to me to evade my question. "I was honestly certain they knew where it was. I didn't think they were using me to find it."

I flicked my gaze up to Liam. "I'm very tempted to say *I told you so*."

He flashed me a pained smile. "Go ahead. Say it."

Lucas sauntered in then, shaggy-haired and shiny-eyed. "Back from the dead so soon, Clark?"

I shook my head in amusement. "Would you rather I have haunted your ass, Lucas?"

"Did you just . . . did you just"—he slapped a palm against his chest—"*swear*?"

While Sarah rolled her eyes, I snorted. "I'm happy to see you, too."

"You gave us quite the scare last week." A genuine smile now graced Lucas's lips.

"Wasn't my intent."

"Can you tell Matt it was? 'Cause I sort of have a bet going with him that you did all that for the attention."

I gawked at him.

He smirked. "Kidding."

"So I got you something," Sarah interjected, digging into her enormous Mary-Poppins handbag. "I got *us* something."

She pulled out a firetruck-red silk bomber jacket.

"Wow that's really . . . *red*."

"Wait for it." She flipped the jacket around. On the back, in flowy white embroidery, was written Boulder Babe. "I have a matching one for myself. Obvs."

My eyes—or rather eye—dampened again.

"I suggested Boulder Bitch, which would've been species-accurate, but this one" —Lucas pointed to Sarah—"vetoed my proposal."

Sarah gave him the stink-eye, which made laughter burst out of me. I never thought I'd laugh about anything containing the word bitch, but hey, I hadn't thought I'd die and come back to tell the tale.

"Do you love it?" Sarah asked, her wild curls glinting in the sunlight.

"I love it."

"Good."

The sound of someone knocking had all of us turning toward the open door.

Why was Ingrid Burley standing on the threshold of my hospital room? When August walked in behind her, I realized they must've bumped into each other in the cafeteria, because they were holding matching takeaway coffee cups.

"Hey," she said, watching him bring me one of the coffees. "I'm sorry for bargin' in here, but I heard you were finally awake."

I wrapped my fingers around the warmed paper cup, unsure as to why she was in Boulder in the first place.

"Ingrid's the reason I managed to unite the packs," Liam said, as though he'd heard my thoughts. When I frowned, he added, "She brought us the Sillin."

Ingrid shrugged. "That's what allies are for." She drew her fingers through her long, glossy strands, working out a tangle. "I'm just glad we made it in time."

Perhaps I should've been thankful the Rivers had aided us, but it nagged me that she'd used it as an excuse to fly out here with Nelson. More importantly, though, why was she still in Boulder a week after the duel? Was she still holding out hope for August to change his mind?

"Congratulations," she said.

"Thank you." I offered her a stiff smile.

"Are you heading back to Tennessee today, Ingrid?" Sarah asked.

"Not sure yet." She took a sip of her coffee, glancing over the rim at Liam. "Might stick around a few more days."

I squeezed my lips shut to prevent myself from asking why.

"Liam, can you and I talk a sec?" she asked.

Liam nodded, then cupped the nape of my neck and rested his cheek on my forehead. *I wish I had been the one to deserve you.*

My heart jounced at the sound of his voice in my mind. Unlike the link connecting me to August, the one connecting me to Liam hadn't shattered.

I ducked my head out from underneath his. "I heard you," I whispered, remembering another time when I'd spoken the same words to him with the same amount of wonder.

He frowned. "Why wouldn't you have heard me? You're my wolf."

"I just thought . . ." I glanced up at August who stood so rigidly he looked carved out of wood. "I just thought that link might've been gone too."

There's nothing more powerful than a bond to an Alpha.

I craned my neck to look at Liam.

Nothing, he repeated, gaze leveled on August.

I felt like a fly caught in a web belonging to two equally big and possessive spiders. But it wasn't my life or my heart I feared for; it was theirs. I couldn't split myself in half, and even though I loved them both, I loved them differently.

I set my untouched coffee down on my bedside table and wrapped my hand around the one August had fisted at his side, prying his fingers open until they relaxed and twined with mine.

"See you later, Liam." I smiled at him, but all I got in return was a sharp nod.

He backed away.

As Ingrid trailed after him, I called out, "In case I don't see you again, Ingrid, have a safe trip back, and say hi to your family from me."

She looked over her shoulder at me, then at August, then at our hands. "I will," she said, offering me a weak smile.

Once the door was closed, Sarah loosed a breath. "Well, that was a little awkward."

"And this is why I advocate polygamy," Lucas said brightly. "And orgies. Everyone gets what they want, or rather, *whom.*"

Sarah smacked his thigh.

"*Ow.* What was that for? I'm allowed my opinion," he muttered. "It's my constitutional right."

"When you're going to say stupid shit, use your inside voice," Sarah said.

"*Stupid shit?* How was that stupid?"

"It was unhelpful," she said, gaze pinging between August and me.

Greg blustered into the room then. "Got here as fast as I could."

I'd never been so happy to see the pack doctor. One, because I was anxious to get my bandage off, and two, because I didn't want to talk about our tangled love lives anymore. I sensed Lucas had been trying to lighten the atmosphere, but his quip had the adverse effect. August's grip had become bruising, as though my former mate was afraid that if he let go, I would venture away.

I'd moved him the night of the duel. Perhaps if the link still connected us, August wouldn't have felt so threatened, but now that it was gone . . .

"Glad to see you awake, kid." Greg squirted some disinfectant into his palms and rubbed them as he approached my bedside.

I tried to smile, but a bolt of nervousness shot through me.

"So, I'm going to take a look under the bandage."

Take a look underneath it? "Is there a chance it's not coming off?"

As his fingers inched up to the gauze, he seemed to realize we weren't alone. "You mind giving Ness and me some room?"

"Sure, doc," Lucas said.

Sarah rose from the bed reluctantly. "I'll be right outside."

"Want August to stay, Ness?" Greg asked.

My heart started pounding double-time. "I-I . . ."

August's motionless body finally came alive. "I'd like to stay." He dipped his chin into his neck to peer down at me. "If that's okay with you?"

Greg waited until I acquiesced before proceeding to remove the bandage. As the strips fell away, and cool air touched my newly exposed skin, I shivered.

August let go of my hand and skated his palm across my back to drive warmth into my chilled skin.

Greg gathered the fallen gauze and chucked it in the garbage. He lifted his fingers to my face again, I assumed to remove the last of the bandages, but he simply prodded my cheek.

"You're not going to remove everything?" I finally asked.

His hand arced down slowly. "I did, Ness."

He must not have, though, because something was still obstructing my sight. I raised my hand to do it myself. When my fingertips bumped against my lashes and the slick surface of my eye, I turned to marble.

62

The weight of my surprise made my numb fingers glide down a hardened ridge that tapered off into smooth skin.

Greg was saying something, but his words banged into my eardrums without penetrating. I flung the sheet off my legs and got out of bed. When the balls of my feet hit the cold linoleum, my head spun. Two sets of hands wrapped around my upper arms to steady me—Greg's and August's.

The tan-colored wall swam in and out of focus. I shrugged their hands away, then padded into the bathroom in my hospital gown.

Cold air snuck through the papery fabric, wrapping around my bare skin, bringing more goose bumps to the surface.

I flicked the switch on the wall, or thought I did, but my fingers whispered through air, missing their mark. My second attempt, though, was successful.

Light flooded the tiled space that had been scrubbed with so much antibacterial soap my nose twitched. I stepped in front of the mirror, wiped my right eye to clear it of the blur. As my vision sharpened on my reflection, a breath stumbled through my parted lips.

I raised my fingers to my face and traced the two centipede-like violet scars that started at my left temple and curved over my lid and cheek, arcing toward my ear. But the scars were hardly the most alarming thing about my face. No, what truly distressed me was the paleness of my blue iris and black pupil.

I swallowed back the lump rising in my throat. Crying over my appearance and loss of vision felt so silly considering everything.

I caught movement and turned to find August leaning against the door. I palmed the left side of my face to hide my disfigurement.

"Dimples . . ."

The pity coating his tone had me bristling.

I sidestepped him and returned to Greg. "Will my eyesight come back?" I asked, my voice surprisingly firm.

Eyes crinkling with grief, he shook his head. "Your scarring, in time, will become fainter—Liam's has already improved, but he's Alpha so you can't really compare your healing capacities—however, your eye won't improve. The corneal abrasion was too deep and drops of Morgan's blood came in contact with your aqueous humor."

Humor . . . What a strange term for something that was decidedly not funny.

"Do you see anything at all?" he asked.

"No."

He nodded.

Heat glazed my cold spine. Instead of leaning into August, I took a step forward, bumping my shins into the gray base of my hospital bed.

Greg shot out a hand to steady me. "It'll impact your depth perception. You're going to have to relearn how to move your body in space. It'll probably take some time, time during which you shouldn't drive and should exert extra caution on stairs."

My heart pumped blood that felt like sludge through my veins. "How long?"

"Weeks. Months."

Air pulsed through my nose as I thought of my new car. With my hand still covering half my face, I sat on the firm mattress. "Can I still shift?"

"I pumped you with quite a lot of Sillin, so you might not be able to for a while still." He tipped his head toward August. "Shouldn't be too long, though. August can already shift again."

"Completely?" I asked, watching August's jean-clad knees.

"Yes." August's voice was as tight as his locked joints.

After a beat, I asked, "Can I go home?"

"Yes." Greg rose from the bed. "I'll go get all the paperwork in order." His hand dropped to my shoulder and squeezed lightly. "If you have any questions for me, you have my number."

Lowering my gaze to the shiny linoleum, I nodded.

Once Greg left, August crouched in front of me to capture the attention I was withholding from him. His hands coasted over my kneecaps that were wedged together, the bones grinding into one another. I hadn't yet seen the rest of my body but sensed I'd lost too much weight.

"Dimples . . ."

"Is Jeb back?"

August sighed, probably not wanting to discuss my uncle right now. "He's at the inn with Lucy, putting it in order. Liam gave it back to them." August tried to tow my hand off my face, but I resisted. "You don't have to hide from me."

I didn't say anything . . . I couldn't. The lump had grown too much to speak around it.

"Ness . . ."

I turned my face away and stared at the dancing boughs of the oak tree, trying to settle my churning thoughts.

August's knees clicked as he rose. For a long moment, neither of us spoke.

Then, "Can you ask Sarah to come back in here? Just Sarah. No one else."

A moment later, his footfalls petered out. While I waited for her, I wondered if she'd already glimpsed my face without the bandage.

When her lavender-and-silk perfume replaced August's heavy, heady scent, I turned. Making sure no one else was in the room and that the door was shut, I lowered my hand and exposed my ruined face.

Her gaze didn't waver in surprise, didn't widen in horror. It remained steady on mine. I guessed she'd known what to expect.

"You know what's insane?" she finally said, blowing a puff of air out of the corner of her mouth. "It's how ridiculously pretty you still are in spite of your battle scars. Here I thought I'd finally have a chance to outshine you."

Tears tracked down both my cheeks. My left eye was inept at capturing images but not at producing tears.

"Oh, sweetie." Sarah dropped down on the mattress, making it bounce a little, and then she wrapped her arms around my neck and hugged me close.

"I know it's stupid to be angry about this, seeing as I could be dead, but it sucks," I whispered.

Sarah pressed away. "It's not stupid. You're allowed to be angry. I don't think it would be healthy if you weren't." She combed a lock of hair behind my ear, exposing more of the horror.

"Everyone's going to stare."

"Everyone already did."

"But not for the same reasons."

"You're right. Most people are probably going to wonder how you got your scars. Better come up with a good story that doesn't involve a duel with a massive wolf. You don't want to frighten the townspeople." She smiled, but it didn't reach her eyes.

Her perfect eyes and her smooth skin.

"I can't drive. Not for a while. Depth perception," I added glumly.

"Good thing I'm an exceptionally great chauffeur *and* we go to the same school."

"Sarah . . ." I pressed my trembling lips together. Tears circled around them and dripped down my chin, plopping onto my hospital gown.

"What?"

"You're not going to spend your days driving me around."

"Why not? I love driving, and surprisingly enough, I love spending time with you. It's a win-win for me."

A knock on the door had me quickly wiping the tears on my sleeves and finger-combing my hair to shroud half my face.

"Ness?"

Jeb . . .

"Should I let him in?" Sarah asked quietly.

I nodded. "But just him." I didn't want to see Lucy. If she'd even come.

Sarah hugged me again before getting up and letting Jeb inside. "Do you want me to stay, Ness?"

"No. I'll call you when I get home."

"I meant in the room. I'll be out in the hallway. It's a real party out there."

I grimaced. "Can you get everyone to leave? I don't—"

"Say no more. Your wish is my command. Bye, BB."

"BB?"

"Short for Boulder Babe." She winked before pulling the door open.

I eyed the red jacket. If I hadn't been scarred, it might've amused me to wear it, but now . . . now people would surely laugh if I donned it.

"Ness!" My uncle barreled past Sarah and reached my bed before she'd even closed the door. He hugged me so tight it squeezed an *oomph* from my lungs. "I think I've aged a decade in the past week. Between you and Lucy." He didn't mention Everest, but I sensed my cousin was never far from Jeb's mind.

"I heard you got the inn back."

"Thanks to you." He let me go, but then his hand moved to my stringy hair. I let him tuck it behind my ear and inspect the mutilation. His lips pressed so tight they vanished completely in his thick beard. "If Liam hadn't burned her body, I'd—I'd . . ."

"He burned her body?"

"Yes. So she could rot in hell next to Aidan."

Had that been his reasoning, or had Liam worried the silver in her blood would contaminate the soil? For whatever reason he'd done it, I was glad she was well and truly gone.

"I saw Greg signing the discharge papers. Ready to come home?"

I nodded, but then asked, "Which home, though?"

He smiled gently, skating his palm over the side of my face that wasn't injured. "Whichever one you want? You have many now. I kept the apartment. August got a team together to clean and repaint your house, so it's ready too. And the inn, there's always a room with your name on it. It's completely up to you, honey."

"Where are you staying?"

"Wherever you'll be."

I smiled at him. "You don't need to take care of me anymore, Jeb."

"Who's going to take care of me?"

"I'm half-blind." My voice was a cracked whisper.

"You're half-sighted." He combed another lock of hair behind my ear. "And the best way of taking care of a person is to spend time with them and love them. You're really good at that."

"You have Lucy now."

"And what? I can't have *two* women in my life?"

"I know she apologized, but I'm not ready to live with her."

"Then you won't. She'll stay at the inn. And I'll stay wherever you want to live." He stood, extended his hand, palm face up, and waited for me to latch onto it. When I did, he said, "So where shall we go?"

"The apartment," I said without hesitation.

It had been a safe haven, unlike the inn, unlike my parents' house. "I might need some clothes though . . ." I tipped my head to my bare legs poking out of the hospital gown.

"Of course. Let me run back and get you some. Give me a half hour."

After Jeb left, August let himself in again. Draping my hair over the ugly wound, I sank down on the bed and gathered my hands between my knees.

"Everyone's gone," he said, coming to sit next to me.

"Except you."

I felt his body stiffen. "Did you want me to leave?"

"You don't have to stay."

He crooked a finger under my chin and lifted my face. I slid my chin off its perch and dipped it back against my neck. "Why won't you look at me?"

"It's not that I don't want to look at you," I whispered. "It's that I don't want you to look at me."

He sighed, a deep, rattling lungful that softened the line of his body, and then one of his arms hooked my knees and the other curved under my arms. He scooped me up and deposited me with the utmost gentleness onto his lap.

"I don't want you to stay with me because you feel pity, August," I said, nestling my head in the crook of his neck.

He snorted, sliding his hand through the back of the gown and running his fingers delicately over my spine. I felt something stiff press against my thigh.

"Because that's the reason I'm staying with you," he said softly.

"How can you still desire me? My face is—it's . . ." Tears crept down my scars and pooled in the corner of my mouth.

"It's the face I want to wake up to every morning and fall asleep watching every night." August's hand settled on the small of my back. "Besides, I'll remind you that I'm scarred too."

"Not your face."

"No, not my face." He tucked me a little closer still, locking both his arms around my juddering ribs. "Your scars are a piece of you now, and I love all the pieces of you, Ness Clark."

A loud sob scraped up my throat as I burrowed deeper into this man who'd always tried to keep me safe, and who, when he'd failed because I'd pushed him away, had risked his life so I could get mine back.

"You're the love of my entire life, August Watt," I whispered against his neck that smelled of wood and spice . . . that smelled of home.

EPILOGUE

The sunset dripped through the evergreen needles, showering the forest with a crimson glow that turned the rough trunks tawnier. I was still in Colorado, but miles away from Boulder.

When Sarah had caught me crying into my pillow after I'd failed, for the fourth morning in a row, to make myself a cup of coffee—I'd poured the scorching liquid all over the countertop and down my legs instead of inside my mug—she'd booted my butt out of bed and taken me on a road trip to a cabin that belonged to her father, but which he apparently rarely used.

We'd told next no one we'd left—just Liam, Jeb, and Evelyn. Evelyn because her heart would've given out if she thought I'd run away, Jeb so he knew I was safe, and Liam because he could track us, and I didn't want him to give my location away to August.

Sarah believed I'd taken her up on the trip to regain my footing in this new world, but that wasn't the reason I'd gone with her.

I'd gone because I was ashamed.

The morning I spilled the coffee on myself, August had cleaned up my mess. He'd cleaned up most of my messes since I'd been home. And although he never once complained, it wasn't fair to him. Which had been the second reason that propelled me out of Boulder . . . out of his life.

He had everything going for him. He didn't need to be saddled with a girl who couldn't manage to fill a glass, who knocked into furniture, who tripped because she constantly miscalculated the distance between her feet and the raised threshold of a doorway. Perhaps, one day, my brain would catch up with my two-dimensional vision, but until that day came, I didn't want to be anyone's ball-and-chain.

As I rocked in the hammock hooked between two great spruce trees, I twirled an aspen daisy between my fingers, marveling at the petals' lilac shade. I'd picked it with Sarah before she'd headed into town for some fresh produce.

Even though I could never hate you, if you break my heart again—

When I break yours, it breaks mine.

We'd been gone three days, and I'd spent all of them thinking about August, reliving tender moments we'd shared, but then I'd close my eyes to force the memories away, because the pain of being without him made my broken heart hurt more than my broken face.

A car engine rumbled up the long, dusty drive. I imagined Sarah was back. I got down from the hammock to help her with the groceries, but froze when I saw it wasn't a red Mini that had pulled up but a gleaming navy pickup.

Was her father visiting?

When the driver got out and slapped the door shut, the daisy tumbled from my fingers.

In spite of the sunset burning behind the man, darkening his body, there was no mistaking my visitor.

I supposed I would recognize August in the darkest of nights, his shape as familiar to me as my own.

He eyed me a long moment before opening the backseat of his new car and lifting a duffel bag. "You can run, but you can't hide, Ness Clark. Not from me," he said, his back still to me.

Words stuck in my throat as he turned. I wanted to ask him how he'd found me, but did it matter? I dropped my gaze to the bag clutched in his fingers, then looked at the road, wondering if my friend's car was about to make an appearance.

"Sarah will be back in the morning," he said, reading my thoughts. "Unless you were looking at that road to assess how fast you could get away."

I snapped my attention back to him.

"We need to talk, so don't run. I *will* chase you, but I'd rather not have to do it after the last three days I've had."

As he drew the door of the house open, I finally found my voice, "You said that if I broke your heart again, you'd stay away from me."

He paused on the threshold. "Apparently, I can't."

I winced when the door banged shut behind him.

I DIDN'T GO INSIDE RIGHT AWAY.

I let him settle.

I let his anger settle.

Even though nothing tied me to him, I could sense his irritability seeping through the grayed plank walls of the cabin.

Pulling down the sleeves of my red silk bomber jacket, I waited for the sun to dip completely and lacquer the woods in darkness before heading inside. The air held a chill that made goose bumps spring across my skin. Granted I was only wearing a bikini under the jacket, having spent most of my afternoon drifting around the infinity pool on an inflatable pizza slice, trying to make sense of my life, of what I wanted to do with it now that I had it back.

A single lightbulb burned in the loft-style living area—the copper pendant over the granite dining table. August was bent in front of the fireplace, coaxing a fire to life. He didn't acknowledge me when I came in. Didn't glance over his shoulder as I took a seat on the couch behind him.

He poked the blackening logs. "When you disappeared with Sarah, I told myself you'd left because I couldn't give you what you needed, but then, when *no one* would tell me where you'd gone, I realized you'd left to get away from me." He finally straightened and turned around. "What did I do to make you run?"

"You didn't do anything." Slipping my hands between my knees, I tucked my chin into my neck, hoping the barrage of hair blocked the sight of me. "I left so you could get your life back."

"My life back?" His voice was so shrill it made me look up.

"You don't need to take care of me, okay? Nothing binds us anymore."

His green eyes flared.

"Ingrid—"

"I don't want Ingrid, Ness!"

I recoiled from the harshness of his voice.

"I'm sorry." He spoke quietly this time.

Heat snaked under my lids, blurred the crackling fire.

He came to stand right in front of me. "Thank you for giving me a choice. I didn't realize that was your intention."

I swallowed.

He crouched so his face was level with mine and stole my clammy hands from between my knees, cocooning them in his warm ones. "But, Dimples, I don't want anyone else. I want you. Just *you*."

Sobs stumbled inside my chest. "You say this now, but in a couple years"—my voice broke—"when I still can't fill a cup or drive a car—"

"I'll just say it again."

I bit my wobbly lip.

"Besides, I have no doubt that you're going to be back behind the wheel of a car soon."

"You don't know that," I murmured.

"I do." He hunted my face with his emerald eyes. "You're much too willful to give up hope, or your independence, for that matter." He raised one of his hands to my face to push back my long blonde strands.

I let him look his fill. Maybe if he looked long enough, he'd realize he didn't want to wake up to this face.

When he leaned over and kissed my spoiled cheek, my wet lashes swept down, stayed down. A part of me still didn't understand how he could stand the texture of my scars, much less the sight of them.

"I'm not sure what I have to do to convince you that I can't live without you, Ness." His words pulsed against the tip of my nose. "Bringing you back from the dead would've been enough for most girls."

My lips twitched. I opened my eyes to find his agonizingly gentle ones set on mine.

"Is it because I can't give you any daughters? Is that why you're pushing me away?"

A chuckle burst through my trembling lips. "I love boys too, you know."

He smiled, but then he grew so serious that my laughter wilted. He unfurled his long body, tugging me up in the process. "Will you come home with me? Not tonight. But tomorrow? Or the day after?"

Pressing my lips together to stop their shaking, I nodded.

"Good. Because I have this piece of land."

"By a lake?"

"That's the one. And the only thing standing on it right now is a palm tree."

My head jerked back a little. "You planted a palm tree?"

"Had to have something to build our house around."

Our house? Had this man ever envisioned his life without me?

"I'm starting to have a surplus of houses," I whispered raucously.

"As long as you only have one home."

A fresh wave of emotion slicked my eyes. "Oh, August," I croaked, throwing my arms around his neck.

His calloused hands slipped under the silk fabric of my jacket and pulled me close, pressing my body against his as though to seal me into his skin and erase the distance I'd put between us. Moment after moment passed in this quiet communion.

As the logs crackled in the fireplace, I filled my lungs with his familiar scent and my ears with his heartbeats. How I ever thought I could give up this man was beyond me.

The tendons in his neck flexed under my fingertips. I lifted my head off his chest and craned my neck as his mouth arced toward mine. He kissed me long and deep.

When he started on my neck, I rasped, "Want to go for a swim?" Between what he was doing to me and the fire, I was dangerously close to overheating.

I felt the curve of his smile on my skin. "I didn't bring any swim trunks. Hope it won't be a problem."

I had to clear my throat before I could answer him. "No problem at all."

Keeping his eyes on mine, he unbuttoned his flannel shirt and chucked it on the couch, revealing a torso honed to such incredible perfection that my hands trembled as I removed my jacket and draped it over the arm of the couch. As he lowered the zipper of his jeans, I walked toward the sliding glass doors and dragged them open, then crossed the stone deck and dove into the dusky pool to cool down.

After I broke the surface, I pushed my hair off my face and stared up at the moon that was brilliant and full, illuminating the dark world surrounding us. A moment later, arms wrapped around my stomach and pulled my back against a rock-hard chest.

A rock-hard *everything*.

"You're missing the pack run," I said.

"I'm here with you. Beats any pack run." He rested his chin in the crook of my neck and inhaled me slowly. "God, I've missed you so much."

"I can tell. That thing's going to end up bruising my spine."

"That thing?" He snorted.

I turned around to flick him.

He smiled roguishly at my fingers before backing me against the tiled wall and scooping me up. "To avoid any bruising."

He was no longer my mate, and yet I desired him just as much as when he had been. Locking my eyes on his, I rocked against him slowly.

He gripped my thighs to steady me. "Careful, sweetheart."

I tilted my face to the side to study his expression. "Why? We're no longer mates . . ."

Hurt darkened his freckles. "You're my mate in all the ways that count, Ness Clark."

"I didn't mean—" I held on to his shoulders, my pale fingers crimping his brown skin. "It came out wrong." I linked my arms around his neck. "I love you," I whispered. "Never doubt that."

Keeping one hand underneath me, he brought his other up to tuck a wet lock behind my ear. "I didn't doubt it until you left."

Raindrops began to fall from a dark strip of cloud that moved across the bloated moon, the droplets glittering as they plinked against the glassy surface of the pool.

"I'm so sorry," I whispered.

He cupped my jaw and kissed me. And for a long, *long* moment, that was all we did. And it was perfect and beautiful, but I wanted more. I craved more. So I moved against him again.

He ripped his mouth off mine.

Before he could speak, I said, "I'm not in heat." Sarah had taught me to use my sense of smell to determine my cycle since oral contraceptives didn't work all that well on werewolves.

A vein in August's neck began to throb faster.

I shrugged. "In case you wanted—you know . . ."

"In case I wanted to make love to you in this pool?"

Heat crept up my neck. "Yeah." *So much for using the pool to cool off . . .*

He shifted his hold on me until we were lined up, then his thumb brushed my skimpy bikini bottom aside before settling against my pulsing flesh. As he waited for me to make the next move, he swiped his finger over me.

Heart pounding like my wolf's when she scented her prey, I slid him in, inch by slow inch.

His thumb stilled against me, and a shudder went through him. He closed his eyes. When he opened them again, they glittered as wildly as the stars rioting around the storm cloud.

"I moved your body," I said. "We never talked about it, but I moved you."

"I know, sweetheart. Almost got me killed." He glided himself out and then dipped back in.

I shot him a sheepish smile. "Seems like I'm almost getting you killed a lot. Are you sure you're not better off without me? You'd surely live a much longer life."

August's expression became edged with so much fury and pain that I caressed his jaw.

"I didn't mean to make you angry."

"There is *no* version of me without you, okay?"

"Okay."

"It's you and me, Dimples. Always has been and always will be."

Between the feel of his thick, silky flesh, the scent of spice and rain lifting from his skin, and the timbre of his voice, my heart thundered in my chest. He dragged my body away, then thrust into me, causing the pounding to travel lower. As the rain fell harder, it created a cacophony that drowned out everything but the sound of our hearts.

His lips claimed mine with such violence that our teeth knocked together. My legs clenched around him as a thrill began to build in my core, and then a moan tumbled from my mouth straight into his as the sensation overrode my entire system. He pumped harder, and I clawed at his back, the orgasm exploding inside me, striking my veins and muscles, battering my sinews and bones, scorching my skin.

He deepened the kiss, his teeth catching on my bottom lip. As the taste of warmed copper coated my palate, a new wave of pleasure clapped against my thighs and rushed through my limbs, making me gasp his name.

His rhythm turned brisker, more urgent, rough grunts scraping the walls of his throat, causing the flutter behind my belly button to transform into full-on drumming.

"Sweetheart," he rasped a second before my body undid his.

The water around us rippled, and then it began to glitter as though it were drizzling stars instead of raindrops. It was so beautiful. Everything about that moment was so beautiful. I wanted to immortalize it in my mind for all the years to come.

Still surfing on the wake of my orgasms, I stroked the nape of his neck, watching his features crinkle and smooth as he poured himself inside of me.

Our first time had been special, but this time . . . this time had been spectacular. I hoped it had also been good for August. Maybe he'd had better. I grimaced at the thought.

"I have never had better," he whispered huskily. "*Never.*"

The blood drained from my face. Had I spoken out loud?

August blinked. And then color leached from his skin as he looked down at the water that still glittered wildly around us. ***Oh . . . shit.***

I blinked, because his mouth hadn't moved to form the words, and yet somehow, I'd heard them. "Did I—did you—"

My navel pulsed harder than my core and heart put together.

Was the link back?

I think . . . I think . . . His voice surged inside my mind.

"I can hear you. Why can I hear you?" I asked, barely louder than the plinking raindrops. "Did we just . . . did we just *consolidate* the link?"

Sadness furrowed his brow. "I think—God, I'm so sorry. I know you didn't want this." He pressed his forehead against mine, his fingers digging into my thighs. "I'm so sorry," he repeated.

For a moment, I held perfectly still, absorbing the significance of what had just transpired. Then, without using sound or breath, I said, *I'm not.*

He lifted his face off mine.

"Are you actually sorry, August?"

"No." His forehead had smoothed. "But I've wanted this . . . Well, I've wanted this since the tether snapped into place." He shot me a sheepish smile that made him look more boy than man, but then he shifted a little, and I felt him harden inside me again, reminding me that he was all man.

My man.

His smile turned devilish as he tugged on the tether, reeling my body in until he was fully sheathed inside. *That's right, sweetheart.* **Your** *man.*

I laughed. "I can't decide if I like this new skill of ours or fear it."

"Why would you fear it?"

"Because I'll have no more secrets."

"Planning on keeping things from me now, are you?" He grunted, so I flicked him, which just intensified his amusement.

"How am I supposed to surprise you with anything if you can read my mind?"

I'll act surprised.

I rolled my eyes but grinned.

For a moment, neither of us spoke, neither out loud, nor through the new connection that had opened between our minds. We simply contemplated each other.

Then, "You look happy tonight, Dimples. Are you?"

I cupped his jaw, roughened by stubble and years, and even though I didn't need to sound the word, I spoke it out loud for the moonlit land to hear. "Terribly."

ACKNOWLEDGMENTS

You might not believe this, but it wasn't my intention to write a love triangle. Originally, *The Boulder Wolves* was supposed to be a duology (Ha! Like I could ever fit all my twists and turns inside two books . . .) and Liam was supposed to die at the start of book 2. Well, I loved him too much to kill him off, so I adapted my storyline to fit him inside.

And that's how I ended up with a love triangle.

Anyway, all this to say that I didn't mean to do this to Ness, or to you.

I hope you've enjoyed this series. Thank you for running along with my wolves, for your heartfelt messages and kind reviews. I hope you'll join me on all my next adventures.

Thank you to my own true mate for putting up with me. For making my life sweet and beautiful, each and every day. For taking me on adventures even when I want to stay home with my computer.

Thank you to my children for inspiring me and for filling my life with your shrill voices and contagious laughter.

Thank you to my family for buying my books. Even if you never get around to reading them, I appreciate your support.

Thank you to my kick-ass beta readers—Katie, Astrid, and Theresea. I love you girls so darn much.

Thank you to my publisher, and to my fabulous editor, Krystal, who never fails to challenge me, and to Monika for another gorgeous cover.

Thank you to all the members of my **amazing** Facebook reader group (OLIVIA'S DARLING READERS). Your engagement and enthusiasm never cease to delight me.

ALSO BY OLIVIA WILDENSTEIN

YA PARANORMAL ROMANCE

The Lost Clan series
ROSE PETAL GRAVES
ROWAN WOOD LEGENDS
RISING SILVER MIST
RAGING RIVAL HEARTS
RECKLESS CRUEL HEIRS

The Boulder Wolves series
A PACK OF BLOOD AND LIES
A PACK OF VOWS AND TEARS
A PACK OF LOVE AND HATE
A PACK OF STORMS AND STARS

Angels of Elysium series
FEATHER
CELESTIAL
STARLIGHT

The Quatrefoil Chronicles series
OF WICKED BLOOD
OF TAINTED HEART

The Kingdom of Crows series
HOUSE OF BEATING WINGS
HOUSE OF POUNDING HEARTS
HOUSE OF STRIKING OATHS

YA ROMANTIC SUSPENSE

Masterful series
THE MASTERKEY
THE MASTERPIECERS
THE MASTERMINDS

YA ROMANCE STANDALONES
GHOSTBOY, CHAMELEON & THE DUKE OF GRAFFITI
NOT ANOTHER LOVE SONG

ABOUT THE AUTHOR

USA TODAY bestselling author Olivia Wildenstein grew up in New York City, the daughter of a French father with a great sense of humor, and a Swedish mother whom she speaks to at least three times a day. She chose Brown University to complete her undergraduate studies and earned a bachelor's in comparative literature. After designing jewelry for a few years, Wildenstein traded in her tools for a laptop computer and a very comfortable chair. This line of work made more sense, considering her college degree.

When she's not writing, she's psychoanalyzing everyone she meets (Yes. Everyone), eavesdropping on conversations to gather material for her next book, baking up a storm (that she actually eats), going to the gym (because she eats), and attempting not to be late at her children's school (like she is 4 out of 5 mornings, on good weeks).

oliviawildenstein.com
olivia@wildenstein.com